IN THE WORLD

IN THE WORLD

WORLD

A NOVEL BY

George P. Elliott

New York · The Viking Press

First published in 1965 by The Viking Press, Inc.
625 Madison Avenue, New York, N.Y. 10022

Published simultaneously in Canada by
The Macmillan Company of Canada Limited

Library of Congress catalog card number: 65-19267
Printed in U.S.A. by the Vail-Ballou Press, Inc.

The lines (p. 224) from "Voyages, II" from *The Collected Poems of Hart Crane*, Copyright © R, 1961, by Liveright Publishing Corporation, are quoted by permission of Liveright, Publishers, N.Y., and those (p. 41) from "September 1, 1939" from *The Collected Poetry of W. H. Auden*, Copyright 1940 by W. H. Auden, by permission of Random House, Inc. and Faber and Faber Limited, London.

For Nora

IN THE WORLD

I

· 1 ·

The first ten years they were married the Royces had often agreed that they were better guests than hosts, but then in their middle age they discovered that they liked giving parties. They did not give a great many, perhaps four a year, but they came to enjoy themselves more at their own parties than at other people's.

Each had an explanation for the change. Alfred, as he was disposed to do, saw it as the result of a combination of causes, of which the chief, to be sure, was their house. This was the house on San Jacinto Way in which they had lived since just before the war. Beth saw no reason to look beyond the house itself: the housewarming had been the most successful party they had given up till then, and though there had been some dullish ones since, they had had no bleak fiascos like a few of their earlier ones, the kind after which Beth did not even empty the ashtrays but dragged off to bed, sometimes in tears. Alfred's talk about their finally accepting adult responsibility, about the confidence of experience, about the altering climate of the times, did not faze Beth.

"Well, *why?*" He was still dashing his theories about their parties against her rock conviction. "You're so stubborn, Beth. Very well, what are you being so stubborn about? I know it's a nice house, I like it as much as you do, that's why we bought it—because we both like it. But what's so special about it for parties?"

She did not know. "It's the size." She had no theories. "It's a good size, no matter how many or how few people there are." She did not really want to know. "We used to have quite different friends than we do now, but it's always been the same story. Mary Louise has noticed it too."

3

"She has indeed. She has a good eye for such things."

"Are you insinuating something?"

"Insinuating! I'm complimenting her. At least that's what it sounds like to me, 'she has a good eye.' As a matter of fact, I think we have much to be grateful to her for."

"Oh?" She glanced up from cleaning her nails.

"Yes. I wish Shirley at least could be coming this evening. She could give Nancy some moral support. Nancy hasn't talked to me about it, but I get the impression that she is a bit uneasy about Jean-Louis."

"You can hardly blame her. They're thirteen, and she's never even seen him."

"I don't blame her. I just wish Shirley weren't so loyal to her mother."

"Well, you wanted Horace," Beth said with a little flourish of her head. "What did you mean, we ought to be grateful to Mary Louise? Of course we should, but you seemed to have something special in mind. I thought you were Horace's friend."

"Oh, Beth, how often must I tell you, I like them both, I refuse to take sides."

"I notice it's Horace you invite to your parties—with his wife of the moment."

"And you invite Mary Louise to yours. That's what I meant, we ought to be grateful to them both for not making us take sides, for both remaining our friends."

"For pity's sake, dear, we are talking about grown-up people. They aren't children."

"How many divorced couples can you say this of?" Alfred insisted.

"It's true," she said heavily, blinking her eyes slowly, "nobody coming tonight fits your little category."

"In your own experience," he said as though he had not noticed her sarcasm.

"The Burnhams," Beth said without conviction.

"When did we last see Cynthia?"

"Leave me alone. I've got to go make the aspic."

"Anybody else?"

"I do wish Mary Louise would remarry."

"No red herrings!" said Alfred. "You see, I have the theory that one of the reasons our parties improved when they did was our dividing them up. Your guest lists make good parties, mine make good parties, only different. Combined, not so good. And the first time this became an issue was at our housewarming party—Horace or Mary Louise."

"That was a bad fight."

"It was indeed. It nearly ruined the party for both of us."

"We nearly didn't have one."

"Exactly. So we drew straws, and it was your party. A great success. Mary Louise came—Horace did not bear a grudge. Tonight he'll be here—Mary Louise holds no grudge."

"You see," said Beth. "Horace is your special friend."

"Not so! I invite him to keep the balance of your inviting Mary Louise. The point is, we owe the balance to them."

"Alfred! Look at this house! It's a beautiful house, good for parties. It's as plain as the nose on your face about this house. Sometimes I wonder how you could ever have been any good as a lawyer or a professor."

"So you have said before, my dear."

She glanced at him. "Aw, I'm sorry." He looked furious at this. "I didn't hurt your feelings? Good. All I'm getting at is this—you ought to let the house loom more."

He whinnied with constricted laughter. As he walked toward his study, he sang in Wagnerian tenor: *"Beloved Beth . . ."*

"I mean loom in your mind!" she called after him.

"I mean mind, body, and soul. *You'll be my death."*

San Jacinto Way was a short, winding street half a mile north of the campus in Berkeley. The street curled on a deep ledge part way up the range of steep hills against which the city backed to the east; some of the houses on the uphill side of the ledge, among them the Royces', had a glimpse of the Bay and the Golden Gate. The long-time residents of the street were well agreed that a panoramic view of the Bay was vastly overrated and that, if they were forced to live in the celebrated, extremely modern cliff-hanging houses farther up on the hill, they would not enjoy the panorama assaulting them from the west but would be forced to protect themselves from it. They thought it ostentatious to pull back the curtains and expose the grand view to a guest's involuntary admiration. They preferred to let him find for himself the bonsai maple in the dented copper tub, the bird-of-paradise plant below the terrace, the fact that a disarrayed hillside garden was composed entirely of California natives. You could know one of the regulars for a year before learning that two Nobel-Prize-winning scientists lived on San Jacinto. You would very likely be taken to peek through a grape-stake fence shielding a house made in the Japanese style, set back from the street; in front of it rose a handsome Monterey cypress, under which the ground was swept smooth; in the gentle obscurity of the tree you could see in profile, on a low blue ceramic base, a wooden Kwannon whose original infolded peace had been weathered by centuries into a different but no less lovely quietude. You would discover that the house was occupied by

5

Thomas Durkheim—a retired Justice of the United States Supreme Court, over ninety years old, who had known Theodore Roosevelt, had served on the bench with Holmes, and had been a thorn in the side of F. D. Roosevelt and the New Deal—but what your San Jacinto friend took you to see was the house, the tree, and the image. In a Spanish-mission-style house lived a Chinese who was an Oriental art goods importer and who taught a seminar in Chinese porcelains. In a Swiss châlet lived the six-foot-five-inch Oxford-educated grandson of a cannibal and his six-foot-four-inch University of London wife; he was here for a year teaching economics and ethnology in the newly established African Studies Program. Except for Justice Durkheim—and for a used-car dealer named J. J. "Texas" Ranger, who wore rodeo hats and flashed "Howdy" at his neighbors with undauntable cheer—everyone on the street was or had been connected with the University, for the most part with one of the letters or arts. Most of Berkeley was an unexceptional, middle-class, early-to-bed American city, right-angled, noisy, characterless. San Jacinto Way thought of itself as set off, a quiet, cultivated ledge of the true Berkeley. Most of the old-timers had come from New England and a lot of them from Boston.

After a brilliant career in law school, Alfred Royce had gone to Washington as Justice Durkheim's clerk for two years, the first two years of the Depression. When Durkheim, feeling his powers waning, retired a couple of years before the war, he returned to Berkeley, where he had lived only when he was a student working his way through the University in the 1870s, and bought the Japanese-style house from the estate of a deceased classics professor with whom he had studied Catullus. Childless, his wife long dead, he lived alone, with a spinster niece for housekeeper. Alfred, his nearest friend in the Bay Area, had become acquainted with San Jacinto Way through calling on Durkheim. At the upper end of the street he had seen the white frame house for sale and had discovered that the down payment was reasonable. The house had won Beth instantly. They had bought it. Through their three daughters Beth made acquaintances among neighboring mothers, but Durkheim remained Alfred's only friend on the street. Since the war Alfred had taken to calling on the old man every Saturday afternoon and reading to him. At first he had also attempted to keep him up on current legal matters, but it was stories the old gentleman wanted, tales, *The Decameron,* the *Odyssey,* the entire *Arabian Nights, Don Quixote.* He was half blind, he wore a hearing aid, his bluish hands shook, a gold fob always hung from his vest pocket, he wore spats, he had once known as much about corporation law as any man alive. Yet what he wanted to hear, rocking back and forth in his early-American rocking chair, smiling and wheezing and sometimes clapping his hands, was tales, the bawdier the better. Sometimes he would recite an especially indecent line from Catullus and wheeze with delight.

Occasionally Beth invited a San Jacinto couple to one of her parties. Alfred had long since quit trying to fit them onto his guest-lists. "I would have them, my dear, but I find them incongruent." "Oh, Alfred, for heaven's sake, incongruent." There the matter rested.

The Royces' house was on a deep lot that sloped quite abruptly down from the street. Only the garage and Alfred's study were on the street level, five steps higher than the main floor of the house. The garage and study, together with a couple of Douglas firs and a wooden gate, effectually sheltered the patio and the main part of the house from the casual glances of passers-by. On the north side of the patio, connecting the study to the main part of the house, the Royces had added a large bedroom for themselves; it had a fireplace, three casement windows facing south, a dressing room for Beth, its own bathroom. When it was first built, Nancy was not yet five, and Beth felt uneasy having her sleep alone in one of the three rooms on the lowest story; and regularly after her parents moved up to their remote privacy Nancy trudged up to them in the middle of the night, seeking consolation. But she overdid it: twice she wrung their hearts by announcing that she was afraid she was going to die in her sleep down there; the third time her voice was a touch histrionic, and she clambered into their bed with a complacent sigh. Alfred grumbled. "Oh, come on now, Nancy." Beth carried her wailing down to her bed, tucked her in, and kissed her warmly but only once, saying she did not want to see her again till breakfast time. The commotion had awakened Lizzie, then fourteen, who had been both overjoyed and stricken to inherit the big room which her parents had used while their wing was being built. She came in in her pajamas, told Nancy peremptorily to quit crying for a minute, took her mother out into the hall, and made a deal. "Since I get the biggest downstairs room for my own, it's only fair for me to take care of Nancy when she wakes up." She told Nancy the arrangement and made it clear that she wasn't a bit impressed by Nancy's supposed fear of dying in her sleep. Nancy gave each of them a shrewd glance, issued the perfunctory bellows required by honor, and settled down. Doors were adjusted. Beth and Alfred slept in tranquillity.

On the main floor were the kitchen and dining room, connected by a double-sized doorway, and the long, handsome living room. The house had been designed by Orestes Stull, who for forty years was the most celebrated architect of private residences in the Bay Area. Typically his houses were of redwood, but this one was of pine planks, with a cedar shake roof and a good deal of plaster on the interior.

7

The house was agreeable enough outside and in, but except for the living room it could have been the work of any one of fifty architects. Only that room had the Stull irregularity and charm of proportion. It was rather long for its width, and the gabled roof with exposed beams was slightly lower than one would expect. The result was a commodious informality, and the Royces had so disposed their furniture as to make intimacy possible. Along the western side, relieving any sense of narrowness or constriction, extended the gallery—a sort of long alcove with casement windows, an enclosed sun-porch giving both upon the cascading garden and, over and between two topped redwoods, upon the Bay itself far beyond. On the eastern side of the living room, French doors opened directly onto the patio. In good weather one lunched in the patio, sunbathed, or took tea; parties circulated freely in and out. But there was no sense of that indoor-outdoor living which had by then become so fashionable in modern design. In that Stull living room, though it was not gloomy, being painted a light off-gray and having a good many windows, one felt securely enclosed in a shelter, protected from the out-of-doors. Partly the low eaves created the sense of shelter, partly the proportions of the room, partly the fact that one stepped into an alcove to enjoy the western view; but not the least of what created this sense was, against the south wall, the old-fashioned brick fireplace with a mantel and a hearth.

The house had a central heating system, and it almost never drops to freezing in Berkeley. Nevertheless, the Royces burned a couple of cords of wood a year in their fireplace, and when they had guests they would build at least a small fire, sometimes when the evening was so warm that they had to open a door or window and waste the heat.

· 2 ·

The first to arrive were Chantal Bigonneau and her son Jean-Louis.

"What!" said Chantal. "No one else is here? Oh, Professor Royce, I must apologize to be early. Yet is it not after five?"

"Ten past. And please, in my own home, don't call me Professor Royce. I would prefer Alfred."

"No. For me it is impossible."

"Then Mister. I teach only the one seminar. Strictly speaking I'm not a professor but a lecturer."

"Ah, but at the associate-professor level. You see—I know, I am in the secrets." She worked in the office of the Law Department.

"Well," he said, "Mr. Royce, how's that?"

8

"No. Someday Alfred, yes, I hope so. Mister, never. I am stupid. You will forgive me? I came to this country too late to learn all sorts of things. Slacks, for example, I push my legs, but they won't go in them. You can't teach an old bitch new tricks, no?"

Beth had come in from the kitchen to hear Chantal's last remarks and could not help laughing. Alfred, who had intended to jump over them with no more than a blink of the eyes, was caught up in Beth's laughter. Chantal, who knew perfectly well how "bitch" was commonly used in English, presently joined them, delighted that they were enjoying openly what they took to be her blunder and that they were tactful enough not to correct her.

Beth called down to Nancy, who yelled that she would be right up.

Jean-Louis stood by his mother at attention, his slacks sharply creased and without a wrinkle, his sports jacket properly buttoned at the second button, every gleaming hair in place.

"You will pardon me, Mrs. Royce. I told Jean-Louis he must wear a white shirt and a tie. He said no, it's June, we are to dine at buffet, he'll be out of doors. As you see, he wears a sport shirt, open at the throat. This is not bad?"

"Of course not, Mrs. Bigonneau. You'll see. The men will all come in ties and jackets. But it's warm today, so most of them will take off their jackets, then their ties, if Alfred does first. He usually does."

"Good. Nevertheless, we are early. Yet I asked. Professor Royce, I asked Myrtle in the department office. She said to cocktails one is half an hour late, to an evening party half an hour to an hour or even more, but to dinner one is on time. So, you have a buffet supper and say come at five! Confusion!"

Nancy came clattering up the stairs and into the living room in simulated eagerness, and, when she joined them, panted more than was needed. Seeing Jean-Louis, she was sorry she had spent so much time ironing the pink dress she was wearing. She was big for thirteen, taller than her grown-up sisters, and Jean-Louis was scarcely as tall as his mother, who was a tiny woman.

"We have a Ping-Pong table out in back," she said. "Do you play?"

"I know how, thank you. I am not very good."

"Well, come on. I sometimes beat my father."

"Then you shall beat me with no trouble."

"We'll watch you from the window," said Alfred.

"Be careful, Jean-Louis," said his mother. "Remember what I told you."

"Come on," said Nancy. As they were starting downstairs the adults heard her ask him, "What school are you in?"

"Garfield."

"No, I mean this year, not next." This was the first weekend of their summer vacation.

"Garfield," he repeated. "I am now in the eighth grade."

"Yikes! I'm going into the seventh. You must be smart."

"I consider it advisable for the future to study hard, especially languages."

Chantal lifted her shoulders and lowered her eyelids. "What shall I say? His father was not pompous, I think I am not. Regard. But he's a good son."

Beth was a bit on the tall, rangy side, and her face was round and regular enough to threaten prettiness. When Alfred was courting her, twenty years before, he had mentioned once that there was no sort of beauty he admired in a woman so much as a severe handsomeness. She had let her blond hair grow and ever since had worn a coronet of braids as severe as she could manage. It did not make her handsome, but at least it rescued her from the cuteness to which her features made her liable. Chantal was the sort of consciously "feminine" woman of whom Beth was disposed to be suspicious, careful of her hair and clothes, charming of voice. She was slight of build and quick of movement. Her face was by no means beautiful, yet the alertness of her large dark eyes and small mouth informed her features with what sometimes struck one as beauty: *une belle laide.* Moreover, Beth was disposed against every sort of quick, easy intimacy, such as a mother's complaining of her child to a stranger. Yet Chantal won her out of hand. Chantal's complaint about Jean-Louis, which in another woman might have seemed intrusive, in her seemed humorous honesty without the slightest personal appeal; and her femininity was pure. That is, like the husky burr of her voice, it was an aspect of herself of which she was clearly aware and which she would use when and as she decided, nor would she decide to use it to seduce. Beth had heard Alfred talk about his part-time secretary for a semester, and she had set herself against this moment. Now she unconsciously squeezed Alfred's arm in pleasure as great as his, in gratitude for his bringing Chantal to share with her.

Beth asked a question of the sort she usually abhorred. "Your husband did not come to America with you?"

"He died in 'forty-four. In the mountains above Grenoble." She made a round-topped gesture as though placing him deep in near mountains. "A viper stung him, they had no doctor. Well, it's better than being shot by the Germans. Many have been."

Beth restrained her conventional impulse to say, "I'm sorry." "It was an honorable death."

"He was a small man, Jean-Michel, but you should see how he carried his head." She tried to show them. "Better. With *panache,* no?

You understand, *panache*?" She folded her arms, shrugged, and sighed.

Alfred offered her chilled white wine, beer, or gin and tonic with a slice of lemon and a sprig of mint.

"Ah, I must look. The beer, if it's any good I prefer it, but most of your American beers are not so good, I think. Your California wines are good, but today I like beer. Please, may I look? It is not rude, what I do?"

· 3 ·

The two older daughters, Lizzie and Sybil, came up from their rooms together when they began to hear men's voices. Alfred had told them that the core of the party would be some students from his seminar in the theory of law, those who were still in town after the end of term. But the men that the girls found already gathered disappointed them.

There were three friends of the family: Aldo Ramsey, a courtly professor of money, a bachelor to be sure, but middle-aged; Horace Skellings, who was fifty, with Virginia, his fifth wife, who was much nearer Lizzie in age but acted as though she were of Beth's generation; and Woodrow Ravagli, a youngish millionaire, with his wife, Kay. And there was Hugh Hansson, a decorative-arts student at the University who was like a country cousin to them; he had lived all year in the shack at the bottom of the lot, working four hours a week in the garden for his room.

Three students arrived together: Brewster Adams, who was not an inch taller than either of the young women, and they thought themselves short, and two Marcuses, Fisher and Turnipseed. Alfred had not warned them: Turnipseed! How could a man named Turnipseed be anything but funny? Fisher looked possible, but the Turnipseed rubbed off on him through the shared Marcus.

A striking man showed up, Leon Kalish, whom they had heard Alfred mention as his star student. He was lean, square-shouldered, and tall, with black wavy hair brushed exactly where he wanted it; his features were so strong and well proportioned as to give him the effect of being handsome, though his face was blotched by eczema; his clothes were conventional but good, and he wore them with conscious pride. But he brought with him a girl to whom he seemed attentive, Robin Farquhar. To be sure, her face was pocked with acne scars, but, like Leon, she dressed with flair and carried herself with a confidence that made a good impression.

Brewster or one of the Marcuses . . . Lizzie dove among the married women and talked curtains. Sybil made herself as busy over

11

the olives and bread and cheese as she could, but an amiable Marcus cornered her—she was not sure which, and giggles kept rising in her, like bubbles in cake batter, at the thought he might be Turnipseed.

About quarter past six two promising men without women arrived. Alfred greeted them at the French doors, and it was clear that the black-haired dandy was introducing the tall, round-shouldered, shambly one to Alfred. Lizzie glanced around; Beth was not in sight. "Excuse me, some new guests just came in," Lizzie said to the matrons and left them among their upholstery. Sybil too felt an access of hospitality. "Oh," she said to Turnipseed-Fisher, "please excuse me. Daddy has some new people." She grabbed a dish of olives and reached the open doorway at the same time as Lizzie.

Lizzie was a forthright, chunky woman of twenty-three with a broad good-natured face and harsh blond hair cut sensibly short; her clothes were usually too tight for her because she was always about to lose some weight and seldom did. Her weakness for snappily dressed men was a family joke, and she had once confessed—rather, announced—to Sybil that she could not resist a man with "bedroom eyes," that is, with slow, heavy eyelids. This dandy, Joseph Thompson, not only had heavy eyelids but was in beautiful physical condition, and his features were odd and interesting. Her eyes round as a kitten's, she took his arm—with a glance at Sybil, who gave her a tiny nod—and bore him off to introduce him around.

Sybil was nineteen, with trim round tennis-playing arms and legs, conventional hairdo and make-up, and a pert face of a kind for whose prettiness age alone provides no remedy; wrinkles merely wreck it. She was dreamy and vague; she liked drifting into things and seeing what came of them. The slouching stranger, Roy Carver, looked vague too but sharp-eyed; his forehead was complicated with puckers; she thought he knew how to have a good time. A fun-loving man with hidden problems—good. She tugged at his sleeve, chattering vaguely up to him. He smiled at her complicitously, and she began the round of introductions.

It was one of Alfred's principles that no party should be so large that every newly arrived guest could not be introduced to all the other guests and then—after the introductions, not before—given a drink. Even now, long accustomed to this procedure, both Lizzie and Sybil felt their father's eye on them. Lizzie gave him an indignant frown; he gave her a quick nod of approval. She was only the more incensed; she would introduce Joe Thompson because it was the right thing to do, not because her father had his eye on her. Sybil did not react to Alfred's watchfulness either by looking at him or with a conscious emotion; but, on the pretext of taking Roy Carver out back to see the garden, she neglected to make the most important introduction of all, to her mother.

Sybil and Roy found the Ping-Pong table deserted, and played. With a paddle in her hand Sybil lost her vagueness. She paid no attention to Roy's verbal pleasantries but bent to the game with that concentration which had made her the family champion. He smoked as he played, he moved as though loose-jointed and indolent, he congratulated her on especially good returns, he beat her by five points.

"Another game?" she said.

"Oh, let's not. We'll get hot and sweaty."

"I suppose." She sat on a garden bench to put her sandals back on. "I don't get you. You said you were just a fair player. Well, I know I'm better than fair, and here you beat me."

He touched her nose delicately with a forefinger. "You have beads of sweat on the bridge of your nose. Charming."

Combativeness and pleasure in being stroked grappled in her, neither able to throw the other. "Come on, let's join the party."

"Wait." He touched her arm. She turned, making what would have been a frown if her face could have wrinkled. "Your hair." He made a couple of deft passes with his hands, and then quickly described both her ears at once with delicate fingers. "That's better."

She shivered with a voluptuousness she refused to yield to. "Who is that little Frenchwoman you knew already?"

"Chantel Bigonneau," said Roy. "You don't know her?"

"She's my father's secretary or something. How do you know her?"

"A man I know brought her over a couple of years ago."

"Oh," said Sybil vaguely again. "He brought her over."

"She had no money, of course. I don't think they got married, but I never really asked."

"Didn't that other fellow you came with say you were a reporter?"

"For three small labor papers, for A F of L councils. Big stuff."

"My father's a labor lawyer. At least he was."

"Your father is a lot more than that."

"Oh?"

"I'm thirsty," he said.

Halfway up the stairs she turned on him. "You know, Roy, I don't like to be beaten so casually."

He grabbed her hand and pressed it to his chest. "I promise never to beat you with a paddle again but only with a baseball bat."

Usually she liked flirtatious silliness like this, but now she pulled her hand away. "You're not even glad you beat me." She started up again.

"Wait." He ran up to her. His face puckered and his voice deep-

13

ened. "I like you. I want you to know that I think you put up a swell fight. If you really want to, after supper we'll play another game. Okay? You put on shorts and a sport shirt and tennis shoes, and we'll really play. I don't want to give the wrong impression. Chantal—she's my friend's girl friend, or former girl friend maybe, nothing to me. You see, Sybil? I'll play lefthanded and I'll really give the game all I have."

"Lefthanded!"

"You must believe me." He looked as though he might be going to cry. "I don't want this thing to come between us. I'll hold the paddle with both hands if you insist. Sybil! Please!" He sucked in his breath. "I thirst. Beer. Beer."

She ran away from him.

She found Lizzie near the fireplace with Woody and Kay Ravagli, listening to Joe Thompson. As she was approaching, Joe stuck his tongue out, not at her, and put his thumbs in his ears and waggled his fingers. They laughed.

Lizzie whispered to her, "What happened to that Roy?"

"He's a goofball," Sybil whispered. She made a tiny gesture at Joe. "What's he talking about?"

"I," he said looking at her mildly, "was explaining how certain ancestors of mine raise their children."

Sybil blushed. "Oh, you overheard me. I'm sorry."

"No, I saw your finger sort of point at me. You see, I intend to be a trial lawyer. Nothing," he said gravely, "must escape me."

For a moment the four of them were stiff with uncertainty at how to take this statement of his. What he said was true and important enough to stand without irony, if he was sufficiently humorless. None of them knew him well enough to be sure how solemnly he took himself. Then Lizzie laughed. Her laugh was always loud, but now, because of the uneasy delay, it was too loud; she brayed at him. Woody stuck his pipe in his mouth and gave a quick frown. Kay and Sybil glanced at Joe. He was looking at Lizzie appreciatively and chuckling. The two women joined the laughter, but Woody stayed out of it. Joe rolled his eyes at him slowly and winked.

"What do you mean," said Sybil pertly, " 'ancestors of mine'?"

"I mean some naked little kink-heads I read about that have them a sacred tree, the best I ever heard of."

"All right," said Sybil, "I bite. What's so special about it?"

"Any child touching it can't be touched by his parents—you know, can't be. Big taboo. And any child that climbs up in it can't even be spoken to by any grown-up. Now that's what I call civilized."

"Great," said Lizzie.

"I don't know," said Kay. "They're probably horribly brutal with

14

their children. They need it for a safety device to relieve their guilt."

She and Woody, after months of discussion, had just that week hired a maid to look after their children. Kay strictly saw to it that the maid was lenient with them—"permissive," in the jargon of child-raising. If the maid had done anything so reactionary as physically to punish one of the children for disobeying a rule—for example, spanked him for running over to the couch and turning a dish of oat-meal upside down on it—Kay would have got Woody to fire her out of hand. Kay could not do the firing herself, but Woody, having been used all his life to servants in the house and employees in the office, had assured her that, whenever she needed it done, he could ease a servant out so smoothly that she would hardly notice.

"Oh, Mrs. Ravagli," said Joe to her, "you've got it all turned around. That tree keeps them from being brutal, and they know it. Look what a power they give their children. Any child gets up in those branches and shouts and wails and complains about his parents till the whole world knows what they did, and they can't do a thing about it at the time and they can't punish him afterwards for what he said up there."

"You see," said Woody, "what Kay had in mind was that if the parents were kind and loving in the first place there wouldn't be any need for the tree."

"Why, yes," said Joe slowly, "that is true. Like if Eve hadn't eaten that apple we wouldn't need to wear clothes, and here all us Jews and Christians are dressed, dressed."

This time everyone laughed but Kay, who studied the problem.

A hand with an apple appeared in front of Sybil. She glanced over her shoulder. Roy's face, grinning, was so close she started back with a grunt. She made a noise like a cat spitting. "I don't like you," she announced clearly and walked off.

"Sybil!" Lizzie called sharply and went after her. "What do you mean, saying such a thing?"

Sybil realized that by walking away she had let them see she meant what she'd said. She turned back. All she needed to do to her face in order to look amiable was to raise the corners of her mouth, which she did.

"Well, he made me mad. He goes and beats me at Ping-Pong and then won't give me a chance for revenge."

"Oh, that Roy," said Joe, shaking his head, "he's a caveman with the ladies."

"Come on," said Roy to Sybil pleasantly. "If you want me to beat you eleven to nothing, all right I'll beat you eleven to nothing."

"Judges!" Sybil cried. "Come on, I want judges." She ran ahead, and they all followed.

Nancy and Jean-Louis were in back of the garage, sitting on the ground, chatting.

Leon Kalish was telling a long joke in a Yiddish accent to half a dozen people on the sun porch.

Marcus Fisher was in a corner, looking at a book of photographs.

Alfred, seeing him alone, was on his way over to talk him into joining some of the others, when the telephone rang. He glanced about; seeing none of the girls at hand, he answered it.

An operator with a cute drawl said that Houston was calling Mrs. Alfred Royce.

· 4 ·

He found Beth standing in the doorway between the kitchen and the dining room, her right elbow resting in her left hand, the back of her right thumbnail clicking against her front teeth. She was surveying the food and dishes heaped on the table and sideboard.

"Oh, that Mother," she said to Alfred. "Why does she always call at the wrong time? She has a genius for it. Somehow when Papa was alive the calls came at a better time. Here, Alfie, carve a few slices and then ring the gong. I think things are ready. Where's Lizzie? Oh well, she'll show up if you need her. She knows where everything is."

"Go on," he urged. "Your mother's waiting."

"I don't want to."

"You have to."

"It'll take forever."

"Use the extension in my study, dear, and take your time. Lock the door so you won't be disturbed."

He gave her a shove of a pat on the shoulder.

As soon as she was gone he threw open the doors and called. In no time he was besieged by outstretched plates, and he sliced the cold ham and hot roast beef with a flourish. Jabber and clatter filled the room, and everyone exclaimed how wonderful the rice casserole smelled—cooked with olive oil, garlic, and sweet basil. The Grenache rosé was the most popular of the wines he had opened, and the three bottles were emptied fast. Horace offered to open another, and, though to let a guest, even an old friend like Horace, open the wine was not to Alfred's liking, he let him, being busy supervising.

The orange sunset made the room mellow.

Before he served his own plate, Alfred stepped among his guests, making sure they wanted for nothing. They were scattered through the living room and gallery, on the floor, on chairs, on steps in the patio, and they kept telling him not to worry. "I'm not worrying," he would answer, "I am caring." He meant that, at the luckiest, worry is but allayed, trickles off, whereas care can be fulfilled and so ease the mind.

Leon and his girl, Robin, were side by side on the floor of the sun porch.

"What a sweet man he seems to be," Robin murmured to Leon, and he murmured "Yes."

"Professor," said Chantal, who was near them on a straight chair, "you have counted your flock? We are all present? All grazing?"

Leon looked at Chantal sharply. Because she was older than he and not obviously attractive, he had paid no attention to her. But what she said, especially after Robin's savorless praise, pleased him. He saw in her another who cherished Alfred, this good man, who was delighted even to know him. They were a society so secret, Alfred's true admirers, that they scarcely spoke of what they shared, so Leon felt; they knew one another by their glances.

Alfred was a tall, fat man, but his fat was so evenly distributed that people had an impression of his size which "large" or "well-fleshed" satisfied. He was physically indolent, a sitter and reader, but he moved, as now among his guests, so lightly and quickly, his weight forward on the balls of his feet, that people thought of him as a vigorous man in good condition.

"Is his voice always like that?" Robin asked.

"What do you mean?" said Leon, frowning. "Is it always high? It's naturally tenor."

"No, no, I mean does he always sound interested?"

"He is responsive, if that's what you mean. I've never heard him sound bored, if that's what you mean, even when he must have been bored. In seminar I've heard him dismiss a stupid idea someone put forward, but never in a dismissive voice, if that's what you mean."

"You needn't be so aggressively defensive."

"You're getting at something. What?"

"Lord, Mister," said Robin, "I just wonder what he's really like behind that impressive front. He's interesting. Do you mind if I like him?"

"So it's a front, is it."

But Leon could not put much into this last statement. He too breathed the intellectual air of the age and unthinkingly assumed that behind the façade everyone *really* was different from what he seemed, *really* was worse than he seemed. Though Leon himself did not hesitate to remind another of the weakness, disease, malice in those the other loved and admired, of the coils of feces moving in the hand-

somest and sweetest-smelling body, he now resented Robin for practicing what he practiced. Her assumption that the soul was struc-
turally hypocritical violated his experience of Alfred. Even so, being
psychologized enough, he did not trust his experience and so attack
the assumption, but looked with suspicion at his experience of Alfred's honest goodness: Leon assumed that his understanding of his
experiences had been distorted by some hidden wish in his own
buried, *real* self.

"You have mayonnaise on your chin," he said coolly.

Robin offered him her chin, which he wiped with his paper napkin.
She touched her forefinger to her lips and then to his. He wiggled his
nose at her. During this byplay they watched each other like hawks.

At each of his parties Alfred found occasion for a toast. He stood
for a moment now alone at the dining table, debating whether to offer
the toast before he ate. Beth would miss out on it if he did so, to be
sure, but it seemed to him that the moment was right. The mood of
the party was quiet and easy; people had been drinking for a while;
the general friendliness had not yet begun to form amorous clusters.
He decided not to be so formal as to go about making sure that every
glass was full; anyone with an empty glass could borrow a sip from a
neighbor to drink the toast.

He filled his glass with dark red cabernet, stationed himself sidewise in the doorway between the patio and the living room, where
everyone could hear him easily, and raised his glass. Those who saw
him shushed the others. Those around corners moved to where they
could see him.

"Friends." When he was excited his voice rose and his articulation
became clipped. "I have a very pleasing announcement to make." He
caught a glimpse of Beth peeking out through the Venetian blinds in
his study. He held his glass up in invitation, but she shook her head
and faded back out of sight. "Brewster Adams"—Brewster, who was
perched on a stool next to Virginia Skellings' knees, started, blushed,
pointed to his chest, and said "Me?" with his lips—"Brewster received word a few days ago that as soon as he passes his bar exam in
the fall he will receive a year's appointment as clerk to Chief Justice
Stankle in Sacramento. This is particularly fortunate since it will permit Brewster to discover by inside experience whether he wants to go
into politics. Shall we drink to his deserved good fortune?" He asked
Brewster if he wanted to say anything; he did not.

In the form of happy encouragement Alfred limited their roistering
by giving them permission for it. By accepting the gift of his permission they made decorum their responsibility. He promised dancing in
an hour and a half or so, after the dinner had settled. Then they
toasted good fellowship and cheered and laughed.

18

Alfred was sitting on the piano bench by Aldo, enjoying Horace's description of an absurd dispute, originating over a cat, which he had just arbitrated between the Inland Seamen's Union and a Stockton barge company. Alfred had put his last bite of beef in his mouth when the telephone rang. He was grateful to Sybil for getting up immediately and going to answer the extension in the back hallway.

"Horace," said Aldo, his eyes behind his rimless glasses crinkling with anticipation, "I am reminded by your story of the tugboat cat of an adventure I had with a cat that got stuck on a fire escape. I was living in New York at the time. Where's Beth, Alfred? She has a proper aversion to felines. This anecdote was made for her."

"Beth!" Alfred started up and looked around. "I assumed she was still on the phone. But it just rang again. Where can she be? Excuse me."

He darted about, not finding her among the guests. He went into the back hallway.

"Daddy," Sybil said, "it's Chrissy, and she and—"

"Where's your mother? Have you seen Beth?"

"I don't know where she is. Anyway, Chrissy and Rose are asking me to go over, they're not doing anything. So I thought, why can't they come to the party? You don't have enough women, Daddy. There are three men left over." She whispered. "You even invited old Elsie for old Aldo, but Lizzie and I have five—if you count Hugh." Her voice came back up. "So why can't they?"

He looked at the mouthpiece of the telephone, which she had left uncovered while she was talking to him. He did not like Chrissy, and Sybil knew it. He was tempted to refuse Sybil's request just to punish her for this stratagem she was using on him with such disingenuous innocence, her face and voice all childish eagerness but the mouthpiece turned in his direction. Still, it was true that two more lively nineteen-year-old girls would help the party when the dancing started. He said that of course the girls could come, he would be delighted to have them. As he said this he gave Sybil a look meaning that she had not got away with anything. She blushed a little and half turned from him; her voice was audibly false-eager as she relayed the invitation to Chrissy.

He found Beth in their dressing room standing motionless in front of an open suitcase, a high-heeled black shoe in each hand. Her hair was coiled on top of her head and she was standing erect as a caryatid, eyes cast down, scowling. The suitcase was nearly filled with

19

her clothes and toilet articles, neatly folded and tucked away. She glared at him. "They won't fit in anywhere," she said furiously. She burst into tears and dashed the shoes into the suitcase.

He asked her what had happened. He tried to take her in his arms, but she was all elbows. He nearly danced a jig about her, making broken little gestures toward her. Then her shoulders sagged and she wailed, "Oh, Alfie," in a softened voice. He could embrace her.

"Mother's dying. She had another stroke this afternoon. That was Miss Pritchett who called. I didn't want to spoil your party. Oh, Alfie, she's in a coma. An oxygen tent."

He tried to lead her to the bed, but she balked. "I must finish packing. There's a plane to Houston from L.A. at midnight. I've got to catch it."

He recognized the clutching fear in her eyes. But he could not think of any way to help her that she had not already seen to. She told him that she had to be at the Oakland airport no later than eight-thirty and had ordered a cab to come fetch her at seven-forty-five. He started off to tell the guests what had happened. She caught him.

"Darling," he said, "it's only a party. They can go home or go to the movies, whatever they want. It's not seemly to be having a party at such a time."

"No! The cab will be here in half an hour. Send the girls in to me to say good-by. That's all." She burst into fresh tears. "Don't make me feel guilty for spoiling your good time, everybody's. Mother may not die. Sometimes they don't for a long time."

He called the taxicab company and canceled the order.

"Oh." She sobbed. "I'm sorry. Thank you. Thank you for helping me cry. I couldn't cry. I was just standing there, I couldn't seem to move. My tears are so salty." She smiled at him, lips quivering, eyes still clutching at him. He still did not know what they were clutching for.

· 6 ·

By three-thirty the two girls had straightened the house, emptied the ashtrays, rinsed and stacked the dishes, put away the food. Sybil, the drifty, pretty one, was in bed a minute after they had gone downstairs. Lizzie, the resolute, stubby one, spent a good fifteen minutes in a ritual of ointments and cleansings. Then, though she was the advocate of regular hours, she pulled her robe around her and plunked herself on the foot of Sybil's bed.

"Sibling?" Lizzie said.

"What do you want? Oh, my God, you want to talk."

"I was thinking about Granny."

"I doubt it." Sybil spoke from the irritation of one who has been yanked from sleep for no good reason, but she was immediately conscience-stricken at what she had said. "Okay, Liz, I'm sorry too."

"You know, Mother's going to inherit that house and furniture, to say nothing of all those stocks and bonds."

"Elizabeth! You've flipped. I thought you were gone on Indians." Sybil buried her head under her pillow.

Lizzie bristled, as she always did at the faintest breath of criticism of her beloved Pueblo Indians. "What are you getting at?"

Sybil sighed, resigned herself to talk, and propped herself on her pillow against the headboard. "You're always yattering about how wonderful it was the way they did without money at San Refugio—"

"It *is* wonderful."

"Sure, and here you are at four in the morning talking about inheritances."

Lizzie nibbled a hangnail. "It's not the money, sib, it's the effect on Mother. I was pretty young but I still remember the effect of that oil well she got from her grandfather."

"Oh, Lizzie, forget it. Tomorrow! It'll keep. I'm sleepy."

"At least I'm glad I was able to see Granny last week. She was so pert."

"Is it my fault I'm a history major," said Sybil, "and have to stay in Berkeley while you get to go gallivanting on field trips?"

"Who said anything about fault? I just said I'm glad I saw her before she—you know."

"Well, what do you have to say it to me for at four o'clock in the morning? Just to make me feel guilty, that's why, and I don't like to feel guilty."

"Sybil! You're being silly."

"If I'd been an anthropology major I'd have seen her too, and if you'd been a history major you wouldn't have seen her. So you don't deserve so much credit."

"Nobody was talking about credit."

"I haven't seen her for two years." Sybil's voice had become reflective. "Since that summer she came here on the train for a visit. She's a jolly old gal."

"What did you finally think about Joe?"

"Aha. Now we're getting down to business. I hate him."

"Oh," said Lizzie.

"The only person at the party I hated more is that friend of his. Roy Carver. They're slippery. They scare me."

"At least they aren't milksops like that Brewster you spent so much time talking to."

"Oh, I don't know," said Sybil vaguely.

"Personally, I think there's a lot to Joe. Don't you think so?"

"There's plenty to him all right. Plenty."

"Can't you imagine," Lizzie said around another hangnail, "say, having him kiss you?"

"Imagine it! He's a pro, can't you even tell that? Kiss! Why do you think they both scare me?"

Lizzie nibbled for a while. "Hugh certainly took a shine to Turnipseed."

"Oh, they'll be *close* friends, darling." Sybil flapped her hand, batted her eyes, and smirked.

"Do you think he's really like that?"

"Hugh or Turnipseed?"

"Hugh. Or both of them. I hadn't gone that far. They don't either one walk like fairies or make those gestures like you just did."

"Not in front of us, they don't. How do we know what they do by themselves? Did Hugh ever once make a pass at you in the whole year he's been living here?"

"He's always touching me when he talks," said Lizzie.

"A pass, I said. Roy Carver made a dozen passes at me tonight and he never touched me once."

"No, I guess Hugh never did. I can't say I missed it. Still."

"He and Turnipseed," said Sybil with relish, "certainly didn't seem to mind not having a woman to dance with. Chrissy worked out on them and got strictly nowhere, and if she gets nowhere there's nowhere to get."

"You talk about your dear friend as though she were a gold-digger."

"Go to bed!" said Sybil. "Leave me alone! I say all sorts of bitchy things this late at night. It's practically dawn."

"That Robin Farquhar . . ."

"Who?"

"Robin. Leon's girl friend, the one with bad skin and teeth like so." Lizzie put her forefingers to her open mouth, suggesting eyeteeth pushed out like little tusks. "If you called *her* a gold-digger I'd see what you meant."

"Oh gosh, Liz, take it easy. You aren't sleepy, you got no excuse for being a bitch."

"Did you see who she worked out on?"

"Not especially. She was talking to Woody for a while."

"Talking, little sibling? She was giving him the old rub-down with the eyes and voice. What the Koyala call making bitch-in-heat eyes."

"Yeah? I liked her, sort of."

"I hated her," said Lizzie. "And who was the one other man she

22

gave with? Horace. He's old enough to be her father, and bald, and she was really massaging the old boy's gonads. And what have Woody Ravagli and Horace Skellings got in common?"

"Money?"

"Millions and millions. That operator either has a nose like a bloodhound or else she did her homework fast as soon as she got here. Daddy wouldn't have told Leon who he was inviting to the party ahead of time, so she couldn't bone up first."

"She couldn't have just happened to like them?" said Sybil.

"Impossible. Of course, I'll admit that maybe what really attracted her most was that they were both married."

"She didn't go after Daddy."

"Oh, Daddy," said Lizzie. "What an idea."

"He's not so bad," said Sybil. "In fact, I think he's very distinguished-looking."

"He was just the next-best-looking man at the party, that's all. He's so polite, that's what keeps the Robins off. Anyway, how do we know what she'd have tried if he'd been alone—say at a party at somebody else's house and just having a good time?"

They ruminated for a while.

"The sinister thing is," Lizzie said, "I think she's intelligent."

"Boy, Liz, when you go after a girl you really take your tomahawk with you. Maybe she just happened to like them?"

"Sure. Some people find they can only build a beautiful love on a foundation of rocks. Good solid twenty-four-carat rocks."

"Eh," said Sybil. "She spent most of the time with Leon. I kept my eyes peeled."

"He looked nice," said Lizzie. "I wonder what's the matter with him that makes him like her."

"Oh, go back to your Indians. Didn't you like anybody?"

"Joe asked me out tomorrow to a movie."

"Gee, hot ziggedy dog! A double feature? And a hamburger and Coke afterwards?"

"Enjoy your callow jokes," Lizzie said. "They mean nothing to me. There is more to that man than meets the eye."

"I'll say this much for him. There's a lot that meets the eye. He's about as sexy a hunk as I've met in a coon's age."

"Coon's age. Why did you say that, I wonder?"

"An expression!" said Sybil. "I speak American! Are you going Freudian on me at this hour?"

Lizzie nibbled. "He said something about how he was passing through this white world, and it didn't make sense unless he was using 'passing' with that special meaning."

"A lot of what he said didn't make sense. So?"

"You know, Negroes pass when they can be taken for Caucasians."

"Yes, teacher, I know."

"Do you suppose he really is a Negro?"

"Elizabeth Ann, beware. You aren't on a field trip. This is real life you're talking about."

"That's true. Well." Lizzie shook herself and stood up. "Time to go to bed."

"Rah-ther," said Sybil.

"Did you hear what that Frenchwoman said to her son?"

"No, I did not hear what that Frenchwoman said to her son. Tell me, Rastus, what did the Frenchwoman say to her son?"

"Brewster and Aldo were going on and on about salaries and income taxes. It was a bore. But that boy of hers—what's his name?"

"Jean-Louis."

"Yes. Jean-Louis was fascinated and hung on their every word. Once he asked his mother what one of the words meant. Then she said to him, loud enough so everybody around heard, that if he ever began thinking about money all the time she would put him out of her house and never let him come back in again."

"Did Daddy hear her be rude?" Sybil's voice floated.

"No. He hadn't got back from the airport yet."

"Oh, well, if Daddy didn't hear I guess it doesn't matter."

"What about Aldo and Brewster?" said Lizzie sharply.

"Good lord, they're supposed to know all about money, aren't they? If they don't know that some people have bad thoughts about it, they'd better begin learning. I'm all for her, actually. I think money's a bore. You've got to have it, of course. Like water. But you don't have to talk about it much."

"*I* think she's nuts. She just said that to attract attention. Money is terribly important. That's why I like the Koyala so much—they got rid of it."

"Oh." Sybil writhed. "All my life I've been hearing how you're the logical one."

"What did I say that was so funny?"

"Just think over your last sentences. Go to bed and think them over. Go!" Sybil slid under the covers and shouted something unintelligible.

Lizzie laughed with a touch of embarrassment. "What I mean is—"

Sybil poked her head out. "Go to bed! You're out of your mind."

"Anyway, I got a date out of it."

"And I didn't? Sadist! Monster!"

Nancy yelled. Both young women looked stricken. Lizzie went into Nancy's room and soothed her with promises to be quiet.

Sybil was back to sleep before Lizzie came out of Nancy's room. Lizzie lay awake till dawn, thinking about Joe. She wondered especially why his laugh sounded so strange—full, yet measured, at once sensual and forced, ironic in tone even when there was nothing apparent to be ironic about. She speculated on what his problem was.

· 7 ·

Leon slept till noon the next day and woke up angry. The sky was still leaden with the usual morning overcast. The weather was not exactly chilly, but there was too much breeze to suit him. He stood in front of the hot plate in the bathroom, unable to decide whether to reheat some rancid-smelling coffee or wait the half-hour it took to make fresh coffee. He opened and drank a can of prune juice and put the old coffee on to reheat. Out of habit he made up the daybed on which he slept, and he got dressed; but he thwarted habit by not shaving first thing after breakfast. Not shaving was for him an excess of slovenliness. He brushed his hair, searched his face in the mirror, brushed his teeth, and stood over his desk, waggling his jaw irritably.

This was the moment he had prepared for for months. His teaching duties at St. Anselm's College were finished for the year; he had taken care of every detail of his domestic affairs, down to getting the carburetor of his old car adjusted. But now that he was about to sit to his task, he did not want to. He had passed his preliminary examinations and got along well with the professor who was directing his dissertation. Moreover, he felt fortunate in comparison with most of his colleagues: he thought the dissertation was worth writing. He often said that he would have made the study and written the book even if there were no question of a Ph.D. and a career of college teaching at stake. His subject was "Political Theories and Practices of Four Renaissance Thinkers—Machiavelli, Calvin, Ignatius, and Bacon." He could read the languages, and he was fascinated by the similarities and differences among the four men. The topic was sufficiently unorthodox and loose to have occasioned dispute in the department, and it had finally been approved mostly as a sign of the committee's confidence in him to do a good job, however lacking in scholarly circumscription it might be. That had been two springs ago. Even as he had been doing the core of the reading last summer, he realized that he could play with the elements of his subject easily and solemnly enough to get his degree with little pain, but he also came to realize

25

that if he was to write a book that mattered he would first have to put his own ideas about society into order. He had to have his own theory of the state before he could hope to say anything important about theirs. This discovery had come early in the fall, when he had just begun at St. Anselm's and was absorbed by the problems of teaching. He had, therefore, postponed further work on his dissertation and gone late into Alfred Royce's seminar in the philosophy of law, to clarify his own thoughts. Now, after the most exciting course he had ever enjoyed, he was wonderfully clear about Alfred's opinions; he thought those opinions were right; he thought he had made them his own. But at this long-prepared-for moment, waggling his jaw and scratching his right buttock, he did not want to sit at his desk and write the first sentence.

His thoughts had flickered toward Robin a few times since he had got up. Now they dwelt on her. The more he thought about her behavior at the party, the angrier he became. He dialed her telephone number, but there was no answer.

He had had difficulty with Calvin. His committee had given him a dozen (thickheaded) reasons for not including Calvin in his study. The more opposition he had run into, the more stubbornly he had defended his choice—and had also complained to his friends about how the faculty's unimaginative pedantry was threatening to smother him. Now, after a year of stagnant victory and two semesters of Alfred's seminar, he was no longer attracted to Calvin. Yet, out of stubbornness, he had not seriously contemplated dropping Calvin and finding another to take his place. Such a reversal on his part would look like a victory for the pedants' judicious counsels and also would make him appear to have fought that battle merely for the sake of winning it. He felt aggrieved that he could not make an honest change of opinion without losing face. However, instead of actually changing his opinion and getting to work, he nursed his grievance.

He had a mind which comprehended logical connections firmly and rapidly but which seldom made images. Now, however, seated at his desk, his jaw on his fist, staring at the magenta desk-blotter before him, an image appeared unsummoned in his mind: of Robin's face tilted back in laughter at one of Horace Skellings' no doubt fatuous jokes. Leon felt his head throb and flush hot. He had talked with Skellings just enough to type him as a goatish old bureaucrat with nothing but a repertory of stories to recommend him. He had been sufficiently bothered by Skellings to ask Alfred a more personal question than was strictly proper—how long Alfred had known Horace. When he learned that the two had been in law school together, Leon forgave Alfred for having Horace at the party: loyalty to an old friend would excuse a worse offense than this. But he could not forgive Robin for playing up to Horace. What especially bothered him about this unwonted image was the way her mouth moved. The flesh of her face, because of the acne pocks, was not very expressive, but her eyes and mouth he found animated and charming. Her lips seemed rather small in her broad face with its almost heavy jawline, but they were perfectly defined and smooth, or seemed so by contrast with her uneven skin. One expression, which her lips sometimes assumed when he separated from her after a long, deep kiss, he had felt was peculiarly his, just for him: a soft, voluptuous, involuntary motion as of a rich red flower closing for the night after a day of warmth and bees. Watching her lips at these moments moved him to a pure erotic pleasure as nothing else had ever done. It hurt him with pleasure to see her mouth, after having opened to him in full trust, fold into itself again—hurt him flatwise between the heart and the stomach. Yet the image of her that was now assaulting him, which he took without question to be an image from memory, showed her mouth unfolded in laughter at Horace's stupidities exactly as it unfolded to Leon's kisses, and then showed it slowly folding again to Horace as Leon had until then seen it fold only in the privacy of their embrace.

At two-thirty he dialed again, intending to call off their date for dinner that evening. There was still no answer. His agitation would not permit him to remain seated or even to stay in his two-room apartment. He shaved and then walked up the steep hills to Parktilden Village to call on Peter Hazen, a sociologist he had met that spring. Peter was not at home. This straw of frustration broke the back of Leon's weak rage. He collapsed in laughter, lay on the lawn for a while, basking in the sun, and strolled home. At six-thirty he dialed Robin's number again, hoping to get out of the date, not because he was still hating her so much as because he just wanted to be alone. Her roommate, Amanda Lily, answered; Robin was in the shower; he sighed and told Amanda Lily it wasn't important, he'd come by at seven.

· 8 ·

Robin had been awakened by Leon's first call, but by the time she had stumbled across the room he had hung up. She had such difficulty collecting her wits when she first woke up that she often failed to get to the telephone when it yanked her from sleep. Usually such a failure upset her. What had she just missed, perhaps forever? But this morning she dropped the instrument back into its cradle with a "Pff"; she had been spared the effort of being charming before coffee. Robin had packed a number of her mother's principles intact from child-hood: a lady never yawns in the presence of a gentleman; a man who neglects to hold a lady's chair at table is no gentleman; always answer the phone "with a smile in your voice." Today Robin did not worry at having missed the call, but yawned and practiced stretching as Francis, her drama teacher, had taught her. "Like a cat, darling, not like a stiff old bitch, like a cat. Arch your back, arch your fingers, arch your throat. Then go limp. Like a cat." Of course she felt like stretching first, but practicing the luxury made her enjoy it the more.

She went through her morning routine automatically, and by the time she had shaken herself together she knew with satisfaction that she was feeling fine. She had graduated from college; she was getting away from stale Berkeley; limitless possibilities opened before her speculations. She did not know exactly what she was going to do, after visiting her mother for a few days; but nothing she could think of seemed less than exciting to her. Her keenest impulse was to go to Detroit and get a job on an assembly line. Francis had wounded her by saying (to a "candid" friend, who had passed it on to Robin as soon as she had got her in the company of their competitors) that Robin was too ladylike and couldn't be any good as an actress until she knew what *real* people were like. Besides, she was tired of academic, intel-lectual men. Leon was all right, she liked him fine, in fact she loved him quite a lot. But he picked at things too much. What she wanted was men who didn't get sidetracked by little things but drove for what they wanted. She wanted them to let her do most of the talking but not pay too much attention to what she said. Working stiffs, factory workers, real men.

All roads eventually led to New York—to off-Broadway little the-aters, preferably in Greenwich Village, where informed audiences went to artistically serious productions of experimental and classical plays. Still, even her goal was not tediously fixed but danced with possibilities. Perhaps she would turn, after making her off-Broadway reputation, to Broadway itself if its commercialness and vulgarity were not hopeless; perhaps even to television. She would have to wait and see. Meanwhile, everywhere she looked she saw approaches to her shimmering goals. Her immediate problem was to decide which of the many ways to take. She was going to turn her back to the past, that was certain—to her family, the university, Berkeley, Leon, Cali-fornia. A new start, and New York was her destination. Experience in the theater or experience in life, which did she need more? Which theater should she go into first? Which part of "the field," as Francis called life outside the theater, should she explore first? She always tried to be cool and rational when she thought about it, but her imagination would get so caught up with the excitements of following out one or another of the possibilities that she would forget that her career was supposed to be seriously affected by whichever choice she made now. Anyway, secretly she did not want to make the big choice that she often talked about so brightly; she wanted to make herself available to whichever possibility came along first. She took it for granted that her getting ahead in the theater would depend upon a few key men far more than upon training or talent, and she could not possibly know ahead of time who these men would be or what they would want of her. She kept as her secret motto what Francis had written in the one-volume Shakespeare he had given her after her performance as Ophelia: *Readiness is all.*

Now, still in her pajamas, she realized she was daydreaming and sprang from her chair and went to take a shower. She had a week's work left before she could go home to visit her mother and then take off for the East. Her job was transferring research data onto IBM cards for a botany professor; because she was allowed to set her own hours, she had worked little toward the end of semester, promising to finish off the job after finals were over; the time had come for her to keep her promise.

When she was putting on her eyelashes the telephone rang. She sat with her hand on it while it rang three times; then she answered.

"Darling!" It was Francis. "Mudge *wants* me!"

"How wonderful for you! Who wants you?"

His voice lowered. "Mudge Arena Theater."

"Really!" She had never heard of it. "How thrilling. When?"

"I must be there June twenty-second. And they say I can pick my own assistant."

"Oh, Francis, I can't say how pleased I am for you. It's the break you've been needing."

He purred.

"What are you going to do?" she said.

"Stage manager, and they've left it open about which show I'll direct. Of course, I want *Bunny Boy*. We'll see. Isn't it exciting?"

"You deserve it, Francis. You've stuck to your guns. It's the beginning. I feel it in my bones. It's the beginning for you. How many shows are there?"

"Six. The first one opens July Fourth. Nothing much, you know, summer stuff, froth for the holidays. But they're thinking of Strindberg for later. They mentioned *The Ghost Sonata*. Can you imagine? But it all depends on the adaptation. They hope to get Tennessee Williams to do it. He owes so much to Strindberg, you know, and he's a Saint Louis boy himself. We'll see."

29

"But Francis, adaptation? You always say what butchery is done in the name of adaptation."

"*Tennessee Williams?* Darling, this is summer stock." His voice became cold and his diction clipped. "I want you to come with me."

"Me! Francis! I thought—Harold?"

He sighed. But his voice remained cold and clipped. "Harold is sweet, he has lots of ability. But I need somebody I can absolutely rely on. You have never let me down. I've never heard of your letting anybody down. You know, Robin, you have a reputation worth having. Now I can't guarantee you a part. In any case, you know what I think—you should go into the field for a while. Saint Louis offers plenty of opportunity if you want to stay there—factories, offices, the South. . . ." His voice sank. "Merrill Oxford is expected."

"Who? I missed the name."

"Merrill Oxford. We expect him for three shows in August. We're committed to the tune of a thousand dollars at least."

"Would I get paid?" she asked.

"Keep. Transportation. Lagniappe." She could imagine how his free hand tossed. "There's the one thing, Rob. If Merrill does come, *I* want to get to know him."

"Naturally," said Robin. "So do I."

"I mean specially. You know."

"Aha, AC-DC, is he?"

"Mmm?"

"You mean he works on both sides of the street?"

Francis fluted. "Rob-bin! I should have given you Emily Post, not Shakespeare. Really."

"Oh, Francis, I am sorry. But you have always been so open, so nonconformist. Harold?"

"That's what I mean, you must go into the field. You've been in the groves of academe too long. Truth truth truth, shout shout shout. Now, working people—they know there are some things one *just does not say*. They will teach you. You will come, Robin? I haven't made a mistake, have I?"

"Of course I will come, Francis. Dear Francis. This is the nicest thing anybody ever did for me. Of course you haven't made a mistake. I won't let you down."

"I know that. It's just . . . Well, you sounded just a wee bit blunt? I thought of Harold. Oh, I did. But he's so bitchy, and this is such an important summer for me."

She kept assuring him till he sounded mollified.

As she finished making up her face she decided to do what she had been putting off for over a week. She made an appointment for that same afternoon with a doctor to find out if she was pregnant.

"How do I look, darogòy?" Robin asked.

She was wearing her plum-colored sweater with her roommate's quilted skirt, which was dark yellow with tiny plum-colored flowers on it.

Leon studied her. "Twirl." She obliged. The skirt belled prettily. "Good. But you need heels."

"Oh," she said complainingly, "ballet slippers are so much more comfortable."

"With that skirt you need a trimmer line to your legs. Try heels and let's see."

She put on one black pump and one white one.

"Charming," he said. "With another costume?" She pouted at him. "Come, come, you're being frivolous, Robin. Two white shoes, please."

She looked him over as severely as he had done her. She intended to annoy him by this, but he waited seriously for her comments. She trusted his taste in clothes more than her own, and costuming was too important a matter to be petty about.

"There's just one thing wrong," she said. "You've got a hole in the seat of your pants."

He shrugged. "A cigarette hole? Who sees it?"

"I do. It's bothered me for weeks. Take your pants off and I'll mend it right now."

"What if Amanda Lily came in?"

"She took off with Pirkle ten minutes before you came."

He muttered as he took off his trousers. "Amanda Lily and Pirkle. Really, Robin, how's it possible? You made them up. What would they name their child?"

He took out the telephone directory and began thumbing through it for outlandish names. They entered brightly into the name-game. He kept chewing the inside of his cheek. She was concentrating more than was necessary on her sewing.

"Lyoshka, where are you going to take me to dinner?"

"Spenger's."

"Oh, Lyoshka, Spenger's." She stuck lower lip out and made it tremble grossly.

"Last time you said you liked it."

"It's fine," she said. "But I had my heart set on going to the city. After all, you know—Saturday or Sunday?"

"You're really and truly going home?" She nodded. He sighed. "I know it, yet it hasn't sunk in all the way. But that's why we're going to Spenger's. I don't want us to waste our last nights on movies and such like."

"Do you love me?" She had finished the mending and was smoothing the trousers on her lap.

When, as now, she asked this question in a properly flirtatious voice, he could say in a similar tone that he loved her; he said it now.

"Well, then," she said in the same voice, "we can have one nooky first and then go to a good restaurant in the city."

"Ah, honey." He knelt beside her and caressed her. "I'm so hungry. I got up late, and I had no lunch. You know, we must never spoil it." He kissed her.

She was rather hungry too, and it was kissing and murmuring she most enjoyed—though what came afterwards was lots of fun too, of course. She sighed, and they kissed again, not separating their mouths for three or four minutes.

"It's so hard to get you to spend money on me," she said.

"That's not what my bank balance tells me."

"Really?" she said eagerly.

"Yes, really. Let's go."

She hung on his arm.

· 10 ·

As they were sitting at a table in the half-filled barroom, waiting to be called to the dining room, they saw Joe and Lizzie come in. Leon started to wave, but Robin caught his arm.

"Let them find us," she said.

"You dislike them?"

"It's a little game," she said. "I want to see how they react when they discover us. What gives with the fellow—isn't his name Joe Thompson?"

Leon nodded. "He didn't say much in the seminar. He was in the Air Force in the war."

She clasped her hands and her eyes sparkled. But she did not look toward Joe. "He's a hero?"

Leon shrugged. "I just learned about it last night myself. Roy was telling Chantal and that bore you were making up to so much."

"Oh, Leon. You mean Horace. I was just flirting with him the least little bit right under his wife's eyes. Here they come. I wish it wasn't Lizzie. She doesn't like me."

Yet it was Lizzie who spotted them and suggested that they join them. She would have preferred to remain alone with Joe, as he with her, but she had acted from a reflex politeness which often made her behavior more friendly than her feelings. She knew this about herself so dimly that she could giggle as though innocent over her sudden rudenesses.

As they were still standing, Joe mentioned that he and Lizzie had more or less been planning to call on Chantal after dinner; Roy would be there. Leon eagerly asked if he and Robin could join them, and Robin, though he had not sought her agreement, said she would love it too. Joe went to phone Chantal, and Leon went to tell the headwaiter to find a table for four instead of two.

"Tell me, Lizzie," said Robin with a straightforwardness that appealed to Lizzie, "did I disgrace myself last night with Horace Skellings? Leon seems to think so."

"Oh, I don't know. Disgrace?"

"Please be honest. I know we aren't close friends, but I'm asking you this because I feel you will be honest with me."

Lizzie made a blank face, thinking, We aren't friends of any kind, close or otherwise.

"Leon says I made eyes at Horace," Robin said. "I mean—yes, of course I was enjoying myself with him. But he's so much older—he's older than my own father—it didn't mean a thing."

"It didn't?" said Lizzie. "Virginia's under thirty, you know. She's his fifth wife."

"God! I didn't know," said Robin. "Please, I want to apologize to your whole family through you. I had such a good time, and I liked your father so much. I'm ashamed of myself."

"Nobody's keeping score on you. Forget it."

"But you wouldn't have flirted so much with him, would you?"

"Me!" Lizzie snorted derisively. "Good lord, no." At this left jab in the belly, Robin's eyes fell. Lizzie giggled. "It's different for me. He's sort of like an uncle. I've known him all my life. Besides," Lizzie went on, crossing with a right to the jaw, "I wouldn't *ever* flirt with a millionaire."

"Oh God, he's a millionaire."

Lizzie liked Robin the better for her gasp when she said "Oh God"; she thought she was ashamed. But then a little inward smile wandered onto Robin's lips, as though some suspicion was confirmed, and Lizzie did not know what to think. She was beginning to like Robin a little, without disliking her any the less.

At dinner Robin said to Joe, "You were a fighter pilot?"

"Fighter pilot! Oh, Mrs. Thompson, look what your son done done. I was nothing but a radioman in a bomber."

"Oh," said Robin, "nothing but! Tell me about it, what it was like, what you did."

33

"Well," said Joe.

"Did you get any medals?"

"The usual—an Air Medal and two or three Oak Leaf Clusters."

Lizzie was not sure whether Joe's reluctance to answer Robin's questions was caused by natural modesty or a dislike of being pressed. She rather thought it was the latter. But she wanted to know what he had done in the war, and as long as Robin would get the blame for pushing, if blame there was to be, Lizzie did not stop her.

"I bet," Robin said to Joe, "you did more than just complete some successful missions." He laughed. "Come on, Joey, what was it like?"

"Well, I'll tell you. Nervous. Bad on the nerves. Waiting to go on a mission was jittery, and taking off with a full load was as bad as having a dentist fill ten cavities without Novocain, and sitting up there with flak on every side was bad, and having a Messerschmidt on your tail was real bad. It was just about all nerves. No muscles to speak of." He had put down his fork and knife.

Robin reached her left arm across the table and squeezed his hands. "I never talked to a real hero before."

He grunted. "It's over and done with now. Hero? I never met one, myself."

Lizzie was not easy at seeing Robin touching Joe, even above the table. She turned to Leon. "What branch of the service were you in?"

"Merchant marine." He dusted off some oil-tanker anecdotes for them, and they finished the meal in light spirits.

"Joe." Robin's voice dawdled.

Lizzie watched her closely. She was addressing Joe too often and too winningly.

"Joe, what kind of a lawyer are you going to be?"

"A good one, I hope. Any ambulance I chase, it's going to be a Cadillac ambulance."

Lizzie was so engrossed in watching Robin smile that she neglected to laugh at his joke. It seemed to Lizzie that Robin's face was a lumpy, impassive mask of a woman in her thirties, in which nothing moved but the sensitive lips and brave eyes of the twelve-year-old girl wearing the mask. Thinking of Robin as wearing a mask allowed Lizzie to assume the stance of anthropologist. Lizzie had a strong natural curiosity, which she used anthropology to strengthen; she thought it gave her a franchise greedily to peer into other people's souls.

Robin asked Joe again which kind of law he was going to specialize in. As she sat listening to his answer her mouth made first a lopsided, winsome smile at his facetiousness (he expanded on how much he would have liked to go into canon law) and then settled into a bow of repose, making occasional tiny twitches of interest at the corners as he became serious (he would have to start out with his uncle, who more or less specialized in income-tax law, but what he aimed for was to become a public prosecutor).

Lizzie, her curiosity unleashed and her zest for categorizing swollen, watched Robin with intentness. She saw these movements of Robin's lips as expressing a girl's shy flutter at getting an attractive man to pay some attention to her; the real Robin was timid and sweet, only the mask was bad.

The men were watching Robin's mouth and eyes too, but they were feeling what they saw and returned their feeling in their seeing. Theirs was a small, undifferentiated, erotic pleasure of which everyone was conscious.

That the men should find and show such pleasure in watching her, Robin accepted as natural, like the odor of roses in the Codornices Rose Garden, through which she had walked on her way to campus for two years. Lizzie's round stare made her bristle, if only because it was alien and unexpected. She kept track of those round blue eyes and at the same time tried to follow what Joe was saying about insanity and free will. Her lips became motionless and slightly thinner. She saw that she was losing the men's attention but not Lizzie's.

"You know, darling," she said up to Leon, snuggling his arm, "there's something I don't understand. You told me Professor Royce is a specialist in labor law? And you aren't much interested in labor law? And here's Joe interested in criminal law? Well, what could Professor Royce tell you fellows that you were so impressed by him? Because there's no doubt," she said to Lizzie, "they are very impressed."

"The philosophy of law," said Leon, flipping the end of her nose with his forefinger, "and a fish restaurant is no place to explain what that means."

"You know, Lizzie," said Robin, "I think you are the luckiest woman. Your father is so respected, and he's always a gentleman."

"Yes?" said Lizzie.

"How do you know whether he's always a gentleman?" Leon asked.

"I saw him at a couple of parties by himself, a while ago."

"Oh yes?" said Lizzie.

"You never told me," said Leon.

"The things I haven't told you, Lyoshka, liubeémy . . . He liked to drink."

"He got tiddly?" Lizzie asked.

"Tiddly! He got swacko," said Robin, and Joe laughed. "What impressed me so much was once I went out to the kitchen and there he was flat on his back on the floor, singing away in Italian."

"*Lasciatemi morire*?" Lizzie asked, chewing a nail.

"I don't know," said Robin indifferently. "There were three or four people around."

Joe began singing Monteverdi's song in a voice surprisingly thinner than his speaking voice. Lizzie, who was having a touch of hay fever, scrubbed her nose with pleasure.

"That's it!" Robin murmured, clasping her hands. She did not in the least remember whether that was the song Alfred had been singing. "Only louder."

When he finished, Leon, aggrieved, said to Robin, "Why didn't you ever tell me about this before?"

She shrugged.

"You know," Leon persisted, "how much I admire him."

She shrugged again and said to Lizzie, "Anyway, I think you're the luckiest girl I know. My father got drunk too, but it was different. When I was four years old he left my mother for a gallon of angelica, and the last I heard he was living with a new gal every day or two on Skid Row. That was several years ago."

She felt Leon's arm press her hand, and saw Lizzie's face blank as a cow's. It was Joe she was not sure of: she did not know whether his slumping down a little in the booth and lowering his heavy lids indicated withdrawal or sympathy. She had detected remnants of a soft accent in his speech.

"My folks," she said to him, "came from the South, and my mother always told me how important it was to be a lady and associate with gentlemen. I know that's awfully old-fashioned and strange nowadays, but I do enjoy being in the company of gentlemen."

"Well, now," said Joe, "gentlemen. It's just a good thing times have changed. If they hadn't, you could be owning me right this minute."

"You mean," said Lizzie avidly, "you have slave ancestors?"

"Yes, my dear, like most people I have slaves perched in my family tree. The difference is, I *know* they're in mine. I know the name of one of them—Emma. She had six children by her husband and two by her owner, and my grandfather on my father's side was one of the two bastards. They lived on a plantation east of Jefferson, Mississippi, and that owner's name was Farquhar too."

"Imagine!" cried Robin. "My folks came from Louisiana."

"Let bygones be bygones," said Joe.

"Just think," said Robin, "here you have slave ancestors, and Leon's parents were Russian Jews, and my mother's father's folks were Orthodox and came from Serbia. That's where I get these broad

36

cheekbones and this wide pelvis." The men's eyes followed the small gestures with which she accompanied these words. Lizzie was filling with something to say. "Lizzie, you're the white Anglo-Saxon Protestant of the group. How does it feel to be a Wasp?"

"Oh," said Lizzie hastily, "my name wasn't Royce originally. I took Daddy's name, but my real father was a black Irishman— O'Hare, Bing O'Hare."

Lizzie was hurt by Leon's reaching over and patting her on the shoulder and by Robin's victorious laughter. Joe laughed too, but in his complicated manner, and he shoved her with his shoulder in an affectionate way, which meant she had been silly.

"Shoot," said Joe, "this reminds me of a cute little castle I saw in England. It wasn't too far from the base, and on a nice afternoon when I could get me a ride I'd go over there and walk around a good deal. It still had a moat, with lilies and geese. What was the name of it? Bodleian? No, Bodiam. It looked like a castle out of King Arthur and all, there on a hillside with pastures and a village and a copse or two. Of course there weren't any roofs left, but from a ways off it was the nicest little walled castle you ever did see. I thought about it a lot, I don't know why. The nobility that used to live there were the most important for miles around. And why? Because they lived in *it*. That's the great thing. You take a wide open countryside and build a pretty prison on a certain spot, and then you tell everybody, 'Nobody's allowed in here but us and our friends,' and lo and behold, you become the most important people in that country. Everybody wants in. All those free people out where it's beautiful and easy, they want into that prison. That's what that castle was like inside, a prison. Lizzie, what's the matter with you, girl? Robin so nicely puts you into Castle Wasp and calls you a lady, and here you rush out to be on the wrong side of the moat with us peasants."

"Ha!" she cried. "And where do you want to be, in or out?"

"In, Lizzie, in. That's the place to be. All those marauders and invaders and who knows what else. In! In!"

Robin pretended to join in the laughter. Lizzie and Joe were rocking into each other, and she saw they were set against her. Leon did not seem to realize how they were cutting her out. She held his arm the tighter, as though with delight and affection. He bent, still laughing, to rub noses with her.

· 11 ·

Chantal lived on a short block on Sixty-third Street. The front of the gray house was absurd: the lower half was conventionally right-

37

angled, but a fat curve took off the left corner of the upper story, and on top of the right corner there perched a would-be tower with the contours of a vat surmounted by a gigantic dunce's cap. Chantal and Jean-Louis lived in the upstairs flat, the rooms of which were comfortably large but furnished in landlord's nondescript. Robin, Lizzie, and Joe were content to go through the dining room with no more than a glance and to join Roy and Jean-Louis, who were playing checkers in the arc-sided living room; but Leon stood at the doorway, still in the dining room, studying the two rooms. Chantal, polite, stood with him.

"Are we in Berkeley or Oakland?" Leon asked her.

She gave him an odd glance. "I'm not sure," she said in apparent seriousness. "I know that *they*"—she pointed at the five in the front room—"are in Oakland. Come with me, please." She touched his elbow, and he followed her into the kitchen. *"Voici.* Now we are in Berkeley. The city line goes through the dining room somewhere. You see? Such is the foolishness of the law—drawing lines, drawing lines. Shall I make coffee, Mr. Kalish?"

"That would be fine, Mrs. Bigonneau. This is a very agreeable kitchen."

She made her quick little shrug of absolute dismissal.

He glanced through the open door of Jean-Louis's room. "The rest of the house is so-so, adequate. But the kitchen has a certain old-fashioned character. I like it. It's livable."

"Good enough. Should I better serve wine? Yes. But I have only *vin ordinaire.* What you call it? Dago red."

"Coffee, truly," he said and winced to hear himself talking like a translation from the French. "It is too soon after dinner to serve alcohol."

He stayed, leaning on the oven, watching her make coffee.

"Mr. Kalish, what is so interesting to you about my apartment? I'm not so interested in it myself even."

"I'm about to move, and I want an idea of what I might be able to get. I want more space than my student room in Berkeley, and more space normally means less beauty for the same money."

"Space, yes. Seventy-five dollars a month." She visibly decided to be more friendly with him. "I like this flat because I could take in a lodger if things got bad with me. Two lodgers, even—a *pension.* I would stay in Jean-Louis' room, and he would stay on this little back porch." She shrugged. "As it is, I work for Professor Royce, and Roy takes dinner with us. He pays me fifty dollars a month, whether or not he eats every dinner. I make by."

"Make by," he muttered. "Ah, make do, or get by."

"You are a teacher, no? Please, don't blush. I appreciate corrections. Get by, good. Thank you."

"Perhaps if I got a place in the neighborhood I could take dinner with you too?"

She shook her hand loosely in front of her chest, in the French gesture meaning "too much."

"I am sure you are a good cook, Mrs. Bigonneau."

"Yes, I am a good cook. Jean-Michel, my husband, demanded that I be a good cook, and I enjoy it. But it's so much work! Moreover, Roy is my friend's friend. We will see."

Leon stepped onto the back porch. He returned, looking puzzled. "It sounds like there's a factory in this neighborhood."

"There is! Indeed, yes. Mr. Kalish, this is a bread factory two doors away. All night the blowers grind and roar. You do not imagine. On Saturday nights I never like to go out to a party or a movie, because the factory is quiet. I must stay home to enjoy the silence. Not a bakery—no. A bread factory. And what kind of bread? French bread that was never seen in France. Eh."

"That's terrible." He cocked his head. "It's always there in the background, isn't it? Like a nagging worry."

"Exactly, sir. Bread and anxiety—I feel myself so modern. My situation is most existentialist, no?"

Her large soft brown eyes, musical voice, and hard intelligence pleased Leon enormously; and she could cook well. He assumed that she and Roy were lovers, at least from time to time, and this made her the more attractive to him.

"Here, Mr. Kalish, if you please. If you will take this tray in, I shall bring some panettone. It isn't much, but something. You caught me—how do I say?"

"Unprepared?"

"No, no. An idiom. Ah, with my pants—" She clapped her hand over her mouth, and they both laughed. "It is rude. Pardon me."

"I'm serious about boarding with you. Fifty dollars a month, whether I take every meal or not."

She puckered her lips. "If you promise to correct my mistakes in English—maybe. Roy is bad, he doesn't help me."

Resolving that he would not correct her, he said that he would.

As he turned with the tray in his hands Robin appeared in the doorway. He saw with resentment that her eyes were "sizing up the situation in the kitchen" even as her voice was cheerily asking how she could help, and he got a vindictive pleasure in seeing Robin's eyes blink and drop when Chantal told her brusquely to go back into the living room.

39

Leon imagined a conflict in Robin's face as Lizzie did. But, having eczema himself, he saw the lumps on her skin as no more than the consequences of disease. The conflict which he had gradually formulated, and to notice which by now severely irritated him, was between her delicate, winsome mouth and her ever-watchful eyes. At first, six months before, her mouth had been a rose of inestimable beauty and her fearful eyes evidence of a wounded soul needing him for shelter. Now her mouth was the lure which enticed him into that destructive female possessiveness of which her cold, watchful eyes gave evidence. As he carried the tray past her he thought with satisfaction that in a week she would be leaving for good. The whole affair could die a natural death without his having to hurt her. He did not blame her for being at once attractive and possessive, any more than he blamed her for having a large bristly mole on her voluptuous belly down over the appendix. What he did blame her for was not having the mole removed by surgery, and not having the possessiveness extirpated by psychoanalysis. If she were not about to leave, he would have felt himself forced, in self-protection, to tell her what she ought to do. As it was he would be spared that thankless task. Meanwhile he allowed himself cold, reproving glances, which would get him into some trouble with her but no more than could be repaired later by the ardent kisses of impending separation.

Once they were settled with the others in the living room, he paid little attention to the conversation but bent his antennae toward Chantal, seeking virtues in her. He was especially pleased by the promptness and the absence of protest with which Jean-Louis obeyed when she told him to go to bed. Leon fantasied the pleasures of having dinner here every night, or, if not every night, as often as she would have him.

· 12 ·

" 'There is no such thing as the State,' " Lizzie declaimed.
Leon flopped.
Lizzie was sitting in a straight chair; her legs were so short that only her toes touched the floor. Without rising, she marched straight up to Leon. "That's Auden, and you'd better listen. 'There's no such thing as the State. We must love one another or die.' He's the poet that speaks for the age. When he says something like that, you discover that's what you'd been thinking all along."
The couch was a three-quarter mattress and springs pushed against the wall, covered with a brown blanket and ornamented with three little orange pillows. Chantal was perched erect in the middle of it

with her legs folded tailor-fashion, and Roy and Leon were stretched practically supine on either side of her, their heads propped at a sharp angle to their bodies. Leon flopped again, by crossing his legs the other way, but still did not say anything to Lizzie.

"That's right." She pushed her chest out at him and waggled her head, nose to nose at ten feet. "What he means is that there shouldn't be any such thing as the State. It's wrong."

"Oh now," said Joe, "I don't remember the poem too well, but I take it Auden's not a fool. It's like saying there shouldn't be any such thing as fog. Well, you know, there it is. No use complaining, as the limeys say."

Lizzie turned toward him. Her posture and voice were no less belligerent than they had been toward Leon. " 'We ought to get rid of the State,' something like that, 'we wish it wasn't there and we ought to get rid of it.' And we ought to, too." She kicked her short legs back and forth like a child.

"You're all wet," said Roy. "You'd be surprised how often poets mean what they say." Roy had been lying there chain-smoking and seemingly bored. Now, his voice was light, quick, and insulting. "Auden meant it literally."

Lizzie stopped swinging her legs and puffed.

Joe forestalled her. "Yeah?" he said to Roy. "Then I was wrong —he is a fool."

Leon, having been irked by Lizzie's energetic bumbling, waited to see what Roy would make of this challenge issued by her defender, Joe.

Roy got up in a single continuous movement, yet without taking his hands from his pockets. He managed to appear as indolent on his feet, pacing, as he had looked on his spine.

> "All I have is a voice
> To undo the folded lie,
> The romantic lie in the brain
> Of the sensual man-in-the-street
> And the lie of Authority
> Whose buildings grope the sky:
> There is no such thing as the State
> And no one exists alone;
> Hunger allows no choice
> To the citizen or the police;
> We must love one another or die.

That's clear enough, isn't it? What people call the State is a lie, and what matters is love, personal love. He's romantic? All right. Sentimental? All right. But the main thing is—the State is a lie and we've got to destroy the lie."

41

"That's what I mean!" Lizzie cried. "Wasn't that what I said? I meant to."

"No, honey," said Roy indolently, "that wasn't what you said."

"Well, I did mean to. Now the Pueblo Indians, they never had a State and they wouldn't have anything to do with ours if they could help it. You don't have any idea how wonderful it is to be with people who don't base everything on a big lie."

"Oh, yes," said Roy, "I have an idea."

"Watch it, Roy," said Joe.

Roy glanced at him, then stepped toward Lizzie. "Do they love one another like crazy?"

"No," she said stalwartly. "Just about the right amount."

"That's good." He nodded. "I'm glad of that." His entire manner changed. "For *them* it's good. If there's anything good left for *us* to do, it is to destroy the State."

"You're an anarchist!" cried Lizzie.

"Is it possible to be anything else?"

"Tya tya tya," said Chantal.

"Well, now, Carver," said Joe, "I find it possible to be a Republican."

"A Republican!"cried Lizzie. "You mean I was taken out to dinner by a Republican!"

"You were, madam. The party of Lincoln is the party for me, and the party of the Southern Democrats is not the party for me. So I am a Republican."

"So shortsighted," Lizzie said and showed every sign of settling into a lecture about changing times and politics as the art of the possible and why one should be a Democrat.

"Kill," said Roy in a voice appropriate to "Take it easy." Lizzie glanced up at him, not comprehending; her mouth opened as he went on in the same voice. "Kill. It's necessary to kill. Things have gone too far."

Leon was fiddling with a paper match. He did not look at Roy. He was no longer flopping. "And then?"

"After the State is demoralized?" said Roy, standing over him in a slouch. "Destroy it all. Begin all over. Local government in small communities, true democracy. Nothing else is fully human."

"Tya tya tya," said Chantal.

"If you would sit down," Leon said to Roy, "and quit bullying everybody, maybe we could have a civilized conversation."

Roy cocked his head to let the cigarette smoke drift up without getting in his eyes, and remained silent.

Leon suddenly leaped up. "All right, square john!"

"Here!" said Chantal. "You will sit down, both of you. This is not the way to do. Sit. Very well." As they subsided, she muttered, "Politics, always it is like this."

Roy reclined again, seemingly as relaxed as ever. Leon sat up, awkwardly twisted, and began explaining what the State really was.

"No!" said Chantal. "Perhaps it would be better that you should both go. Now you talk ideas. In half an hour who knows what you will be saying. Doing?"

"Oh, Mrs. Bigonneau," said Leon, "I promise not to raise my voice."

"It's so much fun," said Lizzie and made an O of her mouth. "Please."

"Roy?" said Chantal, and he shrugged. "I don't trust you. Tya. But go ahead." She shifted back on the couch, out of the line of fire. By having made the debate formal, she had made it difficult for them fully to realize the insult latent in their stances. She did not look worried.

While Leon was pontificating in such large phrases as "the structure of social will" and "the State as the personification of the law," Joe lolled over in his chair toward Lizzie and whispered in her ear, "Now you know what your father's been saying all year in seminar."

"These are Daddy's ideas?" she whispered eagerly.

"In a nutshell," said Joe.

"Oh good. They're so exciting."

"Revolution, yes," Leon was saying. "I'm willing to dispute revolution." Suddenly he withdrew and focused on his fingernails. "I ought to be."

"What do you mean?" cried Lizzie.

"I was named after Trotsky," he said. "I was born the day Lenin died."

Roy propped himself on an elbow. "In Russia?"

Leon nodded. "My mother was related to Trotsky's wife." Having studied a nail with ferocity, he bit it with pedantic care. "My grandfather was a *narodnik*. He was supposed to have been implicated in the assassination of the governor of some prison in the Ukraine. Anyhow he was executed for it."

"Kill," said Roy in the same "Take it easy" voice.

"And be killed," said Leon, "for what? For a better State, yes, or the hope of one. But to destroy a State which doesn't exist anyway, in order for this non-State to dissolve itself and become a Stateless, Godless society which is really the Earthly Paradise . . ." He fanned his face.

"Logic is the opiate of the intelligentsia," said Roy.

"You know what I'm going to miss so much?" said Robin. She had not spoken for a long time; everyone now turned to her, a bit surprised. "This weekend I'm going home for a while, to my mother's in

43

Bakersfield, and there won't be anybody around with two ideas to rub together. It's so restful to be among intellectuals, because here everything is society's fault, and at home most everything will be my fault again. Oh, Lyoshka baby, come home with me just for a day or two, to bridge the gap."

Joe and Chantal began laughing. Lizzie gave a snort of laughter and tried to explain about the individual's responsibility to society, but Joe's and Chantal's prolonged laughter swamped her out. Leon gazed at Robin with cold speculation. Roy's look wished to kill; he took up the coffee pot and went to the kitchen.

The sound of a door closing came from the kitchen, and Chantal went to see what he was up to. Presently she returned. "Unforgivable! He went home without saying good night. Even in your free-and-easy country, without politeness, isn't that rude? Unforgivable."

Joe found that he was awfully sleepy, and, shortly after he and Lizzie had left, Robin remembered the typing she had to do in the morning.

"Mr. Kalish," Chantal said at the door, "dinner four days a week, yes? We will work it out." She shivered. "Roy Carver, brr."

· 13 ·

"What was that four days a week stuff all about?" Robin asked in the car.

Leon did not answer her for a moment, debating whether to tell her the truth. "I've decided to move to a larger place. I'm tired of eating in the lousy restaurants, and you know how bad my cooking is. So I'm going to take dinners with her." He expected Robin to act offended, or at least upset, by this. Instead she moved over in the seat and snuggled against him. In gratitude he garnished the story. "I don't want to stay in my present place after you've gone. It'll be sort of empty, sad. Roy eats there, and he says she's a good cook."

"Roy! You're going to be pals with him after this big fight you had?"

"At least," Leon said, "he doesn't have a career all mapped out in front of him. That's something. Lawyers, teachers—he doesn't have everything wrapped in cellophane already, with a pink ribbon around it."

"You're sweet. That Bigonneau woman looks like she doesn't have everything wrapped up either. She's so French. Why do you suppose she came to California?"

"I have no idea."

44

"Well, I forgive you, darling. I have no intention of remaining faithful to you either after I go away."

"I believe," he said severely, "that she already has a friend."

"But does he eat there?"

"I don't know. No, I don't think so."

"Liubeémy, I wish you luck."

"Luck!"

"I hope she helps you bridge the gap. Please come to Bakersfield with me and help me bridge my gap? It's the same gap, sort of."

"I'll think about it."

"Good. That's settled."

"Do you know why I like you so much?"

"Tell me," she purred.

"Because you don't pretend to be good."

"Isn't it good not to pretend?"

"The best."

"Then I'm good because I don't pretend to be good."

"You're not good, you're terrific."

They were at a stop sign. She turned his face to her and kissed him. "Lover," she whispered, "take me quick."

Because her words did not come from the heart and did not arouse in him concerns of the heart, he allowed them to inflame him sexually. They rode the rest of the way to his place without speaking. There, they enjoyed themselves at a vigorous textbook job of making love. She pretended to share not just some of his pleasure but all of it. Because he did not know she had pretended this, he felt satisfied. Because she thought he was satisfied, she was content.

She had stayed overnight with him a couple of times, but it was a narrow bed. Besides, she could not get to sleep for quite a while after making love, and she had found a certain excitement in leaving his room late at night, a college girl, and walking home alone, fondling the secret of what they had just done.

She slipped out of bed and dressed quietly, so as to disturb him as little as possible. As she was ready to leave she kissed him on the forehead and lightly smoothed his hair. He murmured good-by to her.

He came awake after she left, and lay contemplating himself with melancholy. He was ashamed to make loveless love. At first he had thought himself in love with Robin, but now he believed that what had originally excited him about her had been the prospect of their having a safe love affair. He swore to himself not to make an overture to Chantal unless he was sure that they could and would love one another. "We must love one another or die." The melancholy he was presently feeling was a kind of dying.

45

14

Robin hoped that Amanda Lily would not be home yet; she wanted
to stand in front of the mirror and practice "making a mouth." Leon
had scolded her sharply the night before, after the Royces' party, for
having made up too much to Horace and Woody. When she pressed
him to explain what had offended him in what she had done, he was
at first general and angry, but then dwelt on the expression of her
mouth. He complained that he had seen her, while talking with
Horace, make the same "mouth" she made with, and for, him alone
after a long kiss. He had many times told her how he loved her
"mouth," how it thrilled him; he seemed to feel she had betrayed him
by doing it with Horace. Because she did not know what it was she
had done, but could see how powerfully it affected him, she wanted to
learn how to do it at will. As an actress, she ought to be able to do it
for effect. But Amanda Lily was already in bed, asleep.

Robin lay in bed, practicing in the dark. Perhaps it would be better
to practice without watching herself, since in actual life she would
never see it herself. The night before, they had kissed several times.
She tried to feel how the muscles of her lips moved when they
"made the mouth," but Leon had told her she had not once made it
when she tried to. She was vexed to think she might never be able to
do it at will. She owed it to her acting career to learn how. In bed now,
she tried again and again. The trouble was that she needed Leon to
tell her when she had succeeded, and he was so jealous of it that she
was afraid he would tell her she had not done it even when she had.
Something about her had made a strong impression on Horace, that
was clear—not that making an impression on a bald old married millionaire was of any importance. Still, it was fun to be able to.

15

Lizzie draggled up to the kitchen just as Sybil was pulling out a
tray to load her breakfast on.

"Oh." Lizzie groaned. "It isn't fair. Two eggs, four strips of
bacon, two English muffins with butter and marmalade, coffee with
cream, and you won't gain an ounce. And if I have anything more than
Shredded Wheat and half a banana with skim milk, I'll put on a
pound."

"Well, big sister, don't you worry. The Koyala like their womenfolk substantial."

"Wait for me, Syb. I'll be ready in a jiff. Did Mother call last night?"

"She said Granny rallied for a while and she talked to her for a few minutes."

"I'm glad for Mother," said Lizzie. "How did she sound?"

"Daddy said she sounded under control. They talked for ten or twelve minutes. He wants to answer the phone every time it rings."

"That's nice. You know, they really are the most married people."

"Oh," said Sybil, "it's not all peaches and cream. Like that time during the war when Daddy spent four or five months in Washington. I bet that wasn't all business."

"Of course they have troubles," said Lizzie with a superior air. She looked longingly at the half-banana she had not sliced onto her Shredded Wheat, and then put it aside. "Being married is a way of handling trouble together—the way they do."

"Hmph," said Sybil and took her tray.

Nancy was sunbathing in the patio, wearing dark glasses with wide white shafts studded with rhinestones. She was propped on her elbows, in front of her a horse magazine on which she was spinning a twenty-five-cent piece, and she had on nothing but a sort of diaper with gaudy polka dots.

"Nancy!" Sybil cried. "You're indecent."

"What's the matter?" Nancy said. "Men?" She pressed flat onto the sunbathing pad, her head craning around comically. "Quit scaring me, Syb. I know what I'm doing. See?" She flipped the ends of her bikini top over her back and snapped them together. "Quick as a wink."

Lizzie appeared and sat on a bench. "Hi, kiddo."

"Liz," said Nancy, "isn't it all right if I sunbathe here without a top on? Sybil's trying to make me ashamed."

"Of course it's all right, sweetie. You lie on your back and we'll tell you if anybody starts to come. Don't pay any attention to *her*. You know what she's full of—Sybiling rivalry."

"Pss," said Sybil and waved a piece of English muffin drooling with butter under Lizzie's nose.

Nancy spun her quarter again. "What is money?"

"A medium of exchange," said Sybil, who had just finished a course in economics. "It makes it easier for people to pass things back and forth all over the country and even the world."

"Yeah?" said Nancy and rolled over onto her back.

"The main thing," said Lizzie, "is to realize that money stands for some actual work somebody does. It's a symbol."

"Yeah?" said Nancy. "Then why do I like it so much?"

"Because you're a brat," said Lizzie.

"Yeah?" said Nancy. "How was your date?"

"Wonderful," said Lizzie and twiddled her feet back and forth under the bench. "It was just about a perfect date."

Nancy's face, like her body and all its members, was slim, long, and regular, the skin tan and with scarcely a blemish. The modeling of the cheek- and jawbones gave an impression of straightforwardness; yet by the slightest narrowing of the eyelids and the faintest smile she could give the impression of knowing connivance. "Plenty of canoodling?" she asked with this sly expression.

"What?" said Lizzie, sitting even straighter. "What's that?"

"Hanky-panky in lovers' lane."

"Do you have to be so common?" Sybil asked.

"Well, what does she mean by a perfect date, then?" Nancy said in the voice of an aggrieved child.

"I mean good conversation," said Lizzie. "That's what I mean. We had a sort of a party. We ran into Leon with that Robin at Spenger's—"

"Is Leon the tall handsome one?" Nancy asked. When Lizzie nodded, she rolled up her eyes, crossed her arms on her chest, and sighed voluminously.

"You know," Sybil said to Nancy, "I'm trying to enjoy my breakfast. Do you have to be so corny?"

"Well, anyway," Lizzie went on, "we ate dinner together and then we all went to Chantal's place—you know, that Frenchwoman."

"Jean-Louis's mother?" Nancy cried rapturously. "Did you see Jean-Louis too?"

"Oh yes. He and Roy Carver were playing checkers."

"I bet Jean-Louis won."

"No, Roy beat him."

"Alas," said Nancy weepily, "my defeated hero."

"If you don't shut up," said Sybil, "and talk like a human being, I'm going to pour coffee on you."

"That'll make Lizzie happy, anyhow."

"Make me happy? Why?"

"Because," said Nancy, "you like people better the browner their skins are."

Lizzie bellowed.

"Well," said Sybil, "there's something to that. From the mouths of babes."

Lizzie bellowed again.

"Last night," Nancy said, "I mean the night before last, I heard Horace say to Aldo that you had the most advanced case of reverse race prejudice he ever saw."

At this, Sybil looked sharply at Lizzie, who stopped chewing and just sat there.

Nancy glanced about quickly. "Well, he did."

Sybil put down her plate, went to the faucet, turned the hose on full force, and soused Nancy, pad, and magazine. Howling, Nancy fled through the French doors into the house. Lizzie shushed loudly. Sybil tiptoed to the faucet and, as she turned it off, kept an eye cocked on Alfred's study.

A blind went up, then a window, and Alfred's frowning face appeared. "I have nothing against your eating breakfast in the patio, but I must repeat—"

"I know, Daddy," said Sybil, "and I'm sorry. But Nancy was being obnoxious. Now go back to work, and I promise it won't happen again."

He blinked, blew them a kiss, and pulled the window and blind down again.

"Do you suppose he is actually working?" Lizzie asked.

"Why not? He always does. Oh, you mean because of Granny."

"And Saturday, and no school, and June sunshine."

"You know," said Sybil, "how he saves dull stuff for times like this."

"But his light was on when I got home at half past twelve. I bet he didn't go to bed till all hours."

"And you didn't even go in and chat with him?"

"Oh." Lizzie looked stricken. "I should have, shouldn't I? You know how we don't bother him, Mother always tells us how he works best at night? Well, I just wasn't thinking."

"So," said Sybil. "What gives with Joe? Is he passing?"

"I asked him, and he said in some states he's a Negro and some he's not. In Oregon he is, but in Tennessee—I think it's Tennessee— he isn't. Can you imagine that?"

"Yes."

"Well, it's awful."

"You mean," said Sybil, "it'd be better if all the states had one stupid bad law instead of forty-eight different stupid bad laws?"

"In a way. You'd know where you were. I hate all this crookedness. Who wants to go around living in a jigsaw puzzle all the time? Anyway, his great-grandmother was a slave, and her master had his grandfather by her illegitimately."

"So he says."

"What?" cried Lizzie. "Of course Joe's the one who said it. What are you getting at?"

"All his other ancestors are white except that slave woman? How come that slave mulatto bastard got married to a white woman? What state was that in? That ain't the way I heard it. Don't forget, Dizzie, I just took a course in the causes of the Civil War."

"Oh, for heaven's sake, does everything have to belong to a historical pattern? Statistics! Didn't you ever hear of individual differences? Anyway, I invited him to Sunday breakfast at ten—before I thought, that is. Naturally I had to take it back. But do you know why he couldn't come? He goes to High Mass every Sunday at eleven!"

"Lizzie," Sybil said in admonition, "remember about Catholics."

"He's an Anglo-Catholic."

"What's that?"

"I'm not too sure. Maybe they believe in birth control and divorce."

"Lizzie."

"And that Roy—he's weird. He's an anarchist, he really believes in bombs."

"So he says."

"Oh, Sybil, what a pain in the neck you are. Don't you ever want to know how amazing people are?"

"I got a date for tonight. I was reading a mystery story about nine o'clock last evening, and who phoned me up for a date? Brewster."

"Brewster? That feisty little guy with big glasses? He seemed nice."

"Oh, he's nice. Mother would just say he's *so nice*. But I sure don't know where you get that feisty bit. He's going into probate law with his brother. He already knows all about wills and bankruptcy and missing persons, I don't know. Lizzie," she wailed, "if he keeps coming around I'll probably learn to love him and I'll never find out if the world is amazing or not. He's my fate."

"I am your fate," Lizzie sang to the opening bars of Beethoven's Fifth Symphony, "please let me in."

"Save me!"

"Roy's certainly different. Get to know Roy."

"Not him! I'd rather have a wall-to-wall husband like Brewster."

"Well, I don't want either one of them."

"Thanks," said Sybil.

"I'm sorry."

"Are you going to fall for Joe?"

"Heavens, no," said Lizzie. "But he is interesting. Schwesterlein, why do you always think of marriage the first time a fellow calls you up for a date to the movies? I don't get it."

"I can't help it. It's just a reflex." She made a comic-book expression of distress. "Do you know what I'm going to be when I'm fifty years old? I'm going to be a married old maid."

The telephone rang. They sat waiting to see if Alfred would call one of them or Nancy. When he did not, they just sat. It was a quarter of an hour before he appeared in the doorway of his study.

"That was Beth. Her mother died a little while ago."

"Oh," said Lizzie in a small voice. "How long will Mother stay in Houston?"

"At least two weeks, maybe three. She must turn things over to a reliable lawyer and break up the house." He was audibly moved. "I would have gone if she had wanted me. She was determined to do everything herself."

"Of course," said Sybil. "How did she sound?"

"Fine," he said, turning to go back in. "Just fine."

"What about Donald?" said Lizzie.

"He will be let out to go to the funeral. But Beth is the executor of the estate." He closed the door behind him.

"What about Uncle Donald?" said Nancy.

They turned. She was leaning against a post, only her head, shoulder and upper arm showing. Lizzie glanced at Sybil, who shrugged.

"He's in prison," said Lizzie. "He's an embezzler."

"I thought he was a high-school principal," said Nancy.

"He was, but he was caught embezzling. Stealing school funds. They sent him to prison for a year."

"Come on out, honey," said Sybil. "The pad's dry."

"Mother's voice wasn't fine at all," said Nancy.

"What do you mean?" cried Lizzie *sotto voce.*

"You listened on the extension!" Sybil whispered

Nancy stepped into the double-width doorway, slim, taller than either of her older sisters, her contours already beginning to be female, in plain view of anyone who might come to the gate, stark naked.

"She was sobbing," Nancy whispered. Lizzie and Sybil registered shock at her nudity, but they did not move while she told them her clandestine information. "She sounded desperate—you know, the way she does sometimes. And she kept telling Daddy she loved him."

They drove her back downstairs to her room, saying harsh things to her without raising their voices, and made her promise to get dressed. They returned to the patio.

"What's got into her?" Lizzie asked.

"It's the Peterson in her coming out." Sybil was breathing hard.

"I mean," said Lizzie, "maybe it's serious. I never saw her do so many bad things all at once."

"Maybe Granny's spirit entered into her. Granny was a mean old witch."

"That's not funny at a time like this."

"Not a stitch on! Eavesdropping!"

"She hardly knew Granny Peterson at all," said Lizzie. "Why should her death upset her? Goodness, she was way over seventy."

Sybil's face wore a look of discontent. "Last night," she said unhappily, "I went down to my room a while after Nancy went to bed and I heard her crying, so I went in. Mother forgot to say good-by to her Thursday night."

"Why," said Lizzie, "that's not so. I saw Mother kiss her myself, right in the hallway by the linen closet. She was downstairs with Jean-Louis, and he came up with her when Daddy called, and Mother *did* kiss her good-by."

"She somehow doesn't think so. Which is peculiar."

"I'll go right down and set her straight."

"Wait!" said Sybil. "Take it easy on her, Liz."

Lizzie's face crumpled into lines of sympathy. Though she was considerably plumper than Sybil, her face was not so firmly gay. "Oh, the poor damned kid."

But her sympathetic intentions were gummed up by what she found when she went into Nancy's room: Nancy, still naked, was standing on her head in the middle of her bed, slowly scissoring her long legs back and forth. Lizzie rather peremptorily told her how Beth had kissed her good-by before leaving for the airport. Nancy, upside down, legs solemn as antennae feeling the empty air, gravely watched her and thanked her politely when she had finished.

· 16 ·

Robin was lying on her back on the front seat, her head propped on Leon's right leg. From time to time as he drove he would pat her affectionately or she would rootle her head against his side. Her bare left leg was bent and erect, and her right leg was balanced onto the left knee. Leon had not seen her in shorts before. She had heavy thighs which the line made by shorts thickened. Where her skin had not been enriched by sunshine, it was mostly white—not the light pink and beige of the "white" races, but untinted, without hues. Leon enjoyed inspecting her body nude; he derived a lascivious pleasure from the contrasts between the colored areas of her flesh and its dominant pallor, a pleasure of the sort he got from *fin de siècle* drawings of wicked women wearing nothing but arm-length black gloves and black stockings with purple garters. But nothing was less lascivious, more antiseptic, than the light blue shorts and sleeveless T shirt he had found her in that morning. He had looked at her costume with disapproval. "Ha," she said, "this is what the native women wear in Bakersfield. And I'm a returning native."

The drive down the center of the San Joaquin Valley was devoid of interest. The roadside towns were without exception sleazy. The most the fields alongside the highway had to offer was an occasional expanse of green. The huge ranches into which the fertile valley was divided were less like farms than like industrial undertakings. Even to a motorist's eye a rationalized ten-thousand-acre peach orchard laid out to a surveyor's transit is obviously no place where people live and have their being but a species of factory or production line. The mountain ranges bordering the valley were invisible, so that the landscape was of a prairie without the prairie's vaulting sky. Seen from above, the haze which obscured the mountains had a rather lovely quality, faintly opaline because of the dust and industrial wastes in the air. But in the midst of this haze, as Leon and Robin were now, one was chiefly aware of how it dulled the sunlight without reducing the heat, and how it blotted out the already constricted horizon.

"You know," Leon said, "this entire valley is as bad as a desert. There has been nothing but aridity and uniformity since we left the Coast Range."

"Aw, now, Lyoshka, haven't you seen even one pretty thing?"

"Not one. Have you?"

"Two. Your eyes."

He squinched them at her.

"Let's get our minds off where we are," said Robin. "We'll be there soon enough. So. Does your Ph.D. thesis matter to you awfully?"

"Yes. No, not really. Getting a good job, of course, but that's about all. Here," he said severely, "let me say what I mean. The dissertation as such does not matter a bit to me except as a sort of union card. But the subject matters enormously, and I am going to do all the justice to it I can."

"Gee," she said, "I hope when you get your degree you get to wear a robe with rabbit-fur facing on the lapels."

"What?"

"For academic hair-splitting."

For lack of anything better to do, he gave more laughter to the joke than the joke had given him amusement.

"So," Robin said, "it *is* important to you?"

"Working on the subject is."

"My God, still at it," she said. "What I'm trying to do is to make you make me feel good. If you're taking time off from doing important work to come home with me, then it means something special. See, my dopey darogóy?"

"Oh, it does mean something special. Very." He flipped her nose. "Also, I've been stuck. I can't seem to get started writing."

"That's a fast left hand you got there, mister."

"What?"

"What you give with your right hand you take back with your left, quick. To take time off from work when you aren't working anyway . . ."

Because it was true and because she sounded humorously rueful, he made a caricature of a Jewish shrug.

"Okay," she said, "why are you stuck?"

"It's funny," he said seriously. "I've done all the essential reading, I've given the subject a lot of thought. Still, all week I've been sitting at my typewriter and not getting a word down on paper."

"Tell me about it."

Because she did not know or care much about his subject but would understand what he said if he said it well enough, he talked carefully. She asked him a few questions to help him in his search for what he meant; she did not do it to learn what he had in mind but for the pleasure of helping him. At first, while he was talking about his four brilliant men and the century in which they were set, ignorance kept her quiet. But as he moved into ampler realms of speculation, she found it possible to play the role of eagerly questioning disciple. She was guided less by what he said about society and the state than by the quality of voice in which he answered her and elaborated on his ideas. She followed him as far as he had gone, till "absolutely" and "without a doubt" began to stud his sentences. But because he did not speak with a finality in his voice commensurate with that in his words, she allowed her questions to keep floating against him, as twigs in an idle stream nudge against a waterplant whose root is still holding and then drift on their way.

"Do you know what's wrong with your ideas?" Robin asked in a light voice. Knowing that she was intruding, she waited to hear his response before she decided whether to withdraw into joking or to trespass further.

He did not take her seriously. "If you can summarize my main points, I'll listen to what you think's wrong with them."

"Oh, I could summarize them. I got a B average. What's wrong with them is, you haven't made them all yours."

This he did take seriously. "You mean I sound as though I were parroting Alfred?"

"No."

"As though I said what I didn't believe?"

"No. You're not a hypocrite."

"Because I assure you I do believe that what I said is true."

"You sounded to me like you believed some of it and wanted to believe all of it but weren't yet sure."

She glanced up. From the vantage point of his lap, his dark face appeared to scowl severely and his rather small mouth to be pursed tight.

He was waiting to see if she would apologize. If she did, or if she showed any obvious signs of pleasure in his discomfort, he would discount what she said as frivolous and malicious. He was aware that she was looking up at him. Presently he glanced down. She was clearly not concerned about what she had said so much as about possible trouble from his reaction to it. He looked back at the road.

"You know, Robin, this is one of the most important things in the world."

She laughed abrasively, then cupped her mouth with her hands. "Now hear this: Whether Leon Kalish knows the exact truth about political theory is one of the most important things in the world."

"You are both facetious and unkind," he said icily.

She sat up and moved against the door. "Go ahead and be stuffy. By the time you stuff a Ph.D. down inside your already overstuffed shirt, you're going to be really stuffy."

He kept the silence for half an hour. When he saw a highway sign, BAKERSFIELD 8 MILES, he glanced over at her. She was asleep.

"Robin bird," he said, not without tenderness, and tugged at her arm. "I've been mulling over what you said, about my sincerity." He glanced at her again and recognized on her face the lost expression with which she always woke up. "There may be a sense in which you are on the right track."

"When I was in the eighth grade I learned something I never forgot." In her voice, despite the noise of motor and wind, he detected a hint of delicate woe like that now in her eyes and on her lips. "I had Mr. Carillo for civics, and I'll never forget what he said one day. He was young and all us girls were madly in love with him. They wouldn't take him in the Army because of his heart. He had to quit teaching a couple of years later. Mother sent me a clipping from the paper two or three years ago when he died. One day my girl friend Peter and I went into his office to ask him whether it was our duty to vote when we grew up, even if we didn't like any of the candidates. We didn't give a hoot about it, naturally. We just wanted a chance to talk to him and we neither one had the nerve to go in alone. He gave us the good-citizen line, the way we knew he would. So we put up a big argument, to drag it out as long as we could. 'Suppose,' I said, 'just suppose we had to choose between Hitler and Tojo for President of the United States. Aren't they both awful? I couldn't stand either one of them. Just suppose.' He said that in America we'd never have such a choice, but if we did we'd certainly have to choose Tojo. Always take the lesser of two evils. That's pretty much what democracy comes down to, he said, having to choose the lesser evil all the time. You can see why we liked him so much, and he had the neatest little mustache too. Then he sort of gazed out the window and made a funny little gesture with his hand—like this. 'Just remember, a hundred years from now it won't make any difference in the world which

55

way you vote.' I can't tell you how much that has meant to me."

Leon did not say anything when she paused. He felt deflated by that banal, nihilistic idea, as though a huge hypodermic had been eased into his soul and had vacuumed out his vitality in one suck. In his adolescence he had written some science-fiction stories full of callow metaphysics and horror. He looked back at them now with contemptuous indulgence; he had been "going through a phase." But one of the speeches had stuck with him and came to mind now: "After all, Spingarn, we are nothing but lice on a mudball which is whirling around a middling star in a middling nebula at the edge of everywhere."

"Whenever I get the blues," Robin went on, "or get to worrying too much about what I ought to have done instead of what I did, like, say, about some of the things you and I have done together, why then I just say to myself, 'Little girl, don't get so worked up. In a hundred years it won't make a speck of difference one way or the other to anybody.' "

They were coming into Bakersfield.

· 17 ·

Bakersfield was an offspring of Highway 99 and the surveyor's transit.

Traffic going south on the great highway stopped there to rest before the push over the mountains to Los Angeles. Northbound traffic rested from the effort it had just made. Bakersfield existed to feed fuel into travelers, wipe them a bit, and dispose of their detritus—to keep them moving.

Oil fields and industrial agriculture had added enough people to the town to have made it a city. Statistically it became a city. The thirty-five thousand people who lived there contiguously referred to their aggregate as a city; so did the Bureau of the Census; so did the mapmakers. But it was not a city such as men had made in previous ages. It was not arranged for the ancient reasons—protection, whim, geography, beauty, caste—which, by combining to hold citizens in and turn them back toward the town center, made it seem that the city had a heart, a soul. Bakersfield's low shoebox houses were set at a considerable distance from one another and square to the wide straight streets; downtown was where the buildings were larger. The city was laid out in accordance with that obscure obsession for right angles which had settled upon American town-making a couple of centuries earlier—it is singularly appropriate that the Father of His Country was a surveyor—and which later suited the convenience of automobile movement to perfection. The arrangement of things in Bakersfield was such that people did not take walks. Whichever way they looked, the streets came from and led toward flat land and gray sky, and these blanknesses kept the streets swept clean of almost everything but cars. Bakersfield might have been designed for the welfare of cars, to which, like service stations, the human beings were accessory.

Bell View Mobile Homes and Bell View Trailer Park was an establishment at the edge of the highway south of town where trailers were sold, repaired, and parked. Robin's mother, whose name was Ida Kuczinski, was in charge of sales; also, four evenings a week the owner of the entire establishment left her in charge of the park. The owner was Mike Kuczinski, Ida's fourth husband, from whom she was now divorced. Because her trailer was also the lived-in model to be displayed to prospective buyers, it was in the number-one plot, the one closest to the entrance on the left, next to the lot containing trailers for sale. Mike's trailer was established in number 48 plot, the rearmost one on the right. Mike and Ida were agreed on not speaking to each other except on business. But this agreement presented a difficulty: they had to appear cordial before others, to put on a good front. They saw each other in the office off and on, where at any moment a customer or tenant might walk in. They kept running into each other on the lots, where curious wives at trailer windows could always be watching them, especially since they were known to have been once married. If they met downtown—in a store or cocktail lounge—they could never be sure who was looking at them. Even in their own separate trailers they were in reach by telephone. Only when driving their cars were they immune. When they passed in their cars they pretended not to notice each other, though Ida, without moving her head, would glance at Mike sideways to see who was with him.

Bell View Trailer Park was the first in Bakersfield to be equipped, not for transients staying only a few days at most, but for permanent renters planning to stay for months at least. For nearly five years not one of the forty-eight plots had been vacant for as long as a week. Three of the mobile homes had been standing on blocks since they were first put on them toward the end of the war. It was a feature of Bell View that each plot should be provided not only with water, sewage disposal, and electricity, but also with its own picket fence and lattice arbor, even for those families who had no dogs or children and planted nothing. However, most had a few potted geraniums at least, and nearly everyone, encouraged by Mike's promise to have the handyman mow it, started a patch of lawn at one time or another—to abandon it soon to its united enemies, sun, adobe, dust, and crabgrass. The trailer park was laid out in the shape of an E, with three dirt streets leading from the highway to a transverse back street. The trailers were parked alongside the fence and arbor constructions, which were fixed at exactly equal intervals and at right angles along the three laterals and along the back of the transverse. At the back end of the center row of plots there was a cement-block laundry-and-shower building, and beside it there were a slide, a teeter-totter, a large sandbox, and a climbing maze constructed of half-inch pipe joined at right angles. Along the back row of trailers there was a row of tamarisks, half of which were stunted and dying, and lining the highway were a dozen eucalyptus, which in the late afternoon cast some shade over the lot. Up from the wash house stood the tallest television aerial in southern San Joaquin Valley, and its guy wires ran out to the corners of the trailer park like ribs of a shelter.

In addition to the plot number, everybody except two unsociable couples from Vermont, who did not even use the automatic washing machines, also put a name over the arched gateway in each picket fence; the Vermonters had taken down the ones they had found there. Robin's mother's was called Ida's Hida Way.

She was like a smaller, slightly blurred version of Robin. Her face, unpocked, was prettier than Robin's, if one did not notice the eyes.

"I am very pleased to meet you, Mrs. Kuczinski," said Leon in his most gracious voice and leaning from the hips. "Robin has told me so much about her wonderful mother that I just had to meet her. So, here we are."

"My God." She moved abruptly to one side, but erratically, not decisively as Robin moved. "Who's this you've brought me, Robbie? Emily Post's brother or something? Jesus, mister—you got me scared to call you by your right name even. The least you can do is call me Ida." She flapped her hands at him. " 'Mrs. Kuczinski'—hell, that's just an inconvenience. Come on, what's your name again?" She tapped her ear. "I'm sort of hard of hearing."

"Leon Kalish."

"Okay, Leon." She snuggled his arm as though they were on a date, and waggled her head at Robin. "Let's be friends, okay?"

"Certainly, Ida."

" 'Certainly, Ida.' " She gave him a dark glance and then threw her arms around Robin, who was standing pigeon-toed on the stoop. "It's so good to see you, lambie pie! It's so good, I can't tell you. Maybe he'll limber up a little after a while, do you suppose?" She took his near arm at the elbow and shook it till his hand flapped like a rag. "That's better." She kept flapping his arm and Robin's together and against herself as she talked. "That's much better, children. Let's go in." There was a confusion at the doorway because she refused to let go of either one of them or even to quit flapping their arms. The interior of the trailer was neat, clean, and air-conditioned. "You know, Leon, I'm going to be losing my little girl. She's my onliest one, too. She keeps talking to me about running off to New York. What's the matter with California, honey? Hasn't Hollywood got everything you could ever hope to find in New York, and close to home too? 'The theatah.' Hell." A few tears spilled from her eyes. "That's all right. Go off and leave me. I been left before, plenty. You got to learn to expect it, Leon. You know that? In this world. Come on, kids, we need a drink."

She made a direct line to the galley, where she took out whisky, glasses, Seven-Up, and ice; she poured the bourbon and mixer efficiently.

"What an amazing sense of room," Leon was saying. "From the outside I had no idea a trailer could be so spacious. It's like an apartment."

"It's the biggest size," Robin said. Her voice was bright, thin, and brittle.

"Not any longer it isn't," said Ida. "That was Christmas, honey. You've got out of date already. Christ, nowadays even the Army's out of date every six months. They've got a bigger one now—trailer, I mean. Three states won't let it through on the highway, not even when they pull it with a licensed tractor. How d'you like that? Three states that I know of, and I'm as bad out of date. . . . Leon, you know what? You'll never believe it. To get from here to my home state, which is Louisiana, you know how that trailer has to be hauled? Through Kansas. I'm not kidding you, it has to go clear up through Kansas. That's what Pierce told me."

"Who, Mama?" Robin wailed.

"Pierce." She distributed the drinks, keeping her eyes on their hands. "Come on, sit down, you're tired from the trip. Guess who lives in Twenty-three, baby? You know, The Rattler's Roost? We got names for every living unit, Leon. We think it's sort of cute."

"I noticed," said Leon.

"Yeah," she said, wrinkling her eyes at him. "He smiles. What's he up to, Robbie? College professor. Ha. 'I noticed.' "

"You mean, Mama, that Pierce is back? He's actually living here?"

"Now, you watch your tone of voice. That's no way for a girl to talk about her own second father. I ask you, Professor, is it? He's got him a new wife too, a Yankee, an honest-to-goodness Yankee from Maine."

Ida's course, which resembled that of a very slow particle in a cloud-chamber, took her near the galley again. She went in and made herself another drink.

59

Robin leaned over to Leon next to her on the couch and whispered, "Pierce used to be my uncle, then he was my father. He's the one that seduced me for a raspberry milkshake."

"What?" said Leon. He sat up and glanced around. "What?"

"He's the one," said Robin.

"I don't understand what you're talking about," said Leon.

"Don't believe her," Ida called from the galley around the corner. "Raspberry milkshake, right? She's been hipped on it ever since she was nine. 'Mama, he made me go all the way.' She told me a year later. As though he'd do a thing like that. Why, she was so innocent she didn't even know what the words meant. 'All the way.' Probably a French kiss, maybe. Don't blame him either. She was the cutest little old bunny you ever did see. I'm telling you, Leon—round, and tan all over, and so innocent."

Leon stared from one to the other.

"Oh, Mama," said Robin brightly. "You've had one too many already."

"Pierce is a good egg," said Ida. "He's oversexed, I'll admit that, but Pierce's all right. I just didn't love him enough. You know how that is? How it goes out on you? Pfft. I don't hold anything against him. A man can't help it how sexed up he is."

"But this is shocking," said Leon.

"What is shocking?" said Ida harshly. She planted herself in front of him. "Are you going to stay here for dinner? Let's go to dinner at the Waikiki, Robbie." Ida kept staring down at Leon. "Are you Jewish?"

"Yes."

"I knew it! I can always tell by their noses." She sat on his knees. "He's the best-looking boy you ever brought home, Robbie. You really are. I could go for you myself."

A car honked outside, and a man whistled.

"Mike. The son of a bitch. Who does he think I am, he can just whistle at me? Men." She put down her glass, went over to the door, and leaned half out, holding the door open so that the cool air escaped. She spoke in cordial tones. "Who do you think you are, you fat bastard, honking and whistling when my daughter just got here? My daughter is a college graduate, which is more than any Kuczinski ever has been or ever will be. And she brought a college professor home with her. I am entertaining. We are going out to dinner, thank you. I won't be receiving this evening."

"I just wanted to drop by," Mike said in a hoarse, apologetic voice. "I just wanted to see if she got here all right. I'll take over tonight, Ida."

"Thanks, Mike. That's sweet of you. It's just the honking. 'By now." She came back in to the two young people rigid on the couch. "You got to excuse me, Leon." She smiled lopsidedly. "I'm not really this bad. I mean, not all the time. I got to go lie down for a while. So." She wobbled her hips around. "Till the Waikiki—aloha." She had no sooner gone than she reappeared. "Robin. I got so worked up looking forward to having my little girl come home, I slipped myself a couple extra ones. You know? She's had it rough, Leon, remember that. I'm a busy mother. But I always did love her. You know that? I always will too. Raspberry milkshake. That's rough. It really is. 'By now, kids."

· 18 ·

Robin sat still, waiting for Leon to do something. He did not make a move, but stared into the empty tumbler he was tilting back and forth between his knees. She wanted to touch him but was afraid he would flinch if she did. Once he had flinched at her touch. She had not blamed him; she'd thought she must have somehow deserved it. But she could not stand it.

Leon was locked between two unrelenting and irreconcilable impulses: the obligation to treat Robin gently and the urge to get away. About the moral importance of the first there was no more question than about the emotional strength of the second. But to run was blatant cowardice. He occupied himself with a futile search for justifications for leaving—for getting away from the trailer, Ida, Bakersfield, Robin. He was so busy doing this that he neglected to do anything to show Robin that he meant kindly by her.

"Why don't we go swimming, Leo?" she said in a low, slow voice.

It would get them away from the trailer at least. He responded almost fulsomely and gave her an uncle-ish sort of hug.

Robin adjusted the Venetian blinds, and they began to change into their swimming suits in the living room.

"I do not want to sleep here tonight," Leon said.

Hearing the coldness in his own voice, he glanced at Robin. Her eyes fell, and her lips made a tiny smile of pain.

"All right, darling, you don't have to. The couch opens out to a three-quarters bed. That's all. You're welcome."

"The reason I don't want to is that I couldn't rest, having you in the very same room, practically, without being able to have you in bed with me."

She knew by his elaborate, if strained, manner that this explanation was mere gallantry, the truth being unsayable. She pretended to take the gallantry as the erotic compliment it pretended to be. Since they both happened to be naked at the moment, she made an obscene gesture, to which he responded obscenely. So his kindness reached her.

Half a mile toward town they found a swimming pool which was part of a new motel. The pool was a long rectangle made of light blue cement and bordered by six feet of grass-green cement. A middle-aged couple in bathing suits sat under a black and orange beach umbrella at the shallow end of the pool, watching a tan chubby little boy. He was splashing, calling to them, and swatting one or another of his five inflated bright-colored plastic toys: a duck, a ball, a life-saver and life-raft big enough for him to use, and a fish.

Leon checked in at the motel so that they might go swimming free. Before, when he had taken little pleasure trips, he had stayed in old-fashioned cheap motels in which one could cook. His room here was the first he had stayed in which was without a character of its own but had been preassembled in that featureless, smooth, coast-to-coast style called contemporary. He was impressed by its apparent elegance, which he thought of as functional, that is to say, having large uninterrupted planes related to one another by crude arithmetic or by chance. But he was suspicious that it had been designed to impress, rather than to delight with beauty or comfort.

"Tovarich," cried Robin, assuming the advertising posture of housewife ecstasy, "this is a suite! A one-room suite! This is the stuff that suites are made of!"

"Not despite its absurdity," he declaimed with a raised forefinger, "but because it is absurd." And he joined her in enjoying the edge-less, eight-dollars-a-night meretrix.

In a few minutes their pretended-actual admiring became strained, and they ran to the pool. The little boy squealed and invited them to play with his toys with him. The middle-aged parents were smiling benignly. Neither Leon nor Robin was particularly fond of children, but playing with the boy would make it possible for them to relax without having to talk about anything that mattered. They played.

Later they lay on the green cement, sunbathing.

"I wonder," said Robin toyingly, "how long it will be before we see each other again."

He played. "Months? Years?"

"I promise to write. Do you?"

"Faithfully. Once a week."

" 'I'll love thee, puss . . .' " she said, cuing him into a line from a musical farce she had acted in that spring.

He joined her. " 'Till marriage do us part.' "

They hooked little fingers.

"I'll be in New York when you get there," said Robin.

"I haven't been east of the Rockies since I was five years old. Why should I be going to New York now?"

"You are hardly flattering, sweetheart."

He looked at her mouth to see if she meant it. She did. This irritated him.

"I bring home a hundred and ninety a month ten months a year. Who'll pay for this trip?"

"A convention? Business? They like you at Saint Anselm's. There are always professional meetings going on. Maybe they'll be calling you to Washington for consultation."

He did not laugh as she intended. "I'm not positive what I shall be doing next year," he said.

"Then come with me to the Casbah, *chéri,* and I will show you such things—"

"I am thinking of going to law school. After all, Saint Anselm's is just a stop-gap for me. I'm so overloaded with work. I can't do a really good job teaching."

She was determined never if she could help it to put up with another discussion of the pros and cons of working for a Ph.D. Whether the arguments were cynical, idealistic, or self-deluding, they always seemed the same and were always dull.

"Did I ever tell you about the time Alfred Royce made a pass at me?"

Leon's response was gratifying.

She told this story.

That winter, on the Friday before Christmas vacation, she had gone with George Falconetti to a graduate students' red-wine party in the shambles of a mansion down on Telegraph Avenue. She and George had been on the point of breaking up—it was at the very next party she'd gone to that she and Leon had met and hit it off so fast—and she had been greatly taken with Alfred. He was the center of the party's life for a couple of hours, singing folksongs and arias from operas by himself or with whoever would join him, telling good stories about cross-examination tricks and surprises, flying high in a fierce argument about the dangers of socialism. (The more justice the less freedom, and the less freedom the less life and love. "So," said a bug, "so love is what it's all about, like in a ladies' magazine?" "Not at all," cried Alfred, his nose in the wind. "Love is only one of a multitude of things it's all about. All I mean by love is that without which our life is not worth living." The bug's legs waved in the air for a while, but no one paid any further attention to him—except Alfred, who from time to time turned to him solicitously and made sure the pin on which he was fixed was still well secured.) Robin had stayed near Alfred, at once avoiding George and making him jealous, and she had liked Alfred more and more. He had an appetite for pleasure and knew how to satisfy it. But he drank too much wine. When a girl in black tights began walking on her hands—chiefly, Robin thought, so her skirt would fall over her head and she could show how elegant her hips were—Alfred challenged the world to do a standing flip. George did one without taking the cigarette from his lips. Alfred went over and landed flat on his back. The wind was knocked out of him for a moment. Robin helped him into another room to lie down quietly and rest. The others said he needed to sleep it off for a while, but she was solicitous and kept going in to see to him. When he came round, she was on the bed beside him. His hand rested on her knee and then slid up her leg under her skirt and caressed her thigh. Sitting up, he kissed her right on the mouth. Then he said—she repeated every word—"I wish you were not a marvelously attractive woman. I must get one of the young men to drive me home to my wife."

She had expected this story to tickle Leon's sense of humor. Instead he almost cross-examined her, going over every detail. She kept telling him it had been harmless and boozy, it just showed that his idol had natural impulses like everybody else. But Leon kept pushing her as though something important was at stake. "There's something unlike Alfred about it, something surreptitious, dishonest. I don't get it." "For heaven's sake, darling, nothing happened. It was friendly. I liked him for it." Leon seemed to settle for this; at least he quit pestering her. "You liked him for it. Good. And after all, it was you he was with, not me."

What she had not told Leon was that she had been flirting with Alfred outrageously all evening and that when he had been waking up on the bed she was lying beside him, her head on his big chest and her arm across his waist. He hugged her affectionately, and in the confusion of groping to hoist himself up, his hand indeed slipped under her skirt and grasped her thigh near the crotch. "Oh," he said in a voice that could have continued equally well into apology, withdrawal, embarrassment, or erotic play, but instead went into grave affection and courtly compliment, "how lovely." He had then put one arm around her shoulders, taken her face in the other hand, and given her a kiss at once sensual and friendly—not somewhere indefinite between them but both fully at once. All this Robin knew but did not tell Leon. Except for her flirting, which she knew would annoy him, she did not omit any of this in order to mislead him, but because she did not understand what had happened. She did not know what all she felt toward Alfred. He had seemed at that time to both like and desire her, and though he had suggested that he was taking flight to the safety of his wife, Robin assumed that it was something else that had moved him. But because she could not imagine what else besides fear, respectability, or monogamy could have moved him, and because she was sure that he had felt real desire for her and had known that she was responding to him, she remained mystified. She held the memory to herself, hoping some day another party would bring them together again and clear things up. The only other time they had met had been at the party at the Royces' house the week before. Then, she had not even been sure he remembered having met her the first time. This only increased the mystery: if he had been that drunk at Christmas, then it had not been herself he was responding to at all, he had just been behaving out of habit.

There were two serious errors in her remembering. The first was this.

Just after withdrawing his hand from under her skirt, Alfred had suddenly peered through a rift in the fumes, straight into her eyes for a moment. Next he closed his eyelids as though in pain. Then he embraced and kissed her. She remembered that it was along about this time that she had felt a melting, falling sensation in her chest, but she forgot that this feeling came just when she had been looked into. Because she did not know what had happened, she remembered only the emotion attending what had happened; and, emotion being the shapeless clay it is, she had mistaken her feeling for just another amorous thrill. She could not imagine that anyone could really look into her and then kiss her with affection.

Her second error of memory concerned his leave-taking. He did not say, "I wish you were not a marvelously attractive woman," as she recalled and repeated. What he said was, "I find the flesh marvelously attractive, young woman." He was not fleeing from his desire home to his wife. He meant to tell Robin that he was going to his wife full of it, and he meant Robin to take this as honest enough of him but rather low, animalish. She had not been able to understand his meaning—indeed, not even the very words he used—because, for a husband married to the same woman long enough for them to have grown children, the action was too loving for Robin to credit. In such an act, she thought—she did not think so much as assume without knowing that she assumed—in such an act, generally speaking, love must be the veneer for lust, cowardice, and betrayal. Nevertheless, she did not feel that Alfred was cowardly or treacherous.

Her convictions about him contradicted her convictions about men at large. Yet as she told Leon about him, Alfred began sounding like ten thousand other men. Maybe, if she kept on making him sound like ten thousand others, her impression of his differentness would quit perplexing her and somehow go away.

"Leon," said Ida, hugging his arm, "will you excuse me just a minute? I've got to hie me to the little girls' room."

"Not at all."

He started to get up from his chair as she was getting up from hers. She had been using his arm for leverage, and she staggered back into her seat. He apologized.

"Hell," she said, "it's my own fault. I been around hillbillies like Mike so long I forgot what good manners are. So excuse *me*. You know, Rob, he's real Continental. You know?"

"He was born in Leningrad," said Robin, "which was Petrograd at the time. It used to be Saint Petersburg. How cosmopolitan can you get?"

"You see?" Ida looked at Leon admiringly. "Don't I spot them?"

"Come on, Mama, let's go to the powder room." Robin's voice was still bright, but her eyes were obscure and her mouth was wistful. " 'By now, Leo, I'll be seeing you in my dreams."

Her remark was so inappropriate that Leon scowled. A Midwest waitress in a zippered sarong came by, and, though they were about to order dessert, Leon ordered a double Scotch for himself.

"You know, Mama"—Robin was checking her make-up in the women's rest room—"how I said I'd go—how I *want* to go and visit Uncle Dolph and Aunt Charlotte in Saint Louis this summer?"

"Yes." Ida was intent on fixing her hair.

"Well, I will too, and I want to see that house where you lived when you were a little girl. I'm going in and look all around."

"That's more than I'd do. Suit yourself."

Robin did not respond. Ida looked over at her. Robin was staring at herself in the mirror.

"What are you doing?" Ida said.

"I'm practicing widening my eyes. Francis said I should develop my eye muscles for expressiveness."

Ida peered into her mirror and began making melodramatic faces at herself. Two spike-heeled blondes came in. Ida calmed her face and spoke quietly to Robin.

"What were you driving at with all that Saint Louis jazz?"

"Nothing."

"Come on. I'm your mother. I know you."

"You weren't interested." Robin stood up. The other two women were watching them out of the corners of their eyes. "Let's go." Ida did not move. Robin continued, "I thought since I'd be doing something for you, sort of, maybe you'd do something for me. Forget it."

"Tell me."

"Don't paw Leon. He hates it."

Without a word they returned to the table.

"Well," said Ida as they took their seats, "are we beautiful, Trotsky?"

"Trotsky?" he said.

"Sure, Leon from Leningrad. That's my Trotsky."

"Oh, Mama."

"You think I don't know anything? Ask me, go ahead, ask me. You think because I never went to your snotty old university I never learned anything, don't you? Ha. Leon, listen to me. Don't ever have a child. Don't misunderstand me, they're wonderful. They get to you. They get to mean the world and all to you. They snuggle right next to your heart. And then . . . They're sidewinders. When you aren't looking." Her left hand darted out, and the nails of the first two fingers jabbed into the back of his hand on the table. "Oh, I'm sorry." She glanced as though guiltily at Robin. "I forgot and touched you. My daughter said I wasn't to touch you. Here." She took out a handkerchief, carefully grasped his arm by the jacket sleeve, and inspected the tiny indentations her nails had made. "I'll wipe it off." She made light, caressing strokes with the handkerchief. "This is what I used to do when Robbie got a bump. Remember, sweetie? I'd wipe the hurt away with my magic cloth?"

Another waitress came to take their orders for dessert. She was not wearing a sarong but over each ear she had a gardenia pinned in her hair, the foil-wrapped stems jutting forward and up. On Ida's recommendation each ordered an Oahu Original—fresh papaya with pineapple sherbet, synthetic non-fattening whipped cream, and grated coconut.

As the waitress was clearing their table and wiping the crumbs off, Ida noticed the glass in which Leon had had his double Scotch. She picked it off the tray where the waitress had put it, and held it up, as though offering a toast.

"Aha, Professor, there's still some unmelted ice in it. Circumstantial evidence. You snuck yourself a quick one while we were in the little girls' room. Well, Robin Adair, you did all right after all. Between the two of us we're making a human being out of him. Okay, Professor?" She held the glass up to the waitress. "I'll have one myself, thank you."

"Robin?" said Leon.

"Thanks, I will."

"One more all around," Leon ordered. "Right away, before dessert."

"Look, kids, I like you, I like you, I really do, both of you. I'm a third wheel. This is your last night together. Take me home. Go on, you got things to say. I won't watch the clock, Rob. Stay out as late as you want. Have fun. That's what it's all about, isn't it? Have a good time."

· 20 ·

By the time they had dropped Ida off at her trailer, Leon wanted nothing so much as to go flop alone on his firm, flat motel bed, sleep till morning, then get in his car and drive off before a thought or feeling could rise in him. Much whisky; heavy food; Ida; the long hot drive down from Berkeley—they were oppressing him. But because it was their last evening and also because he was pitying her for her mother, he did not cut Robin off when she made the usual erotic suggestions. She said she wanted a Bakersfield sequel to the dinner. They drove out of town till they found a field of alfalfa, parked by it, and necked.

At first their necking was calm and friendly, suitable to the smell of alfalfa and sound of frogs and crickets. But as Leon declined into lethargy, Robin became more energetic. "Come on, corpse, I'm going to breathe some life into you." He responded to this sally with a disgusted grunt. Before long she was in a frenzy of caresses and panting. "Take me home, lover, take me quick, take me hard." He pretended that he thought these words were sincere and that they aroused him. In the obscurity her eyes were wide and white, their centers black.

As he drove toward the motel in silence, he was dreading the coming encounter. He reminded himself to avoid looking at her back, where two large pimples were coming to a head below her left shoulder blade. She would undress too fast. Sometimes that excited him. Tonight only to think of it offended him; it seemed aggressively intimate.

"False intimacy"; the phrase was Alfred Royce's. He must have meant by it something like a woman's thrusting her naked self on a man.

The previous fall, during the second meeting of the seminar, Alfred had insisted at length on the necessity of the law's concerning itself with acts which were reasonably unambiguous.

"As you might expect, nowhere do the codes have more difficulty than with sexual proscriptions. It is perfectly understandable, however absurd, that there should be an ordinance in Los Angeles forbidding even man and wife from copulating in a shower bath. And it is equally understandable that there should nowhere be statutory sanctions against one of the commonest but by no means one of the least serious of the perversions, false intimacy. Indeed, so far

68

as I know, it lacks even the minimum legal status of terminology."

No one asked him just what he meant by the phrase, and at that time Leon was too busy making up his mind both about Alfred and about the subject of the course to deflect his attention to a definition of an incidental term. This one had stuck in the back of his mind, and he now thought of it gratefully. The too easy gift of the flesh; Robin's presenting her entire naked body to him when what he wanted at the most was to hold hands; her zeal to go to bed with him the first time he had taken her out, which was only the second time they had met . . . Of course, he was in it too, he had let her do it, he even enjoyed it. But the main thrust he blamed on her.

When he drew up in front of his motel room he embraced her and whispered, "Let's take it easy, darling." He did not expect to overcome his lethargy, but he hoped to assuage his growing irascibility.

As soon as he had locked the door of his room, she pulled him down on the bed beside her. "I can't wait to take off my clothes. Pretend you can't wait. Take me as we are. Be rough with me."

A flash of rage cleared his mind and gave him energy. This was a thrust of intimacy beyond falseness. "You are not ready," he said coldly.

"I am, I am."

"I mean, your diaphragm."

What she answered to this seemed to him utterly inappropriate to her writhing and moaning.

"I am immune to you, lover, you have vaccinated me. Vaccinate me again. Please."

"What are you talking about?"

She stopped and reared her head to look at him blackly. "It's all right. It's safe. Don't you believe me?"

"Of course. How can it be safe?"

"I'm pregnant." Her voice was a parody of soap-opera breathlessness.

He said, slowly and in a somewhat deeper register than usual, "Oh my God." In the silence that followed he did not think about what she had told him but about the soap-opera, slick-magazine-story, Grade-B-movie phrase he had uttered in an intonation that he did not think belonged to him. It rang in his ears like the sound of a cell door being shut. Even though he was thinking this, remotely, he next said in the same hollow voice, "What shall we do now?" This phrase, which he did not think belonged to him either, he heard clang like a bolt locking him in.

What he had said was unexceptional: "Oh my God. What shall we do now?" It was himself alone who had uttered these words in a false voice. Yet, by dwelling upon the utterances as romantic signs of imprisonment, he managed to consider himself put upon, innocently victimized, trapped by circumstances.

He was sitting on the edge of the bed, his elbows on his knees, his head bent. Her legs tailor-fashion, Robin was sitting erect in the center of the bed. They were half averted from each other.

"I wasn't going to tell you till"—she gave a little shrug—"afterwards."

"You are considerate," he said, "for lack of a better word."

"I didn't want to spoil things for us till I had to."

"Christ on a crutch," he said. "You're bankrupt."

They looked at each other. When she saw the cold contempt in his eyes, the appeal went out of her manner.

"I hope you're not," she said in a harsh voice.

"There's only one way out," he said.

"Which is?"

"You don't want marriage any more than I do."

"And?"

"You *can* have the child if you want. Plenty of people want to adopt."

"That is my decision, apparently."

"Not just yours. You are positive you are pregnant?"

"Yes."

"You can have an operation for about three hundred dollars." He named this sum because he had heard someone mention it once, and because he had about that much in his bank account. "I'll make the arrangements, of course, but it'll have to be around the Bay Area, where I know people."

"I will do it. Send me the money."

"But I want to do it. I should."

He put some energy in the plea and looked at her. She turned her head toward him. Her face was without expression, and he could not interpret the blackness of the pits of her eyes.

"I do not want you to," she said. "And it does not cost three hundred dollars, it costs nearer five hundred. I've found out. Take me home."

When they drew up at Ida's trailer, Robin opened the car door and said, "Don't bother to get out."

"I'll put the check in the mail Monday as soon as I can get the loan. If anything goes wrong I'll wire it."

"Wire it anyway—five hundred. It's surer by wire. I'll be here till next Wednesday. Good-by."

They embraced rigidly, and without a kiss.

"Good-by, Robin. This is the only way out."

She laughed harshly.

II

· 1 ·

"Daddy?"

Alfred shoved his chair back from the desk and swiveled around. "Nancy?"

"Do you mind if I ask you just one question?"

"Of course not, honey. Come in, come in."

"When is Mother coming back?"

"She hasn't said, dear. Don't just stand there with the door open. You'll let the flies in."

"A month?" she said, closing the door behind her.

"Oh, heavens, no. I'm sure not that long."

"She's been gone a month already, and you didn't expect that."

"Not quite a month. It does seem like it, doesn't it?"

"Well, tomorrow?"

"No. Maybe another week or two. There are quite a few legal matters she has to deal with, and family to see, and her mother's house to break up."

"Break up?"

"The things in it. Give some away, sell some, have a few pieces shipped home here—you know, to remember her mother by."

Nancy came along a bookcase, trailing her finger on a shelf. "Daddy? Does everybody get in a legal tangle?"

"What an idea! Where did you get such a notion?"

"Well, I heard Kay tell Mother that Woody was in a legal tangle, and I heard Horace say the labor movement was in one, and now Mother is in one."

"All right, you've had ten questions. So now go play."

"What are you doing this morning, Daddy?"

"Writing a book, as you well know. Leave me alone."

"The same book, on legal tangles?"

"No, it's not on legal tangles and you know it's not on legal tangles. Go! Leave! Scoot!"

He was roaring but he was still in his chair. She circled him till she was across the desk from him. She pointed at the blank paper in front of him. "You're not writing at all."

He sighed. "Most of the time what I'm doing is deciding. I have to decide what to write down on paper."

"Don't you erase and cross out? I do when I write a composition for school."

"Not much. I decide ahead of time, in my head, what to say and how to say it. You learn that after a long time."

"Tell me what the law is, Daddy. I want to know."

Her manner was so sincere that, even knowing her artfulness, he would have been fooled, had she not been so elaborately badgering him until that request.

"No, I will not tell you what the law is." He got out of his chair. "You must get out of my study—now."

She quickly turned an unsealed, stamped, addressed envelope on his desk around so she could read the writing.

"Why, this is to Mother. You aren't writing a book at all, you're just writing a letter to Mother. Tell her something for me. Tell her she's been gone too long."

"Why don't you write her, dear? She'd love to hear from you. She misses you. Why don't you do it right now?"

Nancy gave a little shrug.

"Do you miss her, sweetie?"

Nancy shrugged again.

"Well, go do what you wish, but you must go."

"I'm bored, Daddy. This is the most boring summer. Even Syb and Lizzie think so."

"Are you lonesome for your mother, Nance?"

She pushed air rapidly from one cheek to the other, staring at the tip of his nose. "Sometimes I get this funny feeling in my stomach. I hate it."

"Maybe we should go to a doctor. Where is it?"

"Oh, Daddy, no! It's not any place exactly. If she'd come back it'd go away. But don't tell her that! Don't tell her that!" She came around and rubbed against him. "Daddy, what do you do while you're deciding what to write down?"

"I just sit here. A lot of the time I look out of the window. I either look up into the trees or else I roll the chair over here a ways sometimes and look down into the patio."

"You don't pace around like the genius in one of those movies?" She put her hands behind her back and goose-stepped up and down. "Or do exercises, or even just smoke a pipe?"

"No, I just sit."

"How tense."

"Tense! Just sitting?"

She dissolved onto the floor (her gym teacher that year had been keen on Modern Dance), arms self-consciously akimbo, unconsciously graceful. "See, relaxed." She leaped up and sat in his chair with one elbow on the desk, her chin on the heel of her hand, and her legs entwined. "See—you."

He laughed, recognizing the parody. "You've been spying."

"Tra la la, la la." She ran to the door and squinched her face at him.

"Look, Nancy, at three this afternoon we'll go to the city—to the aquarium, then ice-skating at Sutro's, then to a Chinese restaurant for dinner. Okay? Four of you may come, you three girls, but *you* are the one that gets to invite one of *your* friends. Now go tell your sisters."

"Do they *have* to come?"

"They have to be asked, of course. Four of you in all. Go."

He heard her whooping down into the lower regions of the house. He sat back to his desk and began writing with a pen on a sheet of typing paper.

"Dearest wife,

"Nancy just came in forlorn, asking for you. You are needed at home, by all your children. I would call you except that we are both so businesslike on the telephone, I always feel inhuman. The legal matters can be handled by mail. You have done your duty and more than your duty by your kinfolk there. You have had plenty of time to decide how to dispose of your mother's effects.

"Let me tell you what Nancy said."

From the patio Lizzie's voice called, "Dad."

He rolled over a bit and glanced through the Venetian blinds down at her to see how she was looking. Though she was the daughter not of his flesh, she was dearest to him, she seemed by some perversity of things least strange to him, he was easiest with her. But he was also afraid of her sometimes, as he was not of the other two. She was standing in the sun, her skin strikingly pale, legs apart and fists on her hips, blond hair loose, "stocky and cocky," as he liked her best. He raised the blinds and the window and stuck his head out.

"Lizzie-O."

"Is what Nancy says true? Are we going to Sutro's?"

"Sure. Coming?"

73

"You bet. Syb's not. She's got a date—with a shnook, I think."

"With a what?"

"A shnook. Brewster Adams. He took us both to a movie once, so I know whereof I speak. Not one of the blessings you have showered on your daughters, Father dear. But Sybil's going out with him. Maybe she's going to rescue him from himself."

She blew Alfred a kiss and skipped back in.

He went back to the letter he had started to Beth. It now seemed to him dense with obscure reproach. He lifted it to drop it into the wastebasket, but then read it over again. Though she wrote every other day, she had not yet made it clear to him what had been keeping her there so long. He was not really worried about Nancy, but he saw no justification for Beth's staying away any longer; finally she would give cause for genuine worry about the child. He continued the letter as he had begun it.

"The real reason," the letter concluded, "I want you to come home is to cook. What have you done to your daughters, Elizabeth my love? Sybil understands all about the broiled hamburger. Lizzie is an adept at macaroni and cheese and more than competent with chili con canned carne. Nancy is second to none at heating a can of soup. We can all fry eggs. But a stew? Your oatmeal meat loaf with mushrooms? Your Stroganoff? You are needed, you are wanted, you are missed."

He saw the flippancy of this conclusion as a way of putting himself at an affectionate disadvantage with her. He had known her over twenty years and still could suppose that, because she enjoyed such a tone when in the mood for a frivolous party, she would enjoy this facetiousness of his in this letter now. He sealed the envelope with a certain flourish and sang a ditty from Gilbert and Sullivan.

· 2 ·

At about nine o'clock in the evening a week later, Alfred and the girls were on the San Raphael–Richmond ferry, returning from a two-day visit with the Ravaglis on the Mendocino Coast.

The previous winter Woody and Kay Ravagli had moved into the house they had built in Berkeley on Churchill Court, a short dead-end street on a ledge up the hill from San Jacinto Way. This house, in a modified Japanese style, was already so celebrated for its beauty that they had been forced to erect a fence with a locked gate to protect themselves from the stares of sightseers. It had quiet, privacy, and a superb view. For Kay its chief drawback was its nearness to the Hill, the steep slope where the University's radiation and parasitology

74

laboratories were clustered. To be sure, the Ravaglis' house was screened by trees from a view of these large buildings, which were uninteresting to look at; but she found it a source of irrational uneasiness to be neighbors to people she feared. She had met some of them at parties or during intermissions at concerts. Before she found out what one did, he usually seemed agreeable enough, but after she knew what he did she would see him as wearing the traits of his type like a uniform. In her mind these scientists, many of whom were famous, were devoted to acquiring the most potent knowledge in the physical world, but impurely: the most obvious social result of their knowledge was unimaginable damage. They might have begun as seekers of pure knowledge, but now they were careerists. On the Hill, she had heard, they spoke of a Nobel Prize as something they "gunned for." Their wives were often alert, decent, warmhearted, and concerned with matters of conscience. Kay kept meeting them because one of Woody's companies had important electronics contracts and because Woody's brother Ted worked on the Hill; he was in charge of studying the long-range effects of a plague bacillus now tamed enough so it would not kill most of its victims but only knock them out with dysentery for a few weeks. Woody agreed that all this fascinating activity was deplorable, but he saw no reason why it should affect them any the more for taking place just beyond the trees from their incomparable house; also he thought it tiresome of Kay not to have raised her objection before they moved in. She was ashamed of being silly; she would not say another word if only he would get them a place to go to on weekends and for the summer. So he bought a six-hundred-acre sheep ranch above Stowes Landing. The ranch operated at a loss, in a way that made it profitable for him on his income-tax statements to enter that loss against his varied huge income. They were spending the summer there in a big old ten-room collapsing shack high above the sea. When they had moved to Berkeley the previous winter, they had also kept their San Francisco town house in Pacific Heights, renting out all of it but the servants' quarters. They had converted these quarters to a four-room apartment which they used whenever they stayed late in the city, in order to avoid the fatiguing trip across the Bay late at night. It was especially convenient for Woody, who often had to stay in San Francisco on business till late in the evening.

Alfred and his daughters were the only passengers in the ferryboat restaurant.

"You know," said Lizzie, "I think all that money is just wasted on Kay. She doesn't know what to do with it."

"*You* would?" Nancy said, grinning.

"Of course not," said Lizzie. "It would just get in my way. None of us would be any better than Kay."

"Oh, I'm not so sure," said Sybil.

"Don't be silly," Lizzie said. "What do you want that ten or twelve thousand dollars a year won't buy? Which is what your husband will make."

"I don't know," said Sybil, "yet. It'd be fun to find out."

"No, it wouldn't either," Lizzie said. "You'd just worry, the way Kay does."

"Well, I know what I want," said Nancy. "I want horses and stables and grooms and an airplane."

Lizzie said, "Sure, but do you know who would really know how to enjoy money? Mother."

"Well," said Alfred, "go on, I'm fascinated."

"Oh, Daddy," said Nancy. Her sympathizing only pretended to be mock-serious; she squeezed his hand with genuine warmth.

"You're not implying, are you," said Sybil to Lizzie, "that Dad would have made Mother happier by making more money?"

Lizzie nibbled a hangnail and frowned into her coffee. "Yes, I guess I am." She gazed at Alfred, her blue eyes untroubled. "Just as Mother would make you happier if she liked to take trips as much as you do. One's as unimportant as the other—like so." She held thumb and forefinger about the thickness of a toothpick apart. "Yea big."

This was a family joke, but nobody smiled.

Alfred was nodding and squeezing his chin.

Sybil left without a glance or nod. She could be seen through the dirty windows, hair and skirt whipping, walking the deck, not looking in.

Nancy leaned against her father, hugging his arm, gazing at Lizzie blankly and unswervingly.

"What's the matter with everybody?" Lizzie asked indignantly. "I'm not really criticizing you, Dad. You know that, don't you?"

He kept on nodding at the same slow rate.

"Money, for heaven's sake," she went on. "What good is it except to buy what you want? That's absolutely all there is to it. That's why I like the Koyala so much. They won't have anything to do with money, even now. All these feelings us Westerners attach to money —they're so illegitimate, so unnecessary."

She continued to develop her theory about how Beth would learn to move around from house to house, buying things, living luxuriously one week and carelessly in a cabin the next, giving herself over to the fun of variety without being nagged by "Should I?" as Kay was. Alfred responded, but with such cues as to move her apparent theorizing in the direction of open fantasy. After they had driven off the ferry and were riding up into Berkeley, he kept her fantasy bounc-

76

ing. But while he was doing it he was speculating on what there might have been in his response to Lizzie's statements to stimulate the other two girls to behave as they had behaved—and were still behaving, for they said nothing all the way home, just sat watchfully listening. He was distressed to think it might have been something in his attitude toward money that had caused them to act this way, for he professed to himself an attitude as contemptuous as Lizzie's toward the misuses of money.

· 3 ·

The lights were on in the house.

"Mommy's home!" cried Nancy and flew out of the car before it had stopped. "Mother!" she screamed as she ran.

"Impossible!" said Alfred. "She wrote that it would be Sunday definitely. Sunday at five-thirty."

All the same, he too ran in as fast as he could, neglecting, like the girls, to take any of the baggage with him.

When he got into the house he found Beth standing by the dining table with the girls upon her. Hugh was standing on the other side of the table, shyly smiling. Beth stretched her free arm over Sybil's shoulder.

"Oh, Alfie darling, why weren't you here?" She hiccuped; her eyes were wet; her lips smiled. "I don't know what I would have done without Hugh. I was so disappointed. The house was all empty and shadowy. I just went down to Hugh's cabin, and there he was, and we ate together and he's been telling me everything, where you were and all. Oh, he's a Godsend. And it's so good to see you, darling." With this she broke down into tears. The girls released her, and she buried her face in Alfred's bosom. "So silly. I'm sorry to be silly like this. I just wanted to surprise you. I wanted to come home early and give you a surprise."

Nancy's eyes were spilling over too. Hugh's arms were twining and untwining in front of him like amorous snakes. Sybil and Lizzie were grinning. Alfred felt hot tears in his own eyes, and words began spurting from his mouth.

He began telling about a machinists' strike at a precision-instruments plant named McKee's; Horace had decided to arbitrate the dispute himself, both because the dispute was unusual and because McKee's was making high-priority instruments for secret weapons. He began moving with Beth into the living room, and the girls followed.

77

When Hugh started to slip unobtrusively out through the kitchen, Beth called to him with undue urgency; she wanted him to come in with them and sit around the fireplace.

"Oh, I do want a fire," she said.

"But it's not cold," Alfred answered.

"I'm chilly." She extended her hand toward Hugh, who, blushing, put his hand in hers. "Do go get some light pieces of wood, dear Hugh, and build a little fire. I would like it so much."

Hugh's happiness to do this for her struck Alfred hard. They had always been scrupulous not to encroach on him.

"Honestly," said Beth, "I mean it, what I said about Hugh. He was a life-saver for me this evening."

Seated on the couch, arm around her, Alfred told her what Hugh had been doing in the garden while she was away. He had firmly fixed the stepping stones winding down the right side and had started another compost pit as she had been wanting him to do. But Hugh would be leaving for New York in a couple of weeks; he and his best friend had decided to try their fortunes there; his friend had a friend who dressed windows in Saks Fifth Avenue. While Alfred was talking on, praising Hugh's work and watching him lay the fire in a pleasing meticulous pattern, he was imagining Hugh day after day alone down in the cabin cooking on the hot plate, not included. They had never invited him to dinner or parties except when an extra man was needed; he had not complained, never tried to intrude; he had stayed by himself, having a friend in to visit from time to time; quiet, reliable, eager to please, eager to say the arrangements pleased him, but not included. Now he sat at the side of the hearth, turning to glance at the fire from time to time, beaming at them all.

"Mommy," said Nancy, leaning against her, "do you know what I did up at Stowes Landing? Cathy was sick in bed, and Kay let me take care of her."

"Big deal," said Sybil.

"Wonderful, sweetie," said Beth. "Do you like Cathy?"

"She's the nicest little kid ever. Kay doesn't have any help up there, so I helped. Do you suppose I could go stay the rest of the summer if they want me to?"

"Oh, great," said Sybil.

"You're just jealous you didn't think of it first," said Lizzie to Sybil. "If I wasn't going on a field trip, I'd like to do it myself."

"Can I, Mommy?"

"We'll see, dear." Beth squeezed Nancy, and she wriggled.

Alfred began describing their stay at the Ravaglis' ranch, which Beth had not yet seen, and the girls chimed in to correct or amplify what he said. They overlapped and contradicted and supported. His voice grew louder and higher as he talked over them. His arms were spread to touch them all four.

Hugh in his chain-knit sweater was rocking on his hunkers on the hearth, smiling and hugging his knees.

· 4 ·

At midnight Alfred insisted they go to bed. No one wanted to, but everyone agreed that Beth must be tired.

"Don't unpack a thing, Mother," said Lizzie. "Just climb right straight in bed. I would."

"I would too," cried Nancy.

"Yes, but you'll sleep better if you wash your teeth first," said Sybil.

"Good night, my angels. Good night, Hugh."

Alfred straightened up the house for the night, locked the doors, and answered Nancy's call to come tuck her in; she was lying in bed, stiff and wide-eyed. He took his time to do these things, hoping to find Beth in bed when he went up to her. He found her standing un-dressed in front of the full-length mirror built into the inner side of the closet door, craning over her shoulder at her back. He stopped and spread his hands.

"My Cranach wife."

"What?" She looked around at him, still scowling.

"There was a Cranach nude at the de Young last month. I'd never really looked at him before."

"Don't be mean to me, Alfie."

"Mean! His women are beautiful—like you. Sloping shoulders, high-breasted, long willowy body."

"They're pretty, they have sly eyes, they don't have big red blotches in the middle of their backs, they're young. Look at this face." She slapped her jaw hard. "Beat up. Bags under the eyes." She squeezed her cheeks, then threw herself in his arms and hung from his neck.

"Just a couple of little pimples."

"My hips are getting thicker."

"The face I love, bags and all."

She reared back in his arms, her hands on either side of his neck, her forearms parallel on his chest. She smiled a little, but when he leaned to kiss her she averted her mouth. The superficies of his mood were gathering together, to deepen toward desire.

"Another thing," she said, "what was that big pitch about Nancy? She looks fine to me. What were you doing anyhow in that letter?"

"She is fine. I wanted her to stay that way."

"You got me so worried and guilty and mixed up. Everything seemed to be going against me all at once."

"You're home now," he said, "you can take it as easy as you want."

She snorted. He released her, and she turned away.

"You want me to cook all the time. That's what you wrote—come home and cook." Her voice was humorless.

"I was trying to be funny. Maybe it was a poor joke."

"No 'maybe' to it."

"But," he said sharply, "it was not such a bad joke as to deserve your bearing down like this."

She had put on her pajamas and now stood staring into the open suitcase on the floor. "I'm not even going to brush my teeth," she said defiantly. Then she kicked the suitcase. "I'm sick of this house. There's no room in it for anything. Look, I even have to put the suitcase on the floor because there's no space in this dressing room. And this." She jerked the pull-cord on the Venetian blind. "It's been broken like this for a year."

"But we never pull this blind up. You know that. We can adjust the slats, which is all we need."

She gave him a black look and went to bed. When he got in, she flounced over with her back to him.

For a time he lay rigid, staring at his duty, unable to move toward it. He saw clearly that he ought to comfort and cherish his wife, whose unkind behavior was no more than a symptom of a profound unhappiness; but he felt himself held locked by the emotions of frustrated desire, rejection, and resentment. She made a jerking movement with her leg and uttered a long sigh, both of which irritated him. But when she breathed in after the sigh, her breathing was rough with little catches as if she had been crying, though she had not, and he began to thaw. Without warning, she kicked her heel back against his shin twice, hard enough to hurt but gentle enough to be taken as friendly. And it occurred to him that what he most wanted, so far from either sort of stagnant righteousness, whether pity or resentment, was to gratify his desire; this he could do only by arousing and gratifying her desire.

He cuddled himself against her. "Spoons in a drawer," he murmured and she wiggled appreciatively. That had been a tenderness of their honeymoon, for years now neglected and half-forgotten. He was forty pounds heavier, and even though his fat was well distributed he did not fit her still-unthickened body as he felt he might be fitting it. For a time she did not seem to be responding to his caresses. Then she flipped in his arms like a fish. They strove together with a harsh force which he did not recognize or even like but which he rose against and with and through.

· 5 ·

"Syb?" said Lizzie from the doorway.

Sybil looked up from her novel petulantly. But when she saw that Lizzie was hesitating even to come into her room, she spoke with concern in her voice. "What is it, Liz?"

"You heard Mother talking to me in my room just now?"

"I heard your voices," said Sybil. "I didn't listen."

"Do you know what she was talking about?"

"Come in, for heaven's sake," said Sybil. "Have a seat, be friendly."

Lizzie responded to this jocularity by stepping just inside the door and closing it behind her. "She kept talking about how she could use my room. I distinctly got the impression she'd be glad if I moved out instanter. Lord, I'm going to leave home soon enough as it is. Doesn't she even want me to come back for a visit?"

"Yesterday she came in here and told me how I needed another chest of drawers and a couple of chairs."

"But she wasn't trying to get rid of you the way she is me."

"Burying me with furniture is a good beginning," said Sybil. "I like my room the way it is. This is a big house. We have a basement to store stuff in. I fixed my room myself, and she knows I want it just the way I want it."

"You really don't think she has something against me?"

"Pff," said Sybil. "You know what she did to Nancy, don't you?"

"When?"

"Last night. She told Nance she couldn't go stay with Kay and Woody this summer and take care of the kids."

"Why not?" said Lizzie indignantly.

"Because she might need her to lean on. That's what she said."

"Well, that shows who she prefers."

"Prefers!" Sybil said. "Nancy cried herself to sleep."

They stared at the floor.

"Do you suppose," said Sybil, "Dad knows what's going on?"

"Let's go see."

They went, rather heavily, up the stairs and into Alfred's study. He was not there.

They heard a car draw up and stop on the street in front of the house. Sybil peeked through the slats of the Venetian blinds. "Hey,"

81

she whispered, "it's that handsome guy at the party with the fast chick. Alone."

Lizzie peeked too. "Leon Kalish."

As he got out, a low, snappy British sports car drew up with Joe Thompson in it.

"Oh my God," said Lizzie, "Joe's half an hour early."

"Early for what?"

"Picnic."

"Well, go get ready," said Sybil.

"I want to watch."

"Say," said Leon to Joe, "hello. We meet again."

They exchanged greetings and, after Joe had pulled off his brown gloves, shook hands. They began talking about Joe's green MG.

Leon was carefully dressed, but as usual there was a flaw in his appearance, this time the beginning of a hole in the right elbow of his well-pressed jacket. Joe was wearing a motoring cap with an adjustment strap at the back. They stood chatting, both of them gazing at the MG, kicking a tire from time to time, rapping a fender. Leon was the taller of the two and lean.

Joe had narrow hips and wide shoulders. When he unbuttoned his tweed jacket, the girls saw he was wearing a tattersall waistcoat. His plain brown shoes were scuffed, but because everything else about his appearance was immaculate it was clear that he had studied their neglect. As they talked he pulled out a briar pipe with a metal stem and began filling it from a leather pouch. When he clenched the ivory mouthpiece between his teeth and lighted it, Lizzie sighed.

"Even so," said Sybil, "I think Leon is handsomer. Those imperfections on his skin—they make him more interesting."

Lizzie winked.

"Well," said Joe, "it looks like we'll have to go in your car. No use taking two."

"What?" said Leon. "Where?"

"Wherever we feel like. Personally I had Muir Beach in mind."

"What are you talking about?" said Leon. "I'm here to see Alfred."

"You are? I assumed you and Sybil were going with Lizzie and me on our picnic. Sorry." He laughed.

Leon straightened up, looking severe, and took a step back.

"You want to?" Lizzie whispered.

"Sure," Sybil answered.

"Let's see if Leon wants to."

Joe was doing a sort of stationary shuffle, shifting his weight from one leg to the other, moving his feet a little without lifting them from the ground.

"Well," he said, "I don't know what the girls have in mind or anything, but if you won't be too long talking with Alfred I know I would like it if you came along."

"Impossible," said Leon stiffly. For a moment he stood like a statue, and Joe, eyes lowered, danced inside his clothes. Then Leon visibly relaxed. "As a matter of fact, I've decided to quit work on my dissertation and get a law degree. The law has come to fascinate me."

"The law? What about *practicing* law?"

"Well," said Leon decisively, "I want to talk to Alfred about that."

"You don't like teaching?"

"Yes, I do. And I think I would keep on liking it. But the law, you know, the law is wonderful. There's nothing like it."

"You're coming to the right man," said Joe. "Alfred's your boy. But then, you know, the law's been around a long time, it'll wait another day or two. Now what if Sybil is home and willing? This very afternoon?"

"Girls!" said Alfred sharply from the doorway. They jumped away from the window. "What are you doing?"

"Joe and Leon are out there, Daddy," Sybil whispered. "Please."

"What were you doing in my study in the first place?" he said in a voice that seemed to them loud.

"A picnic," Sybil said. "We may all go on a picnic."

"That's not what I asked."

"We came," said Lizzie, trying to sidle by him to the door, but he blocked her way, "to talk to you about Mother, but it's not really important. Come on, Syb."

"Wait." He deliberately closed the door and then sat at his desk. "What about your mother?"

"It's nothing, Dad, really," said Lizzie. "We just wondered if you'd noticed how frenzied she is."

The two men walked into the patio and rang the bell. The girls ran to the windows on that side of the study, gesticulating silently. Beth answered the door, smiling and seeming at ease.

"See," said Sybil, turning, "she looks just fine. We've got to go, Dad."

"What did she do that caused you to come up?" His face was unresponding but not hostile, the countenance of a lawyer gathering evidence. "I need to know."

They told him.

"Now, Daddy," said Sybil, "do *us* a favor, will you please? Leon told Joe that he's here to talk to you, but everybody wants him to come on the picnic, so can we just tell him you're too busy to talk to him? Tomorrow afternoon instead?"

There was a perceptible interval while the lawyer's face became the face of their father again. They hardly waited to hear what he said but ran down into the living room.

Their mother, in her gardening clothes, without make-up and with a streak of dirt on her forehead, looked happier than they had seen her since the evening she had arrived home. They acted surprised to see Leon.

"I only came by," he said, embarrassed to be saying the same thing so many times, "to talk to Alfred, if he's not busy."

"Oh," said Sybil, wide-eyed, "we just were up in his study and got kicked out. When he's really working it takes an earthquake to make him stir. But I'll go ask him if he wants to see you."

"No!" cried Leon with the appearance of horror. "Of course not! I wouldn't dream of disturbing him."

"Well, now," said Joe, laughing his full rich laugh, in which nevertheless much was being held back, "there's nothing holy about writing a book. Not that I'd pester him myself, but, you know . . ."

"You do it your way," said Leon coldly, "and I'll do it mine. I'll telephone him and make an appointment, as I should have done today. It's my own fault."

"Oh," said Lizzie, "he can see you tomorrow afternoon at three."

Leon frowned. "How do you know that?"

Lizzie started to explain, but Sybil, fearing her forthrightness, slid in front of her words. "We went in just as you two rang the doorbell and so he told us he didn't want to talk to anybody till tomorrow at three. But we said we were going on a picnic, and he kicked us out. You can come with us, can't you, Leon?"

"There's plenty," said Lizzie. "We'll just throw in some more cheese and fruit."

At Leon's complicated yielding, Joe began chuckling and carried first the three women and then Leon with him into laughter.

A quarter of an hour later Alfred heard the voices of the four young people in the patio, soprano and baritone mingling, the words unimportant. He looked out at them, the men so dandily dressed, the girls in bright skirts and blouses, carrying bags and blankets. In the doorway, smiling, Beth waved and called good-by. The gardening smudge on her forehead made her look furiously worried.

· 6 ·

Alfred turned back to his desk, hoping that Beth would leave him undisturbed for at least two more hours. He anticipated some sort of elaborate trouble with her; he was not sure what would provoke it or what it would be about, but he recognized in her the signs of the need

84

to quarrel. He felt rushed. A time of obscure oppression stretched ahead. He intended to spend that afternoon making up his mind about his book once and for all.

When he had begun it more than six years before, he had been clear about its subject, which was described by the title, *Foundations of Labor Law in the United States*. For three years or so he had been content to remain within the limits set by that title, and had published as articles much of what he had written. He knew from experience what he was writing about. He had assisted in the drafting of the National Labor Relations Act in 1935, and he had been a special legal adviser for the California State Council of the American Federation of Labor up till the war; he had been appointed by President Roosevelt, shortly after the United States entered World War II, to a committee of five to establish emergency labor regulations, and for the duration of the war he had served as chairman of the Pacific Area of the War Labor-Relations Commission (the WLRC) and as the Secretary of Labor's adviser for Western affairs; since the war he had twice served as special arbitrator in labor disputes, once in a Midwest Teamsters' strike and the other time in a nationwide Big Steel strike; he had advised several California industries on establishing a better labor-management policy, telling the management, for $100 a day, what it seemed to him an adult of good will should have known anyway. During the war he had begun teaching a seminar in labor law at the University, in good part as an intellectual relief from his bureaucratic duties on the WLRC. He enjoyed teaching this course so much that he continued it after the war; from the discussions in that seminar came the ideas for the book he was now writing. The book and the seminar continued to be the core of his professional life. To hold them he had rejected offers of many sorts: from an industry to run its labor-relations department (at a salary more than five times his present income); from the national headquarters of the Steelworkers Union; from the National Labor Relations Board, the Federal Conciliation Service, and the California Fair Employment Practices Commission; from the University of California to teach as a full-time professor of labor law; and from the University of Michigan to set up a school of labor relations. Each time he turned down these offers of power and money, his book became more important to him. Each time also, as he knew, the book acquired more repute in the world, a repute which the articles that appeared in journals sustained. Nevertheless, as he sacrificed more and more to the book, he came to look at it with an ever colder eye.

After three years he had begun to enlarge its scope. From labor law he began to move out to positive law, and he began dropping first "labor" and then "in the United States" from his title when he thought of it; it became *Foundations of Law*. When he became aware that he was repeating himself in the labor seminar, he attempted a course in common law for a couple of years. But it had not shaped up well. This past year, over the opposition of the department, he had insisted on conducting a seminar in the philosophy of law, and here he found what he had been groping for. He had never been more pleased by a job of work than by that seminar. The book too had been changing over these past three years, and it was this change that was forcing him to a decision.

For a time he had persuaded himself that in the last half of the book he would be able to go on to something larger than his original subject, using labor law as a mode of entry into a consideration of positive law generally; and insofar as the later chapters were taken as exploratory, rather than definitive like the earlier ones, he had succeeded. But during the past year, excited by his seminar, he had lost his balance in the book and had moved from a consideration of certain aspects of positive law to an investigation of the tensions between positive and ideal law and toward a consideration of the nature of law itself. What really excited his mind now was inquiring into the nature of social justice, of the State; and just at the further brink of the State, the chasmic wildernesses *society* and *human nature* invited his explorations.

For months he had been assuring himself that the large speculative section he had written would provide an unorthodox but satisfying conclusion to the book he had begun. Now he sat staring at the one-page outline which he had made the day before, and he saw the book as a shambles. The last section not only did not conclude anything; it was a bungled beginning to something vast and vague: man, the law, justice, truth, the One, the All. Gas. Meanwhile, his original book, on American labor law, had been pretty well finished a year before. What did it amount to? A hill of beans. Gas and beans. There already were adequate books on labor law, and it was a subject which deserved no more than fairly good books. What service would his somewhat better book perform? Further his reputation, chiefly. To some extent it would place labor law in the general context of American law, but any professor worth his salt would do that in a course on the subject. In all conscience he should scrap the tiny, local book he had written and stake everything on the one big, timeless book which would be his life's work—knowing that it might very well turn into philosophical vapor and, if he was lucky, dissipate into learned bibliographies and library catalogues all over the Western world for a generation or two.

"Now then," he said aloud and gave his head a brief nod. His voice was abrupt but reasonable, as when he was explaining the path of good sense to one of his children. He went on in silence, but gesturing. "If I permit myself to go on thinking this way I will do nothing, or else I will undercut anything I do so that it will come to nothing. Conceivably I might write a book that will weather the ages. Meanwhile, I have written a useful one. This one right here is useful." His forefinger jabbed the one-page outline on the desk in front of him. "If I were teaching an undergraduate lecture course on problems of labor-management, I would assign it as a text and be grateful to have it there to be assigned. Very well. I shall throw out this last section"—he set aside the pile of manuscript—"write two or three thousand words of conclusion, and have it typed up in final form. In fact, I'll get a typist started on it Monday. As for the other, I shall do the best I can. My subject is positive and ideal law, and it is worth the best years of my life." He settled back in his chair and took a deep breath. "But," he said aloud and raised a finger. He continued in silence again. "Suppose I do the big job badly when I might have done a more modest task well. Three years: I give myself three years. If in three years' time I have written nothing better than this,"—he flipped the discarded section with the back of his fingers—"I shall abandon the project, without dishonor, and do what I know I can. If I cannot be superb, I shall be useful."

In earnest of this, he picked up the bundle of discarded pages and held it over the wastebasket; but in a moment he shook his head, pulled open the bottom drawer of his filing cabinet, and tossed the pages loosely into the vacant space back of the dividers. He glared at the closed drawer, puffing. Then he rushed out the front door of the study—being careful to close it quietly behind him so as not to attract Beth's attention—and strode down San Jacinto Way to visit Justice Durkheim.

He thought he was so solid with good sense that he would not need to mention his decision to the old man. Also, he glowed with satisfaction at the epigram "If I cannot be superb, I shall be useful." To be sure, he knew better than to store it up and use it in public. He felt solid with good sense.

In fact what he was doing was protecting his study—his book, his mental work—from that voiding force in himself which was capable of exhausting significance from anything, as it had just been emptying his book of value. The manifest way this protecting appeared to him was in a surreptitious determination to keep Beth away from his book and out of his study, although in fact Beth had never shown signs of wanting to intrude on his work. What he really feared was that she was going to start a quarrel of such a kind as to embolden in him raids by that voiding force which was already too well established in his soul.

"Well, Alfred," said Justice Durkheim, who was sitting in back of his house in the sun, "you're looking proud of yourself. You must have done something good today."

"I've decided to finish my book this week."

"Decided? I didn't realize one could tell a book when it was done. I thought it told you, like bread in an oven."

"It was really finished months ago, a year ago. I'm going back where I started adding things on in the wrong direction and put an end to it."

"Good. Back to labor law. The way you've been talking you were going off into philosophizing. You don't have the brains for it. Plato took care of all that."

"I'm afraid, Thomas, I'm going to philosophize in my next book. Positive law is only part of it."

"Positive law," the old man said. He was tapping his fingertips together, and his watery blue eyes were staring at Alfred without expression. "Musical music. What other kind of law is there? *The* law, not positive law—what's the matter with *the* law? Natural law was all right till science gave it a merciful death. Divine law? Theologians. Ideal law? Philosophers. *The* law. You're a lawyer. Who do you think cares about your theories? Talk to lawyers. They'll listen when you talk their language. Do you know what professional philosophers are talking about these days? How to talk. If you start philosophizing, that's what you'll wind up doing, talking about how to talk. *The* law, Alfred. It's hard enough to know what *the* law is."

"You're right. That's what I must do, describe it. I'm giving myself three years to do it. But in my own way."

"Three years, is it? Then I've got something to live for." He tinkled the silver bell on the stool beside him. "By God, Alfred, I'll make you read your claptrap to me as you write it. I'll even listen to it. Damn. Here's a man who can write legal English so it can be read, and he wants to theorize instead." His niece came out, a thin, tall old maid with a smile crucified on her anxious face. "Irma, my dear, would you be so good as to bring me my calendar." Blinking, she left. "Alfred, three years from this day I'm going to remind you of your vow. You are under oath."

They sat in silence till Irma returned with his desk calendar.

"Is this the one you wanted, Thomas? Or was it the appointment book?"

He had meant the five-year appointment book but he remembered that he had said "calendar." He did not smile at her or pat her hand, as he occasionally did, but gave it to her straight: he looked her severely but directly in the eye and said, "You're perfectly right, my dear." Acquittal was the dope to which she was addicted. Several times a day she got him to judge her and find her not wanting. She went back into the house a little higher in the shoulders than she had been when she had come out.

"Sometimes," said Alfred, "I find myself thinking about first things. It's a common human activity. Didn't you ever fall into it?"

"Rarely. Not for more than fifty years. This is the wrong century for it. Lord help me, they don't even know how to write bawdy stories any more. What a century. Foundations—you're always putting 'foundations' in your titles. Get away from foundations, man. There isn't anything under them any more. No rock."

"I'm going to see for myself."

"You'll never get to the Supreme Court philosophizing."

"I don't wish to get to the Supreme Court."

"Yes, Alfred, you do." When Alfred began swelling with suppressed expostulation, the old blue eyes blinked and the lids stretched a little. "And a healthy wish it is. Three years. Good. Then the federal bench for you."

· 7 ·

As Alfred walked around Justice Durkheim's house to the front gate, he nodded at the Kwannon under the cypress and said inaudibly, "Why does he have you in front of his house?" Then, looking back from the gate and seeing the statue on the bare ground against the graceful house, he changed his question: "Why did he move into your house? That's much better." He walked along the street swinging his arms. "He wants me to take his way. And a house like that is what it leads to, is it?"

Nancy, long of limb, in shorts and sleeveless blouse, was jogging down the street. At sight of her father she veered to one side and glanced at him slyly. "Hi, Dad," she said noncommittally and showed no signs of pausing.

"Nance!" he ran across the roadway and caught her arm. "You've got an overnight bag. Where are you going?"

Her face became puckered and mean. "I wish I was running away from home."

"Oh?"

"I'm going to spend the night with Shirley. *She* said I couldn't, but I'm going anyway."

"You are disobeying your mother?"

Nancy dropped her head.

"Come," said Alfred and started to pull her with him.

"Wait a minute!" she cried fiercely and wrenched her arm loose from his grasp. "She knows where I'm going. She didn't really try to stop me. She just said I couldn't and when I said I was going to any-way she said 'Oh, all right.' "

They glowered at each other.

"Daddy?"

"What?"

"You know she won't let me go up and take care of Cathy and Tod this summer?"

"She never told me. She must have a good reason."

Nancy dropped her eyes. "Oh?" she said, mimicking his inflection. "Ask her yourself and see how good it is."

"What did she say?"

She looked at him in triumph. "Oh, Daddy, I'm not a tattletale. You taught me yourself never to tattle."

Because he knew he was in the wrong to ask her the question, he could not estimate how much in the wrong her teasing was and did not trust himself to reprimand her for impertinence without being too harsh.

"Go! Get! Wait! Did Shirley tell Mary Louise you're coming? It's all right with her?"

Nancy shrugged and ran off down the street.

By the time he went in the back door of his house he was livid with rage.

· 8 ·

"Beth!"

There was no answer. He heard water running in their bathroom. He ran up the stairs and paused for a second outside the bathroom door. She was not showering but using the washbasin. He rapped on the door sharply.

"Beth!"

"Tell them I'm washing my hair."

"It's not the phone. I want to know about Nancy." He tried to turn the knob; it was locked. "Nancy!"

"She's spending the night at Mary Louise's."

The water began running harder than ever, and she began singing.

He gave the door a kick and rushed across the bedroom toward his study. He opened the first of the double doors he'd had installed and had his thumb on the latch of the inner door; but then, instead of pushing it open, he backed off, remembering his determination to maintain the sanctity of his study. He pushed the door to behind him as hard as he could. But the fit was tight; so far from slamming, it did not even completely close.

The kitchen was cluttered with dirty pans and dishes. He saw with bitter satisfaction that it was after five o'clock and that there was no sign that Beth had started to prepare dinner.

Cold sandwich meat, he thought; carrot strips and pickles. What a wife.

The telephone rang. It was Horace, suggesting that if they weren't tied up they might like to drop over that evening and play some bridge with Virginia and him. Alfred made his voice as politely regretful as he could, but when he came to put the receiver back in its cradle he slammed it down.

When he found himself, as he roamed the house, reluctant to step into the sweet calm of the patio or to stand on the gallery and look at the pearly tranquillity of the Bay, he worried that his anger was dying down. To stoke it, he went into the kitchen and began washing dishes, a chore he had abandoned years before.

"Alfred," said Beth from the doorway, "for heaven's sake, what are you doing?"

He glanced at her over his shoulder without speaking. She was fluffing her hair with her fingers and shaking her head. She was wearing an old workshirt of his, the tails of which hung down below her knees, and there was a towel across her shoulders.

The Saturday afternoon before he had asked her to marry him, he had gone by to see her and found her with Lizzie, who was two, on the porch of her garden cottage, dressed like this and drying her hair like this. Lizzie had stretched her arms out to him and crowed when he appeared, and Beth had waved and giggled.

Over the years he had seen her thus so many scores of times that the original image had worn down, as, by the strokes of the worshipers' fingers, a marble Bambino is worn down to a wraith in the Holy Virgin's arms. But now, quickened to her, he felt again the homely dearness. Annoyed with himself for this yearning, he turned back to the dishpan and plunged some cups and saucers into the suds.

"Alfie, you're white around the lips." She was hovering near, afraid to touch him. "What happened?"

"Did you tell Nancy she couldn't spend the night with Shirley?"

"I told her I didn't want her to, but when she acted so disappointed I let her go. Why?"

What she said was so reasonable and likely, and her tone was so patient, that he was almost reduced to temperance. But his anger rallied. He turned from the sink and pulled off the apron.

"The important question is—why did you tell her she couldn't spend the rest of the summer with the Ravaglis in Mendocino?"

Her mouth became stiff, but her eyes vague. "I don't want Kay to be imposed on. After all, Nancy can be so persuasive. She can talk circles around Kay if she really wants something."

"Woody was for it too."

"They're so *nice*. I just thought I'd protect them from being encroached on. Nancy, you know—Nancy knows how to get her way."

"I was there," he said. "You were not. Why didn't you consult me? Kay and Woody are going back up day after tomorrow. Nancy must tell them yes or no tomorrow."

"I will not be cross-examined. When you can speak to me like a human being . . ."

He grabbed her by the upper arm as she was turning to leave. "What reason did you give Nancy for not letting her go? You hurt her."

"Let go of me." He did so. "My God, here I've just barely got back from my mother's funeral, and my daughter, my baby, wants to go away from me. She doesn't love me."

"What was the reason, Beth? What did you tell her?"

"Why's it so important to you whether she gets a month's free vacation? Are you so cheap?"

"What reason did you give her, Beth?"

"I told her the truth." She tossed her head defiantly.

"Which was?"

"That I might be needing her. That she could be a great help to me."

"Needing her? For what?"

"Lizzie's always rushing off somewhere or other on her field trips. Sybil—oh, you know. She's sweet, I love her so much. But she's hard to get hold of. Somehow I feel closest to Nancy. I lean on her, in a way."

"So you told her you needed her to lean on. My God, Beth." He moved heavily into the dining room and sat, staring at an ashtray. He half hoped she would go off now, for he needed time for his anger to metamorphose into whatever it was going to turn into; but she came slowly after him. "What about leaning on me, wife?"

"Oh, darling, don't be silly, it's not the same. I don't want to just depend on you."

"And what do you expect to come up, for heaven's sake? Your mother has died, yes, but she'd been sick a long time, she wasn't young. And there aren't any difficulties over the will." He glanced at her sharply. "Are there?"

"No, no!"

"Donald isn't causing any trouble?"

"Oh no, it's going right along. Legally."

"Very well then, Beth. I'm giving Nancy permission to go. I'm going to call the Ravaglis now and tell them so. When you are in the mood to tell me what trouble you expect so great that you need a fourteen-year-old child to lean on instead of your husband, all right, I want to hear. But till then we're going to let the girls lead a normal life."

"You're a bully!"

He slammed the kitchen door behind him. As he stood in the hall, dialing and talking with Kay, he heard Beth open a bottle and pour herself a drink, pound the kitchen table with her fist, and sob.

He wanted a drink, but he did not want to speak to her, as he would probably have to do if he went into the kitchen to get it. He dialed Mary Louise's number; Shirley answered, and he asked for Nancy. As he was telling her to be sure to come home early the next day and get ready to go up with the Ravaglis, Beth opened the kitchen door and stood in the doorway, staring at him blackly.

"Now what?" she said.

"Would you like to go out to dinner?"

"Don't try any of your sweet-talk on me. Now what?"

"Now what *what*?"

"We're alone. After weeks of separation, husband and wife are alone. Their ever-loving children have gone off and left them to-gether. What are you going to do about it?"

"Confusion." He did not recognize her. He wanted to go away, but there was no place to go to. His study was not far enough, and she could follow him there. Besides, he did not think that contemplation would do much to set the confusion of his feelings in order. She was thwarting even his impulse to sympathize with her and cherish her. "No more of this." When he saw her respond to this statement with a sneer, he started to walk toward her, not knowing what he was going to do or even what he was feeling. He saw by the widening of her eyes that he was going to hit her.

She backed against the sink, her right hand groping for a place to set her glass down safely. "Alfie?"

He was raising both arms stiffly as he stalked her. Because she looked so frightened, he would not be able to hurt her. He brought his arms down in a clumsy way that landed his hands on both her upper arms in a half-blow, half-grasp, and he repeated this furious caress three times.

"Don't ever speak to me like that again." He stood in front of her, puffing.

She looked up at him after a while and spoke in a subdued, railing voice. "Now you've shown what a strong man you are, go out and let me fix supper."

He squeezed her arm as hard as he could with one hand, then poured himself a tumbler of red wine and went out to the patio. There he sat in the slow fall of the day, no longer riled by confusion of feelings, but not at peace.

· 9 ·

As they were eating their supper of hot canned spaghetti and cold sandwich meats, Alfred mentioned that the Skellingses had invited them over for a game of bridge, and Beth said that was awfully nice of them but she had a lot of ironing and mending to catch up on. He was relieved; no longer furious, he was not quite sure why he had refused Horace so firmly. He looked forward now with pleasure to spending the evening alone with Beth, reading to her or playing word-games with her as she ironed. When they finished eating, he found something smooth and symphonic on the radio, took out a book of complicated crossword puzzles of a punning sort Beth was good at, and established himself in the gallery, where she liked to do the ironing.

She did not come and she did not come, and he heard no sounds from her. Puzzled, he went up to their bedroom, calling softly in case she had fallen asleep. She was in the dressing room, bent over her fingernails. She did not glance up at him.

"I'll be down after a while," she said. "I've been neglecting them for ages."

He retreated, baffled. He could not recall when he had last seen her putting polish on her nails. In fact whenever one of the girls walked around waving her hands stiff-fingered to dry the nail polish, everyone else made fun of her.

Horace had once said he'd divorced Myrna, his fourth wife, because for hours before they went out to dinner or to a party she would traipse around the house in a slip, barefoot, her hair in curlers, her face greased, her toenails red, waving her hands like a bug on its back, and for some reason or other grimacing as though to keep her teeth dry. Now here was Beth—up to what? Horace's account of Myrna had once made Beth laugh till the tears came. Alfred opened a magazine and jumped with thrashing energy into the shallow waters of an article on the deer population in California yesterday and today.

When she came down he noticed nothing untoward in what she was wearing: a faded blue denim skirt, a dark blue T shirt, and a pair of huarachos that Lizzie had brought back from New Mexico and tired of after a while. And for a couple of hours, in the most amiable way, they worked on a crossword puzzle, digressing, laughing. When he brought in a tray of tea and gingersnaps and spread the cups and saucers on the table behind her, she stepped over to him where he sat and softly patted his hair. "Thinner and thinner, Alfie. Hurry up and lose it all on top. I just want you to have a fringe like a monk. It'd be fun to be married to a monk." Under this surface of pleasantness he speculated on why he had been so perturbed by her polishing her nails. Maybe they were dry and cracked. Maybe she'd just felt like it. What was the matter with him anyway that he should be so suspicious and jittery?

At the sound of a car door slamming and of happy voices, Beth said, "Oh dear, I'm all sweaty and messy," and ran off to her dressing room. Alfred sat thinking how easy it would have been for him to interpret this concern for her appearance as evidence of some peculiar impulse in her; instead, he now saw it as demonstrating her desire to come out attractive and pleasant after her sojourn in gloomy places. When she came back down with fresh lipstick on, her hair nicely brushed, and a silver thunderbird pendant on her chest, he complimented her on her appearance, and she blushed.

She put away the iron and ironing board; she rolled up the sprinkled, unironed clothes into a fat sausage; she stacked the piles of ironed things over on the window bench out of notice; she cleared the tea things off the table. And still the young people had not come in. She went to the front door and called, "Lizzie? Sybil?" There were the sounds of good-bys, of motors, of backing and starting, of laughter; then the girls came down the patio steps and burst into the living room.

"What a picnic!" cried Lizzie. "It was the best picnic I've ever been on in my whole life!"

"The food wasn't so great," said Sybil.

"Oh, food. What about the spirit? You're so materialistic sometimes."

"I put the water on for coffee," said Beth. "Why didn't the boys come in? Didn't you invite them?"

"They're not boys, Mother," said Lizzie. "They're men."

"Besides," said Sybil, "it's ten-thirty."

"Ten-thirty!" said Beth. "When did that ever keep either one of you from bringing your young men in?" Her face betrayed an unreasonable distress. "These seemed like particularly nice ones, too."

"They are more than nice," said Lizzie. "Especially Joe. They're real men."

"They're all right," said Sybil. "We invited them in, Mother. The reason they didn't come was that Leon is scared of Dad."

"Oh, lord!" said Alfred.

"He is," said Lizzie. "You said you didn't want to see him till tomorrow at three, and wild horses wouldn't have dragged him in to-night. Joe wanted to come, though."

Alfred would have laughed and let this pass, had he not caught a black glance from Beth.

"As I recall it," he said, "it was you girls who decided I wasn't to see him till tomorrow afternoon. If I am not mistaken, you, Sybil, said the words, though both of you were in on it."

He watched Beth closely as the girls stuttered their explanations. She looked at them briefly, with blame in her expression, shrugged irritably, and began picking up the bundles they had dropped helter-skelter.

"None of that martyr stuff," said Sybil brusquely. She seized her mother from behind. "Get to work, Liz."

Lizzie wrenched the bundles from Beth's arms. "This is our job, Ma."

Beth looked for an instant as though she was going to tongue-whip them; but then she gave way. They moved toward the kitchen, chattering.

"Joe's coming by for me tomorrow at noon," said Lizzie.

"Are you falling in love with him, darling?" said Beth.

"Mother!" said Sybil. "That's the sort of question you taught us never to ask."

"I know," said Beth. "Are you, Liz?"

"Anyhow," said Lizzie, "it doesn't matter if you did ask it. People like me don't 'fall in love.' It's childish. It's passé."

Alfred sat alone, trying to order his thoughts about Beth's behavior. If she had silently blamed him but not the girls, he would have taken it that she was angry at him for some reason or other. But she had blamed the girls too. So she must have wanted to see Joe and Leon. Why? She hardly knew them. Her concern for her fingernails, her hurry when they'd heard the car pull up, her anger when the men had not come in—all this seemed to point to her being somehow or other taken with them. Alfred remembered that she had looked happy, too, when waving the young people good-by earlier in the day. Then he caught sight of "she doesn't love me any more" among his thoughts and clobbered it over the noggin and stuffed it back in a hole out of sight.

There was the question of her not wanting Nancy to go up with Kay and Woody for a month.

This was a bad puzzle he was working on; there seemed to be more than one way for the parts to fit together.

10

"Where are we going?" Lizzie asked when they had finished lunch. "I thought we'd take a walk," said Joe. "Okay?"

"Where?"

"Just around here." He paid no attention to the disappointment in her "Oh." "You know, chick, I'm from the flatlands myself. I just want to get a notion how you three-dimensional people up here live."

"You're all gussied up," she said maliciously. "Is that the way they do things down on the flatlands, dress to the teeth on a nice warm summer afternoon?"

"I just came from Communion."

"Oh, really! What church?" She knew her reaction was rude, but she was glad the words had got out before she'd had time to stop them. "You don't have to answer if you don't want to."

"True," he said sardonically. "It's in the Constitution."

"I mean . . ."

"I go to Saint Dunstan's. Do you know anybody that goes to church, Liz?"

"I used to. I even went myself for a while, to the Unitarian church. I don't know whether I know anybody now or not." She thought for a couple of hundred feet. "No, I guess I don't. It's not a Berkeley custom."

He laughed his slow, painful, contagious laugh.

"You laugh," she said severely. She pulled herself up straight, like a suffragette, though she was wearing, as usual, a rather tight skirt; and she strode as though she were marching, though her hips swung somewhat amply at every stride. "Maybe you don't realize that the Bay Area has the lowest rate of church attendance in the United States."

"And the highest suicide rate."

"Correlation is not causation." She looked up at him triumphantly. "So there."

"So what's new? Seen any good TV shows recently?"

"Yes, as a matter of fact, I did."

"Do tell! You mean your father has a TV set?"

"He doesn't, but I do." She scowled up at him. "And why shouldn't I? I bought it with my own money."

"That's all right, baby. All I meant was, the way he laid into TV one day in class I didn't think he'd even allow a set in his house. You see how wrong I can be."

"Why, he even comes down to my room and watches it sometimes. I let him."

"You *let* him!"

"He never comes into my room without asking my permission."

"That's your idea?" he said.

"Not particularly. It's just the way things are done in our house. And it's the right way, too."

"So what was the good show you saw?"

"A panel discussion on the role of the social sciences in a changing world."

He groaned and mock-staggered.

"What's the matter with you, Bugs Bunny?" she said. "You don't think the social sciences have a role? Or don't you think the world is changing?"

"You bet your boots it is. But I'd rather watch a wrestling match."

"Daddy watches sports mostly. Of course, all TV is good for is serious discussions and sports."

"Lordy, lordy," he said, holding his hands palm forward on both sides of his head and trembling them like a vaudeville darky. "You missed your calling, Lady Liz, you missed your calling. You should be working for American Can. I worked for them one summer, and I know just the very spot on the line for you: packaging. In one hour you'd do the mostest, bestest packaging—of *anything*—in the history of the American Can Corporation nationwide. And labeling of course. Neat? Oh my lord, she's neat."

She stopped, fists on her hips, and when he grimaced mock-repentantly at her she punched him as hard as she could in the belly. Taken by surprise, he gave a genuine grunt of pain. When he bent over, she hit him again, in would-be karate style, on the side of his neck with the edge of her soft hand, and then ran back down the road.

He followed her at a distance till she slowed to a walk. Then, when she was going by trees at a bend in the road, out of sight of any house, he caught up with her, taking her hand. She tried to yank it free, but he pulled her to a stop. He hoped she would look at him defiantly, so he could apologize by losing a fight with her. But she just stood there, not looking up at him, steadily trying to pull her hand from his.

"I'm sorry, Lizzie. I didn't know you well enough to say what I did."

"Oh, so you're that sort, are you?"

"What sort?"

"A betrayer. The kind of person that makes friends and then hurts them. You only say hurtful things to a person when you know them well."

He dropped her hand and stepped back a half-pace. She turned from him toward the thicket rising from the hillside below them. He made himself speak clearly.

"That's not what I meant. I'll say it again. I didn't know you well enough to say what I said."

"And you never will."

"Which way do you want me to take that?"

"Oh, good lord, can't you take anything straight?" She glared at him over her shoulder. "Take it any way that hurts."

"They both hurt. One means you'll never let me get to know you very well, and the other means no matter how well I get to know you I'll never have the right to tease you."

"Oh." She broke off a twig. "I guess I didn't mean either of those exactly." He moved beside her, waiting. "I can see how you might think I did." She looked at him. When she saw the light in his eyes, the frown of thoughtfulness on her face turned into a frown of anger. "What I meant was, don't ever call me dogmatic. People have been calling me dogmatic for years, and I hate it. I can't help being dogmatic any more than you can help . . ."

"Than I can help what?"

"Oh, moving the way you do."

"How's that?"

"I don't know. Like a leopard or something."

"I'd tell you what you move like," he said, "if I knew you better."

They began strolling up a side street. She did not accept his gambit. He had intended to say she bounced along like a plump little bunny, but he caught himself back from this indiscretion and said nothing.

"Well," she said finally, "you didn't know me well enough this time yesterday, but maybe you do now. Tell me."

"The way you were running up the road back there a while ago reminded me of a moose."

"A moose!"

"Yes, a moose. Have you ever seen one run?"

"Of course not."

"Well, I have."

"Where?"

"Idaho."

"Don't they have big stupid faces?"

"I was talking about the way they run."

"And last evening on the beach you called me an artichoke."

"All prickly and succulent. Yes."

"So," she said sternly, "I'm a dogmatic artichoke that moves like a moose. What in the world sort of creature do you . . ."

But his laughter began to dissolve her indignation, at first into blunt snorts and then into peals that mingled with his.

When, as they began to stroll on, his hand took hers, her fingers laced through his and returned their pressure.

"My, I like these houses," he said. "Don't you?"

"I guess so. Some of them."

"You're so cool? I think they're wonderful."

"Good. It's just that I grew up with them sprouting up all around. Maybe I'm choosy."

"Yes, you are," he said.

"Is that good?"

"I'm not sure yet. Probably."

Halfway up the steep slope above them a redwood house with window walls to the west was cantilevered out from the hillside, jutting free of all foreground toward a stark panorama of the Bay, the Marin hills, and Francisco.

"I was born in Atlanta," he said, "and when the depression came along after a while my folks moved to East Oakland, down on the flats, below Fourteenth Street."

"What did your father do?"

"Factory hand. Still is, for that matter. Used to be a metal handler, and then during the war he operated a drill press for a while, and even a lathe. He's not as young as he was, and nowadays he's riding a fork lift. He's steady. Well anyway, all I ever grew up among was shoebox houses. The only beautiful building I saw till I was grown up was church."

"Episcopal?"

"Yes. They're mostly very beautiful. Mother went to church every Sunday and took us kids. I got three sisters. Mother died when I was fourteen."

"Didn't you ever go exploring? You weren't all that far from Piedmont and the hills, were you? Or San Francisco, for that matter?"

"You know, where I grew up, us kids were sort of like sparrows. We had our little area we kept guard over, maybe a few blocks, and every so often we'd go flying out and look around, when we got big enough to drive cars especially. But on the whole, all we knew was our own little bailiwick. We were *scared*. Sure, we'd drive through Piedmont sometimes, even up here in the Berkeley hills, but we wouldn't see anything. We couldn't *look*. You know, if your father hadn't invited me up to your house the way he did, and if you weren't here with me, I wouldn't be able to look at these houses here right this minute. They *cost*. Oh," he said, "Lizzie. Oh dearie me, Lizzie baby, I do want money in the worst way."

11

For some reason she suddenly felt bursting with good feelings and went bounding up the road ahead of him.

Moose, he thought. Hell. That plump little rump? She ought to be eaten up for her own good.

She thought that to want money was ignoble. She had no idea why Joe's confession that he wanted it so much made her feel happy instead of disgusted or, at the most, sympathetic with him; she ran ahead partly so he would not take offense at seeing how broadly her face was beaming. Here he had just insulted her; apparently he was part Negro and passing for white, a surreptitious sort of thing to do and moreover an evasion of his ethnic privileges and duty; he went to church; he wanted money in the crassest, most bourgeois way imaginable; yet she was practically dancing for him.

"Oh, Joe, it's such a beautiful afternoon that it just makes me feel wonderful. Don't you?"

"I do," he said.

He caught her hands, and they began revolving toe to toe, leaning back, held on each other's stretched-out arms.

They were in a driveway that turned sharply and led to a car shelter consisting of a flat roof on four pipes. Down the hill through a terraced garden a path of stepping stones led to a long, low house among trees.

"I'd even settle for that," he said.

"There's no view from here in this valley."

"It's pretty, though. I'll take it."

"Yes, pretty," she said with scorn. "All you'd ever want to do in a house like that is clip coupons and sniff roses."

"There are worse fates."

"It's not real," she announced. "East Oakland is real. The Pueblos are beautiful *and* real."

"You ever watch the quiz shows on TV?"

"A few."

"What did you think of them?"

"Gunk. Some of the people certainly knew a lot."

"Well, they answered a lot of hard questions all right. I got me a forty-second cousin works for one of the networks in New York. He was out here recently, and he said they're starting up the biggest giveaway show in history this fall. I mean *money*."

"So?"

"Lots of money."

"I think it's disgusting."

"What is? Easy money?"

"Giving away money like that. I wouldn't—"

"Oh now, Liz, take it easy, baby. This may be set up as a team show—man and woman. The least you can make, even if you crap out on the first throw, is five hundred smackeroos apiece and a free trip to New York."

"Disgusting. Money should matter."

"Matter! What do you think I've been talking about? Of course it matters."

"I mean, people shouldn't get all mixed up about it. You know?"

"No, frankly, I don't. What I was trying to say—before you turned on that Mixmaster you got in your head instead of a brain—was that if I could get me a partner, like you for instance, we would have a good chance of getting on the show. If they want partners, that is. Anyway, it'd be worth a try."

"*I* don't know anything."

"Indians?"

"Even if I did know anything I wouldn't do it."

"It's possible to make fifty or sixty grand. Somebody will."

"Oh, for heaven's sake. Oh, that's indecent."

"That chick Leon brought to your father's party . . ."

"Robin."

"Yes. Well, I understand she's gone to New York."

"I wouldn't know," she answered. "But she'd do it all right, if there's any money in it."

"Maybe. You don't know her?"

"I just met her twice. She'll do it. If she knows enough to answer any questions, that is."

"Oh, well," he drawled, "I gather from my cousin that people have been known to perform marvels. I expect Robin wants the money."

"I expect she does," said Lizzie and spat. "And that's no way to treat money."

"It's not holy, you know."

"No, and it's not feces either. Whatever the Freudians say, it's not feces. I may not know exactly what it is, but I know that it is important. This all upsets me, I hate it, let's talk about something else."

"Well, for crying out loud."

"You're all mixed up, you know. I just can't imagine—"

"All right, all right, lay off. That's enough. We'll talk about something else."

They walked along for five minutes before they began talking again. The first subject was the chances of war with Russia; the next was the weather; the next was the way the press was covering a notorious murder trial. At this point they found themselves on the road home, hurrying.

· 12 ·

"You must forgive me," said Alfred, "if I don't advise you. You catch me at a bad time."

Leon jumped to his feet. "If I had known—"

"Oh, sit down." Alfred was tilted back in his swivel chair with his feet on the edge of his desk. He flapped his hands at Leon, who eased stiffly back into his armchair. "It's not that I'm reluctant to give advice. If you ever want to know whether to marry such and such a woman—"

"Like Robin?"

"Sure—don't marry Robin. No, there's a special reason why this is a bad time for you to be asking me whether to devote yourself to the law or to teaching. I'm asking myself the same question. How can I tell you what to do when I haven't even told myself yet?"

"Oh, come off it. You do both."

"I'd like to think that I've chosen both professions, with a steadiness and largeness of blah transcending the blahness of blah, blah, blah. But the suspicion is beginning to bother me that what I have been doing is refusing to commit myself fully to either teaching or the practice of law."

When someone came to Alfred for advice, he was careful to connect himself with the question, to make it clear that he had similar difficulties himself.

"What about your book?" said Leon.

"Oh, my book." Hearing the impatient dismissal in his own voice, Alfred realized that he was in danger of deflecting the conversation to himself entirely. "I'm giving it to the typist tomorrow."

"I mean," Leon pressed, "you have committed yourself there, surely."

"Justice Durkheim yesterday— Please, enough of this. This is bad of me."

"Please, please," cried Leon with a note of distress in his voice. "What did he do? This matters to me."

Alfred bit his lips together, then spoke dryly. "I told him I was going to give myself three years to write the book I really want to write on the law. He made me realize that by setting a time limit I wasn't fully committing myself. An escape hatch, always the escape hatch. He said he'd have something to live for for the next three years just to hold me to my resolution. He'll do it too. He thinks I'm no philosopher. He wants me to become a judge."

"But this is shocking." Leon bounded from his chair and began pacing. "You're a man of—a man in—" He waved both arms. "No good can come of this. One must know what one wants if one wants to . . . Look, Alfred, you know Roy Carver? That fellow at your party in June?" Alfred nodded. "He's a reporter on a labor paper. I've got to know him pretty well in the last few weeks. We both eat at Chantal Bigonneau's."

"The girls were talking about it."

"I board with her four dinners a week. She cooks like—well, like nothing I ever dreamt of. Anyway, the better I get to know Roy the more I don't want to be like him. He's never *in* anything; he prowls around the edges, peering and poking and making jokes. Sometimes his jokes are also very intelligent observations. Of course he's a journalist, it's easy to see him as an outsider. But my point is, I'm too much like that myself."

"Well," said Alfred, "he's involved in the McKee strike."

"He knows all about it," said Leon, "he knows the union officials involved, he's talked to the pickets and the management. That's not the same thing."

"You've seen him recently?"

"What are you getting at?"

"How can you be so sure of the extent of his involvement in the strike?"

"Naturally I'm interested," said Leon. "Roy's told me a lot about it, and I went down with him last week to see the plant and the pickets. I assure you I wasn't a bit further out of it than Roy was. There I was—a complete stranger to everyone, no official connection to either labor or management, no real emotional commitment even, since I tend to favor unions but this union is loopy on this issue. And Roy was saying hi and what's doing, men were nodding at me. Yet they didn't let him get any closer than they let me."

"Physically, you mean?" said Alfred.

"Physically too," said Leon, "but mostly I meant, well, socially, personally. I'm not exaggerating. Talking died when he came up, they look at him without expression. Of course they looked at me suspiciously, but when I didn't do anything they just ignored me. Suspicion, ignoring—nothing's worse than blank looks at a man who is not a stranger. And then a couple of evenings ago Chantal's friend Harry Evans showed up. He's the one who brought her over from France. I don't really know a thing about him—where he came from, what he does for a living, what he stands for. But the way he asked Roy about the strike was *committed*. He telephoned somebody Roy told him about, some sort of official, not in the union, I don't know in what—Zagri, some name that sounded like Zagri—and the way Evans talked he was already *in* things. You see, Alfred, more and more I'm coming to think that the great question of our time is commitment. We must commit ourselves." Leon paused, frowning, at Alfred's laughter. "I'm serious. This is a major problem."

"It's the way you put it—we must commit ourselves. That is what one says of a man who is voluntarily entering a mental hospital: he is committing himself."

Leon glowered and sniffed. "A judge, Alfred—you a judge? By definition a judge is not committed to anything concrete. One cannot be committed to anything so abstract as the Law. 'The best lack all conviction, while the worst are full of passionate intensity.' That's **the** trouble, and we've got to do something about it."

"Conviction too now," said Alfred. "So that's what a judge does. Lacking conviction and commitment, he sits up there and convicts and commits others."

"You think that's a joke. Well, it isn't. It's the sober truth. Pilate was a judge."

A red stain spread from the bridge of Alfred's nose up onto his forehead and part way down his nose and onto his cheeks under the eyes. He carefully removed his glasses and laid them on the desk in front of him.

Leon recognized these signs from a couple of episodes in the seminar. He feared that if he paused at this moment he might back down before Alfred's anger. So he plunged on.

"I don't know whether it's true for all judges at all times, but for you it must be. You a judge! You uncommitted! What a violation. The man who would want that for you must be a fool." He half expected Alfred to hit him; he did not know what he would do if he did.

"Tell me," Alfred began, then stopped for a moment till his teeth quit chattering. "I'm curious about this Harry Evans you mentioned."

"He has great personal force. Look, Alfred, I'm sorry I—"

"Tell me, what do you think he's committed to?"

"I'm not sure. He doesn't exactly open up. He's a friend of Chantal's, so I assume he's on the side of the angels."

"Ah. What does he look like? How does he talk?"

"Broad shoulders, a rather dingy effect all in all, wears a dark suit and a poorly knotted tie, scuffed shoes, drinks too much, raspy voice, intense light blue eyes that look over to the left most of the time and then catch you all of a sudden. Why?"

"What does he have to do with the strike?"

"Nothing that I know of. He's just interested."

"Ah. And what's so odd about the strike itself?"

"The men claim it's a question of seniority. Their own officials tell them they're wrong, their contract gives management the right to appoint any foremen it wants to. Roy says it's obviously a question of race prejudice. The men will work with a Negro but they won't work under him. You know the situation? McKee's promoted a Negro to foreman, with less seniority than three whites. There seems to be no doubt that he's the best machinist in the shop. He has a degree in mechanical engineering. But the men deny that race has anything to do with it."

"What do you think it's all about?"

Leon shrugged. "That department is making bombsights these days. Maybe the men don't like making bombs."

"Oh?"

"I'm being funny."

"Ah." Leon's version of the strike differed from the one Horace had told Alfred chiefly in that Leon did not speculate so much on the strikers' hidden motives as Horace, an experienced conciliator, had done. Alfred decided to use Leon as a source of information. To be sure, Leon would not like discovering that he had been used without having been told he was being used; but at the moment Alfred took a certain pleasure in the thought of Leon's feeling offended. Anyway —so Alfred justified himself—Leon would be a better informant for not knowing that his information might be satisfying more than Alfred's personal curiosity.

"You know, Leon," Alfred said in a relaxed way. But it was a studied relaxation. "You know, this case promises to be of interest. I'd appreciate your letting me know about any further developments. It seems to me that something new is in the air. The labor movement is in process of changing. My book will be obsolete by the time it's published. No, that's too strong; it won't be obsolete, it will be historical, about past history. Oh, to be sure, the same laws will still be applicable, the various officials in labor, management, and government will go on behaving as though everything were as it has been. Meanwhile something strange is stirring. There is a lot of talk in intellectual circles about labor seeking larger social goals—bread-and-butter issues are no longer the real thing for many unions, better pay is just a substitute satisfaction for a malaise whose origins are completely different. But this is all *ought* talk. *Ought* is the curse of liberalism. This analysis of the labor problem—you know the sort of slogan, New Challenge for Labor—it's intelligent enough, so far as it goes; maybe it's even right. But I want to know what's actually going on. What are the men actually moved by? What are they using the unions for, now that they have most of what the unions were made to get in the first place, wages and hours? One doesn't speak of 'the business movement.' I'm beginning to think that the labor movement is as archaic as states' rights. You see my area of conjecture? I'd be interested in anything you pick up. I'm in the dark. This Evans fellow, for example, what about him?"

"Roy worships him."

"Good. What about the men? Does he have any followers— No, are any of the men under his influence? Or is this all spontaneous?"

"I get you."

"Is there any person secretly behind it all? Any idea?"

"Okay. I'll poke around."

They lapsed into silence.

There was the sound of the gate opening and two pairs of footsteps going down into the patio. "Oo-hoo," called Lizzie, "we're here."

Leon bounded up with the energy of relief and went to the window.

"Joe and Lizzie," said Alfred, wanting to keep Leon from calling out. "Let's go down to the living room and have a drink with them." But he did not get out of his chair.

Leon started for the door, then stopped. Alfred was waiting.

"You know why I said so much, Alfred. It's no excuse, I realize. But everything that happens to you matters so much to me that I just didn't control myself."

"I have observed that frequently those who come seeking advice are also bursting to give it."

"Thank you, Alfred. Very gracefully done. That's not all there is to it, of course."

"No, that's not all there is to it, but it'll do. I need a gin and tonic."

They went down.

· 13 ·

As Alfred was mixing the drinks and the others were talking, the telephone rang for Hugh. Beth called out from the gallery window, but there was no answer from his cottage.

"Oh lord," she said. "Lizzie dear, would you go see if he's home?" When Lizzie ran off, Beth spoke to Joe and Leon. "We haven't had three calls for him all year. He doesn't abuse the phone privilege. I'm sure this call is important." She fluttered, without humor. "I'm upset because Nancy—that's my youngest—has just gone off with the Ravaglis to their ranch for the rest of the summer. It's her first time away from home, really." She smiled wanly, beseechingly. "Of course I'm just being silly. She couldn't be in better hands."

Leon, covering his embarrassment, began telling her about a summer camp where he had once been a counselor. She hung on his words.

Lizzie found Hugh asleep, roused him, and sent him up to the phone. On her way back into the house she looked into Sybil's room and found her at her dressing table, chin in her fist, staring out the window.

"Syb, don't you hear the men? Joe and Leon!"

"I hear."

"You're all dressed. Come on up."

"You know who's coming for me in half an hour."

"Brewster? I thought you said you like him."

"I do. We're going to a progressive jazz concert, which I expect to enjoy, and then to the New Pisa for dinner—at least I'm going to plug for the New Pisa because I know I'll enjoy that—and then some foreign movie. *And* he'll kiss me good night. So I don't want to spoil things by talking to those goons before he comes."

"Sybil! You liked Leon well enough yesterday."

"Phooey. He's patronizing towards me."

"What's the matter, didn't he kiss you good night?"

"No, he did not, and I wouldn't let him if he tried."

Whereupon, without a glance in the mirror, she got up and went upstairs with Lizzie.

"You're here!" cried Leon when she appeared. "What a treat!" He put his arm across Sybil's shoulders familiarly but not amorously. She did not pull away but leaned stiffly. "You know, that was the best picnic I've ever been on in my life. Mrs. Royce," he said to Beth, relinquishing his hold on Sybil, "you have two of the most charming daughters in the world, and if I do not say three I am sure it is only because I scarcely know Nancy." He held up his glass for a toast; the others raised theirs. "To Beth Royce, for the happiness she has caused to come about, and may she have many more years of happiness herself."

With this toast Sybil moved back up against him. As he drank he glanced down at her, and she wrinkled her nose at him.

Beth cried a little, her lower lip trembling as she smiled. "That's the nicest thing that has happened to me in I don't know how long."

Joe, who had assumed that Leon's speeches had been mere flattery, was amazed at their effect on these people, who he had supposed were too sophisticated to be soft-soaped. Alfred's eyes looked moist, and Lizzie was smiling fit to burst.

Hugh came sidling out from the kitchen, his arms intertwining.

"Mrs. Royce," he said tentatively.

"Come in," said Alfred, "good lord, come on in."

108

"I do hate to interrupt, but it's sort of urgent. Mrs. Royce, maybe you'd like to step out in the kitchen with me for a minute?"

"Nonsense," said Beth, taking him by the arm. "You must join us. Alfred, Hugh needs a drink."

"You see," Hugh said, "that was Robin, and I—"

"Who?" said Leon somewhat peremptorily.

Hugh's head swiveled toward Leon and at the same time drew back on its neck away from him. "I said Robin. My friend. Why?"

"Sorry. I knew a Robin. Can't be the same person."

My Robin," said Hugh, his head both turning and moving toward Beth, "called to say that we have a ride all the way to New York, and we can stop over in Iowa! Robin and I do all the driving, and our transportation won't cost us a cent. It's an elderly couple going to Europe, and they are afraid of planes and *she* can't stand trains."

There were general congratulations, and Hugh beamed.

"Why are you so glad," Lizzie asked, "to stop over in Iowa?"

"Mama, of course," he said with a tiny frown.

"Your father's a farmer?" said Beth.

"Half the time." Hugh waggled his eyebrows. "The other half of the time the government pays him *not* to farm. He's in Montana. It's Mama I'm going to see in Iowa, if you must know. She's with the county recorder in Ottumwa. Well, I'm sure none of you are interested in my family history. *I'm* not. What I have to tell you, Mrs. Royce, is that we are going to leave first thing tomorrow morning."

"Not so soon!" cried Beth with undue distress.

He looked terribly upset, and the girls reassured him that the harm he would do by leaving next day would not be irreparable. Beth said so too.

"Joe may be going to New York before long," said Lizzie and was gratified by the scowl Joe cast her.

"Who knows?" he said. "I'll look you up, Hugh."

"How can you look me up?" said Hugh snippily. "I don't know where I'll be myself. I hardly know a soul in New York."

"Leon knows someone there," said Sybil and was gratified when Leon looked at her sharply. "Have you heard from your Robin since she left?"

"She'll go to the YWCA when she gets there."

"Oh!" cried Hugh. "Now I know! Francis's Robin, the one who was so good in that Wilde thing Francis did last year, *Lady Windermere's Fan*. Was she here at the party? I wish I'd realized. She was so good, I wanted to tell her how good she was. I thought she was going to Saint Louis with Francis this summer, to the Mudge Arena Theatre."

109

"She went," said Leon curtly. "She was in three of the productions. She just wrote me, she's on her way to New York."

"I'm sure she won't still be at the Y when I get there," said Hugh anxiously. Then he brightened. "But they'll be able to tell me where she is. I must be sure to look her up." He became aware that he was the center of all eyes and that some of those eyes were cool. "Well, I know I'm just boring you all to death with so much me. I must go pack and clean up now."

"Oh," said Beth, "you are so neat and clean, Hugh, don't give another thought to cleaning the cabin."

"Hugh," said Lizzie after he had started to leave, "are you going to try to get on a quiz show?"

He wrinkled his nose and shifted his shoulder.

"Joe's going to," said Lizzie. "Maybe he could get you on."

"No, thanks," said Hugh. "Thanks just the same. There are limits."

Lizzie snorted at this slur, but Joe shook his head at her.

Beth went with Hugh, insisting, over his protests, on helping him.

"Well," said Joe and rose, "I guess I've got to be shoving. I've got to see a client at five in East Oakland. I haven't passed the bar yet, but my uncle lets me work with him. This guy I'm going to see is an old pal, and I don't know too much about what he wants, but I've got to go talk to him over a beer."

"In a bar in East Oakland?" Lizzie asked greedily, her sentence loaded with the unspoken words "real life."

"Sort of. A joint we used to hang out in when we weren't old enough to suppose to. Iggy's Igloo." He spoke with obvious reluctance and he was moving toward the door.

"Income tax?" said Sybil, her voice friendly and her eye as malicious as Lizzie's. "Didn't you once say your uncle is in income-tax law?"

"More or less, but mostly he's a general practitioner, as you might say. Well, I've got to get going."

"Come on," cried Lizzie, "tell us who you're going to see."

"Lizzie," said Alfred, "this is a professional matter."

She stuck her tongue out at her father. "Oh, come on, Joe."

"Well, he's mixed up in this McKee business," said Joe. "He's one of the machinists that got passed over when a Negro was made foreman."

"Oh," said Alfred, his face displaying every sign of eagerness but his voice neutral, "that must be especially interesting to you."

"Oh, I don't know," said Joe.

"Daddy," said Lizzie, mocking him, "this is a professional matter."

Joe looked down his nose at her, then back at Alfred. "It depends on what he wants and what I can do about it. All I know is what he told me over the phone, that it doesn't have anything to do with the union or the management as such. So, I don't know."

Joe and Leon told the girls good-by perfunctorily, but the voices with which they kept talking with Alfred at the door were animated.

Sybil made a little face and started to go back down to her room, but Lizzie pulled her up into their father's study.

"What're we coming up here for?" Sybil whispered.

"I want to hear what they say about us. Sssh."

Lizzie quietly raised the window on the street side of the room and adjusted the Venetian blinds so that no one could see in.

"What if Daddy catches us?" Sybil asked.

"Maybe he won't."

In fact, after Alfred took leave of Joe and Leon in the patio, he went to the window in the gallery and stood staring at the city. He was trying to imagine what was going on at McKee's. Then he tried to understand the emotional currents and undercurrents among the group that afternoon, and failed.

He saw Beth carry a straight chair out of Hugh's shack, then fetch a rag rug, shake it, and hang it over the chair back; and he remembered something that she had said yesterday. She had spoken in a reflective way, thinking aloud; the sentence had not been apropos of anything they had been talking about; he had been thinking of something else, so he had not really paid attention. But now the words returned. *"Where* am I going to put everything?" What could she have been referring to but the possessions she had inherited from her mother? But when she had left for Texas she had asserted vigorously that she would sell everything she did not give away to relatives and her mother's friends, for she did not need or even like most of her mother's things. He heard Beth's carefree laugh. Why on earth should helping Hugh get ready to leave make her so cheery? Then he tossed up his hands in a shrug.

Outside the study by their cars, Leon and Joe were chatting before driving off. The girls were behind the Venetian blinds, listening.

"I think," Leon asserted, "that I'm going to law school this year."

"Yeah?" said Joe. "It's not much fun. I thought you liked teaching."

Leon began talking about importance to society, commitment to central issues of the time, and intellectual integrity.

"Yeah, sure," said Joe. "Well, I got to go now."

"I admire you, Joe. You know what you want."

"Well, I know what I got to have. Alfred, now—he's free to have most anything he wants. That'd worry me."

"Alfred is saintly," said Leon.

"He's what?"

"He's the saintliest person I ever knew."

"Man, watch those huge words," said Joe. "You got to be careful where you lay them down. You drop one that size down the well, you splash all the water out. Now watch it."

· 14 ·

Lizzie was so amazed both by what Leon had said and by Joe's response that she had to clap her hands over her mouth to keep her giggles in; she rolled back onto the floor. Sybil, when neither of the men laughed at what they had said, scowled furiously, raised a slat, and peeked out at them.

"Oh my God," she mouthed silently.

Lizzie questioned her with a frown. She beckoned, and they tiptoed off into their parents' bedroom.

"What is it, Syb? What are they doing?"

"I can't stand either one of them. What fools."

"They are pretty hard to take. Joe's a big letdown to me."

"And who's coming up the street but Brewster," said Sybil. "He looks like a worse fool than either of them. Do you want to go to the jazz concert?"

"Sure. But three's a crowd."

"I'm sick, Liz. Do me a favor. Go with him in my place. At least you'll get kissed good night."

"Sybil! Really!"

"If I'm going to go the Brewster route, I'm going the full distance —Marcus Turnipseed or nothing. I'm sick. Good-by and good luck to you, Brewster Adams. Thanks loads, Liz."

Lizzie, waiting alone in the patio for Brewster, decided to be unkind to him. He was a short, stocky man with a crew cut and obtrusively perfect teeth, and he was carrying a gardenia corsage. She was more than unkind, she was brutal. She told him in one sentence that Sybil was sick but that she would take her place, if he didn't mind. But after a moment of confusion ("I'm sorry she's sick, I'd be delighted if you would come instead"), he beamed so openly that Lizzie blushed. Laughing, he gave her the corsage

"You know," he said, "when a man seems to choose between two attractive sisters he's afraid of having offended the one he did not choose. And here you are as friendly as can be, and so is Sybil for letting me take you instead of her. Now, no matter what the future brings, I feel we'll always be friends, all three of us."

What he said struck her as being so forthright and sensible that she was ashamed of her unkind intentions and forgave him his flat, accountant's way of putting things.

On the way to the restaurant after the concert, he mentioned that he thought of specializing in inheritance law, if he did not go into politics after his year at Sacramento. She spoke with contempt of bourgeois property obsession and told him how the Koyala could not understand what the term private property meant, even after they learned English, but thought of things and land as there for the use and benefit of all the people. He said that was wonderful, but he was descended from Adam and Eve: he had a free will. And nothing fascinated him more than trying to make up his mind about the will of the dead, which was nowhere more clearly expressed than in what they chose to do with their property. Again she felt ashamed by the seriousness beneath his dullness, and she drew him out in an argument so warm that it carried through dinner and they skipped the movie entirely.

When Lizzie got home, Sybil, in pajamas, came into her room as she was undressing. "Did you go to the New Pisa?"

"No, Chinatown," said Lizzie.

"Well, how was everything?"

"I can't stand cool jazz. It's too nervous. I like a good old physiological beat I can dance to."

"I like it," said Sybil.

"Good for you. But we had such a wonderful argument we didn't even go to a movie."

"What about?" Sybil asked glumly.

"Free will and life after death and property and inheritance."

The more Lizzie glowed about the evening, the glummer Sybil became.

"Did he kiss you good night?"

"Yes, and he's a lot sexier than I'd expected."

Without a word Sybil left. Lizzie thought she heard her sobbing in her room, and shrugged.

· 15 ·

Leon went up the back stairs and greeted Chantal in the kitchen first thing upon entering.

In her blue smock, standing at the stove, she was stirring something in a saucepan.

"Ah." He groaned ritually. "What odors. Chicken?"

"Is it not Sunday? Of course we have chicken."

"I smell something new in that sauce. What a woman for chicken."

"That's true."

"And no false modesty to her either."

"If it is said, 'Chantal Bigonneau is a perhaps meager little woman with a sharp nose,' one must say it is true. If it is said, 'Chantal Bigonneau knows many excellent ways to cook chicken,' one must also say it is true." She shrugged. "Go, you will divert me. They're in there already."

"They" were Roy Carver and Harry Evans, talking in the living room. At the sound of Leon's voice saying hello to Jean-Louis, who was playing solitaire at the table in the dining room, the two men fell silent, but they greeted Leon amiably enough when he joined them.

Evans was a paunchy, half-bald man of medium stature, dressed in a blue suit and white shirt that looked as though he had slept in them. His left sock was on upside down, the heel up on his instep. There was always some part of him in motion; he would be scratching his ear, clicking his teeth, half humming, or, if nothing more, jiggling one of his big toes in its shoe so that the calf of that leg would be twitching, as it was doing now.

Roy was slumped down on the couch, meticulously tearing a paper match to bits. Debris from other matches was scattered on the couch beside him.

"Why are you mad at Chantal?" Leon said in a soft voice. Roy cocked an eyebrow at him. "You're making a mess on her couch cover."

"That's true," said Evans to Roy. "None of the stuff seems to get onto you." But it was Leon, not Roy, whom Evans glanced at with hostility.

With a wide sweep Roy brushed the bits of paper onto the floor. Then, staring at Leon, he took the cigarette from his mouth for the first time since Leon had come into the room, fished a shred of tobacco from his lower lip with his tongue, spat it in the direction of Leon's shoe, put the cigarette back in the corner of his mouth, tore a paper match from a fresh packet, lit it, immediately blew the flame out, and began tearing it to bits, which he let fall onto his shirt. For some reason these trivial acts absorbed the attention of all three men.

Evans gave his head a little shake and turned to Leon. "Where have you been?"

Despite a certain note of demand in Evans' voice, Leon took this request as an effort at politeness after Roy's obscure behavior.

"As a matter of fact," Leon said, "a little while ago I was talking to a young lawyer, and he was about to keep an appointment with a man involved in the McKee strike."

Roy did not react, but Evans rolled forward in his chair, his scowl heavy with demand.

"This man," said Leon, "is one of the three with seniority on that Negro who got promoted over them."

"And what does he want his own lawyer for?" Evans asked. "What's the matter with the union lawyer?"

"I don't know," said Leon. "To be exact, this guy I was talking with won't be a regular lawyer for another month or so, but he's working with his uncle. He's a friend of Roy's."

"Oh?" said Roy.

"Joe Thompson."

"Ah," said Roy.

"You can get in touch with this Thompson?" Evans said to Roy, who nodded. "Good. I'd like to know what is going on. Tell me, Kalish, what time was Thompson's appointment for?"

"Five," said Leon.

"It's six-thirty," Evans said, "too soon to call him. After dinner, Roy."

Leon knew this about Evans.

During the war he had served in the OSS—it was in that service that he had come to know Chantal's husband in the Dauphiné Alps, and so Chantal—and once he had garotted a German sentry with piano wire. His hands were long, the fingers deft and quick. He would play melancholy love tunes on his guitar for hours, and if others were singing along he would not stop playing till they begged off. He had been captured by the Germans one evening, and before he was rescued in the middle of the night a Gestapo officer had had holes drilled in each of his teeth; through one of the upper molars the torturer had pushed the drill so hard that it had gone up through the root and the cheekbone; for quite a while afterward when he breathed through his mouth he could feel air whistle up into his sinus.

He was saying that the malaise troubling American workers now should not settle into union affairs. Such a mix-up would pollute the labor movement, which ought to preserve the limits of its historic task, the economic betterment of the workers. To be sure, this task is not as important as it used to be. But even though the importance of unionism is being reduced both by its own success and by the postwar shifts in the balance of social forces, its original function is still important and must not be corrupted. The malaise among the masses comes from their not knowing who is to blame for what is wrong. Something has happened to Wall Street as a symbol. Some unions are actually becoming big investors! The Red-hunt now under way is going to fizzle out. Communism is too remote to be a good enemy for the American masses because it is invisible to them; there are hardly any American Communists left. How many Americans are personally acquainted with even one Communist? An enemy you cannot see exists in your own mind; he becomes part of yourself. The worst aspect of modern warfare is that we seldom touch those we kill; we commonly do not so much as lay eyes on them. The spirit of the age calls for new symbols for the masses, above all an enemy they can get their hands on. The historical mission of a leader at this moment is to give the masses a true enemy.

"Whatever a Jew is," said Leon, and his voice stuck, so that he had to clear his throat. "Whatever a Jew is, I'm one. Remember Hitler? He gave the German masses a true enemy—Jews. What you say makes me uncomfortable."

Roy averted his head, his lips curling. But he glanced at Evans and, seeing him respond to Leon patiently, contented himself with a sniff and lit and blew out another paper match.

"I'm not talking about scapegoats," said Evans. "I said a true enemy. Didn't you hear me?"

"I didn't think you meant Jews," Leon said. "But who *are* the true enemy?"

Roy allowed himself a small smile.

Evans shrugged, and rolled back in his chair. "That is what the leader must show. If the masses weren't so confused they wouldn't need a leader." He closed his eyes, his face retaining its amiable expression.

The meal began badly. But the men respected Chantal and knew she permitted no unpleasantness at her table; the food was excellent; and the Napa Valley white pinot which Roy had provided, "for the occasion," was declared by Chantal to be worthy of comparison to a modest Burgundy. Presently the men warmed up. By the cheese course they were amiable again.

Evans tapped his wrist watch and glanced at Roy, who went to the telephone.

"I told Joe," Roy reported back, "we'd drop by his place in a little while."

"After coffee," said Evans. "Did he give any notion what the worker he talked to wanted?"

"Libel," said Roy. "The guy says he's being libeled for prejudice against Negroes. He says prejudice hasn't got anything to do with it."

"It's as bad as that?" said Evans, rolling in his chair.

"As bad as what?" Leon asked.

At first Evans did not address himself to anyone in particular. His blurred voice was somehow thicker, more menacing. "The worker has become so bourgeois that he's concerned with a libel action. Against who, by the way?" Roy shrugged. "We'll learn. Is the worker concerned about his fellow worker, the Negro, whose life is being ruined? Not at all. And certainly not about his union. His property feelings are hurt, he says he's being libeled." Evans now addressed himself exclusively to Roy. "We must get everything out of Thompson we can."

At this moment Leon decided, and knew he decided, to become a lawyer.

· 16 ·

As Leon was walking home Roy's car drove past him; neither Roy nor Evans waved. This event confirmed him in his resolution.

If he were a lawyer, men of action would seek him out. Who pays attention to a college teacher of history or political science? He would be in on things, not an outsider, a commentator.

Moreover, he could never expect to make much money as a college teacher, and he would probably be needing a good deal of money before long to help his mother. She was housekeeper for a rich family in Pasadena; she sent most of her money to her sister and brother-in-law, who had been in Argentina for many years, unable to gain entry to the United States; her arthritis was getting worse. Leon was formally very correct with her, but there was no warmth between them; she had been warm with no one since Leon's father had killed himself in '37. When his mother should have to quit working, he knew she would not come live with him, even if he was married at the time to a wife who would not object to caring for an ailing mother-in-law.

To be sure, he knew that there were five hundred more lawyers than taxi-drivers in San Francisco; he had seen scruffy civil-service attorneys who lacked even the energy to be college teachers; he had seen the one-desk dusty office of an offal-picker of a lawyer in El Cerrito, and he knew there were hundreds like him. But these were the failures, the unlucky. They had nothing to do with him. He was brilliant and young.

The thought of discarding all the notes and pieces of the dissertation that he had been so vigorously not-writing this summer now fired him, and he ran the remaining block to his house, burst open the door to his rooms, and rushed to his desk. He threw the cards and papers into two wastebaskets, carried them out back of the house to the garbage can, and dumped them.

Elated, he rummaged through his desk, looking for anything he might have missed the first time through. He found nothing of that sort, but he did pull out two letters he had received in the past few days.

The first was from Robin in St. Louis. When it had arrived he had skimmed it and tossed it in a drawer. He ran though the first three pages of gossip again—productions she had worked in, all-night cast parties on the Mudge grounds, a bohemian night club called the Hanging Gardens—and read the last paragraph with care.

"And so, Leonochka, the season is over, my first summer stock. 'Her modest beginning pointed the way toward—' What? Toward the assembly lines of Detroit? Toward a long apprenticeship in little theaters doing the classics and serious modern plays? Toward a brilliant career as the foremost costume designer in the history of the American Theater? No! Toward the 51st Street YWCA in New York City and a part-time job (hopefully) as somebody's Girl Friday. Heute St. Louis, morgens New York!

"Your everloving co-parent,
R.

"Don't worry, next time we meet—wherever—whenever—whyever —we'll be *former* co-parents."

He tried to read it as though he knew nothing of the woman who had written it, and he despised her. The self-conscious posing was not cute and winning; it was not even pathetic. It was just despicable, the posture of brittle cuteness assumed because she was so false that no natural pose was possible for her. That parody of the Nazi slogan, *Heute Europa, Morgens das Welt!*—what did it reveal? The people it occurred to her to compare herself to were the worst the world had ever known. He remembered something Alfred had remarked during a digression on insanity one day in class. The subject of the discussion was a woman who had committed a murder provoked by a letter she had received from her lover. "The view I take of it," said Alfred, "is that she was sane. She was shocked because she had never seen him before. In his presence she had been hoodwinked by passion, by his charm, by her own guilt—one can't know what-all. Here, in this letter, she sees his mind naked for the first time, and she is appalled by its sliminess. The record does not say whether he was an attractive man sexually. I would bet a good deal that he was." Leon saw himself seeing Robin's mind naked for the first time and appalled by its ugliness. How wise Alfred was, as usual. Enough of her. If they should ever meet again, it would be no doing of his.

The other letter was from a fellow graduate student, a dull dog named Paul Sterne, who had been perched on a mountain in the Siskiyous for months, fire-watching and working on his dissertation. He wrote that he had a job for the fall in Presley College, a girls' college in the hills above Richmond, eight or nine miles north of Berkeley. How would Leon like to split the job with him, so that they would both make enough to live on and get their dissertations written? The opportunity pleased Leon. The pay was no better than at St. Anselm's, but the atmosphere would be more agreeable. Not that the brothers who ran St. Anselm's were pious or sanctimonious. But they were out of things. He felt himself stagnating there, in a backwash. Presley should be much more lively. An eminent Protestant theologian, a German refugee, lived on campus and taught a bit. The girls were not from the petty bourgeoisie as the boys at St. Anselm's were, with no higher goals in life than baseball, TV, two cars in the garage, and wangling a reserved seat in heaven. The Presley girls would be from the cultivated classes; they would have something to talk about worth the trouble. Good. He would quit St. Anselm's—they did not really want part-time teachers anyway—go to Presley, and start in at law school right away.

Thought of Roy and Evans interviewing Joe rose in his consciousness, but before it got past "What for?" he put it down again. He stretched out on his bed, hands clasped behind his neck, staring out the window up at the faintly colored overcast, and turned his thoughts toward Alfred.

He was sure Alfred was going to make the same choice he had just made—leave the deadening cloisters of academia and go out into the world of affairs. He imagined himself Alfred's son-in-law, visiting Alfred and Beth on Sunday afternoons, calling him up for advice on points of law (Alfred would be a federal judge, of course), bringing the grandchildren to San Jacinto Way for Thanksgiving dinner. (Sybil? Lizzie? Maybe he would wait and see how Nancy turned out.) There was nothing he would not do for Alfred. He would learn from him how to be a father, a husband. He said to himself, "Alfred is my world."

· 17 ·

When Evans fell silent, Roy, who had been saying hardly anything, spoke in his negligent way.

"Why are you holding out on us, Joe?"

"Who said I was holding out on you, Roy?"

Evans gathered himself again. "In other words, Joe, does this friend of yours think there is any organized intention behind the slanders?" When Joe shrugged, Evans went on. "Well, what do *you* think?"

"No," said Joe. "I assure you, Harry, I believe you when you say it's important for you to understand what's going on, and I'd do anything I could to help you. I don't know of any organization behind this libel business any more than I know of any organization behind you and Roy, except Roy's newspapers, of course, and whatever it is you're a journalist for, I believe Roy said you're a journalist? I appreciate your candor with me, and I'm trying to be equally candid with you in return."

Evans rolled to his feet. "Let's go, Roy." At the door he turned to Joe and said with a grimace, "Thanks all the same."

In the car Roy said, "Zagri should be at his place. Want to go see him?"

"Why not?"

"Fuck Joe Thompson," said Roy.

"Which side is he on?" said Evans. "From what you said about him, I thought he was on our side."

"He used to be. Now he's a lawyer. He's playing both sides against the middle. He's on the side that pays the most."

"Those who are not with us are against us." The wheeze of Evans' voice was full of menace. Then he made a *pfft* with his lips. "Does Chantal know him?"

"She talked to him once or twice. She said he was an eel."

"That does it." He made a garotting gesture.

"You trust her reactions that much?"

"I've trusted her with my life."

Roy wanted to say that there was a difference between saying "I trust her reactions" and "I trust her with my life," but the finality of Evans' manner forbade his comment. Before long this small impulse of Roy's submerged under gratitude to Evans for having put a stop to the incessant yatter which occupied his mind. Roy often felt that, in his mind, both a high intellectual concern for distinctions and the merest word quibble were nothing but yatter; and because Evans alone had the imperial power to resolve this exhausting internal disputatiousness of his, Roy wanted more than anything else to submit to him formally, to find a way to put himself into Evans' hands, to oblige the conqueror to rule. But, at the moment, it was enough for him just to feel quelled. The ruling would come in due course.

Dr. Zagri owned a big old house in West Oakland. Most of the rooms in the house he rented out as little apartments, charging the tenants just enough to maintain the place in decency. The three high-ceilinged rooms in which he had lived and had his office for twenty years were malodorous and unwashed as always, but half the walls of the two he lived in were crowded, as they had not been till recently, with large paintings full of unidentifiable violence.

"My God, Zagri," said Evans, "are you going in for psychotherapy these days? I thought you were a GP."

"These are *my* paintings," said Dr. Zagri. "I've taken to relieving myself on canvas."

"Relieving yourself!" said Roy. "You know what that sounds like?"

"The words were mine. Gentlemen, you don't like my paintings? Very well, sit here with your backs to them. I'll give you some red wine, and you don't need to look at them." He poured the wine and arranged the seating while they continued to walk about, inspecting the paintings. He was a round little man with a ball-shaped head; he wore old felt slippers and a brand-new purple bathrobe with blue satin lapels; his voice was at once gruff and apologetic, and he was chewing on an unlit half-smoked cigar. "Come, sit. You are unkind. Sit with me." They sat, but Roy moved his chair around so that he could glance at the paintings from time to time. "I'm over sixty. You, Harry, you are about to be middle-aged; I'm about to be old. Roy, you are dry behind the ears already. We're all three Americans? You are Anglo-Saxon Protestants, I am a Rumanian Jew. Did you ever hear anything good about Rumania? No, not for generations has good been said about that country, where I was born. So. I'm on the winning side in two wars, the war against the Fascists and the class war. But what happened to the victory over the Fascists? Where's the peace? And the class war—I'm not sure of the victory, I don't see it anywhere. Yet where has that war gone? I can't see it either. Lack of war is not peace; of course not. Here we are, lacking war and peace both. Where are we? So. In war I know who to hate. In peace I don't have to hate anybody too much—I mean politically, everybody like Democrats and Republicans, family squabbles only. But now I'm full of war hatreds and I don't feel like squabbling. Yet who to hate? The Russians? Absurd. The physicists for making the bomb? No, I can still see straight: they are tragic, one does not hate tragic heroes. The Communists? No doubt, but most of them are Russians, and I can't hate Russians. All the Russians I ever knew I liked, more or less. Communism maybe? Maybe. But I'm crude, when I shoot I must see somebody fall down, the right person, the one I shot at. Where's this ism? 'Let the ism step forward!' But no ism steps forward. How can I shoot at it? So, I make these paintings. Harry, tell me where you have been and what you are doing here now. I'm glad to see you."

Before they had talked together long enough to discover whether they were going to recover what they had lost to time, there was a rap and the door opened. A lean black woman of thirty or so stepped in, unremarkably dressed except for being barefooted.

"I'm sorry, Doctor." She backed halfway out. "I didn't hear you had comp'ny."

"What is it, Helen?" he said, not standing up.

"She won't get to sleep, and I wondered if you . . ."

Dr. Zagri squeezed his nose. "All right. I'll be up in a little while. You give her a sugar tit, Helen?"

"Mm yhh."

"You give her something to suck on. She hurts."

"Yhh mm," she said, leaving.

"Helen!"

She opened the door again and stared at him without expression.

He went to a cupboard and rummaged around. "Here." He gave her a pacifier, a pink plastic disk with a rubber nipple sticking out of it. "You give her this. I know she's not a baby any longer, but you try it. Keep Philip away from her."

Helen clutched his hand. "She don't sleep."

"After a while."

Roy had taken a pile of blank labels out of a box on the table, the sort of gummed labels put on a package to be sent by parcel post, and was riffling them with a calculating air, like a card shark deciding which trick to pull.

"So, Roy," said Dr. Zagri, sitting again, "we haven't been seeing you for quite a while."

"At the tea parties?" said Roy. "I've lost interest in social gatherings."

"It's true we drink tea. It's even cheaper than coffee, as you know. Why do I explain to you? So, what have you been doing?"

"Shooting."

"Shooting? Hunting?"

"No, target practice."

"But you were a soldier."

"I spent the war reading maps and writing reports," said Roy. "I'm practicing small arms. You want to know what triggered me? One afternoon last winter I was standing on the corner of Twelfth and Clay, waiting for a bus. My car was broken down and I had to get out to San Leandro. It was a nice day, and a lot of people were standing around waiting for buses—Negroes, whites, Mexicans, men and women, two or three little children. There was a woman selling tokens, in a bus-company uniform. She was loud and strapping, a big mouth with lots of lipstick, a white woman. She was joking with a cabbie, his cab was parked nearby. She was doing all the talking, and he was laughing too hard and nudging her every chance he got.

" 'You know the cab driver killed a man the other night?' she said. 'It was the other guy's fault. It always is. He was old. They don't react quick enough like that. Anyway it's too bad he wasn't a nigger. He wasn't, was he? You know what we say up at the carbarns when a guy comes in and says he had a wreck? We all get around him and

122

say, "Hey, did you kill him?" If he says yes, you know what we say then? We say, "Was he a nigger?" And if he says yes, we say, "Good, that's one less of the monkeys." '

"They laughed. Before I knew what I was up to, I let my feelings go towards those Negroes that were standing around and heard what she said. Pity, the fallacy of pity. Then I spat on her fat ass. She heard me spit and she didn't see it land on the pavement, but she didn't feel it either. It made a streak on her skirt. When she looked around at me I wanted to call her some name that wouldn't sound weak or phony. All I could get out was, 'You, you.' She and the cabbie moved off a few steps, and their voices lowered. My bus came in a little while, and I sat in it trying to think what I should have said to her. There wasn't anything good enough.

"We were going along East Fourteenth, and all of a sudden the bus stopped and the driver got out. Everyone watched him; he picked up a large rubber ball that had rolled in front of the bus, and tossed it into the arms of a little girl on the curb. The child's mother came running out of a store and scolded and hugged her and waved to the driver. He got back in the bus, looking a little sheepish. There were two shoppers sitting in front of me, and one said to the other, 'Such a mother, not watching her child better than that.' 'Trash,' said the other one, 'and this driver is trash too. He could have swerved around the ball. We won't get home till suppertime like this. Why didn't he run over it?' It's the sort of thing you get used to in a city. But that little gesture of the driver's had got to me somehow. It seemed to help make up for what that woman had said back on the corner, and here these two fat-necked women sneered at him. I nearly killed them. In some way I hated them even more than the token-seller. What she had done was viler than what they had done, but I loathed them more. The first thing I did next morning was to go to a pawnshop and buy a pistol, and I've been practicing out in a quarry above Richmond ever since. Which is why I don't come to your tea parties any more."

Helen came to the door again. She was wearing slippers and an old sweater.

"She take it for a while, Doctor, but she cry anyhow. She skeers me, she don't cry loud enough, just so little, whimper, like she been beat. Nobody ain't beat her."

"I'll be up in a minute, Helen. Now go look after her." She disappeared. "I won't be long," he called after her. Then he turned back to the two men. "The child fell downstairs and broke her arm. Nothing serious. But when I went to fix her up, I found out she had syphilis. She's six years old. When I discovered it, I saw by Helen's eyes that she knew about it. But all she said was that Philip had sores like

123

these, there must be something in their blood, their father was no good. Philip is eight. I checked him over down here in my office, and I found out from him that he gave the syphilis to his sister. He doesn't know who he got it from. Their father abandoned them four or five years ago. I never knew him. Helen is a day worker. I'm treating the children, of course. But she puts all her worry into that little broken arm. Wait for me, I'll be right back." At the doorway he turned back and said, "The trouble is I don't know how to tell Helen because she already knows it."

Roy jerked his head after Dr. Zagri. "He's going in for heart in a big way."

"Well," said Evans to Roy, "he was one of our good men. I'm sorry we've lost him."

"Let's get out, now," said Roy. "No, wait a minute." He returned to the table, took out his pen, and printed meticulously on one of the labels he had been riffling:

FROM THE ARTIST'S COLLECTION
NOT FOR SALE

Then he licked it and pasted it in the middle of the largest painting, on a broad magenta zigzag slopped across dark blue splatters and pink blobs.

· 18 ·

The Royces did not make a point of eating breakfast together; they prepared what they wanted when they wanted it. The next morning, when Alfred, Beth, Lizzie, and Sybil found themselves seated at table at the same time, they all smiled a little more than they felt like smiling.

"Well," said Alfred, "what are you ladies going to do this morning?"

"Don't ask," said Sybil, wrinkling her nose.

"*I* am going to finish my book this week," he declared.

"I'm still waiting," said Lizzie.

"I hope Nancy's all right," Beth began vaguely.

"Oh, Mother," said Sybil, and Beth shrugged apologetically.

The telephone rang, and Lizzie leaped up.

"Speak of the devil," said Beth.

"Hardly—I've been expecting it for days," said Lizzie as she ran out.

"Besides, it may not be for her," said Sybil.

"All right, so I'm always wrong," Beth said.

"I'm useless," said Sybil. "This summer is just the most useless summer. I'm so useless, do you know what I'm going to do this lousy perfect morning? Read a science-fiction novel."

"You might at least read one in French," said Beth. "Keep your French up."

"Oh, Mother."

"We're going!" cried Lizzie, bursting in. "We've got permission! It'll count!"

"Where are you going?" Alfred asked.

"Northeastern Nevada for two or three weeks. You know, I told you all about it last month. Remind them, Syb. I've got to rush."

"You're not going right away?" asked Beth in alarm, clutching Lizzie's arm.

"Half an hour, Mother dear."

"I need you."

"No, you don't. If there's one thing I know how to do, it's how to get packed in twenty minutes." Lizzie ran off.

"At least she's busy," said Beth.

"At least," said Sybil.

"My," said Alfred, "you two are mean this morning. Green eyes?"

"I don't know," said Beth. "I suppose all this poking around into Indians amounts to something."

"Dad," said Sybil, "you once said something I took to heart. You said one of the hallmarks of maturity was to know the difference between work and busy work. Well, no busy work for me. I'm just going to lay around all day a-readin' about rational carrots. Leave the dishes, Ma. I'll redd them up sometime before lunch."

The telephone rang again, and presently Lizzie called from downstairs that it was a moving company for Beth.

She sprang up and dashed through the kitchen. In a minute she called back into the dining room, "They'll be here in half an hour. I must go out and spray right away. The aphis on the cotoneasters are terrible, the worst I ever saw."

"The aphis on the asters," Sybil chanted in waltz rhythm, "and the space ship in the time warp, and the grave mounds of the Shoshones, and the general theory of labor law, and this is the way the world wags."

Alfred did not know how he was supposed to laugh at this. Watching her healthy, compact, all-American-girl body as she walked away, he could not imagine she was doing more than some sort of complicated collegiate spoofing. Yet if he had said such things, he would have been dancing on a high-wire over a dark pit.

Shortly before nine Lizzie kissed everyone good-by and went off in a station wagon with three other rosy young women. Alfred was established at his desk, the Venetian blinds tilted up, his attention focused on his work. When the van backed up outside he paid little attention, prepared to blot out the movers' sounds for twenty or thirty minutes.

After an hour and a half he could ignore them no longer, especially since they kept making a lot of paper noises right under his window. He stepped into the bedroom next door; there the Venetian blinds were tilted down and a window was open. He looked out. The patio was strewn with wrapping paper; there were two piles of folded olive-green pads by the bonsais. Beth was standing at the wide doorway to the living room, her left hand across her brow. The two men were standing by a large mahogany sideboard, one of them folding a pad, the other looking at the ground before him.

"It's so big," said Beth.

"There's just one more chest and some straight chairs," said the man with the pad. "Then we've got her whipped."

"I don't know where to put it," she said. "Do you really think it won't go in the dining room?"

"No, ma'am, it won't."

She sighed.

He dropped the folded pad on one of the piles and stood with a hand on the sideboard. She disappeared into the house.

"Maybe she's going to start an antique store," said the other man. "She'd better."

They exchanged a glance and shook their heads gravely.

Alfred looked around the bedroom. There were three pieces of furniture he had not seen before: a large bureau with a marble top, a full-length swinging mirror in a dark frame so heavy and broad it seemed squat, though it was seven feet tall, and a peculiar chair. It was rather elegant from the seat up—the back was of two-colored inlaid wood —but it looked clumsy from the seat down, with a solid skirt of curved, veneered panels. He investigated. The skirt and top layer of the seat swung open. It was a commode.

"Biedermeier!" cried Beth from the doorway.

Alfred jumped back from the absurd chair. "What? What?"

"It's a Biedermeier commode, Great Aunt Clara's Biedermeier commode."

Beth looked at him with a desperation he thought to divert with a little joke.

"Poor thing," he said, pointing at the empty commode. "It hasn't got a pot to pee in."

She broke into rigid sobs and hiccuping recriminations.

For weeks afterward Alfred, seeking the crucial choice which his legal training supposed, went back to this moment. It came to seem to him that his response to her hysterics caused the subsequent troubles by not preventing them. It did not fully cause them, of course; but one who has the power to divert strong emotional forces from a destructive course and fails to do so permits the destruction they produce, and to permit is to help cause. He later believed that he had had such diversionary power at this moment and had failed to use it.

He should have slapped her as he felt like doing. From experience he knew her immediate response to a blow: she would have collapsed, thrown herself onto the bed in a soft heap and wept for half an hour or so, then emerged after a while, perhaps after having a little nap, contrite and willing to be affectionate. He should have followed his impulse and slapped her hard, then have gone into the rest of the house and seen—what he did not have to see to know—that the house was cluttered with furniture from her mother's house, and have ordered the movers to put it all in storage, where it would stay till he and Beth had agreed upon which pieces to keep and which to sell. There would have been prolonged battles over this, and she would have hated him for a while; but the pieces would have discharged, as it were, their potent force, either by disappearing into antique stores for cash or else by being incorporated, a few of them, into the household, made an ordinary part of the family's life. That way, Beth would have been rid, painfully but cleanly, of the obscure involvements which these handsome, unnecessary things brought with them and held in life.

Moreover, Alfred himself, had he allowed his raised right arm to fall as it trembled to do, would have, so he came to believe, had the confidence to continue in the stern, resented measures which the circumstances demanded. He could not later pretend to himself that he had not appreciated the importance of the moment. He knew, as one knows in the thick of action, what he should do. He knew in his muscles, prepared to strike back in natural resentment against her crazy, blackmailing emotions.

Most of all he remembered her eyes. From within the mask of hysteria, they were appealing for help, and he recognized that appeal. There was only one help he could have given, the one his body moved to offer: responsive anger, measured violence.

Instead, he dropped his arm across her shoulder, held her tight, let her tremble a minute in his arms, got her into her dressing room and onto a gentleman's chair with a piece of twine still on one leg, told her not to worry but to let him take care of everything, and closed the door. She was left in quiet while he got the movers to put the sideboard and remaining furniture in the garage. When he returned to her, she was grateful and subdued, she kept telling him how sweet he was to her, and she said with tearful smiles what a goose she had been. All was smooth and sweet.

His worst humiliation was that afterward he could find nothing by which to exonerate himself for what he had done, had not done. There was not even an extenuation of the sort one can use as an appeal for sympathy: he could tell no one about it. He disapproved of a man's hitting a woman, but not unqualifiedly. He pitied Beth's distress, but nothing like as much as he resented her histrionics. The real reason he had done the easy thing was to avoid trouble. He did not want to face her immediate opposition or the long struggle over the inherited furniture; somehow, if he comforted her, the difficulty might all just go away. Worse, and he could never make up his mind just how large a part this played in his decision, but too large, much too large, he had not wanted the two movers in the patio to hear him slap his wife and her cry.

It was not for a few weeks that he made up his mind about why he had failed to do the right thing at that moment. Once he had made it up, he never changed it but started upon a long course of reparation, always goaded by the shameful knowledge (never mentioned to anyone) that the troubles which befell them he had permitted, finally, out of sheer pusillanimity.

· 19 ·

After the movers had left and he had soothed Beth, Alfred got her to lie down, promising to bring her a cup of coffee. The pot was empty. He called down the stairway to Sybil; there was no response. He filled the kettle and put it on to heat, washed out the pot, and put fresh grounds in the basket; then he looked into the dining room. The impression of crowded clutter made him breathe heavily. He went into the living room; there was a huddle of eight cardboard barrels in front of the piano. On the gallery, blocking the view from the living room, stood a six-shelf bookcase with glass doors, the panes of which were cracked.

He ran downstairs for Sybil. The door to her room stood open. She was not there. In the middle of her room stood a pretty, low white vanity and two ruffled stools. "Sybil?" He peered into Nancy's room, which looked normal, and Lizzie's, in which two tall flat crates leaned against the wall. There was no special reason for Sybil to have stayed; he did not need her help exactly; yet her being gone agitated him. The year before, Nancy had learned about bats, how they constantly orient themselves by emitting supersonic squeaks. She had called Alfred her daddy-bat, because he was constantly calling out to Beth, to the girls, keeping track of everybody all the time, wanting their respondings. Now no one answered. Hugh had left; even the cottage was empty.

At the thought of the cottage, Alfred ran down the garden, bleating, "Sybil?" as he ran.

She was curled on the bed with a book in her hand, and when he stood in the doorway she gazed at him with utter blandness. "Yes?"

"I wondered where you'd gone. Everything is upside down."

She said nothing; she neither frowned nor smiled.

"Beth is badly upset. I'm glad you're home."

"I'll be there for meals." She pulled aside the tan curtain that hid the makeshift closet; her clothes hung from the rod, her shoes were on the floor. "I've moved down here."

He did not know what to say. He felt like crying.

She just looked at him.

He left, saying, "Everything's all mixed up. A bad time. I'm sorry."

When he was halfway up the path she called from the doorway. "Yes, Sybil? What is it?"

"You know how I'm fed up with Cal? Okay for me to see if I can get into Presley? Rose has transferred."

"Go ahead." He waved aimlessly as he turned to leave.

"Thanks. I'll get right on it."

As he was putting Beth's coffee things on a tray, he heard Sybil's motor scooter start up and racket down the street.

"Here you are, my dear, fresh and hot."

But Beth was not in the bed. She was on her knees by the huge mirror, rubbing a finger along a scratch on one of the walnut stanchions.

"Put it over there, will you. Look," she cried. "They gouged it! They're butchers."

He saw no chance of a reasonable discussion about what should be done with the furniture.

"Alfred, come here, look what they did. Morons!" She glanced up to see why he had not joined her. "What's the matter? Don't you believe me? Just look here."

"Obviously it is scratched. One expects a certain amount of damage when moving. You must itemize the damages."

"You're so cold. How can you just stand there like a judge? Lawyers, brrr. Don't you care?"

"About the scratch? Not much. What I do care about is having that monstrous object in the house at all—it and the rest of the junk."

"Oh." As she glanced over her shoulder at his legs, one corner of her lip quivered like a dog's. "So you don't want me to accept my own inheritance?" She stood up, keeping her head averted, sat on the edge of the bed, and poured some cream in her coffee.

As she moved, he caught sight of himself in the mirror. Because it was slightly tilted, he looked shorter; the reflection was sharp but rather dark. The dark, squat, looming image was quite menacing, left leg advanced, right arm crooked back, fist doubled, large head swung forward. If he had had a rock in his hand at that moment he would have hurled it at the glass. He shook himself and moved toward the door, out of sight of his reflection. When he spoke he kept his voice in a low register.

"Beth, it's impossible to keep most of these old things which are cluttering up the house."

"Cluttering. Junk."

"You know that, don't you? You must get rid of them immediately."

"Get rid of them."

"Sell them, give them to friends, call Goodwill, I don't care what. Meanwhile they can be stored in the garage."

"It's greasy! Not on your life!"

"I am going to call the movers and have the men come back and move everything into the garage, Beth."

"No, you are not, Alfred."

"Sybil has moved to the garden cottage."

"So? Maybe she wants to have some quiet for a change."

"You had no business putting those things in her room."

"So you mean I've driven my own child out of her house?" When he did not answer she pressed the back of her hand to her forehead and half closed her eyes. "Answer me, Alfred. Is that what you meant?"

"If you tone it down forty-seven decibels—yes. And she's going to transfer to Presley College. She decided that too this morning."

"I'm glad *some*one in this family makes decisions that meet with your approval."

"I only mentioned the business about Sybil to bring home to you the effect of all the furniture nonsense."

"Yes, Alfie, I know you, Alfie, I know how your virtuous little motives are only for the best. You just have the welfare of others in mind, don't you? Shit on you, husband. You wanted to make me feel bad, and you did make me feel bad, and now I'm damned well going to make you feel bad. It's going to take me a while to get these things settled into my house. I'm not so far gone, *yet,* but what I realize there's more than we can absorb. Something's got to give, and meanwhile you've just got to suffer a little bit, a teensy-weensy bit, okay? It's going to take me a while to find out which things I want and which things to get rid of. But I have a hunch it's some of *our* stuff that's going to go. Mother's is mostly a hundred times better. The china alone—"

"Eight barrels!"

"Eight barrels, yes, eight barrels. So?"

"Beth, it's not just your decision. Running the house has always been your province. I never really challenged your authority there, you know I haven't. But there comes a point—"

"Did I put anything, even one little stool, in your holy of holies?"

"My study? No."

"Okay, buster, go back into your thinkery and think, and leave me to run my house my own way."

"Our house. 'This house is the property of Alfred Stephen Royce and Elizabeth Peterson O'Hare Royce.' "

"Law, law, deeds, titles, escrows."

"Joke, wife. I was making a joke."

"I know, I know. Lord, but how I know when one of your jokes is in the air. I recognize all the symptoms by now. But since you raised the question, I just want to get one thing straight once and for all."

"No! Leave it alone."

"I don't care about deeds and titles. What's that got to do with anything? Dust in a drawer. Whose money paid for this house?"

"Beth, let it lie. We've been through this"

"My money, left to me by my grandmother. My mother's mother."

"That was the down payment. All right. It's our house."

"Down payment! In other words the heart of the thing. That without which nothing, cardunc."

"In five years the mortgage will be paid off, right? All the mortgage payments have been made by me, right? The money for the new room came from my earnings, right? Our house."

"The new room you paid for is your study, right? Your study is where you are undisputed master, right? King of all you survey. Go think and leave me alone."

It was at this point that he hit her. She fell back onto the bed, spilling a few drops of coffee. She covered her face with her crooked arm and just lay there.

Neither the blow nor roaming around the house glaring at the intruding things vented his anger. He would have gone up to his study, had she not taunted him to. As his anger subsided a bit, he became aware of a dread far worse than the anger. She had never gone this far before, even when most hysterical, and certainly never in so short a time.

He telephoned Horace and arranged to meet him at one at the Fly Trap for lunch. He would clear his mind by talking about the McKee dispute. He called Joe, who told him about his interview the day before but not about the visit from Evans and Roy. Alfred had the obscure feeling there was something else he should tend to, but he could not think what it was.

He almost overcame his dislike of driving. Though he didn't drive a car if he could help it, the irritation of waiting for buses now seemed to him nearly strong enough to justify his driving across the bridge, but not quite. After he had walked a couple of blocks toward the bus stop the swarm of thoughts settled enough for him to become conscious that he was walking with the usual springiness of step. He was glad to discover that his natural good spirits had not been overwhelmed.

· 20 ·

"Salad!" said Horace. "I thought the reason you always wanted to come to the Fly Trap was to get mutton kidney chops."

"It is. But today I'm not very hungry."

"You aren't dieting, that's for sure, not with crab salad and mayonnaise." Horace was a tough, wiry little man, bald, tan, who kept himself in good condition. For twenty-five years he had teased Alfred for being fat. "Still, all things considered, Alfred, you're looking good."

"Any interesting cases coming up?"

"Not many," said Horace. "Yesterday Shirley was over having dinner with us, and she mentioned something that Nancy had told her. Apparently Beth has been kicking up since she came back from Texas?"

"Nothing more than you might expect."

"Shirley got the impression Nancy was troubled."

"It was a little thing—whether Nancy could go up to the Ravaglis' ranch and look after their kids for the rest of the summer. So she went up yesterday, and everything has settled down." Alfred hoped that Horace dropped his eyes because the answer had satisfied him, not because of the omissions in Alfred's story. "What's new on the McKee case? Need an arbitrator?"

"You interested?"

"Maybe."

"We're going to be called in tomorrow, as a matter of fact, if things don't straighten themselves up. I thought you'd dropped out of arbitration."

"It's summer. I'm on the last two pages of my damned book." He shrugged.

"It's a messy case," said Horace, watching him closely, "and not too interesting so far. Bad temper mostly. A liberal management, a responsible union, well-off workers."

Alfred had a hunch that if Horace knew what Leon had learned he would have taken the dispute himself.

"As a matter of fact," said Horace, "I was going to have to take it myself. Everybody's on vacation. You can have it if you want it. There's a bigger one brewing in the aircraft industry, much bigger. I'll keep that one."

"Good. I wouldn't want a big one anyway. I'd appreciate a local one like McKee's, short and sweet, to keep my hand in."

"It's yours. How's Beth? When you didn't come over Saturday night, I thought maybe . . ."

Alfred let the pause hang, expecting Horace to say something he could seize on and refute. But Horace left the sentence dangling.

"Well, her mother's death upset her more than I thought it would. They hadn't been close for years, but they corresponded. And there was her brother Donald. They let him out for the funeral, so he raised as much hell as he could—nothing of any consequence, just emotional turmoil."

"*Just* emotional turmoil!"

"Well, things show signs of settling down before too long."

"You know Juanita?" Horace asked, and when Alfred frowned he added, "My second, the one that *really* didn't take, my bride of a year. You know what knocked us for a loop?"

"I never got to know her very well," said Alfred.

"Or like her a bit. A puritan with hot pants. Excuse me, that's vulgar. But true. She's the only one of the five I regret. The others—things just didn't work out right. The other three, I mean. Virginia and I are still clicking a hundred per cent—well, ninety per cent, eighty-five at the very least. Anyway, what got in our way, with Juanita, was a farm she inherited from her father, a chicken ranch up near Petaluma. He died a couple of months after we were married. You know, this was 'thirty-three, when everybody with two dimes to rub together was starting a chicken ranch. Her mother was dead, and her father left this miserable little ten-acre place with a house and furnishings and some sheds and equipment and four or five thousand chickens And Juanita and her brother Samson—can you beat that for a name, Samson Taylor?—the old man left no will, so they divided it fifty-fifty. Then the fight began. Did we need half a chicken ranch, with a market value of five or six thousand dollars by stretching the evaluation till it squealed? Let's face it, even in the Depression I was wealthy. 'Give Samson the whole damned thing,' I said. She hated me for that, really hated me. She wouldn't settle for less than half the value of the place in cash. He couldn't fork up more than enough for chicken feed for a month. It was already mortgaged pretty heavily. He had a lousy job in Oakland, he wanted to move his family up there and try chickens. One of his boys had something wrong with his bones, needed lots of sun. Okay, so a chicken ranch is a fool's choice, still Samson was an okay guy and he wouldn't take nothing from nobody, no, not him. Every once in a while Juanita'd drive up to the place—we got a guy to look after it during probate—and come back with a piece of furniture. A good piece, naturally. Samson got madder and madder. I tried to pour oil on the troubled waters, and his wife was decent. Things showed signs of settling down, as you put it. And then I pulled the real boner, the marriage-buster. I offered to lend Samson the money myself, at one per cent a year, no time limit. He'd have taken it too. But pfft—Juanita left me. She said I'd destroyed her! The slut."

While listening to Horace, Alfred was aware that he was being invited to confide, and he was weighing, even as he enjoyed the story, the pros and cons of telling Horace about Beth. On the whole, he thought he ought not. Mary Louise was Beth's closest friend, and Alfred had always been scrupulous not to speak ill of either Mary Louise or Horace to the other, or to allow either of them to take sides in any altercation he might be having with Beth. He was quite sure that Mary Louise and Beth gossiped a lot about Horace and Virginia, and very likely about Alfred's own shortcomings, but their gossip never became admissible subject for conversation in his house or presence, nor did they try to foist it upon him. Yet Beth's egregious behavior in surreptitiously intruding so much of her mother's furniture into their house would become known soon enough among all their acquaintance, and Horace might legitimately interpret Alfred's not telling him about it in the natural course of conversation as unfriendly reticence. He decided he would do well to mention it now, casually and lightly.

"Fortunately Donald can't raise any legal fuss. He already got more than his share of the inheritance in cash. What Beth got was the house, which she's going to sell, and her mother's furniture and dishes, which she's very fond of."

"Good, I'm glad to hear that. What's she doing with the furniture and dishes?"

"At the moment a good deal of it is in our house. We haven't decided how much to keep yet."

"Aha. How long has it been there?"

"It was just unloaded this morning, as a matter of fact. The house looks like an antique shop. I'm having the stuff stored in the garage for the time being."

"But it's in the house now?"

Alfred knew that he had said enough and more than enough, and he knew Horace was prying too much. But the ease he felt from confiding was too sweet for him to deny.

"All over the house."

"And she agrees to having the stuff stored in the garage?"

"Not so's you'd notice it. But it will be."

"Aha. You know, Alfred, I'm leery of giving advice. I don't need to tell you. One of the reasons I am leery is because of something you said to me in law school, the first year we got acquainted. Here you were, four years younger than me, laying down the law already. You always had a judge side to you. But I never forgot what you said. The important thing is, you lived up to it. I've never known you to give advice till you have both sides, all ten sides. There's just one area where I dish out advice free, and I'm going to serve you up some now. That's marriage. Why? Because I'm a four-time loser. Who'll believe me? Who'll take me seriously? Especially you. My advice to you, Alfred, is: go home and make her move that stuff *now*. Use every low sophistry in the book. Just don't delay and don't give up. Bully her. Threaten her. Tell her you'll leave her. Do it."

"As a matter of fact, persuasion won't work. I tried it. I had to hit her."

"You beat her?"

"Slapped her hard a few times. You couldn't really call it beating. The children were none of them in the house."

"Alfred." Horace reached across the table and grasped his hand. "My friend."

"It's pretty vile, I admit, but sometimes I—"

"You did it. I always suspected you were a great man. Now I know it. I never had the nerve to sock a single one of my wives. You know that? Not one. I'm a worm. Good man, good man."

"It's a sign of weakness, of course. I know that. Still."

"Sure, sure." Horace squeezed his hand hard. "I'd like to be weak like that sometimes. Christ, Alfred, now go home and get that furniture moved."

· 21 ·

Alfred went by the department office on the campus to pick up his mail; none of his colleagues were around to chat with. The bookstore he liked to browse in was closed for summer inventory. The only familiar person in the café he looked into was a mathematics professor named Devereux; a stern young woman was explaining something to him and scribbling on a paper placemat. Alfred went by the University police office and tried, unsuccessfully, to talk the sergeant out of a parking fine. In the library neither of the magazines he wanted was on the shelves. He had a cappuccino in the northside coffee house and then, every excuse used up, walked home.

The living-room floor was half covered with shredded newspaper. Three of the barrels were emptied. There were piles of china on the dining-room table, and Beth was at the kitchen sink, washing piles more.

"Well, my dear, you've not been idle."

"Where did you go?" she asked pleasantly.

"To the city. I had lunch with Horace."

"Isn't that funny," she said. "I'm going down to visit Mary Louise for a while this evening myself."

"Not so funny. She's your closest friend."

"And he is yours."

"My oldest friend, at least. I was seeing him about the McKee strike. I'll be arbitrating it."

She held the edge of the sink with both hands and threw her head back in constricted laughter.

"What's the matter?" he cried. "What are you laughing at? What did I say?"

"Nothing, nothing. It just struck me, under the circumstances—the thing you want to do is arbitrate." She shrugged and shook her head.

"Well," he said, "what about dinner? It's five-thirty. And why isn't Sybil helping you with all these dishes? Isn't she home yet?"

"She's down in the cottage. I don't want any help now. This is the Spode."

"You mean we're not going to be allowed to eat off it?"

"Only on special occasions. What do you think?"

He was breathing a bit harder. "Well, what about dinner tonight?"

She turned back to the dishpan. "Would you mind dreadfully taking Sybil out to a restaurant? You both like Mexican food, and I don't. Why don't you go to the Yucatán? I want to get everything cleaned up and put away as fast as possible. I don't like all this disorder a bit more than you do, and I'm just as sorry as you are that we have to have it. When you come back from dinner, the front room will be swept up, I promise. The dining-room table will be clear for breakfast. I won't go to Mary Louise's till everything is straightened up. I promise. I'm going to get everything done and decided just as soon as I possibly can, so we can get back to normal. I want everything to be shaped up by the time Nancy comes home. Lizzie's gone. Sybil's down in the garden; nothing bothers her anyway. Bear with me a little while. Really, it will all get straightened out if you just have patience. Okay?"

Her appeal was too heartfelt and reasonable for him to dismiss.

As he sat in the patio, enjoying a gin and tonic, he inspected her argument as though he were a judge and it had been presented to him by a trial lawyer: it looked good.

A woman inherits a houseful of antique furniture and china from her mother. Although she does not need it, she likes it for its own sake, and although she has not been close to her mother for years, she wants it to remember her mother by. She gives some to relatives and has the rest shipped home. She wants to try it out in her own home to see which pieces to keep and which to sell. It is true that she did not warn her family that she was going to do this. She was troubled because she never intended to keep the things and did not know she was going to keep them until the time actually came. She is embarrassed to have changed her mind. She was moved to it by being with her mother at her deathbed and by having the furniture actually there to dispose of. When it arrives at her own home her husband becomes so angry that he beats her. Despite this, later in the day she pleads for his forbearance for only two or three weeks until she shall have decided what to do with the possessions; then the household shall be restored to normal, only with some handsomer things in it than before.

Against this case, his own complaint seemed whiny and flabby, one neurotic accusing another of being even more neurotic. There was no doubt that Beth was flamboyantly neurotic at the moment; the behavior of the girls would attest to that to the satisfaction of any judge. And Alfred as husband knew beyond argument that, even during her last, rational, irrefutable appeal for his forbearance, the desperately potent emotion in her voice had little connection with what she was saying. It was his clear duty, seeing this, not to allow his responsive feelings to sway his judgment. If he found himself walking out on her, as he had done during the troubles that had followed their buying the house originally, he must take himself firmly in hand and walk right back. At the very least he must think of Nancy, who was only thirteen, a bad age for her father to default. He was too irrationally responsive to Beth; he must not let his actions be governed by his emotions.

As he sat motionless, a hummingbird buzzed down for some sips from the fuchsia blossoms. It hovered a moment, looking at him, then shot up into the obscurity of the redwood branches above the garage.

Having put plenty of gin in his drink, he consciously indulged in moralizing. A clean, decisive act, he thought, without concern for motive. Thank God for birds.

· 22 ·

Mary Louise had once been proud of her sexiness, but now, having given up on men, she had turned blowsy and rather fat. She derived much nourishment from a good grievance, and divorce and psychoanalysis between them had kept her well provided. She did not whine or rail; she was often humorous, even cheery, about her grievances, and she never gave resentment its rein. But she did like to dump, as she put it, and to have her friends dump on her. She taught third grade, and during summer vacation was used to letting herself go. This summer, however, Shirley had been having an access of thirteen-year-old respectability and loudly deplored her mother's slovenly ways. They had reached an agreement: Mary Louise would not wear housecoat and slippers later than ten in the morning if Shirley would not criticize her for drinking so much beer, and they would do the dishes together after every meal.

"Do you know what he said then?"

"Nothing?" said Mary Louise with a lopsided smile.

"Not nothing," said Beth, tilting the can till the beer almost spilled. "Nothing would be an insult, and I'll say this for Alfred, he's never insulting."

"That's something."

"At least you can get your teeth into an insult. Give me a good insult any day. There I am groveling on my knees to him, and what does he do? 'Very well,' he says in this cool, polite way. 'Very well.' Then he makes himself a tall drink. Doesn't even offer to make one for me—not that I could have had one, with my hands in the dishpan up to my elbows. 'Very well.' And out he goes into the patio and lounges back in the deck chair as though he didn't have a care in the world. I started out once to say something, but when I saw him stretched out there gazing up into the trees, I didn't trust myself to say a damned word. 'Very well.' "

"Okay, Beth, baby, but I have heard worse, you know. More dire? No?"

"Such as?"

"He didn't beat up on you, after all. They do."

Beth smiled in a knowing way. "Maybe. He's so cool, so right, so self-righteous."

"Why did you smile like that?" Mary Louise leaned across the kitchen table, where they were sitting, and squeezed Beth's arm sym-

138

pathetically. "You're holding out on me." She peered into Beth's eyes eagerly. "Did he beat you?"

"And the pay-off was, when he and Sybil drove off to the restaurant they were laughing like they were going on a date. They didn't try to talk me into going with them. Sybil is about as warm to me these days— What a fish I bred. What were they laughing at? What's so funny?"

"He did beat you. Didn't he?"

"Not tonight he didn't. He never beats me after two in the afternoon." Beth's forehead had been made lumpy by anxiety, and her cheeks were no longer firm and round. But her mouth was supple and expressive, and her eyes bright and quick. Now, with the fun of teasing Mary Louise, her voice became light and merry too. "Just a slap on the bottom. That doesn't count against him."

"But the funny way you smiled when I said he didn't beat up on you." Mary Louise was outright pleading. "What did you mean, smiling that way?"

"A whack or two? I was bitchy to him this morning. I would've whacked me if I'd been him."

"So he did. The bastard."

"I really was bitchy. I mean it."

"You know what I'd like to give you, sweetie?"

"A beer."

"Sure." Mary Louise fetched a beer from the refrigerator, opened it, and set it in front of Beth as solicitously as a nurse bringing medicine. "Sure, you need lots of beer. You deserve it. You can stay here all night if you want to, honey. There's no earthly excuse for a man beating a woman. They're stronger." Mary Louise opened her hands and eyes wide, shrugging at the same time. "What I'd just love to give you, if I could, would be a short course."

"In what?"

"Therapy. I think you're reverse-projecting." She clapped her hand over her mouth in mock-consternation. "Whoops. You don't like the tongue. I speak in tongues myself. What can you expect? My great-grandfather was a Micmac. Traumas, traumas."

"So you think I need to be analyzed, eh?"

"Some. Don't you?"

"Pfft," said Beth. "What in hell is reverse projection anyway?"

"My own contribution to the science. Projection is when you attribute your own motivation to somebody else. So reverse projection is when you attribute somebody else's motivation to yourself. Twenty-five bucks, please."

"Mary Louise, it's a good thing you're so batty or I'd hate you."

"Go ahead, hate me, it's included in the fee. So, when you say you were bitchy, you say it because Alf acts as though he thought you were bitchy, and you accept his evaluation. You reverse project."

"Why not just call it inject and cut the corners?"

"Oh, no no no no!"

Mary Louise began a long, pedantic, muddled disquisition on psychoanalytic theory. After Beth was reasonably sure she had got far enough from Beth's motives so that she was not likely to swerve back to them, she interrupted her.

"Did Horace beat you, Mary Louise?"

Mary Louise's mouth twitched in an odd way. She finished her can of beer in a draft and got another.

"I never knew the details of your break-up with Horace. Remember? Alfred and I were having a rough time along about then ourselves."

"He pushed me around once."

Beth was aware of Mary Louise's resistance to these inquiries about facts; emotions and motives Mary Louise was promiscuous with, but she was shy with facts. Beth resolved to take only one further step.

"Did you leave him or did he leave you?"

"He left me. What do you think churned up all that childhood stuff? Nine thousand dollars' worth of couch work. Desertion."

"Well, by God, if Alfred ever leaves me I'll never take him back."

"Talk, big talk. Go ahead and talk, sweetie, maybe it'll make you feel better. Go ahead, dump on me all you feel like."

"I won't! I swear I wouldn't dream of taking him back!"

"You mean it? You think you mean it."

"After he left me? The rat. Never!"

"You and Alf aren't like Horace and me. Don't get confused, Bethie. 'Just remember this,' " she sang, " 'life is no abyss.' Insert a canceler. Remember what I say, you two love each other and always have and always will. You can't help it. I don't say it's good, though it is, you know that. I just say it is. *Fiat. Dixit.* You're stuck with the so-and-so. Just remember I told you. You two are stuck with each other in the worst way. Which is the best way, I guess, in this world. Cheer up, honey, I love the rat too, sort of. Don't give him an inch."

· 23 ·

When Alfred got home next afternoon he found the three empty barrels in the patio. Taking this as a hopeful sign, he stacked them in the garage. But when he went into the house nothing else looked altered, not in the living room or in the gallery or in the dining room or in their bedroom. He began calling out for Beth and heard no response. He rushed downstairs. She was sitting on the edge of Lizzie's bed, reading a letter; there were many envelopes and cards scattered on the bed beside her.

"Here you are!" he cried in a pouncing way.

"Hello, honey," she said, putting the letter back in its envelope. "I hope your day was profitable."

"I read letters all day."

"Letters! Whose?"

"Do you know where Sybil is?" she said.

"Not since breakfast. Why?"

"Dinner. I just wondered whether to make dinner for one or two. Idle curiosity."

"You're not eating again, my dear?"

"Nope. Is Sybil going to deign to eat with us? That is the question."

"I assume she is."

"I don't."

"We needn't wait dinner on her. Whose letters are all these?"

"Lizzie's."

"You've been reading Lizzie's letters?"

"I read Mama and Papa's this morning. It just about killed me. They *loved* one another, could you have known that? Physically, I mean."

He sat down. "You mean, you found your parents' letters among your mother's things and brought them home with you?"

"There never seemed to be a good opportunity to read them in Houston. So I stowed them away in that vanity that's in Sybil's room now. I never really knew my parents, that whole side of them. I can't tell you what bitter thoughts I've had about them sometimes, Papa more than Mama. After Bing—you know—and Lizzie came, Papa was awful to me, simply awful. I never forgave him while he was alive. Mama never cleared him for me either, when she talked about him. Alfie, I can't tell you what it means to me to have read those letters. I'm too much like him. I see it now, but I never even guessed it before."

"You've kept them?"

"No. I burned them in the fireplace, every one. It took hours. I cried."

She smiled. He did not smile.

"What about these letters here?" he asked.

"Oh, Lizzie's a regular pack rat, she keeps everything. She still has a valentine she got in the first grade."

"And her love letters?"

"Sure."

Beth smiled again, and again he did not return her smile.

"And Sybil's letters? And Nancy's?"

"No," she said.

"How could you go through her letters without her permission, Beth? That's a terrible, terrible thing to do."

"Because I'm a terrible, terrible person. Didn't you know that?" She looked at him belligerently as she spoke, but when she finished she began fumbling the letters together. Then she stacked them back in a drawer in Lizzie's desk. "All right, all right, so I shouldn't have read her goddamned letters. She shouldn't leave them lying around if they're so precious."

"We have always taught the children to respect one another's privacy, and I thought they always did."

"It isn't *that* awful. Lay off, will you? She's my child."

"She's a grown woman."

"Obviously she's a grown woman, so you can quit overcompensating *now*."

"What? What? Overcompensating? What do you mean?"

"You don't need to be *so* protective and *so* considerate of her. She doesn't need it any longer now she's a grown woman."

"You mean, I favor her over the other girls?"

"Alfred, you don't need to favor her any longer because she's not your child. Isn't that what you were telling me—that she's not a child any longer, not even my child? Well, that certainly lets *you* off the hook. So leave me alone. If I want to do wrong to her, she can take care of herself. By your own reasoning."

Beth was not overwrought in manner, or obscurely pleading, or flagrantly offensive. She seemed confident of herself and of what she was saying.

Her confidence gave her statements an impact on Alfred which any excess of emotion would have reduced. If she had spoken passionately, her words, however accusing and unjust, would not have carried their ordinary meaning. But these words she meant, she knew what they meant, she had thought about them, she thought they were true.

Neither had ever before impugned, by the slightest inflection, the other's love for the children.

By their eyes, when they looked at each other now, they recognized that they were going in a direction which they had not taken before and which would, if they continued, break them up. At that time they went no further but had a nervous dinner. Beth sat at table with him and ate some jellied consommé, and Alfred told her, in more detail than was interesting, about the dispute he was arbitrating.

Not long after daybreak Alfred was awakened from sound sleep by a shout from Beth. He was capable of sleep-talking, rational and wide-eyed, for a minute or two about how he definitely was going to get up right away, so that none of his womenfolk believed he was actually awake until he was at least sitting up. Now Beth's cry brought his head off the pillow. "Yes, my dear, of course. What? What?"

She was sitting bolt upright. "Go away!" she declaimed. "I said for you to go away!" Her right arm waved at the door to Alfred's study. She was scowling at the mirror, which reflected, from their angle, the hall door and the gas heater. She yielded to the gentle pressure of his hands and lay down. He watched her till mutters quit coming from her throat and her eyes were no longer flicking about under the lids.

He felt both logy and wide awake. In such a state, which was rare for him, he was subject to assaults of ego thoughts: I am very important, I am more important than people show in the way they treat me. When he recognized these pests and saw that they could not be kept out of his lying-down head, he heaved himself up onto one elbow and then, with an inaudible groan, got up.

As he was sitting at the dining table, waiting for the left-over coffee to reheat, Sybil came in the front door.

"What are you doing up so early?" she said.

"I woke up," he answered. "Where've you been?"

"Up all night. Do I stink of cigarettes?"

He sniffed her hair. "Some. You don't look too bad."

"Well, wait till I get myself a glass of orange juice and I'll tell you all about it."

She had a long, spritely story about a beach picnic and an old movie and tea from a samovar. He kept trying, and failing, to understand why she found her story so amusing.

She had stayed up all night, talking with Morrie in his ratty place over a bookstore south of campus, and every hour or two Sheila would phone and complain about how she couldn't sleep. Morrie and Sheila had gone together for four years—since they were juniors in high school in Cleveland. Sometimes they lived together, usually they didn't. They were unswervingly faithful to three things: to ideal free love, to the importance of marriage, and to each other. Sheila lived two blocks from Morrie, and usually when she had insomnia she would go to his place (her landlady would not let her have men visitors). But last night Sheila had had to stay home and write a term paper and kept calling him up to complain about her sleeplessness.

She'd thanked Sybil for staying up with him, because by dawn he was often down in the dumps and would threaten to go off and join the Army, "get it over with."

"It sounds like a pleasantly foolish way to spend the night," said Alfred. "And now you'll sleep without dreams. At least I've found that I have fewer dreams when I sleep by daylight, and not very bad ones."

"And how's McKee's?"

"Fascinating." He too was hearty while telling his story. "The wonderful thing is that the management men, McKee and Brady, are just like the union negotiators, Flanagan and Pellegrini. They all four came up from the working class, they're all meat-and-potatoes bargainers, none of them understand what the dispute is really about. Neither do I, for that matter, but I do know it's not about wages and hours or ordinary contract matters."

"How do you know?"

"A hunch."

"But, Daddy, you told me once that wages and hours were what unions are good for."

"That's exactly what's wrong with these negotiators. They're fighting according to old-fashioned but legitimate rules they know inside out. There isn't any other way to carry on an industrial fight, at least no way I know of. But something else is happening here. You see, everybody involved has plenty of money. They aren't worried about getting enough to eat or decent clothes. Their big economic problem is which kind of new car to buy next year, a Ford or an Oldsmobile. Yet there is a terrible uneasiness. Perhaps no one, not even the men themselves, knows why."

"Isn't it race prejudice?"

"You say that so coolly. The very fact you can be so cool and open about it makes me doubt that this is the main issue."

"You're as bad as mother. What have *I* got to do with it?"

"Not just you, not just you," he said hastily. "Everybody treats the racial trouble so offhandedly. He's the only Negro technician in the plant. There's no real threat. He's like the Army's one nigger general. North, South, East, West, the niggers damn well know their place, honey, and everybody sees to it that they keep it."

"Daddy."

Every so often he feared that her face was impenetrably pretty. Now, by her eyes and the inflection of her voice, he knew she was shocked, and he liked her the better for being reassured that she was not pretty all the way down.

"Which bothers you, what I said or the way I said it?"

144

"Both," she said. "If it's true, you shouldn't be so cynical about it."

"Right. Back to McKee's with me."

"Well, I'm bushed." She started toward the kitchen. "See you later."

"It has something to do with money." He seemed to be speaking mostly to himself.

But she paused at the doorway. "What does?"

"This labor trouble, the malaise among these workers."

"But you just said— Oh, Alfred, you're just a crazy mixed-up kid."

"I've been thinking a lot about money recently."

"De Tocqueville was right," she said. "I thought he was all wet, at least about *my* family."

"What are you referring to?"

"He said Americans were obsessed about making money." She looked cool and humorless.

"I didn't say I was thinking about making money," Alfred said. "I've been trying to understand what money is and what it stands for."

"Accumulated labor. Years ago Aldo told me Marx was right, and Aldo is a full professor of money."

"Sure, sure. It's like saying love is sex."

"Oh? You're comparing love and money? Love is to sex as money is to . . . ? Oh, Daddy, you're hopeless this morning. It's late. See you around."

"Sybil! Beth and I are going out to dinner tonight, with Horace and Virginia."

"Ripping. I'll make out. Toodledoo, old thing."

For a few minutes after she had gone he was furious at her for being so slippery with him. With Beth, yes, but why should she elude him? He was open with her, he made no unreasonable demands on her. Just before he began to think she might really be cold of heart, he declared to himself that it was best for her spiritual economy now to withdraw from her parents' troubles, and he resolutely swiveled his attention toward money.

The open-end proportion Sybil had flipped at him would not close. He was not troubled to think that love arose from sex. A simile he had come across a long time before had helped him across three or four stinking swamps of debased Freudianism: healthy love is like a tree with its roots deep in the rich soil of sex. He had long diverted himself—it now seemed nothing more than diversion—by thinking of respects in which money was society's equivalent to love: it was an expression of mutual need and trust; the more refined it became, the more necessary to civilized life and at the same time the more subject to perversions; to learn about it was mostly to learn one's ignorance about it. And now a pretty daughter, who surely could not have appreciated what she was doing, had ruined his speculations with a proportion. Money was like a tree with its roots in what? Avarice? The social instinct? Too abstract! Vapors! Physical soil was the only kind of soil. A tree with roots in air!

Safely wrapped in this quarrel with himself, he managed to shave, dress, and get out of the house before Beth had awakened. It was only seven-thirty, and his first appointment was at ten.

· 25 ·

"Do I think *what* was handsome?"

"The house." He spoke with more exuberance in his voice than in his heart, resolutely not hearing the tone of her voice. "The Fowlers' house."

"What kind of a joke are you making, Alfred? I'm sorry, I didn't have such a rip-roaring time as all that. Jokes . . . It was a stucco cube, just a stucco cube with a good view of the Golden Gate. A respectable, uninteresting house."

"I meant the interior, the furnishings actually, especially the living room."

"You mean it!" she said.

"That high ceiling, the copper facing around the fireplace, the drapes, the tables, the whole living room made a strong impression, as strong as any I remember on first acquaintance."

"Another cube! A white cube of a room! It was like being inside a cube of sugar all evening. And the furniture was ghastly."

"Oh, come on, Beth. You like the Ravaglis' modern furniture. What's wrong with the Fowlers'?"

"How can I begin explaining to anyone so stupid? I knew you didn't have any taste when I married you, but I thought you'd picked up a little in the last twenty-one years."

"Control yourself."

"Do you know what your mouth looks like when you say things like that, all puckered up? 'Control yourself.' Like an anus."

"You had too much to drink."

"Not half enough I didn't." She looked out the car window for a while. "I'll try just once more. When Kay chooses and places her furniture, she does it because she likes it. The same with Mary Louise. The same with Virginia even, though she has shaky taste. I haven't

seen Kay and Woody's place up in Mendocino yet, but I already
know one thing about it—I will feel at home in it. That Fowler
woman—everything she did she did because some interior decorator
said to, or some ladies' magazine. That monstrous, expensive, cheer-
less, overheated sugar cube with a view . . . Let me out of the car.
Stop!"

"Don't be absurd."

"Stop, or I'll open the door and jump out."

"You will not. We are on the Eastshore freeway, and I will not
even slow down till we get to the Berkeley exit. I shall stop on University Avenue only if a signal turns red against me."

The third signal they came to was red. When the car stopped, Beth
got out and started trotting down the side street in the direction away
from home. It was nearly one in the morning. Alfred drove around
the block and was waiting for her at the second intersection she came
to. She jerked the back door open, slammed it after her, and lay on
her side on the back seat.

"You are a bad, bad husband."

"You are the best judge of that, as I am the best judge of the kind
of wife you are."

"Judge! Judge! Is anybody home *bei dich?* I said you were a bad
husband and you talk about judges. Don't you care? Did you hear
me?"

"Yes, I heard you. Yes, I care. Am I a bad husband because I happen to like the way the Fowlers' house looks and you don't?"

"You idiot. After all these years I still can't get through to you.
I'll try again. You had no business making me walk. It was bad of
you."

"But you wanted out of the car! You jumped out of your own accord. It wasn't my idea."

"I can't stand being in the same car with you. I can't stand it.
Don't you know anything? A good husband would have gotten out
and let his wife have the car to drive home in. You let me walk alone
in a strange neighborhood, hoodlums, God knows what."

His anger made him tremble. Not trusting himself to drive well, he
shifted into second and crept the last few blocks to their house.

"And you are a bad father," she was saying. "You play favorites.
You've always been so bloody kind to Lizzie. You let Nancy go off
for the summer practically the day I come home. Sybil has turned
against me. Did you know she didn't come home last night?"

"Yes, I knew it."

"I wonder who she's sleeping with. Some Negro with a goatee, I
wouldn't be surprised."

"So? If he is a Negro with a goatee?"

147

"Who cares what I think?" The car was just going into their driveway. She reared up on the back seat and clouted him on the back of the head. "When did you ever care what I thought? You've always been so considerate, so kind. You are a monster, Alfred Royce, you are a pitying monster. All I ever hear is how thoughtful you are, so patient. Monster!"

He poured himself half a glass of whisky, drank it neat, and went to bed in Lizzie's room with his arm across his eyes. He tried to understand what Beth had been getting at or what was really bothering her, and failed to think of anything more complicated than that she just didn't love him any longer.

Presently he heard the door open. She was standing in the doorway in her pajamas.

"What're we going to do about it?" she said in a low voice.

He did not want even to try to understand what she was talking about. "Sleep. I have a hard day ahead of me tomorrow."

"Honey, you didn't like that house, did you? Tell me you didn't."

"I liked that house quite a lot," he said, "and I especially liked the way the living room was furnished."

The next time he lifted his arm the doorway was empty, the door still open.

· 26 ·

Thursday, Alfred got home after six. He stood in the patio a moment, watching Sybil come and go in the dining room as she set the table, and listening to her and Beth chatter; their voices sounded amiable enough. The five barrels by the piano remained unopened.

"Hi, Daddy."

"Hello, Sybbie." He stood in the kitchen door, uncertain whether to kiss Beth as he normally did on coming home. Her greeting was pleasant enough, but she did not turn to him from the salad she was preparing. "What's for dinner, honey?"

"Lasagne, salad, and a honeydew."

"How's the arbitrating, Daddy?"

"Oh, the whole dispute is petering out. Nothing more's coming of it than a gripe about working conditions. It'll be settled tomorrow, probably; something will be settled anyway. Bah."

"Mom, do you want me to pour a pitcher of red wine?"

"There's a gallon of white in the icebox," Beth said.

"Which shall I get?" said Sybil.

"Alfie, red or white?"

"White," he said happily. "I need something cool. I'm going to wash up and put on a sports shirt."

"We'll be sitting down in half a minute," said Beth.

He whistled as he changed and smiled in the mirror.

As Alfred was serving he said, "Lizzie should be here. You know how she loves lasagne."

"How she loves to eat, period," said Sybil. "And from what I hear, the Shoshones don't cook so good."

Alfred and Sybil laughed. Beth did not laugh.

"Do you know what?" said Sybil brightly. "Let me tell you what I did last night. We went to the Noble Savage after dinner."

"Where?" said Beth.

"The Noble Savage, down in Emeryville on San Pablo. They have folk singers on Monday, Tuesday, and Wednesday. Anyway, we went there—"

"You and who?" Beth asked.

"Brewster."

"He's the proper one?"

"None other. I had him all taped as a solid citizen. You know, when a girl says she's looking for a husband, that's Brewster. Hubby, the perfect hubby."

"God," said Beth.

"But let me tell you. He's quite a surprise. We went there about nine-thirty. It's sort of a barn of a place, with lots of little tables, with a chianti bottle on each one with a candle in it, you know, gobs of candle drippings on the sides of the bottles. There weren't more than half a dozen tables with people at them, all up near the stand, but the singer was using a mike anyway. Isn't that the nuts—a PA system when everybody is within thirty feet of her? She was a Japanese girl in black slacks and a turtleneck sweater and she was singing old English ballads, not too good but it was fun. So we sat at a table and ordered beer."

"But you're not twenty-one," said Beth.

"This is Emeryville, Mom. After the girl was through we looked around, and there, two tables away, was Roy Carver, you know, that slippery character that was here at the party in June. He was with a seedy-looking old guy with an unlit cigar in the corner of his mouth. They came over to our table, and Roy introduced us. The old guy was named Doctor Zagri. Roy got Brewster and him to arguing about television. They were both for it, but they disagreed about what it was good for. I didn't pay much attention. Television is a big blah for me, and they were getting along fine. Roy kept glancing at the door. After a while, he got up and said he had to go, he had an interview. I caught a glimpse of a short, baldish man in a ratty blue suit in the doorway. He was just turning to go back out. I guess Roy went with him. Doctor Zagri—I never did find out what kind of a doctor he is, medical or what—anyway, he didn't seem surprised when Roy took off with that guy in the doorway. In a little while two mixed couples came in that Doctor Zagri knew, and they pulled up a table and sat with us. The next singer was awful—no voice, old popular songs. So we all went to Doctor Zagri's place, way down in West Oakland.

"In the slums?" said Beth in alarm.

"Sort of," said Sybil. "Anyhow, he's got this real crazy apartment with lots of big paintings in it he did himself. They don't look any worse than most of the paintings you see in the museums when they have a contemporary show. He had a jug of dago red, and we divided up, men against women, and did charades. The great thing was, Brewster was terrific at it. I wouldn't have believed he had it in him. He just stole the show. It got so we all just wanted to give him things to do so we could watch. He even moved like a dancer sometimes. He could get down on the floor and wriggle around through the chairs like a snake. His voice would go up to a silly falsetto or way down in the cellar. You know, there's more to old Square John than meets the eye. He's as square as a soda cracker but he's got something. He dances like a dream, too. We didn't get home till three-thirty. Imagine, good old Brew, every mother's dream son-in-law, dancing at a bohemian party in the colored district till three in the morning."

Beth's face had been unresponsive during this recital. After it was over she stared at the table, laid her fork down on the plate, and slumped.

"I want a glass of ice water," said Alfred in a cheery voice.

Sybil went to the kitchen to get it. Beth looked after her balefully and without a word got up and went through the living room, up to their bedroom, slamming the door behind her.

"Now what did I do?" said Sybil from the kitchen door with an empty tumbler in her hand.

"No one will ever know," said Alfred crisply.

They finished the meal in a hurry.

"Please clean up, my dear. I'm going to my study."

"If you don't mind," said Sybil, "I'm going out tonight. Is that all right?"

"Of course. Have a good time."

There was a long silence.

"What's the matter with her?" Sybil asked almost in a whisper.

He stared out the window for a while. "There are so many possible answers . . . I keep juggling them. Which is silly of me. But I've got them going and I don't know how to stop them from flying around. Well. There's one thing I am sure of—none of you girls are in any way responsible for your mother's troubles. Okay?"

"By-by, Poppy."

He went into the study through the outside door, so as not to have to go through the bedroom. He was as full of mixed emotions as he could be without giving way to them.

In an unbroken rush he finished the last chapter of his book, his right foot tapping or his tongue clicking on the roof of his mouth as he wrote.

As he was reading over what he had written, with cold distaste and with the knowledge that it did what it was supposed to do, Beth came in.

· 27 ·

"I've just finished my book," he said.

"What difference does that make?" she said.

"It's a load off my mind."

"You can't imagine how little it would have mattered in the scheme of things if that book had never been written at all."

He began jabbing his thigh with the eraser end of a pencil. He was sitting erect at his desk. The left side of his lower lip hung out a little. With his head turned a bit to one side, he watched her, not taking his eyes from her face.

She stood leaning on the file cabinet in a tense parody of nonchalance. Her head was cocked to the left as though she had a stiff neck. Mostly she looked at something else, but every so often she dragged her eyes up to his face. At such moments she concentrated her gaze on the bridge of his nose.

"You never liked this house," she said, "not really."

"What makes you say anything so preposterous?"

"There are signs. Oh, you think you like it. That's an old Royce trick. 'Put a good face on things.' If I heard your mother say that once I heard her say it a thousand times."

"That's right, you did. And now my mother is dead."

"Not in her darling little sonny boy she's not."

"Lay off Mother. She did you no harm."

"Not directly, perhaps. I'm sorry. The week after we moved into this house you left me. If memory serves."

"That's gone. Let go of it. That was years and years ago."

" 'If you can't forgive, forget.' Jesus, she used to say that too. Well, not me. If you can't forgive you can't forget, and vice versa."

"If that were true we'd all be in hell."

"Ah, now he's joining the human race. Right, friend. We all are in hell."

"At least you don't have to talk about it. There are things one does not talk about."

"You bullied me into swallowing that for ten years, and for ten years I never talked about it once."

"About what?"

"It."

"Not even to Mary Louise?"

"I just got through saying I never talked about it once. Don't you even believe me any more?"

"I believe you."

"And it didn't work. So, we're going to talk about it now."

He did not respond.

"And that little cutie pie you played around with. Not that she matters a good goddamn."

"I didn't exactly leave you, Beth. We separated for a few weeks. You wanted me to go as much as I wanted to go."

"Oh yes, you did exactly leave me, Alfred," she mimicked. Then she sneered. "I lived here in this house—our home, remember?— with my three children and you went down in Oakland to live with your cutie pie—"

"That is not true."

"Well, you went away *and* you had her. What was she, a stenographer or something?"

"A practical nurse."

"Practical nurse! Christ, couldn't you even rate a registered nurse?"

"With fallen arches and varicose veins."

"A sense of humor he loads me with on top of everything else."

"Beth," he cried, "what are you trying to do? Drive me away?"

"Again? You mean again."

"Yes, again."

"Look, you bulled this house through. I wanted to put Grandmother's money into blue-chip stocks, remember? And you insisted we buy this house. You found it. You sold me on it. You didn't listen when I wanted to back out of the deal before it was too late. You never let me forget you were making the payments over the years and all I contributed was the down payment. *I* drove *you* out! That's the way you've got it all fixed up in your righteous head, is it?"

"I said we had to make that money an active, integral part of our lives. I said you mustn't hold out on me."

"It was my inheritance."

"Your grandmother hadn't seen you since Lizzie was born. You thought she hated you, and then she up and willed you as much as her other grandchildren. That's why we had to neutralize the money, take the charge out of it, ground it. We agreed the best thing to do was to buy a house with it. As for my not liking this house—it's not just that

I like it, I think our family would not be the same without it and would be worse off."

"What do you think I brought all this antique junk home from Mother's for? Your same old theory—'make it part of our lives.' I don't like her stuff, don't you even know that? Some of it's all right. There are some handsome pieces. But they aren't me. Still, I can't repudiate my mother just because she's dead. I'm too old to try to get rid of her again. I've got to live with her for the rest of my life. And you hate me for it, you all hate me."

She began crying and sat in a straight chair. When he stepped toward her she jerked away from him. She accepted his handkerchief. He sat back at his desk. Presently she wiped her eyes and looked up at the bridge of his nose, her face contorted.

"There was one thing you said last night," Alfred began, "that I didn't understand. I can't get it out of my mind."

"Welcome to hell." She was grinning. "Where things won't get themselves forgotten."

"What?" he said. "Oh. I'm not blaming you, I simply want to know what you meant."

" 'There are things one does not talk about.' If *I* go poking around, that's what I get dished out to me. But if *you* do it, it is only because you want to 'clarify the situation.' You are absolutely beyond . . .'"

This time when he thrust the pencil down, his elbow bumped on the arm of his chair so that he jabbed himself in the testicles. He had to close his eyes against the pain, rigid to hold himself from doubling over.

"You implied," he said, his eyes still closed, "that I favored Lizzie over the other girls and that I did so for some sort of peculiar reason."

" 'The poor little bastard.' "

"She was not a bastard."

"Legally she wasn't—lawyer. I was legally married to Bing and legally divorced, and I've never seen the dirty rat since. Here I was, two thousand miles from home with a fatherless baby. You were good to me, Alfred."

"I was not 'good to you.' "

"All right, you weren't good to me. I'm so stupid it took me twenty years to see what else you were to me. Do you know what opened my eyes? Mama's death. She knew what I'd done and she was mean to me for it, but when the chips were down she came through. And you, you don't even want me to take what my own mother gave me! You never loved me, you pitied me! Mr. High and Mighty! I hate you, how I hate you, you'll never know how much I hate you! Oh God!"

They began shouting. She cried without hiding her tears. He paced irregularly, both fists clenched white. They had never before used such tones of voice to each other.

It happened that Alfred's hand was on the receiver when there was a call. At the first ring he lifted it in a sort of reflex, though Beth was railing at him. Seeing that he had lifted the receiver, she stuffed her fist in her mouth to quiet herself and bit her knuckles in a frenzy of frustration.

"Yes?"

"Alfred?"

"Speaking."

"What's going on?"

"Who is this?"

"Horace, for Pete's sake. What's wrong with Beth?"

"She's upset."

"From the sound of your voice—"

"What is it you want?"

"Have you been listening to the radio?"

"In the name of God, no, I have not been listening to the radio."

"All right, all right. McKee's home was bombed half an hour ago. McKee is critically injured, and Brady is dead."

"Dead! You're not serious."

"Killed. There's no clue. I talked to Macouillard."

"Who did it?"

"Wake up. I just said nobody knows. Get over here. Pull yourself together, man."

"I'll be there in a few minutes."

When he hung up, Beth spoke. "What's up?"

"A bomb has been thrown. Everything's changed. I've got to go to Horace's. It's the dispute I'm involved in."

"If you go out of that door now, you don't ever need to bother to come back. I won't have you back. I'm warning you."

"Indeed. This is a real emergency. Our little altercation can wait. What's it about, even? A man has been killed."

"I am sorry a man has been killed, but there's nothing you or I can do about it. Don't leave."

"It's important for me to do what I can."

"I mean it. You'd better not walk out on me now. We have things to settle."

"Don't kid yourself," he said as he stood at the outside door. "If we ever separate again, I will be the one who decides to do it." He went out.

She ran to the door and caught it before it had closed. "Too late!" she screamed. "Two months ago I would have believed you, you could have bullied me with that. But you're behind the times! Things have changed!"

She slammed the door as hard as she could. Her knees supported her into the bedroom but gave way before she reached the bed. She collapsed onto the rug, weeping, but also impatiently waiting till she should regain her composure and strength so she could do what she had to do.

· 28 ·

Alfred stayed with Horace less than an hour. He declined every invitation to talk about Beth. They stayed with settling the strike and advising the union officials. They were public servants conferring.

He let Horace think he was rushing back to Beth. In fact, he was suffering from intolerable curiosity. He felt absolutely positive that to understand the bombing he would have to know the true cause of the strike.

By a filling station he found a pay phone in a sort of glass sentry box, installed himself in it, and dialed Roy Carver. There was no answer. Leon—no answer. Chantal—her voice sounded odd, and she said she had no idea where Roy was and thought Leon was at a movie. Then he called Joe Thompson, who sounded relieved to hear him and wanted to talk. They met in a bar.

"The thing about this cat—you know?—that wants to bring the libel suit," Joe said, "he told me a story that really cooled me. It just makes me wonder what people think libel is. He says there's a guy at McKee's, an old neighborhood buddy of his, that's going around spreading the story that he, my client, is against the Negro that got jumped in rank because he's got race prejudice, whereas that's obviously a lie, he tells me, because he's got a colored brother-in-law. How could anybody with a colored man in the family have race prejudice? Then he goes on to explain to me how this old buddy of his was at his sister's wedding with the colored fellow. He, my would-be client, got loaded before the wedding—too much marriage cheer, he called it—and sort of cut up at the ceremony. When I asked him what-all he did, it seems he interrupted the preacher, he exchanged punches with the groom and insulted his sister. He laughed when he told me —you know—man to man. This colored machinist that got promoted —there's nobody on earth he respects more; it's just the question of seniority, it's the principle of the thing. So let's sue for libel. I inquired around a little and talked to Roy about him. This cat's not the troublemaker, nobody thinks. But you know, I think troublemaking's

155

gone sophisticated too these days. My hunch is, this cat's the idea-man, as it were, and the so-called troublemakers are the front men for him, without even knowing they are. All they do is spread the trouble; he really does the making of it. Mind you, I don't have an iota of proof, this is just a hunch I've got."

"Damn," said Alfred. "It seems to boil down to plain old racial prejudice."

"Not so plain. Fancy, I'd say."

"All right, devious race prejudice."

"Maybe," said Joe, "it has something to do with the bomb parts they make at that plant."

"But," said Alfred, "the men think of themselves as contributing to the future. So I've been told. Everyone agrees they're proud of their jobs."

"Sure. Have you taken a peek at the future recently? Like what you see? Myself, it scares me shitless sometimes. These machinists aren't dopes, you know."

"You're doing a lot of interpreting, Joe."

"That's right. But I didn't accept the case. I'm not being a lawyer, just a private citizen, sort of an innocent bystander."

"I wish I had a better interpretation," said Alfred. "In fact I'd set-tle right now for any other one this side of treason."

· 29 ·

When he got home the lights were off in the house and Sybil's motor scooter was not parked in its niche.

In the patio he came upon a cardboard carton containing his shoes, the typescript of his book, and some odds and ends from his desk, and also a suitcase, which he opened. In it, neatly packed, were most of his clothes and toilet articles.

The front door was locked. He laughed painfully, holding his key that unlocked all the outside doors of the house. No. He would not humiliate himself by having another scene with Beth. He picked up the carton and the suitcase and put them into his car. She was intoler-able, and he was leaving her. This time for good. He hoped she was lying in bed listening to him laugh.

In fact, she had gone to Mary Louise's, drunk a lot of brandy, and was now asleep on the daybed in Mary Louise's living room.

A flock of alternatives swirled into Alfred's consciousness, so that he had to stop the car before he had gone half a block. Where would he live? How would he get all the possessions he wanted, snapshots, books, the canister of raw sugar that he liked on his breakfast food, letters, his file cabinet, his swivel chair? Who would get the unabridged dictionary, the lithograph Aldo had given them for a wedding present, all the presents given them in common? She would! She had the house, the children, the furniture—God, yes, the furniture—she would get everything! And their friends—they would have to divide up their friends. How? Where was he to go now? And the girls—he would have to get hold of Sybil, then go up to the Ravaglis' place and see Nancy. Woody and Kay would no doubt want him to live in their Berkeley house till they returned, or maybe Woody would offer him the San Francisco apartment to use. What should he do then? Meanwhile the McKee disturbance would need all sorts of attention. Why should he worry about it, though? Anybody else could do as well as he; it was nothing to him, really. What publisher should he send the book to? What if he were offered a federal judgeship?

He peered out of the car into the quiet, dark, gentle street for help. He discovered that he had pulled up in front of Justice Durkheim's house, and he felt clearly and unambiguously ashamed of himself. He had no business, even unconsciously, making the slightest move toward anyone else in this trouble, which was strictly between himself and his wife, had no business substituting, by even the most devious gesture, this nearly dead old man for his dead father: to do so was puerile, irresponsible, and weak.

He drove to a motel north of town and fell asleep almost immediately.

He dreamed he was wearing a white wig and sitting in a tall judge's chair. He was trying to get some surface transport workers to explain the cause of a strike which was half paralyzing the city. They kept insisting that they were not striking against *her, she* was striking against them. "But why? It doesn't make sense. Why?" "She had so much income this year that she's taking everything out on us." "You're talking nonsense. You're keeping things from me." "If you don't like what we tell you, quit butting into our business. We didn't come here of our own accord. Leave us alone, the buses will be rolling before long." "The subways are crowded as it is." "Crowded!" The workers roared with laughter. "You said crowded, did you!" They rolled on the floor. "People are dying in them every day, that's all." When he leaned forward in the chair to reach the gavel, which was big as a mallet, he discovered that his feet did not touch the floor. He quit trying to restore order and gave way to spasms of laughter.

But when he woke up enough to realize where he was and why he was there, he discovered the spasms were great dry sobs. For some time he lay on his back, unable to stop. His eyes felt swollen with tears, but none came.

III

On the evening of the bombing Leon had discovered he had a cold in the head and set about his ritual for curing one. The important first steps were heavy steaming and a hot toddy, then to bed early to sleep the clock around. Though the telephone rang three times during the evening, he did not answer it.

The next day he covered his head with a blanket and breathed steam once each hour; he took aspirin by the clock; during the course of the day he drank exactly one quart of fresh orange juice and more than a quart of weak tea without milk. By six o'clock he felt even better than he'd known he was going to feel and was in the best of spirits as he walked over to Chantal's in the mild air with a light scarf around his throat. He had not read a paper or listened to a news report on the radio for more than twenty-four hours.

Leon felt the better because of an analogy he had come upon during the afternoon. When he was not ministering to his cold he had prepared for a freshman course in American institutions he was to begin teaching at Presley the next week. He had to look carefully at several textbooks, all written in thick, gummy prose. Leon was not wincingly sensitive to clichés; indeed, he felt comfortable in well-worn phrases and resented the preciousness of colleagues who dismissed as gassy cliché formulas he liked to use, "it might very well be the case that," for example, or "the present world situation." But too many hours of political-science jargon had made his mind feel thick and heavy. Then in one of the texts he came upon an essay by a professor of English in a college he'd never heard of, and his mind cleared. The essay posited the axiom that without language man is but a super chimpanzee and then devoted itself to a diatribe against organs of mass communication. It concluded with the assertion that in the United States there were untold millions of people who were less than human because the debasement of their language by the mass media had rendered them unable to think. Gleefully Leon extended the blame for this debasing to include writers of social-science textbooks and gave himself over to cruel fantasies.

The kitchen was cold. He looked into Jean-Louis's room, where he heard a murmur. Chantal was curled up on the boy's bed, listening to him read. She did not look up when Leon appeared in the doorway. After a couple of sentences Jean-Louis stopped reading and greeted him with a politeness unadulterated with the slightest warmth. Leon felt straight-armed.

"Chantal, are you sick?"

"Forgive me." Then she said something to Jean-Louis in French and rolled over facing the wall.

"Please," said Jean-Louis and took Leon out onto the back porch. "Maman is very low since last night. You'd do her a favor to tell Roy not to come tonight either."

"And Harry?"

The boy shrugged.

"The three of us might go out to dinner together? No? Well, I'll telephone tomorrow. Be sure to let me know if there's anything whatever I can do."

The boy shrugged again.

Leon went off, not very worried. He assumed that Chantal was suffering an unimportant female depression, though he had not known her to give way to one before, and that the deadness of her voice and the coldness of Jean-Louis's shrug were no more than their rude politeness, of which he had caught glimpses from time to time and which he thought of as French.

Roy was not home.

In front of the bar and grill Leon went to, the racked newspapers had the bombing in the headlines. As he ate his meat and potatoes he read two versions of the event, both of them full of speculations about the extent of the striking union's complicity in the act.

He was excited by his nearness to an act of labor violence. Leon held the view, conventional in his intellectual world, that all strides in man's long advance were a consequence of rebelliousness. He also held, uninspected, the emotional twin of that view, that a rebellious act was a blow for freedom and surely did more good than harm. He thought of his father, whom he could hardly remember, as a rebel against rebels, a rebel true to rebellion—one who rebelled even against the successful rebels, for they had lapsed into authority, a martyr to rebellion who risked his life and lost his health, dying in exile and poverty, angry and idealistic to the painful end. Now, Leon would be able to look at rebellion plain, in the flesh. He would track the marvelous beast to its lair and know it.

The door to Roy's rooms was usually unlocked, but tonight, when he went back, Leon tried it and found it locked. There was no response to his rap.

From the telephone on the wall by the front door of Roy's rooming house, Leon dialed the Royces' number. Having got a busy signal, he drove impatiently to their house.

Sybil answered the door. She did not invite him in but stood in the doorway, telling him that Alfred was not home. He felt she too was straight-arming him, as though he were a door-to-door salesman.

"Would you ask him to call me as soon as he gets home?"

She nodded.

"You know," he said with as much eagerness as he could muster, "this bombing may be a very significant episode. I think it may very well mark a turning point in radical politics in our time. What does Alfred think?"

She shrugged. "I haven't talked to Daddy about it."

"I'll be home all evening. I'm preparing a new course I'll be giving at Presley. You know I'm teaching there this year?"

"I heard you mention it to Daddy. Or Daddy to Mother. Or somebody to somebody."

"How is your mother?"

"All right. Well, I'll tell Daddy you called, next time I hear from him."

"Hear from him! He's not out of town, is he? He's right in the thick of this whole thing."

"I don't know where he is."

She stepped back and began to close the door. Because her face was pretty and her voice friendly, as they always were, he was confused into reaching out toward her.

"Sybil, please, what's going on? You're mixing me up."

She looked at him exactly as she had looked at him on the beach when he had been teasing her flirtatiously. It was also exactly as she had looked at him when she was displeased by a coarse joke he had told in the car on the way back from the beach, but he forgot this and remembered the flirting.

"I beg of you." His manner was mock-serious except for his voice, in which his real seriousness showed.

"Daddy moved out last night, and I don't know where he is."

As soon as she said this her glance dropped and a shadow of displeasure crossed on her face. Against his stammer, she closed the door. He raised his hand to knock, but dropped it and turned away.

He sat for half an hour in his car in front of the house before driving home.

· 2 ·

When he returned he felt chilly, and his nose was stopping up again. He wanted to steam for a while, but he felt ashamed to be pampering himself when everyone else was in serious trouble of one kind or another. He shut the windows, which he'd left open to air the place out, and went to bed.

Twice during the night he got up to take his temperature, at once fearful and hopeful that he was delirious; but the thermometer read slightly below normal. Both times he dialed Roy's number, without answer.

He kept trying to direct his thoughts onto the idea of rebellion, and to think of the assault on McKee and Brady as a rebellious act. But his consciousness was dominated by unwanted images: of Chantal turning her back to him; of Sybil closing the door on him; of Alfred at the head of the seminar table, drumming the table with his fingers, eyes flashing; of his mother, for some reason; of Robin. He had scarcely given Robin two thoughts since she had left. He'd paid to get out of that trouble; she'd written that he had nothing to worry about, and that was that. Yet erotic images of her kept coming up again and again. But there was nothing amorous about the emotions accompanying them—anxiety, revulsion, aggressive concern. He kept having to labor to recall her name each time her image returned. Thoughts of Alfred kept agglutinating and separating. He kept repeating that Alfred was the victim of God only knew what female craziness. But his emotions hardly responded to the thought, not a hundredth as much as to the memory of Chantal's rolling over on Jean-Louis's bed toward the wall and of her dead voice.

The ideal of rebellion-as-a-duty had long been a foundation rock in his life, and Alfred as the good, responsible man had come to be another. Now the bombing began to dislodge the one because Leon could not see any social end for it to have served, and Alfred's leaving his wife began to dislodge the other because the act seemed to Leon, whatever his busy intellect said, to reveal a fatal flaw in his idol. The two masses of surcharged thoughts were caroming around in his mind, knocking things over. Worse, they crackled with hostility toward each other. What was rebellious about Alfred? Leon had got along for months without having that question confront him.

Just before dawn he had the illusion that a woman was getting into bed with him. He thought it was Robin and embraced her with a great outflow of erotic tenderness. As he fondled her body—he had appar-

162

ently forgotten how large she was—he gradually realized that it was a man he was caressing. He was too horrified to look at the face and broke out of sleep with a moan. It was beginning to be light by the time he had entirely quit shuddering and could slump back into sleep.

· 3 ·

On the way to open the door, Leon glanced at the mirror to make sure his eyes were still puffed up, and as soon as he had let Joe in he blew his nose. He spoke as thickly as he could.

"Sorry to drag you all this way, Joe, but you can see what a cold I've got."

The truth was that he had got Joe to come to his place because he did not want to leave the telephone. Alfred might call.

"That's all right," said Joe. "I don't mind too much. Anyway, it worked out for the best. Hey, good lord, you aren't this sick. It's a nice day out, and you've got it so stuffy in here I can't breathe. You don't mind if I just open this window halfway and sit by it? Man, you must think you're dying the worst way. You don't look so bad to me."

Leon was relieved to open all the windows. He pretended to be surprised at the mellowness of the fresh air and said that breathing it made him feel better. Just as his pretended pleasure in fresh air covered a genuine relief to be putting off sick ways, so his pretended hypochondria, which he had assumed to justify his getting Joe to come to him, covered a genuine worry about something obscure and important in himself.

"You see," said Joe, "on my way over to this godforsaken back alley you hole up in, I thought I might as well stop by the union headquarters and see if I could get anything out of my client. Hey, you know, he really is my client too. I got the notice yesterday. I passed the bar, I'm a legal lawyer now. How's about that?"

"Congratulations. So what's the union doing, denying everything?"

"Worse. They're really denying it. They aren't a bit glad it happened, not even secretly. You know this joker that's been paying me, he's dropped the whole libel bit; all he's interested in now is clearing his name. I'm pretty well out of it, naturally, from here on in. That sad sack, he seems to think there ought to be a law somewhere to restrain people from gossiping. I'm just hanging around for the fun of the thing, really. You see, there's a finger of suspicion pointing his way on the bomb bit."

"The big finger?" said Leon, poking out his middle finger and jabbing it at Joe.

163

"Just the little one, maybe, but a finger, all the same. You know the impression I get? These guys, all these union guys, don't give a hot fart who was killed, they just don't want to be thought in on it. Not for the sake of the union or the labor movement or anything like that, and heaven forbid it should be because killing people is bad. Not even for their own necks, really; at least none of them look to be worried about the police. What's really eating them is, they don't want to be thought unrespectable. It isn't respectable to throw a bomb at your boss. You see, nobody has a notion who actually did it, and meanwhile these innuendoes are sort of slithering around all over everybody, and naturally the obvious place to look for a suspect is in the union. Even the union stiffs are looking at each other sideways once in a while. Well, all I know is, if it was a union member that did it, what the cops and the DA and San Quentin do to him is nothing to what his brothers are going to do to him for having their respectability asperged."

His pained laughter was so ample that Leon, against his inclination, joined him and felt the better for it.

"Who did you talk to at the union hall?"

"Various people. Not too many, actually. The main one was a guy named Clark something. I'd met him at a couple of parties here and there. He's a so-called reporter for the McKee house organ, and he isn't exactly received with open arms around union headquarters, but he was there anyway, and they let him be. You see, each one of them knows *he* didn't do anything, and if one of the others did it, then let that other one get it in the neck. It's instructive, Leon, it really is, to see what it does to people to not know who their enemy is and suspect their brother. Anyway, Clark wasn't getting too much of anywhere, and neither was I, to tell the truth. So we went to a greasy spoon and had some coffee, and he did some interesting talking. Have you seen Roy the last couple of days?"

"Roy? No, I haven't."

"You eat with him, don't you?"

"Yes. I haven't been able to reach him at his place."

"Neither has anybody else, including his office. So Clark said, anyhow. Isn't this a funny time for a reporter on a labor paper to take a powder?"

"What are you getting at?"

"Well, Clark was full of wild conjectures about some screwy outfit he calls the Comrades. He says that's not their real name but that's what the local group call themselves. They drink lots of tea and talk about attentats. You ever hear of such a thing?"

"Sure, attentats run in my family. They're schemes to assassinate somebody."

"No, well, what I was getting at—how does the whole set-up strike you?"

"It sounds like a lot of malarkey to me, romantic hokum."

Leon's eyes were on his hands. From hints and pieces, a conspiracy was putting itself together in his mind. He did not know whether Joe knew about Harry Evans. He did not know what or who might be implicated, but for some reason he did not want to tell Joe what he was suspecting. He was aware that Joe was watching him closely.

"You knew Roy," Leon said sharply, "before I did."

"We horsed around town together. We never settled down to a serious political discussion."

"Yeah," said Leon. "It's all up in the air. I still think we ought to go talk with . . ." He trailed off.

"The DA?" Joe asked incredulously.

"I was thinking of Alfred."

"Yes, Alfred." Joe's voice had suddenly become so expansive that Leon looked at him in surprise. He was beaming. "Good old Alfred. I called their number last night. I had the same idea, to sort of set things in order, as you might say, by talking with somebody that has his head screwed on the right way. So who do you think answers the phone? Lizzie."

"She's back already?"

"No less. (You know Alfred's moved out?)"

"(So Sybil told me.) Well, I'll be damned. Did she have a good time? How're the Shoshones?"

"Not so hot. They let her down bad. You know what those copper-plated buggers are doing to our Liz? They're gallivanting around in pickups like a bunch of farmers. Dodge pickups mostly. For some reason she seems to be all stirred up because those degenerate post-pre-literates got Dodge pickups. I asked her what make station wagon it was those four cute little Cal scientresses drove up there in to poke around amongst the natives—a Ford? were they outclassed?—and Liz reached right down the mouthpiece and right along that wire and right out my receiver and jerked my rumdy ear off."

They both laughed altogether harder than was necessary.

"I love her," Joe went on, "I absolutely love that little pillar. She does me good. She's so solid about what's what. Like the way she told me I couldn't speak to Alfred because he'd moved out and nobody knew where he was, well, naturally I was thrown by this, I wasn't expecting anything like it. So I blurted out—you know, the way a person does when he's off guard—something to the effect, 'Is there another woman? What's happened all of a sudden?' I don't know just what I said, it's not my style, really, you know, butting in. The way she'd said it, though—so stalwart, as you might say, upright-

165

sounding, matter-of-fact . . . And she'd only been home for three or four hours herself, it was all new to her." He shook his head admiringly. "So anyway, her answer was what did me in completely. I'm hooked on her, you know, I really am. She said in this chunky way of hers, 'There's nothing so surprising that Alfred and Beth should separate for a while or even divorce. It is a normal pattern of behavior among Wasps of their socio-economic level.' Can you imagine that? Oh, what a pillar of salt she is! There she stands, but solid, looking out over the cities of the plain with a scowl on her face, and I'm just wandering around like a crazy mixed-up wild ox or something. I don't know what's what half the time, and the other half I'm too busy to care. So every once in a while I go over and lick her, it makes me feel better, it's nourishing, she's nice and salty and I lick her, she's a landmark. Did you ever know anybody like her? My goodness, my goodness, I guess I'll get going right over there to San Jacinto Way and refresh myself. She said she was going back to New Mexico before long, and I'm afraid those Pueblocitos she's so goofed on might just keep licking at her till she melts away. I'm crazy about that stupid girl, I really am."

Leon forgot he had a cold; Alfred's separating from Beth looked more ordinary than alarming; who threw the bomb was a detective's problem, not his. He took everything Joe said as the fantasy of high spirits, including Joe's declarations of affection for Lizzie. Therefore, when Joe stood up, Leon assumed he was going to leave, probably to go chat with Lizzie for a while.

"Come on, Joe, don't go, stick around for a while longer, sit down."

But Joe had only got up to pace. His face was heavy. His voice was quite altered, taut instead of relaxed. "Money," he began. "I'm in shit up to my armpits and I need money to get out."

The melodramatic shift in voice and subject made Leon smile in appreciation of a trial lawyer's histrionics. But if Joe was putting on an act, Leon could not detect any staginess in his comportment, and what he said was not too fantastic to make good sense.

"So how does a person go about getting money in this cesspool of a society we're in? By being part of it, of course. That is seen to. Especially for a lawyer. Which I chose to be of my own goddamned ignorant free will. You remember what Alfred said a lawyer was one day? A node of the social will?"

Leon shook his head.

"He just said it in passing, and you wouldn't be interested since you're going to be a teacher anyway."

"No! I'm going to start in law school right away. I've decided to become a lawyer."

"More fool you. I don't know if that 'node of social will' bit means a bloody thing, but what it means to me is—to get ahead as a lawyer you got to have all the contacts you can manage and you got to work within the procedural set-ups society has evolved. In fact, you got to be part of it *so* much it becomes part of you. By the time you get the money which was to get you out of the stinking cesspool, it won't do you one mother-loving bit of good. You'll carry the stink with you, you'll have the shit in your blood forever."

"Money isn't the only way out."

"It's the only way up and out, if you don't have angels to give you a lift, and I don't. There's a few ways down and out, like heroin, or being a bohemian or some sort of criminal. Maybe I just don't have the nerve, maybe I'm a coward, I don't know. But I do know I don't want to make the down-and-out route, I'm just not a bum at heart, my father was the debt-paying type, and my mother respected him and so did all his other children and so do I. What I want is to sail around in a trimaran with two masts, leaning back in my seat with a cigar between my fingers and a bottle of champagne when the water's smooth enough to pour a glass, and I want Lizzie along, upright there beside me, scowling back at Sodom and Gomorrah, so's I can reach over for her now and again and grab me a lick. Now skimming around like that takes money, nothing else but."

"You're taking a very naïve view of money if you think it's not essentially social in its—"

"Don't bug me, Leon, just don't bug me. I know as many theories of money as the next man, and none of them explain to me what money is. I don't care what money is, I just care what I can do with it. But I've got to get some right away, quick. My soul can't afford to wait. Another couple of years, man, and I'll be down there on my knees with the rest of the bourgeoisie on Sunday morning, meaning what I say. 'We have left undone those things which we ought to have done, and we have done those things which we ought not to have done, and there is no health in us.' Lord, have mercy on my soul."

"You're optimistic if you think you can hold out for two years."

"I know it. Two months is more like it. Two weeks maybe. Hell, I may be there already, for all I know. I felt so bad this morning I went to Mass. It didn't help."

Leon swallowed and blinked. "I didn't realize you were a Catholic."

"I'm not." Joe's voice became easy again, and his eyes veiled. "I'm Episcopalian, high church, and I didn't know of any Episcopal services on a Saturday morning this side of the cathedral and maybe not even there. So I went to Mass in a Catholic church. That Latin, it's too much. There's nothing like the Book of Common Prayer, man, to tune you in for a while. So I'm going to New York in a couple of weeks."

Up to this point Leon had been trying to follow Joe. But at this sudden inexplicable turn, Leon withdrew in irritation. "Yes?" he said coldly and watched.

"You know these TV quiz give-away programs? Well, this way and that I've got myself booked for one. It's the big one, the big new one. It goes to over a hundred thousand dollars, if they like you."

"What does liking have to do with anything?"

"Who was the third governor of South Dakota? What was the antler-spread of the Irish elk? I mean, they got to like you."

"Who are 'they'?"

"The gods, as usual. So I'm going for broke. I figure to clear me fifty thousand bucks and then go skimming around for a while."

"You could do me a favor while you're in New York."

"Sure."

"Look up Robin."

Joe just blinked slowly. "What do you want me to tell her?"

"Nothing special. She's trying to get into the theater. She has no friends or anything."

"You just want me to see how she's doing and report back to you?"

"Not really. I don't know. I'm not sure why I brought the subject up. I haven't written to her. I don't even know where she's living." He spoke with severe disapproval. "Forget the whole thing."

"It depends on how long I'm there." Then, while Leon was lighting a cigarette, Joe, without any other preparation, said, "My God, it's two-thirty. Be seeing you"—and went out the door.

It was a moment before Leon realized he had actually left. He rushed out into the hall, leaned over the rail, and called to Joe.

Joe stopped on the main floor and smiled up at him. "I didn't realize what time it's got to be. Miss Royce will have been kept waiting. That cannot be. Roger?"

· 4 ·

An hour later, burning with impatience, Leon telephoned Horace Skellings, who said that he was in communication with Alfred and that Alfred was all right. Leon could not hold himself to the thank-you the occasion called for, but went so far as to say that he hoped the breach between the Royces was not permanent. Horace, in his hasty and yet rather portentous manner, said that all he knew about it was that they had had a disagreement over furniture; and he begged to be excused, since he and Virginia were about to go to the city.

The five-o'clock news announced that a farmer near Nevada City had been arrested early that morning in connection with the Brady-McKee case, because the license-plate number of his car was that of a person wanted for questioning; also, the farmer's car answered the description of the wanted car, a light green '47 Chevrolet two-door sedan; however, the farmer was released shortly after noon, when it became clear that his license plates had been switched sometime recently, without his knowledge; search had been intensified in the area of the foothills and the Sierras.

Roy Carver's automobile was a two-door Chevvy in two tones of light green, and Leon thought it was a '47. He went over to Chantal's immediately.

Chantal was sitting, hunched over, at the kitchen table, picking at a piece of yellow cheese and a crust of bread. On the table, beside the saucer she was eating from, were four short fat sausages and an unopened can of sauerkraut.

She glanced at him, then stared back down at the cheese. Her features, naturally small and close together, seemed to him now pinched, wizened.

"I said I would call, but I wanted to see for myself how you were." She did not respond. "Is Harry around?" She shrugged with her face only and gave her head a tiny shake. "I thought you ought to know that Roy probably won't be coming for a while."

"Oh?" She glanced at him. "Roy is tired of eating here? I am surprised."

He told her what he knew of Roy and what inferences he had drawn.

"Aha," she said. "No doubt you are right."

Her left hand, with a crumb of cheese between thumb and forefinger, remained suspended halfway between the saucer and her mouth. He waited for a long time to speak again, till the hand had moved either up to her mouth or down to the saucer. She became aware of the bit of cheese and looked at it severely; then, to Leon's relief, she ate it.

"Where's Jean-Louis?" he asked.

"*Alors.*" She shook herself and stood up. "Two sausages will be enough for you, Leon? Three if you wish? Four? As you see, I had Jean-Louis get enough for Roy too."

"You are not eating?" She shrugged and flicked the cheese. "And where is Jean-Louis?"

"Oh. He's out to dinner." She laughed. "The first time since we come to America he goes out to dinner alone. And where? To a birthday party. Let me tell you. It's across the street, a Negro girl named

169

Pearl." She looked at him expectantly. "That is not strange—Pearl? She's so black."

"It's a common name."

"So. Today is her thirteenth birthday, too old, one should suppose, for such a party. But observe, there are ten children there, two white, Jean-Louis and a girl from his class in school. This white girl is a little bit crushed on him. Anyhow it's very proper, home movies, and hamburgers and I don't know what for supper—ice cream and cake, to be sure, *c'est de rigueur,* a white cake, if I know anything about Pearl's mother, with little white candles standing in pink sugar blossoms. He would never have gone, but she lives right across the street and of course one can never refuse the hospitality of a Negro, that is understood. Therefore"—she made a tiny, humorous gesture at the sausages and sauerkraut—"as you see, dinner is not inspired. I didn't know who would be here, perhaps no one."

"Let me take you to a restaurant for dinner."

"No!"

"I'm sorry. I'm sorry I even mentioned it."

"Pardon me, I was brusque. It's only that I don't want to leave the phone unattended."

Seeing his telephone anxiety mirrored in hers, he found her silly and dear. Joe had been very anxious too, but his attitudinizing, his staginess, had kept Leon at a distance. Leon enjoyed stagy posturing when it was a question of having a good time or a love affair, but not for something serious. Chantal seemed to him genuine, she rang true, she was all of a piece. He wanted to help her.

But just because she was all of a piece she would not appeal to him for help and he must reach out to her. He realized he had to be very careful, for he was not sure what sort of help she needed. He decided to try a sort of cross-examiner's question on her, fearing that it might drive her off but not knowing a better way to approach her.

"What is Harry's connection with the Comrades?"

"Ah. The police have found you?"

"No. A friend who knows a reporter. You have been bothered by the police?"

"They have not found me yet. Or else they prefer to spy. Who can say? Perhaps they are in the basement now, listening for my bell to ring. Tapping the wires, no? Still, I guard my telephone."

She was assuming his complicity. But he did not know what he was supposed to be part of, and he was not sure how to inquire without revealing the extent of his ignorance.

"Harry?"

"If it were not for Jean-Louis," she said, "I would think only of Harry. So I tell myself, at least. But now I think mostly of myself

170

because what happens to me happens also to my son. He wants to go back to Grenoble. Why shouldn't he want it? His father was a hero there. But it won't be so simple. When the police find Harry, then they will drive me back to France. You see?"

He could think of nothing but Harry Evans and the Comrades and their effect on Chantal. He spoke as though he knew much more than he did, hoping that she would let drop comments which would clarify his understanding; but she accepted his assumption of knowledge and revealed nothing.

Distressed for her, not knowing the extent or nature of her involvement, he burst out in an emotional voice, "What can I do to help?"

She glanced at him with coldness, then turned her back on him. "Change the past. That would be a good start. Just one or two things suddenly not there in the past. Eh? That would help very much."

He went into the living room and thumbed through a picture magazine till she called him to dinner. She did not sit with him as he ate. When he called good-by through the closed door of her bedroom she did not respond.

· 5 ·

For a night and a day and a night Leon suffered knottings and cloggings and grindings without remission. He no longer had even a cold to divert his attention.

Nothing he thought about was sure. He was nearly but not quite sure that Roy and Evans had done the bombing; that he could help Chantal, though he could not think how; that Alfred could explain everything to his satisfaction. As Sunday wore away and Alfred did not call, Leon's doubts about him grew; he felt betrayed, neglected, resentful.

The center of his thoughts was the bombing. He could not make sense of it as an act of rebellion. What the plant made was worth rebelling against—mechanisms for bombs and rockets, military secrets—but McKee and Brady were not the ones to attack. They were no more responsible for those things than any two workers in the plant were, and not much more responsible than any other two voting and taxpaying citizens in the country. He could not see, at all, what idea had been attacked when those two middle-aged men were assaulted. Many times he muttered the words "wanton nihilism" to himself. But he could not admit the possibility that a rebellious act of such gravity could be morally wanton.

The Russian nihilism he had been reared hearing about was of an extreme and exalted idealism. His mother had always spoken of the violent nineteenth-century anarchists as being admirable and coura-geous, her own father the bravest of them all. Leon also knew about pseudo-nihilists such as the Czarist double agent Azev, who informed the secret police what the terrorists were up to even as he was helping in the assassinations of grand dukes and governors, but such nihilists were negligible, playboys out for kicks, material for cheap thrillers. He could accept even the nihilism of insanity, such as Hitler and nazism; dreadful as it was, it had its own logic. But there was no place in Leon's mind for the notion that any event could be without sufficient explanation. "Wanton nihilism" was an emotional formula without intellectual significance, as he thought. All the same, the term kept repeating too often for comfort, as though it signified something he should attend.

The McKee-Brady incident answered to none of the categories of meaningful nihilism. Because Leon could see no possible good the bombing had accomplished, he could imagine no idealistic motive for it. Knowing Evans and Roy as he did, he did not think of them either as madmen or as daredevils. He found himself looking again and again at rebellion as such, and the oftener he looked the narrower its limits became.

"Rebellion" shrank so disastrously that he even found himself looking at his father's martyrdom. His mother had always spoken of his father as a martyr to the purest ideals of rebellion, and Leon had heard no one else who had known him say anything to challenge his mother's version of his father. But his father's main acts, so far as Leon knew, had been to flee a tyrant, which was not rebellious but prudent; and then when he was sick with tuberculosis, poverty-stricken, exiled, hopeless, to kill himself, which was pathetic but not very noble. Leon's strongest memory of his father was of his com-plaining in a petulant voice that the tea his wife had brought him was too hot, too strong, not sweet enough.

Authority was crushingly anti-life: Leon had been set in this atti-tude for so long that he could not, even now when things were turning upside down in him, challenge the assumption that you are wrong to keep power even when you do right with it. So far from challenging the assumption, indeed, he could not even formulate it. Such a formu-lation was what he wanted Alfred to provide, so that he could look plain at what was troubling him. "A question that does not imply its own answer is not well put." It was this aside in seminar which had won Leon, and the qualifier to the statement Leon had attributed to Alfred's modesty. "Like any aphorism, this is too neat. But I hold on to it, it's encouraging." But Alfred did not call.

A mediator, Leon thought at one point in the middle of Sunday night, a conciliator. A friend to enemies. Nobody's friend too much.

"There's much to be said on both sides. We must keep an open mind." I'm glad he hasn't called me up. He would try to persuade me it's all right not to take sides. Leon's resentment of Alfred relieved him of some of the anguish of indecision. He was proud that at least he did not fool himself into not taking sides—even though he himself was not sure what the sides were, much less which side was right and which wrong.

By the time Alfred actually called him—Monday morning as he was about to leave for his first class at Presley—Leon was able to be firmly courteous and no more than that. He was careful to hesitate a moment before agreeing to have dinner with Alfred that evening. Alfred was staying in Woody Ravagli's apartment in the city, and Leon pretended that it would be awkward for him to take the time to cross the bridge.

At dinner he was prepared to guard his guesses from Alfred's "mediator" probing. Instead, Alfred, drawn, jittery, drinking too much wine, asked nothing about the case and did not mention his separation from Beth.

"I've never been so confused in my life," Alfred said. "I'm probably going to be invited to serve as a federal judge before long. There was a day—less than a month ago, for example—when the invitation would have overjoyed me, and I'd have accepted or declined according to my wish, my whim, really. Now I don't dare accept. The law no longer seems adequate to deal with what matters to me. Politically, that is, in social matters. Nazism, for example, the Nuremberg trials, the responsibility of groups and nations and organizations—the law is inadequate. This bombing, if only it turns out to be an act of political idealism, at least, it'll remain manageable. That it should be a part of the class struggle is too much to hope for. I fear it'll turn out to be neither idealism nor class struggle. The class struggle is becoming identical with the race struggle. So? Is that mixed up in this? I don't see it. Whom have I been mediating between? Enemies? Not at all—partners, more like. I've never spent my time more frivolously than on this assignment. I should've been playing chess instead; it's relaxing. What has happened to the classes? Maybe the trouble is that we really are turning into a classless society, and it is monstrous. But no, that's absurd. There are still the few to say, 'Do so-and-so,' and the many to do so-and-so because they're ordered. Maybe it's machinery, the engineers. Suddenly ruler and ruled are huddled together on one side, and these new men, these outsiders, come along and say, 'Here are things that will do what you want. Just tell us what you want. If you don't keep us busy with new desires, we will make more things which will make you have unsuspected desires.' Suddenly it's

173

very important to know what you want. It used to be that you had few choices and just wanted. Now you must know what you want. You are turned free to want. But this is not a political problem! It's moral, metaphysical, religious, psychological, who knows what. Yet here it is in politics. One must pass laws about it. Leon, am I making sense? Please, where am I?"

Leon drove home, thinking of a phrase Alfred had used as they were standing on the sidewalk saying good night: "A personalist revolution, I and thou. Does that make sense? I don't know." A personalist revolution—one must begin by relating in a new way to one's neighbor.

He was thralled again to Alfred.

· 6 ·

The next morning before class Leon was chatting with his office mate, a freckled man named Simkin who had been in California only a week. Leon was amused by Simkin's exaggerated praise of Wisconsin, where he had just got his Ph.D.

"This bay of yours, everyone makes me say how beautiful it is, and of course it *is* beautiful. But it's vulgar. Too much of any good thing is vulgar, and this bay is too big. There's a proper size for everything, and this is ostentatious. You know how big a body of water by a city ought to be? About four or five miles long and a mile or two wide, the size of Lake Mendota in Madison. On a nice Sunday you can stretch out on a campus lawn and see the whole lake at once, watch the boats, maybe a regatta. That's civilized. I was doing it two weeks ago and I wish I were doing it now."

The head of the department walked into the office and asked if everything was all right. She was a short, stout woman of fifty, who had insisted after the first interview that Leon call her Fran. She wore plain suits and flat-heeled shoes; her straight hair was short and unadorned; her manner was gruff.

"These children are mostly from sheltered homes," she said. "They're naïve. But they're interesting kids, once you get to know them. The first week's the worst. I've been in the teaching racket for twenty-six years—thirteen of them here at Presley—and every blessed summer I forget all over again how ignorant the children are. They're so ignorant they're stupid. That's our job," she said, chuckling, "to wise them up." After a few more pleasantries she started to leave. "By the way, fellows, there's sort of a custom here. We leave the office door open during conferences. No discrimination against men; it applies to us women teachers too."

The moment she had gone out the door Simkin muttered, "It especially applies to some of us bull dikes."

Leon was delighted by the quickness of Simkin's spite, but he was a little shocked. "You really think she's one?"

"She lives with the physical-education teacher, the one with the baritone voice."

"How do you know?"

"School directory. They have the same address and phone number."

"The president seems like a nice motherly type."

Simkin writhed a little. "After the no-dating pitch you say this? You Californians—"

"I was born in Russia. What no-dating pitch?"

"You mean she didn't slip it to you with a smile—'Here at Presley we don't encourage student-faculty romances'?"

"That seems proper enough. I wouldn't dream of taking out a girl in one of my classes."

"So I have to have the president *tell* me not to? And how come she feels called on to tell me and not you?"

Leon was excessively severe in his manner with his eleven-o'clock class. He thought the girls in it were indifferent to what he said or ever would say and were satisfied with themselves. The one that might have been called pretty was chewing gum with her mouth open.

At lunchtime he avoided the faculty room. He was so full of anger he was afraid he would not be able to be polite if he happened to sit at the same table with the president or Fran. He walked to the corner hamburger joint, but the twitter of dozens of girls kept him out. If he had not needed the money, he would have quit the job that very day, regardless of the black mark on his record; he was not going to be a career teacher anyway. Trying to decide whether to drive somewhere to eat, he realized that his stomach was knotted almost painfully, so that he would be better off not eating. The thought of Simkin's sarcasms refreshed him.

He went to the periodical room of the library, where there were several overstuffed chairs. To his relief, he saw nobody else in the room. But when he went over to the far corner where the out-of-town newspapers were shelved he noticed a girl curled up in a chair facing the wall; there was no magazine on her lap. She made a gesture of avoidance, ducking her head even farther and slightly raising the shoulder next to him. He leaned over and peered at this one who wanted him as little as he wanted her; some day he might be introduced to her or find her in one of his classes, and he wanted to recognize her as a possible friend.

"Sybil?"

She raised her head a little but by no means looked him in the face. "Yes?"

"Sybil Royce? You're going to Presley and never told me?" He was so amazed that he was slow to reproach. Her head sank a little, and he thought she was ashamed. He squatted in front of her. "It isn't that bad," he said indulgently. He put a finger under her chin and tilted her face up. She jerked her head aside, but before she did so he saw her cheeks were stained with tears. "Oh," he said in a low voice. "Pardon me." He stood.

Her left hand tugged at his pants leg. "Don't go." She looked up at him, neither smiling nor frowning. "You're the only one in this god-forsaken pep school I could ever talk to. 'Rah rah rah,' " she whispered. " *'Go team. Ye-e-eah Presley!'* "

He took out his handkerchief as he squatted again and offered it to her. She scoured her face with it harshly.

"You're the prettiest girl on campus."

She hissed at him. "Cheerleader pretty. I know all about it. You know the only reason I wasn't a twirler in high school? I've got every-thing it takes—face, figure, coordination, peppy peppy peppy. I even borrowed a baton a couple of times and tried. I could do it. Two weeks in that summer camp they've got for twirlers down in King's River Canyon, and I'd be out there between halves in those black cowboy boots, the star of the show. Twinkle, twinkle, little star, for a couple of minutes."

"There are worse fates." He smiled.

"But that's *my* fate." She had spoken too loud. She hoisted herself up and peered around over the back of the chair. No one else was in the room. He pulled over a straight chair and sat beside her, in a way that would look unexceptionable to anyone who might see them. "My parents protected me from it while I was living at home. It wouldn't even occur to them that a daughter of theirs could be a drum ma-jorette. I just couldn't ever have done it to them. But it's my fate. Here I come to Presley, and what is it? A pep school. Twirl girls."

"And where are you now? Alone in a corner. So you've got a soul after all."

"Look, that Robin of yours . . ." Sybil grinned at his scowl. "She came from Bakersfield, didn't she? Well, if I'd come from Bakersfield I'd have been a twirler for years already and it'd be all over with. My doom would be sealed. This way I'm just postponing it."

"You're being cute," he said severely.

"I can't help being cute," she whispered. "Haven't you been listen-ing to me?" He saw her as an angry kitten. "Look," she said, "you're peeved at me, and I can tell it. That blotch on your forehead is red-dening up a little, you're sort of sneering in an uncle-ish way. You've got a face. The end of your nose is knobby. When you laugh your mouth gets sort of shapeless and big. You've got a face a person can live in. Can you even imagine what it's like to see a Kewpie doll every time you look in the mirror?"

He blinked. He opened his mouth, then closed it without saying anything.

"So. I've got through to you. Hot damn." She stared at him. "Did you ever see a middle-aged cutie pie? Well, I've got a cousin in Texas who looks the way I'm going to look when I'm her age, and I've looked at her hard and it's terrible. She's still got a good figure and legs. She's getting a little stringy—you know, the tendons are beginning to show a good deal, like in her neck, not too bad but enough. But her face is so *cute.* "Why, I declare, honey child, she's the cutest thing.' It's a little lumpier than it used to be, maybe, specially around the eyes, but she's still mighty cute. She's a living doll."

"Even her eyes?"

"No, not her eyes."

He took Sybil's hand in his, meaning to play with it. But, realizing in time that no sort of play would do now, he squeezed it with more warmth than he had thought he felt. He was looking at her eyes at the time, trying to read them and not being able to. When her hand returned his hand's pressure, he felt in his heart a response of the kind he had not felt since he was in high school in love with his pretty young civics teacher, and his response was the deeper because he could read nothing in Sybil's expression. At the same moment both of them looked down at their hands, which then, timidly, drew apart.

"Have you tried doing very much with make-up?" he asked. "A lot is possible."

"Oh, Lizzie and I tried all sorts of things, naturally. We both of us look sort of Halloweeny with anything interesting on."

"I picked up a good deal of information from Robin. You know she was in theater and she had those bad acne scars. She had a lot of skill and imagination." A couple of girls came into the room, chatting. When Leon glanced at them they quit talking and began to browse along the magazine shelves. He was leaning forward toward Sybil, whom they could not see, and though he knew they kept glancing at him covertly, he continued to lean toward her and speak in the same quiet voice. "Saturday about five, why don't I come pick you up? You put all your cosmetics in a bag and meet me at West Gate. I don't want to sit around the dormitory waiting room with a bunch of callow youths. I'll be waiting for you at West Gate at five sharp. We'll go out to dinner somewhere, and then go to my place and see what can be done in the way of make-up. Okay?"

"At your place?"

"Anywhere you say." She said nothing. "San Jacinto, if you'd rather. Lizzie is home now, isn't she?"

"If she hasn't left for New Mexico already." She rolled the back of her hand in his waiting palm.

"Well?" he said.

"All right, your place." She looked at him and spoke earnestly. "Should I wear black tights and ballet shoes? Are we going to a coffee house, when I get all made up, and have espresso?"

His impulse to laugh at her assumption that he wanted her to look bohemian merged instead with his tenderness for her and swelled it.

"No, no. No costume, Sybbie. Who knows what you'll come out looking like? I'll sit you on a straight chair and cover you completely with a sheet except for your head. *Real* make-up stuff."

"Fun." She uncurled, put her purse under her arm, and straightened her blouse. "You know, I had a lot of envy for Robin ever since that party last June. I just hated everything about her. And here I'm going to be accepting something from her that might be pretty important to me, and all I feel is grateful. Isn't that funny?"

He wanted to take this as a declaration of love, but was not sure she meant it as such. He would have held her hand again, but one of the browsers had drifted too near. He had to let Sybil leave unread.

· 7 ·

"Leon," said Chantal, "what is there suddenly about Jean-Louis? You glance at him many times. You say very little this dinner, yet you look happy and you glance at Jean-Louis. He looks the same to me."

"The potatoes are excellent," said Leon.

"Potatoes." She made a little face. "The simplest marinade possible. Here, potatoes, have as you wish."

"Maman!"

"You want potatoes too? Wait."

"But I had only one helping and he's had two already."

"Here, here," said Leon. "Excuse me, old boy. You know, that was a good game of football you were having this afternoon."

"Football!" cried Chantal.

Jean-Louis scowled, blushed, ducked his head, and helped himself to the rest of the potatoes.

"Sure," said Leon. "I was going by the school grounds this afternoon and I heard him. He was choosing sides. He was one of the captains."

"C'est vrai, chéri?"

"Oui, maman."

"Tu es capitaine?"

"Aujourd'hui seulement."

She began scolding him in French. Leon gathered that he had disobeyed her by playing a dangerous game.

"But it was touch football!" Leon said. "No one gets hurt, they run, that's all. He was a very fine captian. The other boys called him Lou. They wanted him to be their captain, even though he was the smallest. He's quite fast."

She listened and went back to scolding. But Jean-Louis was obviously not taking her harshness too seriously, because she could not keep a little smile from her lips. Leon imitated Jean-Louis, pretending to quail under her wrath. Leon felt positively good about Chantal's pleased anger because it was a bursting out of the shell she had cased herself in.

She sent Jean-Louis to his room. On the way from the table he stopped by the sideboard and openly, with proud defiance, looked over the apples, picked the largest, and went out, polishing it on his shirt sleeve. She did not stop him.

"He's manly," said Leon.

"He is a child!"

"He's a child who's becoming manly."

She sighed. "And American too."

"And American too."

"This is good?" She watched him.

"I think so."

"Hm." Then she cocked her head and frowned. "Leon, why are you so happy today?"

"I learned that there was more to Jean-Louis than I thought."

"Pfft." She turned to her coffee.

"I also learned that there was more to a pretty girl than I'd thought."

"Ah."

"Not just any pretty girl. Alfred Royce's second daughter."

"Nancy? You know Nancy? Jean-Louis's friend?"

"No, not Nancy. The second girl, Sybil."

"Sybil is Alfred's first daughter. You don't know even that much? Lizzie had another father. I betray no secrets."

"You'd rob a man of his favorite child on a technicality like that? You're worse than a lawyer."

"Come now," said Chantal flatly. "It matters who a child's physical father was."

"It matters if you let it. Alfred didn't let it."

"Alors."

"Getting back to why I'm so cheerful—I think I've figured out how to help you."

"Help me! So. You are happy, then, because you are foolish."

"We must talk. But we can talk only if Jean-Louis won't interrupt."

"I don't wish to discuss this subject. *Fini.*"

"What time does he go to bed?"

"Nine-thirty, ten at the latest."

"I'll come back at ten-thirty."

She shrugged, apparently as indifferent as she had ever been.

"Chantal, you will be sent back to France if Harry is discovered to be implicated in this McKee business. So you told me."

"I talk too much. I know nothing for sure."

"I can keep you from being deported, if you wish to stay."

"You can? Interesting. How?"

"I offer you marriage—a legal marriage."

"Oh, good God in heaven. You are indeed a fool."

"We must talk about it." She did not respond. He stood across the table from her. He realized that she might withdraw from him absolutely, but he was too keyed up to worry about this possibility. His manner was solicitous and firm, without apology or anxiety. "May I return at ten-thirty?"

"You look so young, even younger than usual. Why should I bother to upset myself for a young man's foolish impulses? You think I would permit you to sacrifice yourself? No, you may not come."

"*Maman!*" called Jean-Louis from the door to his room and said something in French.

She glanced at Leon bitterly. "You are as bad as he is. Boys."

"Marriage," said Leon. "Marriage and then divorce. You must consider it. I've already thought about it."

"Boys! They don't leave the heart alone!"

"I don't offer anything to do with the heart. I offer—"

"Marriage has nothing to do with the heart!"

"I offer you citizenship."

"*Maman!*"

"All right, all right, *bébé,* I'm coming. You come too, Leon. Everybody's grabbing at everybody all the time. There's no peace. Come on. Why not?"

"Till ten-thirty."

"Imbeciles!"

Leon studied constitutional law until a quarter to ten. Then he stepped into the unlighted kitchenette of his place and looked across at the bedroom window of the rear apartment of the house next door. A newly married couple had moved into the apartment recently, strapping, bland young people with whom he exchanged the time of day in the driveway once in a while, and he had discovered two weeks before that almost every night at this time he could spy on their going to bed. The blind was now still drawn, but by the light from inside the room he saw that they were beginning.

He read a few more pages and went back to the window. The blind was still drawn. It was ten. If they did not hurry, he would be late to Chantal's. But that was not possible! He stood at the sink, quivering with irritation at them for choosing this night to be tardy.

The light went off. The young man, in his pajamas, raised first the blind and then the window halfway; then he disappeared. The young wife was sitting before a dressing table brushing her long hair, and the bathroom door was part way open, reflecting light from within the bathroom, so that she was dimly illuminated. She was wearing a loose robe, and her gestures were easy and slow. From occasional gestures of her head, it was clear he was lying in bed watching her. After a while she got up from the stool and, with quick movements, facing her husband and in profile to Leon, she took off first her underpants and then her robe, both of which she carefully laid on the stool; she bent forward and took off her bra, and in the same motion with which she laid it down picked up her nightgown and pulled it over her head; then she went into the bathroom and pulled the door closed. Leon knew that it would be at least ten minutes till she came out again. She would open the door wide and stand in the doorway a moment, in her frilly white gown, her hair down her back, smiling at her husband before she switched off the light.

Leon looked at his watch; it was ten-thirty already; cursing them for being so ordinary, not even beautiful, he ran out. Why didn't they keep their blind drawn till all the lights were off the way decent people were supposed to? They were exhibitionists, surreptitious exhibitionists, the worst kind. Well, bad weather would come before long and teach them to keep their window down far enough so they would quit provoking their neighbors.

"Why are you puffing?" said Chantal. She was seated at the dining table, on which the dinner dishes remained as they had been.

"Haven't you got up since I left?"

"Ha," she said dryly and took a sip of cold coffee, "we might as well be married. We're bourgeois enough. 'Why did you do this? Why didn't you do that?' No, I have not been sitting here all the time. Jean-Louis is asleep."

"I had no right to ask you that. It was just that I was surprised to find you . . . I ran over because I didn't realize how late it was getting. I was reading law."

"Leon! You have gone to that trouble? To find out the legalities even of this preposterous marriage you dream on? I am touched."

For a moment he considered letting this flattering version of why he was late stand unaltered. But then, with the severe air of one obliged to the unpleasant task of setting the record straight, he rendered a version which was less flattering but only slightly nearer the truth.

"The law about deportation is plain. As the wife of a veteran, you would almost certainly not be deported but could become a citizen within a short time. I already knew that law. This evening I was reading constitutional law for a course in law school. It was a case concerning a libel suit against a newspaper, brought by a candidate for high political office."

"Tya tya tya. You were correct, my friend. It was nothing to do with the heart you offer me, if you could be late over such a matter. A libel suit."

"If," he said stiffly, "I offered you marriage for sentimental reasons, you would quite properly reject my offer as insincere. I repeat: I offer the one legal assistance I know of by which to keep you from being forced to go back to France, and that's all. There's no question of our living together. Pardon me, that's not quite accurate. We would have to live together for a time, to convince the authorities. I'd move in here with you. But of course we'd have separate beds. Then, when it's safe, we get divorced."

"You spell out very clearly that I mean nothing to you as a woman."

He breathed hard, glaring at her. "No, that was not what I was spelling out, and it's unfair of you to take it as such. I thought your affections belonged to Harry. My feelings have no business becoming involved in this arrangement, nor have you any right to inquire into them."

She looked genuinely contrite. "Pardon me. What you say is perfectly right. I had no business. The truth is, Leon, I am so upset I don't know any longer which is which. I am tempted. If you were not such a good man, I would accept, probably. But I cannot, from you. You have no idea what you're getting into."

"I was born in Leningrad. My parents escaped to China when I was five. When I was nine they came to this country, illegally. They were devoted to free-thinking; they never got married. My father shot himself. He was in bad health; everything was wrong with the world. I have no brothers or sisters. My mother works as head housekeeper

182

for a rich family in Pasadena. She supports herself, and when she is too old they will probably take care of her. I am a citizen. I served in the Army. I have a small salary, but enough to help out financially if you need it. In a couple of years I'll be a lawyer. Then I should begin to make more money. In any case, I can provide free the legal advice on our arrangement. I don't know what else to tell you about myself. I am grown up. I know what I'm doing."

"Almost," she said, "I am convinced. Look, my friend, for all you know I want to remain out of France because I'm wanted for murder, embezzlement. You know so little about me."

"I know all I need to know to make my decision."

"The egoism of the generous! What about me? Do you know all I need for you to know? Do you think there's nothing I could tell you about myself which would make you change your mind? You are that romantic?"

"Of course there are things that would make me change my mind. I am not a total fool. It's just that I don't believe *you* have any such thing to say to me."

"You tell me about yourself but you don't let me tell you about myself. What kind of honor is that? All one way! You would drown me! Romantic!"

He was happy to have her scolding him. "Tell me what you wish me to hear." He disposed himself to listen with attention. "Actually, it'd be a good idea for me to know more, in case they come around asking questions."

"Again you pour generosity on me. You should know about me for *my* good! I give up! 'Madam, will you marry me?' 'Sir, first let me introduce myself. Then ask me.' Impossible!" She shook her right hand in front of her chest, then held it out to him and rose. "Come, let's go into the living room."

Before they separated to sit down, she on a chair, he on the couch, their hands pressed firmly in conscious affection.

He could not help comparing this handclasp with his holding hands with Sybil at noon, this one full of open friendship, that one warm with amorous promise, neither of them hiding anything, both of them chaste. This comparison, from which everybody came out well, only increased his happiness. He watched Chantal draw into herself, this time not to hold him out but to collect her strength that she might reach toward him, and he felt that she was the person in the world whom he trusted most. He could not imagine she would ever let him down. At the same time, he was looking forward to allowing himself to fall in love with Sybil. Strengthened by such pure affections, he felt himself already emancipated from corrupt women like Robin, to whom he had always been attracted against his better judgment.

"Do you know why," she began, "I'm able to tell you what I had never intended to tell anyone again?"

"Does there have to be a reason?"

"There *is* a reason. It is because of what you said about Alfred and Lizzie, something about how it only matters, paternity, if one lets it matter. I know how you feel about Alfred, of course. Who does not like this man? For such a person, it might seem easy to be father to another man's child. But you meant it also for yourself. It did not seem strange to you."

"Oh, Jean-Louis is . . . You know . . ."

"Wait. You go ahead too fast. I'm not thinking of you as Jean-Louis's father. He's too old for that. He is mostly himself already. I haven't tried to be father to him, mother only, let him have such father as fate gives him. Enough." She stopped.

"His own father," said Leon softly, "was an admirable man, and Jean-Louis knew that. That's helped him a lot."

"No. His father was a scoundrel. He seduced me. Jean-Louis knows nothing about that. He knows nothing about his father."

"I thought . . . You have spoken often of—Jean-Michel, wasn't that his name?"

She sighed heavily. "Yes, that was the name of my husband. He was not the father of Jean-Louis. He married me one month before Jean-Louis was born. And not from pity, from love. I knew it even then." She shrugged. "To be sure, I would have married him though it were nothing but pity. My family would not have me. I disgraced them. They never spoke to me since. They never saw Jean-Louis, though they lived twenty-five kilometers from Grenoble, for generations in the same house, respectable little merchants in Vizille. So. It was to the *pension* of Jean-Michel's aunt that I went when my father put me out of the house with two thousand francs. He loved me, yes, Jean-Michel. I told him the truth when it became clear that he thought of marriage. Now I tell you the truth, though you do not love me. It is the marriage offer that opens my mouth. To Harry Evans I did not tell this. With him it's never a question of marriage. Of a passion perhaps? I'm not sure. An odd passion, at any rate. What has passion to do with friendship? Yet we began as friends and now, for two or three years, we are friends again, companions. To be sure, we sleep together from time to time. Can one visit an old passion with a friend? What nonsense."

"Chantal," Leon began after a silence.

"No, don't interrupt. No questions, please. I'll tell you what I need you to know. The one thing, who Jean-Louis's father is." She sighed again. "I had a cousin named Luigi. His mother was my mother's twin sister. His father was from Turin, a traveling salesman. One

184

knows the type. He deserted my aunt after two children and went back to Turin. Later he became a little functionary of the Fascist Party. I didn't know my cousin Luigi well. He was five years older than I. We lived in the same town, yet we had nothing in common. Perhaps my mother made me suspicious. He was thin and quiet, with sharp eyes like a squirrel. Very young, his mother sent him to the Jesuits. He became a novice. He went to seminary. He would be a priest, it was well understood. Pfft. I didn't think about him twice. Then, the summer I was sixteen, he came home to visit for a couple of weeks. I was a solitary child, full of romances. I did my duties, and read, read, read. One day we took a bus up into the Dauphiné Alps more farther than I had gone. Luigi wanted to visit a village still from the Middle Ages, Besse. Why not? I had been nowhere. To me it was a grand adventure just to go with my father to Grenoble for half a day. Besse sounded romantic, from George Sand perhaps? Hugo? Who can say? But it must be very romantic. So we went, and it was romantic enough. We had more wine for lunch than I was used to. It was hot and clear. We came to a stream on the mountainside with a pool. We lay down to take a nap. Luigi had talked not much. When we walked we sometimes would hold hands. I was a little bit terrified of the mountains and the old women with black gowns of Besse. I was happy to sleep for a while beside my cousin the baby-priest. I woke up with cold water on my face. Luigi was laughing. I thought it was raining. I sat up. He was in the pool, naked, and splashing the icy water on me. I had seen men urinate all my life. What's that? Pfft. He waded out into the water till it was to his stomach. He wanted me to come in. Perhaps I would have if I hadn't seen him naked. That frightened me. It wasn't romantic. I think, now, if I'd taken off my clothes and gone in too, he would have been satisfied. He too would have been consterned. A woman is an agent of the devil; still, it's hard even for a baby-Jesuit to see a skinny girl nude, with goose-pimples, and think, Aha! Lilith! No. But I, I was alarmed to see him naked *en pleine vue du bon Dieu,* and I fled a little way. He dressed and caught me presently. He talked of nature, of duty, I don't know what. I shrank but listened. It was a long way home. We talked so much we did not walk fast. We were not yet home when it was dark. We bought some bread and cheese. There was a great moon. He spoke of his doubts in seminary." She shrugged. "It was the first of three times only. Then he had to go back. He swore he loved me. He was pale and nervous, with quick eyes. Then, when I knew I was pregnant, I told my mother the truth. She told my aunt. Luigi was summoned. He denied everything. Yet it was observed by all that he did not look me in the eye, ever. Nevertheless I was expelled from my family, and he is a priest, in Chambéry when I last knew. In France I have no friends but in Grenoble. Yet there are those implacable ghosts waiting to reproach me there. Jean-Louis would learn his father is a priest. How could that be prevented? No. And I have no other resource. Harry rescued me, as it were. I inquire very little into that fortunate passion. So, Leon."

They agreed to go first thing in the morning to the city hall and begin to do whatever was necessary to get married. They promised each other faithfully to get divorced just as soon as it should be safe.

When Leon was about to leave he took her by the shoulders, bent down, and kissed her on each cheek.

"No," she said, frowning. "Who knows what is right in such a case? Still. One little real kiss, my fiancé."

He chuckled, and took her in his arms, intending to kiss briefly and formally. To his surprise it was, as she had said it would be, erotic. It lasted longer than he had expected. He drew away from her in confusion.

"So," she said and stroked his hair gently. "You don't know exactly what to think. Good." She laughed genuinely, so that her upper lip revealed her teeth for a moment, as it did only when she was very amused. "Just as long as your charity is not pure, *mon cher époux.*"

· 8 ·

"Lizzie! Come in, honey. You don't need to ring. I've told you, if the door's unlocked just walk on in, I'm home."

"I know, Dad. But still, I feel funny barging in on you *here.*"

They hugged and kissed.

"Put your things there—anywhere. It's so funny to be visited by you. I can't get used to it. Nancy came over Sunday. At first she sat there so unnaturally. She was 'paying a call' on her father. It's so wrong, so wrong. Here, please, sit in the comfortable chair. I'll make some coffee. Or would you rather have a highball? How are you, honey? It's good to see you."

"Daddy, for heaven's sake, why are you so wild? You're running around like a chicken with its head off. What have you been doing to make you so wild?"

"Writing. I'm working like a madman. I've never done the like before. I came across a book that set me off. It was the most fortunate timing. I was all ready for that book, and lo and behold, it appeared. *Njal's Saga,* a wonderful story, Icelandic, about law and anarchy. Man must have the law, you see, because of the alternatives, which are so much worse. Man in society, that is. Of course I'm not saying that in so many words in my book. Instead, I'm putting into order the fundamental structure of our system of law. Why? To demonstrate that this structure will be strong enough and yet flexible enough to hold out against the forces of disorder. Of course it cripples us, this legal order, the state. But the alternatives! I say none of this. It's what my book is *really* about. Sneaky, huh? I work very hard these days, here in this handsome apartment. I didn't know I could work so hard so long. It's funny that you should say I look wild. Wildness is exactly what my book is against. Civilization, that is what I am for. Domestication."

"I just meant excited, churned up. You look like your thoughts were somewhere else."

"Okay, I understand. It's so good to see you. You've had dinner?"

"Oh sure. Mother made Spanish rice. I drove over. I have three subjects to talk about."

"What else? The good fairy always bears three gifts."

"They aren't gifts, for Pete's sake, they're just topics to talk about. The first isn't even that, it's just news. Irma walked up this afternoon and told Mother that Justice Durkheim is failing and keeps asking to see you. He can't get out of bed any longer."

"Ah. Thank you. I am sorry to hear it. I will go tomorrow. Let me see. I have not been to see him for two weeks, have I? Dreadfully remiss." He cleared his throat. His manner had become severe and proper, but his fingers were trembling so much that the column of smoke rising from his cigarette was wavy. "Well. How is everybody? How's Nancy?"

"Fine. She's a tough cooky. You don't need to worry yourself over her. She'll always land on her feet. Syb's okay too."

"And your mother?"

"Fine, just fine. She's keeping busy."

"Good, good, I'm glad. You are a jewel, Lizzie. How is she really?"

"Fine, Dad. I said it already."

"Of course, of course, I believe you. I just want to know how she really is."

"Why don't you go see for yourself?"

"See for myself! Don't be ridiculous. We're separated. We'll probably get divorced sooner or later. I remember what my father said to me when his nephew and niece got remarried after a divorce. 'Son, if I ever leave your mother, there's one thing I know. I'll never speak to her again.' "

"I've heard you tell that story before. He never did leave her, did he?"

"No, no. She died a couple of years later. He never remarried. He was busy till the week before he died."

"The relevant point is, he didn't leave her. Dad, the tone of voice you ask about Mother in, you haven't separated from her except physically. I'm not the only one to notice. Sybil does. Nancy never says anything, but I bet she does too."

"All right, all right." He closed his eyes. "Let's drop the subject. I haven't seen her in a month. You know that."

"One last thing, then I'll shut up."

"Don't shut up! I want you to talk. It's just that sometimes you tread—a little heavily?"

"Yes? I wanted to say that Mother asks about you the same way. She swears when she does it and calls you all sorts of bad names. But it's the same really."

He rushed around the room, adjusting ashtrays. "Lizzie, you must learn to take off your spiked boots when you walk on a man's . . . A drink? Here, I forgot to get you a drink."

They were quiet while he poured two strong highballs.

"Well, now, what other gifts do you bring, my good fairy?"

She scrubbed her nose and held back her irritation at his good-fairy joke. "I've definitely made up my mind to go to New Mexico right away. Tomorrow."

"Wonderful. You have a position lined up at San Refugio?"

"That's the catch. I can't be sure of anything till I get there. The Koyala distrust anthropologists. I don't blame them."

"Neither do I."

"What? What do you mean to imply?"

"Anthropology seems to me the most arrogant enterprise since theology."

"You mean *I* am arrogant, Daddy?"

"Colossally arrogant, darling. In complete assurance that you understand human nature, you preach the doctrine that there's no such thing as human nature. I'm sorry to have interrupted you. Go on."

"I'll come back to this later."

"I'm sure. But go on for now."

"Well, in a nutshell, I have hopes of being able to make enough to live on there, but I can't be sure for a while."

"I will of course help out. How much do you need now? Will a hundred dollars do till the first of next month?"

"Oh, thanks, Daddy, that's more than enough." He went to the desk and took out his checkbook. "I feel like a heel. I always swore that as soon as I graduated I'd be on my own. Here I am full of a fresh B.S. and already begging for help."

"Not begging."

"Mother offered to help out. I don't know how you two have fixed

188

things up financially. I thought I should speak to you before doing anything."

"I'm glad you came to me, honey. Beth would be glad to give you the money, and she has it to give. But then she would resent me for having allowed her to do so."

He tore off the check and held it out to her.

"I'm confused," said Lizzie. "You want to give it to me to keep her from resenting you?"

"Partly. Mostly because it just seems to me the right thing and I want to."

She took it.

"I'm still confused. Wasn't it an ordinary inheritance? Was there something horrendous about Granny's will I don't know about? How could it cause all this commotion?" She began biting her nails.

"It was a conventional will."

"I wish," Lizzie burst out, "the Koyala would make me a member of the tribe! Not just an honorary member, the way some tribes do. The Koyala don't have any of those, so even that would be something. But a real member. If I were a Koyala, I wouldn't ever have to think about money again. I hate to think about it."

"Beth's inheritance was property in other forms than money, most of it."

"Daddy." She spoke as gently as she could, mindful of his admonition. But her eagerness showed. "Is it really true, what Mother says, that you won't come back home so long as the furniture she inherited is in the house?"

Very fast, he thumbed mentally through the complexities and qualifications surrounding this question. "That's not all there is to it."

"No. But is *that* much true?"

"Yes."

She sighed with obvious relief. "Well, that's a big load off my mind. Off Syb's mind too. At least you and Mother agree on the main thing."

"Agree on the main thing! What on earth are you talking about?"

"You agree on what you're quarreling over. I'm convinced that mostly when marriages break up it's because the two parties don't really know what they're fighting about."

He brayed with laughter. "Oh good lord, but you're presumptuous." He threw his head back and laughed harder and longer than he had laughed since he had left home. "Thank God for Lizzie. For all I know, you're right." He saw she was hurt by his laughing at her, but he did not moderate it. "Daughter, daughter, the Koyala need you."

"No, they don't. I need them. For a while anyway. There are lots of things I've got to get straightened out."

"Oh oh oh." He could hardly catch his breath. "You do me good. Don't go. Stay here. I need you."

Offended, she stood up.

"Here, honey, pour me another drink. I'll stop. I'm sorry. I'll get hiccups if I don't stop. I'm stopping."

After she set his drink down on the stand beside his chair, she stood in front of him with her fists on her hips. "Well, aren't you even going to placate me?"

"No, no," he said. "After all these years, Liz, I'm not going to begin flattering you now. So just sit down and tell me, what is the third gift you bring me?"

"Huh. Good fairy indeed. You're losing your sense of humor, old man. Calling me a fairy." She sat down, pleased with this little sally, which she had refrained from making for so long. This was the best time for it anyway. "Well. You know Joe?"

"Joe Thompson?"

"He took a bus for New York this morning."

"That surprises me. I thought he was so involved in the McKee business he'd want to see it through."

"After the strike was called off? No libel suit? And especially now they've caught the bomber and the union is clear?"

"I suppose. What about Joe?"

"Incidentally, he sort of hinted once that Roy Carver might be involved." She waited; he did not respond. "Hint hint."

"I have no idea whether Roy is involved or not."

"How long has it been since you talked with him?"

"Weeks."

"Joe says he thinks he's disappeared."

"Ah."

"All right, Alfred, you can take your wig off. I'll drop the subject."

"Very well, my dear. So Joe's gone to New York."

"To be on a TV quiz program."

"He really meant it, then."

"The trouble is, Dad, he doesn't know where he's going to be staying there, and I can't be sure I'll be in San Refugio. What if I have to go to San Leandro and live, or even Santa Fe?"

"I understand. You want to be able to get in touch with him."

"I want him to be able to get in touch with me if he ever wants to."

"Letters have been known to be forwarded, honey."

"I don't trust the post office. Remember that time it took an airmail letter three weeks to get to you in Washington they forwarded from Berkeley? And Mother, well, she's sort of absent-minded sometimes. She might forget to readdress a letter."

"Especially when it comes from Joe Thompson?"

"Why doesn't she like him?"

He shrugged. "She doesn't think he would be a good husband for you."

She snorted. "That's for me to decide. Besides, who's talking marriage?"

"I must add, dear, I don't think he would be a good husband for you either."

"Or that I would make him a good wife, I suppose?"

"That's quite another matter. I had thought of that too, yes. I think that would be much more likely, you being what you are."

"Really?"

"But please don't marry him."

"The subject has never come up." She tried to look haughty and succeeded in looking feisty. "Besides, as I've said a hundred times, I am certainly not going to get married till I'm at least twenty-five, if ever."

"Good."

"You know how everybody keeps moving around these days? Joe's going, I'm going, nobody's staying put any more. Anyway, I hope it's all right for me to have told Joe he could find out from you where I am?"

"Of course it's all right. Of course I'll answer the moment I hear from him." Alfred had been planning to move out of this apartment of Woody's within a week or two. He knew that his staying was no great imposition on Woody, that Woody was positively glad to let him have it. It was far better than any place he would ever rent for himself but it was not his own, he could not arrange it as he wanted. "Did you give him my address at the University or here?"

"Oh, here. This way fewer mailmen will handle Joe's letter. You're going to be here for a while, aren't you, Daddy? Just three or four weeks at the most?"

"Of course, of course, honey. I just wanted to know where to expect it." He spoke expansively and saw her gratitude in her eyes. He was stuck for another month in this too excellent place where there were almost no noises of other people to relieve his solitude. At this rate he'd get his book finished by the end of the year out of sheer desperation. He laughed. "I hope Joe makes a pot of money and goes off to the Riviera for a couple of years and blows it gloriously."

"That's the cultural pattern, all right. But somehow I doubt if he'll fall into it quite so pat. He's sort of religious, you know. Actually I'm going to be very interested to see what form his extravagance takes."

He almost said, "If I didn't know you, I wouldn't believe you existed." But he realized in time that this was too unkind altogether. Still, he could not let this silliness of hers pass unslapped. "I wonder what the Koyala would think of a man's making a fortune by answering some insignificant questions in public, as a way of advertising a chemical which keeps women from smelling the way they naturally smell? A fortune as large, perhaps, as the total income of the tribe in a decade."

She stuck out her tongue at him. "You don't think," she said in a small voice, "that I've thought about that?" She scrubbed her nose hard. "I've got hay fever for some reason."

When, after a while, she stood at the door about to leave, she spoke almost shyly. "You're getting thinner."

"Yes," he said brightly. "I've been talking about losing weight for years. This is the perfect opportunity to practice what I preach."

"Don't lose any more. Please? You look better plump."

"Just ten more pounds? Actually, honey, you might think of dropping a few yourself." He patted her thigh. "You'd look trimmer."

"Don't you like me the way I am?"

"I love you the way you are, but that's not what I was talking about. I was—"

"But that's what matters. Isn't it?"

"Oh my God!" He flapped his arms. "Oh dear God in heaven. What shall I do with this daughter of mine who's driving me crazy?"

He beat her softly and hugged her. "Have you any idea when you may be back?"

She shook her head and hurried up the walk with her head lowered.

That night he had even more difficulty than usual in sleeping. He had enough whisky in him to fall asleep, but he woke up two or three times. He would be straining to hear one of the girls coming in late; then, hearing only distant noises of the familiar, alien city, he would lie in lethargy for a time, thinking very fast.

· 9 ·

Justice Durkheim's house was in the shape of a broad U with shallow wings. The exterior wall of his small bedroom was mostly of glass. He had had Irma pull his bed, as always when he was confined to it, over by this window-wall, to which she had rolled up the bamboo slat curtains. His head was propped on two hard pillows with brown covers. The bed consisted of a single-width cotton mattress on a sheet of thick plywood standing on four square wooden legs. There was a bamboo stool near at hand with water and paper handkerchiefs on it; there was a small wicker chair, for one guest; and there were two earth-colored pots, one for trash and cigarette butts, the other containing an exquisite bonsai maple which Irma would put outside for a few hours on a good afternoon.

When Alfred came in, full of solicitous greetings, the old man smiled wryly and made a little gesture with the fingers of his right hand, indicating that Alfred should not come touch him but should sit in the wicker chair. It was the gesture of a baby pushing an unwanted piece of food off his tray, a tiny, petulant, stubborn gesture. At first Alfred obeyed; but almost as soon as he had taken his seat he leaned forward and held in his warm hands that cold hand with its horny nails. The old man slowly blinked. "Tell me what you are doing, Alfred." His voice was dry and exact, and he spoke with effort, slowly. The skin of his face was not wrinkled and loose so much as drawn taut over the bones, with fine crinkles, and his nose stood out like a small beak.

Though Justice Durkheim did not smile when he spoke, his lips being drawn when at rest into a shapeless contour, and though his voice was as expressionless as his mouth and watery eyes, Alfred nevertheless believed it was the right thing to have taken his hand. "I am working." Alfred shrugged. "Nothing new. But I came to see you, not talk about my work."

"I have an hour, half an hour, of living in me at the moment. The rest of the day I shall spend dying." The old head rolled on the pillow so that he was looking back out at the yard and trees. "This is the place to die, Alfred. See to it that you die right here, at this very spot in this room. I reflect on custom from time to time. I've been one of the guardians of the customs, and here I am not dying according to the custom of the country. Yet I don't feel that I am betraying a trust by dying this way. I haven't the strength to make something of this thought. The spiral."

Alfred did not know what the old man meant by "the spiral," and thought either that his mind was wandering or that he would explain when he felt like doing so. Meanwhile Alfred gazed out the window at the trees beyond the garden fence. A copper beech dominated the view, a wide-spreading tree with leaves, each of them lovely, so separated from one another that they did not compose a blur of foliage but remained many light creatures. Well beyond the beech there were three deodars in a row, and from the downhill corner of the lot rose a redwood tree over a hundred and fifty feet in the air. Rising beyond these there was a hillside of indistinguishable greens, and the view was crested by a line of eucalyptus with delicately moving members. It was beautiful, of course, but Alfred could not imagine himself looking at it for long at a time, year after year. One got used to anything, certainly to nature. Yet this old man, whose eyes were already filming over, seemed to be feeding on this long-familiar sight—not just with the clutching desperation of a dying man, but tranquilly and assuredly, as Alfred had seen him feed on it for years.

"I did almost nothing to the other half of the garden," said Justice Durkheim. "It's the part everyone exclaims over. The only thing I have against it is the exclamations. The rock garden is what I like most. I put a desert tortoise in there once, but it crawled away. I'm glad now that it did." He lapsed into silence again.

The garden was contained within the U of the house. Defining it on the open side, there was a fence of vertical, unpainted boards, weathered silvery gray, the grain waving down them like hair. The far half of the garden was planted in moss, a few shrubs, and a flowering plum; it was focused on a large, rough boulder against the fence, on ledges of which, as on ledges of a cliff, four bonsai pines were situated in heavy celadon pots. A path consisting of three round cross-sections of a redwood tree sunk into sand divided the planted half of the garden from the near half. This near section, the one Justice Durkheim was speaking of, was a square of pebbles, in the center of which were two smooth river boulders, one upright like a long egg on end, the other on its side like a bent torso without limbs. A few leaves and twigs lay scattered on the pebbles, and against the fence leaned a long peeled gray pole with a slight jog two-thirds of the way up it. Otherwise there was nothing to look at but the uniform river pebbles, grayish or brownish, without spots.

"When I first came here, those two stones were absent, and there were three swastikas with many arms drawn in the pebbles. Also it was kept clean of debris. I disliked the swastikas. They were impure forms, because of the Nazis. I knew that a spiral was well thought of, so I drew one. But I was troubled by the clutter. I didn't know how to start it perfectly. Also the corners of the square bothered me. How to get the spiral into them? And I didn't see how to keep the pebbles clean every day without too much work. Then Beth gave me those two large stones."

"Who?"

"Your wife."

"Beth gave you those? Did you tell her you wanted them? I don't remember anything of the sort. I never even saw them before, except here. I thought they always were here. Are you sure?"

"My dear Alfred." The old head rolled back and the old eyes blinked. "I believe the two of you went on a vacation up to the Feather River Canyon one summer. She brought those stones back in the car and put them in her garden, where I admired them. I once mentioned my dissatisfaction with my rock garden. She brought them down one afternoon, in Nancy's little red wagon, and left them by the front door. I was taking my nap at the time. She told Irma. I never thanked her for them. When I had placed them where they now are, I had Irma call her. She came down, and we agreed they were in the right place. We had tea and talked about them."

"Well," said Alfred and took off his glasses. "Aha." He smiled uncertainly and half hiccuped. "Really." He blew his nose.

Justice Durkheim looked back out again.

"Once those stones were placed, it was possible for me to trace the spiral, without concerning myself with the imperfection of its beginning and ending. And for some reason I was no longer concerned over the twigs and leaves that fell on it, until they got thick enough to make a real clutter. Making that garden—no, drawing that spiral—was the one important act I have done since I retired. Those stones made it possible."

Alfred looked at the spiral. He could not see where it began—on the other side of the two center boulders, presumably—and the outer limit of the curve was set by its butting into the fence; the square corners were without markings. He had seen this spiral many times but had never really considered it. He wondered whether by chance he had never heard it mentioned in his presence, or whether he had failed to do what Beth had done, pay attention to Thomas's comments. The spiral was a shallow, regular furrow in the pebbles. If he had not been told these curved lines composed a spiral, he would have taken them for concentric circles. He could not imagine contemplating this simple form. He would not have believed that Thomas actually cared much about it one way or another, had he been told so under any other circumstances, nor would he have believed that Beth had any understanding of such matters. But he knew that in fact Thomas loved this house and this garden, chose to look at this garden as he lay dying, and had no conceivable reason now to be joking about a matter he said was important. Alfred could not imagine what went on in Thomas's mind as he contemplated that spiral, except that he was sure it had little to do with intellect. Alfred would have dismissed such lucubration as silly, self-indulgent pseudo-mysticism, had he not heard of it from this man whom he knew to be neither silly nor self-indulgent nor pseudo anything. And there seemed not to be the slightest breath of mystical double-talk in the old man's statement now, as there never had been before. He was just explaining the way he did things, and he wanted Alfred to do things this way, not because it was his way or the right way or even the way to something else, but because it gave practical satisfaction. "Drawing that spiral was the one important act I have done since I retired." Alfred got up and charged about the room.

"Do me the favor of sitting down," said Justice Durkheim. Alfred sat. "I have about enough strength to listen to you for ten minutes at the most, and I don't want to squander what I have, watching you pace."

He lapsed into silence, staring at Alfred. His head drew in a bit and he hunched down under the covers. From years of sunning, his skin was brown and leathery, and though it was rather tight across his face, it was loose on his neck. Dry brown folds appeared on his neck as his head drew in.

"Are you feeling cold, Thomas?"

"I'm never warm. There are three things I want you to tell me about. The most important will take too long. If you were living at home where you ought to be, you could come see me tomorrow morning for a while and talk to me then. It's damn inconsiderate of you to be living in the city at this point."

"I'll come by every morning, till you—get well."

"Till I die."

"Or till you die."

"Thank you for saying that, Alfred. I have been fearing I would find it distressing to hear those words uttered by anyone except myself. Dr. Myer is being mealy-mouthed with me. They don't sound so bad. Have you decided to become a judge?"

"No. I'm writing hard. I like my seminar."

"Ass."

"Teaching is an honorable profession."

"You skitter around too much. You need something to hold you down. A heavy load of responsibility, say. You think there's something wrong with being a judge? It's unimportant?"

"On the contrary. I doubt that I'm worthy."

"That." The eyelids closed. "No one is worthy. You are worthy."

Alfred waited for the brown leathery eyelids to open, but they did not. After a while the lips puffed a little and parted at one place enough to let out air with a barely audible sigh. They closed, the covers over the old chest rose a bit, and another tiny sigh escaped through the lips. Alfred tiptoed out.

· 10 ·

While riding on the bus across the Bay, Alfred had played with the idea of walking up to his house after leaving Justice Durkheim's. Nancy would be in school, and Sybil was living at Presley. If Beth saw him and he had to speak to her, he would have a good excuse for being there—Lizzie's departure. That morning when packing his briefcase he had, without really thinking why, put in a book he had bought in a secondhand bookstore for Lizzie, an 1898 collection of photographs of Pueblo artifacts, with commentaries by two Indian Commissioners; he had no idea whether it was anything more than amusing, but he knew she did not already own a copy; he had forgotten to give it to her the night before. What he could do was to slip the book into the mailbox, which was inside the front gate, and quietly walk away. Of course he was not going to do any such thing. He had been so sure he would not that, as he rode along on the bus, he did not bother to tell himself so more than once or twice, but abandoned himself to the conscious fantasy of visiting the house for a brief look. All the same, as he had walked down the path to Justice Durkheim's house, he had wondered whether he would turn uphill or down when he came back out. While he had been with the old man he had not thought about the matter.

He closed the gate; then, without exactly deciding to, he turned uphill.

The house was unchanged. The flowerbeds were still moist from a watering the day before, and the paths were swept. There were no sounds from within the house. Perhaps Lizzie had already left. Perhaps Beth was driving her down to the railway station now. Or maybe they were both in the dining room, having coffee. Or both still asleep; it was only ten-thirty, Lizzie always liked sleeping late, and Beth had often done it during times of stress. When he opened the gate to step inside the garden and put the book in the mailbox, he stepped on a whistling rubber duck a child had dropped on the path. He leaped at the tiny scream, hastily pulled open the front door of the box, pushed the book in, slammed the door shut, and hurried away, banging the gate behind him.

His leg muscles ached to run, but by a great effort he kept himself to a fast walk down San Jacinto Way. He was also careful to keep his head high and a smile on his face. When he passed a middle-aged woman walking up the road, he was careful to greet her.

A block later, the expression on her face was still sticking in his mind. He could not remember who she was, though he must surely have seen her scores of times. It was not the face but the expression that remained, an expression of astonishment. Perhaps he had said something untoward? He could recall the tone of his voice as he had spoken to her—a sort of light babbling—but not what he had said. When he shook his head with impatience at himself, a smear appeared on his glasses, and he realized that tears were streaming from his eyes. He dashed them away as he strode along, and when he passed a little boy on a kiddie car he sang hello. The boy sang back.

He had decided to spend the day at the library, looking up references for the chapter he was writing, and at his office, preparing for seminar the following day. On campus he ran into no one he knew. By twelve-thirty he had done the library work. He found no one in with whom to have lunch. He ate a hamburger in a student hangout. There was noisy chatter in assorted jargons—gossip, school talk, football guessing, pronouncements on ultimate values. He tried to be amused by the vitality; instead, he was irritated at the triviality and pretentiousness. He felt excluded, albeit from something he did not want to be a part of.

In his office, he prepared for the seminar in less than half an hour. He always thought it would take him hours to plan what to say in class; actually it took him only a few minutes to prepare, for all he decided ahead of time was the general subject for the day, not what he was going to say about it. He was afraid to walk into class without knowing what he was going to say. Yet when he had been new to teaching he had sometimes planned thoroughly and such classes had always fallen flat. To be sure, sometimes a class failed when he went in with no plan; but it was only when he was discovering what he thought as he spoke that a class had a chance of succeeding. He sat for quite a while in his office, hoping that someone would come in to chat, if only the other part-time professor he shared it with, a dry corporation man whose specialty was patent law. He kept cursing his luck at not having the sort of mind that needed to order a subject thoroughly in advance; then he would at least be kept busy at bad times like this. As it was, he could teach well only as he kept his mind continuously alive, and at the moment he felt like dying for a while. He would have, too, had it not been for those sixteen students who would come at four next afternoon to listen to him talk for a couple of hours. If only they would not really listen, he could just tell them what other people thought, or what he himself had once thought. But they did listen. And the way he talked made them listen. He was trapped into living up to himself.

He thought of Nancy. He had thought he was trapped into living up to his best as a father, and here he had let Nancy down. Lizzie and Sybil were grown up, but for him to leave home was to let Nancy down badly. He tried to think of Beth with resentment for having forced him to fail in his duty to Nancy; but here, surrounded by law books, he could not pass any excuse off on himself. Whyever, he had done it. He wanted to cry. In this office tears would not flow. He could not bear the thought of spending the evening alone.

He called Horace's office; Horace was out of town. He called Virginia. She sounded, as always, frightened when she answered the phone, as though she were expecting bad news.

"It's just me," he said.

"Alfred?"

"Sure. I thought maybe I'd drop over this evening, if you and Horace aren't busy."

"Horace's in Stockton at a hearing." Her voice was warm and full. "He should be back by six-thirty or seven. So come over whenever you're ready and have supper with us and stay the night."

"Fine. I'll drop by when I'm finished here on campus, four-thirty or five. Ginner?"

"Yes?"

"Why do you answer the phone so scared?"

She laughed uneasily. "I'll tell you sometime."

He had asked her this before once or twice, and she had put him off. He resolved to get it out of her today.

He read magazines as long as he could stand to, and left the campus for the Skellingses' at a quarter to four. It was a half-hour walk up into the hills.

Alfred had first known Horace in law school. Though Horace was born owning enough of the Sacramento Valley to make him rich for life and though he wanted to go to Paris as other rich young Americans were doing in the twenties, he had decided he had better get his law degree first or he would never get it. He had thoughts of going into politics. But Alfred, though four years younger, had so impressed him that, after less than two years on a European fling, he had returned to California, started a general practice, and before long found himself serving as the legal adviser for some unions who could so little afford to pay that they had never had counsel before. Horace had bulled the friendship through every adversity of separation and falling out, even through periods when Alfred wanted to let it drop. The severest trial had been in 1940, when Mary Louise was divorcing Horace. It was at that time that Alfred finally made up his mind once and for all to stick with the friendship no matter what, forcing Beth, who loved Mary Louise, to remain at least in the cool reaches of politeness with Horace. Beth could not abide Myrna, the one Horace had married the day after Mary Louise's divorce had gone through, but she had not shown her feelings too openly; Virginia, who came after Myrna, she admitted she might have liked a lot, had she known her as the wife of another man. Alfred disapproved of Horace's dealings with women and found him somewhat dull company. But Horace admired him so steadfastly he could not escape. Horace had gone into labor relations because of him, had served on the War Labor-Relations Commission because of him and served well, and had endowed a scholarship in labor relations at Cal because of him. A few times, when Alfred had done something sleazy, Horace had said nothing but simply looked let down. Over the years this had happened half a dozen times.

Alfred had seen that same look in his daughters' eyes when he had half broken a half-promise, say, or offered a bribe. He had seen it in the eyes of students, especially Leon's watchful dark eyes, when in class he had covered over a confusion or an ignorance with a charming sally.

He could not bear that look, and the worst thing about it was that it required him to strive always to be at his best.

There were plenty of those who did not look that way when he was sleazy—Aldo, for one. They seemed to like him none the less for his imperfections and even to expect them. He approved of a friendship which understood and then accepted. But it was not to Aldo's tolerance that he was walking up the streets now, it was to Horace's demand. "Be thou worthy of my trust."

He tried to think of Beth's attitude toward his lapses. She did not look hurt or let down, yet neither did she accept them tolerantly. She was sometimes accusing, sometimes forgiving. Who was she that she dared blame him for his weaknesses? They were no greater then hers. Rage poured into him, as though she had just that minute been laying into him cruelly. That morning when Thomas had spoken of her, Alfred had softened toward her and felt he had been wrong to leave her. Now, drenched with anger, remembering, he felt justified in having left her.

He rose onto the balls of his feet as he walked, and smiled at everyone he passed. When he rapped at the Skellingses' door, he was glowing and full of energy.

· 11 ·

The house was a pink Mediterranean villa which Horace had built early in the Depression to please his second wife, Juanita. The day they were to move into it, which was also their first wedding anniversary, Juanita ran off with a prizefighter from her mother's native town, a Sinaloa village in the hills above Mazatlán. Though Horace had been shocked enough by her betrayal to take nearly three years to remarry, he had not been too shocked to move into the house and make it his own: Juanita had not tainted it by living in it, and he, not she, had worked with the architect and builders. While he was making up his mind whether to propose to Mary Louise, he was tipped in her favor by the jolly way she took his story of Juanita and the house. Thereafter, whenever he was looking over a woman as a prospective wife, the most reliable touchstone he had found was to tell her the story and show her the house. Two young women had eliminated themselves early from his considerations, one by disparaging the house, the other by melting all over him with sympathy for what wicked Juanita had done to him. Myrna passed easily; she had lived the sporting life herself off and on, and had run into Juanita and her boxer. "What do you expect from a meatball like that?" And the house met her chief requirement: it was good for big parties. But Virginia had pleased him most: she'd called his bluff.

He had known her for a couple of years around the WLRC, where she had risen in three months' time from the typing pool to Disputes secretary to Alfred's private secretary. In this capacity she'd made Alfred the most envied executive in the Federal Building: she was at once marvelously efficient and voluptuous. Alfred had been so undeviatingly correct in his relations with her that every rumor about their having an affair died of malnutrition. They were not even hurt by the lies of their devoted enemy, the Madame Defarge of the agency, a weasel-faced, pigeon-breasted, parrot-voiced senior economist named Georgina Wilkins, who spoke of herself as a refugee from Alabama and who spent a good deal of her time rocking in her leather-covered swivel chair, chewing hangnails and watching. After a week of hearings in Los Angeles, she came back swearing that she had seen Alfred let himself out of Virginia's hotel room in the small hours of the morning with his shoes in his hand. But almost no one believed her, and even those who did were chiefly amused by speculating on why she had been snooping around the hotel corridor at that time of night. Most of the conjecture was about why she hated them so much—whether one or the other had snooted her somehow, though they'd never snooted anyone else, or whether it was politics. She was a fellow-traveler, and Alfred had more than once been heard to insist that "Russia, not Marxism, is our ally," a distinction that was not always made by liberals during the war, when Stalin was "Uncle Joe" and "the democracies" included the Soviet Union. To be sure, Alfred, despite his open anti-Marxism, did nothing to disturb the handful of Communists or fellow-travelers on the staff; they too were disgusted by Georgina Wilkins' slanders. The one thing sure was that her face was never more pinched and pallid than when she saw Alfred step out of his office to tell Virginia, whose desk was in the corridor by his door, to do something or hand her some papers, or especially when the two walked together to the meeting room, chatting pleasantly, the handsomest couple for miles around, though a couple for only the time it took them to walk a hundred feet of carpet past the crowded desks.

Horace had spotted Virginia, while she was still down in Disputes, as the best-looking woman in the agency; but her reputation for efficiency kept him at the distance of ogling comments on her figure. What he saw of her taking minutes at the board meetings, calm and alert, held him at that same distance. The most he expected was a kiss and a feel behind a filing cabinet at an office party. Then, one afternoon in the board room, as the eleven members were waiting for Alfred, the chairman, to come and start the meeting, one of the industry members, a Long Beach oil man with a gravelly voice, recounted Georgina Wilkins' tale of the hotel corridor as a big joke, and when Alfred and Virginia came into the room the men were still laughing and looked at the two with indulgent, suppressed lewdness. "What is it? What is it?" said Alfred, sniffing for whatever was mingled with the laughter. "I just told a dirty joke," said the oil man. "It wasn't so funny. Let's skip it." Thereafter Horace began watching Virginia more closely, talking to her now and again, watching Alfred deal with her. For a while he thought that Alfred was so correct with her, so abnormally correct, because he had detected something dangerously wrong with her; but then one day he caught Alfred's gaze lingering on her splendid rear end as she walked out of the office. Horace watched her for her own sake and decided that her efficiency would not necessarily be of the kind to drive her into a career, unless luck went against her, but could make her a model wife and household manager if she put it to the proper uses. He spent several weeks making the first overture. She was correct but sharp: with her, a man was either out or in, and all the board members were definitely out. When at last Myrna went off to Reno for a divorce, Horace was careful to tell Alfred about it within earshot of Virginia. A week later he invited her to go to the symphony with him; he had an extra season ticket. He said this with a little shrug and glance that meant he knew she knew why he had the extra ticket, and he said he hoped she liked Mahler. She said, very coolly, that she did not know who Mahler was. He liked the tilt of her head when she spoke; he explained. She said she was sure she would not like anything by a man who composed a whole series of soulful songs about the deaths of children. So Horace promised her a Mendelssohn piano concerto too, a Haydn symphony, and dinner at a place he knew which somehow or other could be relied on to have good roast beef in spite of the meat rationing. She laughed and accepted.

The third time he took her out he told her the story of Juanita and the house and invited her to come and see it.

"Hmp," she said, "you're testing me, aren't you? I don't like your stinking little trap, old man." Her tone was agreeable enough, but he was forty-five and she was twenty-four. He bridled. "If I ever do see your house, I'll like it or not, as I please. I don't want to have anything put between me and my pleasures. But I'll promise this—I'll tell you the truth about what I think. If I ever see it, that is. Which won't be for a good long time at the soonest, till I get this stink out of my nostrils."

When he recovered from his annoyance he was so pleased with her for having called him on this test business, which he recognized she was right about, that he proposed before she'd seen the house.

"Where would we live?" she asked.

"In my house, of course," he answered.

"How can I answer before I've seen it? Supposing I don't like it?"

She liked it all right, though she demanded a free hand in having the kitchen remodeled and in doing what she wished with the garden, and she stipulated a generous household and personal allotment for which she would not be accountable. Then she thought the whole thing over for three weeks and accepted him. As for sex, once all the arrangements had been settled, she was as generous about making love as her open and easy manner had promised she would be.

"Alfred," Horace said, "she's the best. This time it's for keeps. She knows what she wants and she doesn't get it confused with anything else. I'm learning from her. We'll be married as soon as Myrna's divorce goes through."

"For the first time," said Alfred, "you're not in love. Right?" Horace nodded. "That's a loss."

"Sure, a loss. No more pink cellophane. This is mature love, Alfred. This is for keeps."

"I can't give you anything less than my best wishes. Blessings on you both. She's a good woman."

"You don't need to warn me. I tell you, I'm learning. I'm growing up. This is mature love. I'm going to stick this one out. I'm tired of alternatives."

· 12 ·

Alfred found her weeding in the garden, in sneakers and a blue denim smock.

"Here you are, Papadaddy," she called up to him, brushing the dirt off her knees. "You came at just the right time. I'm ready to quit and have a drink of something cold. So put down your briefcase and take off that hot coat and give me a good hug. I bet you haven't hugged a woman for weeks. It shows in your eyes."

As he took off his suit coat, she took off her gloves, pulled off the sweat-band which she had been wearing around her forehead, and shook out her hair. She spread her arms out to him, but as he stepped toward her she said, "Now, wait a minute, Alfred, not with that thing on." She took off his tie and undid the top three buttons of his shirt. Then she snuggled up against him, her shoulders rounded toward him, her face nuzzling his chest. "You're nice and steamy, the way I like a man best." Her voice sounded as though it were about to burst with laughter. She leaned her head back—she was six inches shorter than he—and gazed at his mouth.

Even since she had married Horace Alfred had maintained a certain distance with Virginia. With many of his women friends, with Kay Ravagli, for example, or with all four of Horace's former wives, he was used to demonstrating his affection with warm embraces. But with Virginia he had never broken the habit of strict propriety formed during the two years she had worked as his secretary. Sometimes, mellow at the end of a party, he would give her a good-night kiss on the cheek. Moreover, as she said, it had been weeks since he had hugged a woman, except his daughters, who seemed to have become at once stiff and listless in his arms.

Virginia's openly sensual embrace found him defenseless, and he sank into the kiss so far that when he pulled away from her he had to clutch her upper arms and keep his eyes closed for dizziness.

"That's better," she said, jiggling his sides with her hands. "Stretch out there on the garden chair and I'll go make some cold lemonade." But when he opened his eyes and looked at her, blinking a couple of times, she put her arms around his neck. "One more kiss first. I haven't kissed a man with a beard since I was eighteen. It's so sexy. It makes me feel deliciously perverted."

Whatever in him the first kiss had not had time to conquer, the second stirred and quelled. She left. He took off his shirt and reclined on the chair. The sun was warm on his skin, the breeze cool. He had been able to refrain from adultery for more than ten years, since Nancy was a baby. He had been sure he would never commit it again. But now, waiting for Virginia to come back, he realized that whether he made love with her depended on her, for though his conscience would not let him press her to it, his desire would not let him resist he will. He also realized with a mild amazement and an even milder regret that he wanted not to resist, though he knew, remotely but nonetheless surely, that desire for him was only a part of her will, the only part he liked.

Shortly after she left, sweet and tasteless dance music began coming out of a speaker hidden up under the eaves. Usually he found this outdoors canned-music system that Horace was so proud of, like most of the music on Horace's hundreds of records, vulgar but innocuous. At the moment he found that it rather fitted his mood. He gave a snort to think what this said about the quality of his mood, but he did nothing to change it.

In half an hour Virginia returned, hair brushed, wearing sandals and a square-cut brown cotton dress, washed, without a trace of make-up on her face. As she poured the lemonade he said that she looked beautiful.

"You know the first time you ever complimented me on my appearance?"

"Good lord, what a thing to remember. Was I as stingy as all that?"

"Not with the other women you weren't. One day I even heard you tell Winifred she looked good." Winifred was the old-maid Disputes Director. "Maybe you were relieved to see her in something besides that blue wool suit she always wore. But me? Never. Not once."

"You were my secretary."

"So? I wanted to have a crush on you so bad, but you wouldn't let me."

"Are you sorry?"

"I was then. Not till my wedding! I had to come stand in front of you in a white satin wedding dress, bringing you a piece of wedding cake on a plate with gold around the edge, before you would even tell me I looked good."

"Was that the first time? I remember how you looked at the wedding. It was extorted from me. I simply could not help myself. Will you forgive me, Ginner?"

She glowered.

"This is splendid lemonade, my dear. You must have made it from fresh lemons."

"From that Meyer lemon tree there. And the sprigs of mint are from the mint patch by that faucet near the side door. And there's a couple of jiggers of Curaçao in it for sweetening."

"What a lucky man Horace is."

"Horace! You sit there holding a glass of lemonade I made for you, and you tell me how lucky another man is. For years I've been hearing what a great fellow Alfred Royce is, and by God it seems to me the main thing he is is a spoilsport."

"There's something in what you say." But she was not interested in diluted contrition from him. He put down his glass, leaned forward, hoisted her ankle in his left hand, and stroked the smooth underside of her strong brown leg with the right. "I think you understand why I never complimented you on your appearance before you got married." He might have said this much on his own motion, though probably not. That he went on, he felt—and secretly enjoyed feeling—was because of her will. "I was more powerfully attracted to you than to any other woman I had ever known." That did not quite satisfy her, but he would submit no further: he would not bring the tense up into the present, *and I still am*. But, in mock submission he bent down and lightly kissed up and down her shin.

He could not tell whether the quick *frisson* that accompanied her squeal at these kisses was forced or genuine.

"I've never been browsed by a man with a beard before. It's delicious." She held out her arm to him. "Here, more." But, smiling, he lay back in his chair. She caught his hand and put it to her face, pressing the fingertips into her eyes and kissing the palm. Then, snuggling his hand against her throat, she said, "You're a pretty good old Papadaddy anyhow." He saw by her eyes that she recognized his distaste at these cutie-pie ways she was putting on. She winked and let go of his hand. "When did you start the beard? It's great."

"I don't know. One weekend after I moved over to Woody's place I forgot to shave for several days, so I just let it keep on growing. It's still sort of scraggly."

"Only on the cheeks. You might shape a goatee out of it, a sort of oval goatee. Like this." She leaned forward and outlined it with her finger. "You'd look very distinguished. We'll wait till Horace comes home and ask him what he thinks."

With her mention of Horace, Alfred concluded that the flirting was over. He felt both disappointed and relieved.

He did not want to lose this new and risky intimacy with her entirely. "Tell me, Ginner, why do you sound scared when you answer the phone?"

Her eyes dropped, and she sat still. He could inspect her face closely. Her smooth cheeks were full but uninteresting, without lines. Her eyelids were very large, and the line of the lashes, when her eyes were downcast as they were now, was clean, slightly tilting at the corners so as almost to meet the long sloping line of the well-defined brows. She wore her hair drawn straight back from her forehead, which was broad and low. She was flicking the tip of her tongue up and down between her lips. Normally he would have found this an act of no consequence, if he had noticed it at all; but now, sexually alert and stayed, he found himself fascinated that this mouth, whose sensuality his own mouth had recently proved, should be so small in that large face, these lips so thin and sharply outlined.

"You probably don't remember," she began in a small voice, "but a month after I began working for you I took a week of sick leave."

"No," he said gently, "I'm sorry, I don't."

"I was worse than sick. It was the one time in my life I ever seriously thought of killing myself. When I first went to work at the agency, I was engaged. He had a personnel job in the Richmond Shipyards. He was Four-F. He told me the Army rejected him because he had diabetes, but I don't know. When all the trouble and bombing was going on at McKee's this summer, I heard you and Horace mention his name once—Sterling Medgar."

"The editor of the McKee house organ? Sort of a loose-jointed fellow? Very bright? Talks with a drawl?"

"He's the only man I was ever in love with."

"Not Horace?"

"Of course not, any more than he was with me. Or you with me now, or me with you. I promised myself I'd never fall in love with anybody ever again, and I never have. You can't teach anybody anything, they have to learn it for themselves. My mother kept telling me not to get love and sex and marriage mixed up together, but I paid no attention to her. I knew better. Well, I learned the hard way. I loved him so much I kept telling myself that marriage would cure our sex troubles. They weren't all that terrible, I kept telling myself, just a matter of adjustment and experience."

"You were living with him?"

"Just sleeping with him. I listened to my mother that much anyway. I wasn't such a big fool, even then, as to think of marrying a man I hadn't been to bed with a good deal. We neither one had much experience, but I knew we weren't doing so well. The trouble was, he liked to twitch my clothes up while we were talking about something else, or run his hand under my dress in more or less public places, like in a restaurant booth, and I hated it, I just hated it. He didn't really want to go to bed unless he'd done a lot of this twitching stuff first. He'd sort of snicker, too. Only, when he did this it chilled me, so I could hardly ever enjoy intercourse. He wouldn't talk about sex, ever, so we couldn't talk over what was wrong and what to do about it. Which was probably just as well, I suppose, but I sure worried at the time. And I worried a lot about what I should do to make myself more attractive for him. Then we got engaged, and everything seemed to pick up. We went back to the way we had been at first, before the twitching started. He took to undressing me after we got engaged, not just pulling at my clothes but really undressing me, at the right time, and we made love the way it ought to be done a few times. I was sure I was right and marriage was the answer to everything for us. Then one Saturday he stood me up. He'd done that a couple of times before. Once he was too busy winning at poker, and the other time he forgot to tell me he was going with some buddies up to Reno for Labor Day weekend and gamble. Both those times we hadn't been getting along too well. So this time I was upset, especially since our date was to go out househunting. As soon as we found an apartment we were going to go to the secondhand stores for furniture. We were going to be married in less than a month. Our big problem was whether to blow ourselves to a brand-new bed or not. We only had three hundred dollars saved up between us. I didn't hear a word Saturday or Sunday. I was worried that he'd gone off gambling again, and I was mad. Sometimes I sort of hoped he'd lost all his money and was ashamed to come tell me about it. That way I'd have a hold over him to make him let me manage the money. I knew I'd have to do that if we were ever to make do. Only, how was I to get him to let go of it and give me the reins? Then Monday morning about eleven I got a phone call. I was typing up a letter for you at the time."

"You remember that?"

"It was to Justice Durkheim. He was in Washington on some war-time commission or other. You'd just gotten a letter from him, and when you dictated the answer I took it all straight. Only, at one point you put in a couple of *double entendres* close together. I thought maybe it was my dirty mind. I didn't know you too well then, and you were so serious when you dictated that letter to me. Well, I answered the phone and a man asked to speak to Miss Virginia Lavros. I said I was she, and he said he was somebody or other on the San Francisco Police and was I acquainted with Sterling Medgar. I'll never forget the way I couldn't get an answer out. He said, 'Hello, hello,' and jiggled the receiver. Finally I could get something out of my throat. He said Sterling was being held, but I could get him out on a hundred dollars' bail. He wouldn't tell me anything more except that Sterling was being held on a charge of indecent exposure. So I went down and bailed him out. He wouldn't look me in the eye. The first thing he said to me, out on the steps, was that it was all over between us. He sounded miserable but at the same time angry with me. He said he never wanted to see me again. I didn't beg him to come with me or patch it all up again or anything like that. He really and truly never wanted to see me again, I could feel that. And somehow I could feel that he blamed me that things had gone wrong between us. I blamed myself too. I thought I'd failed to make him good in bed and I'd never have a second chance unless he wanted to give me one. And he did not, for sure. But I did plead with him for one thing, to tell me what had happened. Not why, even—just what did he do? Apparently it took place in a movie house on Market Street, in the lobby, with an usherette somehow. He really looked at me with hatred when he got through mumbling this to me. I had tears pouring down my face and didn't care. This was all on the steps in front of the city jail, you understand. Then he went away and I've never seen him since. He never even paid me back the hundred bucks. When I heard you and Horace mention him, I felt sort of panicky for a minute or two but then I just felt sorry for him, the poor sad sack, and I wondered if he ever got married. But at the time I was really hit. I wished I was dead. I even walked out on the bridge one afternoon so I could jump off if the spirit moved. It didn't. But, as I say, one good thing came out of the mess—I never got sex and love and marriage mixed up again. Mother was right. Two of them at a time is a handful, all three and you've got murder."

"What did your father say?"

"He was a mortician."

"I know, I've heard you mention that. What I meant was, did he agree with your mother about love and so on?"

"He took off when I was thirteen. That's when she got started on the sex-love-marriage bit. Her mistake was she loved him. All I ever remember him ever to get enthused over was corpses. He let me watch him put cosmetics on a dead old woman once. He ran off to Phoenix and started a new business. I used to have daydreams sometimes. I'd be eloping, and me and my boyfriend'd be hightailing it through Arizona, running out on Mother, and we'd have a car accident, and my body would be taken into my father's mortuary, and wouldn't that be the surprise of his life! But then he'd prepare me for the casket so's I'd look as good as new—you know, a living doll— and I'd lie there like a jewel in a case and everybody'd come look at me. Well, you'd expect a mortician's child to have morbid thoughts, it's natural. I got over them when I got over Sterling. I don't get things mixed up any more. Horace has been a big help to me."

· 13 ·

At ten they were still seated at table.

"Horace," said Alfred expansively, "you and I are sidetracked. If we stick with labor much longer, we're going to find ourselves way out in the middle of nowhere with our hats on. It's time we made a change."

"Oh-oh," said Virginia, getting up. "It's time for you two to go into the living room."

"We'll help clear table!" cried Alfred, leaping to his feet.

"Sure, you'll help, by getting out of my way. Git."

"Madame," said Alfred, bending over her hand courtlily, "for that superb dinner, I salute you."

"You mean it was up to Beth's standards?"

"At her very best."

"That," said Horace, "is a compliment, honey. For him, Beth is *it*."

"Pardon me," said Alfred, "I said 'at her best.' And this dinner of yours, my dear Virginia, was just an impromptu weekday affair. The uninvited guest?"

"Not so impromptu," said Horace. "She keeps things on hand, chicken stock, shallots, the best fruit in season."

"Don't disillusion him," she said. "I want him to think I'm wonderful."

"I do."

"Go! Git! You're in my way."

As they strolled into the living room, Horace pulled out two cigars. "Here, have one. You like her, don't you?"

"A bit more than that."

"Here, take one. My cigar man assures me they're mellow but robust. The combination intrigues me. I know what you think about cigars, but try one."

Alfred accepted one.

"I'm leaving day after tomorrow for New York for a week or so," said Horace. "I'd like to leave her with you while I'm gone."

"Horace! What are you doing to me? You want me to gain back all the weight I've lost? Here I am in the best shape I've been in for years and you want to fatten me up again. I can't resist such wonderful food, you know that. With such wines? Impossible."

"You need a woman. It shows."

"Oh, that. If that's all. Sure. Say, this is a good cigar."

"He's a reliable man." They settled into overstuffed chairs. "What did you mean, we're sidetracked in labor?"

"Labor doesn't matter the way it used to," said Alfred. "It's more or less got what it wants. Which turns out to be not very much."

"A decent living for ordinary working people and some time for themselves? So what's wrong with that?"

"What it stands for. I had thought—we'd all thought—that those who were to be released from the bondage of drudgery and poverty would aspire to high civilization, or at least to luxurious civilization. Instead they aspire to nothing. They've put themselves into a new figurative bondage, possession. They have to possess the very instruments which released them from the old literal bondage. Release the slaves and they become serfs, release the serfs and they become workers, release the workers and they become machine operators. I've had it."

"Oh, I don't know whether you've had it yet or not," Horace said. "What happens to the operators when the machines start operating themselves?"

"The masses, the pure unleavened masses, modern mediocre mass man. God help us all."

"So, what's the new area? Race relations?"

"No! They're essentially the same as labor relations. It's always good to remedy an injustice, and God knows the Negroes and Indians in this country have suffered even greater injustice than the workers ever did. That injustice should be remedied, yes, and by the racially oppressed themselves. It will be remedied. This time the law will lead the masses. In a generation it will have brought the bulk of the people up out of the worst public forms of racial injustice. But the law will do it mostly for the wrong reason."

"Oh? There's a wrong reason to do it?"

"For national prestige. That's wrong enough. Racial prejudice weakens us in world politics. It spoils our national image abroad, as the manipulators put it. That's a vile reason."

"Still, if it gets done . . ."

"But that's only one of the reasons race relations are out of the mainstream. What do the oppressed want? From labor we know the answer. Mediocrity. A washing machine, a house in the suburbs, respectability, a little trip in the summer, hundreds of dollars' worth of presents under the tree every Christmas morning, a nation that is a winner in the power games, ugliness, miles upon miles upon miles of civic ugliness. Do you know the worst thing we rich whites did to the poor and the dark-skinned? After the first big enslavement and expropriation, that is. Killing and stealing—sometimes I think those are not so dreadful as what we did next."

"Pardon me. *I* didn't do any of this. *We?*"

"How many acres of California did your grandfather get by cheating that Spanish grandee, whose ancestors took it by force from the Indians?"

"All right," said Horace resignedly. "I don't always follow you when you get on one of your mystical kicks. Who's responsible for what? But don't forget, you enjoyed this expensive dinner we stole from the Digger Indians as much as I did."

"Right," said Alfred with glowing eyes. "I don't refuse injustice and violence. I live in the world, as you do. But one thing that is not a necessary part of the world is bad dreams, and the worst thing we did to those we oppressed was to rob them of whatever dreams they had of their own and give them false dreams which could come true. They are coming true. Material plenty—in another generation nearly everyone will have it, Negroes too. Better to have pie in the sky, a thousand times better; then you can die hoping. I'm not sure that anything in this life is worth getting. Maybe everything whatever crumbles to dust when you finally get hold of it. I don't know. But I do know that the American dream does. That generations of men should have devoted their lives—that you and I should have devoted the best years of our lives—to attaining what we thought was so beautiful and turns out to be mediocrity itself . . ." There were tears in his eyes, and he was smiling. He took off his glasses and wiped them on his handkerchief. "Damn, damn, damn. And do you know"—he started up again, dropping his glasses into his lap and raising both fists over his head, his bent arms rigid—"what the worst lie of the dream was? The lie that gave us Americans the enormous energy to turn out all that we have turned out, the lie that has released incredible power? The liberal lie, that remedying specific injustices will make the world just. That the world can be made just at all."

"Alfred," said Horace in the comfortable tones of after-dinner discussion, "you shock me. Aren't we lawyers? Don't you teach the philosophy of law? Haven't you considered becoming a judge? What's the law for, if not justice?"

"To keep us from killing one another, of course," Alfred said in a bedraggled voice, sinking back into the chair. "To make walled villages in the wilderness, that we may survive."

"You've been without a woman too long. You need—"

"I know," said Alfred, flapping a hand at Horace, "I know, I know, I know, I know."

They sat for ten minutes, gazing out the picture window at the lights of the city, which were softened and ambered a little by a light smog down over the flat stretches of Berkeley, blotting out all but a few lights of San Francisco. Distantly the phonograph finished a record of saxophone waltzes and began one of nightclub folksongs.

"Our city," said Alfred, "from a certain distance, it is so beautiful. There must be something I'm not taking into account."

"That's right," said Horace. "And I'm glad you know it."

Virginia came in and stood between them. She held out a hand to each, and each raised a hand to her.

"That's the way I like it," she said. "I'm going along now, okay? I feel like washing my hair and taking a nice long hot bath."

She kissed Horace's shiny brown skull, and he slapped her flank. Then she bent over Alfred and kissed him sensually on the mouth.

"Good dinner?" she asked, still leaning over him.

"Marvelous," he answered. "You're marvelous to me, you're both wonderful."

She left.

"I mean it," said Horace. "It'll give me real satisfaction to think of you looking after her while I'm away." He leaned forward and squeezed Alfred's leg, looking up into his eyes. "She told me once she'd never have dated me that first time if I hadn't been your friend. I never forgot that. I'm full of gratitude to you. You mean a lot to her too."

"You're crazy," said Alfred. "You're both absolutely crazy. I don't want to hear any more about it. I'm tired. I don't want to get worked up. I'm going to bed."

"I'll stay here and finish my cigar. You know where your room is."

Alfred could not relax while he could hear Virginia moving about. He kept half expecting her to come into his room. He kept thinking that Horace had been offering her to him to live with for the next week or so, and though he reproached himself for his lascivious thoughts, he could not repress them. It was not till long after he heard Horace go to bed that he fell asleep. He slept badly.

At dawn he was awakened by the telephone's ringing. Horace talked on it a while, then made a call. Alfred was trying to sink back into sleep when it rang again. He got up and dressed.

He found Virginia in the kitchen making breakfast. She was in her dressing gown; her hair was fluffy and not in curlers; she looked at her best, except that her eyes were puffy.

"That was a call from Washington," she said. "Horace has to catch the eight-o'clock plane."

The taxi honked while they were still at table.

At the front door, Horace kissed Virginia good-by, then shook Alfred's hand hard.

"Keep an eye on her, Alfred. She wants you to."

"Yes," she said.

"Oh my God," said Alfred squinching his eyes comically. "It's so early in the morning."

He watched the taxi drive away with Horace, then closed the front door and turned to go back into the dining room to finish his coffee. Virginia was standing in front of him, her robe slightly open, revealing her pink nightgown with white ruffles at the throat.

"Alfred?"

"Yes?"

"Let's go make love right now." She took his wrists and pressed his hands onto her heavy breasts.

He moaned. "What? What are you talking about? In my friend's bed that he's barely out of, with his wife?"

"All right, in your bed, with *me*."

"My God, my God, I can't. All right, but not here. I can't in this house. We'll go over to Woody's apartment in the city. After my seminar this afternoon. I'll go see Thomas this morning, then go to my seminar at three. Then I'll come back here and we'll go over to Woody's."

"Listen," she said, "I'll come pick you up on campus and we'll drive right over, and maybe we'll make love first and then go out to dinner, or maybe we'll go out to dinner first and then make love.

We'll see how we feel. Oh, Papadaddy, it's going to be the best holiday anybody ever had. I've waited this long, I can wait a few more
hours."

· 14 ·

"I had a bad night," said Justice Durkheim in a whisper. "I wish I
had a pain to complain about. I could neither sleep nor wake. I kept
creeping around in my own mind, which I know too well. Nothing
new to look at. Complain to me about your wife, Alfred. It will do me
good."

Alfred had resolved he would never do this. "My wife doesn't understand me"—he would not succumb to that banality.

For a moment he glared at Thomas for tempting him, and breathed
so hard he was almost snorting. Then it occurred to him that whatever he said would be burned up with the old man's body. Moreover,
maybe his complaining really would be a relief to Thomas, maybe this
was not a lawyerish trick to get him talking. For some reason at that
moment his arms and mouth remembered intensely the ardent embrace with which Virginia had taken leave of him twenty minutes before. Such indignation at Beth roiled up in him as he had never been
conscious of before except in the thick of conflict when she had just
said or done something to hurt him. He began talking.

Wherever he started, he always came back to Beth's inheritance.
The first few times he spoke of it, he was analytic and understanding,
but after a while he was openly complaining and abusive. The old
man did not respond in any visible way. Alfred found himself working to produce some reaction on the brown old face, and finally he
got one, a slow blink of the leathery eyes and the faintest of smiles on
the drawn lips. He stopped to recall what he had said to produce this
smile. "I'm not vain enough to suppose that I've been without fault in
our marriage. I have a thousand flaws and I know it. But in balance,
in point of fact, there's just one essential reason we broke up, and
that is the manner in which Beth handled her inheritance." All right,
he was saying, "It's not my fault, it's hers," and Thomas was smiling
at the banality. But it was true! It was her fault! "It's the act that
counts. It's the act that can be seen. The act can be known if anything
in human affairs can be known. And this was her act."

"You say nothing about bed."

"That's a matter," said Alfred in a rather clipped way, "about
which we have never disagreed. We have never let a third person into
bed with us except literally—in the person of one of our babies."

"I beg your pardon," said Justice Durkheim loud enough for a faintly ironic inflection to be audible. "Is Tony St. Clare in town?"

He was one of the United States Senators from California and lived in Oakland.

"Congress recessed last Friday. I suppose he is."

"I want to talk with him as soon as possible. Try the phone now. If you can't get him, see if you can locate Cecil Scowecroft." This was the Senator's brother-in-law and the Chief Justice of the state Supreme Court. "I'd thought there was nothing left for me to do. It turns out that there is after all."

He lifted his right arm and, holding his right wrist steady with his left hand, he sighted down his right forefinger at a spot between Alfred's eyes and bent his cocked thumb down, making at the same time a tiny click with his tongue, as though he were shooting.

Virginia was in the parking lot waiting for Alfred when he came out from his seminar. He was wrought up from the class, which had gone well; he did not enjoy driving; she was seated behind the wheel of the car and he knew she was a good driver. Nevertheless, he opened the door on the driver's side and said, "I'll drive, if you don't mind." She moved over with a little shrug. "Let's go to the apartment," he said, "and have a drink." She said fine. They did not talk much on the way over and then only about trivialities of the road.

Once in the apartment they did not pause for a drink but made love immediately. He expected to fail the first time, from excess of ardor, but she joined him in his excess. After a long quiet dinner and a walk, late in the evening they made love again, and again when they woke up next morning.

The third time, in addition to a perfection of pleasure, he thought that something strange happened, but he did not know what.

She seemed glad that he would be gone for the day. She wanted to idle around, shopping for food and preparing dinner. She told him what kind of wines to buy. He could see no change in her manner with him. She met his attempts at intimate tendernesses with a long neutral look or a kiss and wink.

"You're late," Justice Durkheim said.

"Half an hour. I was delayed by an accident ahead of me on the bridge. Did Tony get here?"

"On the dot at eight-thirty. We did our business in twenty minutes." He blinked at Alfred. He was sliding down under the sheet already, neck wrinkled, eyelids heavy. "I'm sorry I wasted that energy on something that gave me less pleasure than listening to you would have given me. I wanted to hear about the McKee bombing."

"I'll tell you what I know."

"Go ahead. I'll hang on as long as I can."

"Everything about the case is obscure, down to exactly what happened. Evans denies that Carver helped him, but Carver disappeared the day after and his car was found hundreds of miles away. The license plates had been switched. The other car has not been found yet. Evans has produced no car for himself to get away in. Or take my own personal involvement. My daughter Sybil has been seeing a lot of Leon Kalish, the best student I ever had or expect to have—I brought him to meet you once. Good. But Sybil's been showing lots of signs of strain. I can't be sure whether it's because of her new school, which she does not much like, or living in a dormitory, which she hates, or her parents' separation, which she never mentions to me—terribly artificial, since I can't bring the subject up with her somehow—or Leon, something wrong with her connection with Leon. She talks to me about him every time I see her. She seems to be pretty much in love with him. But she hasn't completely broken off with another man who is in love with her but who is dull as dishwater. Leon has not called me up or come to see me since I left Beth. Why? Does he disapprove of me? Is he hiding something? I would call him and have him to dinner with me and sound him out, except that I've learned an odd thing. I ran into Paul Fenstermacher at the Guild one evening. We had a couple of drinks together. He's been District Attorney for Alameda County for six or seven years. We were rivals in law-school days. We get along all right, bump into one another every year or two and talk a while. He's on the McKee case, naturally, and he began sounding me out on Leon. I praised him to the skies, but I was wondering what was cooking. Well—I know Leon has been boarding with Chantal Bigonneau, a Frenchwoman whom I knew as a secretary in the Law Department at Cal. She quit this summer. I don't know how she earns her living now. Leon and Roy Carver both boarded with her. I assumed that Paul is interested in Leon as a lead on Roy. But he asked me about Leon's love life. Naturally I did not mention Sybil. I did mention a girl Leon went around with last spring, till she left for New York this summer. And I mentioned Chantal. He asked me to tell him everything I knew about Chantal. At this point curiosity got the better of me. I offered him a swap—my what for his why. He told me that Leon and she were married nine days after the assassination, and that this was not generally known. I was dumfounded. Paul might or might not have known about Sybil. I told him the little I knew about Chantal. The crucial question, obviously, was how she got to this country so soon after the war, who sponsored her. She indicated to me once that it was an OSS man she had gotten to know during the war, but I knew nothing else about him. When Paul and I were saying good-by I had the strong impression that he was on the verge of telling me something more and then decided not to."

"And Evans," said Justice Durkheim, "is merely a madman."

"Not merely," said Alfred. "He may be mad, but not merely. In any case, I'm interested in the system of madness he's caught in. But I have so little to go on other than guesses and hunches. To tell the truth, I rely more on bull sessions with students than on anything else, late at night after we've been drinking too much. So I've developed a theory. Not a theory—a hypothesis. I'd be willing to bet that Harry Evans is a romantic, a real romantic, a genuine rebellious romantic. He can't stand the oppressive order of modern societies. He thinks that what he hates is injustice, but really it's more than that, it's deadening order he hates. In the thirties he was a wild radical, not a Communist, not even a Trotskyite, some splinter group so crazy and secret and tiny that when the war came the FBI didn't even have a file on him. He got to be some sort of secret agent against the Nazis and did an excellent job. But after the war, what? Destruction and waste had not impoverished ordinary Americans but enriched them. The only Americans more deadly dull than the Communists were their persecutors. All the other radical subgroups were disintegrating into respectability or lunacy. The labor movement at least was left for him to hope for, a sluggish group, maybe, but one that by its very nature is opposed to the bourgeois order which is deadening everyone and everything. Right? Absolutely wrong. It turns out that what the labor movement is willing to settle for is third-rate bourgeois order. It's striving valorously to become a facsimile of its adversary and is in process of succeeding. Understood? Here is the McKee strike. By one desperate gesture Evans hopes to turn it from a local peeve on the part of rich union members against a rich employer—the real issue is respectability—turn it into a symbolic blow. After all, the union was originally part of the IWW. The true target for the workers' strike in this case should be to oppose the production of the precision mechanisms for making rockets, for the only social function of rockets is folly and destruction—like the atom bomb. In his mind, logically the true purpose of the bombing was to arouse spirit in the strikers, to return them to their duty as rebels. Conceivably, sixty or seventy years ago, this action on his part could have had such an effect on the strikers. But in those days the government was not engaged in massive lunacies, nor were the workers so fat. What his act accomplished was to disrupt the lives of a few score people and to provide a topic of speculation for a few thousand more. I doubt that it will provoke a counterreaction even from the government security officers. He may very well be judged insane and not even executed for what he did. If he is executed, it'll be for nothing more than murder. He wanted passionately to goad some of his fellow men to turn against that which was drugging their souls, to drive them to live until they died. But they weren't interested, they preferred to breathe the fumes of security. Isn't it clear, they say, that many who live die young? Besides, living hurts so much."

"So he killed one man and crippled another," Justice Durkheim whispered.

"They were to be sacrifices, and he was to be another. But no one believes in that political religion any more. After all, to an outsider a sacrifice is nothing but a kind of slaughter and the sacrificing priest nothing but a kind of butcher."

Alfred paused and realized that Justice Durkheim's eyes had been closed for some time. Yet he had spoken recently.

"What else?" said the old man. "I can still make out what you're saying."

"Nothing else, really." But he snorted.

"What's that?"

"I really have no business telling you this. Horace Skellings went East yesterday, and Virginia is staying with me while he's gone."

The eyes snapped open. "You took her?"

Alfred shrugged and nodded.

"With Horace's knowledge and consent?"

"Implicitly."

"You've actually had her?"

Alfred nodded again.

"Splendid. Tell me about it. Or do you have this same rule of exclusiveness with your mistress as with your wife?"

"Well," said Alfred, "honestly, Thomas, it seems to me . . ."

"You know, I was thinking yesterday, after you told me what you had against Beth." His voice died away. He blinked and swallowed, then started up again. "Carrie died a little over forty years ago. I never exactly intended to be true to her memory. It seems to me I could never find another woman I wanted, and I was always so damned busy. Do you realize I haven't had a woman since before the First World War? Living fossil for you. At least you aren't a fool the same way I've been one. Tell me about Virginia. I saw her once at the St. Clares' swimming pool. From the rear she reminded me of the first mare I owned. A sorrel. Splendid animal."

"Well," said Alfred, "insofar as it is a question of pleasure, I have no complaints."

" 'Insofar as it is a question of pleasure,' " Justice Durkheim whispered. "That's a good beginning. God have mercy on my soul, Alfred

Royce, but you can be the . . . 'Insofar as it is a question of pleasure.' "

His voice became inaudible. His lips ceased to move but held the traces of a smile.

Alfred said to himself: It's not as you think, Thomas, not that way at all. Then he told his story as though he were adapting it from *The Decameron*.

· 15 ·

"A Special Delivery letter came for you at noon," said Virginia. "It's there on the mantel."

"From Joe. Good." He tore it open. It contained a note for him and another stamped, sealed envelope for Lizzie with the address left blank. "I must go right out and mail this to Lizzie. He's going to be on TV Monday evening. That's the day before Horace comes back."

"Is he the tall one at your party in June that looks like a sleepy panther?"

"You might say. He's going to be on a give-away quiz program."

"So much for him. Hurry back. I made you a coffee cake. The coffee'll be made in ten minutes."

That was as close to a conversation as they were having. Alfred was made uneasy by the lack of conversation, but Virginia seemed content with this, as with all their other arrangements.

She prepared food for him, it seemed to him, constantly when he was there, and served him in little domestic ways he had never been served in before. Sexually he had not known he could be served as she unrelentingly served him.

He wanted to say that he was logy with fatigue, but she did not let him. She touched him, and he could not say it.

The next morning, when he knocked at Justice Durkheim's door, Irma answered, weeping. The doctor had just left; Uncle Thomas was in a coma; it was only a matter of hours now. Alfred asked what his last words had been. Since Alfred had left the day before Irma had not been able to make out more than a random word or two— "water," something like "trouble," "home" or "homes" or "Holmes."

Alfred sat by him as he died. Justice Durkheim had ordered the doctor not to use any artifices whatever, even oxygen, to keep his body breathing longer than it wanted to breathe after the last sinking had begun. Irma came in from time to time. There was nothing to be done. Alfred tried hard to look at the rock garden, really to look at it, but could not. At one o'clock the death rattle began. In ten minutes it ended.

Irma knew the arrangements he had made for the disposition of his body: the undertaker, the niche in the columbarium in which his ashes were to be deposited. The funeral was to be held in the nearest Episcopal church. "It's the church of the ruling class," he had told Alfred when Alfred, fresh in Washington, had been inveighing against the tedious hypocrisy of Episcopal services. "I joined it when I was elevated to this bench. You can be scornful of it because you were born into it."

To Irma's gratitude, Alfred undertook to make the necessary telephone calls. No matter whom he was talking to, he kept wondering whether he should telephone Beth or walk the half-block up the street and tell her in person. Finally he telephoned her.

Her voice was neutral till he told her what he was calling about. Then she broke down and began to cry gently. They talked for quite a while, with tentative warmth. He said he would call for her Monday at ten and they would go to the church together. She thanked him. "Oh please, please, Beth. Thanks? No."

It seemed to him extraordinary that he should be warmer with her now than he had been since he had left home. After two days of flagrant, voluptuous adultery, where was his guilt? Where were the pangs of conscience?

He told Virginia, in a somewhat lofty manner, that he was still distressed from Justice Durkheim's death and wanted a quiet evening alone. She was sympathetic and understanding and went off to a movie. He read for a couple of hours in the scrapbook he had compiled of the opinions which Thomas had written during his years on the Supreme Court, most of them majority opinions. Then he went to bed and to sleep. When Virginia came to bed she touched him, and with a groan of reluctance that became a moan of desire he fell into lovemaking.

He needed to be away from her every day for several hours. She was tranquil and self-contained as always, her voice was filled to bursting, and she laughed joyfully over little things. He reproached himself for his fears and decided he simply lacked the aptitudes of a lover. He wished Horace would somehow be obliged to come home early.

He asked Virginia if she did not have errands to run.

"I'd planned to do a lot of shopping while Horace was away," she said. "He's always telling me I ought to. But I hate to. Just food and drink, that's all I enjoy buying." She wrinkled her nose at him.

"Won't your women friends miss you?" he said.

"What women friends? Do you have any idea what women like to talk about? The only one I know that I'd want to be friends with is Beth, and she's devoted to Mary Louise. Probably I'd have liked Mary Louise too if I'd ever known her. You know, Alfie, I'm only half a woman, the man's half."

"Oh?" he said indulgently.

"I'm barren."

"That's true."

"Women talk about children all the time, or bridge, or house-decorating. My mother goes shopping at least twice every week of her life, and every day between Thanksgiving and Christmas. After Christmas she has two weeks of taking things back, maybe three. Did you know that Kay Ravagli took a ceramics course? This was after she married Woody, who could buy Horace out five times over. She wanted to make pots to put in special wrought-iron brackets she ordered from Morocco, to hang on the wall and put dead weeds in— very special dead weeds, of course. She gave me two of these rigs for Christmas. Don't tell me she didn't give Beth some?"

"I've seen them in the patio."

"Kay's a nice girl, but how could I ever be friends with her? She spent a whole afternoon telling me about the pots. I told her I'd rather watch her make them, but she never asked me to."

At first Alfred had thought that Virginia abandoned herself when they made love, like no other woman he had known, and that this transport was, as the contemporary authorities agreed it should be, the high authentic good of sexual passion.

But, quite rapidly, his opinion changed. This change began with his becoming physically conscious of the disparity in their ages. To be sure, he was only seventeen years older than she, not old enough to consider himself in her father's generation necessarily. Still, the thought occurred to him that literally he was old enough to be her father, and it connected with that image she had given him from her fantasy, of herself a corpse in her father's hands. In her lover's arms there was nothing corpselike about her hot and plunging body. All the same, Alfred kept having the notion—and at the same time repudiating the notion as far-fetched and even mad—that, when she was transported from her body by passion, nothing came to occupy it in place of her gone self and that the galvanized body he embraced for those few moments each time was vacant as a corpse. This notion he could dispose of rationally, but the experience which produced it was not accessible to argument or denial, being of his flesh and feeling. He might not be able to deny the experience but he could trick it.

Her behavior in the early stages of making love and all the rest of the time they were together was recognizable enough. She was the same woman he had known for years as his private secretary and as his friend's wife. If he found her passion alarming, then it was only his pusillanimity that he should be concerned about. Always before he had conceived of lovemaking as a meeting of man and woman for mutual pleasure and, frequently, for spiritual exchange, as intercourse. Now, to be able to last out these days with Virginia, he conceived of a lovemaking as a sort of realm created (like a marriage) by the man and woman, but separate from them too, a realm which each entered severally. The strange realm which he and Virginia created together was more glorious than any he had created with other women, and he resolved to explore it to the limits of his power, whatever Virginia herself might be doing there, whether she was there or not. This trick worked for a while.

The trouble was that, between times, he kept thinking of Beth. The realm of their lovemaking was narrower, less dark and gorgeous and reverberating—less accessible, even, since a good deal of the time they failed to create much of anything when they embraced. But when they did manage to make a realm of love, what they both did there was to look for and sometimes find one another.

After the funeral, Senator St. Clare asked him to come back to Justice Durkheim's house and be a witness to the reading of the will, but Alfred refused somewhat brusquely and said he'd call about it next morning. He drove Beth home. She wanted to drop him off at the campus or near a bus stop, but he insisted that he go home with her and that they have a bite of lunch together. He did not tell her that he had driven the Skellingses' car over and parked it a few blocks away.

"I'm surprised," she said, "that Horace and Virginia weren't at the funeral."

"Horace is in New York. I suppose Virginia didn't think she knew Thomas well enough to attend by herself."

"Did she go with Horace?"

"No. Why?"

"I've called her three or four times and got no answer."

"Really? How's Nancy?"

"How is she ever?"

"She's been seeming a little cold recently," he said tentatively, "with me."

"An iceberg," said Beth, "with razor-sharp edges."

They ate too fast. The lunch gave no opportunity for small talk— liverwurst sandwiches, pickles, and milk. Not that Alfred wanted an epicurean repast; he was not really tasting what he ate. The only subjects on his mind—their separation, Nancy's withdrawal, and Thomas's death—were too large to chat about; besides, he did not know

222

what he wanted to say to Beth about the separation and was afraid that if he began to talk his tongue might somehow betray him. Moreover, being in his own house was confusing and upsetting.

He stood up from table to leave. Beth remained seated.

"Alfred, there's something I think you should look into. It concerns Sybil. She won't let me talk with her any more, not really."

"Nor me."

She glanced at him. "Is that true?" He nodded. "I thought she would with you. Even so . . . You know Jean-Louis Bigonneau. He has begun taking dancing lessons from Mademoiselle Sylvie, and he seems to be taking quite a shine to Nancy. He took her to a movie Saturday afternoon, and they had dinner at his house. Leon Kalish drove her home at ten o'clock. Everything was fine, except that she says Leon is living at Chantal Bigonneau's. Jean-Louis told her. She was not clear whether Leon's room is separate from Chantal's, and I didn't want to pry. Perhaps he's only a lodger. But isn't Sybil seeing a good deal of him? That's my impression."

"Aha," he said and promised to go into action immediately.

He felt remiss at having done nothing, and grateful to Beth for recalling him to his duty in this matter of Leon and Sybil.

She repelled him when he tried to kiss her good-by and gave him a look of such trembling fury as would usually have meant hours or days of trouble. He was glad to be reminded, as it were, of his reason for having left her. He walked down San Jacinto Way, rising on the balls of his feet at every step and flourishing his head from time to time.

"Seven-thirty!" Virginia said. "That was just when I planned to serve dinner, and I've made such a dinner for you. Can't we skip it?"

"Now look, it'll just take half an hour. Why don't you stay here while I sneak over to the Spindrift and take it in? I'll be back by two minutes after eight."

"If you go I'll go. But everything's ready! Oh, the Spindrift's a fun place. If we have to watch a bloody TV program, that's as good a place to do it as any."

The Spindrift was a new bar which Alfred had gone to a few times because it was the closest to Woody's apartment. It was chic and *louche* but not very expensive; not having been mentioned yet in the gossip columns, it was not yet fashionable. The façade was tongue-and-groove planks painted with a gray wash, and it had one large window so designed and illuminated as to make a passer-by think he was looking into an aquarium tank. In this window was a stuffed seal with its nose pointed straight up, its rear flippers on sand and its fore flippers propped on an arching piece of driftwood. On the back wall was painted an imitation parchment scroll on which in black uncial letters with red majuscules were the lines from Hart Crane's poem:

O minstrel galleons of Carib fire,
Bequeath us to no earthly shore until
Is answered in the vortex of our grave
The seal's wide spindrift gaze toward paradise.

The proprietors, who were also bartender and waiter, were two slim young men called Bric and Brac. At signs of interest in the décor, they would explain that, except for the furniture, they personally had salvaged from beaches everything in the place—the bits of glass, the nets, the oar, the glass balls, the driftwood, the shells. There were six tables, the rear two of which commanded a view of a small television set recessed in the wall a couple of feet above the floor. If asked, Bric would, with a not quite imperceptible sniff, turn it on with the sound very low.

There was no one else in the bar. Alfred ordered two Pernods and had Bric tune in the give-away quiz program for them.

The master of ceremonies was introducing the two contestants, Joe and a prissy-mouthed little man wearing rimless spectacles. Joe gave the impression of being even handsomer than he actually was, but his face was stiff, the smile wooden. When he walked over to one of the two glass sentry boxes in which each of the contestants stood during the show, Virginia said under her breath, "He walks like zombie." From then on everything he did struck Alfred as unnatural.

Bric set their drinks down, then stood between them a moment, frowning at the television screen. The first question was being put to Joe.

"He's a friend of mine," said Alfred.

"Well," said Bric, going away, "it's a living. I suppose."

Nothing whatever was pleasing about being in this place, yet Alfred could not manage, even at such provocation, to consolidate his bad feelings into anger at Bric. He sat in a lukewarm stew of emotions, watching Joe debase himself.

"At least," said Virginia during the second commercial, "he knows a lot."

"That last date he worked so hard to remember? All that scowling and clutching? It was in the seminar paper he wrote for me in the spring semester."

"Let's get out of here."

He paid, leaving no tip.

He opened the door of the bar just as a tall square-shouldered woman was entering. He and Virginia stepped to one side. Behind this woman came Mary Louise and a woman research biologist named Michael who had abetted her at the time she was leaving Horace and had ever since remained her other best friend and certainly her heaviest drinking companion. There were stammered and aborted salutations.

"Who," said Virginia as they hurried up the street, "was the tall gal?"

"I don't know. I've seen her."

"Mary Louise is sure to tell Beth, isn't she?"

Virginia had not answered the telephone or the doorbell during the days she had been staying with Alfred, though they had not gone to out of the way restaurants, thinking it all right to be seen together in public. He had thought, from her attitude, that he had imposed these precautions on her against her will; but now that they had actually been seen together he was gratified and relieved to see that she was disturbed on her own.

"If Mary Louise doesn't, Michael will," he said. "Husbands are her natural enemies."

"You must beat them to the punch with Beth."

For some reason he suddenly felt quite gay. "All right, Ginner, fine." He took her arm, and she looked up at him first quizzically, then laughing. "Let's forget it. Let nothing spoil the chicken cardinale and Montrachet awaiting us."

And in fact he rose with her up from the meal slowly and without reluctance into the quick of lovemaking.

Some time in the obscurity of the night he struggled out of a dream in which he was standing on the edge of a deep pool about to dive in. He found himself on the bed facing Virginia, kneeling erect with his hands pressed together and held at the level of his forehead. In his confusion he thought his posture was one of prayer. Virginia was lying flat on her back with her arms at her sides, naked, the covers down around her knees. He quit breathing. It seemed to him that he was praying beside her dead body. Then her eyes opened, she smiled, her hand rose. She touched him, and he fell.

The lovemaking into which he plunged seemed to him a vast, quick, blurred realm which he was powerless to get out of by any means whatever except an orgasm. This he labored painfully to attain, fearful that it was no longer within his strength to reach it. Finally in desperation he simulated an orgasm, and in the simulation attained the real thing. But he had forgotten about her so utterly that when, gasping out on firm land again, he heard a woman's voice call him heroic, he did not at first know who she was. Even when he recognized her, he had no notion what she was talking about. He heard her breathing alter as she fell asleep.

225

Without sobbing or wiping his eyes, he lay on his back, weeping for loss of Beth.

· 16 ·

After Virginia had gone home next morning, Alfred telephoned Chantal and asked her if she could help him get in touch with Leon.

"Yes, Professor. He's at Presley now, teaching. I'll tell him to call you when he comes back. He is rooming here now."

"Are you working, Chantal? We could certainly use you in the Law Department again. The place hasn't been the same since you left."

"You are very kind to say it. I have a job in an insurance office five hours a day. Dead dull. Oh dear, very dull. But it's nearer home and it pays better. Perhaps you will come have dinner with us? I will speak to Leon."

"I should be delighted. I understand Jean-Louis and Nancy are becoming friends."

"That is true. She's taller than he. He aspires, that one, no?"

Senator St. Clare, when Alfred phoned, told him that Justice Durkheim had bequeathed his property to Irma in the form of a trust fund to be administered by Alfred—all but the house, lot, and furniture, which went to Alfred. It was to make this provision in his will that Justice Durkheim had called St. Clare to him the day before his death. Originally he had bequeathed to Alfred his library, about $20,000 worth of common stocks, and fifty shares in an abandoned silver mine which he had bought, his first investment, in 1888.

Alfred called Irma and said that he would go by the next day and for her by no means to think of moving out of the house.

The rest of that day—it was drizzling—he spent in the apartment trying to think, but he kept stumbling over the image of Thomas mock-shooting him with cocked finger. All he could make of Thomas's will was a big practical joke, which he kept prowling around. Thomas's reasons for playing this joke remained just out of reach of Alfred's understanding, as did the consequences to himself of this joke.

He emerged from his seminar the following afternoon less discouraged than he might have been, for, though it had gone badly, as he'd expected, he had got through the full two hours, as he'd feared he might not.

Horace was waiting in the corridor—short, muscular, big-mouthed, bald, smiling Horace. Alfred blushed deeply. Having no other escape, he would have fainted if he could.

"Alfred," said Horace as they walked out to the parking lot, "I want you to know how much I appreciate the way you've taken care of Virginia. I had a wonderful trip, she had a wonderful time too, you're looking wonderful yourself."

As he kept on talking, Alfred thought bitterly how little his oldest friend knew him if he could be telling him sincerely that he was looking wonderful. A death, a wife lost, moral confusion, nervous exhaustion—how could he look wonderful? Horace was a thick-skinned, stupid, coarse-grained immoralist.

"You know that Robin Farquhar?" Horace went on. "Is she in New York?" Alfred nodded. "She had pock marks on her face. Right?" Alfred nodded again. "It's got me puzzled. Twice on Monday I saw a woman I would have sworn was her, only no pock marks. Thicker in the middle, but maybe that was the winter clothes. The main difference was no pock marks. Her face looked red in a funny way, only smooth, with a few lumps, sort of, on the cheeks. The first time, she was in a cafeteria in the Forties in Times Square, with two men. One was that kid you had living in your garden cottage last year."

"Hugh Hansson."

"And the other was Joe Thompson. This was the afternoon before his appearance on TV. Stupendous! You saw it? Well, I didn't greet them. I was not by myself. They came in and talked half an hour and left. They looked intent on something. Say, where am I taking you? To the city."

"No no. I'm going down to Chantal's for dinner."

"Great. So that same evening I was at Romeo Salta's, and in came two couples together. The men were maybe sixty. One is a corporation man from Chicago. I don't recall his name, Mac something, but I've seen him many times. His women are always well-dressed, real clothes horses. They don't talk much, they just sit, and people look at them. So there was Robin with him! Five thousand bucks' worth of dresses and furs and jewelry, and she wore it. . . . Mmm. She looked me right in the eye once, but I don't have the faintest notion whether she recognized me—not a flicker of a lid. Of course, I'm not quite positive she was the same woman. The voice was the same, the laugh was the same."

The first thing Leon said when Alfred walked in was that he was looking better than he'd looked for months.

At his wince, Chantal laughed her harsh laugh. "Professor, pay no attention. You look terrible. So." Then she really gazed into his eyes. "No, not terrible. Healthy, tuned up—toned up, what does one say? But tired, without rest."

Leon was clearly living in the apartment, but there were no other signs that they were married nor did Jean-Louis seem to be treating him in a special manner.

After dinner, while they were still at table, Alfred asked Leon how Sybil was doing at school. Leon showed no signs of embarrassment but opened warmly about Sybil and undisguisedly spoke of going out with her. Chantal spoke of her briefly but admiringly. She had come to dinner a couple of times.

"Pardon me, Professor. She is so American toothy-toothy, I was put off. But she has a soul. Yes. You must be glad of her."

Chantal ate almost nothing. She had lost weight, and she was dark around the eyes. Her mouth was somewhat more tight than usual. But her voice sounded as light and clear as ever.

· 17 ·

Late in the afternoon before Christmas, Robin and Hugh were in a westbound bus going seventy miles an hour on the northernmost highway in Montana. At that speed the bus rode smoothly, taking the corners and dips with grand sways. Robin was next to the window on the north side of the bus. She shivered and huddled away from the window.

"Oh, but it's cold."

"Cold?" said Hugh. "Here, trade seats with me. I certainly don't want you to get cold."

"I'm not cold. *It* is cold."

He reached across her and felt the side of the bus. "Don't be silly. There's lots of heat for you."

"Look at that wind. It's cold, Hugh."

"Maybe," he said tentatively, "it's because of your condition?"

She started to laugh harshly, then made the laugh good-tempered. "No no, little hubby, no no."

At the sound of a gust, they looked out.

They were on a slight rise in the prairie; the sky was fairly clear, and the sunlight was coppery: the view afforded a sense of the hugeness of the frozen plains. The wind had swept the fields more or less clear of snow. Occasionally, at fences alongside the highway, there had piled up dunes of dry snow, and the wind blew thin veils of snow dust off these dunes, in some places enough to obscure the edge of the pavement. There was little traffic; the bus did not slow down for these patches, where the road seemed to be a waving sheet.

"It was ten below," said Hugh, "at that last place we stopped at in North Dakota."

"That's twenty degrees colder than I've ever been before."

"But *you* aren't cold," he said anxiously.

"What do you mean, I'm not cold? Who knows what I am if I don't? I am too cold."

"Do you think it's bad on"—he made a little pointing gesture at her belly and raised his eyebrows—"that one?"

"It will be if this keeps up much longer. Three days on a bus. God."

"We'll be there in forty-three minutes by my watch."

"How will we recognize it?"

"No way," he said. "It's just like all the other wheat towns. Anyway, this is only the fourth time I've ever been here and the first time in the winter. Oh."

At the interjection she glanced at him; he looked as though he wanted to cry. She wrinkled her nose impatiently. "Well, it's your idea we're here, honey chile, not mine. Crockett, Montana, is the last place on earth I was ever expecting to spend Christmas."

"It's not my idea at all. You know that. It's my father's doing. Anyway, we're not coming here because it's Christmas. I'm bringing you to meet him. You knew that before we"—he giggled—"got married. That was the bargain."

"I'm keeping my part of the bargain. Your father. You're always saying how you can't stand him."

Hugh gave a little sniff and shrug. "I'm not going for his sake. I'm going because I believe in keeping a promise, and I promised him I would bring my bride home. That was the last time I was visiting him, two summers ago. I thought it was a big joke. *Me* with a *bride*! But it meant a lot to him, and after all he is my father, even if he is a lout. So."

"Didn't he give you a car that time?"

Hugh nodded with closed eyes. "A Chevvy convertible. Naturally I sold it the day I got to Berkeley. I ask you, which is worth having, two season tickets to the opera for two years in a row, in the Grand Tier, with a dinner for Robin and me at Amelio's before and a hot chocolate or an apéritif afterwards, or a necking teenager's dream of callow bliss? I just ask you."

She patted his hand. "Why did you look so unhappy a minute ago when you said this was the first time you've visited your father in the wintertime?"

"It wasn't because it's winter. It was just that I suddenly thought, We're almost there. And we won't have time to visit Mama. Will we? And you would love her, I know you would. She would be so happy to meet you. We've come all this way—we couldn't work it in?"

Robin shook her head slowly.

"It would kill Mama to learn we came here and didn't go to Ottumwa. I'm all she's got, you know. Oh, I loathe and detest Crockett. That's why they broke up, when my father inherited this ranch from his uncle. Mama wouldn't leave her home and all her friends for this godforsaken place. She wouldn't even come look at it. So he picked up this Eileen in some saloon or other and married her, and now they have two children. And the way they live . . . You won't believe your eyes. I wouldn't be surprised if they have a juke box in the living room by now. That the kind of values they have. If you cut off their supply of rotgut whisky they'd die of spiritual malnutrition—no *spirits*. Isn't that an awful pun? It's Mama's. She calls Eileen his concubine. Don't you adore 'concubine'? The delicious ways it resonates in the antrums, as Francis would say. 'Darling, I do want you to meet Eileen. She's my father's *con*cubine.' "

"Now listen, Hugh, we've got to be back in New York by December thirtieth, and that's all there is to it. It was a two-way bargain, and you've got to stick with your end of it."

"I told you I keep my promises," he snapped.

"We've got to be all ready for the Institute New Year's Eve, and I've got to rest up for the occasion. So we can't even dream of going to see your mother."

"I *said* we couldn't. You don't have to talk to me as though I were a mental defective. I have a BFA, which is an F more than you have." He stuck his tongue out at her.

She decided to play his game. "Well, a BA in theater arts is a lot more scholarly than a BFA in decorative arts. I know more than you do."

"Oh, is that so."

"Yes, that is so."

"Hmph."

They played angry, not looking at one another or saying anything.

"Is that Crockett?" Robin said after a while.

Hugh looked at his watch. "It must be."

"It looks sort of like a cathedral town in the Middle Ages."

"Oh, Rob-bin! Honestly!"

"You know, with the houses all huddled around the big tall building."

"It's nothing but a grain elevator."

"You see, it elevates!"

"Rob-bin, please. That's just the way grain is stored. Still, maybe you've got *some*thing. After all, that's what my father raises grain for, to store it in elevators."

"What do you mean, he raises grain to store it? People eat wheat, and so do cows."

"Ha," he said, sniffing, "so much for a BA. Your economics are perfectly disgraceful. The government pays my father a great deal of

230

money *not* to raise as much wheat as he can, and what he does raise is mostly just stored in government vaults or bins or whatever they are, because there's too much already."

"You're kidding me. Aren't you kidding?"

He shook his head with a superior, sincere expression on his face.

The highway entered the town alongside the railroad tracks. There were gas stations, auto repair sheds, cafés, and small frame houses. The streets were wide and laid out at right angles. The houses were set well apart. There were a few shrubs and bare trees.

"It just occurred to me," said Hugh in an awe-stricken voice. "My father is as useless as I am."

"Oh, Hugh." Robin impulsively reached for his hand. But when he snatched it away she saw her impulse had been mistaken. He looked proud.

· 18 ·

When they stepped into the drugstore which served as the Crockett bus station, there were shrieks from two children on stools at the soda fountain. They darted among the adults in the store, crying "Hugh!" He dropped the suitcases, bent over a little, and caught the children in his arms.

"Doris, sweetie. Why, you have some lipstick on. Don't you?" She was eight; she giggled and hid her face in his side. "Hi, Davy, you're taller by inches!"

"Pow!" cried Davy, who was six. He hit Hugh as hard as he could on the front of the thigh. "How's that for a sock? Pow!"

A barrel-bodied man shorter than Hugh had made his way to them and was standing to one side, legs straddled, hands in his mackinaw.

"Hi," said Hugh, looking up from the children but not letting go of them. "Robin, this is my father."

His big hands stirred out of the pockets and flopped against his legs. He grinned and ducked his head.

Robin was conscious that they were being watched, indifferently by a few of those milling around in the store, but attentively by the three clerks. The woman at the soda fountain was leaning on the counter, to the neglect of her customers, one of whom was rattling his cup in his saucer. She was studying Robin without a smile.

"H'lo," said Mr. Hansson.

Normally Robin would have said hello in return and have waited for him to make the next move. But with those watchful eyes on her she could not let the scene peter off as it was threatening to do.

"Karl!" she said with a throaty enthusiasm which, she had discov-

231

ered, worked on men in public places. She threw her arms around his shoulders, gave him a loud kiss on the corner of his mouth, pressed her cheek against his gravelly cheek, and leaned back. He was hugging her by then, and smiling and blinking his eyes. "It's so wonderful to meet you after all the wonderful things Hugh has told me about you."

"Yuh," he said, "I don't know. Well, kids, let's bundle up. Eileen swore," he said to Hugh, "she'd have supper waiting for us when we got home. It's Christmas Eve, so we have ham and sweet potatoes."

When he saw the car, Hugh crowed and flapped his arms. "A Cadillac! Look, a powder-blue Cadillac!"

"Yuh," said Karl. "You like it? We go back and forth so much, and it's comfortable."

Robin joined Hugh in singing its praises.

They went south for fifteen miles down a darkening road. Whatever else was happening or being said, Davy sat in the corner of the back seat next to Robin, watching her almost without blinking, occasionally sucking his thumb, not speaking, playing his fingers in the fur collar of her coat.

The house was in a swale a hundred yards off the county road, with two medium-sized fir trees posted in front and several larger black-limbed deciduous trees around the sides and back. It was a two-story white frame house with a screened front porch. Thirty steps from the back door was a corrugated-iron Quonset barn. The floodlight in the back yard was on.

Karl drove toward the door of the barn. The children jumped out of the car and opened the barn door for the car.

"Well, kids," he said as he was closing the trunk of the car, "take the newlyweds on in. I'll do the chores up quick so I won't have to come back out after supper."

"The real reason," Hugh whispered to Robin as they lagged behind the running children, "he wanted to stay out here was so he wouldn't have to see Eileen gush. Of course she doesn't always gush. It depends on how much she's had to drink. But when she does . . ."

They entered directly the warm, large, odorous kitchen.

The kitchen was divided into two parts. The smaller, outer part consisted of an enclosed pantry and a wood-floored entrance, which was given over to boots, coats, a shovel, a shotgun, a double-edged ax, and a bucket. The larger, inner part, the kitchen proper, was linoleum-floored, brightly lit, and painted white. All the big objects in it had white enamel surfaces—table, sink and drainboard, stove, refrigerator, cupboard doors, dishwashing machine. There were two spoons and a fork on the drainboard next to the stove and a white enamel double-boiler on the stove; except for these there was no visible sign of cooking.

Eileen stood at the edge of the linoleum, greeting them in a nasal contralto voice, her hands smoothing her spotless apron. She was a short, stocky woman of thirty who had never been in a city larger than Denver but who studied a women's fashion magazine. Her features were rather plain; by applying pancake make-up she had blurred them out fairly effectually; she had then drawn and painted in lines which would have been becoming if they had been identical with the outlines of her natural features; the effect she achieved was of a pretty girl surprised. However, without really altering this expression, the flesh beneath the immobilized prettiness would from time to time make quick small motions, anxious cues to which the code was lost. She was put out to recognize Robin's coat as vicuña, though it was in fact a merino imitation of vicuña. But she was gratified to think that Robin's coiffure was a disheveled version of her own perfectly lacquered one. She was quite right in thinking that Robin's hair was disheveled not because of the long bus ride but because Robin wanted it that way; what Eileen did not know, because she had not believed it when she had read it in her magazine, was that to wear this coiffure disheveled was itself of the highest mode.

When Robin reached both hands out to her, Eileen began saying, even as she squeezed Robin's hands harder than necessary, that Robin must give her the beautiful coat to hang in the closet under the stairs with a sheet around it. They had a contest of protestations about how carefully to treat the coat. Eileen won.

Robin hoped to lie down, perhaps even to nap, before supper, but she had no sooner washed, changed, and stretched out on the bed than Hugh came to their room to fetch her. Karl was stomping in the vestibule of the kitchen, and as soon as he had washed his hands they would sit down to eat, though it was not five-thirty.

Eileen apologized for the meal, saying that on Christmas Eve they took it easy, saving up for Christmas dinner. In the center of the dining table was a huge platter on which was a baked ham with pineapple rings all over it; around it on the platter were roasted Irish potatoes, candied sweet potatoes, and carrots. There were soft white biscuits and a mound of home-made butter, a pitcher of milk for the children and a pot of coffee for the adults, and a lemon chiffon pie. Everything was on the table at once. Davy said the blessing without pausing between words, in a tiny voice, palms pressed together; he did not pretend just to peek but openly stared at Robin beside him. "Our Father, we thank thee for this our food. Bless it to the good of our bodies for Jesus' sake. Amen." Hugh and Robin poured milk and coffee, Karl carved, and Eileen dished up. Doris was full of questions about the bus ride.

As they were finishing the pie, Eileen spoke in an artificial voice. "The children must go to bed very, very early tonight. Santa Claus visits us early because we are so far north and he has so many children he has to visit before morning."

Doris made a tragic face at her and cried, "You promised!" She looked at Robin, who did not know what was up. Then she slid out of her chair and hid her face against her mother's shoulder. "Mommy, please."

They whispered.

Doris came around to Robin and with one forefinger stroked the cuff of Robin's pale yellow blouse. "Tell about the wedding."

"You mean, where it was?"

"All about it."

Robin glanced at Eileen. She was smiling fixedly; the right side of her lower lip twitched a little.

"It was in a church."

"A big church?" said Doris.

"Pretty big, but not nearly the biggest one in New York. Not too big. Just the right size." Robin glanced at Hugh, who was frowning. "But we'd better wait till tomorrow, when there's lots of time."

"Just tell me one thing so I can dream about that one thing all night. A good thing."

"Well, it's called the Little Church around the Corner, and actors get married there. It smells good. And that's absolutely all for tonight. You see, Hugh and I weren't able to bring you any gorgeous Christmas presents, because there wasn't room on the bus for what we wanted to bring. So I'll save the wedding till tomorrow for another present. How's that?"

"That's the best Christmas present I ever got," said Doris.

"No, it isn't," said Davy. "*She* is the best present. She's my Christmas present. She's my big sister. Pow!" He hit Robin on the leg, then laid his head on her lap, sucking his thumb.

Robin was in bed when Hugh came into their room.

"Don't look," he said, and she turned toward the wall.

When he got in the bed he lay stiff on his back clear over at the edge away from her.

"I hope," he said "you can get us out of that lie you got us into. That perfectly unnecessary lie about the wedding."

"It was just to give her something glamorous to think about. Will it do her any harm, now honestly, Hugh?"

234

"Don't call on me to corroborate your story. I just may tell the awful truth."

"Oh, now, it wasn't so awful. Really it wasn't."

"A justice of the peace in *Yon*kers! Not awful!"

"I'm sorry."

"You should be."

"I like your family."

"You would."

"At least they're a real family."

"They act like one because they're scared of you, that's all. And *you* started the whisky flowing! Why, Robin, why, oh, why did you say anything? They might have gone to bed sober for once."

"I meant it. I needed a drink to relax me. And they were looking so pathetic, I knew they wanted one. You know, Eileen sort of opened up a little, putting the presents under the Christmas tree."

"After six jiggers of Bourbon, you mean."

"Oh, Hughie," she said, turning over. "You shouldn't be so hard on her. She keeps a clean house and tends her children."

"Compulsive neatness. Obsessive, maybe. And another thing, you let Eileen believe your coat was vicuña. Where in the world would you get a vicuña? That's not a bad question, you know, even for merino. Where, indeed?"

"I opened the door one afternoon, and there was a delivery boy from Bonwit Teller. Seriously, though, Eileen likes a little romance too, and so I gave her some."

"But it's a lie."

"Look, these little fibs aren't going to cause you any trouble. We won't be married forever. I'll probably never see your folks again. Meanwhile, let them dream."

"I just don't like it a bit."

"What do you think dreams are made of, the truth?"

He flounced over with his back to her.

· 19 ·

They ate breakfast quickly so as to get to the presents right away.

"My," said Robin, though she had said it the night before, "it's such a beautiful tree. And so fragrant." She broke off a needle and sniffed it. "How far did you have to go to get it, Karl?"

"Yuh, well, I used to, but they aren't so good around here. The Indians sell this one in town. Anyway, I save money. I don't travel all over looking. I just pay five dollars, and they do the work."

"Now everybody take a seat," said Eileen. "And Hugh is going to pass out the presents, aren't you, Hugh? Davy and Doris, you be sure to put the wrapping paper between you in one pile, and don't throw away the cards, so we'll know who to send thanks to Santa for for everything. There are so many packages," she said proudly to Robin, "because my brother and sister have four each. Of course we have to send twice as many to them. But we can afford it, so we don't mind."

Davy got a wind-up furry bear that walked, several pieces of candy, nuts, an orange, a little phonograph (Doris had one of her own), three records of patriotic songs sung to sweet orchestral accompaniments, a gun-belt with an imitation six-shooter in the holster, a real BB rifle, a large comic book of Bible stories, knick-knack toys, and clothing. Doris got a baby doll that had genuine human hair and that wet its pants, candy, nuts, an orange, six records, of which one was of bird songs, a birdwatcher's guide to the north-western United States, a card game called "Bible Folks," toys, and clothes, including a two-piece bathing suit.

Two hours after the presents were opened, Karl had gone out to do the chores, Eileen and Robin were in the kitchen preparing the dinner, the two children were staying, as they had been admonished, in the living room with "all those wonderful presents," and Hugh was wandering back and forth from the kitchen to the living room.

Once Hugh found Davy lying on his back with his head propped on the toy bear, sucking his thumb.

"It's too much for you, isn't it, little brother?"

"Pow!" said Davy, whipping out his pistol. "I'm Davy Crockett. I really am. Pow! Pow! Crockett is my middle name."

A bit later Hugh missed Doris in the living room and found her in her bedroom, lying on her back and staring out the window at the gray sky. He squatted beside her. There were traces of tears at the corners of her eyes.

"What's the matter, honey? Is Christmas too much for you?"

She did not respond.

"Did you get too many things all at once? I know how you feel."

"Robin promised she was going to tell about the wedding," Doris said reflectively. "So I asked her to, and Mommy said I had to stay here in my room or she wouldn't let me listen when she told. I wish Mommy was the Christ child, because then when she grew up they'd crucify her."

"Doris! You mustn't say things like that."

"I don't, I just think them. It's all right to say them to you, you're my brother."

"How do you know I won't tattle?"

"Grown-ups don't tattle. That's kid stuff."

"You've got me there, kiddo."

When Karl put down his coffee cup, wiped his mouth with the back of his fist, and pushed his chair back from the table, Doris immediately leaped out of the ambush she had been watching from.

"Now! Tell all about the wedding, Robin. Please? Dinner is over."

"Shush," said Eileen.

"Yuh," said Karl. "That was good food."

"The plum pudding was divine," said Robin to Eileen. "I must be sure to ask you for the recipe."

"Ha," said Karl.

"It's canned," said Eileen brightly, looking very surprised.

"They make them better in cans than she does," said Karl.

"Isn't it wonderful what packaging has done for the American housewife?" said Robin.

"It gives me so much free time for myself," Eileen said.

"For bridge, you mean," said Karl. "Yak yak yak."

"Well, our bridge is no worse than your poker."

"Money," said Karl. "Money talks, we don't talk so much. Money."

Hugh was bending forward, a look of pain on his face, his arms intertwining about themselves. Davy was trying to imitate him, but his arms were short and plump; he was chewing his tongue and frowning seriously.

"You promised," said Doris to Robin with tragic anguish. Then she turned to her mother with tears in her eyes. "And I was good all day long."

"When you go to bed," said Robin "I'll tell you all about it for a bedtime story. I'm sure your Daddy and Mommy don't want to hear it."

Eileen's eyes batted, and her mouth made a silent O.

"Well," said Karl with a laugh that sounded as though he were clearing his throat, "that's a good idea."

"That's an awful idea," said Eileen, turning on him, relieved to have someone she could scold. "How do you know what I want? Maybe I'd like to hear it too. And what about your own son? You don't even want to hear about his wedding?"

"Okay, okay, I was just kidding," Karl grumbled. "Go ahead."

"Honey," said Robin to Doris, "just as soon as I've helped your mother do the dishes and I've had time to let this wonderful, wonderful meal settle the least little bit, I'll tell you all about it. Okay?"

"Okay," said Doris sullenly.

"When I grow up," said Davy, who was leaning against Robin and looking up into her eyes, "I'm going to marry you."

"That's the nicest thing anybody ever said to me," she whispered and kissed the top of his head.

237

She spent two hours describing the wedding. Karl left for the livestock after five or ten minutes, but he did not stay out quite long enough and got caught for the last quarter of an hour of the story. Robin filled the church with every religious prop—organ music, incense, gloom, paintings of Madonna and child, sprays of bright flowers, stained-glass windows, robed clergymen, candles—and described every costume in detail.

"That's very pretty," said Eileen. "You know my sister lives near Calgary and her husband teaches hymn-singing to missionaries. They're Baptists."

"We're Lutherans," said Karl.

"*If* you're anything," said Hugh. "Myself, I'm nothing."

"We go every Easter at least," said Eileen. "Now it's time to go to bed, kids."

As she was shepherding them out, Karl said, "They go to Sunday school when the weather's good enough. It's nice for children."

As soon as Eileen came back from putting them to bed, Karl cracked out a quart of Bourbon. By ten o'clock he was pouring the last round from it.

"Squeeze it, Daddy," Eileen said.

"Good to the last drop," said Robin.

"You bet," said Karl, cough-laughing. "Right, Hugh? Good to the last drop."

Eileen and he roared. She was sitting sidewise at the table, her chin on the heel of her hand. Her mouth opened only part way, yet she made a braying noise.

Suddenly Karl slapped the table with the flat of his hand. Hugh and Robin jumped, but Eileen did no more than blink her eyes.

"The way to raise children," Karl announced, "is to let them do what they want till the time comes. Then"—he slapped the table hard again and jerked his thumb in the direction of the children's rooms—"they know it. Right, Hugh? They know who's boss. My children know who wears the pants in this family." Eileen blinked, and her cheeks worked. She sniffed. "Right, wife? Doris knows. David knows. I know how to handle children." Suddenly he glared at Robin's belly, then leaned forward and poked it hard enough to make her wince back in pain. "You aren't prennant already? Are you? Me and Eileen talked about it. I'm a plain man. I like to get to the point."

"Karl," Robin said, "what a thought for you to have."

"What a stomach you have," said Eileen, sneering prettily.

"You mean," said Hugh in a high voice, "you accuse her of going to have a baby already, and we've just been married two weeks?"

238

"Yuh, her and you," said Karl. "I wasn't going to shout about it. It's all right with me. I'm wondering, though."

"Karl," said Robin earnestly, "I promise you that you aren't going to become a grandfather for a long time. Years and years. I need to reduce, that's all. And I'm going to. I take after my mother. All her excess weight goes to her middle too. It just runs in the family. Next time you see me I'll be twenty pounds lighter. I promise."

She made the mouth she had learned with Leon's help. Karl watched her as he would have watched a cow chewing the cud, and he cleaned his teeth with his tongue.

She looked significantly at Hugh, who frowned in annoyance.

"Maybe we should tell them?" she said to him. He shrugged and began plucking at his cuff. "We have a secret." Neither Karl nor Eileen smiled responsively. "We were secretly married in Mexico last June. We didn't tell anybody because we wanted to make sure we could make a go of it first, and anyway we didn't know how New York would work out. Sort of a *married* trial marriage."

Eileen winked at Hugh, who look pained.

"Look!" Eileen cried. "My eye is stuck! I winked and it won't come up!"

Karl and she brayed a time or two. Then Robin mimicked her stuck-eye routine with such exaggeration that they started up again, and she joined them. Hugh smiled too, the expression on his face almost free of disdain.

Robin went up to their room before Hugh and was in bed in a minute. She lay there, crying. As she had told about the wedding, she had seen in Doris's eyes that Doris was seeing her as a fairy godmother conjuring pictures of loveliness, and she wept to think of herself at eight, eager to be filled with magical dreams by a fairy godmother, but having to make do with illustrated books from the public library.

"Robin?" said Hugh, holding the door not quite closed. "Robin? Are you crying?"

"Yes. I'll quit."

He closed the door cautiously but did not let go of the knob. "I'm sorry to have to disturb you."

"I'll stop." She wished she could tell him what she was really crying about, but she knew he would prefer a women's magazine story instead, a warm, simple version of a cool, complex truth. "Your family is so nice. This is the most wonderful Christmas I ever had. With my pretend husband's real family."

"They're putting on a good show for you, I'll say that much for them."

"Don't be unkind," Robin said ruefully.

"Since when do happy families drink like fish?"

"I didn't say they are blissfully happy. I said they were real."

"So, pretend wife, is that something to cry about?"

"For me it is."

He crept in under the covers and lay apart from her.

"Not for you?" she said. "Not even a little bit something to cry about?"

"No," he snapped.

"I was thinking how wicked it would be to break them up. It would just be unforgivable for anybody to do that."

"Don't worry. With *my* father, nobody's outside help is needed. He's an expert at breaking up his family by himself, let me tell you."

"I don't believe he's doing that now. Homewrecking . . ." Her voice faded away. "I couldn't help thinking of the Royces. When Joe told us they were separated, I can't say how awful I felt."

"I suppose you felt guilty?" he said flippantly.

"Yes," she answered softly.

"Of what?"

"Homewrecking, possibly."

"You broke *them* up? My dear Robin, what are you thinking of? You're mad."

"Maybe. I hope so."

"What on earth are you hinting at?"

"I seduced Alfred."

"Oh, for heaven's sake. The only time I ever saw you with him was at that party in June, and he hardly paid you any attention at all, or you him either."

"It wasn't at that party."

"Even if you did seduce—which I don't believe for an instant, he seduced you, more like it, or no, you just did it with him, *if* you did it at all, which I doubt. Anyway, what difference would it make? What did you do, give Mrs. Royce a blow-by-blow of the whole thing like a real bitch?"

"No. I don't even know whether she found out or not."

"You're fantastic, Robin."

"I hope so. Sometimes a person is at a turning point, and one little push at the critical moment can send them one way or the other. If I actually broke up that wonderful marriage, I'll never forgive myself."

"Here, now, let me hold your hand. If I can't hold Robin's hand, I'll hold Robin's hand. How's that?"

"Thanks," she said, entering his game. "Here's Robin's hand. You're sweet, Hugh. When you try."

"In the name of the husband, the wife, and the goly host amen, I

Hugh thy husband do thee Robin my wife forgive, world without end, okay?"

"Okay. But what is it you're forgiving me for?"

"Everything. I absolve thee, my child, that thou art shriven. How about forgiveness for all those lies you told tonight about the wedding?"

"Lies! Oh. Wasn't it a pretty story?"

"There were lots of pretty details, I'll say that for it. How come you know so much about it?"

"I've gone to half a dozen weddings at the Little Church around the Corner."

"Really? You have that many friends in New York already?"

"They weren't friends. I just went and sat in back, out of the way."

"At least it wasn't entirely a fabrication."

"And you notice I didn't have us married in the main church but just in the wedding chapel."

"You're incorrigible," he said indulgently.

"You know, darling, as an actress I have to immerse myself in life in all its richness, as Francis always says, and where do things get any more immersed than at a wedding where actors are really doing it?"

They lay without speaking.

"Thank you for letting me hold your hand, Robin."

"What are you trying to do, make me start crying again? *Thank* me!"

"I mean it," he said. "I like holding hands with you, for some reason. And you did a good job evading that 'prennancy' bit of my father's."

"Do you think they believed me?"

"Of course not. But you kept them from saying so. It's a lucky thing you're naturally long-bodied and thick-waisted."

"You know, Hughie, maybe we're a well-matched couple. Long-bodied and thick-waisted indeed."

"I don't think I want to know what you mean by saying 'maybe we're well-matched.' "

He turned over onto his side with his back to her and did not answer when she said she was sorry.

· 20 ·

"Tell us again," said Doris to Robin.

"But I told you already," said Robin.

"I don't understand the parts you left out," said Doris. "That made it hard to understand the parts you left in."

241

"Again! Again!" cried Davy, butting Robin's thigh with his head.

"It would be nice," said Eileen, her nose giving a wiggle. "If Doris doesn't understand, she'll just plague me with questions for weeks to come."

"Well," said Robin, "I'll go pack first. Don't you think that's a good idea?"

"No!" cried the children.

"We have to get up at three o'clock in the morning," said Robin, "so your daddy can drive us to Crockett to catch the bus. So we have to rest up."

"Supper will be ready in half an hour," said Eileen reproachfully.

"Here comes Daddy and Hugh," said Davie. "Hugh will tell us."

"I know what," said Robin. "Why don't we go into the living room and I'll lie down on the couch and tell you there."

"Good," said Eileen, smiling and batting her eyes. "That'll get them out of my hair for a while."

Robin established the children on the floor beside the couch. Hugh joined them presently, stretching out on the floor, willowy and graceful beside the chunky children. They squirmed away because he had brought the cold in on his clothes.

"It's not like ordinary acting," said Robin. "It's very special. You see, it's a brand-new place that hasn't even opened yet. It opens New Year's Eve, and we're the star performers. It's called the Institute of Modern Living, and I bet you'll be seeing pictures about it before long in magazines."

"On TV too?" Doris asked.

"No. It's very dignified."

"Oh."

"You see, they want us to display the American way of life so everybody will know just what it's like."

"What kind of a way of life have we got here?" said Karl from the doorway. "We're already American."

"Oh," cried Robin, looking back up at him, "you have just about the most wonderful house and family in the whole world, that's all."

"What's wrong with the way we live?" he said.

"Nobody said there was anything wrong with it," she said earnestly.

"All right. So what's all this loco stuff you're giving us?"

"It's like hair," Robin said to Doris, patting the child's curls. "It's just fine the way Mother Nature made it, but it's even better with a permanent wave sometimes. Not better—different. And variety is the spice of life, they say."

"Yuh," said Karl and went away.

"You know," said Hugh to the children, "we're going to show everybody who comes to look at us—thousands and thousands of people—the modern American way to live."

"We'll even have electric toothbrushes," said Robin.

"What else?" said Doris, shivering and throwing out a fat leg.

Till Eileen called them to table, Robin and Hugh regaled the children with an account of the gadgets and novel kinds of furniture that were to be exhibited in the Institute of Modern Living, where Robin and Hugh were to function both as demonstrators of the interior of an up-to-the-minute house or apartment and as a living exhibit, the Young Marrieds.

When Davy came to kiss Robin good night and good-by, he hugged her neck so hard it hurt. She saw that his lower lip was trembling, but she also saw him glance fearfully at Karl. She led him off to his bedroom, promising to tuck him in and sing him a song. There he gave her a long hard-pressing kiss on the cheek and grasped the middle finger of her left hand, refusing to relinquish it. She made a game of his going to sleep, and when he was fully pretending to be asleep she kissed his eyes and slipped out into the hallway.

As she was tiptoeing down toward the living room she heard fierce whispers from Doris's room and stopped by the closed door to listen.

"But I can't. I just can't." This was Doris.

"Yes, you can." This was Eileen. "The rest of us do, so you can. You have to."

"I bet you didn't *really*."

"Yes, I did. It wasn't so bad. It just looks funny. It doesn't feel different—not too different."

"Mommy, please."

"How do you know what it feels like? You said yourself you never even kissed her once."

"So why do I have to begin now?"

"She's your sister-in-law."

"I know it," said Doris. "It's just her face."

"Well, nobody likes it, honey. There's something wrong with the color, that's all. It doesn't feel so different when you touch it."

"I can *tell* it does. It feels awful. To me, it feels awful. Honest to goodness, cross my heart and hope to die. Do I *have* to?"

"Why don't you do this? Hug her nicely and then kiss her on the side of her neck. That way, nothing but your hair will touch her face, and your hair won't mind."

"That's a good idea, Mommy. She's nice. It's just her face. It's got lumps. That's a good idea. You're a nice Mommy."

Robin tiptoed on.

She was merry with Karl and Hugh till Eileen and Doris appeared. When Doris came to say good night, Robin was scrupulous about not letting her face touch Doris's skin, and she saw Doris and Eileen exchange a gratified glance as the child was going out of the room to bed.

At seven o'clock she thanked Eileen warmly for all the warmth and friendliness and said playfully to Karl that she'd be seeing him at three in the morning. In ten minutes she was packed and in bed. For a while she lay flat, listening to the window rattle in the steady wind from the north. Then she turned on her side, facing away from the door, and wept as softly as she could.

"Are you crying again?" Hugh said when he got into bed.

"I'm sorry. I'm trying to stop."

"What is it this time?" he asked warily.

She was convinced that the truth would turn him from her too; yet she could think of nothing better to tell him. She spoke slowly and lightly, in the bitter anticipation of being the cause of her own abandonment.

"I overheard Doris begging her mother not to make her kiss me, because I am so ugly."

"You're being fantastic again."

"She said my face looked lumpy, and Eileen told her there was something wrong with me because of my color."

"Oh, Robin." Hugh found her hand and squeezed it. "What do you care what louts like them think?"

"I had my face scraped twice."

"I know, darling, and the operation was a great success."

"My face looks like a slab of liver with holes in it for the nose and eyes and mouth. It is lumpy on the jaws. I have lumpy jaws," she said with a little would-be laugh that emerged as a hiccup.

"Your face doesn't look nearly as bad as it did with the pockmarks."

"I'm hideous. Children run from me."

"Davy dotes on you. He adores you."

"He's a man."

"Robin. Really."

"I know it's silly to say so, but he is. Do you think I ought to be scraped again?"

"It's too late. The show is about to go on, darling."

"Anyway, I used up all my money on the first two. The doctor said three times would be best."

"You could sell the coat, you know," he said, "if it was really a question of a third one, which it isn't at all."

"I should have done it right away when I got the coat. I don't know what was wrong with me that I didn't."

"Well, it does keep you warm for one thing, and you didn't have a winter coat."

"You know who gave it to me?"

"You mustn't tell me anything you don't want to, Robbie."

"You do know, don't you?"

"I've always presumed it was 'elderly dealer in electronic supplies,' as Joe called him."

"It's the only thing he gave me, except that he took me to dinners and shows, of course."

"Ah."

"I went out with him twice, and he gave the coat to me, and then I went out with him three more times. That's all. Nobody else either."

"Well, well."

"I'm never going to do it again," she whispered. "It's not worth it. Nothing could be."

"How much did the coat cost?"

"I don't know."

"It's probably worth hundreds and hundreds and hundreds of dollars."

"He gave me two dresses and some shoes too. The worst thing was that I believed he gave things to me because he liked me. That's why I took them, because I let myself believe that. I still can't get it out of my head that he really did like me. He said he was grateful and I really believed he was. You see what a crazy mixed-up kid I am. I can't even tell when—"

"Sh," Hugh said and put two fingers gently over her lips, then caressed her face a moment.

She held his hand tightly and began crying again.

The truth was that, had the dealer not been grateful, he would have given her a fifty-dollar bill at the end of the first evening and never sought her out again, since she was not beautiful like most of the women he took with him to display in public places. But she had been merry, if forced-merry, and she was far more intelligent than the women he was used to. Consciously she had accepted his invitation, which had been arranged by another manikin in the firm where they were both employed to display clothes to out-of-town buyers, in order to "get a peek at high life"; unconsciously she had been profoundly disturbed at the thought that she was prostituting herself. As a result, she was so wild and intense that she not only delighted the old man with her company but aroused him from the impotence with which he had been afflicted for some time and then gave him the passive gratification which was all his timorous lust dared. In his gratitude he had given her presents instead of money and had even taken her to a banquet at the Waldorf-Astoria (an honor which, in ignorance and boredom, she had mistaken for drudgery). The fifth evening he spent with her, accustomed to her role, she had turned her intense emotions inward; her gaiety was hollow, and her eyes appealed; his impotence returned, and he had decided not to make her his mistress after all.

While she was crying, Hugh crooned the "Whiffenpoof Song" to her, mostly without words, sometimes singing *sotto voce,* "We're poor little lambs that have gone astray, Baa baa baa."

After a while she wiped her eyes with the sleeve of her nightgown and thanked him for putting up with her so patiently.

"Robbie, would you mind terribly if I touched your abdomen? I'd like to know what it feels like."

"Mind! I'd love to be touched."

"You know, both my hands?"

He tentatively laid one hand on the top side of her belly and slid the other under the lower side.

"Squeeze a little," she said. "It won't hurt me."

"It feels so strange."

"Not *so* strange, huh? After all, there's a woolly nightgown between your hands and me."

"It would be even stranger—nude?" He shivered once. "Do you ever feel it move inside you?"

"I felt him just a few minutes ago. Sort of a flip."

"Do you suppose I could feel it too?"

"I don't know. Not through the cloth maybe."

"Well, the next time it happens you let me feel. You guide my hands underneath your nightgown so I won't touch anything wrong."

She laughed.

"That wasn't a very nice laugh, Robin."

"It was just irony, one of life's little ironies. I never expected to guide a man's hands away from those places because he asked me to."

"That's not a very nice aspersion to cast on me at a time like this. You may not know it, but I'm enjoying this. I might even go so far as to touch your breasts."

"You're sweet, Hugh. You musn't do anything you don't want to do."

For the first time he moved his hands from the spot where they had come to rest on her belly; they moved about a quarter of an inch up toward her chest.

"Just think, here I am with a son I'm not the father of and whom I shall never see. You are going to put him out for adoption, aren't you? For sure?"

246

"Yes. I'll never see him."

"Why don't you keep him for the Institute? After all, one of the things they liked about you is that you're *enceinte*."

"Everybody was against it. A baby is too unreliable. He could get sick. Anyway, he would distract me from exhibiting.'"

"I still can't get it out of my head—"

"Sh. Let's go to sleep."

His hands moved another quarter of an inch. "May I?" Breathing hard, he gradually moved them up till the tips of his fingers had found her breasts; then, as though they were touching eggshells, his trembling hands closed over her breasts, skin to cloth, not flesh against flesh.

"It's so wonderful," he said. "You are so different. I would like to . . . Do you suppose I could ever . . . You are so different from Robin. That's silly, isn't it? You are such a different Robin. I'd never guess how different."

"Here," she said. "I'll turn over and then you can snuggle up against me. From the back you probably can't tell much difference. You can put your hand across me and put it wherever you want to."

"You're so thoughtful. Is this the way husbands and wives do?"

"When they go to sleep, sometimes."

"So this is what it's all about," he whispered. "I kind of love it. I even," he whispered right into her ear, as softly as he could and still be heard, "don't blame my father for leaving Mama."

"What do you mean?"

"You know—Eileen? Mama slept in the other room all the time from him." He shivered. "Don't ever tell anybody I told you."

"Don't worry."

"Especially don't ever tell me."

She undid the three buttons at the throat of her nightgown. Then she took his hand, which he was resting lightly on her belly, carefully directed it onto one of her bare breasts, then made him press her firmly. He sighed and shook. When she let go his hand he did not let go her breast; he even kissed her neck.

"Maybe it's the best thing in the whole world," he murmured.

"It can be if it's left alone."

"You mean, the way neither one of us has left it alone?"

"Sh. Let's go to sleep."

There were banging noises from downstairs, shouts from Karl, a peal of laughter from Eileen, more angry shouting from Karl. Hugh and Robin lay still, their heads raised from the pillows to listen. There was a bang of breaking glass, a squeal from Eileen, a door slamming, and silence.

Hugh jerked away from Robin. He adjusted himself in the bed with a petulant jerk and tugged at the covers.

"If you pull so hard," said Robin mildly, "all the heat will escape and our backs will get cold."

He lay stiff for a moment, then relaxed. "After all, it's not your fault we're here, is it? Poor Robin. What I've put you through. I don't know what came over me."

· 21 ·

When Joe did not answer her ring, Lizzie scribbled on the back of an old envelope, "Am at the Y—if you're interested," and slipped it under the door of his apartment. Then she directed the taxi driver to take her up to the YWCA at Fifty-first Street and Eighth Avenue. Two hours later, having telephoned his number twice without response, she was lying on the bed, staring at the grimy ceiling and wondering if she had the nerve to go out to dinner by herself in New York. Her phone rang. It was Joe in the lobby. She was there in a minute.

"Lizzie, baby, how did you ever get here?"

"Oh, Joey, where were you?"

She had resolved to hold back from him coldly. Holding hands, face to face, each looked into the other's eyes deep enough to see the worry. She fell into his open arms.

"Let's remove ourselves from these precincts of propriety," he said softly, and they strolled, not much noticing, out onto the street and down Eighth Avenue.

"Do you realize it's practically New Year's Eve already?" Lizzie said. "Where were you?"

They began their complicated accounts of change of schedules, and the three airports around New York City, and how frightening New York was when you were alone, and a plane crash the day before in which forty-four people had been killed, and the importance of messages.

"Besides," he said indignantly, stopping in the middle of the sidewalk and giving her arm a painful squeeze, "what did you mean in that note, 'if I'm interested'? Here, looky here." He pulled out the envelope and unfolded it. " 'Am at the Y—if you're interested.' What on God's green earth do you think I was doing sending you a ticket to fly all the way here, and going out to the airport to meet you and worrying myself half sick and taking taxis everywhere? What was in your mind?"

"How did I know?" she said. She reared back her head and gave him a scornful hoot but did not let go his hand. "Here you're a big-time star of television in New York City, with starlets festooned all over you probably. How could I know what you wanted? To show off, maybe. Anyway, you weren't *there* when I arrived, and I've never been here before. It's scary."

"Starlets festooned. Baby, didn't you even read my letters?"

"A girl can't tell when a man means what he says unless she hears him say it and even then she can't always be sure."

"Well, you listen to me. I wanted you to come here because I want to marry you. You hear?"

"I hear."

"You believe me?"

"I believe you." She quit glaring.

"Will you?"

"Yes."

"All right then." He quit glaring too. "This is certainly not the way I meant to do it. On Eighth Avenue." He looked around. "On this block. Good lord, there ain't an honest-to-goodness whore in sight."

"Whore!" she cried, gazing around. "Why did you say whore? Is this a red-light district?"

"There ain't no such animal any more, sweetie, but if there was, this is worse." He nodded at the café they were standing in front of. "Rough trade and switcheroos. The black leather jockstrap gang. Let's get moving."

"And just to think, yesterday morning I was in San Refugio."

"For each man sells the thing he loves," Joe declaimed and laughed his slow, complicated laugh.

"Here they do," said Lizzie, looking about with round greedy eyes. "Isn't it just awful?"

"So let's go down to the City Hall before they close shop, and sign up for a marriage license, and maybe we can even work in a Wassermann test before dinner, though it's pretty late for that."

"You really mean it?"

"I really do, and we're going to get married in church by a priest too."

"All right. I don't have a dress or anything."

"That's true, you don't, so we'll have to get you one. That's what I got you here today for, so you can take advantage of the January white sales that start day after tomorrow. Here, we're going down on the subway."

"Subway too! I'm so excited I don't know what's what. It smells funny." She balked at the top of the stairs leading under the street. "Do we have to, now?"

"It's the only way, baby."

She pulled him to one side and gazed at him coarsely. "You look different, Joe."

"Better dressed?" he said.

"No, you always were the best-dressed man I ever knew. You're just more so now."

"Well, that's mighty kind of you."

"It is not kind. It's just the simple truth."

"I'm surely flattered."

"It is too the truth! The very night after that party where I first met you I said to Sybil when we were going to bed that you were the best-dressed and the best-looking man I ever met. That didn't have a thing to do with my feelings, any more than it does now. It's just a simple fact."

"May the Lord forgive me, sweetheart, but I do believe you mean it."

"I don't see why you make fun of me."

"Each man ribs the thing he loves."

"I guess you aren't so different, but your face looks as though you were."

"You look just the same to me, and I like it."

"Are you really a TV star?"

"Brightest thing in town. See?" Without turning his eyes, he nodded to one side. She saw a half dozen young people whispering among themselves and staring at him. "I'm a three-day wonder, though, no lasting power, nothing but a nova, that's the kind of a star I am, a nova star, just call me Joe Nova. So I'm just going to snatch the dough and run. Come on, if we don't git they'll be wanting my autograph, and once they get started on that route there's no telling what they'll do."

· 22 ·

Lizzie peered out of the window of the cab as it pulled to the curb. "You mean the most fashionable party in New York isn't in a hotel or an apartment but just a big square old house."

Joe groaned. "First of all, it's not the most fashionable party. It's the one with the most celebrities, which is another matter altogether." He paid the driver and they got out. "And second of all, this is not a house, it's a mansion. And third of all, it's a mansion in the East Sixties between Madison and Park. And fourth of all, it's not really a party, though that's what it calls itself; it's really an opening night."

"Well, if I'm supposed to be impressed, I'll be impressed, but there are dozens of houses in Berkeley that are a lot better-looking than this one. And another thing, I still think it was a dirty trick for you to bring me here without any clothes."

She opened her coat and looked down at herself with evident satisfaction. She was wearing a plain white jersey dress without a belt or adornments. It was supposed to be modestly elegant. However, instead of its making her look simple and chic, she made it look like a sack full of flour, with suitable but vague dents and bulges.

"Sweetie," said Joe, in his voice an absolute lack of irony which he affected when he was being absolutely ironic, "there'll be a few formals amongst the two or three hundred ladies present tonight, but mostly there will be ordinary women wishing they looked half as good as you do. You're a duchess, babe, you're my duchess—la duchessa di San Refugio. How's that?"

"Well, let's go in," she said with a little toss of her head, squeezing his arm. "Where is everybody?"

"We're early, that's all. The invitation was for nine, and it's only nine forty-five."

"What a silly custom, being late. I think it's right to be on time. Whose house is this anyway?"

He pointed at a brass plate by the main entrance, on which was etched in square letters:

THE INSTITUTE OF MODERN LIVING
FORMERLY
THE SMARDON TOWN HOUSE

A man in tails and white gloves opened the door for them, asked their names, and introduced them to a woman in a strapless full-length gown who checked their names off on a list and directed them to a girl in maid's costume in the corner behind her. The girl took their coats, giving Joe two tags in exchange, and disappeared behind a screen.

"Oh well," Lizzie whispered as they stood adjusting themselves and looking about, "it's impressive all right. Why don't I just shut up and look? Don't let go of me, Joe." She clutched his arm.

"Here, sweetie, we'll do it this way." He intertwined fingers with her. "I like to feel your naked, naked flesh. This is not exactly the right place to do it, but this is where we're doing it."

The entrance hall contained no furniture except for three black marble benches. Up toward the ceiling there was a mobile illuminated by four amber spotlights, one in each corner. It was a system of bronze wires radiating out from a vacant center; on the wires were studded many-faceted bits of glass, winking reflections as the whole thing majestically oscillated; enclosing the whole was a lacework of white filaments so fine they were not discernible individually but gave the effect of a filmy cloud.

Strains of music drew Joe and Lizzie straight ahead across a transverse hall and into the Atrium, which was the core of the mansion. It was here that partying was to happen, although at the moment there were only four other guests in it. The Atrium was a large rectangle with broad covered walks, almost halls, on the four sides of a sunken garden laid out in symmetrical cobbled paths. However, because of the cold climate, the garden was not open like its smaller Roman original but was roofed over with glass in leaded squares, like a greenhouse. Near the main entrance was a long table with six waiters ready to serve champagne, cognac, or Scotch, and several kinds of canapés.

Joe chose among the three champagnes offered (he chose the brand he had never heard of before, though he had tasted none of them), the bottle was uncorked, and he accepted two hollow-stemmed goblets filled to the brim.

"Caviar, sir?" said a waiter down the table. "And the lady?"

He cooked two little crêpes in a copper chafing dish, then put them on gold-rimmed saucers. On each crêpe he put a dab of scraped onion, some minced hard-boiled egg, and a generous spoonful of beluga caviar, and squeezed over the little mound a few drops of juice from a half-lemon wrapped in one layer of thin white gauze.

They walked up the long side of the Atrium, opposite the side on which a ten-piece orchestra was playing waltz music. By careful promenading, all three couples were managing to avoid each other. Halfway up the corridor on their side was an alabaster bust, made by Rodin, of Phoebe Love Sturge Smardon, wife of the founder of the fortune, Abner Hancock Smardon. At the other end was another serving table identical with the first, except that instead of caviar there was Strasbourg pâté in a long small square loaf built on a dark axis of truffles. Joe accepted two more glasses of champagne and two wafers with pâté.

They went through French doors into a room labeled Playways, with a dozen mechanical toys in it, all of them operating. Three middle-aged women were watching a ten-inch tank climb over a real brick. When it had righted itself on the far side, its turret gun fired a cork. The attendant in a maroon tuxedo fetched the cork, put it back into the muzzle, and turned the tank around. The women shook themselves, nodded uneasily at Joe, who nodded genially in return, and left the room.

"Don't we have a host or anything?" Lizzie said in a low voice.

"Madison Avenue's our host, that's all."

"I mean, some*body*."

"Corporate bodies of majestic power greet you. Great big advertising and public-relations firms, like Patton, Frumenty, and Blackwell; Aware America; Henry Polski Associates; The Mutual Transmission Corporation of America (my benefactors); Wallace and Wallace; you name it, they're *it*. The guy that dreamed the whole deal up, the chairman of the board of the Institute, is St. John Collier, of Aware America. He took them over when old man Smardon bequeathed this mansion to the industry to use in any way that would advance the public interest. Here." He fished out of his jacket pocket a paper napkin he had stuffed in it for lack of a wastebasket. On the napkin was stamped the coat of arms of the Prince of Wales, including his motto: *Ich dien.* "See, that's their motto: 'I serve.' Naturally one does not overlook the fact that serving the public interest is tax-free. Get it?"

"No, I don't. Where is everybody anyhow?"

"Wandering around, looking at things. The joint'll be jumping in another hour or so. Honey, it was the most publicized Triumph of Dignity in modern times that you aren't on television right this minute. *This Hour Together* offered half a million smackeroos just to show your pretty face to the folks way out yonder. But St. John Collier refused, the board stood firm behind him, and Madison Avenue gained a cubit in stature. It said so right in *The New York Times,* so it must be true."

Except for three rooms which were used for offices, every room on both floors contained an exhibit of furniture, household appliances, tools, clothes, or whatever else could be subsumed under "Modern Living."

When they returned to the Atrium after touring the rest of the mansion, they found thirty or forty couples, a few of them near the orchestra, dancing, the rest chatting in subdued voices. Lizzie recognized two movie stars. Several people recognized Joe. People shifted about while talking, darting glances over their companions' shoulders. Lizzie thought the celebrities themselves were glancing about, while talking, more than anybody else; she was proud that Joe, when he brought her another glass of champagne, established himself in a conspicuous position but then looked at her.

"Dig that," he said, nodding to her right and looking at somebody in the sunken garden.

The only people on the cobbled paths were the heavyweight champion of the world and a woman in the handsomest dress Lizzie had ever seen. They showed every sign of inspecting the planting, and they stood in front of the dolphin fountain for some time, not looking at those who were staring at them.

Occasionally someone drifted by to chat with Joe a moment. The subject of conversation was the Institute. Lizzie smiled fixedly. Joe made a point of capping every suggestion offered. After he had got to the point of sending the Institute on tour from capital to capital throughout the world, he took Lizzie by the arm and steered her out of the Atrium.

"It's getting crowded, baby, and I've run out of gas. Let's duck outdoors for a breather."

"But it's practically freezing out and I don't even have any sleeves on my dress."

"Do you trust me?"

"Well, of course, but . . . ."

"Come on, let us seek sanctuary."

Many people had put on brightly colored paper hats, and some were blowing horns.

· 23 ·

The eight-foot doors to the garden entrance of the mansion had been brought from a Lombard monastery built in the fourteenth-century Risorgimento and abandoned in the nineteenth-century one. The wood was cracked and gray on the outside; on the inside its diapered carving was dark and unmarred. The black hinges were studded with wrought nails; the latches were enormous. One of the doors stood ajar. Joe and Lizzie glanced at them, then went through the doorway and down five steps into the garden.

"Oh!" cried Lizzie, waving her hands about in a way that was groping and exulting at once. "It's magical! What have they done? Why isn't everybody out here? It's so quiet."

"That's why it's quiet, sugarlump, because nobody's out here."

"The light! The light!"

It was slightly cooler in the garden than it had been inside—mild and still. There was an impression of unshadowing dusk; yet the flowers and flagstones and shrubs were not only clearly visible, they seemed to glow mysteriously.

"I feel like Dorothy in Oz!" cried Lizzie. She ran around a little maze of paths and back into Joe's arms. "Where are all the tall apartment houses?" She leaned back in his arms and looked up. "Oh, my goodness." She shrank against him. "Oh Joey, look. There's a rainbow at midnight, and all the buildings are gone."

High above the garden and enclosing it on every side, rising continuously from the mansion roof and the outside of the garden wall, arched a light gray plastic dome, which seemed to shed both luminous twilight and faint electronic music; across it glowed a broad pastel rainbow. At one end of the rainbow was a campsite, complete with a clear, running stream and two trees. At the other end was a flat-roofed house with horizontal lines, the facing wall of glass, brightly furnished, having various sorts of area dividers instead of internal doors.

After glancing at the campsite, they went to the house. One other couple was standing at the rail, looking at the exhibit inside.

"Hell's fire," said Joe *sotto voce,* "we're stuck for sure."

"Why? Who are they?" Lizzie whispered, halting him on the path.

"My producer and his assistant, Stan Wrigley and Penny Hardwick."

"Well, if you don't want to talk to them, why don't we just go over to the camping ground till they go away?"

"Because Stan's got radar, like a bat, that's why. He's a bat from outer space. He's a superbat."

Even while Joe was speaking, Stan glanced over his shoulder and recognized him. The two men put on a show of cordiality, but Penny and Lizzie told them to pipe down and watch the exhibit.

"Isn't this the greatest?" said Stan enthusiastically, waving at the dome and the mansion. Then with the underside of his voice he addressed Penny. "Why in Christ's name do we have to watch this act? Those second-rate robots. The flop of the show."

"The woman interests me," said Penny nervously, almost stuttering with apparent diffidence. "I'm not sure how good she is. Do you mind, darling? Just another minute or two?"

"My God!" said Lizzie under her breath, aside to Joe. "It's Hugh. Isn't it Hugh in there, Joe?"

He stroked her hand on the rail and nodded.

"The thing that intrigues me, Lizzie," said Penny, looking at Joe but obviously intending to be heard by Stan, "professionally, of course, is whether that woman is acting or not. I mean, whether she means to be acting the way she's doing. Oh, it's so awfully complicated. Let me try again. Is she that affected at home alone, or is she putting it on for the show, and if she is putting it on, is she doing it because she's such a bad actress she thinks that is the way it should be done or is she doing it because she thinks the situation is so hopeless that nothing but such stilted acting would work?"

"Oh, Jesus Christ Almighty," said Stan. "Come on, people, it's nearly midnight. There's champagne, all you want. Come on."

"You see, if it's the last—if she knows what she's up to—she's worth keeping an eye on."

"Joe!" Lizzie whispered, turning her back on Penny and clutching his arm. "Isn't that pregnant woman Robin?"

He nodded gravely and pointed to the luminous plastic tablet in front of them.

The Young Marrieds	Robin Farquhar Hansson and Hugh Hansson
Architect	Richard Verley
Interior Decorator	Madeleine McLiam
Costumes	Boothby

"Oh!" Lizzie hooted softly, with the inflection less of indignation than of dismay and fear. "They're married. I thought Hugh . . ."

Four jolly couples descended upon them, making rude remarks about the exhibit.

"Let's go," said Stan, and Penny yielded to his tug. "Coming, Joe?"

"We'll see you around," said Joe, shrugging and pointing at Lizzie.

Presently Joe and Lizzie were alone at the rail.

"This is just awful," she said three times. "You should have warned me. She used to be Leon's girl friend. What does it all mean? And her face—her face is different."

Hooters blared. Screams, laughs, toots, and "Auld Lang Syne" came from the mansion. A cruising butler filled their glasses with champagne and wished them Happy New Year. They clinked glasses and kissed.

In the kitchen area of the model house, Hugh went to the refrigerator, took out a bottle of champagne, wrapped a napkin around the neck, and took it into the dining area. Robin meanwhile took from the open-shelf cupboard two goblets with solid stems and put them on the dining table. He took quite some time to unwind the wires and pry off the cork, being careful to aim it so that it bounced off the ceiling into the kitchen area. Robin, hands folded in front of her chest, her lips in an O, moved her feet in a sort of subdued dance. He poured, then carefully placed the bottle between the candlesticks on the center mat. He held up his glass while apparently making a little toast; she tossed her head merrily; they touched glasses and drank, then embraced and kissed as though posing for a Valentine card. They moved on light feet around the bookshelves which also served as dividers; in the living area Hugh placed the bottle on the coffee table and Robin arranged the glasses symmetrically, one on each side of the bottle; then they disposed themselves in the conversation pit and made signs of animation and affection.

"Had enough, babe?" said Joe.

"I can't stand it," said Lizzie.

"Let's go, then."

"No! I want to watch."

"Suit yourself."

The prizefighter and his woman appeared beside them.

256

"Now, what are *they* doing?" said the champion in falsetto.

The woman leaned forward and read the plaque. " 'Gracious living.' That's what it says. They're in there living graciously."

"No shit?"

They pealed with laughter in inflections like Joe's, and he joined them. While they were all three laughing, their eyes met. Lizzie was tugging at him, but he paid no attention.

"You been watching them?" said the champion. "They really doing what that sign says?"

"Lord, you don't think an institute such as this would lie to you, now do you? Sure, they're doing what they say."

"Sitting in a hole in the floor like that?"

"That's gracious living, man," said Joe. "Gracious, gracious, gracious goodness me."

The laughter rose higher than before, and the two moved on toward the campsite.

"You're terrible," said Lizzie, her face anguished. "You were laughing at Robin and Hugh so loud they couldn't help but hear you, and shouting rude things. How could you?"

"Honey," he said with an almost contemptuous indulgence, "they're soundproofed in there so they can't hear a thing we say. And this big picture window all across the front is one-way glass. That's what makes them look sort of remote. And to them it's a mirror. All they see and hear is themselves. They've got kliegs on them. This is a display case, sweetheart, this hasn't got anything to do with real life. They've just got a job, that's all. Don't fret your fat so much."

"That's true, it sort of looks like a display in a natural-history museum, with us out in the dark, and a sloping window you don't see any reflections in, and stuffed animals in a three-dimensional jungle. . . . But they're real people!"

"No, they aren't, Liz. They're just acting that way. For money. It's a job. They're cheaper than robots, which is why they aren't robots."

"Joe, Joe, please, I'm all mixed up, don't joke so much."

"It's hard to tell about young marrieds these days. For instance, would you ever guess that Stan and Penny had just this fall got divorced? They go around together."

"Pooh," she said flatly. "That doesn't bother me. All that means is, they're depraved."

He shook his head. "That's my Liz."

She paid no attention to him.

Robin playfully peeked at Hugh's wrist watch, kissed him on the nose, and tripped over to the sleeping area. She disappeared offstage left and presently emerged in pajamas and robe. While Hugh went off

257

to change, she took the counterpanes off the twin beds, folded them meticulously, and laid them on the big round cream-colored pouf. As he emerged, she was just slipping into the bed with pink sheets. He got into the one with blue sheets. They blew kisses and touched fingers, she snuggled under the covers, he reached out to the lamp on the table between them and turned the switch. All the lights in the exhibit went out.

It seemed to Lizzie, staring into the abrupt blackness before her, that she had not seen anything but had been hallucinating. She buried her head on Joe's chest, trembling.

"Don't stiffen away from me, Joe. Let me lean on you."

"Lean on me? Lizzie Dizzie, what notions you do get. Aren't you my little pillar of rectitude I transported to this city at great expense for me to lean on? I'm supposed to have leaning privileges on you, girl."

"Don't laugh."

"Who's laughing?"

"You'd better be laughing."

"Yeah?"

"I mean it, Joe. They really upset me."

"Damn," he said and enfolded her. "Damn and double damn."

"That's better."

"Do you want to see them?" he asked.

"See who?"

"Robin and Hugh."

"You mean in person?" she said incredulously.

"No less. We're alone out here in the garden, and they may be coming out of that house to go home any minute now. So, if we're here we'll be seeing them—unless there's a back exit for them I don't know about."

"No! No! Let's hide."

"The best place to hide is inside in the party."

"That's too much," she said in a sort of panic. "Can't we get away from here without going through the house?"

"Not that I know of. Come on, babe, we'll go over by the camping grounds and sit on a couple of those phony stumps and turn our backs to the world."

He sat on a stump, and she sat on the ground in front of him, leaning against his legs. The noises of the party and of the city were dim enough so that the sourceless music and the purl of the stream at her feet soothed her.

After a while, stroking her hair, Joe asked her why she had been so upset at the prospect of talking to Robin and Hugh.

"It would take me back to that party on San Jacinto last June,

258

where we first met, and Leon brought Robin, and Hugh and Syb were there, and Roy Carver, and that Frenchwoman and her son, and Brewster."

"So? I had a good time at that party myself. There wasn't anything spectacular about it. It was just sort of a reliable party. You know, 'part' and 'party' are the same word ultimately, and that's what that party was, a part of the good life."

"My parents gave the party." She burst into sobs.

He soothed her while she cried. "Of course they gave it. That's why it was so nice." He talked for three or four minutes till she calmed down. "They're wonderful people, your parents, both of them. They're just having a little trouble at the moment. Things will straighten out for them."

"That's not true," she declared and blew her nose. "They're both out of their minds. Nothing will ever be the same again. And they won't even be at my wedding."

"Mine won't either."

"That's awful. I hardly even met yours."

"Do you want to invite them all?"

"Don't be silly."

"We could."

"Daddy's catting around. He's been seen with other women in restaurants, strange women, his friends' wives, floozies my age, everything."

"Who's he been seen by?" said Joe sharply.

"Friends of Mother's. Sybil told me."

"What friends?"

"Oh, one of Horace's former wives, the one Mother likes so much. Don't you believe me?"

"Sure, I believe you. I just want to know how you know. So this friend saw your father, then she told your mother, who told Sybil, who told you?"

"Oh, don't be so picky."

"It's just the lawyer in me. Was that the way it was?"

"I think she told Sybil directly, not Mother. What difference does it make? All that matters is that he's doing it. And Mother's working as hard as she can to become a drunkard. They're insane, both of them, absolutely insane. And it's all about furniture! Can you believe it? It's all about a vanload of antique furniture my mother inherited."

"Maybe the house'll catch fire and burn down, and everything in it will burn up."

"What a blessing that would be."

"I know an arsonist got out of San Quentin a couple of months back. Want me to contact him? He does a nice clean job."

"Why not? And meanwhile Daddy has inherited another house, Justice Durkheim's, and all its furniture."

"Yeah?"

"He wants to move into it but he says he can't stand to live so near our home. They're really nuts, you know. Here he is, a professor of the philosophy of law, and he's as irrational as a teenager. Didn't he ever even hear of the menopause?"

"Sh. You're working yourself up again. Take it easy, sweetheart."

"Can't we just sneak out a side door or something?"

"Don't think so. We can go through the folks at the party fast."

"Right outside there," she said in a small voice, pointing at the rainbow a few feet above them, "it's so dark. It's so terribly dark. Let's go home."

"No, it's not dark, honey. Tonight of all nights, in New York of all cities, it's all lit up."

"Let's go home quick." She was kneeling in front of him, her elbows on his knees, biting her thumbs. "I can stay with you tonight, can't I, Joe?"

"Well, now, I don't know. You'd better stay at the Y. You know, we'll be married Monday, and I think we'd better wait. I really do."

"Oh, I absolutely agree," she said. Her voice cracked. She cleared her throat and went on in her usual firm manner. "We shouldn't sleep together again until we're married. I didn't mean we should sleep together. I'll just stay on the couch in the front room. You have one, don't you? Or we could sit up if you'd rather. It's perfectly reasonable, you see, for this one night. I'm just overexcited, too many things all at once."

"Well," he said. His eyelids were heavy and drooping.

"Or, if you'd rather, we could sit up in an all-night cafeteria and talk. I just want you to be with me, that's all."

"Sure, baby." He sighed. "All right. I got the show tomorrow night, so I'd better rest up for it. We'll go to my pad and sack in."

There were shouts, calls, and toots from the steps of the mansion, and a woman ran shrieking onto the garden paths.

"Wait a minute," Joe said. "Let's lay low. Maybe they won't find us."

"Here you are rich and famous. And me. Three months ago, in Berkeley, you looked so different. Your mouth especially."

"For Christ's sake, Liz, didn't you ever hear of a time and a place?"

The woman who was running around the garden stopped near them and screamed back to the others on the steps, "No fair! No fairsies! Party poopers!"

"We're flushed out," Joe muttered. "Come on, babe, do what I do, and we'll get out of here alive."

He embraced Lizzie across the shoulders and she put her arm around his waist. They smiled and stared about, waving their champagne glasses, in a parody of drunkenness. They made their way into the mansion, and, in order to avoid the crowd in the Atrium, they went through a series of side-room exhibits to the entrance hall, one against the other when there was enough room to do so without tripping. Out on the steam-warmed sidewalk, they stood under the canopy while a doorman whistled and waved a flashlight for a taxi. They were joined by another couple, who, after a glance and a nod, stood apart with their backs half-turned. For the time it took them to get from the campsite into the taxi, they did not have to say more than "Happy New Year" or "Same to you" to anybody.

IV

When Alfred inherited Justice Durkheim's house, Woody Ravagli expected him to move into it, vacating the apartment in San Francisco. But weeks went by without a gesture from Alfred. In the second week of January it happened that Woody had to stay late in the city four nights running, the fourth time with an Englishman from UNESCO with whom he would have liked to spend a few hours talking seriously in the ease of the apartment rather than at a table in a restaurant. He discussed the problem with Kay. They agreed to give Alfred till the end of the month and then, if he still had made no move, to suggest to him that Woody needed the apartment. But how to do it without offending him?

Woody, having been rich all his life, was impatient of the hurt feelings which his whims sometimes caused others. But Kay—having come of age during the Depression, when her father, a bankrupt real-estate broker, was grateful to get a job, after two years of unemployment, as a middling official in the Bureau of Internal Revenue—was acutely aware that money had the power to magnify a rich man's irritable flick into a blow to break a poor man's bones. Whenever Woody saw the possibility of such negligence on his part, he brought the question to her to decide upon; for, though each time afresh he resented coming to her and usually resented what she advised him to do, he heeded what she told him. He recognized her delicacy in these matters. It had been this recognition which had drawn him to her in the first place.

In 1943 Woody was a member of the War Labor-Relations Commission, Western Division, and Kay was a junior economist in the white-collar section of the department in which employers' undisputed requests for raises for their employees were approved or disapproved. Despite his wealth, Woody was a public member of the WLRC. His views were so liberal that labor was delighted to have him, and the only objections to his appointment had been raised by his fellow capitalists. Kay had no difficulty doing the work of an economist, though it had been psychology she had studied in college, because her job consisted in making rather routine bureaucratic decisions which demanded no special training. In the normal course of things, he would never have become conscious of her existence and she would have thought of him only as the youngest of the twelve Commission members, the one whose beautiful and fashionably dressed wife she had two or three times seen photographs of in *The Chronicle*.

In late November, Woody's wife contracted polio and died within two days. When he returned ten days later to attend a Commission meeting, Alfred, who had attended the funeral, told him that the agency was in double mourning. Kay Sorb had been notified the day before that her husband, a lieutenant on a destroyer, had gone down with his ship in the South Pacific. On the impulse of the moment, Woody had obtained Kay's address from Alfred's secretary, Virginia, and had telephoned his private secretary in Montgomery Street to send three dozen yellow roses and a formal note of condolence to Mrs. Timothy Sorb. Then the gesture quietly faded into the back of his mind, his secretary having no occasion to mention it to him again.

At first Kay was touched by the gesture. Her grief was strong enough for a while to dissolve all impurities. But by the time she came back to work a week later, she was already beginning to resent the flowers—there were too many of them, they were too perfect— and the note of condolence, which was engraved. However, she deplored this ingratitude and brought the card to the job in order to show it to her friends—how thoughtful Mr. Ravagli had been to her, a stranger. But, once in the office, she became suspicious again. Instead of mentioning the card, she compared the signature on it with his on an official document available to her in the files. The signatures were clearly not from the same hand. He had got some underling to sign the card for him. She became furious. All the unanswerable questions surrounding her husband's death found a certain relief in her anger at Mr. Ravagli for this callousness, and for three weeks Mrs. Sorb nourished it unspoken in her breast.

The Christmas office party (the refreshments were paid for by the Commission members but bought and set up by Virginia and another secretary) took place from three to six on December 24. Kay was heard more than once to say that she would stay for the party only because it was expected of her. Some of her co-workers urged her to go home if she'd rather, it wasn't expected of her at all; but she said no, it'd look bad if she didn't stay.

She had one burning intention: to avoid Mr. Ravagli. But at the party itself, no matter where she turned, she kept finding him before long in her line of vision. He seemed to her dapper, a term she thought suitable for a race-track tout, a master of ceremonies, or a gigolo. He showed no signs of bereavement but seemed to be having a good time. He looked healthy, so why wasn't he in the Army or Navy? Because he was so rich?

For the previous three weeks Virginia had been keeping Alfred posted on Kay: quiet, withdrawn, apparently getting along fairly well. All the same, he kept an eye on her at the party. After a while he became aware of the black looks she was darting at Woody. At the time Alfred noticed this, he was well into his third highball; he plunged incautiously.

"Woody," he said as soon as the opportunity presented itself, "do you know Kay Sorb?"

"Who?"

"Kay Sorb. The slender young woman in a green dress over by the drinking fountain, facing this way, brown hair parted down the center."

Woody turned so quickly that he caught Kay's glance. She dropped her eyes and turned aside.

"The one that just turned?" he said to Alfred. "No, I don't know her. She looks as though she had a lot of free-floating hostility." Woody was in the sixth month of psychoanalysis.

"I don't know how free-floating it is," said Alfred, mostly to himself.

"Who did you say she was?"

"She's the girl whose husband was killed in the South Pacific in action last month."

"Oh, yes. I had Vera send her some roses."

"You had Vera send her some roses," Alfred echoed. "Did she ever thank you for them?"

"Not that I recall. I could ask Vera."

"Yes, you could," Alfred muttered. Then, for reasons he could have explained to no one, not even himself, he said to Woody, "I think you ought to meet Kay."

"Why?" said Woody, who had no desire to meet her.

"Manners," said Alfred, taking him by the arm.

In the blur of the noisy party, the words "ought to" and "manners" were clear in Woody's mind; coming from Alfred, they had the force they had had when his parents had used them, "manners" especially. He allowed himself to be introduced to Kay.

265

She was in a group of half a dozen women. Alfred drew her aside a couple of paces to make the introduction. During the first exchange of politeness she was stiff and Woody's graciousness was empty. Four of the women drifted off. Then, hardly knowing what she did, in low, shaking tones, Kay bitterly accused him of having condescended to her as though she were some sort of retainer and he a feudal lord. He was so puzzled that he responded only with concerned curiosity. At his cool response, tears came to her eyes and she said in a voice so low that he had to—and did—lean forward to catch her words, "You have no respect."

"For you?" he said. "You mean, I have no respect for you?"

"For me. For anyone in my position. I don't want to be deigned to by anybody."

He was not quite sure what she meant by being "deigned to," but her accusation hit home.

"Is that true? You aren't just talking, Mrs. Sorb? You must tell me what you mean."

Alfred and the two other women faded away. Woody and Kay were alone by the drinking fountain, each with a glass in hand, leaning toward each other, intent frowns on their faces.

"You got somebody to sign that note of condolence, didn't you? Was it some clerk in the florist's shop?"

"No, my secretary. I meant it—you know, as a gesture of sympathy, you know, my wife too—"

"Yowsah, massa," she said, pulling her forelock. "You's so good to me, boss."

The color drained from his face. "How did you know?"

"Know what? I get kicked in the groin, and how do I know it hurts?"

"This is my nightmare. This is the worst sort of material I've been turning up recently."

Kay was in the second year of her analysis. She understood what this jargon meant and understood also that he was being psychoanalyzed.

"So that's why you're not in the Army."

"What?" he said, stiffening.

"You're a psychological Four-F."

"As a matter of fact, no." He was on the verge of saying, one way or another, that it was none of her business why he was exempted from military service; but he became aware of his stiffness, and it seemed to him that to withdraw, cold and aloof, at this point would be to treat her with exactly the lack of respect she had just blamed him for, would be to pull rank on her. He slumped and spoke apologetically. "I could've done some sort of noncombatant duty, hospital orderly or desk clerk. I thought I could help the war effort more by seeing that my companies operated as efficiently as possible; also by doing what I could here on the Commission. The draft board okayed it. I lost a kidney in an accident as a child. I'm not supposed to drink really." He set his glass down on a chair, making a wry little movement of his mouth.

"Oh," she said. "Oh, I'm so sorry." She huddled into herself, clutching her glass to her chest with both hands. "I had no right. Why did I . . . I'm as bad as you are." Tears of another kind came to her eyes. "Worse. Much worse. I'm so, so sorry."

Woody glanced around for help. But Alfred, head high, was roaming the party, and no one nearby was looking in their direction. Woody was aware of curious stares from two of the Commission members and from a measly sharp-nosed little woman with her hennaed hair done up in spitcurls. He took Kay by the arm and led her around the partition they had been standing against, into a large murky area peopled only by desks and chairs.

A good third of the hundred and fifty people at the party were aware of this event, and Georgina Wilkins did what she could to spread the news among the rest.

In five minutes Alfred asked Virginia whether he ought to go behind the partition and see what he could do. She said they were grown up, for the love of Mike, so leave them alone. Five minutes later he was so disturbed by the buzz of gossip he kept overhearing that he told Virginia he really ought to go see if he could help out. She said that it was none of anybody else's goddamned business what they were doing. He said it was his business because he had introduced them, and anyway they had been so antagonistic when they had first met. At this point Virginia said what he did was none of her business, and she turned her back on him. In much perturbation, he went beyond the partition.

They were in profile against the street window. Kay was standing, leaning against a desk, bent over toward Woody, gesturing in a way that from a distance struck Alfred as attacking, but from nearer by, where he could hear the inflections of her voice, appeared urgently explanatory. Woody was leaning back in a leather-upholstered executive chair in a way that from a distance appeared to Alfred as judging and dispassionate but from nearer by, where he could see the angle of Woody's head and the fingers plucking at his brow, struck Alfred as anxious.

They turned to him gratefully.

"I'll just slip out the back way," said Woody.

"I'm afraid," said Alfred, "the only way out is down the main corridor."

"I'll go with you," said Kay to Alfred. "I really have to leave anyhow."

"I'll give you a ride home," said Woody to her.

"Who said I was going home?" She bridled. When he slumped, she was instantly remorseful. "I'm not going in your direction."

"How do you know what direction I'm going in?" All three laughed at his parody of her bristly manner.

"Okay, I'm going to San Mateo to spend Christmas Eve with Tim's family."

"Good, I'm going to Tiburon to spend the evening with Elsa's family. I'll give you a ride."

"But Tiburon's in the other direction!"

"And I'm not due till seven-thirty." He leaned across Alfred and spoke gravely. "I have done you an injury, Mrs. Sorb. Please allow me, personally, to make this little reparation."

Alfred escorted them down the corridor through the party, and everybody watched. Their colors rose. Woody, who was used to running flash-bulb gantlets much crueler than this one, strapped on his armor of smiling graciousness; it amused him to know that people would suppose he was in process of seducing Kay, and just because nothing was further from his mind he enjoyed lending himself to the appearance. Kay was aware that he was acting dapper again, but now she understood why and did not blame him; also, it made her feel good to know that people were thinking she had been making time with him behind the partition, when she had really been doing just the opposite, bawling him out. Alfred wore a somewhat glazed smile, for he was not in the least sure what it was that he had started with these two; he knew it was not what it appeared to be to all those others, and he even doubted that it was what it appeared to be to Kay and Woody themselves, whatever that might be; he hoped it would turn out all right, but he had a sneaking fear that Virginia had been right and he'd had no business starting anything in the first place. When Alfred said good-by to them at the main door, Woody offered Kay his arm, and she took it.

A year and a half later, after Woody had completed his analysis, they were married. Alfred gave the bride away.

· 2 ·

A week before the deadline they had set for Alfred, Woody and Kay laid their plans: a dinner party for him and two or three others on January 31. They hoped not to be the ones to raise the subject of

268

his vacating the apartment in Pacific Heights; they would give him every opportunity to raise it first.

They agreed to invite Sybil. They debated for some time whether to ask Nancy too, their favorite of the Royce girls and the one whom their children adored, but decided against it because the thirty-first was a school night. Woody wanted to invite his brother Ted, the bacteriologist, a personable young man, timid with women, who spent almost his whole life in his laboratory. Kay would have agreed, normally, but her feelings about the University scientists on the Hill, in the soulless new buildings just beyond the trees south of their beautiful new house, were getting out of hand. She had not told Woody about these feelings yet, for he might want her to go back into analysis and exorcise them as superstitions. She had a physical aversion to any man whom she knew to be devoting his life to bombs or plague germs or such things. Certainly it was superstitious for her to get nervous about eating at the same table with a shy, polite young man of good family like Ted, to dread shaking hands with him so acutely that she devised a dozen subterfuges to avoid the slightest touch from a Hill scientist when introduced to one or when one came to her door as a guest. But though she was ashamed of her superstitiousness, she did not want to let go of it, for, if she let go of that, she might also let go of her conviction that what those men were doing was wicked and that each one of them was wicked to be doing it. She was confused enough already; she did not want to be confused about their wickedness too. She believed in democracy and freedom and social progress, and if there was one institution in the world she detested more than another it was the Catholic Church; yet it was the reactionary Popes who denounced total warfare as wicked and her liberal Presidents, one after another, who heaped honors on the men on the Hill for devising ways to make war utterly and unredeemably monstrous; that was all the confusion she could bear, and more than she could bear. So she evaded Woody's suggestion by saying that Ted and Sybil had already met at a party (she was not absolutely sure they had, but she seemed to remember giving a party to which both had been invited) and had not hit it off very well (which, though a fabrication on her part, was plausible, since so far as they knew the only women Ted got along with were safely married mothers of families). She proposed Jim Sorb instead. Woody, who did not like Jim much, shrugged irritably and told her to go ahead and invite him if she really wanted to, he could stand him if she could.

Jim Sorb was the younger brother of Kay's first husband, Tim. After her remarriage she more or less lost touch with the Sorbs, certainly with Jim, who was in junior high school at the time. He was fourth of the five children of the preacher of a small poor church in San Mateo, the Friends in Christ. The Christian Friends, as they were known, had broken away from the Society of Friends in the late nineteenth century and had returned to baptism and Communion; the theological occasion of the schism, the divinity of Christ which the Christian Friends asserted, had more or less faded away, and the practical question of tithing had taken its place. There were not two dozen congregations of the sect remaining in the country; one by one, down the decades, they had merged with local congregations of the Christian, Unitarian, Congregational, or Evangelical and Reformed Churches. Dr. Sorb's congregation, when Kay had last known, was thinking about merging with the San Mateo Christians, who were doctrinally as vague and morally as lean as the Christian Friends. Dr. Sorb was supporting himself for the most part by running a filling station on El Camino Real, in which the whole family worked. He would lose nothing by the merger; indeed, as the assistant minister in the Christian Church he might hope for a call to some new congregation, say in one of the housing developments that were springing up all over California, where he would no longer have to pump gas and grease cars for a livelihood. There were only thirty-six members of his church left, most of them old, none of them well-to-do. Tithing was the problem. The Christians shared the Christian Friends' abhorrence of alcohol; they too at Communion served unfermented grapejuice in tiny paper cups passed on a tray among the worshipers. But the Christians, a good many of whom were prosperous, thought that church donations should be a matter of individual conscience, whereas the impecunious Christian Friends continued to insist on tithing as a condition of membership. Many of the Christians believed in tithing too, but only after income tax, not before; the Christian Friends were firm that it must come before. Kay remembered Dr. and Mrs. Sorb as a fair, pale-eyed, thin couple, in whose presence she always felt she was somehow falling short, though in fact they had never spoken to her reproachfully. It was just that she kept interpreting their silences, which were often loaded, as reproaches.

One afternoon the preceding September, as she was sunbathing on the lanai, she heard a motorcycle come down their dead-end street and stop, then a ring at the locked gate of the fence protecting them from sightseers. Normally she would not have bothered to answer; the maid was downtown shopping. But wondering who would be coming to their door on a motorcycle intrigued her enough to make her put on her sunsuit and answer the bell. There stood a tall, stooped young man wearing jeans and a half-buttoned flowered Hawaiian shirt and with goggles up on his white crash helmet. She did not recognize him.

"Yes?"

"I'm Jim Sorb." His nose had been broken, he was cockeyed, his complexion was at once weathered and sallow.

"Jim Sorb?" said Kay.

"I remember you all right."

"For heaven's sake! Come on in."

He stepped inside the gate and went no farther. He stood looking at the house suspiciously.

"Well, come on in the house and have some lemonade."

"No, thanks. I just stopped by to say hello. I told Mom I would. I'm going to Cal."

He went another twenty steps, then, coming upon a supine bronze torso writhing as though in agony, he balked.

"Does your father still have his service station?"

Jim shrugged. "They merged with the Christians a couple of years ago, but Pa still can't make a living preaching. I went to San Jose State."

"Oh really? What did you major in?"

"Poli Sci. So now I'm in law school over here in Berkeley."

"You're interested in law?"

"Not particularly."

"Then why . . . ?"

"Money. I'm going to find the kind of law I can make the most money in. All I've got's brains of a certain kind. Then I'm going into that kind of law. I want money."

"Well," she said.

"I hear there's good money in anti-trust cases," he said, watching her closely.

Suit had recently been filed against a company of Woody's which manufactured helicopters, a competitor charging it with monopolistic practices. The case had not progressed beyond the financial pages yet, and Woody, considering it so fraudulent that it would never come to court, had not mentioned it to Kay.

"Fine," she said to Jim. "Good luck."

Jim mistook her ignorance for cool poise and was abashed. "I got to go. Nice seeing you. I'll tell Mom."

His truculence reminded her of Tim, though Tim had been handsome and his manners had been far more polished.

In November she chanced to run into Jim in a stationery store where he was clerking. He blushed to see her and was so polite that, on the impulse, she invited him to come have pot luck with them for supper that evening.

He arrived in a suit, his shoes polished, his hair slicked down, and was so stiff and stuffy that Woody pled urgent business immediately after the meal and abandoned Kay to him. She got him to help her put the children to bed. He asked if there was a guitar in the house; she dug one out of a closet, left over from a folksong enthusiasm of Woody's years before. Jim tuned it as well as he could and sang hillbilly songs to Tod and Cathy so loud and vigorously that they wailed when Kay insisted that they had to go to bed. After they were tucked in, still sobbing, Jim, in direct disobedience of her orders, crooned a lullaby which left the children soothed and which was so gentle and tender that it melted her anger at him.

The real reason she wanted to invite Jim along with Alfred and Sybil was that she hoped he might get them all to singing. Left to themselves, Woody and Alfred usually got all wound up in an abstract philosophical argument on some such subject as whether there could be an ethical commandment valid universally, regardless of cultural differences and local customs. She could neither follow these discussions nor, because their subjects were so exalted and important, cease trying to follow them. She had come to dread the feeling of inadequacy which such an evening left her with, shame at being shallow, confused, and not very bright. Such an emotion could swamp her for days at a time because she had no other sure conviction of qualities in herself to make up for these shortcomings. She did the cooking and took care of the children, but otherwise was without occupation.

· 3 ·

As Sybil was walking down Churchill Court, Jim rode past her on his motorcycle. Without looking at her as she approached, he parked and locked the machine, took off his helmet, held it dubiously by the strap for a moment, then slipped it over a handlebar, combed his hair assiduously, straightened his tie, and stepped toward the gate.

"Hi," said Sybil. "I wouldn't leave that helmet there if I were you."

"Why not?"

"Prowlers. Anyway, the fog may come in and drizzle off the eucalyptus leaves. You're Jim Sorb."

"That's right." He took the helmet off the handlebar and stood swinging it by one finger.

"I'm Sybil Royce. Didn't Kay tell you I was coming?"

"She didn't say anybody else was coming."

"That's a nice bike you've got."

"A BMW."

She made a little gesture which indicated she was annoyed that he could suppose he had to mention the make of the bike to her.

272

Embarrassed, he said, "Best Motorcycle in the World, that's what BMW stands for to me."

She looked at him and blinked once. "How many CCs?"

"Twenty-four liters."

"I don't mean . . . You don't know much about bikes, do you?"

"Not in my head I don't. I just know this one bike. Pa took her in on a bad debt. I know all about her in my muscles, and I own her."

Sybil opened her large handbag and took out a pair of high-heeled shoes, then leaned against the motorcycle and changed from the loafers she was wearing into the heels. As she did this, and he stood by watching her, there was a pleased half-secret little smile on her lips.

She was not just pleased with what he had said or with herself for having successfully provoked him to behave crudely; had she given the matter any thought, she would have considered that this was just the uncouth way he behaved around girls; mostly she was pleased at being engaged with him so soon in a game of "who's on top?" which she saw as having spontaneously started up between them. He, however, saw her smile as evidence of a pretty girl's complacency in having won a tiny victory in the war between the sexes, her victory being to manipulate him into asserting himself; he liked to feel that she, the cunning if smug female, had maneuvered him into the stance of the dominating if bumbling male. Her game was not his war exactly, but their competitions had this in common: neither she nor he could keep on winning regularly except as the other kept on winning too.

· 4 ·

Kay was in the kitchen, preparing lettuce for salad, and the children were eating their supper at the kitchen table. At sight of Jim they yelled, "Sing us songs! Sing us songs!"

"Later," he said, trying to frown but also smiling lopsidedly. "After you're all finished eating."

"Where's Woody?" said Sybil to Kay. "And Daddy?"

"They should be here by now. Woody went down to get him half an hour ago."

"Maybe Daddy's bus is late," said Sybil. "He'll be coming over in the rush hour."

Seated at the kitchen table, pretending to help the children hurry through their meal, Jim was paying attention to Sybil. She was obviously not intimidated by the Ravaglis or their house. He wanted to glean any hints she dropped.

273

"Oh," said Kay, "your father came over earlier. He's in his new house. I mean, the Durkheim house—you know."

"He's there today too!" said Sybil. "Good lord, maybe he's going to move in."

"Do you really think so?" said Kay eagerly.

"Well, tomorrow night he's giving a dinner party there which I have to play hostess at."

"But do you really think he might move in?" said Kay.

When Sybil did not say anything to this, Jim glanced at her. She shrugged at him—"how tiresome it all is." Then she made a little comic gesture of light-dawning.

"I get it. Woody wants his apartment back."

"Well, you know," said Kay, "it's not that he absolutely needs it, of course. We just thought . . ."

"What a slob Daddy is," said Sybil, her expression cheerful but her voice almost sneering. "Everybody says what a grand fellow he is—which he is—but they don't know what a slob he is too. Okay, do you want me to get after him tonight?"

"Oh, Sybil," said Kay, slumping against the sinkboard, taking a deep sigh with fluttering eyelids, and giving her head a little ecstatic nod.

"Jesus Christ," said Sybil in a light, hard voice, "you don't have to dissolve."

Kay turned back to the lettuce and Jim to the children.

"Consider it as good as done," said Sybil, walking out. "I'm going to the john."

Jim pointed at Tod's plate. "Finish them," he said with such authority that Tod, although he was full and did not much like carrots anyway, finished them off in two mouthfuls.

When Jim, in Cathy's room with the two children, was in the middle of his first song, he heard Woody and Alfred come in. Not knowing the right thing to do at that point, he kept on singing. Toward the end of the second song, a long ballad full of snow-white steeds and red roses, Sybil appeared at the doorway. Cathy frantically waved her away; she just winked and stayed.

"Come on, Jim," Sybil said when he finished. "Kay said you got to come join the party."

To the children's complaints, he said, "You heard what your mother said."

"I heard what *she* said," Tod cried. "*She's* not my mother."

"I bet," said Cathy slyly, "she just made that up. She wants you for herself. She wants to be your girl friend, I bet."

274

Jim looked sour, and Sybil said, "Pss."

Tod and Cathy clapped and crowed. "Lovers! Lovers!" Then they chanted, "Look at the lovers go-o! Look at the lovers go-o!"

Woody and Alfred were chatting by the glass west wall of the living room, looking out at the cities and water and bridges spread before them in the evening, lights rendered a soft amber color by smog.

Sybil introduced Jim to her father, and as soon as Woody had begun making conversation politely, she excused herself. "I've got to go to the kitchen and help Kay hatch."

"Hatch?" said Woody. "Are we having chicks for dinner?"

"Hatch a plot, silly. What do you think women are always up to?"

Woody and Alfred laughed indulgently, as they were supposed to, but Jim just gazed at her with an intense and saturnine expression.

"Joke, friend," she said flippantly as she left.

He still did not smile. He took it for granted that she, being a woman, was going to do some sort of plotting with Kay in the kitchen —as in fact she was—so he saw no irony and little humor in her would-be joke. Normally he would have given it a routine smile at least, but now as she left he watched her with the eyes of an abandoned one. He was intimidated by the room, by the house, by the view; his dislike for Woody was largely a mask for fear of him; to have Professor Royce added unexpectedly to these hazards was more than Jim could manage. He did not hear when Woody asked him how things were going, and he gulped his highball down in two tilts of the glass.

Presently the children's cries became importunate enough so that Sybil could plausibly return from the kitchen and in Kay's name lead Jim off to sing them another song or two.

In the hall on the way to Cathy's room he whispered, "Why didn't you tell me your father was Professor Royce?"

"Why should I? He won't eat you."

"But I'm going to be taking his seminar this semester if he'll let me in."

"I thought you were all hot for money. That's what Kay said you said." Sybil studied him when she said this; he responded with a heavier glower and a tiny, abrupt nod. "So why are you taking Daddy's course? There's no dough in the philosophy of law."

"Eh, as long as I'm in law school I might as well take a crack at the best they have to offer."

"You mean Daddy?"

"No comparison."

"It's funny you should think he's the best," she said vaguely as she opened the door to Cathy's room, "because he certainly doesn't go in much for making money."

Breathing hard, he whispered something which the children's squeals drowned and which she did not try to catch.

When she came out of the room again, Kay was watching from the kitchen door across the entrance hall. They waved conspiratorially. As soon as Sybil was back in the front room, Kay yodeled for Woody to come consult with her in the kitchen, and Sybil was alone with Alfred.

"You're looking good, darling," he said.

"Healthy as a pig." She shrugged. "Aren't I always?"

"I didn't say well, I said good. Maybe it's the way you've got your hair fixed—piled up like that."

"That was Leon's idea."

"Ah. It makes your face look thinner. Very becoming."

"I am thinner, by five pounds."

"Aha."

She looked triumphant; he, worried.

"Is everything," she said, "ready for the dinner tomorrow?"

"I've just spent a couple of hours with Irma. She seems pleased to oversee the preparations. If you'll just show up at five-thirty, everything will be ready. You can come, can't you?"

"I warn you, I don't know how to make small talk with a Senator's wife."

"You're not supposed to talk to Faith. You're supposed to listen to her talk. Ask her if she's ever been to the White House, and you won't have to say another thing but oh and ah."

"Irma could do that better than I can."

"Oh no, no, dear heaven, Syb, what a thought. Irma's been to the White House herself, she'd want to compare notes."

They laughed.

"Daddy, have you made up your mind about what you're going to do with the house?"

"No," he said warily.

"Why don't you try living in it a while and see how you like it?"

"I've been through all this with Liz."

"I'm not Liz. I'm Sybil. Remember?"

"Don't be rude. I supposed that you'd have talked it over with her."

"I have not," said Sybil, though she had.

"Ah? The awkwardness, that's all. It would be so close to your mother."

"You could try, at least."

"I could try."

"When are you going to say the word to Mother?"

"Say the word? What word?"

"I don't know what word. All I know is she's sitting there waiting for you to say it."

"What makes you think so?"

"Hunch," she said.

"Ah."

"This I have talked over with Liz. And Nance too. It's not just my hunch."

"You can hardly know what your words . . ." His voice trailed off.

"The reason I asked what you had in mind about the Durkheim house," she said, scratching lightly with the end of a fingernail at a loose thread on his jacket, "was that I gathered from a hint Kay let drop that Woody has been wanting to use his apartment again."

"You're sure?" he said sharply.

She nodded coolly.

"Oh dear, oh dear." He stirred where he sat half-reclining on the couch. It was less that he stirred than that he seemed to try to stir, as though his body were suddenly much too large for him so that it would not do as he wished and all his will was being consumed in getting it to stir just a little. "Thank you, my dear. Perhaps I've been remiss. I have always felt so much at ease with Woody. I guess I've been going along assuming that he'd just tell me when he needed the place back. I haven't really been thinking about the matter, that's the truth. You're positive about this?"

"Yes."

"We'll see."

"Daddy?" She scratched at a brown spot on the back of his hand. "Yes?"

"Will you do me a favor?"

"If I can."

"You know the way you said you've sort of been waiting, without thinking about it, for Woody to make the first move? Well, you ask him about it this evening, or find out somehow, whether I'm right, and if I am, the favor is this: just ask yourself whether, maybe, without exactly thinking about it either, maybe you've been waiting for Mother to move first."

"Oh dear heaven," he said. "Dear God in heaven. You're worse than Lizzie, when you put your mind to it."

His mouth gulped twice like a fish's, and his belly quaked once. But mostly his large body lay inert, his eyelids slowly opening and closing.

The bong of a Javanese temple gong and Woody genial in the entranceway summoned them to table.

· 5 ·

Sybil looked forward to a pleasant dinner. Kay was a good cook, Woody provided plenty of excellent wine, Woody and Alfred enjoyed each other's company, Jim showed every sign of being willing to play a quiet role, Sybil herself was so pleased with her little chat with her father that she had none but benign feelings for everyone. She foresaw no hazard but Kay's chronic anxiety about her cooking.

Kay used only the best ingredients in her dishes, and she was careful to follow a recipe as exactly as she could. But on principle she would not allow Viola, her maid, to help her prepare a dinner, or even to help serve unless it was large and formal, so that she was commonly frantic by the time the meal was served. She was especially anxious when any of the Royces came to dinner; Beth was her ideal as a cook, free-wheeling, irregular, imaginative, almost always successful. It was true that Beth got anybody to help her who could do it without getting in her way, but for Kay every dish was a kind of test of herself. Beth could be badly upset when a dish failed, but mostly she was concerned to get a meal on the table suitable to the occasion —whether a family supper or a formal dinner with five wines—and though she did not enjoy her own dinners as she would have enjoyed them had she not cooked them herself, neither did she feel tested and found wanting every time the meat was tough or the melon overripe.

The first course was a bowl of clear soup with chopped chives floating in it.

After three spoonfuls, Sybil said, "Kay, it's the greatest." It really was very good.

"You like it?" said Kay.

"Subtle," said Alfred, "complex, delicious." He held up his glass of white wine in a tiny salutation. "I toast the maker of soups."

"It's excellent, honey," said Woody. "I think it was a good idea to have chives in it instead of croutons. It's already rich enough. Perhaps they'd have been too much."

Kay's face crumpled. "The chives were a last-minute remedy. I hope they're all right. I forgot and left the croutons in the oven too long. They were all burned."

Sybil and Alfred reassured her.

"Well, you know," Jim burst out, setting his spoon into his empty bowl with a clatter, "it just looked like broth to me, but it isn't. In fact it doesn't even taste like any soup I ever had before."

"Oh," said Kay gratefully, "would you like some more?"

"Sure, if there's enough."

Jim passed his bowl to her, and she ladled from the tureen.

Woody went around refilling the wineglasses from a tall, tapering bottle. When he got to Jim he said, "You don't like this white? Would you prefer some rosé?"

Jim blushed and took up his wide-rimmed, full glass by the stem. He dipped his head down toward the trembling glass, meeting it half-way, and drank deeply. He put it down, and sat back in his chair, not raising his head. "Well, you don't need to all sit there watching me. I never did it before."

"Really," said Woody, refilling his glass. "It's one of the better Livermore chardonnays. I hoped you'd like it."

Jim's shirt collar became a size too large for his neck.

"The reason we watched you," said Sybil quietly, "was because you were blushing so hard."

"This is the first time I ever drank wine," Jim said in a louder voice than necessary. "I've had beer and whisky. In my folks' church they're against wine. They have grapejuice. I'm against all that religious stuff, myself, but I knew a Jew in San Jose that has the same trouble with bacon. Jews, you know," he said, looking around, "can't eat pork. He was raised that way, and even now when he's broken away from all those superstitions and stuff, he still can't eat bacon too easily. The first time he did, he threw up. I'm the same with wine. Oh," he said, sitting up straight and looking at Kay, "don't worry, I don't mean I'm going to throw up, I just mean it's hard for me to do it." He drained the glass. "It's good wine," he said, but the last gulp was not quite down when he spoke, and he choked a little.

It was for Kay or Woody to retrieve the situation. Kay said nothing but began clearing the bowls off the table. Sybil looked to Woody and saw by his eyes that he was restraining the impulse to say something unkind. For a moment she was relieved by Woody's restraint, but then he turned deliberately to Alfred, and what he said troubled her.

"Alfred, what's the inside story on the Evans trial?"

The District Attorney had completed the presentation of the State's case that afternoon; the defense was to open the next morning.

She thought it almost as unkind of Woody to abandon Jim in his exposed position as it would have been to make fun of him. Her sympathy for Jim was so strong that she started to move her foot over and press it against his; but she held back, thinking the gesture might only embarrass him further.

279

For a while she paid no attention to the interchange between Alfred and Woody. She became aware of a pained smile on her father's face. "Really, I have no notion where she fits in all this," he was saying.

"Oh, come on now, Alfred, quit holding out on us." Woody spoke in a conventionally heavy-handed way, with a businessman jocoseness which Sybil knew her father detested. "You knew Carver, you know Kalish very well, you've known her for years."

"Not years. One year in the departmental office. I've seen her two or three times in the past eight months, never to talk to personally."

"Mmhm." Woody blinked slowly.

This was a quality Sybil had not noticed in Woody before. She watched him with new eyes. All he needed was a cigar to puff and wrap his forefinger around in order to complete the stereotype she saw in him now. Then Kay put the hot platter in front of him, and he dropped that role; he became lighter, deft, not thick with power. Still, as he carved the rack of lamb and served the plates, his graceful expertness with the carving tools struck Sybil as a deceptive veneer over a no less expert zeal for throwing people off balance. The dinner party was a wreck at this point, each person concentrating on his own elegant place setting. She took a bite of lamb and one of asparagus and told Kay they were excellent—as she knew they were—but she was not really tasting the food. She thought back and saw Woody as having caused Kay's discomfiture over the croutons, Jim's over the wine, and Alfred's over the trial. Briefly she indulged herself in hating him. But presently she decided to beat him at his own game and to pull the party together.

"I got a letter from Lizzie today," she said.

"Oh, really?" Kay said. "Where from?"

"London still. Lizzie," she said to Jim, "is my sister. She and her husband, Joe, are on their honeymoon."

Jim grunted.

"Is it a good letter, Syb?" asked Alfred.

"Oh, pages and pages. I brought it for you in my purse."

"Thanks, darling."

"I must say," said Woody, "England in the winter seems a peculiar place to go for a honeymoon."

"Where did you go on your honeymoon?" asked Sybil, who knew the answer to the question. The Ravaglis had not gone on a honeymoon because immediately after the wedding Kay had come down with diarrhea for three days.

"Well," said Woody, glancing at Kay, who looked mortified, "when we were married the war was not quite over, so we really didn't have one. I was still on the Commission."

"As a matter of fact," said Alfred, "I can't think offhand of anybody I know who didn't have a peculiar honeymoon one way or another, or else none at all. Beth and I, for example—when we got married we were so broke we could never in this world have had anything like a honeymoon, if it hadn't been for my Uncle Harold. He and Aunt Caroline lived on a sheep ranch up in Mendocino above Stowes Landing—right near your place now, Woody. In fact they may overlap some."

"Really?" cried Kay. "You knew our ranch already? You never mentioned it when you were up this summer."

"No, well, the old house is still standing, but the barn has collapsed."

"Why didn't you tell us?" Kay said. "It's so romantic to think you had your honeymoon right on our ranch."

"No, it's north of your place. Anyway, it wasn't a bit romantic. Uncle Harold and Aunt Caroline had five children and barely enough to live on, but they let us sleep in the barn on the straw. We didn't have anybody to leave Lizzie with; my mother was ailing already, and Beth's mother of course lived in Texas. So we borrowed three sleeping bags and camped out in the barn for a week. We used to go down to the ocean every day. There were lots of tidepools. That's what I remember most, the tidepools. I've never been able to look at them since, not really. What Lizzie liked was the mice. When we went to bed we could hear them rustling in the straw. Beth was nervous about them at first, and she made a big thing of how sweet and friendly they were, so Lizzie wouldn't be scared. Well, of course Lizzie just loved them. The only thing she had against them was that she could never touch them. Once in a while we'd see some, but we couldn't catch one for her to play with. Not that we'd have caught one if we could have —they might bite—but we made a show of trying, for Lizzie's sake."

"What did Mother like best?" asked Sybil.

"Beth? Let me see. The grave markers. There was an old graveyard up the road a ways, and she'd go there and poke around. There used to be a lot of redwood-logging up along the coast back in the latter part of the last century, and a lot more people lived there then than now. They hauled the lumber out in boats. As a matter of fact, we went up to Stowes Landing by boat ourselves. I don't know whether the coastal highway was built then or not."

"Is the graveyard still there?" said Kay eagerly.

"I guess. I didn't really look this summer. The markers were mostly wood, and Beth loved the looks of the weathered wood, that fine gray that comes with the ocean air, and all the grain standing out. She got good at making out the inscriptions. They were almost weathered away. She'd hold the boards up—they were all loose in the ground—so the light would rake across at just the right angle to cast the shadows of the letters and numbers. The one I remember she thought was saddest had four names on the one marker, a young mother, maybe twenty-two or twenty-three, and three children, five and three and one or something like that. 'Died of smallpox.' That's all it said at the bottom. 'Died of smallpox.'"

"How very sad," said Kay.

"There was vaccination in those days," said Woody. "If they'd been vaccinated the way they should've been, they could be alive today, the children at least."

Jim, who had just taken a bite of meat, flourished his fork in a complicated warlike fashion over his head, glaring at Woody, then subsided.

This time Sybil did not restrain her sympathetic impulse and moved her foot over to press Jim's. However, she hit his ankle with the side of her shoe and then pressed a bit harder than she had intended. He gave her a glance signifying, "Was I *that* silly?" Then he looked back at his plate, crestfallen.

Sybil continued. "So Lizzie says that for a while they went to plays and operas and ballets and museums, the way you'd expect. But then pretty soon, she says, Joe began taking them to churches all the time."

"Lizzie going to church?" said Kay.

Alfred laughed like a horse.

"Joe's religious," said Sybil. "He's high Episcopalian, so naturally he's excited to be in England. It's the real McCoy. In fact, I gather that's why they're in England anyway. But it isn't so much that they go to church services. Joe doesn't make her do that, though she does go with him sometimes, she says. The real thing is, he's on this church-sightseeing kick. She says he has books on the cathedrals and little old parish churches around, and they go from one to another all the time and talk about apses and naves and Norman and Romanesque and God knows what-all. This is Lizzie, you understand—my very own anthropological sister Elizabeth Ann."

"I am sure," said Woody, "that she is doing a fine job of observing the Anglican rituals of the natives."

Beneath her father's renewed whinny, Sybil said to Woody aside, "You make that sound funny, but there's more truth to it than you think."

He leaned toward her and spoke softly. "I'm sure. I made a joke because Alfred was looking rather uncomfortable."

She could not tell for sure, because of Alfred's laughing, whether Woody was right or not. By her father's eyes she guessed that maybe Woody was right, and she felt bad. But then, remembering that she was engaged with Woody in a sort of social judo, she thought to herself, It's none of his business if I do make my own father uncomfortable, and she decided to play her trump.

"Wait a minute," she said. "I want to read from one paragraph of her letter."

She fetched her purse from the table by the front door, and as she leafed through the letter, looking for the passage she wanted to read, she told Jim how Joe had come by all his money, over $50,000 after taxes. It occurred to her that what she was going to read would be a thrust not only at Woody, who was rich, but also one at Jim, who wanted to be rich. But so much the worse for Jim: if he was going to have low ambitions, he would have to take the consequences.

"She's been talking about their expenses. They don't do extravagant things, really, and theater seats are cheap and they don't go to night clubs, yet she says the money just melts away somehow. It's London. Incidentally, the letterhead of this paper she wrote on she copped from a hotel they stayed at in some little town outside of London. Don't you just love the name—The Roaring Boy Inn, Seven, the Rumsey Twittens?" Kay joined her in her giggle. "Do you know what a Twittens is? It's a narrow little alley, sort of. 'I'm the Roaring Boy from Seven, the Rumsey Twittens.' Well, anyway, here's what she says about all that money Joe won.

" 'We don't ever talk about all that money of Joe's. Of ours, really, but I don't even feel like it's part mine. Maybe Joe doesn't feel like it's his either, somehow. It was too much too fast. I can't tell you how disorienting it has been. Discombobulating would be Joe's expression for it, but whatever you call it, it's terrible. Money may not be the root of *all* evil but it certainly is the root of *civilized* evil. I kid you not. Take syphilis, for example. You wouldn't think a social disease like that has anything to do with money, but it does. How do you think it spreads, mostly? Money love, that's how. Two or three times Joe has said something about a shower of gold. "I was raped by a shower of gold," he says. Isn't there some Greek legend about a girl who was seduced by a shower of gold? Some stupid god. God, some of those legends were stupid. Anyway, I don't really know what he means by it. I told him, the two or three chances I got, that he did *some*thing for the prize money, it wasn't *just* luck. He answered all those hard questions they asked him. It certainly was a crazy way to get a lot of money, but at least it was a game with rules and he played it. It wasn't roulette, a spin of the wheel. Then he just laughs—you know that funny (funny-peculiar) way he can laugh—and says, "No, it wasn't roulette, it was rape." ' I'll skip a few sentences. Here. 'But when he won't trust me about this money thing, that truly hurts. That isn't background stuff. That's *us*. It keeps us apart. Money is the worst thing in our culture and since Western culture is spreading throughout the world it is probably the worst thing in the whole world. Except for the atom bomb—*maybe*. It gets in the way of love, and the more of it the worse. The more money, the less love. That's silly, of course. It's not the money as such, it's thinking about it, and when you get showered with it all of a sudden (there! I'm using that stupid legend too!) how can you help thinking about it? Sometimes I can't help thinking that money is the main thing people in our cultural milieu think about. The first thing you see in all those old churches we keep going to is a plea for money to maintain the physical plant—the "fabric" is what they call it. They have some funny ways to say things in England and every little place has a name. God and money—ha! Love and money—ha ha!' "

Sybil looked up expectantly. Woody had put on his heavy, power manner again; he blinked at her unresponsively. Jim appeared to be interested, and only interested, as though the passage from Lizzie's letter had been describing odd customs he found it entertaining to hear about. But Alfred's face was bleak and Kay's lined with anxiety.

The two whom Sybil had intended to hit were composed, and the two innocent bystanders were hurt. Woody must have thrown her off balance too. She could not see exactly how he had done it, but he had done it. Here she was, uneasy and remorseful, and there he was, puffing his imaginary cigar.

Jim spoke. She looked at him, ready to lump him together with Woody for being so unruffled.

"Your sister's right. It must be awful to get so much money all of a sudden, for such a silly reason. Luck would be much better. Not that I would turn the money down, you understand. But all the same I wouldn't ever go on a give-away program, not after hearing that letter. It'd be like getting ten years in prison for spitting on the sidewalk, only in reverse. What I meant is, it's just as disrupting to be rewarded for too little as to be punished for too little. Maybe it's worse. The punishment is forced on you and is real, whereas the reward is phony and it's your own fault for yielding to temptation." He stopped abruptly, as though he feared that he had not been making sense.

It seemed to Sybil that he had not only been making sense but had also exercised great tact in speaking as and when he did. Her opinion was confirmed by her father's nodding to what Jim said and by Kay's leaning forward to pay attention to him as he spoke; it was also confirmed, negatively, by the faint smile on Woody's lips as he listened, leaning back in his chair, finger and thumb fiddling at the lobe of an ear.

At quarter past ten Sybil announced that she had to go because of an eleven-o'clock lockout at her dorm. Jim instantly offered her a ride on his motorcycle. She looked at her legs dubiously and said she didn't know whether her skirt was full enough. He said sure it was, and she said probably so but it would be awfully cold with all that cold air whistling around her tonsils, and anyway maybe it was drizzling outside. Woody said he would be glad to run her over to Presley College, or at least down to the bus line, when he drove Alfred down. That decided her. She accepted Jim's offer.

At a stop sign Jim turned his head and said something.

She sat up straight. She had been scrunched down, with her arms around his waist, pressing her cheek between his shoulder blades to protect her face from the damp wind.

"What?" she said.

"I said, it's cold, do you have time for a cup of coffee?"

"Sure. Go left here. I'll show you a diner."

"We don't have long."

"I don't have to be in till midnight. That eleven-o'clock stuff was just talk. I wanted to get out of there."

The diner was deserted except for a car without fenders. At the counter there were two young men in black leather jackets. The juke box was going full blast. The waitress was standing at the candy counter by the cash register, applying polish-remover to her fingernails. On their way to a booth, Jim ordered two coffees.

"What's so special about this joint?" he said.

"Nothing. A girl I know used to run around with a hot-rod gang. They used to hang out here, last summer anyway."

"I'll be darned. You know hot-rodders?"

"She's a math professor's daughter."

"You know," he said, "professors' daughters aren't what I'd expected."

"Which goes to show," said Sybil, "you have the wrong expectations. Like, are you the minister's son type?"

"Who wants to be a type?"

The juke box changed records. The new one was so loud that they gave up trying to talk over it. When silence descended, Sybil said the coffee was good and picked up her purse.

"Say," he said, "I don't have any money for anything fancy, but maybe we could ride over to Diablo some sunny afternoon and have a picnic, or we could go to a movie some evening, or something. Would you like to?"

"Why not?" she said vaguely.

"Come on." He frowned. "Do you want to go out with me or not?"

"Sure." They stood up. "Give me a ring sometime."

"How about a movie this Saturday night?" he said.

"Can't. I've got a date with a guy who wants to propose."

"Oh, for the love of Mike. 'Will you marry me?' See, I beat him to it."

"He means it," Sybil said in a drifting voice.

"But you don't."

"Don't tell me what I mean and what I don't mean."

"Well, if you do mean it . . ." Hissing, he made a rapid cranking motion with his right fist.

She did not know what he intended to signify by this odd gesture, beyond some sort of fierce threat, but she liked his anger. She tossed her head, sniffing, and went out.

They did not speak again till she got off the motorcycle in front of her dormitory, and then all they said was good night. He did not even turn off the motor. He meant the expression on his mouth to be sour and disdainful, but it seemed to her only disappointed, in a way she liked.

· 7 ·

Woody drove back up the hill, hoping that Kay would be willing to make love. If he found her still in the kitchen straightening up, he would go to bed and read till she joined him, when he would be able to find out how she was disposed. The light was on in the kitchen; through the window facing the garage he saw, to his relief, that only Viola was there. That meant that Kay had decided not to feel sorry for old black Viola and do the dishes herself, as she sometimes did after a dinner party, but had gone to the bedroom. He foresaw three possibilities. She might be already in bed in her pajamas, which would probably mean that she was too tense or headachy to feel amorous. Or she might be fiddling around in the nude; she had a sense almost of holiness about the pleasures and benefits of nudity, of sunbathing, lunching, swimming, or just going about the house in the nude (never "naked," always "in the nude"); but he had learned, though it had taken him years to learn it and though he still sometimes forgot what he had learned, that when she was in the nude she reacted to any erotic overture from him as though it were a sort of desecration; once in exasperation he had ridiculed her for speaking of "the temple of

286

the body," and she had cried and railed at him, accusing him of being afraid of the body; now, if he found her in the nude, he would not dare caress her till they were in bed, and probably not then. The third possibility, the one he hoped for, was what he discovered when he went into their bedroom: seated at her dressing table, she was wearing her transparent negligee.

"Hi, sweetie," she said, turning from her nails and smiling at him. "Did Alfred say anything?"

"It's all set. He's moving out this weekend."

"Wonderful!" She held a hand out to him. "Tell me what you both said."

Woody's relief at finding her in her negligee, willing to be caressed, had instantly given way to resentment. She would have to do more than stretch out her arm to him like this to make up for having kept him on tenterhooks.

"There's nothing much to tell," he said, taking off his jacket and tie. "Sybil must've done a good job of softening him up."

Kay had a cigarette going and a glass of red wine on the dressing table. She even had her feet stuck in huge, puffy, frivolous slippers, indicating the luxury of her mood. They commonly went barefoot when they were home alone; the house was radiant-heated by pipes buried in the concrete floor. He took off his shoes and socks and sat wiggling his toes in the thick rug.

"Who brought the subject up?" Kay said.

"Alfred. He thanked me for letting him use the apartment. I said it had been a pleasure and what a fine house Justice Durkheim had left him. He said he was going to move into it. I said everything was working out fine, because I'm expecting a Japanese export man next week and I'd like to offer him the use of the apartment. He said he'd move out day after tomorrow. Everything went as smoothly as I'd hoped it would. No friction of any kind."

He sprawled on a chair across the room from her, watching her push back the cuticles on her nails.

"And what is this dinner tomorrow night?" she said. "Sybil hinted something about the St. Clares."

"Tony wants Alfred to be a federal judge. The only vacancy coming up is in Los Angeles, apparently, and Alfred doesn't want to move. That's all I know."

"Darling," she pleaded, "I've got something on my back, right between my shoulder blades where I can't reach." She let her robe slip down her shoulders. "Come here, Woody baby, and tell me what I've got."

This was more like; he went to her.

"It's just a pimple," he said, touching her back with his fingertips as though reading Braille. "It hasn't come to a head yet, so I can't squeeze it. It's nothing."

He kissed the nape of her neck. She leaned her head back and purred as they rubbed cheeks. He slipped his hands around under her arms and held her breasts through the cloth.

"You don't have a yen for Sybil any more, do you, sweetie?" she said.

"Any more! I never did."

"I've seen you look at her sometimes. I don't blame you. She's pretty and she has a good figure."

She took a sip of wine and held the glass to his lips. He sat on the floor beside her stool and let her give him a drink.

"Sybil's changed," he said. "She's getting hard."

"Oh, gee. A little snippy, maybe?"

"No," he said. "Hard."

"You used to say she was the lightweight of the Royce family." She was unbuttoning his shirt. "How can she be light and hard at the same time?"

"Because she's hollow."

"You're so handsome and strong," she said, "and I've got pimples." She opened her robe and looked at her brown belly with its two long scars. Both children had been delivered by Caesarean section, and she had been warned that she should have no more children. "I'm thirty-five, and I'm not beautiful for you any more, and I've got a pot belly."

"But I still love you," he said. "That's all that matters."

"Yes," she said, "that's all that matters."

As he was kissing her body she stubbed out her cigarette and finished her wine. Then she breathed softly on his ear. The first year they were married she had done this once for fun, and he had shivered and clutched her. He told her that he used to breathe like that on his first wife's ear to make her shiver amorously. In token that she appreciated this solemn confidence, Kay told him that thereafter she would always do it to him as a sign that she was ready for love. However, as it worked out, her doing it became more a sign that she was about to interrupt their caresses in order to go put in her contraceptive. This she now went off to do.

As he lay on the bed waiting for her, resentment at the interruption filled him. She would never make these preparations ahead of time; whenever he had suggested it she had giggled, called him cold-blooded, and wheedled him erotically till he dropped the matter.

As she came to the bed, he seemed to her tense. Smiling winningly, wrinkling her nose and puckering her mouth till he smiled in return, she switched off the one low light, though she preferred to make love with the light on. "See, honey, we'll do it in the dark the way you like to." She caressed him and murmured affectionately till his resentment had melted to desire again, and when he made love to her she went with him as far as she could—most of the way, farther than usual. Then she simulated passion till he was done. Sometimes at this point she would roll over with her back to him, without a word. Tonight she stayed with him, and while he was still breathing hard she began stroking his hair and telling him all sorts of things about how wonderful he had made her feel. She thought that she was fooling him, that he did not know she always ceased to feel much of anything when their lovemaking approached its climax.

He allowed her to think she was fooling him because he did not want to deprive her of the opportunity to make it up to him for having failed him. To disillusion her would not solve her sexual problem; if psychoanalysis had not been able to solve her problem, they just had to live with it. Meanwhile, if she could not be passionate, he would encourage her at least to be affectionate.

"Incidentally," he said as she was browsing his chest, "I liked Jim even less this time than before. Maybe he'll marry Sybil, and then we won't ever have to invite either one of them here again—kill two birds with one stone."

Giggling, she said that he was horrible but that secretly she didn't like them either—though in fact she did.

· 8 ·

The next afternoon at two, when Alfred arrived for his office hour, six students were lined up in the hall to see him. The first was a brilliant sheep-faced young woman who came to thank him for the course and to tell him in sinking tones that she would not be able to take the second semester, as she had planned to do, because her husband was being transferred to Alaska; he would be territorial manager for a large oil corporation; it was such a big step up he could not afford not to take it, and besides if you worked for a big company you pretty well had to go where they sent you; she was almost in tears when she left. The second was a perpetual graduate student in economics, erudite, loquacious, and unable to finish important projects, whom Alfred had heard Aldo groan about for years; when he asked permission to take the seminar, Alfred hesitated a moment over which reason to give for refusing him, a polite evasion or a version of the truth, and decided to give him enough of the truth to keep him from ever coming back. "I'm sorry, but I try to restrict the class to potential lawyers. Occasionally I have admitted a philosophy student or two, when not enough law students have applied, but they were exceptional cases who came very highly recommended." The applicant, who knew that Alfred was a friend of Aldo's, looked at him balefully and, without saying another word, left with head high. The third to go in was Jim, whom Alfred greeted with spontaneous warmth and admitted to the seminar without discussion; he had liked Jim's surly independence the night before, and though a couple of things Jim had said had struck him as original, he would have admitted him in any case as the first promising young law student to apply.

Jim, however, did not know that a vacancy had appeared only ten minutes before he had gone in and that Alfred did not keep a waiting list of applicants, nor did Jim realize that the reason Alfred had not questioned him in detail was that he already knew something about his academic status. Jim assumed therefore that the reason he had been accepted so readily was pull—friend of a friend. The rest of the hour till class convened he sat drinking coffee on the sunny terrace of the student union, scowling bitterly over the corruption of the world. At one point he resolved not to take the course at all, but then he decided that would be cutting off his nose to spite his face. Here he was allowed to take the most idealistic course in law school, for no better reason than that he happened to have pull, when he might be taking some routine bread-and-butter course honestly. He wished with daydream passion that he could clean up the world. Failing that, at least he would seize the first opportunity to get even with Alfred for having let him down so badly.

There were seventeen people at the seminar table.

"We have lost three members of the class from last semester," Alfred said. "Mr. Salz passed his bar and has gone into his father's firm. Mrs. Yount is about to leave for Alaska, where her husband is being transferred. Mr. Ravicelli has left the University. As replacements, to bring the class up to the quota of fifteen, we have, in alphabetical order, Father Ceroise, Mr. Krishna, and Mr. Sorb. The charming young lady at Mr. Krishna's left is Mrs. Krishna, who will accompany her husband to sessions of the class as a silent participant. Mr. and Mrs. Krishna are in this country for a year on a Rockefeller grant from their most recent home, Nairobi, Kenya. Mr. Krishna has studied at the University of London, and he spent last semester at Harvard. He is preparing to teach law at the University of East Africa, which does not yet exist but will surely come into being within the next few years. Meanwhile, he is writing a book—which has to do with game theory?"

Mr. Krishna was a thin-faced, elegantly dressed man, hair perfectly brushed and gray at the temples, head nobly set on his neck, eyes bright and steady; he spoke with British crispness. Mrs. Krishna, round-shouldered, dressed in a soft-colored sari, her lips voluptuously pouting and at the same time humorous, a dark red dot on her forehead, showed no sign of uneasiness but watched intently whoever was speaking.

"That is correct," said Mr. Krishna. "Much work is being done with game theory. Very exciting. Its applicability to law is obvious, but no one has worked out the ramifications satisfactorily as yet. The influence of Holmes at the Harvard Law School is not what I had expected. Here in Berkeley there are Professor Polski and Professor Royce. I was told of them. I am here."

"It's good fortune for all of us, I am sure, that an opening appeared in the seminar this semester." Alfred would certainly have added Mr. Krishna to the class even if it had been full, but he did not want in any way to feed Mr. Krishna's evident sense of superiority. Mr. Krishna responded to this tiny rebuff by the faintest of frowns, at the same time inclining his head as in stately acknowledgment. "Father Ceroise," Alfred went on, "spent five years in China in a mission school. He, along with his entire order—in fact, along with all Catholic missioners, if I am not mistaken"—he cocked his head at Father Ceroise, who nodded—"was expelled last fall by the Communists. Father Ceroise is presently engaged in writing a book on natural law. Father?"

Father Ceroise was a dapper, slight man with waving hair, and his soutane was freshly ironed and well cut; he sat erect, elbows resting on the arms of his chair, fingertips pressed lightly together, and spoke with a blurred accent punctuated by irritable mumbling when a word eluded him.

"Yes, it is a theory of natural law I wish to develop. For years this is my hobby. Now it's my occupation. I am chaplain to the faculty of Saint Anselm's. I have time to study. I shall remain there and write my book finishedly. Not always is general disaster without individual benefit. I have needed the time to work on my book. I have needed to acquaint myself with the Anglo-American common law. Now it's possible, in idealistic circumstances, for me to study these subjects with such a master. Good. I have had experiences with many laws and governments. On my mother's side, I am Walloon. Centuries and centuries of dominations—Germans, Spaniards, Dutch, French, Belgians, Romans even, conquerors. On my father's side, ultimately French. The Napoleonic code, monarchy, despotism, revolution, who knows what? And China—corruption, anarchy, communism. Now the best of all, the common law of England in America. What is behind all these manifestations? Saint Thomas is a guide, he made maps. Perhaps they aren't completely up to date? I must inquire."

Jim was conscious of the patches on the elbows of his sweater, of his unironed corduroy pants, of the two red pustules on his face.

"Our third new member," said Alfred, "is Mr. Sorb, from San Mateo."

Jim was slumped down in his chair. He struggled most of the way up to an erect position, tossed his head to get the lock of long hair off his forehead, and spoke in a voice which squeaked at first.

"I went—" He cleared his throat. His voice descended an octave. "I went to San Jose State, and I'm going to be a lawyer."

"Any special interest?"

"Anti-trust, maybe. I like Mr. Krishna's point of view on games. Law's just a complicated game, and what I want to get from this course is some idea of the rules. Of course all that really matters is how you play it, but I thought maybe I could play it better if I understood the rules better."

Alfred pretended to consider Jim's assertions. Actually he was pleased to see about an hour's worth of argument brewing. The class was scheduled to run till five-thirty, but because the St. Clares were coming to dinner at six he wanted to be home well ahead of time. The first meeting of a class, even one in which most of the members carried over from the previous semester, was by custom brief. What he wanted was about an hour of informal discussion, and Jim had started a good hare.

"I'm not sure, Mr. Sorb, that Mr. Krishna's views are identical with the one you seem to propose. Am I mistaken?"

Mr. Krishna's nostrils were flaring, and Mrs. Krishna, with a slight smile, leaned forward to watch her husband respond.

For ten minutes he explained game theory and its applicability to the study of law. He did not address, or even look at, Jim while he spoke, and the only allusion he made to Jim's statement was "the inevitable distortions of vulgarization to which esoteric theory is liable."

Jim, cowed and furious, was slumped back down in his chair so far that he looked relaxed. He could not think what to say when Mr. Krishna should have stopped. He wished he had never signed up for the class. Trespass and Negligence was dull, but you wouldn't drown in it.

Father Ceroise was bursting to speak. As soon as Mr. Krishna had finished, Alfred nodded to the priest.

For a quarter of an hour, with much ebullience and little clarity, he tried to reconcile Mr. Krishna's game theory with natural law. For a while he kept appealing for agreement to Mr. Krishna, who watched him without a flicker of response. Then he focused his appeal on Jim, who had only the foggiest notion of what he was talking about. The general drift seemed to be that game theory provided the necessary secular rationale to natural law, which had been divinely instituted.

None of this made the least sense to Jim. Happily, he saw by the expressions of the rest of the class that they were understanding Father Ceroise no better than he. He was off the hook. He did not have to worry about responding to this mixed-up priest; instead, he relished in anticipation Alfred's difficulty in picking up the pieces.

Suddenly Jim was aware of Father Ceroise's forefinger waggling at him, impatient and dismissive at once.

"Mister, Mister—pardon me, I don't remember your name?"

"Sorb," Jim said.

"That is why, Mr. Sorb, your view is so offensive. Not because it is practical self-interest. That one can embrace—pff. But because it is in error, in all ways in error."

Jim shook his head and blinked. First this priest surrounded you with a fog of jabber, then when you were good and lost he gave you the old rabbit punch.

"I think—" Alfred was beginning.

"Look," said Jim to Father Ceroise, "I like games as well as the next fellow—chess, handball, poker, you name it. I've got nothing against philosophy. It's a great game. Natural law, positive law, common law—any way you want to play it. But I'm going to be a lawyer. That's work. That's a job for a man. So where do you get off, looking down your nose at a man for his work, a real job?"

He had intended to attack Father Ceroise and perhaps Mr. Krishna too, and both of them showed signs of wanting to counterattack. But when Alfred spoke, Jim realized, to his gratification, that he had been attacking Alfred as well.

"You are implying, Mr. Sorb, that what we are doing in this class is play?"

"Sort of. In a sense. Studying the rules of a game is sort of playing, isn't it?"

"Academic ivory tower, removed from the real world?"

"Right."

This was an attack which Alfred was prepared for and enjoyed defending against. No one had made it the previous semester, so he could enter his defense plea now fully and at leisure, without repeating himself before any of those present. He went to the bookcase and took down a shabby old green volume.

"In book six of *The Republic*," he said while looking for the right page, "is the best version of the charge you are making—a much stronger statement than yours, Mr. Sorb. Ah, here it is. Adeimantus is speaking, a young man, one of Plato's brothers, as a matter of fact.

He's been listening to Socrates turn common-sense ideas about justice and government upside down. He's irritated.

" 'Just as in checkers the less skilful player is finally hemmed into a corner where he cannot make a move, so in this game where words take the place of counters your hearers feel they are being cornered and reduced to silence, but that does not really prove them in the wrong. I say this with an eye to the present situation. Anyone might say now that at each question you ask there is no contradicting you, but that nevertheless, as a matter of plain fact, the votaries of philosophy'—professors? academics?" Alfred interpolated—" 'when they carry on the study too long, instead of taking it up in youth as a part of general culture and then dropping it, almost always become decidedly queer, not to say utterly worthless; while even the most respectable are so far the worse for this pursuit you are praising as to become useless to society."

" 'Well, Socrates replied, do you think that charge is untrue?

" 'I do not know, Adeimantus answered; I should like to hear your opinion.

" 'You shall; I think it is true.'

"You see?" Alfred said, shifting in his chair and looking about at the attentive faces. "Socrates admits the charge. Of course he does. It's obviously true."

Jim half raised his hand as though to request permission to speak, but he spoke even as the hand was going up.

He knew almost nothing about Alfred except what he had observed the evening before. He had decided to take the course on the basis of two comments he had overheard the previous semester. One was by a young instructor who, Jim had heard, had been that vague but glorious entity, a Rhodes scholar. "Royce, of course," he was saying to a student. "He's the closest thing to it we have here." Jim did not know what "it" the instructor was referring to, but he knew it was something important. The other comment he had heard in the stationery store where he clerked twenty hours a week, uttered by a law professor whom he detested. "I hear Royce's book on labor is coming out at last," he said to the man with him. "You realize this is his first book? He's done the best job of parlaying a reputation on the basis of a handful of articles I've ever seen pulled off at this University. That much you have to grant him." "Perhaps," said the other man, "he's good in class? I don't know him, you understand." "Perhaps. The students think so, for what their opinion is worth." Jim had no idea that Alfred had ever considered serving as a judge, and though he knew that Senator St. Clare was a liberal Republican, he certainly did not know that within a few hours St. Clare was going to give Alfred the opportunity to become a federal judge. He knew that Alfred had, during the emergency of war, worked in some federal agency or other. But he would not have believed, if Alfred himself had said it, that any man could seriously find it difficult to choose whether, if the opportunity presented itself, to be a professor or a justice of the Supreme Court.

When Jim spoke his voice was unsteady at first, because he knew that anyone in the room whom he had not antagonized already would surely be so by what he was going to say. When he finished speaking he caught his lower lip between his teeth to keep it from trembling.

"You've shifted the ground. I didn't mean what that guy said to Socrates. I didn't mean that philosophy professors become queer and worthless necessarily. I meant that what we're doing in a class like this is playing around. I haven't got anything against playing around. That's why we're all here—it's fun. But that's what we're doing. We haven't got anything at stake. We're not even playing for pennies, we're playing for matchsticks. What makes it interesting is, we're looking to see what the odds would be if we were playing for real money."

"The game analogy!" cried Mr. Krishna. "You see, a game!"

"Real money," said Jim. "It's just a comparison. When the money is real, it's not a game, in the comparison. What I meant was, a judge acts on the rules and applies them to real life, people's lives hang on what he decides, but a professor or a philosopher just plays around with the rules themselves and it doesn't make too much real difference to anybody what he says about them, except maybe in some indirect, general way."

Alfred assumed that Jim was attacking him personally, in full knowledge of Alfred's situation that very day. He thought Jim had picked up some of the information from the Ravaglis and the rest from Sybil, or all from one or the other; neither Kay nor Sybil was discreet or had any special reason to suppose Jim would use this knowledge for so illegitimate a purpose. Had Alfred doubted that Jim's intention was personal, that Jim, for whatever reason, was intentionally needling him hard, his doubt would have dissipated at the evidence of Jim's biting his underlip and glowering at him.

Alfred liked to think of himself as handling ideas with Socratic playfulness, rising to seriousness without entering into solemnity, and over the years he had, in these seminars, succeeded in striking and maintaining this tone. Now he began his defense Socratically enough, but before long he realized that the tone was shifting. He could not control it. The arguments remained ordered and cogent, but he heard in his voice a passionate undercurrent which had no business being there. He did not know why he had been so maliciously attacked by this bright, uncouth young man whom his daughter appeared to be attracted to, and he was distressed at becoming emotional in a seminar in a tiff with a student. There was no need for him to defend the profession of teaching against an ambitious, impatient youth. Nevertheless, at very great length and with all the eloquence he had, he defended it—not himself as college teacher, but the vocation itself and especially the vocation of teaching philosophy.

After an hour or so, when a joke providentially worked itself into his discourse, relieving the tension, he was able to control the emotion of his voice so that it was congruent with the occasion. But instead of descending then to an easier level of seriousness, he discovered that he had ascended to the highest seriousness of which he was capable, speaking gravely and lightly at once, not without touches of humor. He was able now to look at Jim from time to time with gratitude for having goaded him to ascend to this elevation of intense yet tranquil eloquence, and he was pretty sure, having watched the permutations of posture and expression which Jim had been going through, that he had swayed him and that Jim would do good work in the seminar.

Alfred had deliberately deferred making an overt comparison between judging and teaching, between applying the law and inquiring into its nature, between working as an agent of society's will and as a questioner of that will, until the end of his discourse, so that the comparison should provide formally satisfying completeness. But when he entered into this comparison with which he was going to conclude, he discovered the passion rising in his voice again. This time he knew it had nothing to do with Jim. He did not know what it came from. To allay it, he entered upon a caricature of academic life, its hypocrisies and busy work, the routinizing of intellectual zeal and the comical contests for power, and he turned then to painting a rosy picture of the severe serenity of a judge's life, the unending reminders to him to strive for humility, his service in constructing and preserving the social order itself.

"Yet," he said in conclusion, his voice controlled again, "one must rank them ultimately. Distinction and hierarchy are the very structure of value, as they are of thought. Some things are higher than others, are closer to the best. I mean this not only relatively but also absolutely. I don't mean that one of these two professions is necessarily superior to the other for this or that particular man. I mean that in itself one is superior. This, Plato has argued once and for all. No one is likely to improve on what he has said about the life of the inquiring mind. If he doesn't persuade you, no one else is likely to, certainly not I. Relatively, of course, it is the case that for one man it's better that he should be a judge and for another that he should be a philosophy professor. But what about the man who has a choice?"

At this moment he realized that what he was about to say was the answer to the question Tony St. Clare was going to pose in two or three hours, which was also the question of how he intended to spend the rest of his life. He waited to see what he would say next, knowing that once he had said it, speaking thus with ultimate seriousness, he would stick by what he said and would never have to make up his mind about the matter again.

"Imagine the case of a man equally competent to serve as a judge and as a philosopher of law, an inquirer into the nature of things social. Neither this man himself nor anyone who knows him, let us imagine, can say confidently, 'He clearly should be a judge,' or 'He clearly should be a philosopher.' Let's go further. Imagine that he has in fact had experience as both the one and the other, and has done well in both capacities, to the satisfaction of himself and of his peers. Of course it's not necessary that the divorce be complete. Justice Holmes is the exemplar of the practical man who never ceased to inquire. Let us agree that such a man—a philosopher-king, if you will —can be considered higher than either separately. He is rare. For our purposes, for most human purposes, it's a high enough choice to be one or the other. You see, what I've done is to set up the test situation in which the relative becomes the absolute. What is best relative to the man we've imagined as having to choose must, by the very terms of the problem, be best absolutely. He cannot choose on the basis of preference of competence. There's only one consideration left: Which is more important in itself, to judge in the world of men and affairs or to inquire in the world of ideas? Presumably, some would say one is on a par with the other, flip a coin, do as you want. This strikes me as pusillanimous. My only response to so extensive a relativism is contempt for it as a mask for evasiveness. It becomes mere, and uninteresting, irresponsibility. Others—Mr. Sorb, for example— clearly hold that the practical life is superior to the contemplative one. We're assuming, for the purposes of this final discrimination, that the accidents of the academy or of the bench can be overcome, avoided, subordinated. In some final way, I believe it is true that a judge applies his mind to the immediate circumstance and the philosopher, the philosophy teacher, to the ideas in which such a circumstance finds its meaning. Myself, I don't find it easy to choose between these two modes of contemplation and action. They are both both, clearly—to teach is to act, and to judge is no less to contemplate. Finally, one's decision derives from what one considers to be the highest order of reality. At this point, my duty as a scholarly professor in a mid-twentieth-century American liberal university urges me to present you with the subtleties of Platonism on the one hand, in which reality is purely ideal, or of materialism on the other—pragmatism, maybe—

and then to turn you loose to choose between them. A dogma of the academy nowadays is that the professor's role is to ask the right questions but not to answer them, and Socrates, the great questioner, is appealed to as sanction for this dogma. Well, everyone appeals to Socrates for authority. So will I. I know that I do not know, as he said, but like him I believe I should strive to attain the right opinion —not just to keep it well polished on a top shelf in my study but to tell it, to offer it publicly, to give it to you. Therefore, now, like Socrates I will say what I think is best. I think—I do not know, but it is my opinion—that it is higher to be a teacher of ideas than a judge of actions, because a judge deals only with other people's possessions, or the freedom of their bodily movements, or at the very most their lives, whereas a teacher of ideas is concerned with what is even more important than people's lives—their minds, with shaping their minds. He is closer to them. A judge knows what he has done—altered the circumstances of some men's existence; to be sure, these circumstances influence their minds somehow. A teacher can never know what he has done, but he believes that if he has done anything, good or bad, he has shaped some minds themselves. His responsibilities are the greater, and all the greater because he is responsible to a higher good. The judge is responsible to society, but the teacher to truth. Excuse me. God is coming into the matter, the dissolver of distinctions. Let me try again. The judge is responsible to men collectively, and though that is of a very high order, it is higher yet to be responsible, as a teacher is, to men individually. For the ultimate good of society is not to perpetuate itself or the species but to make you, you, you, me, possible. It of course follows that a bad teacher can do more harm than a bad judge. These are not Plato's opinions, you understand, though his Socrates would agree with these opinions so far as they go. He went further than I go. Socrates said the teacher must not be paid for his teaching. Why? Because a man is primarily the agent of whoever pays him—in my case, the State of California—and the teacher ought to be the agent of the truth only. As Jesus put it, you cannot serve both God and Mammon. Maybe they were right. They frequently were about such matters—those two teachers."

He fumbled his books and papers together, getting the volume of Plato mixed up with the others, and left the room.

Jim hauled himself to his feet, afraid to catch anybody's eye. He was sure they would all be hating him. He was wondering whether he had the courage to go tell Alfred in person he was dropping the course, or whether he had better, out of cowardice, notify him by mail. The more eloquently Alfred had spoken, the more dejected Jim had felt about his own stupid brashness. Why had no one warned him that Alfred was such a good talker? He had not seemed so exceptional the evening before at the Ravaglis'. It would be a sin and a shame for a man who could teach like that to become a judge. If Jim had been alone he would have cried.

"Say, man," said a sporty, crew-cut student whom Jim had not noticed particularly, "you're great for him. Keep it up."

"Yeah? What do you mean?"

"Keep after him, that's all."

"I feel like a fool."

"Don't. He needs you. The rest of us—the trouble is we're just yesmen, or abstract like that padre. He needs you to fight with. You brought out the best in him. You're just what the class has been needing to get it off its ass."

Jim went to the window, pretending to be watching something on the path below, so that he would not have to walk past Mr. and Mrs. Krishna, who were talking to each other in low undertones near the door. His eyes felt hot.

· 9 ·

Wednesday night

Dear Liz,

I'm writing this in the wee hours because I can't get to sleep. So much has happened today I'm all jived up, and I'm home in my old room too, which no longer feels the same, so that bothers me a little. This evening I played hostess for Daddy in his new house. He's about to move into it and live in it! Then, after doing that, I came home and of course Mother was waiting for me and we talked a blue streak for hours. She's wonderful, she really is. Nutty as a fruit cake sometimes, naturally—you know *that,* but tonight she was nuttier than ever once or twice. She's trying to have theories, and all they do is scramble her brains. She's been going to an analyst and of course she doesn't tell me what goes on in the sessions, but she has theories about possessiveness. "An owner of anything is really just a trustee of it," she says over and over, in one set of words or another. So naturally I ask, "Who's he holding it in trust for?" And then the theories start! Zowie! Well, obviously all this furniture she inherited was traumatic for her, and I hope she works through it successfully. You know how we've always been so cynical about analysis because of Mary Louise and a couple of those old crocks she hangs around with? Well, Mother keeps seeing them a lot, but she's got more to her than they do and she'll make it. My hopes are high, after these last three or four hours particularly. Incidentally, she has just stored most of the furniture in the basement and your old room, and the house looks pretty good. Crowded but livable.

It's such a comfort to write to you, Lizzie, because I don't have to keep watch over what I say too much. I can just get it all into what I write you—the way you do in your letters, which are a blessing to me. I'm lonely out there; 750 Presley girls really are a lonely-making crowd.

This dinner Daddy gave—Irma was in charge of it and she was merry as a grig to have something to do. She just lives on in the house. Of course it's convenient for Daddy. Do you suppose he really will *live* there half a block from Mother and Nance? It's just inertia on his part too, that's absolutely all. He had to be pried out of Woody's apartment. So where does he go? To the easiest place even though it's utterly mad for him to be there. You know, Mother's nutty and everybody knows it and so does she. She can even laugh about it. She goes to a headshrinker. Daddy's the wise one. Everybody says so, and of course he *is* wise too, mature, responsible, and all that. But when it comes to doing quiet reasonable-looking *insane* things, give me Daddy every time. Imagine him moving into that house now! Mother was really funny about it last night when I told her. She was mad as hell, but I nearly died laughing. She worked up a whole story of how Irma might break her leg and Daddy would try to tend her but get tired of it after about half a day and call on Mother to come to the rescue. Then she worked up this big farce about which hours it would be safe for her to go down and take care of Irma, and Daddy sneaking his women into the house in the middle of the night, and Mother bumping into one first thing in the morning and him saying she's a nurse. You would really have appreciated it.

Look, don't you dare show this letter to anybody, not even Joe. (If you can help it.) Or you can show it to him, after all he's your husband, but make him promise to carry it to the grave with him. After all, they're our parents.

You should have seen Faith St. Clare's costume!

I perish of sleepiness. Hasta la mañana.

Thursday

What on earth did I mean by that Faith bit? There wasn't anything so peculiar about Faith's costume, basic black with pearls. In fact, the whole evening was a bore and a bust, and if that's what social life is like among political VIPs, count me out. She had a funny big old floppy hat on when she came and she put it on when she left, but practically any hat looks funny to me. Do you realize I never even owned a hat in my life! Do you have one in England? They're so different over there. All I did was what Daddy said and got her to talking about Washington social dos. BLAH.

Well, it had one good effect at least. Brewster is going to be coming down from Sacramento Saturday and take me out. He thinks politics are important, which they are of course, but he's *interested* in them. I must say he can make them sound interesting when he talks about them. He's in on a few State committees—friends of friends—and his judge, Stankel or some smelly name like that, is in on top-echelon Democratic counsels. So, from a hint or two I think he's going to be proposing to me Saturday night after we go dinner-dancing at the Fairmount. "Darling, I love you so much I can't live without you beginning a year and a half from now, after you've graduated from college and I am set up in my career." Well, if there was the least question in my mind about accepting him—which there wasn't—Daddy's dinner last night queered everything. Imagine working like a dog to *rise* to the exalted plane of having dinner with the St. Clares for the rest of your life! Daddy said they're in the next to highest level of society in Washington. And somehow I just don't think Brewster will ever make President. Or Veep either. Maybe the fourth assistant Secretary of Health and Welfare, *if* he's *tremendously* lucky.

So why do I let him come propose? Vanity, sheer vanity.

As a matter of fact, there was one interesting feature about the dinner. You know how indecisive and punctual Daddy is? Well, yesterday he was late and decisive! He didn't get back from his class till after 5:30, when he'd absolutely promised he'd be back well before 5, and also he came with his mind all made up about that federal judgeship, which was what the whole dinner was about. He arrives late, rushes around checking things, only in a halfhearted way, and then he stands at the window in front of the rock garden, breathing deep, and says, "Honey, I've made up my mind." Since I didn't have the faintest what he was referring to, I asked him, and he told me in just a few sentences, very precise and firm. So I asked him what had happened in the seminar that afternoon. He looked at me as though I'd had a feminine intuition or something. It was just common sense. Where had he actually *been* just before he came in? It seems that all this decisiveness was because Jim Sorb had needled him. I couldn't make out whether he was mad at Jim for it or grateful to him. He seemed to be both. Which is peculiar. But like Daddy, I must admit. Who is peculiar way down deep.

Liz, I mean it. You *burn* this letter the minute you've read it or I won't send any more like it. Tell me you've done it. I won't write any more if you don't.

I was going to mail this off to you today but what with classes and washing my hair and one thing and another I didn't get around to it. I went to bed early, before 10 actually. My roommate, Roz, went out with her steady, a frat man at Stanford. She's very proud of him because she's the only girl in our dorm that has a Stanford man in tow. Most of them have a man from Cal, or St. Anselm's, or one or two from State. Anyway, I didn't expect her till all hours, and as a matter of fact she got in at 1:30. But there were still two or three up for her to sigh at before she got to our room, and one of them wormed the Great Secret out of her. She's from another planet, she really is. They all are. *She'd been pinned that very evening!* Yippee.

Here it is nearly 3 a.m. and Roz is lying in her bed sighing at me because I'm sitting at the desk with the light on not letting her get her beauty sleep tonight of all nights. Well, after what just happened, I don't care. You're an anthropologist. You ought to be interested in your peer group at Presley and their tribal customs.

They got me out of bed. They woke up everybody on our floor and we went into the reading room at the end of the hall—two dozen of us, in pajamas and robes mostly, curlers, no make-up, except Roz and a couple of others who'd just got in a little while before. We all sat around on the floor in the dark (the cold hard composition floor, brr). We were cross-legged. Roz was just unobtrusively in the circle —only it wasn't too perfect a circle, sort of irregular, but never more than one person deep. I didn't know what in hell it was all about, and they just told me to do what everybody else did, so I did.

In a little while, when we were all sitting on the cold floor, quiet as mice, in comes Roz's best friend, Debby (thank God she was there or I would have had to do it, because I'm Roz's roommate). Debby had a sheet draped around her like a Roman senator, with her right arm bare and holding a candlestick with a thick candle about six inches long and the sides all knobbly with wax drippings. She was blindfolded. She went into the center of the circle and began to slowly revolve, very serious. The candlelight made everybody look different— sort of spooky, actually. Then all of us began to chant this rhyme.

> Candle, candle, tell me true,
> Who is ready? Tell me who.
> Is *she* ready yet for you?

Then everybody made a sort of clicking—you know, one of the noises people make to a horse to get it going? You sort of open one side of your mouth and pull your cheek away from your teeth in back and the air rushes in with a click. We all did that twice after the chant. When we did that, Debby stopped revolving and the candle began to dip forward at some girl or other. It hesitated a little and then stood back up straight. So then Debby began to revolve again—very stately, sort of, for a chubby little jolly girl. Then the whole thing was repeated over and over. Sometimes the candle would tip pretty far forward and other times it hardly even bowed.

I was so glad Gretchen wasn't there. She lives on our floor but she's home for the weekend, her mother's sick. If she'd been there I'd have caught her eye for sure and we'd never have been able to control ourselves. She's *human* at least. As it was, I farted out loud once, on purpose—nobody reacted even. I can't begin to describe how ludicrous it all was. These dead-serious bridge-playing types chanting in low intense voices and clicking really viciously. And that blindfolded wholesome sweet-sixteen coed going around and dipping the candle. Of course it was all rigged. I knew that, though I didn't know how it worked exactly. (I've discovered since. It seems you can see out underneath a blindfold even when it's tied tightly, so long as the main pressure is on your eyebrows.) It was all so *insincere.* They say college is a training for life. Well, the life these dames are in training for is absolutely unbelievably insincere all the way down.

They went through the whole ritual at least a dozen times, and then came the big climax. Roz! The candle dipped toward her, trembled, pulled Debby over toward her, and then pointed right over at her, spilling wax onto her skirt and legs. I mean, how phallic can you get! I know at least three or four of the girls have had psych courses, and besides it isn't the most obscure thing in the world these days, Freudian symbolism, they've got it in the ladies' magazines. But nobody flickered a lash. Maybe they like to be so blatant? I don't know. I can't figure it out. Because as soon as the wax fell on Roz everybody began to squeal and giggle and oh and ah like it was her birthday cake she'd blown the candles out on and we were all 9 or 10 years old. "You're pinned! You're pinned! How wonderful! Who is He? Let's see it. Show us the pin! Oh isn't it simply excruciating?" You know—silly? Girlish? And two minutes before, everybody was really chanting like savages. It was exciting and at the same time it was ludicrous. Bourgeois maenadism. God.

So that's one for the Koyala, the next time you see them.

If they go through all this brouhaha when they get pinned, *what* are they going to do when they get married? I don't go for your way of getting married either, in a little office in the city hall with the typewriters and telephones going in the next room. Surely there's something in between for the likes of me—you know, neither insincere nor stark? Huh?

Your frantic card just came, and I must say I don't see what you're all charged up about. The answer is yes, Harry Evans is being tried and is refusing to testify (the last I heard), and no, Roy Carver hasn't been heard of since, that I know of. What kind of a honeymoon are you on anyway?

Later

I meant to take this tome out and mail it when Brewster came for me—the nearest mailbox is a couple of blocks away—only when he did come he was a quarter of an hour early, so I rushed to get ready and forgot it.

He proposed, all right, and I turned him down—only I didn't really and honestly turn him down. I left him one little string to dangle on. Of course if he had any horse sense he'd know I didn't really mean it and won't "wait" for him. But about this he doesn't have good sense at all, though good sense is *all* he has about most things. And I knew what I was doing, sort of, at the time.

I feel awful. Why did I let him get to the point anyhow? Then, once he was there, why did I leave any hope? I *am* awful. A bitch.

The truth is, I was meant to be ordinary. Anybody can tell that by just looking at me. You were the first one to say it when you began calling me Cheerleader when I was in the tenth grade. The reason I fought you so hard and scratched your face and bit was, secretly I knew you were right, and *really* secretly I liked it. Only, I go against my own nature all the time, because of the way we were raised. How could any daughter of Alfred and Beth Royce be a cheerleader or any sort of ordinary person? How would they *dare*! That's the whole thing in a nutshell—I don't dare. But the truth is I want to. I want to be a Mrs. Brewster Adams—you know, a Mrs. Anybody. Only, the way I've been trained, I can't stand pinning ceremonies, or Faith St. Clare dinner parties, or living with a man whose dream of glory is becoming fourth assistant to the Secretary of Health, Wealth, and Happiness. But I had quite a good time dinner-dancing last night with him, and he really is a good necker. And I'm a 20-year-old virgin, and I probably still will be a virgin for the man I say "I do" to.

The way we were raised looks ordinary enough, but it's so Goddamned risky. What do *you* do but plunge off and marry a kook like Joe who's fascinating and unpredictable? And *I* behave like a bitch to a perfectly decent guy like Brewster who's never in this world going to do me any harm—he loves me even, in his fashion.

You see? There I go—"in his fashion." He says he loves me, and who am I to cast insinuations on it in any way?

Maybe it'll be sunny tomorrow and Jim Sorb will come by on his

304

BMW and we'll go out to Diablo on a picnic. He said something about it. He's sort of a compromise. And you can't really talk on a bike, just yell and laugh once in a while.

Sunday morning

There's one little thing I forgot to mention which will interest you. *Daddy has a beard!* I must say, he really looks very distinguished. It's a mustache and then it goes down the sides of his mouth and is rounded off at the bottom on his neck like a garden shovel. His fat is pretty well distributed, but I hadn't realized that his chin and neck are sort of shapeless because of the fat. This beard gives his face a lot of shape, and somehow or other it makes his eyes gleam, or twinkle, or pierce, or something like that. He's got this cane, too, which he swishes all the time when he walks. He says he uses it because his back aches, but I don't believe him. The whole effect is too neat.

Well, Thursday morning at breakfast with Mother and Nancy, I brought the subject up, inadvertently, and Nancy and I began comparing our impressions of Daddy's beard and the spiffy way he walks and everything. And Mother got so mad you wouldn't believe it, only with some of that sense of humor of hers too. "He's *my* man," she said, "not yours. And here I've got to learn about him from a couple of upstarts like you. What kind of deal is this, for crying out loud!" So naturally Nance and I poured it on thicker and thicker, and by the time we got through, all three of us were just about splitting a gut laughing.

Nance is wonderful, she really is. Daddy is giving her a trampoline for her birthday. (A week from tomorrow, in case you forgot. Hint hint.) She's already pretty good at it in gym and she wants one at home to work out on. Mother would just as soon *not*. You know how she worries over germs and blind intersections and getting mugged on a dark street and on and on—*Danger!* Still, Nance is good enough, so Mother wouldn't say a flat No. Anyhow, it'll be down at Daddy's house, out in back, where there's enough clear flat space, which there hardly is any of at home. So what could she do but give in gracefully?

I'm sick and tired of the way they don't get back together. What kind of an influence do they think they are having on Nancy? I can't say anything about it to Mother, naturally, or she'd go off like a Catherine wheel. A couple of times I've dropped a little hint to Daddy. All he does is sort of flap his hands and gasp like a fish out of water. Disgusting. I'm just waiting for one of them to tell me it's none of my business. Then I'll *really* let them have it.

Later

This has just been one of those weeks. The only reason I'm not in bed sucking my thumb (figuratively speaking) right now is that I

305

want to write to you. Thank God, Roz is out tonight. She and her dreamboat met at the halfway point—in the city—and they're seeing some Broadway musical at the Geary. O well, it's really just envy on my part. I wish I was doing that too, chintzy though it be. Maybe Jim will come galloping to the rescue on his BMW and sweep me off my feet. Otherwise, who knows? I'll die an old maid. I haven't mentioned Leon before, it's so hard.

We got all involved somehow because he's teaching here and they have this very strong unwritten law about students not dating professors, or vice versa. Of course, Leon and I already knew each other and I'm not in any of his classes and he's sort of a family friend. All the same, you can't help but be conscious of a prohibition like that. We keep bumping into one another here and there on campus; and we always stop to chat and have a cup of coffee if we're free. He's taken me out to dinner and a movie two or three times, but for a date I have to meet him down at West Gate by the drugstore—not surreptitious exactly, but still not the same as being called for in the lobby like an ordinary date. I don't remember very clearly, it was so unimportant at the time, but I can't recall how much we held hands, etc., on that picnic we all four went on last summer. I wouldn't be surprised if he kissed me good-by. It was that sort of a date, anyhow. I remember you and Joe did some smooching, but that sort of always went with you and Joe somehow from the very beginning. *Now* the most Leon ever does is take my elbow when we're going into the movie house or something. The awful thing is, he's married.

He's been very open and aboveboard with me about it. He married Chantal Bigonneau when it looked like she might get into a lot of trouble because of Harry Evans. Leon lives with her but they don't sleep together. "There's never been a question of any of that." Those were his very words. I believe him. He really is doing it just to help her. As soon as the smoke clears away, they'll get a divorce and then she'll be safe in this country. Leon says she is extremely unhappy because of Harry Evans, but she puts a good face on it. She *never* spills over onto other people, not even Leon—which I must say is admirable. In fact, I don't know anything whatever against her, except that he's married to her in this peculiar way.

So all right. We meet on campus from time to time and we talk. Some weeks we meet four times—the four days he's on campus teaching—and I think about it. Other weeks we don't meet at all, and I think even more about that. We never really talk about anything so remarkable or important. It's just that we've got to where we seem to be meaning a lot more than we ever say. This has gotten worse and worse, until lately most of our conversation consists of what we DON'T say. But then you never can be absolutely sure, unless it's said.

And even then, of course . . . I know you know what I'm talking about. I've been looking for other things to get my mind off of him. I began thinking it was all my fantasies maybe. Still, how *could* I feel that way about him if he didn't feel the same way about me? So I tested him. I just dropped a hint, in a cool way you may be sure—I was going to be proposed to Saturday night. He didn't turn a hair. At first I thought that indifference of his meant it had all just been in my own mind, and I got pretty frantic. But after a while that looked advantageous to me. All I had to do was put him out of my mind. So this week I've really been forgetting Leon. I didn't mention him in my letter to you once. I'm so lighthearted in a way. I've been silly and now it's over. Forever. Hallelujah!

Don't forget, sister, keep a holistic view of all those churches you're visiting. Isn't that a scrumptious word? This stupid Mitteleuropa Psych teacher impressed upon us the first day in class that: "Adler's outlook on the human psyche was holistic in counterreaction to the fragmentational tendencies of psychoanalysis." Aren't people incredible? Thank God for People.

· 10 ·

Beth was in the kitchen, peeling potatoes.

"Nancy? Is that you, darling?"

"Jean-Louis has come home with me," Nancy called from the living room.

"I was getting worried."

The slim children appeared in the doorway, in their dance-class clothes but unkempt.

"How do you do, Mrs. Royce?" Jean-Louis stepped forward and held out his hand.

Beth wiped her hands on her apron and shook hands. "Let's go into the dining room and sit down for a while. Do you kids—" She decided to be more formal, because of Jean-Louis. "May I offer you some lemonade?"

"No, thank you," he said, "not for me. We have just come from having tea with Mr. Royce."

"We trampled," said Nancy.

"You what?" said Beth.

"Trampled on the trampoline, and Jean-Louis was wonderful. It was his first time ever, and he did a back twist."

He flushed, and the corners of his mouth twitched. "It was unexpected. I'm not athletic. Yet it seems that I'm quite nimble. Is that the word, Nancy?"

"Nimble, yes, that's what Daddy said. Anyway, another couple of workouts and you'll be as good as I am."

They exchanged bright, appraising glances.

"It's the only way I'm better than you physically," he said.

"You're a better dancer."

"It's the rhythm. You haven't quite perfected the rhythm. You think about it too much. Isn't that odd, Mrs. Royce? I am the intellectual one, except on the dance floor, where she becomes the thinker. But she is stronger than I am. It's humiliating. Today in Codornices Park I ran after her and caught her—it was a little trick, otherwise I could never have caught her. But then when I had a hold of her she made me fall down. See?" He displayed, proudly, his torn trouser leg and the strawberry on his knee. "*Maman* will scold me. I know what she'll say. 'When you were little you did not do such things. What is this, *hein*? Are you in your second childhood already?' But Nancy didn't come off scot-free."

"He twisted my arm behind my back," she said, looking slantwise at her mother.

"May I use your telephone, Mrs. Royce, to call my mother so she won't worry about me? I must go home immediately."

While he was in the back hall telephoning, Beth asked Nancy if he had hurt her arm.

"He twisted too hard," said Nancy. "You can't blame him."

"Who can I blame if not him?"

"A boy hates for a girl to be stronger than he is."

"You don't have to outrun him. You could let him win, you know."

Nancy just blinked at her.

Jean-Louis appeared in the doorway to the living room and made a slight stiff bow. "*Maman* sounded a bit cross with me. I must go."

"Shall I drive you down?" said Beth without enthusiasm.

"Not at all. She said she wouldn't wait dinner for me. Leon must leave early." He shrugged. Then he gave Nancy a little smile. "But it was worth it, to do that back twist."

"Wait! Don't go yet! Mother, he wouldn't believe me. Where was Daddy born?"

"East of Ravendale, up in the Sierras. Why?"

"And why was he born there?" said Nancy.

"His father was a land surveyor for the federal government at the time. They were doing the national forests around there."

"You see, Jean-Louis? And his father was the county assessor while he was growing up, wasn't he?"

"In San Bernardino County," said Beth.

"Which is the biggest county in the whole United States, bigger

308

than Rhode Island, Connecticut, Massachusetts, and Delaware all put together—much bigger. See!"

"It's so amazing," said Jean-Louis, his head high and his eyes cold like his mother's. "Mr. Royce's father was an assessor!"

"What's so amazing about it?" Beth asked carefully.

"It seems so bourgeois."

"Ah? And this?" She waved her arm to take in the house and its furnishings. "What is this if not bourgeois?"

"Civilized," he said crisply and took his leave.

While Nancy was seeing him off, Beth returned to the kitchen, poured herself a tumbler of red wine, and went back to peeling potatoes and slicing them into a flat baking dish. Presently she was giving an unpeeled potato several stabs with the paring knife and muttering under her breath. "Oh, the snot-nosed, patronizing, delicate little half-assed French bastard! 'Civilized!' he says to me. He tells me I'm civilized. The gold-plated, laminated snot-nose! He isn't dry behind the ears yet and he has the nerve to tell me that I am civilized! The bastard!"

"He is not a bastard!" said Nancy from the doorway.

"He is too a bastard," said Beth and took a swig of wine.

"He is not. He told me. His parents got married before he was born."

The almost pleading in Nancy's voice caught Beth.

"You know perfectly well, darling, that all I meant by 'bastard' was that I was mad at him."

"No, I didn't," said Nancy with an odd meekness.

Beth glanced at her suspiciously; but the expression on Nancy's face was as meek as her voice had sounded. Beth repented. "He's the nicest boy you ever brought home, by far. Only, if I have the right to get mad at you, I have the right to get mad at him. You're used to having me shout at you. So?"

"It's different when you say bad things about him."

"Ah. I'll watch it, after this." Beth was afraid Nancy would sidle away, and she wanted her there. She never missed Alfred, Lizzie, and Sybil more than when she was preparing dinner, the most social event of her usual day. "Sweetie, why did you ever get started on the subject of where Daddy was born?"

"Oh, I don't know. Daddy brought it up at tea." She was picking at some flaking paint on the doorpost with her fingernail. "He got talking about what a dreamer his father was. Irma said something that got him started."

"What kind of dreams did his father have?"

"Oh, I don't know. It wasn't too awfully fascinating. He used to

309

say what he was going to do, 'when his ship came in.' Take a trip around the world, mostly. Then he actually got a hunk of money, Daddy said, and didn't go around the world at all. They just put Daddy and Mike and Harold through college on it like anybody else."

"Did Daddy mention where the money came from?"

"I didn't notice. Maybe."

"His mother inherited it."

"The way you did?"

Beth nodded.

Nancy said reflectively, "So that's what he meant, 'Ontology repeats philology.' He explained it but I didn't get it."

Beth laughed. "Ontogeny recapitulates phylogeny."

"Have it your own way," said Nancy irritably. "Is that why you and Daddy aren't living together? Did his parents divorce or anything? Are you two going to do everything they did?"

"No, no," said Beth. She scattered grated cheese over the potatoes with absurdly meticulous care. "No, that's not really our problem. I don't think."

After a minute Nancy said, "Daddy never says anything but good about you, Mother."

"And I suppose I'm always saying bad about him?"

"Well, you say bad about everybody, if you like them."

"Do I really say bad all the time?"

"Pretty much."

"Can't you tell what I really feel about people? You know, like about you, for instance?"

"Mmhm. Sometimes it's hard to tell, though."

Beth filled her tumbler again. "And I suppose I'm a dipsomaniac too?"

"Oh," said Nancy eagerly, "Shirley and I talked about that. We decided you and Mary Louise aren't dipsos at all."

"Great. Thanks."

"You don't drink before dinnertime. There was this article Shirley read in some magazine. It said real dipsos begin drinking first thing in the morning and also they drink just as much alone as in company. So you and Mary Louise are just heavy drinkers."

Beth took a deep unsteady breath, in her heart such a turmoil of emotions she did not know where to look. Chiefly she felt gratitude, as though reprieved temporarily from a sentence she had not known that Nancy had the power to reprieve her from. When Nancy went down to her room, Beth did not try to keep her but finished the preparations with a half-smile on her lips.

They were quiet as they ate, and left the radio on playing soft music.

"Mother?" said Nancy as they were doing the dishes.

"What, darling?"

"Sometimes Jean-Louis kisses me."

"Well, of course, sweetie, and you kiss him too, I hope."

" 'It takes two to tango!' " Nancy burst out and began tangoing around the kitchen, singing the snatch of tune.

"Come on, come on," said Beth, pushing her. "Cut out the monkey business. Here, wipe this bowl."

"Well, anyway," said Nancy, "we don't kiss very often but sometimes we do."

"And enjoy it, I trust?"

"Well, I don't know about 'enjoy.' It's different from enjoy."

"Oh?"

"Sometimes I feel funny. It's scary, only I don't want to quit. We don't talk about it."

"Good."

"But I talked to Shirley about it. You know, she's in love with Cedron."

"I didn't know for sure."

"He's older."

"How old?"

"Sixteen and a half. I said it was puppy love but she says it's real love. She says you can tell, with an older man especially. I guess I'm not in love with Jean-Louis. I'm not sure like she is. But I want to be with him, a lot. Once I dreamt about him. Isn't that love?"

"A little bit, at the very least."

"Puppy love." Nancy groaned. "That's what I thought. Only, Mother . . ."

"Only what, darling?"

"These kisses. Shirley says it's just the same with her. I think about *them* so much. I asked Sybil. Boy, was that a stupid thing to do. She just said I was in love with kissing. Which I suppose is george in *her* circles."

"What? What?"

"I wish Liz was around. Do you suppose it makes any difference to be married? I mean, her talking to me?"

"Yes, it makes a difference."

Nancy sighed. "You know, I'd sure hate to be my own sister's stepdaughter-in-law."

"*What!*"

"Shirley and I figured it out. If Sybil married Leon and I married Jean-Louis, then I'd be my own sister's stepdaughter-in-law."

Beth could not hold back her laughter altogether, though she saw by Nancy's eyes how offended Nancy was by it. "I'm only laughing, sweetie, at the thought of anybody being a stepdaughter-in-law of her own sister. It sounds like Gilbert and Sullivan."

Nancy laughed politely. "Well, it could happen, you know, the way Sybil's going. It's possible."

"Oh? First of all, Leon is already married to Chantal."

"Of course! That's how he gets to be Jean-Louis's stepfather. Anyhow, Jean-Louis says they don't sleep in the same room and he never saw them kiss or hug."

"Ah. And secondly, you kids aren't fifteen yet, so what are you doing even dreaming of getting married?"

"Oh, we aren't. We haven't ever talked about it once," Nancy said.

"So then?"

"So then." Nancy picked at a flake of paint on the cabinet with much concentration. Beth felt like slapping her hand for this, but controlled herself.

"I don't know," Nancy said. "But maybe I could get pregnant."

"Pregnant?" cried Beth. "Have you—"

"Oh, Mother, no, of course not. Anyway, I know all about intercourse. You told me, Lizzie told me, they tell us all about it at school all the time, like. But Cedron told Shirley—he's a biologist, you know."

"Ah. He's a biologist, is he?"

"Yes, and he said that a woman doesn't *have* to have intercourse to get pregnant. So, Shirley and I were just wondering, about these kisses. . . . Could we?"

"No, sweetie, you could not possibly."

"You're sure?"

"I'm sure."

"Cedron is a biologist."

"The only way a woman can get pregnant without intercourse is by artificial insemination, which takes doctors and syringes and lawyers and I don't know what-all."

"You're absolutely positive?"

"Absolutely positive."

"What about the Virgin Mary?"

"Oh, all right, miracles. But not kisses."

"So I don't have to worry about kissing Jean-Louis?"

"You don't have to worry about getting pregnant from kissing him, no. It's one of the joys of love, darling, so enjoy it."

"Well," said Nancy in a still voice, "I thought it really was love. It's sort of wonderful. He won't do it except in special circumstances. Like today—he wouldn't do it in the park because we might be interrupted by some other kids, or on the way up from Daddy's to here because it was a public street. Even when we said good-by out in the patio, it was just a peck, like family. Is that French of him?"

"Not that I know of. But it's sensible."

"Shirley and Cedron do it any old time and place they can. Oh well, I don't know. Mother?"

"Yes?"

Nancy writhed. "It only happens when he puts his tongue, you know, inside my mouth? Is that because he's French? But Cedron does it too."

"No, sweetie, it's not because he's French. It's just natural. It's just part of making love. You're supposed to enjoy it, and I'm glad you do."

"You keep saying 'enjoy.' "

"Any word you want."

"Mother, did you and Daddy used to do—that?"

"Oh yes," said Beth, ducking.

"Do you still, even? I mean, would you still, if . . ."

Beth hunched her shoulders.

"Do you like doing it with Daddy?"

Beth covered her face with her hands, sobbing, and bumbled her way up to her bedroom, where she lay face down across the bed, her face still in her hands. Presently Nancy followed her, cautiously, knelt on the bed beside her, laid her head lightly on the back of her mother's neck, and stroked her shaking shoulders.

· 11 ·

Dear Syb—

You ask me what kind of a honeymoon we are having and well you might! The answer is: a wonderful one, the honeymoon part of it, that is, the sex and holiday part. What I ask myself is: where did this custom of honeymoons come from anyway? What a turgid custom! You've just undertaken what is typically the major responsibility of your life, marriage, and the initiation into it is to go off and be totally irresponsible for a while—or else, you could say you're going off to be responsible to nothing else except marriage, which is just as bad. What bad emphasis! What a puny *rite de passage!* It is amazing, it really is, that society could imagine the best way for newlyweds to adjust sexually is to send them off by themselves on a holiday where they aren't supposed to do anything else but. I mean, you can't *just* have sex all day every day. Of course, in our case everything is all right. We already knew we were adjusted, and as a matter of fact

313

things have just gotten more and more perfect. So that leaves the holiday, and since we're pretty intense tourists the holiday aspect is well taken care of. All the same, it makes me mad sometimes to think "we're *supposed* to be going to a play tonight." Why can't we just go if we feel like it? Because there isn't anything else to do, that's why, except read a book or go to a movie, which we've been doing plenty of already.

The reason I asked you about Roy Carver and Harry Evans is Joe. Two or three times he's gotten all riled up over that murder. He says it's the image that appeals to him. Here is Evans throwing a home-made lead-pipe bomb with his own arm, at two men who are helping to make a missile which is just a "gigantistic" (ugh!) arm for throwing a superbomb. If I didn't *know* Joe so well I'd think he was nutty. I do wish Roy Carver at least was still around Berkeley. (Was he really in on it, do you think?) He probably knows a lot about Evans' motives. Of course Chantal knows the most, but one could never ask her. Maybe Leon has picked things up from her. Why don't you pump him if you can do it discreetly? Or Daddy even? If I just had some motives to go on. What is the psychopathology of it? Obviously he was sick to do a thing like that. But I can't figure out what kind of sickness—*at all*. This way I'm hamstrung when it comes to arguing with Joe. What I want is some good solid psychogenic reason for Evans to have done it, like divorced parents, for example, or a hidden childhood trauma, though that's quite a lot to expect Leon or even Roy to know. Of course our whole society is sick too, but that won't explain Evans' own personal psychology adequately.

You know, England is just awful. How did the English ever amount to anything? It's so depressing. They keep telling us that this is quite a normal winter, which means that by wearing all the clothes you own at once you can keep from shivering *visibly*. And the temperature they keep their buildings! They say you get used to it. Who *wants* to? The Eskimos are much more practical, they keep *warm* inside their skins and igloos. The ethnic way usually is better than the civilized way, of course. Here it is the end of February, and nature is dead. I keep thinking of the flowering fruit trees which are in blossom all over Berkeley, and the birds, and how the hills have been green for three months already, and the nice warm sun in the afternoons— or else I think of the pueblos, Koyala especially, with their *magnificent* vistas and all the cloud activity in the sky—and I feel so home-sick sometimes that I think if it wasn't for Joe I would just die. I think if Joe got a job so I had to live in a place like Chicago I'd just fade away.

I read Joe selected passages from your letter, mostly the ones about Jim Sorb, and he chuckled a lot. Then I followed your instructions and destroyed the letter—though I must say it seems unnecessary to me. What's the matter, little sister? Got a private eye chasing you? At this very moment, Joe is out buying a car. I don't know what kind he's going to get—a cheap one, I hope, our money is just melting away. It seems we're going to take a trip around England, sightseeing. Well, that suits me. I've had about as much London as I can stand. And these side trips we keep making by train and bus are a drag. It's always raining, and you keep waiting for trains and drinking their god-awful coffee or tea in tiresome little tea-rooms, and you walk so much. Somehow it's different taking long hikes in Pueblo country. I've walked as much as 15 or 20 miles there and enjoyed it. But here you keep *dodging* so much, or something, that you don't enjoy it.

Our first stop is going to be Thaxted, a village not far from London. There's supposed to be a nice church there, nicer than average. But the thing that really impresses Joe is a little room where John Ball hid from the king's police for a couple of years—at least that's what a guy Joe got talking to in a bookstore said. John Ball was a priest in the 14th Century (just in case it slipped your mind who John Ball was!) and he was a sort of Christian Communist. He stirred up people a lot and helped to cause the Peasants' Revolt in 1381. He was excommunicated and everything and they finally drew and quartered him. He was pretty impressive, all right, for those brutal times. There was a terrific amount of social injustice, and the peasants had every right in the world to revolt against their oppressors, the lords. But he wasn't all *that* much a reformer, he was sort of hyper-reactionary actually—he wanted to go back to the most repressive sort of Catholic practices. For example, Joe discovered (we went through half a dozen bookstores looking for books on him) that he preached that anybody who was conceived out of wedlock was damned to all eternity. You should have heard Joe chuckle when he read that out loud to me! It was just fiendish. Of course he knows perfectly well that my parents got married at the last minute to legitimize me. I laugh with him but I don't really think it's funny. He shouldn't laugh with me about *that*. So anyway, John Ball was at least against social injustice, which was very progressive in his day, even if his religious views were reactionary. But the thing that really sends Joe is that he hid out in the Thaxted church for two years or so. (It's not in any of the books we got.) "Sanctuary," Joe keeps saying, "sanctuary." Of course it wasn't sanctuary at all, but it was sort of like it in a way; Joe talks about sanctuary so much that I finally looked it up in the encyclopedia. The thing I keep telling him is—after a criminal had been in the church for 40 days, the state would exile him or starve him out. John Ball must have been *hiding*. Joe just glares at me when I say this, though it is perfectly true, and he tells me to quit bugging him.

I hear him coming up the stairs now. I'll pin him down about where we'll be three weeks from now and then I'll mail this right off.

Later

OK—send your next letter to me at Durham, Poste Restante. It seems that's what they call General Delivery in this benighted land. Why do they have to do everything so differently—drive on the wrong side of the road, funny money, rude to each other, Poste Restante! Send it so it arrives no later than March 20.

Love love love,
Liz

"Later" is really two in the morning. I wrote that in case you wanted to show my letter to anybody. *This* sheet of paper is *just* for you.

The thing is, Joe and I had a terrible fight and he walked out on me about six o'clock. I didn't even go down to dinner—not that dinner in this crummy joint is any great temptation. I've just been sitting here waiting for him to come back. I guess he isn't coming back tonight. Where could he be? It's cold out, bitter cold. He doesn't know anybody. Is he in another hotel? Maybe he's really left me. That's absurd of course. Besides, I only have about 7 or 8 pounds. He has the bankbook we draw on. He couldn't leave me like this, flat. He's just mad. But at what? It's awful. Either he has a secret or else he hates me. But how can he hate me so soon? Anyway, I *know* he doesn't. Just last night he was so loving and tender and affectionate, I *know* he wasn't putting it on. Well, but he wasn't putting on this afternoon, either. He's not just ambivalent, he's worse. If I believed in devils, I'd think he gets possessed by a devil sometimes. He must have a secret.

The reason I think so is that there's nothing else it could be, and besides he's dropped hints. Doesn't he trust me? Doesn't he know I would not hold his past against him? It must be something to do with his family or some other woman. It always is family or sex. I know that. Why does he hold out on me? I trust him implicitly. Marriage is based on trust. There's only one thing I haven't told him—you're the only person I ever told. That I had my tubes tied. I'm just waiting for the right moment to tell him, but it isn't something that comes between us. It's just like if I'd had my appendix out and didn't get around to mentioning it till he noticed the scar. The only difference is that I tell him I use contraceptives when I don't. But lord, that's *nothing*. How can he hold out on me? I would forgive him anything, no matter how awful, if he would just tell me about it, but when he

316

doesn't tell me, it is alienating. Doesn't what I'm saying make good sense? Or am I crazy? I told him this about trusting. He just glared at me and his nose twitched. He didn't say a syllable. He just walked out without saying where he was going or when he would be back.

It all started when I told him I had to know where to tell you to send your next letter. He told me to quit pushing him around. Well, of course I wasn't pushing him around at all. What could be more reasonable than a request like that? So I got mad and we shouted around for a while. He said how could he know how long he'd want to stay in Ely? Maybe the cathedral there would be exactly what he'd been looking for all his life and he'd want to stay on indefinitely. So I said, fine, I'd tell you to send your letter to Ely. Then he said that was crazy, Ely was practically the second stop of our trip, we'd probably be out of there in no time. He just didn't want to be pinned down. I cried. I was so mad and frustrated I cried. He was nice. He was re- pentant. He said he was sorry he'd been so unreasonable—of course he *had* been terribly unreasonable. He said to tell you, Durham. Then he went on to say I shouldn't hold it against him too much, he was so heavy-laden. That's when I told him he had to tell me what his secret was if we were to really trust one another, and he walked out on me. So.

· 12 ·

Leon was sitting at the kitchen table, and Chantal was at the sink, peeling carrots. Jean-Louis was gone till early evening, in Tilden Park at a big wienie roast for Nancy and Shirley; the girls had been born nine days apart and had always had a joint birthday party.

Leon took a gulp of air and as he exhaled said breathily, "Chan- tal." He had been preparing for this conversation for several days.

"Yes?"

"I've decided to move back to my apartment."

"Ah?" She rested the heels of her hands on the edge of the sink and looked over her shoulder at him with a blank face. "Jean-Louis has been making too much noise perhaps? Your studies have been distracted?"

"On the contrary, he's a pleasure to have around. I couldn't hope to study harder than this in my apartment alone. You see, it's just that I think it would be better for everybody."

"So. You no longer like my cooking? Why do I make *pot au feu* for tonight? Because you like my *pot au feu*. Perhaps I am mistaken?"

"Oh, good God, don't be absurd. You cook better than ever. Any- way, I plan to keep on boarding with you, as before."

317

"Well, what have I done wrong?"

"Look," he said tenderly, "let's get one thing straight. Your behavior has been impeccable. You never unloaded on me once."

"Unloaded?"

"Dumped your troubles on me."

"That wasn't part of the bargain," she said.

"For example, all I know about Harry is what I read in the papers."

She shrugged and looked up into the corner of the room. She had lost a good deal of weight since the previous summer. Her wrists were bony, her neck showed tendons, her nose was pinched, her eyes seemed larger. Leon had observed these changes with a sort of detached concern; now, looking at her, he saw her as small and scared. As a woman she was quite unattractive at this moment. He had an impulse of sheltering tenderness for her.

"I did not realize," she said, "it mattered to you about Harry."

"Please. It was only an example. I am not fishing. Forget I said anything."

"There's so little to tell. Since he has been condemned, he refuses to see me or even to accept my letters. They are returned to me. Twice I go by bus and taxi to San Quentin. Both times—nothing. Pfft." She perched on a chair across the table from Leon. "He has no relatives, no friends. He refuses to appeal. He will be executed next year, having seen no one but guards and lawyers, to whom he has nothing to say. A doctor who will examine him. Is he too mad to be executed? It's not possible for me to say how mad he is. He was less mad in France, when I first knew him. When he was killing he wasn't mad, I think. Perhaps it's love that makes him mad and mad. Alone, there in the condemned cell, he can kill over and over in his imagination. Me, my letters, we remind him of love. We threaten him again with love, who can say? He and I, we have not loved for years, perhaps only a friendship and a passion. He rescued me, I was grateful. I did admire him, I do admire him, he is courageous. One must be quite mad to get oneself in a position to reveal courage in this age of ours. You and I, we are more normal. We're subtle, not courageous. We aspire to honesty at the most. He was courageous. *Is* courageous. He has no brother, sister, friend. He is alone. Honesty is not enough for that. For that, courage is necessary. I could never have lived with him as a wife—a mistress, perhaps, not a wife, not a true companion. I would have done so, out of gratitude, but I couldn't truly do it. Now, as I am, not loving him genuinely, yet not separated from him entirely, I am in stasis. I am"—she suddenly tightened her arms and shoulders and clenched her face—"locked up. I shall not be unlocked till he is dead. While he's there, alone, alive, unknown to me, something cannot move around in me. Ah," she said, huddling over onto herself, "in California they take so long to kill a man."

"Chantal," Leon said, "do you—did you—" He had not supposed the answer to the question he was about to ask mattered to him. Yet he approached it with far more difficulty than mere regard for her feelings would warrant. He paused a moment in concern and confusion.

She looked at him from her desolation and spoke neutrally. "Yes, Leon?"

"Do you love him?"

"Ah." She gazed at his mouth, her head slightly tilted back. A faint smile moved her lips. "He has the power to pull me down into death with him, I think—some of me. Is that love? It isn't at all what I felt for my husband. When he died, I wept, I grieved, I lived. And Jean-Louis's father, that one who never saw him, the now priest—those were novelistic emotions, they were from Rousseau and George Sand. And you, you—what of you? You are the fourth man in my life. A friend? Just a friend, it appears. I've been deceiving myself." She gazed at her hands; her lips were pursed and drawn down.

"Why do you say such a thing?"

"You tell me you're leaving without a reason. You don't even have the consideration to fight first."

"We never fight, Chantal."

She shrugged. "You see? Who ever heard of such a thing? Half a year living together and not a fight." She looked at him sideways and smiled shyly. "How is Sybil?"

"Why do you ask?" he said stiffly.

"Jean-Louis has mentioned her from time to time. Nancy tells him."

"Sybil has been disturbed by her parents' difficulties. As one of the teachers in her college, and as an older friend of the family, I have talked with her several times."

"Tya tya tya."

"As a matter of fact, I'm going to see her later this evening."

"Heh heh. A professional appointment, no doubt."

"It's a matter of counseling," he said with a sniff. In fact, he was moving out of Chantal's apartment so that he might be free to declare himself to Sybil. "It seems that she has become involved with a young law student who is a brother of a friend of the family."

"Good for her," said Chantal.

"What do you mean by that ambiguous remark?"

"Nothing, my friend. Why shouldn't I be happy for her to have a boy friend? I'm happy for you too. Flossie?"

"God," he said coldly. "My private life is my own business."

"Yes, husband. Well, no more teasing."

"You are a suspicious bourgeoise."

"What else? Didn't I tell you my family were shopkeepers for generations? Well, Leon, I failed to realize, it seems, that you would want to get divorced so soon. I am being ungrateful. We were never completely married, yet I don't like being unmarried from you, either. You're right, it is *louche.*"

He was still snorting as he breathed, though less than before. "When did I mention divorce?"

"*Louche, louche, louche!*" she cried and threw up her hands. "Do it any way you wish. What is it to me? You've done so much for me already. Do what the law approves. I will thank you sincerely."

"You are not kind."

"*Alors.*" She went back to her vegetables. "Pay attention to my words. I mean them. I will thank you sincerely."

He stood beside her, forcing her to look up at him. "We won't talk about divorce until we're both free. You can't be free from Harry till he is dead. I understand. The nature of my involvements is less clear. By then they should be resolved, without a doubt. Meanwhile we must—I believe—we must not get confused. When the time comes for us to talk freely, to act, to move as we wish, then perhaps, one way or the other—who knows?" He waved his arm in a large, violent, vague gesture.

"Leon, my dear friend." She reached up and took his face between her hands. "Here, bend down to me." They kissed. "So. You will continue to eat with me, no? Good. Just remember, from time to time kiss me."

He frowned and blinked.

"If I were the wife of a friend who is to be executed," she said, "would you not kiss her from time to time, in friendliness?"

"But that's different."

"You are so clear about it, *chéri?*"

"There'd be no question of anything but friendship."

"Aha. Who knows? One must allow the heart to confuse itself. That is its nature. Otherwise it will shrink down into itself, from inaction."

"I'm going to go pack my things now."

"I'll call you when supper is prepared."

After they had eaten, he carried down to the car all the possessions he had brought from his apartment. Jean-Louis had not come home yet. He went back up the stairs to say good-by. Chantal was in her bedroom with the door closed. He rapped. She opened it a crack and looked up at him with an expressionless face. He took her in his arms to kiss her warmly, but she was tight and unresponsive.

"I want to cry," he said.
She shrugged.

· 13 ·

"Why are you late?" said Leon, sliding off the stool.

Sybil cocked an eye at the clock above the cash register. "Two minutes?"

"I've been here for ten," he said.

"That's your problem, kiddo. Let's cut out."

Three Presley girls were at the counter, so he suppressed his anger. On the sidewalk he said, "Let's don't start off on the wrong foot tonight."

"Suit yourself." She started to open the door to his car, but he caught it halfway. "Now what?" she said.

"You've been evading me."

"Have I."

"I moved out of Chantal's today."

"Why?"

"That's what I want to talk with you about."

"Well, we can't talk here, so let me get in your ever-loving Dodge."

When they came to a straight stretch of road, he reached for her hand. She gave him a fist.

"Aw," he said, "come on."

"I told you on the phone I felt like going bowling, and here you are heading for the hills."

Though she did not particularly want to bowl, she was all set to make an issue of it. What she really wanted was to avoid necking with him, for fear she would be unable to keep on not caring for him as she was determined to do.

"But I told you I had to talk about something important," he said.

"Well," she said, "here you just take off for the hills without saying a mumbling word. How about some manners?"

"Manners! Why, you self-indulgent twit, do you realize what . . ." He growled. "Jesus, if I ever have a daughter I hope to hell she's not pretty. And I thought you were an exception to the rule, because you don't sleep around. Like hell you're an exception. Manners!"

She tried to take his right hand again, but he would not let go of the steering wheel. He continued to rant, considerably louder than he would have done if she were not making little gestures of appeasement. At one point he waved his arm largely, and she caught it. As though he did not notice, he kept on scolding her, pretty women, womankind, while letting her stroke his hand with both hers. When

321

she felt him soften responsively, she took his right hand with hers as though shaking hands with him but with her middle finger turned in and wriggling suggestively in the palm of his hand.

"Sybil!" He pretended to be shocked. "What are you doing?"

"I'm just as dirty as anybody else."

"You are not," he said almost pleadingly. "You oughtn't to do things like that."

"Oh, come on, you old whited sepulcher. Look, there's a nice dark little old side road. I bet we could find a place to neck down it somewhere."

"Sybil, really."

"Well, where are we going?"

"I have a special place in mind with a great view. There aren't many nights as clear as this. I just hope nobody's there already. Did you know the moon is full?"

She sighed and curled on the seat with her head on his lap. He undid the top two buttons of her sweater and fondled her throat as he drove.

He parked on a point commanding a sweeping view of the wide, silvery, intricate valley of Tilden Park.

"Whew," she said when she sat up, "I guess it's worth it. Why don't you back up a little next to those bushes? Then we wouldn't have to see Parktilden Village."

"I want us to see it."

"But look, over there you'd hardly know there was a city on the other side of the hills, just a few lights from some houses. We could be way inland, up in the foothills, if it wasn't for those hideous towers."

"I don't see any towers. I just see some pretty lights."

"But I know what they're the lights of!"

"And that's why we are here," he said in a portentous voice.

"You know, buster, sometimes—"

"Please," he said peremptorily and began to talk about responsibility and the mature mind.

When he did not even kiss her first, it occurred to her that he must really mean it. She tried to tease him with caresses, but he put his arm around her in a firm, abstracted way and kept on talking. She wanted to say, "Hey, teacher, this ain't no classroom," but then decided it would hurt his feelings so much he would never get around to saying what was really on his mind. His big talk, as she thought of it, was worse than her father's even. At least her father had given her years of experience at turning down the volume till something worth listening to came on. She turned the volume down on Leon now.

322

He had got to sociology and intellectual disengagement, and somehow was working modern architecture in with social commitment and "the new man." He was using Peter Hazen, a new member of the Sociology Department, as an example of everything bad. She had met Hazen two or three times casually, and had no strong impression of him one way or the other—bright, bland, and ambitious, as Lizzie liked to say of new young faculty members from the important Eastern universities.

Then Leon paused, shifted in his seat, and began talking in a voice Sybil tuned in on; also, she recognized the names. He had just learned that Hazen had gotten involved with a professor's wife and her daughter simultaneously. They all lived in the same tower in Parktilden Village; Leon's manner implied that this was a sinister concatenation of elements. The daughter, a girl with whom Sybil had been acquainted for years, had injured herself in a motorcycle accident and then disappeared. Leon said that Hazen had taken up with night-club dancers right away. Then he turned and looked at Sybil severely.

"This whole debacle has brought me face to face with myself," he said.

He did not mention that he had introduced Hazen to one show girl and through him met another whom he sometimes took out.

"I have come to realize," he went on, "that I have never committed myself fully to anyone or anything. Therefore, I've moved out of Chantal's apartment and I'm going to begin divorce proceedings quite soon. Furthermore, I'd like you to think of me as your fiancé. That is, I want to think of myself as committed to you."

"You *what*?" she cried. "Angels and ministers of grace, defend me. Are you by any chance proposing marriage?"

"That was implicit in everything I said."

She laughed shrilly.

"Sybil," he said reproachfully.

"Don't pull the pitiful, for Christ's sake. Shit shit shit." She laughed, screaming. "Well, you can just quit thinking of yourself as committed to me as of two minutes ago because, mister, I ain't having none nohow."

"I really—" he said and reached for her.

She flinched from his hand. "Haven't you got any glue?" she cried. "Sex and duty, that's what you've got. How're they going to hold together without any glue?"

"I don't know what you are talking about," he said in a hurt, patient voice.

"How could you know? Take me home. I want to go back, *now*." She began crying somewhat convulsively. When he tried to reason with her she hit his arm with her fist hard. "Shut up! Shut up! Take me back to my room!" She went on and on, repeating, hiccuping.

He started the car and hunched over the wheel as he drove.

When she had calmed down a little she peeked through her fingers at him and was gratified to see a pained, desolate look on his face. They were through, that much was clear. She was relieved. She would not have to worry about making love with him any more, unsure of how far they were going, unable to resist him, doubtful of what his intentions were, or her own either. Also she was secretly pleased at being so upset. She had never been even slightly hysterical before. Not only was she confident now that she could be as unreasonably emotional as other women, but she had been perfectly right to be so upset. It was all his fault. He was incredible.

She planned to make a polite little farewell speech when they parted, after which nothing—friends, not enemies, okay? But when he drew up in front of her dormitory he began to say something in a voice at once demanding and piteous, and she discovered that she could not utter a word but had to get out of the car almost in panic, lips clenched tight, head bent and shaking no no no no.

Roz was already asleep. Sybil went to bed and cried into her pillow, no longer pleased with herself. Sometimes she hoped that Leon was crying too. Sometimes she wished that he was dead. A couple of times she wished that she had not refused to go to bed with him but was in his bed now or at least in the car petting all the way. She had rejected two men within a few days, word would get around, she would be an old maid. Maybe unconsciously she really wanted to be an old maid?

Roz asked in a thick voice what was the matter. She was able to control her sobbing enough so that Roz only asked once more before turning over and going back to sleep. Sybil wished, unenviously, that she could be like Roz and love a man who wanted to be a part of the world he was going to be part of anyway. She thought bitterly of her parents, who had spoiled her for such men and left her with none but nuts and twitches to choose among. Why couldn't fraternity men be alive? Why couldn't her parents have been wrong about this, as they were about plenty of other things?

She fell asleep.

· 14 ·

"Chantal," said Alfred, pushing himself back from the table and holding his arms out toward her, "permit me to thank you from the bottom of my heart for inviting me to dinner. No, for having allowed

324

me to wangle an invitation out of you, for that is what really happened."

"Why, Professor," she said, "the pleasure is all mine, I assure you." She looked up to him; it obviously made her happy to look up to him.

"*Maman*," said Jean-Louis perfunctorily, glancing at the wall clock, "the *sauce* for the veal was delicious. May I—"

"Ah," she said, waggling her head a little, "one cannot obtain true veal in this country. Why is this, *hein*? Professor, if I'd had more time, perhaps I'd have made a dinner more worthy of the occasion."

"*Maman*—" Jean-Louis began again, but Leon frowned at him.

"Worthy!" Alfred cried. "In the past months, the past eight or nine months, I've become a professional diner-out. It's my chief relaxation after the ardors of study and writing. I've become something of a gourmet of the local cuisine." He winked at Leon, who smiled. "Some of the women of my acquaintance pride themselves, justifiably, on their cooking. Moreover, I've been to most of the best-known restaurants in the Bay Area by now. Therefore, permit me to say: except for an expense-account dinner at Lucien's, where I was taken by a vice-president of the CIO—a man who still wears a scar on his forehead where his head was split open twenty years ago by a goon during a strike for a dime-an-hour raise; when I first saw him at the bargaining table his head was bandaged, his suit was shiny and frazzled, it was a hot muggy day and I remember that his handkerchief was so shabby he arranged it out of sight under the table before he wiped his face with it, and the dinner at Lucien's last month cost the two of us, including drinks, just under fifty dollars before the tip. Well, my dear, except for that dinner, this one is by far the best I've eaten since—well, since. Pardon me, I'm babbling on."

"You are very kind, Professor. *Les Echézeaux* you were so kind as to bring, that would make any meal delicious."

"*Maman*," said Jean-Louis, "may I be excused now, please? I told Barry I'd meet him at the Center at seven for badminton. I'm already ten minutes late."

He had not got up from his chair, nor did he speak in a whining or disrespectful voice. He was eager and courteous at once.

"Ah, well, it's only two blocks. Say good-by to Professor Royce. Then you may go."

After saying good-by politely, he ran out, not slamming the door behind him.

"Be back in an hour!" Chantal called, and he cried something indistinguishable as he ran down the stairs.

"Ah," said Alfred, "what manners! You're a caution to us all, Chantal, all us permissive American slobs of parents."

325

"Pardon me," said Leon, rising. "I'll go over to my place and change, Alfred. Then we can take off. I won't be a quarter of an hour. Okay?"

"You are going?" said Chantal.

"I told you we were," said Leon.

"I know, but . . ."

"I haven't the slightest desire to stir," said Alfred, "for an hour at the earliest. I wouldn't dream of unsettling my stomach at this point."

"The celery root," said Leon to Chantal in an almost shy way, "was masterly. You outdid yourself."

"Which was that?" said Alfred. "I tasted no celery root, at least that I recognized."

"It was the purée," said Chantal, making a gesture of pleased deprecation. "The brown stuff in the pie dish. There."

The men continued their compliments.

"Well," said Chantal, "you've flattered me adequately. You may go now. I have enough flattery to do the dishes by myself without melancholy."

"But I want to sit with you while you do them," said Alfred. "Leon has papers to grade. You gave one of your finals early, isn't that right? Very well, go grade your papers and free your conscience for an evening of indulgence. I'll come over in an hour or so and we'll take our walk. Why not?"

Leon looked relieved. Chantal smiled. Alfred patted his belly.

For half an hour, in pure contentment, Alfred, who had spent eight hours that day in his study working hard, babbled to Chantal about whatever entered his head. She expanded in this radiance, and without for a moment ceasing to look up to him, told him what was weighing on her mind. She knew he would understand her but not give her advice.

She spoke of Harry. "I understand that he should kill those two men, try to kill them both. It's absurd, but I understand his logic. I understand that he should refuse to defend himself in court, that he should scorn to appeal. That too is absurd. He saved everything for his statement after sentencing. You didn't attend the trial throughout? No. I did, of course. He had prepared a speech. They let him speak. It was a good enough speech. But he delivered it—how shall I say? Without conviction. He seemed to know ahead of time that people wouldn't believe what he said, even the little which they might have comprehended. They would convert it into psychology. Of course, precisely. They look behind the political idealism for psychological motives. 'Nothing is as it appears, that goes without saying. All is motive, hidden motive, usually bad.' Bah." She paused, and her face took on a bleak, closed look. "That was the last time I saw him, there in the courtroom. Since then, he refuses to see me or to read my letters that I write to him. This I don't understand. Perhaps it is the absurd of the absurd."

Because she demanded nothing of him and because he was so mellow, he spoke to her with a kind of warm and sympathetic bitterness. "I don't know, of course. I never met Evans. But the absurd, now—it's in fashion. For that very reason I'm leery of it. It's a way of saying—too often, it is used as a way of saying, 'The world is incoherent, I won't even try to understand.' It becomes a way of letting oneself off the hook. You don't understand his cutting himself off from you? Very well, therefore it means nothing? No, no, Chantal, things aren't that simple. Let me speculate. You understand, I am dreaming now. I don't know the man. I'm not really sure of your connection with him. Nor do I ask you to tell me. This way, I remain free to see connections, perhaps I can see the forest without getting lost among the trees, I'm far enough away to make guesses that are comprehensive. Stop me if I am too impertinent or too fantastic."

She left the sink and sat across the table from him, watching him intently, her hands cupped together on the table in front of her.

"Stop you?" she said "Please, I am listening."

"I suppose him as being a man capable of the most intense attachments, but in some profound way afraid of them. I don't understand this configuration from myself, it's alien to my nature. But I imagine that he must turn people he's attached to into enemies if he can. Usually this is not hard, but sometimes he cannot do it. Then he must hurt them, in a kind of revenge for love." He saw her look down into her supplicating hands and saw her mouth tighten. "Pardon me, my dear. Of course the obvious objects of such painful attachment are those who are already enemies. The Nazis were perfect enemies. Perhaps he was never happier than when he was fighting them, especially since he did it secretly, as though on his own. But the world is rich with enemies. In all honesty, it's very hard sometimes not to devote oneself to hating them; so I find, at least. But Evans is a man of pride and intellect. He doesn't allow himself to hate this man or that man for himself only. That's much too petty. He hates the idea which this man or that man embodies. He sees himself a man in a world of avatars. If McKee and Brady had been merely men, he wouldn't have wanted to kill them. Perhaps he wouldn't have deigned to kill them—I suspect he's extremely proud. But they weren't men, they were avatars of capitalism. Therefore, their assassination is an example, not a murder. And so on, and so on. But at the root of all this is a rage against the love which he can't suppress. Rather, he cannot suppress love's needs, so he must subvert love's trust. Society is like love; it is held together by trust and need, yet it sets up prohibitions against the rage and revenge that drive him. Most of his rage against love can be expended in fighting society. Few join him in his war, for it's too total, too personal. He accepts the limitations of his own human body; they are natural. But the moral limitations set by society can be opposed and changed and destroyed, they don't have to be what and as they are, he's against all moral limitation. Love, trust, law—this is the cluster of what he hates. He seems to hate social abuses and injustices like any decent person, but this hatred is only a mask for a hatred of society itself, which in turn is a mask for his rage against love. I don't know how philosophical he is, or what his religious training was, or what his father was like. But I would not be surprised to learn that he hates God passionately."

"That's true," said Chantal and rested her chin on her folded hands. "Once, I remember, when he was already good friends with Jean-Michel, my husband, he learned that Jean-Michel had refuged for several weeks in a monastery in the mountains south of Grenoble. He was furious! How could Jean-Michel have submitted himself to the indignity of hiding behind those monks' skirts? Of course, we were astounded. He said, 'Didn't they love God, those monks?' 'Yes,' said Jean-Michel, 'they loved God. Myself, I don't know if God exists. I don't even care very much. But they protected me from the Germans at the risk of their own lives.' 'What is that but courage?' said Harry. 'One must not be seduced by courage. The enemy is courageous too. God is the ultimate enemy. One must never forget that. His friends are my enemies par excellence. One must not be seduced by their goodness.' Well, of course that was astounding to us. It was like a very bad joke. Seduced by goodness? He didn't mention God again. But I've never forgotten that little episode. How can one hate the good God? That there is no God—yes. That he is not all-powerful—yes. That there are devils too—yes. That God is far away, indifferent—yes, yes. But that he is good and yet I must hate him— how can that be? That is nonsense, confusion. Yet Harry said that. Professor, how do you guess this about him when you aren't even acquainted with him personally? I told you nothing about him, *hein*? Is it Leon?"

"No one has told me anything special about Evans," said Alfred, shaking his head. "I am fantasying. I've made it my profession in life to dream how the world holds together. It is my faith and my hope that reality can be dreamed. Wheee! Bmm bmm bmm wowie! So. I'll come back to earth. Why has Evans cut himself off from you now? His immediate enemy, society, is about to kill him. If he's as proud as I imagine, that fact gives him the strength of opposition. He doesn't want to weaken in his antagonism. Perhaps he hasn't been able to turn you, Chantal, into an avatar of something bad? Perhaps you re-

328

main a person, whom he loves in such a way that he can't quite distrust you enough? Who knows? Obviously, he didn't succeed in hurting you enough to make an enemy of you. But there's more to it yet. Alone, in his cell, he has very little to support him. He will be denied the opportunity to make a great public last speech from the scaffold, such as supported political criminals in the past sometimes. Also, he'll have to wait too long for his last words to make an impact on the world. He is thrown face to face—no, he is posed mind to mind with his purest enemy, God. It is God who is ultimately responsible for the way things are. After Evans is sure he's going to be executed by the minor enemy, he finds himself face to face indeed with the major enemy. He must prepare himself for that confrontation. To be sure, there is no God, there is no life after death. Yet God must be defied to the end and beyond. If Evans saw you, he might weaken with trust, affection might relax his hatred for a moment, his defense might crack, and who knows how far the tender enemy would penetrate? As it is now, he can hold himself rigid right into the gas chamber. *It's all God's fault.* Yet he must sleep. I cannot guess what happens in his soul when he's asleep. Perhaps it's just that I cannot bring myself to think about it closely. That's too painful for me. I am cowardly."

"I too have thought of that, without success."

They gazed at each other a moment. He reached over and held her hands firmly in his. She leaned down and pressed her cheek against his hands a moment.

"If he had not brought me and Jean-Louis to this country, with difficulty, for no reason—that is, for no benefit to himself really—I would know what to think of your theory. But that deed of his, it was gratuitous. It doesn't fit in so well. How can I forget that, even now?"

"People!" Alfred cried, waving his hands. "People! What can you do about people? Of course it won't fit in. Perhaps all he's doing now is avenging himself on you for having allowed him to rescue you. Perhaps it's nothing but psychology. Why don't I shut up? Give me another cup of coffee, and I'll leave."

She served him. Until he rose to leave, neither of them spoke.

At the door she said, "I shall think about your theory. It appeals to me. It appalls me too—that anybody could really hate goodness."

"Not goodness—God. Goodness because God is good."

"Yes. I comprehend with my intelligence, but my heart is afraid to accept what you tell me. That will take time. Yet, I was losing myself before. In the absurd I was lost. I was freezing to death. Perhaps you have saved me? It may be so."

"I am not in the salvaging business," he said in a somewhat hard voice. His eyes puckered and he licked his mustache. "You may use my dream to save yourself with if you can, but I assure you that's not what I made it up for."

For a moment there was an expression of pain in her eyes at this repudiation; then, with the slightest readjustment, her features softened, her body relaxed. His stern look became also sad. Without smiling, they exchanged a look of sympathy. He touched her and left.

· 15 ·

After a fat dancer and a bored one, Mazda was announced.

"She's incredible," Leon whispered to Alfred. "I'm glad you saw those other two first. You'll really appreciate her."

She was slender, lithe, and well proportioned. The belly dance she did was simple and subtle like the music. At first Alfred was afraid of his susceptibility to a beautiful, half-naked young woman performing an erotic dance. But he discovered that, instead of inflaming his sensuality, her motions somehow flowed through the erotic toward esthetic pleasure. Esthetic love? Not sensual indulgence, but love for esthetic pleasure? It had not occurred to him to suppose that erotic pleasure could bypass the conscience, as Mazda's dance seemed to be doing: his conscience was alert to pounce on any vagrant impulse, but none strayed. He could have been watching a sunset.

At the end of the dance, when the audience in the night club was applauding, Mazda gave the only indication that she knew Leon. As she stood in the final position for a moment—her weight on one leg, the other raised a little with the bent bare toes on the floor, body slightly twisted so that there were pleasing lines in her otherwise smooth belly, her arms in the flame position over her head, fingertips touching, head bent to one side—she gazed straight into Leon's eyes. But there was nothing personal about the gaze, no challenging blink, no winking recognition, no appeal for praise, no queening it over him. Alfred could not interpret her gaze; had he not assumed Leon was her lover, he would have supposed her glance had fallen by chance on him merely as a young man in the ringside.

"Wasn't she a marvel?" said Leon out on the Broadway sidewalk.

"A houri," said Alfred. "Lord, it's good to get out in the breeze. Let's walk a while. I'm not used to the gay life, I'm afraid it'll go to my head."

"Isn't she beautiful?"

"Now I understand why the Mohammedans believe women have no souls."

Leon laughed immoderately. "Oh, that's so characteristic of you, Alfred. You Puritan in a liberal's clothing! No soul? First of all she's

330

Greek Orthodox. Her parents are Greeks. And second, she's going to State in the daytime, getting a credential in speech therapy. She wants to spend her life helping children with speech defects."

Alfred flourished his hand and opened his mouth in mock consternation. "Impossible! Lovely! Leon, marry her!"

"She sits in her dressing room between shows, doing homework."

"Credo in unam uxorem et in corpus profanum. Or is it *profanus?* Maybe *profanu,* even. I must be getting old; genders no longer matter to me as they once did."

Leon gave him a hug. Alfred flourished his cane.

An alleyway wide enough for one car ran down from Broadway half a block. Along the center of the alley lay a red carpet. At the end was a marquee advertising the Grubstake.

"That's Flossie's place now," said Leon.

"I beg your pardon?"

"Want to go down and catch her show? She's been going three weeks. It's got to the gossip columns. She's made, for a while anyway."

"One walks on this carpet?" said Alfred.

"Howdy, pardners!" This shout came from a Negro in gold-miner's clothes in front of the Grubstake. It was followed by a yippee. "Right this way to the hottest show to ever hit the Gold Coast! Flossie's Pramenade going on in ten minutes!"

"You know," said Alfred, "I don't really want to go into another one of these hothouses just yet. Flossie is a splendid creature, if I'm not confusing her with one of your other houris. But honestly, I am not impervious enough. It takes practice. Why don't we just walk around for a while and you tell me about her act?"

"Okay. Anyway, there's a five-dollar cover in the Grubstake, and a dollar and a half for beer. As for Flossie's act, it's bad enough to be on TV."

For blocks Leon described it and Alfred gave him a steady supply of grunts and chuckles, assuming he was garnishing the account for effect. In fact, Leon exaggerated little and suppressed what he considered the worst single feature of the story.

Flossie enters, to "Rock-a-by Baby," in a large baby carriage, her entire body except for her head encased in a one-piece infant's sleepsuit, lying on her back, waving her arms and legs aimlessly. The carriage is being pushed by a man seven and a half feet tall, dressed in a nursemaid's costume. He flutters, minces, and oohs, like a homosexual caricaturing a nursemaid. (In fact he is a rather retiring man living with his six-and-a-half-foot wife on a houseboat with a sculptor, his mistress, and their three children.) After a good deal of googooing, the giant feels Flossie's diaper, cocks his head, smells his fingers

331

doubtfully, then feels again and nods and blinks in a pleased way. This is the comic high point of the act. The giant stretches out on a park seat, the lights dim, and both fall asleep. Then to slow, dreamy progressive jazz more like Debussy than like New Orleans blues, Flossie emerges from the sleep-suit like a butterfly from a cocoon. (When the giant was pretending to feel her diaper, he was really unsnapping the suit for her to emerge easily.) She is dressed in a bikini; the diaper-shaped loincloth is fastened at both sides by large gold safety pins. Flossie, heavily tanned, her hair brown, is hard to see in the dim amber light. The loincloth and the narrow strapless band around her chest glow a brilliant phosphorescent orange; her fingernails, toenails, and eyelids also glow orange. She assumes a pose and holds it for a while, moving nothing but her arms in wide slow arcs, so that the audience can figure out what they are looking at. Her appearance is the dramatic high point of the act. For a few minutes she does a shapeless, writhing dance of her own invention. The accompanying music is in a rhythm so much faster and subtler than any sustained dance rhythm could ever be that her motions have almost no connection with it. The lights get dimmer and her motions depart further from the music and from any apprehensible rhythm, until almost nothing is visible but erratic orange streaks. Then the two parts of the bikini begin waving around in the obscurity in a way that means she has taken them off. This is the erotic high point of the act. The pieces of cloth disappear (into the baby carriage), the music reduces to a low saxophone buzzing by itself, the orange spots on her body waver about for a while like fireflies, and then they disappear. The lights and music come up, discovering the giant on the bench and Flossie back in the baby carriage, dressed in the sleep-suit as before. She begins to squall. With much fuss he pulls out of the bag he has brought along a two-foot bottle with a red nipple and shoves it into her mouth. She holds the bottle with both mitts, weaving it back and forth, and makes loud happy gurgling noises. After another feel of Flossie's diaper and much slapstick surprise—batting of the eyes and shaking of the head—the giant begins to push the carriage off, frowns, cocks his head, feels again, rummages around in the carriage under her, and then, triumphantly waving the loincloth, minces offstage.

Alfred found this act, as Leon recounted it, accompanying the story with snickers, meaningless and pornographic in a way Mazda's dance had not been.

The part of the story which Leon had suppressed, in shame before Alfred, was that Flossie had talked to him about her dance in the orange bikini as a work of choreography, applying to it the jargon of modern dance criticism and even hinting once at a new art form emerging from night-club entertainment. Alfred would have taken such talk from such a girl as no more than pomposities floating around in a vain, empty head. Leon, however, thinking that his pleasure in Flossie's act was depraved, considered this theorizing of hers as an ultimate because mental degradation of the human spirit, and assumed that Alfred would so consider it. She had told Leon her new-art-form theory ten days before, just after the first and most important gossip columnist had written her up. Thinking it over next morning, Leon had gradually become so shocked that he had resolved never to go out with her again. He had instead settled upon Mazda. Mazda, however (as he had not told Alfred), had not settled upon him. He had tried to get Alfred to go see Flossie's show so that he might tell by Alfred's reactions whether it, and she, might not be less unacceptable than he thought: he wanted to go back to her. The truth was, despite the "intellectual degradation of the human spirit" that he saw in Flossie's theorizing, it had been the pornographic, meaningless act itself which had upset him. He could not admit this to himself readily because he believed with iron-clad liberalism that pornography existed only in the minds of puritanical hypocrites and that anyway he was above it. Had she been practical or cynical about the act, he would have continued to applaud it, in violation of his deepest feelings, and even to defend it against any charges of meaningless vulgarity ("Of course it is vulgar but that's not the point, the point is . . .").

"You know," said Alfred when Leon had finished and they were walking back into North Beach, "there are only two ways to handle something like this—laugh at it or wipe it out. Nothing in between."

"What do you mean?" cried Leon, stopping on the sidewalk and making him stop. "It's so trivial, isn't it? What does it matter?"

"Exactly. It's so unimportant it has to be got rid of, or else it'll get you all tangled up in such confused, strong emotions you'll never get disentangled."

"Go on, go on."

"Go on? Where is there to go? I want coffee."

"Wait," said Leon. "Why should Flossie's act arouse such tangled emotions? You're right, it does. But why?"

"How do I know? Who cares? The point is this: The moment I begin taking it seriously enough even to try to understand it, I get so riled up I find myself thinking, the civilization which produces and applauds such things deserves to perish."

"Doesn't it? Isn't that the truth?"

"Of course. Of course this civilization deserves to perish. I hope it doesn't: it also deserves to survive. So let's have a cappuccino at Buci's. Is Buci's still there? I haven't been to Buci's for years. They used to have singing waiters before the war—not very great singers, but it was jolly. As I remember it was three or four blocks above Broadway, up the hill from Grant half a block. Come on."

Leon kept pressing past people so as always to be right at Alfred's elbow, as though fearful of missing something.

· 16 ·

Buci's was still there. Alfred and Leon stepped inside and looked around. Nothing about it was the same except the huge heavy bar and cloudy mirror. Alfred made a gesture of withdrawal, but Leon held him. There were a couple of dozen people scattered about the big room. Halfway down it, opposite the bar, was a small stage, on which at the moment a barefoot Mexican girl in blue jeans was singing "Barbara Allen" over a public-address system that made her voice sound metallic.

A waiter wearing huarachos came toward them where they were standing near the entrance—a slim young man with long sideburns, mutton chops, almost. Leon turned to leave, but the waiter called, "Mr. Kalish!" Leon turned back, frowning. "You've come at the right time, Mr. Kalish. You don't remember me. I was in your World History class two years ago. My name was Brother Hortensius then."

"Of course. Good Lord, you look so different."

"I left before I took the final vows."

"Well," said Leon, not knowing how to respond to this, "may I introduce Professor Royce?"

"Professor Alfred Royce?" He looked admiringly at Alfred. "Brother Quintilian said such wonderful things about you."

"Thank you," said Alfred. "A charming man."

"What did he say?" Leon asked.

"Oh, I don't want to embarrass Professor Royce."

"Go on," said Leon. "Compliments are good for the spirit. Secondhand ones especially."

"He said"—the young man spoke to Leon bashfully but clearly— "that Professor Royce was full of wisdom." Then he looked at Alfred, who was beaming uncomfortably. "For Brother Quintilian, that is just about the highest compliment a layman could ever get. He said he wished you were Chief Justice, too."

The girl put down the theorbo with which she had been accompanying herself and announced that she was next going to sing an Appalachian version, "Sweet Barbry Allen," for comparison with the classical Lowland version she had just rendered. She put a dulcimer on her lap, plucked at it a few times, and began singing in a high nasal voice.

334

"Come on, sit down," said the young man. "After her there's a wonderful singer. You got here at a good time." They sat on a bench at a long table, behind two lounging couples studiously listening. "I'll bring you beers."

"No cappuccinos?" said Alfred.

"That's coffee-house stuff. Anyway, beer's cheaper. The next group are bluegrass. They haven't caught on yet. Tonight's amateur folk-singer night. Everybody's hoping to be discovered and get a job. Bluegrass hasn't caught on yet, but they're just wonderful, the girl especially—so genuine."

He left them to get the beer, set it down in front of them, mur-mured in Leon's ear "My name's Calvin Shimp, so you'll know," and withdrew to his station, keeping an eye on them and smiling once in a while.

Now, at last, Alfred began circling in on the subject which he had been wanting to talk to Leon about all evening. They had to talk loud enough to understand each other but not so loud as to bother their neighbors. They had to repeat a good deal; when the music increased in volume they had to shrug and stop; Leon kept glancing around the room at other people; Alfred strummed time with his fingers.

"Yesterday," Alfred began, "I received a disturbing note from Robin."

"From who?"

"Robin."

"Did you."

"She said she'd be out here in a few days and wanted to see me."

"Good," said Leon.

"Why good?"

"Why not? Probably she wants advice, and you're a good person to go to for it."

"But I scarcely know her," said Alfred.

"That makes two of us."

"Oh." Alfred applauded the singer. "I thought you knew Robin well."

"Not really. She's a strange one."

"Have you heard from her?"

"Not since last summer. Why?"

"She hinted that her health was not all it might be."

Leon shrugged.

"She said she'd been having some trouble since her confinement."

"Confinement?" said Leon coldly.

"Surely you could not have missed that?"

"I heard about it."

"Oh?" Alfred could not make out Leon's mood. Normally he

would have dropped the subject after such rebuffs. "It was one of the more celebrated confinements of the postwar era."

"I didn't realize," said Leon stiffly, "that you were an addict, Alfred."

"Of what?"

"Ladies' magazines."

Alfred paused a moment while the first of the bluegrass songs was announced. He decided not to take offense at Leon's rudenesses, for fear of not getting to the subject he was working around to.

"Of course," he chattered, "I hardly keep up with these things out of general interest. But I confess I find a certain fascination to Robin and Hugh's marriage. After all, Hugh lived in our garden cottage, and no one would ever have believed he'd marry any woman, much less an attractive, feminine, intelligent girl like Robin—maybe some beat-up old battle-ax he could sneer at and knuckle under to at the same time. You know how often one says, 'What did he ever see in her?' or vice versa. This marriage was just the epitome of it. And they even had a baby."

"Did they?"

"Obviously. Famously. I even saw it."

"I didn't."

"You know, Leon, the one and only time the Institute of Modern Living permitted TV cameras to enter its precincts? Horace and Virginia had me over to lunch that Sunday, and we watched the tour of the Institute in a sort of trance. There were almost no comments, just a tasteful sentence now and then over the soft music, to indicate what you were looking at if it was hard to make out—a quiet, cultivated voice. The climax was Robin tending the baby in the modern house she and Hugh display. It looked like a fine baby."

"You're sure it wasn't a doll?"

At this Alfred paused a while, pretending to listen to the singing, till he should be able to breathe again.

A strapping young woman was standing at the microphone amid three young men, one playing a guitar, another a jug, the third a washboard. She was singing in a strident voice a ballad about the atom bomb. Her clothes, make-up, and aloof bearing suggested a backwoods woman. Calvin Shimp, at the next break, came over to get their glasses for more beer and told them that he lived in the basement of the same apartment house as the singer and her husband, the jug-player, an Irishman from the Bronx who had spent several months in the back hills of Kentucky and West Virginia, where he had gathered scores of songs and learned to blow jug. She was the daughter of a stockbroker on Montgomery Street and had gone to Stanford for two years. They had met at a hootenanny in bluegrass

336

country the summer before and gotten married right there in Kentucky. Alfred and Leon smiled and shook their heads, and he went away gratified to have given them a glimpse behind the scenes.

"Have you heard from Joe?" Alfred asked.

"Not since he left. Why? Aren't he and Lizzie on their honeymoon?"

"Yes." Alfred could not think of an indirect way of getting to the subject. "Robin's wasn't the only upsetting letter that came yesterday. I also got one from Lizzie. Leon, do you know, or know anyone who knows, very much about television?"

"What do you mean—tubes and antennas and such like?"

"No, no. Actually I meant these give-away shows, like the one Joe won so much money on."

"What do you want to know?"

"Lizzie writes that Joe has told her that the whole show was a fraud."

"So?"

"He says he was tipped off about the questions ahead of time, and so are all the other winners."

"Of course."

"What do you mean 'of course'?" Alfred was so irritated by Leon's manner that he poked him in the arm. " 'Of course'? You knew this all the time?"

"I knew," said Leon haughtily and sliding a couple of inches away from Alfred, "what everyone with eyes in his head knows—that television is fraudulent. I did not know specifically how Joe connived, but the one time I watched his ape act I knew he was either cheating or incredibly lucky, and I mean incredibly. So they're all rigged. Very well. You never watched him?"

"Then you believe this? Lizzie thinks he's losing his mind and that this is a delusion. But you believe it?"

"My dear Alfred," said Leon, "for a man with your experience of the world to permit himself such naïveté is mere self-indulgence. There is only one thing you can be sure of in the mass media, which is that nothing is what it seems to be if it can possibly be faked at five or ten times the cost. You don't really believe that Robin was pregnant and had a baby, do you?"

"But why not? I mean, why shouldn't she?"

"Who knows what the directors have in mind?"

"You mean," said Alfred, "you think it was a false pregnancy?"

"Of course not. A false pregnancy is a term that indicates honest hysteria. This was a hoked-up pregnancy from beginning to end. Robin's no great shakes as an actress but she's certainly good enough to bear a foam-rubber baby."

"Let's go."

Alfred blundered out of the place. He turned up the hill, **away** from North Beach. Leon caught up with him in half a block.

Alfred did not stop till he came to a barrier at a dead-end street. There he stood looking for a while down at the Embarcadero and across at the Bay Bridge.

"But you don't *know* about Joe and Robin?" he said. "You just assume."

"About Joe I assume," said Leon. "About Robin I know."

"You said you had not heard from her."

"Since last summer. But I heard then."

"Perhaps I am naïve. You are right about that at least, Leon."

"It's a phony society. It's absolutely fraudulent all the way through. Maybe the only way to stay pure is not to know too much. You agree?"

"You are awfully hard on Robin."

"Hard on her! If you knew . . . Listen, Alfred, there's one thing I've decided in life, and that is to get the woman I want. That's the one sphere I'm going to be ruthless in. Anyone who interferes with me there, I'm going to ride over him roughshod. I'm not absolutely sure exactly what I want in a woman yet, but I'm nearly sure, and when I find out I'm not going to settle for anything less than her. I'm going to get her, and anybody who stands in my way is going to get whatever it takes to push him out of my way."

"No, Leon," Alfred cried, "don't say things like that! That is the way to certain misery. You must not even think it."

"What are you talking about? I'm determined and I'm going to be ruthless."

"It's not that. Of course one should be determined. But you said you mean to get what you want at any cost. Leon, please, you must try to want what you have. We all must try to want what we have."

It did not occur to Leon that Alfred was referring to Chantal. For a moment he frowned, trying to decide whether Alfred was referring to Mazda or Flossie, but neither of them seemed worthy of such intensity as Alfred had put into his voice. Then it dawned on Leon that Alfred must have been referring to Sybil and was trying to pressure him to stay with her. He spoke coldly.

"It seems to me that you are in the worst possible position to go around dishing out that particular advice. 'You must try to want what you have.' Wasn't that what you said? My God, man, take a good look at the position you are in now."

"Who do you think I'm really talking to, Leon? Why do you think I'm crying now?"

Smiling, in case anyone else should see him, Alfred turned and walked down the hill, swinging his cane like a dandy. He did not wipe his eyes.

Leon caught up with him and tried to apologize. Alfred would not slow down or listen to him, but kept repeating, "My dear friend, O my dear friend."

"You meant Chantal, didn't you? You meant she is the woman at home? We're married, in a way, legally. But you know she's not really my wife. You know that, Alfred?"

"My dear Leon."

In the car on the way to the bus terminal where Leon was going to drop him, Alfred leaned against the door, not wanting to talk. From the confusion of the evening, he was relieved to turn his thoughts to Lizzie, whose letter had been troubling him all day. She was having a bad time with Joe because he was feeling guilty for having cheated. Good. A clean, straightforward moral issue of the kind she relished. She would get along all right.

· 17 ·

"Where are we, Joe?" said Lizzie.

"Well, honey, from the chill in my bones I'd say we're about three or four hundred miles this side of the Arctic Circle."

"Oh, lord, I mean . . . Are we really that far north?" Her eyes widened and she clapped her hands.

"Give or take a couple hundred per cent."

"Why don't we go up to it so we can say we've been in it?"

"Because it's out in the middle of the ocean, that's why. So where are we? Another way of putting it is, we're in what I was told is the best restaurant in Durham."

"Oh, fumdydiddle," she said, "I know that. The only thing in Durham is the cathedral, so where are we to it, north, east, west, or south?"

"Yes. North, east, west, or south in relation to the cathedral, and somewhat below it too."

She dropped her eyes and began swishing her drink around in the glass.

"Come on, pigeon," he said, "don't start pouting on me again."

"You think I'm stupid," she said without raising her eyes.

"Do I," he said in a voice suddenly flat. "Oh, do I. Just quit telling me what I think and everybody'll get along better."

"You *act* like you think I'm stupid," she said.

"You act like you forgot how to laugh."

The waiter came to take their orders for dinner. Lizzie said she didn't feel like ordering, she had no appetite. She wanted Joe to wheedle her into eating, but he only gave a little snort, glanced at her coolly, and ordered a full dinner with mutton kidney chops. If this had been the dining room of the hotel they were staying in, she would have gone up to their room and cried. As it was, she took herself in hand, put on the cheeriest air she could manage, and said that sounded so good she would have the same.

In a little while she said, "Are you still cold, sweetie?"

"Not too bad," he answered.

From the tone of his voice and from the way he hunched forward as he spoke, she took heart and reached out to him again.

"You were in there so long," she said. "I got chilled just being there for matins and looking around. I wasn't in longer than an hour and a half all told. The columns are so big and strong, there seems to be more stone to it than the other cathedrals. Somehow I felt even colder because we were the only ones in the audience."

"In the congregation, maybe?"

"Just the two of us, anyhow, among all those gigantic columns."

"It's the most awe-inspiring place I've ever been in my life," he said.

"Oh, goodness," she said, "not more than Yosemite, surely."

"Well, now, here we are going back to nature again. Take the hot dogs out of Yosemite Valley and put them in Durham Cathedral, and take the choir out of Durham and put it to singing hymns in Yosemite, and maybe I'll take Yosemite. The way things stand, I'll rest content with what's what."

She laughed merrily and kicked him under the table. "You're so witty sometimes."

He had two responsive impulses: "As long as the wit isn't aimed your way," and "It just comes natural to me to be artificial." But during the moment he was choosing between the impulses he decided they were both too unkind to her. They resolved into laughter which she joined.

People at other tables looked at them, at first frowning a bit and then breaking into smiles.

"So, Lizzie. As they say in New York, so what's new?"

She scrubbed her nose. "You mean Sybil's letter?"

"No less. If you haven't burned it already, that is, and forgot what it said."

"You know," said Lizzie, "it's terribly inconsiderate of her to make me burn her letters. Where can I do it? She might just stop to think about that a minute. How can you burn up a letter in a hotel room?"

"Flush it down the john," said Joe.

"Oh, no! That's much too symbolic! I couldn't do that to her. How can she be so superstitious? Suppose I just tore them up and put them in the wastepaper basket. What could any English chambermaid get out of reading them? Nothing what-so-ever. Anyway, she says she can't get anything out of Leon about Roy Carver and Harry Evans, because she isn't going with Leon any longer." She waited for Joe to react to this. He just gave a little shrug. "In fact, she says that Daddy asked her to ask me to ask you what *you* know about Roy and Evans. I guess he's curious."

"Who isn't?" said Joe.

"What'll I write back?"

"About Evans I don't know thing one. About Roy I don't know thing two. Period."

"Okay. But it certainly would be interesting to know why Evans was so rebellious against authority." She sighed. "I don't have the slightest doubt that Roy helped. Do you?"

"Helped kill a man? No, I don't have any trouble believing he could have done that. I'm pretty sure I helped kill a few hundred people myself."

"Oh, Joey, that was so different. The war. No, darling, you mustn't say such things. You must not think them."

They were silent a while. Then she went on. "Tell me about the first time you met Roy."

"It was just a poker game. I told you already."

"I know what you said. What *really* happened?"

"We both had full houses, and I beat him with aces over. That's the gospel truth."

"Oh, come on, Joey, tell me."

"You really want to know?"

She nodded eagerly.

He pretended to think she was playing. He leaned forward; he spoke rapidly, with abrupt pauses; he squinched his eyes.

"Okay, Liz, I'll tell you how it was. We were in this gambling joint in El Cerrito. It wasn't quite legal, but then on the other hand it wasn't too awfully illegal the way a set-up like that would be in Berkeley. There were a couple of dozen men in the room. Nothing but straight poker. Roy and I were at the same table. Over every table a light hung down on a cord from the ceiling, with a green cone-shaped shade so the hands were lit up but the faces were in the shadows. There was lots of smoking going on and the room was thick with it. Not a sound but the shuffling of cards, the chink of chips, the calling of bets. 'Check. Raise you five. Fold. See you.' Once in a while a chair scraped on the wooden floor—someone was going to the john. Nothing but beer was being drunk. All knives and guns had been checked at the door. Three-Finger Torelli personally frisked every man as he came in. Got the picture? No molls. Okay? But for some of us this gambling hall was nothing but a front. Sure, there was a bar which was a front to it. All that meant was, the front had a front. For the poker games all it took was a little mazoola on Saturday nights and the cops wouldn't ask any questions. What if two or three dozen guys asked for the key to the john and disappeared into it when there was already a perfectly good john with an unlocked door for the bar? You know, twenty cars parked on the street outside and one guy at the bar? The big thing—for us—was that there was a basement with a hidden trapdoor in the floor of the special john. Once a week, on Thursday nights, there were classes down there. That's where I really got to know Roy."

Their dinners arrived.

"More later," he said.

She thought there might be some serious truth in what he was saying. "Oh, don't stop! Just tell me one thing: What were the secret meetings about?"

He leaned forward and whispered through clenched teeth, "How to construct homemade bombs."

This decided her. He must be kidding. If there was even a grain of truth in what he was saying she would never be able to sort it out. Her face fell, she put down her knife and fork, she stared at the edge of the table. But then, with a little laugh, she shook herself and decided not to have hurt feelings but to pretend she had been playing too.

"All right, how do you make a bomb?"

"Oh, lots of ways," he said. "I don't want to bore you with the details. We had a textbook by one of those really professional anarchists they had in the last part of the nineteenth century. You know, 'Pardon me, Grand Duke, nothing personal,' wham bam *boom*. I think his name was Most—anyways, we always called him the Most among ourselves. The book was called *The Revolutionist's Handbook,* something along those lines, only it was pretty far out of date. Still, it was useful. Our teacher was a lot like Harry Evans—you know, dedicated? To what? It was quite a lot like the Army, only they weren't so thorough about how to kill, more on who to kill and when to do it. *When* makes all the difference, you realize that?"

He kept up the act throughout dinner.

But the longer he talked the more puzzled she became. He seemed to her to know too much for his talk to be mere fantasy. All you had to do was to accept assassination as a political weapon, and what he said made sense. How could he know so much? He kept bringing Roy into the story, his opinions, his reactions. What about Roy?

One of Joe's comments stuck in her mind.

"Like I said, the textbook was seventy or eighty years old, but Roy swallowed it for the gospel truth. He really believed the truest enemy of the workers was still the bosses. The way my stepmother Margery still believes the earth is flat because the Good Book says it has four corners."

"You're kidding."

"You think?"

"She can't! Why don't you set her straight?"

"Wifie, do you realize that twenty to thirty per cent of the biology teachers in this fair land belong to an association which they've got to take an oath to become a member of, and this oath makes them solemnly swear that they do not believe in evolution but in Adam and Eve? That's our Roy. *Credo in Capitalismus et in unam* lead-pipe bomb."

She joined him in laughing, but she kept coming back to this as Joe talked ahead. McKee and Brady *were* old-fashioned capitalists, and they *had* been attacked with a homemade bomb. And anyway, why shouldn't some anarchists meet in the cellar underneath a gambling hall?

But she knew what would happen if she asked her questions.

What about Roy, though? And Joe himself? After all, she didn't really know all that much about Joe's past. No, but one thing she did know: She'd better keep playing his game now, or she'd not only not learn anything, she wouldn't even have a good time.

They had brandies with their coffee.

They walked back to their hotel arm in arm, talking and laughing, and the narrow street echoed with their Western voices.

In their room they made love slowly and well.

When finally they lay apart, feet touching, Joe turned on the bed-side light that they might luxuriate naked a while, smoking and chatting, as they sometimes did when it was early and they might make love again before falling asleep.

She thought for a minute of asking him playfully the question uppermost in her mind—why had he stayed in a cathedral all day, cold, alone—but she was afraid he might turn against her for this question as he had done the other time she'd asked it, at Ely. She thought she would be wanting to make love again, she wanted to make him happy, she knew she ought to let him work through his problem himself. Nevertheless, she resented having to censor her thoughts.

But she loved him!

"Well, hubby, I guess we qualify for journeymen's cards."

"Lathe operators' union, maybe?" he said. "Technician first class?"

"Technicians hell," she said. "We're artists, we're creative."

"Do tell. I fear me, chuck, you just aren't as up on unions as you might be."

"Maybe not," she said, "but I did read Roy's stupid old labor journals a couple of times."

"And exactly when did you ever hear of a creative artists' union? Technicians is the most we can aspire to in the labor movement."

"All right. It's a stupid movement."

"Didn't use to be," he said.

"Hardening of the arteries."

"Didn't always have."

"Just tell me this," she said. "Why did they strike at McKee's?"

"Who do you think I am, God Almighty?"

"You don't even want to know." She punched him in the ribs. "Is that the truth, Joey? Don't you even want to know?"

"I'd put it a little differently."

She waited. He said nothing but began to rub his leg against hers. She flounced over onto her side facing him, withdrawing her leg so they did not touch.

"Tell me," she said. "How would you put it?"

"Oh," he drawled, "maybe what I'd say is, I want not to know."

"Ostrich."

"A wise bird. The type of wisdom in a dry stretch. Maybe a little slow to learn, but still and all, trustworthy. You know why he sticks his head in the sand from time to time? Not because he's scared, like they say. No, no, never traduce an ostrich. It's because he ran after the horizon a long time before he finally realized there wasn't any fence there, and so now every time he thinks he sees a fence on the horizon he just rests his head in the sand a while so's to keep from running too much. He's resisting temptation. 'I shall not strive to see what cannot be seen.' "

"And another thing," Lizzie said, "what possible motive did Evans have to kill those men?"

He sighed. "No motive, babe."

"Was he connected with the union?" she asked.

"Not that I ever heard. Do you know who sent the biggest floral decoration to Brady's funeral? The union. Do you know how many of the employees in that plant attended the funeral? Over half. Do you know who sent the one letter to McKee in the hospital that broke the old man up when he read it? The secretary of the local, who had worked for McKee for years before he was elected secretary."

"How do you know that?"

"A photographer that worked on the McKee house organ. I spent an evening playing chess with him. We talked some. I can't say I want to spend too many more evenings with him, he's not my type, but I credit what he told me."

"So, what was his theory?"

"Child," Joe said, his voice still humorous but his mouth making a sudden brief rictus, "you got to believe me when I tell you: no theory, no motive, no inside dope."

"Oh, for heaven's sake," she said, "there's always a motive."

"You incorrigible little old internal combustion engine, you. Lo and behold."

He reared up on his elbow, laid her on her back, turned the covers down to her waist, deliberately lowered his face, and kissed her voluptuously, the fingertips of his free hand delicately stroking her arm and breast. Then he lay back on his pillow.

"Oh, darling," she said, sighing, "how come you did that all of a sudden?"

"Why do you think?"

"To take my mind off serious things?"

"*Off* serious things." He laughed too hard. "Scarcely."

"To prove some point then?" she said.

"Not really."

"Just because you felt like it?"

"Right," he said. "Q.E.D."

"Q.E.D. what?" she said.

"Evans threw that bomb just because he felt like it."

"But all you're doing now is to push the question back. Why did he feel like it? See?"

"Honey," he said, "a person's got to quit pushing sooner or later, so why don't you just try quitting sooner? Now?"

"You don't need to be insulting," she said.

He breathed hard, then said softly, "I'm sorry."

She did not really care very much about Evans' motives. What troubled her was the strong, obscure feeling that Joe was holding out on her —a feeling she attached to the Evans case. She *had to know*—the wrong thing. Therefore she nagged.

"You see," she said, "I keep feeling there must be a key missing, and if I could only get hold of the key everything else would pretty much fall into place. Here I've practically got an inside track—

Daddy and you and Leon—and nobody is any help at all. I have the impression sometimes that you know but won't tell me because I'm a woman. You don't think I'm worthy or something."

"Votes for women!" he cried.

"Laugh. Go ahead, laugh. You don't love me."

"Oh, sweet jumping Jesus, lay off."

"I'm just a plaything to you," she said. "You think I'm your doll. Well, let me tell you, Joe Thompson—"

"Shut up!" he said.

She gasped. In the Royce family, "Shut up" was the greatest rudeness. Even so, she succeeded in holding her tongue, though her mouth was puckering and she was glaring at him. But then, saying, "Okay?" in a threatening way, he squeezed her thigh too hard, his thumb digging into the soft inner side so that she jerked and whimpered.

They lay on their backs silently a while.

"I can see," she said, "why Daddy doesn't tell. He has official reasons, he's a mediator, he knows judges and things. But there's only one reason why you don't tell me—because you don't have any respect for me."

Staring at the ceiling, he muttered between his teeth, "God help me." Then he turned toward her and spoke. "Listen to me. Once and for all, listen to me. There aren't enough reasons. If it's important, there never are enough reasons. Maybe there are for the scientists, though from the rumors I keep hearing there don't seem to be enough reasons any more to suit the physicists. Be that as it may, if it *matters,* if it's got to do with us, people, stuff like that there, then you can't find enough reasons ever. There's some reasons, but there's never enough. Got it? Okay. Hold on to it because I've got another point to make. Which is. It's bad enough to try to know all the reasons, but at least it's natural to try and keep on trying. 'I want to know, I got to know'—that's a built-in feature of the creature. But to think you *can* know, to think the reasons are all there to *be* known, that's the sin for which there is no forgiveness, that's the *hubris* for which there ain't nothing but nemesis."

She did not respond, but lay watching him, blinking her eyes rather often. She clearly was not going to rise against him. Gradually he relaxed a good deal. Then he spoke, less intensely but no less seriously.

"That's what I believe," he said. "I believe in God, but I'm not as sure as I can be that there is a God and I know I don't know much about Him. But I'm just as sure as I can be that it's wrong to think you can know *the* reason for something like that strike or that bombing. And lots of other things of a similar nature, lots and lots and lots. So."

His idea seemed to her so preposterous that she took it as a manifestation of some inner trouble of his own. The intensity and the latent insult of his manner only confirmed her in her conviction that the idea was a protective mechanism with meaning only as it referred to his state of mind. Until she knew what was troubling him, she would have to be patient and careful. She slid her hand across under the covers and found and squeezed his hand.

He suspected her of pitying him and pretended to respond to her gesture amorously, in order to obliterate her pity, or at least to obliterate his suspicion.

The one patient, the other evading, they made love only skillfully, enjoyed it only physically.

⋅ 18 ⋅

At three-thirty in the afternoon Beth received a call from Sybil. The front tire of Jim's motorcycle had gone flat on Grizzly Peak Boulevard. Could she come get them? Beth drove up, took Jim, Sybil, and the tire down to a service station where it was patched, and ran them back up. By then it was past five, too late for them to go into the country for the picnic Sybil had packed. At Beth's urging they came down to San Jacinto Way and joined her and Nancy for dinner. Jim looked ashamed but relieved. Beth saw him glancing at Sybil, who looked cool.

They joined her in the kitchen, and Sybil pitched in to help her make a hard-boiled-egg-and-tuna salad to amplify the picnic sandwiches and oranges. Beth spoke to Jim in the doorway.

"This is about as informal a dinner as I ever gave. It certainly wasn't the one I meant to invite you to the first time you came to eat with us. The first time Sybil *let* me invite you, that is. She's been mighty stingy with you, Jim."

"She has," he said with a lopsided smile at Sybil. "In fact, I began to think she was ashamed of me."

"Or of her mother," said Beth.

Sybil did not ruffle. "I believe in letting nature take its course. Isn't it friendly this way?"

Nancy came into the dining room, walking on her hands.

"Wow," said Jim, "not bad. I can't even stand on my head except against a wall."

"This is Jim Sorb, Nancy," said Sybil. "As you can see," she said to Jim, "Nancy is the family acrobat."

"Pleased to meet you," said Nancy and waved her right foot toward him.

He shook it. "A pleasure, I'm sure."

347

"You're the one," she said, stirring back and forth as she looked up at him, "with the BMW motorbike?"

"That's me."

"Syb says it's great."

"I just had a flat tire," he said.

"Give me a ride?" Nancy said.

"When?"

"Now. If the flat's fixed. Is it?"

"Sure, thanks to your mother."

He turned to Beth, who pulled her nose. "Now, Nancy—" she began.

Nancy flipped onto her feet. "Now, Mother. Do you realize that I'm the safest person you know to have a motorcycle accident? I know how to tumble. So do you realize that? Sybil doesn't know how to fall. Do you, Jim? No! See! *I'm* the expert faller around here. So can I, Mother?"

"Just a short slow one, Jim," said Beth. "They're so dangerous."

Nancy grabbed his hand and pulled him out.

Beth praised Jim to Sybil, who began making fun of him. Yet her eyes were not joining the fun. They seemed to Beth somehow yearning and tender at the same time that Sybil's voice was making him seem ridiculous. She was describing a day at the beach and the silly bravado with which he had plunged into big cold breakers which obviously frightened him half to death. As she was going on Beth glanced twice into her oddly yearning eyes, and it occurred to Beth that Sybil was like a girl on a ledge ten feet above a clear pool on a hot day, screwing up her courage to plunge in, wanting to, ashamed to climb down and slip in gradually, too proud to jump in feet first holding her nose, stepping back with arms raised, rushing to the edge, stopping there, teetering, falling back, not quite able to make the all-or-nothing dive.

The meal was full of talk and laughter. They sat at the cluttered table, drinking coffee and eating fig bars.

"Tell me, Jim," said Beth, "I suppose you're going into civil-liberties law?"

"Why do you suppose that?" he said and glowered at Sybil.

"Don't beetle your brows at me," said Sybil. "I never said such a thing."

Beth was hoping she had stirred them up. But Jim turned back to her.

"May I ask what made you think that, Mrs. Royce?"

"Oh, I don't know. Civil liberties are getting hotter than ever, and they ought to be appealing to an idealistic young man. Aren't you an idealistic young man?" Beth overheard in her voice a patronizing quality she had not intended. "That's just the impression I had," she added in a deprecatory manner.

She meant the deprecation to apply to the patronizing tone of what she had said before, but instead it seemed to apply, with some sort of flabby irony, to civil liberties or to idealistic young men or to Jim himself. When Beth saw Sybil's eyes drop and forehead pucker slightly, she felt panicky and turned to Jim to try to make it up to him somehow. But she was unable to say anything, in her confusion at the sight of the extraordinary motions Jim was making.

He was at the head of the table, and she was on the side to his left. He had been leaning toward her a little, legs crossed, sitting sidewise in his chair. After her ambiguous remarks, he uncrossed his legs and sat up straight in the chair, at the same time dipping his head in a long curve away from her; his face, when his head emerged from this dip, was set and his eyes narrowed. If at the same time he had clutched the edge of the table with stiff arms, his posture would have been so melodramatic she could have laughed. Instead, his right hand still held his coffee cup in a rather delicate way, and his left fist was lightly beating his thigh.

"Well, since you're going to be so *ad hominem* about it," he said, and Beth breathed with relief that he was fighting back at her, "I'm going into law to make money, lots of money, and there isn't any money in civil-liberties law."

"None?"

"Who do you think needs civil-liberties lawyers? Poor crazy helpless stupid outcasts that get pushed around all the time. How could you ask them for a fee? Just tell me that—how the hell could I even make a living?"

He made a complicated hailing gesture at Nancy, to apologize for having said "how the hell" in front of her. She, however, having no idea what he meant by the odd motion of his hand, doubled over with giggles. He frowned.

"He's going to be a big-time ambulance-chaser," said Sybil in a neutral voice.

"I am not," he said, looking relieved at last to have her to argue with. "I'm never going to take criminal cases, because I don't want to ever take a case against my conscience, and in criminal law you have to do it constantly if you're going to hit the big time."

"Oh, no," said Beth, "he's not idealistic. Not him."

"That's just common sense," he said, his voice going up half an octave. "It's practical. Nobody can do a good job with a cloud over his conscience."

"Who told you?" Beth asked.

"Nobody had to tell me. I just know."

"Aw, honey," she said, leaning forward and batting her eyes. "Aw, gee, ain't he cute?"

"Now, damn it all, Mrs. Royce," he said, glancing nervously at Sybil, who was frowning at her mother, "you can make fun of me all you want, but were you ever poor?"

"Huh? Poor?"

"That's right. In nineteen thirty-three or -four, when everybody was down and out, were you hard up, even? Have you ever *really* had to worry about money?"

"No," she said, chastened. "At least, I have never had to worry because of lack of money. That isn't the only reason money gets people worrying, you know."

"It's the one I know, like several billion other people, and I don't like it. So I'm going to see to it that I won't have to do it any more."

"At last I've met one," said Beth.

His face puckered and squinched. "Yeah? One what?"

"A young conservative. I've been hearing about how the young people are conservative these days, and now I've met one. You."

"Okay, yes, okay, I'm a conservative, if that's what you've got to be or else be rebellious. Actually most people are neither one nor the other, only it's all the rage to *say* how you're a rebel. There was this girl down at San Jose State last year—her father was a dentist and her mother was nothing awful, a bridge-playing type. I knew about them because they used to buy their gas in our station. Well, she went around rebelling against her parents at school. That's what she said, and everybody else followed suit and said she was too. So what is it she actually does? To rebel, I mean? Get a gun and shoot the Governor? Pass out pamphlets urging students to at least strike against some of the idiotic things the administration of the college is doing? Oh, no. She's much too rebellious for two-bit stuff like that. What *she* does is, she puts on white lipstick, lets her hair hang down without combing it, goes barefoot most of the time, sits around a coffee shop smoking two or three packs of cigarettes a day, and sleeps around with—" He blushed crimson, glanced around, and began stammering. "I mean. I'm sorry—she is a loose woman, that's all, just very loose."

Beth and Sybil leaped in to rescue him from his embarrassment.

Nancy, seeing this as a good opportunity to get out of doing dishes, stood on her hands and walked out.

"So," he said earnestly, "if a conservative is somebody who works within the status quo, that's me, that's what I intend to do."

"You sounded," said Beth, "as though you liked the status quo. Which is really conservative."

"*Like* it?" he said. "Nobody likes it. Who could, most of the time?

It's like people who live in a place where the weather is foul. They don't like it, but it's home. I'll put up with it. Maybe what I'll do is this—I've thought about the matter quite a lot. Maybe I'll make enough money by the time I'm forty or fifty, you know, pretty well along in life—"

Beth winced and shrugged.

"—and I'll just go into civil liberties. Actually I think the American laws are basically sound, they just need to be defended from abuse by the rich. What's wrong with us isn't our laws as such. I'm not too sure just what it is, but I am sure it's not our laws themselves."

"You really think so?" said Beth, deciding to ignore his pomposity this time and take his ideas seriously.

They both shifted in their chairs and leaned on the table, settling in for a good long argument.

"Oh, good lord," said Sybil. She got up and began clearing the table.

Three hours later she had washed and put away the dishes, cleaned up the kitchen, chatted with Nancy in her room, read *The New Yorker,* and they were still going at it hammer and tongs.

She went back into the dining room and pounded on the table with both fists. "Stop! Listen to me! I have a final at nine o'clock in the morning at Presley and I want to study for it and all my books are in my room at the dorm. So take me back, Jim. Now."

"Okay, Syb," he said meekly. "Mrs. Royce, there are a few more things you need straightening out on, but I guess we'll have to save them for another time."

"I've got some straightening irons of my own I'll drag out for the occasion and see how they fit you. Come again soon."

Sybil stood waiting during their pleasantries, impatient and displeased.

A couple of hours after Beth had gone to bed, she awoke from confused dreams, under the impression that she had heard footsteps on the gravel outside the window facing the street. She reared up on her elbows, listening. A latch clicked. She carefully leaned over to the bedside table, opened the drawer, picked up the loaded revolver Woody had given her, snicked the safety, and crept to the window facing the patio. She had to peer slantwise down between a slit between curtains; there was a screen on the window, there was no moon, the only light was the reflection from the lowering sky. She made out the form of a man standing in the middle of the patio. He was holding something that could have been a rifle. She held the pistol pointed in his direction. He took a couple of steps toward the

French doors of the living room and stopped. For a moment she thought he was Alfred; he had the same general height and build, and something about the way he stepped reminded her of Alfred. But then he turned toward the bedroom window and seemed to look up; his face was unrecognizable. Even in the obscurity she was sure it was not Alfred's face, but darker, fatter, wrong. She heard him make some sort of grunting sounds as he stood there. He left as quietly as he had come.

Beth went back to bed but not to sleep. Mary Louise had been shocked when Beth had accepted the pistol from Woody. Now, after this prowler, she felt justified and looked forward to telling Mary Louise about what had happened. Her thoughts went back to the long, intense argument she had had with Jim, and after a while she was furious with Sybil for not showing every sign of loving him and wanting to marry him. What kind of an idiot of a daughter was she if she couldn't tell a diamond like Jim when she saw him! Sybil was so coldhearted and selfish, so calculating. After three or four vagrant hops, her mind went back to the prowler in the patio, and, thinking of the man's strange face, she suddenly was positive he was Alfred; she'd forgotten his beard. The grunts he had been making must have been the sounds of a stifled weeping. She cursed and ground her teeth and could not think what she would have done if she had recognized him. Another surge of anger at Sybil obliterated thoughts of Alfred for a while, but they returned. For a long time she tossed without relief. Then the words took shape in her mind, "When he tried to come back to me, I met him with a gun," and she said them aloud. At the sound of them she writhed with weeping, from which she fell at dawn, exhausted but unrelieved, into sleep.

· 19 ·

Dear Liz,

I have to tell you something about Joe which I'm pretty sure you don't know. It isn't so personal, or private, or anything like that, except that it happened to Joe. From those last two letters of yours, especially that wild one from Salisbury that came five days ago, I get the idea you think he's in pretty bad shape. Traveling only after dark. Staying in cathedrals all the time. The "sanctuary" bit. Turning against you sometimes for no good reason. Writing secretly in his notebook. No interest in sex. His cape. The main thing is—since you want to know the *reasons* why he has problems, you ought to know as many as possible.

I learned about it from Daddy, who heard it last night from Leon —they went out on the town.

You know, it's the most peculiar thing, and I hate it. Even though I'm all through with Leon, and wish I never had got involved with him, and I'm never going to get the least bit involved with anybody like him ever again in any way, and I think it's possible, not to say desirable, that I'll never see him again in my whole life, even so I just can't get my thoughts off of him. It's the most upsetting thing to yearn for something you don't want. What I *really* want is somebody like Jim. That is, what I really want to want.

A couple of Sundays ago Jim took me to St. Simeon's, up above Mill Valley (don't ask me why *either* of us went to a Clementine monastery!) and we watched the monks say, or sing, or perform, or whatever it's called, vespers—I think it was vespers. Anyway, they chanted back and forth, with candles, and I followed the Latin in an English translation. When they got to the prayer of thanksgiving, I cried a little. I know I was being sentimental, of course. Still, everything seemed *just right*. If it wasn't for Leon, I wouldn't be wanting to want somebody like Jim, I would want Jim. Of course I *do* like him very very much now, but you know what I mean, not all the way. Anyhow, to hell with Leon.

He told Daddy that Chantal once told him something about Joe which Roy Carver had told her. Roy was stationed at the same air base Joe was on in England for a while and they knew each other. It seems Joe psiked (sp?) out after 30 missions over Europe and spent 3 months in the mental ward, Section 8 I think Daddy called it, before he was discharged. (Honorably, of course.) What happened was that on one mission he was on there were dozens and dozens of loaded bombers going to bomb Le Havre right across the English Channel, so close they didn't need much fuel and were all chockful of bombs. On a big raid like that, all the planes take formation so that the bombs will drop simultaneously in a certain pattern to do the most damage. All the other bombardiers watch the lead bombardier, and when his bombs drop they push their buttons so all the bombs drop at once, thousands of them. Also, there's an "I" point, where all the bombers take formation and fly straight and steady toward the target. On this raid the "I" point was an old farmhouse out on a cape in Normandy. Everybody was in pattern and there wasn't any flak or fighters. And the lead bombardier made a mistake. He dropped his bombs on the farm. All the other bombardiers knew he had made a mistake, but they didn't give a shit what they blew up, so *everybody* dropped their loads and blew the farm to kingdom come. That night all the airmen got drunk to celebrate (celebrate what?), only Joe lit off for London and stayed drunk for three days. When he got back to

353

the base on the third night, he'd been AWOL, only nobody really cared. The thing was that the next morning he was in such bad shape he couldn't go up with his crew on another mission. Some other radioman took his place. The plane was shot down over Germany, and everybody was killed. Roy told Chantal he has never mentioned this to Joe and Joe has never mentioned it to him, even though he is dead sure that Joe knows he knows about it and also knows about his psiking out because of it.

Who does Joe think he is, Atlas, that he's got to carry the whole damned world on his shoulders? Oh, the poor guy. I hope and pray you never run out of patience with him. He must be intolerable to live with sometimes.

Later

More news—Mother. She's better, even if she is getting goofy. She sits up there emitting smoke about Daddy like a dragoness. Do you know what corn she gave forth with the other day? That when they quarreled over her mother's damned furniture, Daddy said to her "the thing for which there can be no forgiveness." I bet she got that idea out of one of those trashy slick novels she reads sometimes when she's depressed, and now that she's put it into words she's stuck with it.

On to her Project. Mary Louise has a woman friend named Michael, a social worker type, unmarried, but still not too dikey despite everything. I don't think you ever met her; she moved here from San Jose this summer. Michael said there were a lot of underprivileged kids in the Oakland schools who had reading problems but the teachers were too busy to help them enough. So Mother was just sitting at home slowly going crazy—Christmas this year was *bad*—and all of a sudden she volunteered to go down three hours every school day and do what she could to help out. Of course the minute she made the offer (she told me all about it in detail a dozen times) she began hedging her bets. Just three hours every school morning and no more. Only kids in the first three grades. It's a pity people have to be literate to get along in modern society, but since they do have to, they might as well really be literate. Naturally Mary Louise was tickled pink by all this. To her, "underprivileged" is practically a synonym for Negro and Mexican, so Mother was getting in on the anti-racial-prejudice act too. But that bit about how it was too bad the lower classes have to be literate and how fine an illiterate culture can be so long as illiteracy has no shame attached to it, that roused Mary Louise's liberal ire and they've been fighting about it ever since.

All of which is to lead up to saying that Mother has really been coming to life. Naturally she bitches about the kids all the time, but I'm sure the only reason she doesn't go down all day every day instead of just the morning sessions is because she made such a big production about how she was only going to do it part-time, she had a limited goal. (She's great on "accepting your limitations" these days.) She's already promised to keep on working most of the summer—meanwhile shouting at the top of her lungs that she absolutely insists on spending at least three weeks on a vacation, probably up at Stowes Landing with the Ravaglis.

Last week one of the other volunteers was sick and Mother talked me into going down with her. I can see why she likes it so much. If I could just do a better job I'd love it myself. But I feel so helpless. The poor damned brats—it takes so long to get anywhere with them, and to get them to read Jack and Jill you have to get their confidence first. Well, I signed up for next summer, too. After all, what have I ever done that's really worth while in life? So I'm going to live at home and go down with Mother every morning. So so so.

After midnight

People are so much more interesting than psychology.

After the hash and Jello, Roz and I dug in to study. She was on her ed psych and I was on my interlating (interpersonal relationships to you, you peasant). About quarter past nine, we get the buzz from downstairs. It's Jim. Would I like to go out and catch a quick cup of coffee with him?

He never did anything even remotely like this before. Come without phoning ahead of time. Come so late at night. Come the very next day after a date. I was all charged up. I didn't realize just *how* charged up till I happened to catch sight of Roz's eyes as she was watching me get dressed. What was going through my head was: Who's in trouble?

So Roz says to me, "Is he going to propose?" and I say in a disgusted voice, "Come on, Babydoll, act your age." This makes her look more glazed than ever, and when I leave, her lower jaw and eyelids are jess agoin' up and down so *cute*. Which, in the light of subsequent developments, goes to show that I can be as stupid as Roz and bitchier too.

The moment I saw Jim it was obvious he wasn't bringing bad news. He's really a sort of odd-looking guy in some respects, till you get to know him, when he begins to look the way that's right *for him*. Down in the lobby he looked odd in a different way. His eyes just gleamed and pierced.

At first I was let down that there wasn't any emergency. When he asked me where I'd like to go, I said, without having thought it over ahead of time, in a sort of neutral voice, more or less pleasant actually, "Would you like to go call on Mother for a while?"

For some reason I never took Jim around to see Mother till yesterday afternoon, and she and Jim just got along famously. You never were a rival for any of my men, but Mother certainly was for Jim. I don't mean she did anything wrong like flirting. She just plain liked Jim and he just plain liked her, and they argue the same. It isn't that I don't want them to get to know and like each other, I do, but it makes me furious to think about the way he just left me high and dry all evening. I don't trust men. We always kiss good night, naturally, so last night when I saw it coming, I twisted my head at the crucial moment and he caught me just under the left ear. I hope he got hair in his mouth.

Anyway, if he had been enthusiastic to go see her again tonight, I honestly believe that would have been Kaput for Jim Sorb as far as I am concerned. But as soon as I said this, he ducked his head and squinched his eyes and twitched his shoulders and generally acted as though some witch in a cave was sticking pins in an image of him. "Gee," he said, "I just meant a cup of coffee or a beer or something in a joint. If you don't mind. I'd sort of like to find some place on San Pablo where they don't have the juke box on. Anyway it's late to go visiting people—I mean, like your mother." So I said I felt like walking, why didn't we walk down to Shipley's and catch a quick one and then maybe walk up to the stables and back? That suited him fine.

Great. He was out to please. Fine.

So, what does he talk about for an hour down at Shipley's, which was practically deserted, and another hour going up around the stables? Genetics!

It seems he's got all steamed up recently by Mrs. Krishna, who is the wife of a Hindu in Daddy's class. Daddy already mentioned how beautiful she is, so when Jim went on and on about her beauty and charm and intelligence, I just gave him credit for being open and honest. I mean, if he mentioned her without mentioning he felt those things, *then* there would be something for me to worry about. So, the general idea is that Science has given mankind medicine and power over physical nature, but man has not been mature enough to use these advantages properly so that now we have overpopulation and atom bombs. Soon Science will give us control over the genes, so that man will have the power to fix it so there will only be a reasonable number of people and they will be from only the best genetic strains.

No offspring of Alfred and Beth is likely to pass up an invitation as

356

wide open as this one of Jim's. "Do tell! But I'm perplexed. Tell me, honeybun, who all's agoing to see to it the right thing is done with all that gene-type power?" You know what Jim did when I asked him this? He just took off. He zoomed for the moon—and I went trailing after. All the time, we were stroking this nice old mare I jog around on sometimes, a lazy affectionate friendly old girl. And Jim was just zooming out of his mind and I was riding tail on him.

He's not simple-minded, you know. Nowadays, mostly, anybody that's hopeful about the future sounds like a simple-minded liar. "I am here to tell you, my friends and fellow Americans, the future lies ahead! Vote for me!" But somehow, Jim sounds honest and intelligent and *still* hopeful. He believes that man is just about hitting the bottom in self-esteem and so he will use Science to save himself. Mrs. Krishna has given Jim a deep understanding of evolution and the wonderful way it can work through man's own rational consciousness without his even knowing it.

"You mean," say I, "we've got to become a new species of animal?"

"Oh no," he said. He turned toward me away from the horse and took my hands in his. Going down to Shipley's from the dorm he had held my hand too, which was sort of unusual for him. He did it without swinging arms or anything, and when we came near Shipley's he let go. In other words, shy but firm—just the reverse of the usual lunk who comes on strong and then is so ignorant he *asks* May I kiss you? So we held hands, and Jim went on about how man was going to have the opportunity to become himself and realize all his potentialities, to become fully human. And I believe him. I don't remember what-all he said because the next thing I knew he had taken me in his arms and we were kissing. Only this was not like any other kiss. He just *knew,* and so did I.

Do you know what the next thing was he said? In this different voice. "You know, Sybil, I have the feeling our fate is sealed." Isn't that romantic? It's the most romantic thing anybody ever said. And the amazing thing is, it's true! I had the same feeling. If we'd both said it, I guess our fate would truly be sealed, but I had to rush to get in before the midnight lockout. One thing I can't explain is that he didn't once say "I love you." I would never have thought it could be right not to say that. Of course we will say it, many many times, but tonight not saying was the best way of saying.

You know, I meant to tell him what I felt, when he said "Our fate is sealed." But instead what I said to him was, "You think so?" I wasn't cold or hostile or flippant exactly. But still that wasn't what I meant. Yet it was what I said. I would have tried to make up for saying it except you can't make up for a thing like that at a time like that. So I gave him everything I could give in a good-night kiss.

Love love love love,

Syb

You don't absolutely *have* to burn this letter if you don't want to.

· 20 ·

Dear Syb,

It is long after dark and I am probably in a state of shock. My hands are clammy. My fingers do what I want them to do, of course. But I have to *want* them to do it, in some odd way. Half an hour ago, I suddenly looked at my feet and waggled them, to make positive they were all right. Joe hasn't come home yet. He's never stayed this late since that awful time in London when he walked the streets all night. Maybe he's locked in the cathedral. He would like that. Here in England it stays light so late in June. All the restaurants in this city are closed already. I have another envelope sealed and stamped to mail to you, but I am hesitant to go out and mail it. The closest mailbox is on Cardinal Street, six blocks away. Joe might come back when I'm out. If either you or Daddy sent off an answer to my last, they couldn't possibly get here before tomorrow and that would be in Salisbury—which is a long drive on these winding roads with hedges they have. Well, at least we didn't go clear back up to Durham, as he threatened to do. Tomorrow afternoon I'll drive over, if it isn't raining too hard.

So far, we've been like tourists in England. Churches and cathedrals are certainly the best things to visit in this boring little country. More than once Joe and I have been the only people attending a service in a cathedral. Quite often the whole congregation, when there is one, sits up in the ancient wood seats for visiting dignitaries, so as to be close to the priest and each other. It's funny to be sitting in a grand old chair with "The Rector of York" carven on it. Some of the boys' choirs are wonderful and the music they sing is indescribably beautiful. I don't mean there isn't any life in these cathedrals, but it is museum life. Aesthetic. Only, Joe is working hard to make it religious. We never talk about this. But I *know* this is so. That is what is in the other envelope, the proof.

I'm going to go out and mail it right now.

It's mailed. There's no sign of Joe. Why I mailed it was—it occurred to me that if he came back and found me writing *this* letter, that would be as bad in a way as if he found me copying his note-

358

book, so I went out and mailed what I'd copied, just in case. Not that he *ever* reads my letters, but he might accidentally catch a glimpse. I feel ashamed to be so sneaky, but I just had to know. He has been taking his notebook with him wherever he goes. But today it was so warm when we got up that he forgot and left it in his heavy jacket, which he didn't wear. At first I just read it through and thought about it, in a daze, sort of. Then I had the idea of copying out crucial passages to send to you, so you won't think all this is a figment of *my* fancy.

What a terrible terrible terrible religion Christianity is! Repression and torment and denial. It is the most unhappy chapter in man's history, except for the aesthetic element in it, which of course is one of the glories of man. But even at its most beautiful there is always fear in it. They just won't face up to reality. Of course to have no religion might *ideally* be the best for man, but *practically* religion is better than no religion for the good and sufficient reason that it makes all the drudgery and troubles of life seem worth while and relieves you of a lot of uncertainty. But the idea of a *true* religion—that is just monstrous! *My* religion, sure. The *true* religion, never.

The Pueblos have the best religion, and I'm going to make it mine. "Everything both ways." I've said that motto a thousand times, and I still think it's just wonderful. "Love thy neighbor as thyself"—what a terrible slogan that is. Suppose you hate yourself—then what? Or suppose your neighbor is Hitler—who could love him? You can't even *begin* to love your neighbor as yourself the way Christ intended, so you're filled with guilty feelings for failing and with fear of being punished for your sin. Whereas if you lived in Koyala, just because of "everything both ways" and all that goes with it, you couldn't hate yourself and you couldn't have a Hitler for a neighbor. It's perfect, in a way, that Los Alamos is right in the Pueblo country. There it is, the perfect symbol of the destructive potential of science, of pure reason without regard for human values. There just couldn't be anything further from the Pueblo way of life. Yet, it exists, it can't be denied. So there it is right beside its antithesis. You see—everything both ways again. There seems to be a kind of fatality to the whole coincidence. Yet, you know, the Pueblos *are* being corrupted by civilization. They resisted Christianity (both the Spanish Catholic and the American Protestant varieties), the Navajos, armed conquests, science, even anthropologists (ha! ha!). But money is getting them. Not the traders as such—money. The great destructor. Apparently you can't have a civilization without money, at least there isn't one. In that case, civilization is not worth having.

You see, everything about the Pueblo religion makes man the center of his universe. *I* am always the center of where things are. So are

359

you. There are the dead. What do the Pueblos do? If you perform the right rituals, they come back in the form of rain. Isn't that friendly? Take Masau'u, the skeleton god. He is scary because he is the god of death and the underworld—which *are* scary. But he is also a god of fertility. You know how a corpse can become fertilizer? Well, like that. What we do is, we burn up our corpses or seal them in watertight caskets. We don't plant them so they can grow up again as the corn we eat. We put the dead away from us. We cut them off from the community. All that we get rained on by is water.

Oh, I so long to be fully human. I want to be all there. I want to be myself. I am short-legged and sort of underslung like the Pueblo women. But I am so pale and I don't tan well, just burn and peel too much. I would dye my hair black if that would do any good. What about Joe?

Here is this ancient (and hideous) old Christminster full of mouldery old colleges, which *I* go to visit. And Joe just sticks to the Cathedral Church of Cardinal College. He sits there with his red-lined cape wrapped around him, or else he walks up and down and around. Sanctuary. Could he be in there right this minute, locked in? Maybe I should go see. But I'm frightened. Suppose it is locked—what could I do? Stand outside and yell to him? I took him a sandwich and banana for lunch, but I thought we'd go out to an Indian restaurant for dinner. I haven't even eaten anything since noon myself. My hay fever has gotten worse than it's been for years—some peculiar British pollen probably—and I've blown my nose raw.

I hear Joe talking with somebody downstairs in the lobby. This is a small hotel and I'm surprised anybody is there to talk to. I seem to have dozed off for a few minutes. I'll put this in an envelope and hide it.

Liz

· 21 ·

(Syb: I copied this from Joe's notebook.)
"God, God, why hast Thou forsaken me?" Out of my depths the words that arise are the Psalmist's, and those words were there because they are the words that arose out of Christ in his utmost agony. Only, He said, after the Psalmist, "My God, my God." The words that came out of me when I wasn't looking were "God, God." I also said "hast Thou," it is true, but since I was a child I have never been close enough to God to think of Him as *my* God, and certainly not as a father in any sense. Those forms of address wouldn't feel right in my mouth. But "Thou" does feel right. Right but not natural. It

would be wrong for me to call anybody else in the world "thou." "Lizzie, why the hell didst thou—" Still and all, I can't call God "You." "Thou" is unnatural but right for Him. Of course, one way of looking at it is, "Thou" is appropriate just because it is so unique and non-natural: God is unique and supernatural. That is true, but it is not sufficient to explain "Thou." I'm not accustomed to looking up to anyone whatever, so that *for me* there is nothing natural about looking up to Him. And I surely can't address Him as an equal. And there is no possibility of looking downward to Him. What position can I assume when I pray to Him so as to feel natural in it? Really, the only way would be to go out there in space in a rocket where a man floats free, no gravity, no up or down, just a man in the vast inane. Then it wouldn't matter about "Thou" or "You." In fact, there wouldn't even be the vestige of a "He" left, no person. A man goes out into the vast inane, and maybe the vast inane goes into him too somehow, but that ain't *it,* that ain't what it's all *about.* Anyhow, the fact is that I am heavy with gravity, me, here, now, and I may not know where else Christ is but I know that He is in my extremest heart.

How excited I was that Sunday when Papa told me that millions upon millions of the atoms of my body had once upon a time been atoms in Jesus's body. That seemed to me the most miraculous thing I ever heard of, and it made me want to be very careful about being good. It also put me in awe of science for being able to know such a marvel. But it wasn't long till I began to think, "Well, if Jesus's atoms are a part of me, why aren't Judas's too?" They were. And that wasn't so grand. To that Papa said, "Joey, the main thing to hold onto is, millions of your atoms were once Jesus's. Nothing else matters against that simple fact." But that system of his wasn't strong enough to keep my speculations in harness. The next step from Jesus and Judas was to everybody who ever lived before me and a lot of those who are alive and breathing now. Everybody must be part of everybody else, which is confusing. Of course I was only 12 or 13 at the time, so I didn't have the gall to presume there could be anything wrong with the system of science. I could see Papa's system was sort of sentimental about Jesus being part of me, but I liked him none the less for that.

Mama, however, didn't care for all this Jesus-atom business. She did not say much. Mama never had to. She put by 30 shiny dimes with an image of the head of the Statue of Liberty on each one of them. I was running with a bad bunch at the time, sort of tagging along with them really, wanting to get in with them, and I also had Harvey. He was my Sunday school best friend for years and he didn't smoke or anything of that nature. The last I heard he was studying to be a CPA. Well, it got to the point where they told me I could join the gang, only Harvey couldn't. By-by, Harvey. Then I quit going to Sunday school. So Mama took me aside, when she heard these things that I had done, and she counted out those 30 dimes into my hand, one at a time, counting them. "I want you to look at her," she said, pointing to the lady's head on one of the coins. "She's Caesar's wife. 'Render unto Caesar the things that are Caesar's and unto God the things that are God's.' I want you to have these thirty pieces of silver. If you are going to be Judas, you better know it, and the best way is to get paid the right amount for what you do." Well, I was the unhappiest member of that gang, and I didn't last in it a year. I wasn't so bullied by Mama, though, that I let Harvey climb back onto my neck when I got out of the gang.

I just thought of something. There's the reason why I wouldn't ask other than $31 for that old Dodge I had to sell when I was drafted. That Armenian flanger wouldn't offer but $30 for it, and I was so stubborn I wouldn't give way one dollar. I finally had to sell it a week later to a neighborhood kid for $20. Damn that Judas anyhow—he cost me ten bucks.

So, another Reason. There's so many Reasons. Mostly I can get away from them in church. Oh, the goodhearted right-thinking scrubby-nosed chattering little interfering Reasons. They're driving me crazy. Why can't they just leave me be?

(Syb: Then there are pages and pages of theology—grace and sin and expiation and I don't know what-all. Then this about how he can't stand me. He's been keeping this journal for weeks. He has a very neat, clear handwriting, which never gets sprawly like mine. But it's the funniest thing—sometimes his handwriting slants forward and sometimes it stands straight up and two or three times it even slants backward for a while. All three are neat and legible. Once it even changed in the middle of a word. This worries me. As for what he says about me—well, "everything both ways!")

Why did I tell Liz what I did? That was an even worse mistake than doing it. I hoped she would share my burden with me. I thought that was what love meant to her, as it does to me. She must be holding out on me. Everything depends on the involuntary reaction at the moment the confession is heard. Hers was a kind of incredulous laughter. Her whole attitude was: "Nobody *I* love could do such a thing as that." She even put her hands over her ears. (Syb: What a terrible distortion! He must be deeply disturbed mentally. The truth is that I was horrified and felt terribly sorry for him at the same time I felt attacked. Yes, I did put my hands over my ears. I've always done that when I am surprised. You have seen me do it hundreds of times, ever since we were little. Yet to *him* it means I don't trust him. How can I get through to him?) The words she said were all right, I got to give her credit for that, and also she spoke in a good tone of voice. She wants to love and help and sympathize and do all the good works. That's the key to her—good works, *help*. But I don't want good works, I want grace. I want to be trusted. She couldn't even trust her ears. At the time I told her how I'd cheated, I was writhing in that hotel chair, and sweating, and my throat was parched, and she just couldn't take it. I don't blame her. But I can't keep from hating her either, for that look that came into her eyes at *the* moment.

I should have realized this before I married her. When I talked the possibility over with Father Liston, he pointed out the dangers of her secularity. The whole Royce family is secular, of course, but I was seduced by their subtlety. Alfred is as close as a man can get to being wise without God's aid. You got to believe me: I was sort of punned into it. Their house and their manners and their life were so "grace-ful" I thought they were "full of grace." But lack of faith has closed their hearts to grace and mercy and providence. The worst is the cor-ruption of the best. Lizzie has the Royce "gracefulness." She sure hasn't got any personal grace of her own in her body or her dress or her motions. But she has got the tone of moral authority down so per-fect that I overlooked other things: she *knows,* I thought. That's why I didn't invite her to come to New York when I was there TVing. (Syb—Not true! He *did* invite me. I have the letter in my suit-case right here.) I was ashamed to be doing what I was doing there and she would make me more ashamed. Also, after that talk with Fa-ther Liston, I knew I had better avoid Royces one and all. But I liked her so much and I felt so easy in her presence. How can you account for that? So when she came to me in New York and I was so lone-some, I just yielded to her. The loveliness of our fornication was the measure of our sinfulness, which I closed my eyes to. I permitted the lovely mists to blind me. I wanted not to see. But with the marriage sacrament my vision began to be restored to me. And, after all, those Indians she's always chattering about, whatever else you may think about them, they aren't secular by any stretch of the imagination. She doesn't *like* her secularity, it would seem.

Well, all right, so grace did not choose her for its agent of forgive-ness. Still, she might really have helped me. But here too I was de-luded in her. She is secular to the core. The only way she knows to help is psychological—subjectivism, mental illness, adjusting, all that crap. She don't understand Thing One about atonement. She just says to me in this positive voice of hers, as though everything was clear as a bell, "You've got to turn that ill-gotten money over to charity, Joe." As though that was all there was to it! Adjust to society and your psyche will be in good shape again! How's about that?

363

Because Thou hast hidden Thy face from me, she scoffs and says I am full of delusions. Thou hast not found my burnt offering acceptable in Thine eyes, that I dare not sacrifice to Thee yet again, and she tempts me to believe she knows that which she acts like she knows.

I sent $7000 to Papa to pay off the mortgage and buy a good car, and we've spent maybe $5000 on our honeymoon. Did you ever calculate how much it costs to make one H-bomb? Besides, the advertisers were going to spend their money on something anyhow, and the give-away program was nothing but light popular entertainment. If the news ever does leak out, there'll be a mighty portentous scandal, and maybe that will deliver a mortal blow to TV chicanery, which God knows would be a good thing. Why am I so unforgiven? When they gave me the forms to fill out in the Army and I marked the box White instead of Negro, did that little x hurt anybody? I never once, in my adult life, wanted to really hurt anybody. Even when I was dit-dotting when we were going on missions, what I was doing was dit-dots. I didn't want to hurt those people we were up there to drop bombs on. As long as I'm in it anyhow, I'm not going to refuse to put up with the world. For how could I want to overhaul the world unless I was resentful of God for letting it be the way it is? All I wanted in life was what anybody in his senses would allow a person to want and have, and I have done everything in my power to make myself known to God. Yet I have walked out in sin so far I've lost sight of the shore, and I am tiring fast.

(Syb: It makes my heart bleed to see my poor husband so unhappy and not know how to get him out of it. Oh, how dreadful Christianity is for a person in serious trouble! I have thought of explaining Christ as a moral teacher to Joe, but he is so stubborn that I'm afraid he would just set himself firmer against me for it. Sometimes I am amazed at how reactionary he can be when he is being especially Christian. He told me once his stepmother is even more fundamentalistic than his mother was, and she was bad enough. Maybe there is a study of Negro fundamentalism I could read and find out. This next passage is not the last thing he wrote, but it is what scares me most. I don't know how to get hold of the problem so as to help him clear things up. It's so hard to put my finger on *exactly* what's crazy in his thinking.)

It used to torment me why I didn't go RC. Of course when I was talking with a Roman I knew the proper Anglo-Catholic argument: our orders are valid, the Anglican succession was never broken, we are already members of the one true Church. Still, I never fully believed that that point of doctrine was the reason I didn't convert. After all, an Anglo-Catholic is a sort of hybrid between Protestant and Catholic. One way of looking at it, we get the best of both. Another way, we're neither one thing nor the other. There were already plenty of hybrids I've had to be in life whether I wanted to or not, like a Negro White for instance, or an American, whatever *that* is. So why didn't I just opt for RC outright instead of mugwumping on the church fence too? All those Reasons I kept futzing around among were grist for scramble. But I've got the "Why" of it now. And it's not something disguised inside of me, nor is there anything doctrinal about it. It's this: I can't forgive the Church for having failed to burn the greatest and worst heretics of all.

I know the C. of E. was no better at burning: it let Behemoth himself slip by. But by Newton's time things had gone much too far. They may even have gone too far by the time of Harvey and Galileo. The Romans, it is true, laid a hand on Galileo, but it was an infirm hand. Now the Anglicans have a better excuse for having overlooked Harvey: they were busy defending themselves against the Romans. It's an excuse, I know, and not the best one on earth, but it's better than the Romans have. The truth is, I suspect, that once Copernicus had slipped by, all was lost. They were so busy burning witches and Protestants and such-like domestic creatures that they missed Leviathan. There's nothing to complain about in their burning witches and Protestants. That's just what you've got to expect from the material you've got to work with in history, people. But the Catholics in the sixteenth century had the power and the wisdom to kill the scientists when suppression could have done some good, and they flubbed their chance, out of partisan zeal. The sin of omission for which there is no forgiveness. There is only one way to keep the great scientists from doing what comes naturally to them, and that is to say, "We'll kill you if you think such thoughts," and to kill them when they do.

What? Kill the geniuses? Yes, kill the geniuses who think the wrong way. No, not kill them now. Why not now? Because the slaughter could not be administrated. The scientists have proliferated too much and the libraries could likely never be fully purged of their collective memory. There aren't enough available thugs who would and could do the job anyway. For this Final Solution no Hitler will come along, no madman speaking in lying euphemisms. This now would be the genuine article, the really Final Solution, Armageddon itself, which none other than Anti-Christ can engineer, administrate, execute: in other words, for our mortal illness there can be none but a mortal cure. But there was a right time, when the Inquisition had the power and the knowledge and the thugs. But those courageous intellectual geniuses, did they not have the most exalted of motives, to understand some of God's truths? Of course, and they were in every way superior as individuals and as types to those who ought to have killed them. It is not malice or impurity or cruelty or madness that makes a heretic. It is error. And science is wrong, it always has been wrong, it could always have been seen to be wrong.

The results of science are so palpably wrong that I do not have to argue the matter. Oh yes, you do. Well, all right. But later. First, I will establish the nature of the heresy. *Hubris.* Satanism. Man's arrogating to himself that which belongs to God. God permits this error because, of course, without the possibility of such arrogation there would be no free will. The question here is: How can one know what belongs to God and not to man? Another way of putting it: Which are the mysteries that should be left inviolable and why?

An obvious heretic is one who believes there are no holy mysteries but only areas of ignorance. Kill him.

But, historically, he is a late arrival. The early ones were just trying to push back the frontiers of knowledge a little, not to deny all limits, not to civilize chaos entire. Is it not noble to exercise our God-given minds so as to describe, as Copernicus did, the activities of the heavenly bodies ever more accurately and beautifully? Why, in itself, surely, yes, it is noble. And if you grant that, do you not grant all scientific inquiry, right down through evolution to our present-day social psychologists and their psychic tamperings? That's right, you do so grant it. The line demarking the heresy cannot be drawn that way.

You may say that it is each man's highest obligation in this life to save his soul and that science makes it harder rather than easier for most men to save their souls. I believe that is true, but it is a Christian argument only. An argument is needed which will be as valid for nonbelievers as for us.

The only arguments I can think of are moral: Men matter, and men should strive to be themselves. There is no way to prove these platitudes, and if you don't believe them nothing I say means anything to you.

To science as such, men do not matter; they just are, like everything else. Individual scientists, being men, feel that they and men generally matter, but this is, in the judgment of their intellects, emotional subjectivism only. Still, it's a desperate beginning. You can build something on even such vague sentiments. I think, myself, that science ("men just are") is guilty of a heresy against humanity sufficient to burn scientists for. But it is the second platitude which gets to the core of things and for which there can be no remedy but the torch.

If you grant that men should strive to be themselves (whatever that statement may mean, once you drain the high-soundingness out of it), you are obviously assuming that men should be. This is not a subjectivistic sentiment which anyone but a lunatic would share. This is a "should," a moral imperative, from which it follows that no line of action or thought is permissible which will lead to the extinction of man. Therefore, you bigots and thugs, tie Copernicus to the stake and fire the faggots. All you could ever kill, left to your own resources, would be some men, whereas he is giving you the weapons to kill mankind. It is less bad that you should kill him than that you should kill everyone, and this is precisely the power he will give you if you let him alone.

Suppose, however, that mutual fear paralyzes the power-sods who rule us now, and mankind does endure. Yet the thugs' possession of the toys of obliteration—more, the existence of the knowledge of how to construct these toys, more yet, the mere knowledge that such toys have been and can be constructed—this in itself generates anxiety enough to divide us from one another and keep us divisive. And without intimacy and intercourse and community, we cannot become ourselves. Therefore, spit him, you jumping blood-lusters, you'll enjoy yourselves no less roasting him than roasting a gray-haired snaggle-toothed witch, and at least that way there'll keep on being cooks and cookings for a good long while to come.

But even if by some unlikely miracle our fear cures and we again get a chance to love one another some and make communities where we can be human if we choose to be, there's a last danger which there will be no likelihood of escaping. Controlled evolution. Genetic change. Improvement of the species. A change of man's very nature. The end of man by his transcendence into superhominid.

There is a kind of moral justice to Armageddon: we have brought our punishment down upon ourselves. But to seize control of our very natures and to breed ourselves clean of our propensity toward evil and sin, toward stupidity and madness, toward topless ambition and bottomless sorrow, this is a presumption which makes me rave to touch on. I cannot look at it. Let the slavering torturers shred the serene and lofty thinker, that some may be left to become men if they will.

I am probably raving. I fear there are not two other people in the world who would agree with what I have just written, and my wife is not one of the two. She tells me not to be so abstract and remote. I know what she would say to me at this point: "What has science done to *you?*"

There's no use totting up the good things it has done for me. Everybody knows about them. As for any harm from it I have suffered directly, I guess there's none. It's just me as one of 165 million Americans and one of the billion or two citizens of the technologized world. Nothing peculiar to me about it, precisely, yet I find it's all personal just the same. Depersonalized personal, that is to say.

I'm sitting up there five miles in the air dit-dotting and if I don't really extend my imagination I hardly know what I'm doing to a lot of German or French or Dutch men and women and children down in their towns and cities on the ground. And I certainly am encouraged in no way to imagine it, but only to look at my technical job on the one hand and at America's War Effort on the other. It's in between where the living gets done, as the man said, and it's in between where I've got lost. God help me.

I think Mama was a good woman and went to Heaven. Drugs kept her five months past her death in a hell of pain, and maybe in her agony she cursed God before she died and had no chance to repent, so that she may be in Hell for all eternity. But it is sure she suffered five months longer than she had to. I know very well that in the course of nature some have suffered even longer than she did, and I know that I could not have ordered the drugs to be withheld from her, just as I was glad the pain-depressants were given to her. What matters more is that the possibility for such monstrous responsibility should have been made available to us human beings at all. By science.

Because of medicine and sanitation, we are overcrowding the earth. What shall we do, kill people after they are born, or prevent people from being born and so reduce the opportunities for family love?

There is the noise and smog of cities.

There is the poisoning of birds and fish with insecticides.

There is television. I dare not let myself get started on that or I shall be scratching my eyes out.

It's no use saying: "The real problem is in the way men have handled these marvels which science has given us. We must learn to become mature and accept the responsibility for our new powers." It never was a question that scientific knowledge is bad in itself. The sin of science, of the great scientists, was to make unmanageable strength available to those who rule. Who are people. There never could be a way to keep those who have political power from using every other sort of power they can get for their own ends, which are frequently stupid and often evil. Rather, there is one way: change them so they aren't people any longer. That would work, doubtless. The eugenicists are right in that respect at least. Let's tamper with the genes so as to create a race of superhominids with the original sin bred out, along with armpit hair, the vermiform appendix, wisdom teeth, mammae, the hormones of rage, and other vestiges of our shaggy, Pleistocene origins.

I have done that which I should not have done, and I have left undone that which I should have done, and I am in doubt about what I should do next, and there is no health in me. Lord, have mercy upon me.

What makes you think that even the wisest, most theological Inquisitor could possibly have foreseen the consequences of letting Copernicus think? I must address myself to this question later, when I am able. Just now, I cannot.

· 22 ·

By the time the doorknob turned, Lizzie had hidden the letter to Sybil in her purse and was sitting in a straight chair with a mystery novel open on her lap.

Joe pushed open the door sharply, stepped in and to one side, then sharply pushed the door most of the way closed. This entry was one continuous motion, and while he performed it he was glancing about the room. He stood with his hands behind his back, fiddling till there was a click and rattle. His gaze focused on a spot just above the bridge of her nose. His expression was unnaturally blank.

Her legs were so short that only her toes touched the floor.

"Why are you sitting up so straight that way?" he asked her.

She was staring at him with round eyes. "I'm scared."

"Yeah? What of?" He moved toward the closet.

"You."

"Aw, come on." He opened the closet door and reached inside.

"What were you doing downstairs so long, talking?" she asked.

"Telling Mrs. Ball we're pulling out after breakfast tomorrow."

"Are we? For where?"

"That remains to be seen."

He fished the notebook out of the jacket pocket, and as he did so smiled at her on one side of his mouth. "This morning I left this book in that pocket with the spine facing frontward, and now I find it spine facing backward." Turning toward her, he thumbed through it till he came to two certain pages. He spread the notebook at her. "In addition, I left a little drop of stickum gluing these two pages together, and now I find them pulled apart. Liza, you have reason to be scared."

"You tricked me!" she cried. But she did not get up or appear indignant. Her hands clutched at the thin orange-covered book in her lap.

"Now you know." He tossed his notebook onto the table beside Lizzie. There was nothing particularly violent in his gesture, yet when

369

the book went past her head she flinched against the wall and gasped. He laughed. "And now I know too."

"What do you know, honey?" she said.

"Given the opportunity to sneak a peek, you sneak a peek. Like what you saw, baby?"

"Do you really hate me so much?" she said in a small voice. Her hands, one with the book in it, rose to the sides of her head beside her ears.

He was pacing. "It's more complicated than that. I keep repeating to myself, 'The sin, not the sinner. It's her training and her philosophy of life, not her.' But I'm having trouble hanging onto that sentiment, more and more trouble. So what did you learn today?"

"How sick you are."

"Sick unto death. You didn't know that?"

"No, I didn't. What should I do?"

"Do, my little do-good wifie?" His laugh sounded like a parody of his old full, complicated laugh. "Why, make yourself a receptacle for the heavenly dew that falls on good and bad alike." In the corner of the room farthest from her—not very far—he stopped, and pressed himself against the somewhat grimy wall. "Baby, what the hell are you holding out on me?"

The mystery novel dropped to the floor, and she stood up. "What a thing to say." Indignation freed her emotions a little. She stepped toward him, hands reaching. "Joey, my dearest dear one, please."

"Don't touch me!" he half yelled in a falsetto. "Stay back!"

She stopped. She shook her head. He seemed to her to be, both at the same time, trying to press himself into the beaded wallpaper and also gathering himself for a great leap. She gasped through open mouth. "What is it? What's the matter? I must hold you, I must."

"Don't touch me. If you touch me, I don't know what I'll do. I can't be responsible. Don't set me off."

"There's such a look in your eyes." She sank onto the bed.

"You look the same as always," he said. "That's the incredible part of it. The same, only scared some. Okay. Now tell me. What are you holding out on me?"

"What makes you think I'm doing any such thing?"

"I can't trust my reason on a matter like this, I got to trust my intuition. So I trust my intuition, and it tells me, 'Buster, she been holding out on you from hour one.' So I send my reason snuffling around for evidence. There ain't much, but there is some."

"What are you trying to do to us?" she wailed.

"Sweeping down some of the cobwebs that were collecting dust all over our hearts and souls. Maybe we'll survive the operation, and then again maybe we won't, and maybe I'm going about it a good and valid way, and also then again maybe I'm not. But here we go for broke anyhow. I showed you my heart. You read it today, there, in that book of mine. Now you show me yours."

"Don't talk so loud. You'll wake everybody up, and we'll have people banging on the door."

His eyes rolled. "She's right," he said in a subdued, tense voice, "and she's driving you crazy. At such a time she is right about such a thing. Okay, now give."

"Joe," she said and pressed her hands to her bosom, "you are in my heart, just you, darling."

"Too late." His head shook slowly. "Good, but too late."

Tears began to run down her cheeks as from a spring. She did not sob nor did her mouth change expression. She did not wipe the tears. "Look, I swear to you by the one thing that matters more to me than everything else in the whole world, us—I swear that I am not holding anything out on you."

He stepped from the corner and began pacing again. "You're really sincere, aren't you? You don't even know what it is yourself."

She rallied at this charge, and with forefinger raised she began to advance on him.

"I told you not to touch me!" he yelled so loud that she fell back onto the bed. "What you think I been keeping my hands in my pockets for?"

She had not noticed that. She saw by the bulges in the legs of his trousers that his hands were fists. His forearms were trembling visibly. It occurred to her that he might actually kill her. Reared on her elbows, she stared at his gray lips.

"I finally got through to you, did I?" he said. "Okay. Now. Let's begin all over. I'm in a bad way, and one of the reasons is that we are in a bad way, you and me, our marriage. I can't stand this any longer. Okay? I either got to find out what is gumming us up and get shed of it, or I got to take off. And I got to do it now, right this very minute. Now then. There's the obvious possibility, which is that I am such a corrupt fraudulent lying treacherous bastard that I should be cast into outer darkness where there is naught but wailing and the gnashing of teeth, and no woman could abide with me for long unless she was some special new nutty variety of masochistic slob. Or possibly you are the monster. Which I sort of doubt, both ways. From where I stand, it looks to me like we're a couple of people. Just people. Which means we got to give ourselves a chance, and the only way we can do that is to be open and aboveboard with each other. You know? Honest as we can be. Well, I tried to open myself to you. You read what I wrote in my notebook. I know it's hard for you to trust me. Maybe it's just me, and then again maybe it's hard for you to trust anybody.

I don't know. You say what is in your heart is me. I don't know that either. For a while there, I was thinking in your secretmost heart you had a cake of ice. But I was wrong. Ice is clear, it can be seen into. What you've got maybe is mud, cold mud."

Her eyes closed tight, and she rolled over onto her right side with her knees pulled up to her chest.

"Look at me!" he ordered, but she did not stir. He raised a fist to hit her, then dropped it. "Damn it all, Liz, pardon me. Pardon me, please, for saying that. I know it's not true. I did not mean it. It was just meanness speaking out." She was still not sobbing, and the tears were still welling from her eyes. He stood over her, breathing heavily. "Well, pardon me, God damn you."

"I pardon you," she said dully, without moving.

"All right then." He went back to pacing. At every other step he pounded his right fist against the heel of his left hand. "Now tell me this. Is it because I'm a nigger?"

This stirred her. She sat up again. "What?" she said incredulously. "Is what because you're what?"

"Are you holding out on me because I'm a nigger?"

"Holding what out on you?"

"I don't know exactly what. Yourself mostly."

"What possible thing have I done," she said confusedly, "that I could ever have had one least hint of an impulse about racial prejudice? Just one, name me just one."

"All right. I'll name you one. You were overly friendly with Margery."

"Your stepmother?"

"I wasn't talking about Margery Kemp, ducky. How many Margerys do we know between us? Yes, I mean my shit-brown stepmother that everybody else thinks they're doing pretty good by if they can just put up with her. I mean my papa's folly, she who rolls with the holies, that church-mouse with a penchant for slander, and BO to boot. It isn't natural to make up to her the way you did. It looks like reverse race prejudice."

"I just wanted to make a good impression on your folks," Lizzie said. She was frowning as she watched him. She was obviously not concentrating on what she was saying. "Is it a crime for a bride-to-be to try to make her future in-laws like her the one and only time she is ever allowed to meet them?"

"First of all, you weren't a bride-to-be at that time. Second, no, it's no crime, but you overdid it. Third, I don't care for that insinuation that that was the only time you were 'allowed' to meet them. It just happened to be the only time you did meet them, or have met them so far. We haven't been anywhere near our families since we got mar-

372

ried, remember? And fourthly, by gushing and pawing all over Margery, you made a mighty peculiar impression on everybody. I never knew a nigger yet that loved a nigger-lover, not even Margery."

Her eyes closed and she fell on her back. "I'm sorry," she said faintly. Her face squinched tight and she began to sob. She did not curl up again.

He stood over her, squeezing his head between his hands and clenching his teeth. "Here, for Christ's sake. Use it." He dropped his wadded handkerchief onto her upturned face.

She blew her nose and wiped her cheeks. "When I was ten years old, Mother took me to Houston with her to visit her mother. This was the first time she had been home since she got pregnant with me. She wrote to tell her mother she was pregnant. She was afraid to tell her to her face. My grandmother was slow to forgive. She had a housekeeper, Victoria, who she treated like a sort of child, warm and all, but very superior. She expected her to cheat and disobey quite a lot. She was stern with her, but at the same time she was indulgent and humorous. She was always telling stories about Victoria which made her look simple and childlike. Grandmother was bad to Mother too. I hated her. And the more I hated her, the more I liked Victoria. Two or three afternoons a week, right after she did the dinner dishes, Victoria went over to look in on her granny. She was supposed to be over ninety and she had been a slave. She was half deaf and stone-blind, and she just rocked in a chair up in an attic room over where Victoria's brother and his family lived. Victoria had an illegitimate son they had raised for her, only he'd left home by that time. Of course there was not much that Victoria could do for her, but I couldn't help comparing the way she treated her old Granny with the way my grandmother treated her, or even the way my mother and I treated Grandmother because of her own manner with us. Victoria would hug and pat and rub and squeeze and hold hands with her toothless old granny. 'When you get right down to it, Lizzie,' she'd say, 'loving is mostly touching.' That's why I made so much over Margery. I was remembering Victoria. She must have been wrong. I'm sorry I boobooed so badly."

"That's right," he said, "you boobooed badly. You know, those Pueblo Indians of yours must have the queerest arrows in the whole wide world, with points at both ends. I expect that old Victoria of yours just used the ordinary type of arrow they've got in Texas, that points one way only. 'Loving is mostly touching,' meatball, don't mean 'Touching is mostly loving.'"

She nodded. "I haven't had my supper," she said.

"Who has?"

"I've been waiting for you."

"Now listen!" he cried. When she put a cautionary finger over her mouth, he rolled his head back and forth, but he did lower his voice. "Don't you try to divert me! Okay, I never really believed you were prejudiced, but I had to put that nagging suspicion to rest. I must say your story sounds like a Royce woman's story all right."

"Is that good or bad?"

"Both."

"And furthermore," she said eagerly, "you just have to believe me when I say that whenever I'm startled I put my hands up over my ears. I've always done it. You can ask anybody in my family. Apparently it's a holdover from some childhood trauma. It's involuntary."

"So?"

"Therefore, it does *not* mean that I didn't trust you or believe in you when I did that. I mean, like you said in your notebook—that time you told me about how you cheated on the TV program."

"Ah," he said, "you bring that up too."

"Of course," she said. "It's a very big part of our lives right now. Isn't it?"

"And you bring it up at a moment like this?"

"If you get to reach back nine or ten months to the one time I met your folks, I damned well get to reach back three or four weeks to the time you told me about the crime you committed."

"Crime, is it?"

"That's what you called it."

"It's different when I say so," he said half pleadingly.

"No, it isn't."

"Okay, it isn't," he said flatly and paced. "Let's go back to the business of your hands over your ears."

"Let's not."

"Watch it." He stopped in front of her, pulled his hand out of his pocket, and menaced her with a half-crown. "What does this coin stand for? Capital? Accumulated labor? I don't know, and the economists don't tell me much. It's a medium of exchange? Blah. The one thing I know about this piece of metal, because of its shape and design and where and when I am holding it, is this: whatever its economic value may be, it possesses that value because of social trust. Don't try to shake me out of that knowledge. That's the foundation of whatever else anybody's got to say about this big heavy anachronistic stupid coin. The root of all evil, the bourgeois form of power—say what you will, the first thing you have to say is: Money gets its value from social trust. I don't understand it, I just say: That is the case. Likewise, wife, when the person I'm talking to and confessing my secret heart to puts her hands over her ears, that act signifies her personal distrust in me. Wherever it came from in her psyche, no matter what other occasions she does it on, that act at that time means 'I don't want to hear what you have to tell me.' That statement must be the foundation of whatever else anybody has to say about that act, including you. That has always got to be taken into account *first*. Have I made myself clear? Have I got through to you? Anybody home?"

She writhed and pounded the mattress.

He bent over her, his hands working. Then he drew back. He flogged her legs and back with a pillow, saying, "Tell me, tell me, you got to tell me."

She suddenly rolled across the bed, got up on the other side, and made for the door. It was locked.

"What have you done?" she cried. "Let me out or I'll scream for help. Joe!"

"Sit down."

"Toss me the key, now."

"Sit down!"

"I'll count to five. One, two, three, four . . ."

He threw the key at her hard, hitting her on the arm.

Sobbing his name, shaking her head to get the tears out of her eyes, she fumblingly unlocked the door and then stepped out into the unlit hallway. She looked back inside. He was sitting in the armchair with his head bowed. Both hands were clutching and pulling his hair. She stepped back in and closed the door behind her. She looked stupidly at the key, glanced around for a place to put it, then opened the door again and put it in the keyhole from the hall side.

"All right," he said. "I'll behave. Now or never."

"You are trying to ruin everything," she said. "I don't know what you want."

"The truth," he said, "just the truth."

"If I only knew, I would tell you. You need help."

He raised his head and smiled with half his mouth.

"Why don't we go back home to California," she said, "just as soon as possible, so you can go to a doctor? Don't you think so?"

"No, I don't think so. We got some talking left to do."

"About what?"

"That which we agreed never to discuss, I fear me."

"Religion?" she asked.

"Sex," he answered, hissing.

"Oh, sex. Good."

"Good? I thought you were all against talking about it? You said you were."

"That was just because you were," she said. "I wasn't really. Anyhow, I think it seldom pays to bring sex out in the open. But sometimes it is a good thing to, like now. Are you afraid of impotence?"

"No," he said lightly. "Among the many many things on my mind, that somehow just is not included. I was thinking more of baby-making."

"Well," she said in a diminished voice, "sure."

Her face brightened then, and she looked at his eyes for the first time since she had closed the door. She was all prepared to say, "Tell me what I have been doing wrong," but the words died in her throat. Joe's face was contorted. She took a step toward him and crouched a little so that her eyes were on a level with his.

"Joe! Look me in the eye." Whenever he had looked at her this evening, his gaze had held to the spot in the center of her forehead. "Look at me. Please." His gaze shifted down to the level of her eyes, but it still focused between them on the bridge of her nose. "Tell me, what is it? Look at me, darling. You must tell me what it is that's upsetting you so much. Do I do something wrong in bed? I'll improve if you just tell me what to do. Let me tell you this. I never once pretended with you. Truly. I never pretended to feel anything I didn't feel."

"No," he said, laughing with evident pain, "I never thought you were a whore, nor anything near it."

"Is that what whores do?"

"Yes, honey, pretend is what whores do, the zealous ones, anyhow. And this really is one of your two-way arrows: whores do it, *and* to do it is whorish. Okay, okay, thanks, you've given me a little perspective on things now. No, wife, I don't think the rock-bottom worst of you. So."

"Joe?" she said in a little voice. "Have I become repulsive to you, physically? We don't—you know, we haven't for quite a while. Isn't there anything I can do? It's our honeymoon."

His pained laughter had subsided, but at this it swelled again.

She went back to the chair in which she had been sitting when he had first come into the room, and sat in it again so straight that only her toes reached the floor. Her face was drawn, her eyes were large.

"All right," he said, leaning forward in the armchair but restraining himself from getting up. "I'll pull myself together. It ain't so hell-fired funny as all that. You're right. Let me get at it this way. We never talked about children. Why do you suppose we never did?"

"The subject just never came up."

"It often does when people get married. Often."

"Not always," she said. She scrubbed her nose hard.

"Well, what do you suppose I was assuming, that I never brought it up?"

"How do I know?"

"Well, now suppose this was a story you were reading and I was one of the two main characters. You know, a healthy man around thirty years of age, with a decent enough career ahead of him probably, some money in the bank, a churchgoer, not too dedicated to some big-time cause or other. What would you assume about him when it came to the matter of children?"

"Let's not play games, Joe."

"Let's do play this one game, Liz. You'd assume that he'd probably get married and have some children, about two and a half children, I believe, according to the Bureau of the Census. And you'd be right. Now the woman in this story, what about her?"

"Joe, I can't have children now." She was scissoring her feet back and forth, fast.

"You can't? But you always went through the 'I'll be back in a minute' routine and went to the bathroom when it came time for baby-making."

"But I can't."

"So you really don't have any contraceptive stuff in your suitcase. I didn't just miss it, you really don't have any."

"No," she said brightly. "You see, I had my tubes tied."

"You what?"

"I had my tubes tied three years ago."

He seemed to shrink up out of the chair. She ran to the door, but he was not pursuing her. He had plastered himself against the wall.

"Joe? What are you going to do? Joe?"

"Anything else you have to tell me?"

"But this wasn't sex, Joe. Sex is altogether separate. Sex is a thing apart. It is for us, for our relationship. I always think of sex as a necessary pleasure. It hasn't got anything to do with having children, except as a sort of by-product. Babies are accidents. We could adopt a baby if you really want one. I was going to tell you about it at the propitious moment. I was right on the verge of telling you, when you beat me to the punch and told me about the TV business. You see? We're in it together. I wasn't holding out on you. Really and truly I wasn't. I was simply waiting for the right opportunity. Timing is so important. *You* know that so well. Anyhow, I can have them untied if you really insist. Kay Ravagli did after she married Woody, and now they have two fine healthy children. You see?"

As she talked, he pushed himself along the wall toward the bed. When he reached the bed, he stepped up on it, walked sideways on the pillows, and got down on the side next to the door.

"No matter," he said. "This is enough. This is it. There's nothing more you could hold out on me which would matter after this. Don't tell me any more. I don't care. Who did it, your family doctor?"

"Don't be ridiculous. My family don't know a thing about it. I decided I was not going to bring a child into a world as rotten as this. That was my own decision and I'm not ashamed of it for one second. It was *my* business."

"And you aren't ashamed for one second of deceiving your husband."

"That's a lie! I am and always will be a faithful wife."

"You know, I wouldn't doubt it." The contrast between his playful words and the twisting expression on his face so shocked her that she wanted to dash to the door and scream for help. But by then he was closer to the door than she, and he was standing and she sitting. "Cuntwise, kid, you'll do. The kind of fidelity I was referring to is located about ten or twelve inches further up, in an organ you don't know too much about, the heart. Now then." His hand found the doorknob and he pulled himself up straight. "The last thing I have to say to you in this life is this: I hope someday soon you manage to understand what you have done to me. I don't think this is likely to come about unless you become a Christian. But let that be as it may. I hope and I pray that you may come to realize what you have done to me. If not sooner, then later, but sometime, sometime. You just won't ever feel bad enough till you appreciate what you have done, and I want you to feel bad. I long for you to feel bad. Just as bad as you can. As bad as I do. So long."

"I have almost no money."

"Ah yes," he said through the half-closed door. "Money. She's got *some*thing screwed on the right way anyhow. Tomorrow morning, well before noon, sufficient money will arrive for you. Do not fret." He left.

She lay on top of the bed, flat on her back. After a while her eyes were so dry that when she blinked she could hear her eyelids make a soft clicking noise. She did not turn off the bedside lamp. Sometimes she thought she heard stealthy footsteps in the hallway. Once she reared up to see if the doorknob was turning; it was not. She could not bring herself to go to the door, open it enough to reach out for the key, then close it from the inside. Sometimes she lost consciousness for several minutes without knowing she had done so. When she began noticing the sounds of other people getting up, she forced herself to take a bath. She did not think to lock the door. After the bath, sitting in her dressing gown in front of the mirror to put on make-up, she was unsettled by the sight of her face in the glass, especially by the eyes, which did not seem like any eyes she had ever seen before, certainly not her own. She let her head fall sidewise on the dresser between her curved arms and cried herself to sleep.

V

· 1 ·

"But that is not why I came to see you," said Robin.

"I didn't really think it was," Alfred answered.

She dropped her eyes and smiled a little, as though in pain. He was sorry to have hurt her. He had not spoken with rude intention, but her reaction showed him how lacking in friendliness his response had been. From what Horace had hinted, he thought that in New York she had been a call girl or something near it. He did not wish to know any more about her than he already knew. If she had been thrusting herself upon him in any way, his small unkindness would have pleased him, or else he would have done it deliberately. As things stood, he could not refuse to reach out to her.

"It hardly seemed probable," he said, "that you'd drop by Berkeley on your way home from New York just to tell me about The Institute of Modern Living. You are a good *raconteuse*, my dear, and an attractive young woman. I didn't suppose you were so hard up for an audience as to be obliged to seek out a middle-aged law professor to talk to. Tell me why you came."

Robin emptied the teapot into her cup and took a sip of tea. They were sitting in the garden. The shadow of the roof was moving up her legs. She shifted her chair back a couple of feet to catch the mellow sun. She sat up straight in her chair, with her hands folded in her lap, and looked at him. Her glance did not stay on his eyes but flicked to his beard.

Alfred half felt that she was throttling down some sort of terror, but he put the thought aside in annoyance at himself. No doubt the impression had been caused by his disturbance at the change in her aspect. The acne pits were gone from her face; instead, there were some new lumps which had nothing to do with muscle movements or bone structure or anything else organic. She was wearing make-up so heavy as to give her face a masklike appearance. Her eyes did not seem to him to belong to the rest of her face, to her gestures or clothing, or to the way she spoke. They were large and bright and full of an intensity which had no apparent connection with the occasion. Her mouth belonged to her appearance no more than her eyes did; it was whimsical, mobile, appealing. He watched her mouth as she spoke.

"I can't tell you how upset I was when Hugh told me that you and Mrs. Royce had separated."

"That is good of you," he said icily.

"I know it may not seem to be any of my business. But I felt so guilty."

"Ah."

"Yes, and I want to get it off my conscience. Lying there in the hospital, I thought about"—she hesitated—"things."

"In a hospital, one does tend to think about things."

"There were complications after the baby, and the doctor discovered—"

"You really had a baby?"

Startled, she looked him in the eye to see whether he was being sarcastic. He seemed to mean the question. "You didn't know?"

"Everybody in the country knew you appeared to be pregnant, went to the hospital for a few days, then reappeared with a life-sized doll. I—we assumed that since you had a rubber baby you had also had a rubber pregnancy."

"We?"

"Leon, to be specific. It was his idea originally."

"He would like to think that," she said sadly.

"Ah?"

She looked at her knees. "He was the father."

"I'm sorry you told me that," Alfred snapped.

"You don't believe me."

He did not respond.

"I should leave. But I'll say what I came to say." She took a deep breath. "Over a year ago I met you at a party at Throckmorton Manor."

"I used to remember that party with pleasure."

"I encouraged you," she began, then stopped. "It was more than that. I seduced you into making improper advances to me."

He gasped. "You are fantastic. My dear young woman, I remember perfectly well making a friendly little pass at you. I was pretty high, and it was a lively party."

"I'm sorry."

"You mean to say that you could suppose Beth Royce—*my wife* —is capable of falling out with me because I kissed and hugged a girl at a drunken party?" He breathed in snorts. "How very presumptuous of you." He stood. "Please excuse me."

Irma had been hovering in the study. Alfred beckoned her and turned Robin over to her to show out the front door.

He was still breathing hard when Nancy appeared.

"What a pleasant surprise," he said.

"I came to jump while Mommy runs down to the store."

He looked at his watch and frowned. "It's quarter past five."

"She needed some butter and Mary Lou and Shirl are coming to dinner. So is Syb."

"I knew they were coming. For heaven's sake, why didn't she send you down to borrow some butter from me?"

"Well," said Nancy, pinching his ear. "I suggested that."

"Humph. Five to five-thirty is *my* time to use the street."

"What she said was, 'If I have to choose between bumping into him on San Jacinto and borrowing his goddamned butter, I'll take my chances on the open street.'"

"Did she indeed," he said, smiling secretly.

Nancy began jumping.

· 2 ·

"Now I wonder," Beth said to herself half aloud, drew up at the curb, and turned to look out the back window.

The young woman walking listlessly along San Jacinto Way, head bowed so that her face was obscured by her hair, reminded her of Robin, despite the differences in appearance and bearing. Mostly Beth was struck by the chic of her blouse and skirt and the deliberate slouch of her posture; she could have been a model "on camera."

"Robin?" said Beth hesitantly.

Startled, Robin bent over to look through the car window. "Yes?" she said in a cheery voice. "Oh, Mrs. Royce, how delightful." She extended her arm, and they shook hands.

"You have been crying," said Beth.

Robin smiled, shrugged quickly, and dashed the tears from her eyes and cheeks.

"Get in," said Beth. "Let me take you down the hill. You came to see Alfred?"

"Yes," said Robin, "and now I'm going to see Leon. Just drop me near a bus anywhere."

"Don't be ridiculous. I'll run you down to Leon's place."

Beth knew that the usual formulas of greeting and inquiry were called for. "How long—" she began, intending to ask how long she had been in town, why she had gone to see Alfred, how things were going in New York, how Hugh was. Having stopped at a stop sign, she turned to look at Robin and did not complete her question. Instead, at a delicate trembling of Robin's eyelids, she looked at her arm; the wrist was thin and pale, and the hand on the seat between them lay without energy, unalive.

"You are unwell," said Beth.

Robin gave a nod so quick and small, while lowering her head as though in shame, that Beth was not entirely sure it had been a nod of assent. She took Robin's hand flat between both of hers and pressed it. "Is it serious?"

"Hodgkin's disease," said Robin.

"Oh my God. What are they doing for it?"

Robin gave her head a tiny shake.

A car behind them honked. Beth drove on.

"Let me do . . ." Beth began, pulling over to the curb in the middle of the block.

"Please, Mrs. Royce," said Robin, distressed. "It was terribly good of you to pick me up, but maybe I should walk." She started to open the door. "I am upset, and I want to be in control of myself when I go to see Leon."

Beth shifted into second gear and pulled ahead.

"I'll shut up," she said furiously. "It's just so awful. All right, goddammit, I'll keep my big yap shut. That's the least I can do."

In ten minutes she pulled up in front of Leon's house. Robin embraced her with a gesture that was unmistakably calculated to appear impulsive. But there was no necessity for the embrace, since the two women had never been close to each other. Masking as artifice, the impulse was genuine.

"Good-by."

"Good-by."

Robin ran up the stairs with apparent briskness.

Beth sat for a couple of minutes, cursing, weeping, and pulling at the steering wheel with both hands as though trying to uproot it.

· 3 ·

Robin knocked on Leon's door as she had used to when she had come to his apartment the year before: three light quick raps and a heavy one. When she heard Leon coming to the door she put on a bright face.

He opened warily, scowling. "Robin? It is you."

"Please let me *in*," she sang in a voice as deep as she could make it.

He was supposed to reply by singing "You are my *fate*." Instead, he stepped aside and motioned her in with a forefinger; he said nothing; there was a look of distaste on his mouth.

"I was so glad you were home when I phoned," she said.

"You should have written ahead," he said.

"I wanted to surprise you."

He was elaborately polite about seating her. "Mrs. Hansson. Well." He smiled cynically. "What kind of a husband is Hugh?"

"A legal one. I understand you are married too."

"Who told you that?" he said severely.

"Oh, just a little bird."

"Who?"

She smiled and looked around. Nothing had changed but the books. "Everything here's so familiar," she mused, "that I feel strange."

"No red herrings. Who told you?"

"You are so reliable. So conservative and reliable."

"Knock it off, Robin."

"Even the way you dress me down is the same."

"Who told you I was married?"

"To Chantal. Right?"

He remained stony-faced.

Alfred had told her. When she had mentioned early in their conversation that afternoon that she was going to visit Leon, he had told her that she should be prepared to look for him at Chantal's, and why. But Leon seemed so displeased by her visit and especially by her knowing of his marriage, that she did not want to inculpate Alfred.

"Francis," she said.

"Who is she?"

"Francis, Mr. Cross-Examiner, is a he. He's the director of the University Theatre. Remember?"

"Oh, the fairy. How in God's name would he know anything about my private life?"

"His sister has a daughter in some folkdancing class." She was improvising on a theme from Alfred's conversation. "It seems her best friend knows Jean-Louis Bigonneau and Nancy Royce."

"Them." He studied a hangnail. Looking up, he leaned forward and scrutinized her face. "What on earth did you do to it?"

"Had it scraped a couple of times," she said. "They told me three times would be better, but my money ran out after two. Isn't it improved without the pockmarks?"

"No, it is not improved. Where did you get the money to have the operation performed?"

"I used the money you gave me last summer."

"Oh," he said, "you used the money I gave you last summer. Then I take it you had a natural miscarriage."

"A natural birth."

"You mean to say you actually had the baby?"

She nodded. "We are co-parents."

"Then you deliberately," he said, "took my money under false pretenses."

"No, no. It was just that when things got right down to the point I decided I'd rather spend the money having a baby than killing it."

"That's a lie. What you just said a minute ago was that you used the money to get your face scraped."

"I wanted to look—less unattractive."

"I see. And Hugh—where does he get in on the act?"

"Poor dear Hugh. He wanted to keep the baby even more than I did. I never saw the like. Do you want to know what I named her?"

"It was a girl?" he said. He was pale and trembling.

"Gretchen Dolores."

"God in heaven, what a name."

"Don't you like it? I thought it shouldn't be either Russian after you, or English after me, or Scandinavian after Hugh. None of us three are real honest-to-goodness parents to her. I think Gretchen Dolores is a lovely name."

"Gretchen Dolores Kalish. A mishmash. Where is she right this minute? Outside in a taxi?" He went to the window and looked up the driveway. "Or is Hugh nursing her in New York?"

"She is with a very nice couple in Westchester. They will give her a lovely home and all the advantages, much, much more than we could have done."

"You know them?"

"No, no. The agency never lets the two parties know each other's identity. I never even saw Gretchen." She was crying and smiling. "This is not the way I meant to do it, Leon."

His mouth was twisted.

"I don't hate you," she said.

"Who's talking about hate? You're different. I can't put my finger on how you've changed exactly. But I can't understand the connections you make any more."

" 'The man who solves the problem of communications,' " she said, " 'will save the modern world.' I remember the father of my daughter used to say that."

384

He smiled a little but quickly resumed his scowl. "Still and all, there's something very odd about you."

"Yes," she said, "there is."

"Well, what? What makes you think you know what I'm referring to?"

"I am dying," she said.

"Cut the melodrama."

"I'll be dead within three or four months at the outside."

"You're kidding."

She shook her head.

"Robin, please don't exaggerate. This goes beyond the limits of teasing. What do you have?"

"Hodgkin's disease. It's incurable."

"Are you in pain?" he asked.

"Hardly any, yet."

For a while he just stared at the floor. Then he looked at her. Because of the melancholy composure with which she watched him, he became aware that he was grimacing in a foolish manner.

"My God," he said, kneeling before her and burying his face in her lap, "forgive me, forgive me. I have been cruel. This is unspeakable." He began sobbing and beating her legs softly with both fists. "Damn, damn, Robin, oh, forgive me."

"I came to ask your pardon," she said, smoothing his hair. "But things didn't turn out right. So, now I ask it."

He raised his head presently, and began to touch her face and throat and arms. "Truly, darling? Incurable?"

"It took me a long time to work up the courage to knock on your door. That never happened before."

"Why, why?" he said, now so warm to her that he forgot the tone of voice with which he had answered her on the telephone.

"I beg your pardon, Leon, for having our child without your knowledge, and for adopting it out."

He flailed, stammered, and embraced her. They cried in one another's arms awkwardly for a few moments. Then he released her and buried his face in her lap again.

· 4 ·

As Beth drove home up San Jacinto Way, she was clenching her jaws, neck, and shoulders; her hands gripped the steering wheel so hard her knuckles were white. Robin was the fourth person Beth had known who was near death. The other three had been members of her immediate family; their bodies and faces bespoke their maladies; she had learned through doctors that they were dying. In those cases her anger had fed her sorrow. Robin, on the other hand, was a person with whom Beth was only slightly acquainted, though she knew a good deal about her, and by appearances alone Robin might have been having no more than a touch of the flu. Now Beth's sorrow was balked in its reaching out, so that it fed her anger. If she were being drawn by a horse instead of operating a machine, she would have flogged the horse; if she were a slave-owner, she would have been ready to flog a slave. Her justified sorrow for Robin was like a too small vent, through which all her rages tried to roar at once. She was sufficiently in control to drive slowly, in second gear; the street was used like a country lane by children, and there was a Great Dane asleep in the middle of it now.

Up the road on the left side, in front of the gate to Alfred's house, Irma was waving her hands. To Beth, Irma had as much quality as a dish of tapioca pudding. Beth did not want to restrain her anger by so much as the small neighborliness it would take to wave back; white-lipped, she resolutely held her eyes straight ahead.

"It's Nancy!" Irma cried, waving harder. "Nancy fell!"

Beth turned toward the fence to park, but in confusion trod the gas pedal so that the car lurched forward. Irma gave a little shriek and wrung her hands. The car skidded, bucked, rocked, and died, its front bumper touching the fence and its rear end skewed into the road a bit.

Beth poked her head out the window. "What's this about Nancy?"

"Oh dear," said Irma, "I hate to . . . The doctor is on his way. She fell."

"Where is she?" said Beth, getting out but still not stepping toward the gate.

"On the couch. She's so pale. You know how tan she is. I call her a little Indian. But she's so pale now. Alfred is afraid she cracked her ribs."

"My God," said Beth, striding toward the gate. She was glaring at Irma, who stepped aside.

"I wouldn't be at all surprised," said Irma, "if she broke her arm." She was confused among distress for Nancy, fear of Beth, and hopeful anxiety over the meeting of Beth and Alfred. Her mouth worked and trembled. "Right below the elbow."

Beth did not even ask her how the accident had happened but ran to the front door, which was ajar, and called Nancy's name.

"To the right," Irma said solicitously, trotting down the path after her.

"In here, Beth, here," Alfred cried, his tenor voice like a bugle. When she entered the room, she looked first at Alfred standing by the couch on which Nancy lay. He was erect, stricken, and obviously glad she had come.

Nancy said, "Hello, Mommy," in a rather feeble voice. But her eyes were alert on her parents.

"Darling, darling," said Beth and knelt by the couch. She was still tense, her muscles were all set, but she was no longer rigid as she had been. "Let me see." Nancy's left forearm was bruised and swelling. Beth touched it with her fingertips, and Nancy winced. "What about your ribs?"

"I can't be sure," said Alfred. "Myer is on his way."

Beth lifted Nancy's blouse. There was an ugly bruise beginning across the budding left breast.

After touching her and sobbing a little, Beth looked up at Alfred and said without accusation in her eyes or voice, "What happened?"

"She was practicing a forward twist on the trampoline and slipped or stumbled or turned her ankle or something. She landed with her lower half on the canvas and her chest on the bar. Then she flipped off, heels over head, and landed flat on her back in the gravel. It knocked the wind out of her. I was watching at the time."

"Oh," said Beth, "that must have been terrible. But you got to her right away."

"Instantly," he said. "And Irma called Myer in no time at all. Luckily he was about to leave his office. It all just happened three or four minutes ago."

"You don't think there's anything serious?" she said.

His shaky composure broke. "I don't know. She got so pale. I think she passed out for a few seconds. I told her not to talk. It's so hard to know about an internal injury. They tell you not to change their position after an accident, but I carried her in here before I remembered. Could I have made it worse? Do you think?"

At this point Sybil entered. After her came Mary Louise, with Shirley clinging to her mother's arm. The three stood at the foot of the couch, concentrating on Nancy, with quick glances at Beth and Alfred.

In the five minutes till the doctor arrived the talk was trivia about Nancy's accident, and the charged emotions seemed directed toward her but were mostly generated by uneasiness and anticipation about Beth and Alfred. Beth had something to do, stroking Nancy and warding everyone else off, and was the least agitated person in the room. Nancy watched carefully when pain did not shut her eyes. Alfred was vibrating internally, like a tuning fork.

When Sybil first came in she became pale. Presently she flushed, then went pale again. She was not much worried about Nancy, whom she knew to be tough physically and possum when hurt. She had

387

brought with her an agitation of her own, and what her parents did now mattered to her profoundly. The previous night Jim had asked her to marry him the following summer. She had not been able to say yes or no. When he had finally departed in anger, he had demanded that she give her answer by tonight. She still had not been able to make up her mind, and it seemed to her now that only if her parents showed signs of reuniting would she be able to say yes to Jim as she wanted to do; if they showed no such signs, she would want to say yes just as much, but she feared that the word might not be able to get up out of her throat and that Jim, who said there are some things you can't be half-and-half about, would drop her. They had talked on the grass till two in the morning about whether they loved each other the right way the right amount—mostly about whether she loved him enough. Then he had gotten up onto one knee and said, "Look, I'm not asking for a hundred per cent pure distilled love with a lifetime guarantee. I'm asking *you* to marry *me*." When she started to talk about what marriage meant, he cut her short. She would have said yes at that moment if he had kissed her or even held her hand; but he stood up, cleared his throat, and spat in the lake; she said nothing. He was coming by for her tonight after work; he had a new job, as a janitor in a sports store in Oakland.

Once, as her parents looked at each other, their glance held longer than it needed to, and Sybil steadied herself by pressing her legs against the arm of the couch. Fortunately the motion went unnoticed, except by Shirley, who secretly slid her foot over a few inches and touched Sybil's.

Dr. Myer came. He was a small half-bald, quick, dry man who had known everybody there for years. Before he bent over Nancy he glanced about, twitched his nose, and ordered everybody out of the room.

"Not me?" said Beth.

"The child's got to breathe," he said. "My goodness, let the child breathe."

Nancy took an exaggerated breath, and everyone laughed.

"That's my girl" said the doctor and began to inspect her arm. "Now tell me what happened," he said to her alone.

In the dining room, where everybody congregated, Irma in a stage whisper offered cheese and crackers.

"God, crackers," Mary Louise muttered. She was so irritated by Irma that she parodied the old maid's whisper more spitefully than she had intended to. She changed to an undertone. "No, thanks, but I could use a shot of straight Bourbon."

Beth had walked over to the window and stood with folded arms, staring out at the trampoline. Alfred was halfway down the table, half facing in her direction.

"What a contraption," she muttered. "Why can't they just do stunts on mats the way they used to when I was in school?"

Sybil drifted past her father, saying that Dr. Myer certainly did not seem alarmed. Alfred followed her on down the room to Beth.

"Have you heard from Lizzie when she's coming home?" Sybil said to the air between them.

They shook their heads dumbly. Each saw the anxiety in the other's eyes. All three looked out the window.

"Robin!" Beth burst out. Alfred shushed her. She clapped her hand over her mouth and rolled her eyes furiously. "It's awful," she whispered between her fingers.

"What is?" said Sybil.

"Did she go see you too?" said Alfred to Beth.

"I picked her up as she was walking down the street from visiting you," said Beth, glancing at his beard. "She was crying. I took her to Leon's."

"What in the world is she doing in town anyway?" said Sybil.

"That's a good question," said Alfred, sniffing.

"A good question!" said Beth. "The poor goddamned girl. You should be honored that she wanted to tell you—."

"Honored!" he said. "If you had any idea . . ."

"What's going *on*?" said Sybil.

"She has Hodgkin's disease," said Beth to her. "It's a kind of cancer, of the lymph, I think. It's fatal."

"Oh, good lord," said Sybil.

Alfred became so pale and staring that both the women clutched him. "She didn't tell me," he said. "Dear God in heaven."

"She didn't?" said Beth. "What did she come see you for, then?"

"I was so cruel to her," he said. "You took her to Leon's?"

"Yes. What did you do?"

"She's there now," he said, starting. Then he stopped. "But I can't leave!"

"Nancy's in the best of hands, Daddy," said Sybil.

"No! I have to wait and see. Oh, my God."

"I would just like to know—" Beth began, and left off at sight of the doctor in the doorway.

There was nothing to worry about. Nancy had cracked her arm, but he doubted that it was more than a simple fracture. He was quite sure her ribs were all right. X rays were in order. He telephoned the hospital to arrange for them.

"No ambulance?" said Beth.

"Heavens no," said the doctor. "Look, really, this isn't one per

389

cent as serious as a strep throat. Calm down. She can walk perfectly well, with her arm in a sling." He turned to Irma. "Have you got an old scarf to make a sling out of?"

In five minutes Nancy was standing up, to a small chorus of approval.

The doctor told Alfred and Beth to take her on down for the X rays; he would be along in half an hour to read them and prepare the cast.

Out in the street Mary Louise noticed how intently Sybil was watching her parents put Nancy in the back seat; Sybil was leaning forward a little and chewing her lower lip.

Mary Louise gave her a little thump on the arm. "Come ride with us, Syb, we'll tail them down to Herrick."

Sybil nodded but kept watching.

As soon as Nancy was established in the back seat, Beth dug in her purse and handed Alfred the keys to the car. She had commonly done the driving when they had gone out. But on any special occasion Alfred would take over the wheel. He did not have to ask for the keys now, nor was there the slightest hesitation in her giving them. She even took the opportunity to look at his beard more closely, and she smiled a little. They drove off.

Sybil did a whooping dance around Mary Louise's car, to Shirley's scandal.

Mary Louise had seen the key incident too, and when Shirley whispered to her how awful Syb was being, considering poor Nance's broken arm and all, Mary Louise just hugged her and beamed foolishly. When Sybil got in, Mary Louise had to blow her nose before she could drive.

In the house Sybil had been telling herself she would have to telephone Jim from the hospital to call off their date. Now her feet were dancing of their own accord on the car floor, and she could hardly wait for ten o'clock to bring him to her.

When they had gone a few blocks in silence, Beth said, "Alfred, why did Robin come to see you?"

He leaned back in the seat till his arms were stiff to the wheel; he half turned his head, keeping his eyes on the road. "She told me about Leon and about the baby."

"Is Leon?" Beth said.

"Yes," he answered.

"Is Leon what?" said Nancy from the back seat.

"Nothing, dear," said Beth.

"Nancy," said Alfred, "as soon as we get you into the X-ray room, I've got to rush off to see Robin for a few minutes." He reached his right arm over the back of the front seat, groped about till he found Nancy's knee, and squeezed it. "I won't be gone more than half an hour at the very most. I promise. I'll be back before Dr. Myer has even started the cast, and I'll certainly take you home. But I was terribly rude and unkind to Robin. I didn't understand she was suffering. Maybe she wanted to tell me about it, but I didn't let her. You see, darling, I just have to go see her and tell her how sorry I am. All right?"

Nancy looked up at her mother, who winked.

"All right, Daddy."

Once he got Nancy and Beth settled in the hospital, he had to whinny and glare in order to brush past the nurse who was trying to herd him into the business office to fill out forms. "Emergency. Stand aside. I'll be back."

· 5 ·

By the time Alfred knocked, Leon's emotion was impure. The complex of feelings which had made him kneel to embrace Robin had united into pitying woe. However, he had never before embraced her —her familiar and perfumed body—with any but sexual intentions. When she had gone off to St. Louis and New York, he had uprooted all erotic thoughts of her and thrown them in the compost pit of experience to rot away. That afternoon when she phoned him, he was so irritated at having her rise from the past that he nearly went away to avoid seeing her; he remained because he wanted to make it clear once and for all that he never wanted to see her again, and also because under the usual brightness of her voice there was a quality of thin remoteness he did not recognize. Now, embracing her, he began to desire her, even though her voice and motions were not provocative in any way. He worried: if the sexual game were to start, where would it stop short of intercourse? Indulgence had been their custom. Yet for him now to release desire and consummate it would be a monstrous parody of love, an unspeakable indelicacy, mere gross habit. What was to stop them once they began? He feared the slightest erotic gesture from her, even a playful one, and this fear made him clutch at her with his hands rather than encircle her with his arms, gently beat her legs instead of stroking them.

When the knocking began they both froze.

"Is the door locked?" Robin said with her lips.

Leon nodded.

After a pause, the doorknob rattled and turned, and Alfred called, "Leon! It's me, Alfred."

Leon looked at Robin with a shrug and frown indicating: What's going on? She was shrinking in terror, like a child being stalked for punishment. He took her face between his hands and kissed her sadly on the forehead.

"Does he know you're here?" Leon whispered, and she answered with a quick little nod. "I'll let him in."

She grasped his arm, as though in fear of having him get out of reach. Then she took two paper handkerchiefs from her purse and gave him one.

He stood, and they averted their faces to blow their noses.

Alfred seemed to be two sizes larger. He rushed into the room, flapping. His eyes blazed, and his voice soared clear. He pulled a chair up beside Robin's, took her hand, and spoke with tears running down his cheeks. He did almost all the talking, told Robin he had been insensitive and hard of heart with her, told them about Nancy's accident and how he had to rush back to the hospital right away, returned to his callousness with Robin that afternoon. From time to time she murmured, a little smile arose onto her lips, and her eyes brimmed with tears which did not spill over. Leon stood nearby, watching gravely. Despite Alfred's apology, there was nothing depressing in his manner. The energy with which he talked excited everyone. He spoke crisply and clearly as always, yet so fast that it was like babbling. He even told them how wonderful he found being with Beth again. The moment he said this, he stopped, licking his lips, looking at them with a kind of amazement. He shook his head, pressed his eyes with the heels of his hands, then spoke to Robin.

"You're going to see your mother?"

"I leave on the midnight train," she said.

"You will be coming back to Berkeley again," he said.

She shook her head.

He breathed hard, pressed her head sidewise to his chest, and stood. He bumbled with Leon's hand on the way to the door and left with a clarion sob.

"What an exit," she said admiringly.

Leon suppressed what he automatically felt whenever he heard a criticism of Alfred, and asked her in a neutral voice what she meant by that.

"I always think of Alfred as being so natural," she said. "Isn't that funny? Here he is a hundred times as intellectual as I could ever be, and he doesn't live next to nature at all. Yet he seems so natural. That's his great strength, even if he is so weak."

"So weak?"

"With women. A woman can just wrap him around her little finger."

Leon swallowed that and decided it was less glib than it sounded. It was not true, of course, but it was perhaps less than altogether untrue.

"He's been separated from his wife for months," Leon said, raising an eyebrow.

"I'd bet my eyeteeth that if she hadn't wanted him to leave her he'd still be living at home."

This was a sort of extrapolation of something Sybil had hinted once. Leon scratched under his collar.

"You know, Leochka—do you know what I realized this spring? God is a director and it's up to us to do the parts he has assigned us." She glanced at him as though she expected to be hit. He took her hand. She bent quickly and brushed her lips on his knuckles. "You don't think I'm loony? I know you don't believe in God. But you don't think I'm crazy to?" He shook his head. "Well," she went on, "Alfred does a lot of ad libbing when it doesn't matter, but in any big scene he's always in character. That's how he gets away with things like that theatrical exit just now." Leon nodded seriously. She felt that he was listening to what she said. "My trouble is that I always kept trying to improve on my lines. It's become a habit. I've even lost track of what my true lines were. In fact, things have got to such a point that the only important lines I am sure of right this minute—the only ones—are to tell you that I should never have said I loved you. I was just improving on my lines when I said that." She could not interpret the expression on his face. Expecting pain, she hurried on. "I don't mean I hated you or anything bad, Leon, please don't take it that way. It's just—"

He put his fingers over her lips, patting them.

"I know, I know," he said. "We both lied."

Silent and untouching, words and bodies alike untrustworthy, they looked into each other's eyes, for the one time in their acquaintance without a pane between them.

She collected her things and got up. Relapsed into politeness, he urged her to go out to dinner with him; it was the least he could do. She declined.

"I'm going to see Francis before I leave. I have to. I'll grab a bite with him somewhere."

"Why Francis?"

"He was good to me. He would be hurt if I didn't say good-by to him. Of course I won't literally say it. He'll just realize it was good-by when he hears—what's happened."

"And you're going to be in Bakersfield?"

She nodded.

"But you loathe the place. Robin, you must come back here to Berkeley. After all, they're always making new discoveries. The best doctors and hospitals are here in the Bay Area." He shrugged, and his face twitched. "It may take a long time."

"I'm going to spend my last days with my mother. I've made up my mind. Good-by." They touched hands. "Don't come down. Stay here at the door. Please. Francis's place is only half a dozen blocks away. I want to go by myself."

· 6 ·

Leon went to bed that evening in a state of exalted pity. His emotion was not diminished by regret that he and Robin failed to embrace in true love, but strengthened by gratitude that they had been honest enough not to attempt a false embrace.

In the dark of the night he awoke, gagging from a bad dream. His mouth reeked with the taste of rotten crab. In the dream he was sitting alone at a table in a chic restaurant on Fisherman's Wharf. He was served a huge boiled crab but no wine. Sitting at the table next to him was Santa Claus in a long black gown; when no one was looking, Leon snatched his bottle of chilled rosé. Satisfied, he tore off a crab leg, cracked the shell with a nutcracker, and took out a large bite of pink, succulent-looking meat. But after he had taken it into his mouth and chewed, he found it was putrid. He tried to spit it out. In his haste to pour a glass of the robbed rosé to rinse his mouth with, he hit the side of the long-stemmed glass and broke it. When he awoke, not only the taste of the spoiled seafood but the slime of it as well coated his mouth.

To free himself of the revulsion, he deliberately turned his thoughts to Robin. He intended to refresh himself with the friendliness of their chaste embrace; instead, he was revolted at having held that diseased and dying body. The revulsion which the dream had left in his mouth spread as a cringing of skin and muscles, especially of his arms and chest. "Cancer means crab," he thought, and writhed and shook.

At the center of his consciousness was a tiny, intense bulb of shame that his disgust for Robin had obliterated his pity for her. For it was not her body itself which had revolted his sight, smell, touch; it was knowledge of the still imperceptible corruption in her flesh. The knowledge which had generated the pity had also generated the disgust which overwhelmed the pity, and he was ashamed.

When his emotions receded, leaving him stranded on the bed, he lay wishing that he was dead. In exhaustion he went back to sleep.

394

In the morning he awoke with an imperative desire to see Chantal and hurried over to her place as soon as he had pulled his clothes on. She had gone to work already, and Jean-Louis had left for day camp. Leon felt a taut apprehension almost great enough to send him to the insurance office where Chantal was working; but he controlled himself and went back to his room, where he felt in no immediate danger. He set about to study some enormously intricate cases of trust-busting.

· 7 ·

During Alfred's absence from the hospital, Beth became more and more annoyed with Mary Louise and Shirley. Sybil stayed quiet, sitting or standing a little apart, watchful, composed. But Mary Louise burdened Beth with warm worried looks, a sudden squeeze of the hand, soft down-slurring inflections. Without humor to cut it, her sympathy was sticky sweet.

In their klatches that year Beth had come to rely upon Mary Louise; now she found her hard to put up with. Beth now felt acutely that most of Mary Louise's sympathy had been unacknowledged self-pity working for both of them: Mary Louise's sympathizing could be so copious because a good half of it was really for herself, and Beth, by not stanching that flow, let it serve her as though it had originated within herself. Each seeing herself in the other, they had mutually encouraged themselves in this confusion. The result was that, with the aid of a quart or two of wine a day, each was managing fairly well to evade the shame of acknowledging how she was wallowing in self-pity.

Going in and out of the hospital rooms and corridors, looking after Nancy, Beth had no use, even spurious, for self-pity. She had Nancy to cherish; she had Sybil's supporting presence; she had Lizzie always in the back of her mind (and she was thankful to have refrained from telling Mary Louise of her worries over Lizzie); and she had Alfred about to return from a mission which she admired him for undertaking and which she had avoided explaining to Mary Louise. Mary Louise, by clucks and frowns and pats, was casting doubts on Beth's competence at a moment when Beth felt stronger and surer than she had felt for ten months. Outside herself for the time, she saw how badly their mutual self-pity had muddled her understanding of her friendship with Mary Louise. When she had mentioned that friendship to the psychoanalyst she was seeing twice a week, she had spoken only of how supportive Mary Louise had been. He—the dullard!—had not commented on her glowing account of the friend-

395

ship. Now she thought vindictively of how she would enlighten him at the next session: the true nature of what she got from her friendship with Mary Louise was self-regarding self-consciousness, not support. Of course he would say, "Tha-at's right," as though he had known it all along. Then, just to mess her up all the more, he would ask if both aspects of the friendship could not be true at once, on different levels, as it were. Well, shit on him.

At the moment Beth's irritation was directed at Shirley. Shirley was a fat, poised, tenderhearted girl who collected beetles. All her life other children's mothers had been saying of her, "Shirley is no trouble at all." She seemed to Beth to be like a particle: attached to the nucleus of Nancy, Shirley rushed about with much animation; around the nucleus of her mother, she revolved inert. Nancy on the hospital bed in pain seemed to Beth to have more independent life in her eyes than Shirley had in her whole body always an inch from her mother's, slumping like a sack of sand. Her one redeeming attribute was her lovely fresh, eager voice. So what is she doing with it? Beth thought. Sighing. She glared at Shirley and snapped out, "Well, say something."

"Wha'?" Shirley said, blinked, and sagged. Mary Louise poured unction.

Just as Alfred hove into sight down the corridor, Dr. Myer emerged to describe what the X rays revealed: a crack in the ulna. He said he'd have Nancy rigged out in a metal splint in less than half an hour, and then they could all go home.

In the general excitement Beth seized the opportunity to get rid of Mary Louise and Shirley.

"Sybil dear, why don't you go on ahead and fix some soup for Nancy? I have a quart of chicken stock in the freezer." She told her what vegetables to add to it. "Nancy needs something light, but she needs something. All she had for lunch was a peanut-butter sandwich and a glass of milk. Do you mind, darling?"

Sybil addressed Mary Louise. "Can you take me home?"

"Of course, of course." Mary Louise beamed at being given something to do. Then she turned to Beth, beginning to frown.

Beth intercepted the sympathy. "Thanks so much, kiddo," she said to Mary Louise. "And maybe it would be better if Nancy had lots of quiet tonight. I'm going to put her to bed just as soon as she has her supper."

"I understand," Mary Louise said. "We won't hang around. I'll get in touch tomorrow." She squeezed Beth's arm, then turned toward Alfred.

Beth was down to her last gram of patience: if Mary Louise had completed the yearning gesture she started to make toward Alfred—a

396

pat, a squeeze, a quick embrace, even—Beth would have said something rude.

Sybil had started down the hall. Mary Louise converted the gesture into a vague wave at Alfred, wheeled, and followed Sybil. Shirley never got out of reach of her mother.

"Let's go in," said Alfred. "There's no reason why we can't watch him apply the bandages."

"All right, but just a second. You found Robin at Leon's?"

He nodded; his mouth twitched.

"How did it go?" she asked.

He made a little gesture, meaning, How could it go? "Leon looks badly shaken. She won't come back to Berkeley, she says. She's going to her mother's tonight. She is going to kill herself."

"Kill herself! How can you say such a dreadful thing?"

"I don't know. I just said it."

"But what indication did she give?" Beth was trembling. She touched his arm with both hands.

"None I could define exactly." He put his arm around her and began moving toward the room where Dr. Myer was tending Nancy. "Come, my dear, let's go be with Nancy."

"It might be the best thing for her to do," said Beth. "Mightn't it? Before the pain . . ." Her body was rigid, yet did not resist the pressure of his arm.

"Come. Nancy needs us."

· 8 ·

As the car was approaching the garage, Beth said to Nancy, "You'll want some soup now, won't you, baby? Syb's getting it all ready for you. Want to sit at the table to eat it?"

"I'd rather go to bed," said Nancy.

"Right," said Beth, "and a good thing too."

"I'll help," said Alfred, getting out of the car.

When they had got her into her bedroom, Alfred fetched pillows and a bedside table while Beth helped her into her pajamas. She got the trousers on her all right, but ran into trouble with the blouse. The left armhole was too small to take the splint, and Nancy refused to keep her bent left arm under the blouse, complaining rather petulantly that it rubbed against the bruise on her chest.

At this point Sybil arrived with a tray bearing soup, crackers, and milk.

"Here you are," she said breezily and sized up the situation. "Wait a min, Nance. This is just what my blue kimono is for." She fetched from her room a silk kimono with gold braid frogs for buttons and enormous sleeves. She held it up for Nancy's approval. "Like it? Good. It's just right for you. So now it's all yours."

"To keep?" said Nancy.

"Sure," said Sybil and helped her on with it.

"Where did you get it?" said Alfred. "It's handsome."

"Mother," said Sybil, buttoning the frogs. "It was in one of the trunks she brought back from Houston."

Beth blushed and moved toward Nancy's bed. Before she got there Nancy asked Sybil to arrange the tray for her. Sybil sat on the edge of the bed, helping her. Neither looked at Beth, who stood by, as ineffectual as Alfred.

"Jim is coming for me at ten, you know," said Sybil.

"All right," said Nancy. "You can stay with me till ten. Anyway, I'll probably go to sleep. It hurts."

"Your arm?" said Sybil.

"No," said Nancy with unaccustomed shyness of manner. "My bosom."

"Oh sure," said Sybil. "I bashed one of mine once, and it all cleared up as good as new. No one could have told the diff a couple of months afterward."

From the change in Nancy's eyes and the slight wiggle with which she adjusted herself down into the pillows, it was clear that Sybil had just relieved her of a worry much more troubling than any pain she had been feeling.

Beth and Alfred exchanged a glance of comprehension, and Alfred raised an eyebrow toward the door.

"Good night, darling," said Beth. "I'll be right upstairs if you need me."

"Good-by, girls," said Alfred. "See you tomorrow."

At the top of the stairs the awkwardness they had been diligently postponing caught up with them. She no more wanted him to go than he wanted to, but she could not even bring herself to ask him to stay for a cup of coffee. For lack of better, they drifted to the French doors opening onto the patio and stood there in the soft light, watching a towhee in the birdbath.

Alfred jerked back into the room and began pacing about it, went out onto the gallery, into the dining room, through the kitchen, and back into the living room, touching things as he went and making little noises in his throat. Beth observed him, wanting she did not know what, not moving.

"It's so unnatural," he was saying. "I fit. I've got so used to not fitting that now I feel strange. Unnatural, unnatural. The house is hardly cluttered at all. Beth!" he cried. "Where have you put your mother's stuff?"

"Shh," she said, pointing downstairs toward Nancy.

He flapped and whispered, "Where is it all?"

"Come on," she said, led the way up the bedroom, and closed the door behind them.

In their bedroom he slowly wheeled. "That mirror is your mother's. And the gentleman's chair—you had it re-covered, right? Anything else?"

She shook her head.

He was riding upon his emotions like a surfrider coming in on breakers. "What has happened to all that furniture and stuff?"

"Stuck around the house." She shrugged indifferently. "Given away. Sold to antique hounds. Bernstein has given me *some*thing for the twenty-five bucks an hour I shell out to him."

"The twenty-five bucks *I* shell out."

She glanced to see if he was smiling. He was, a little.

"I've had to mortgage Thomas's house," he said, "to pay the soul-sucker. Do you realize—if Doctor Bernstein only worked twenty afternoons a month eleven months a year he would still make twice as much as I ever made, and probably ever will make in any one year in my whole life?"

"Do I realize it?" she said. "What do you think I've been grinding my teeth down to stubs for?"

She bared her teeth at him and gritted them fiercely. They looked perfectly normal.

"All right," he said, "I don't begrudge him a penny of it, anyway."

They glared at each other.

"The gouger," he said.

"The leech."

"The bourgeois shaman."

"If only he wasn't a Jew," she said, "I would call him a Shylock."

"The Shylock," Alfred said.

She looked at him with round eyes and pretended to clap her hands over her mouth. "Oh, Alfred, what you said!"

At that moment they wanted to embrace, but each was too fearful of the other's rejection to make the slightest overture. They dropped their eyes.

"Well," he said, shifting his weight.

"Before you go," she said, "what have you heard from Lizzie?"

"Nothing since the cable last week," he said.

"Did the cable explain anything?"

He shook his head. "It just said she had to have money to get home on. I cabled five hundred dollars to her."

She nodded. "She could have been here two days ago. Sybil got a letter from her three days ago."

"Syb wouldn't tell me what was in it," he said.

"Me either," Beth said. "She was vague, that maddening way she can be."

"All we can do is wait to hear from Lizzie."

"I'm afraid so," she said. "It's miserable."

"The quintessential bloody flux," he said.

"What on earth," she said, "has got into Joe? I always thought he was so handsome and humorous, and he just walks out on her in a foreign country. Do you suppose she did something awful?"

Alfred shrugged, and they both shook their heads.

He took a deep breath. "I'll call tomorrow morning to see how Nancy is coming along."

"Or I'll call you," she said.

They went into Alfred's closed, musty study. He darted around like a bird, then rushed to the outer door.

"Beth," he bugled as though she were not ten feet away but in another part of the house, "we must talk about the future. This is not the occasion for it, I realize, but we must make up our minds about the future."

"Like about what?" she said. "All your gay ladies, for example?"

"Gay ladies! What in heaven's name are you talking about?"

"The usual," she said.

"Beth, I solemnly aver that during the entire extent of our separation I have had dealings with no gay ladies."

"Not even one?"

"Not even one," he said.

"How's Virginia?"

He flushed, swelled, and waved his arm. "Mary Louise!" he trumpeted. "She told you about seeing me with Virginia in a restaurant, didn't she?" Beth nodded. "Good old Mary Louise. The scandalmongering bitch."

"All right, so Mary Louise is a gossip. Who isn't? Come on, tell me, how *is* Virginia?"

"Look, while Horace was in Washington for a week, I took her to dinner near where I was living, the Spindrift. It's chichi and depressing. We went once. She had come over shopping and I took her to dinner, and I would expect Horace to have done the same with you in my place. You know, if everything—"

"All right, Alfred, your ladies aren't gay. So how's about some respectable ones?"

"Beth, no, no, we mustn't start this up again. It's so irrelevant. Let bygones be bygones. We must concern ourselves with the future."

"The future, you dope!" she said. "Where in God's name do you think you're going to find the future except in the past?"

"Ah, oh," he said, "yes, ah, oh my God."

He rushed to her and took her in his arms. She hugged him with her elbows at the same time she was beating his back with her fists.

"Fool," she said. "Idiot. Ass. Nut."

He started to kiss her, but she suddenly reared back. She tried to free her arms, but he would not let her.

"The beard," she said. "It feels funny. It scratches. It doesn't feel like you at all."

"I'm a new man," he said.

"Are you really?" she murmured. "I wish I was a new woman. I'm sick to death of being myself."

They kissed.

It became a fully erotic kiss, but he did not repeat it. Sybil might call them at any time, or burst in on them. Unable to make love now, afraid of recriminations if they started to talk any more, unsure of Beth, Alfred left.

After she ceased glowing, Beth became angry with Alfred for having gone away so soon. He had been playing with her. Well, she would not be so sentimental again. It was just that she was lonely and upset; her defenses had been lowered, and he had taken advantage. They were well separated, and she would start thinking seriously about divorce soon. Then she remembered that he had mentioned having mortgaged Thomas's house in order to pay for her analysis, and her anger revived and redoubled. Whose fault was it he didn't make enough money to take care of his family properly? Besides, if he had been a good husband she would not have had to see an analyst anyway. What was he trying to do, make her feel guilty for having to go to a doctor? As though she could help herself! He couldn't detest the whole thing half as much as she did. To hell with him.

Alfred meanwhile was anxious over whether she really knew about his affair with Virginia, which he thought of with shame and remorse. He wanted to go back to Beth, wanted her to take him back. What a very great pain in the neck Mary Louise was—a sower of discord, an interferer, a manhater, an injustice-collector, a victim-lover, a sentimental slob.

· 9 ·

Sybil was halfway down San Jacinto Way when Jim on his BMW came around the turn. On impulse she stopped where she was, her back to the streetlight, alongside a tall hedge, visible in a white pull-over sleeveless jersey shirt, knee-length pink shorts, and white tennis shoes and rollover socks. She had the urge to tease-test him by getting him to look at her without knowing who she was, so that she could find out the way he looked at strange women. He would expect her to be waiting at home and would probably not recognize her here with the light behind her. He had once spoken contemptuously of wolves. Sybil did not particularly like being sized up and whistled at by strange men, but neither did she mind it much. What she did mind was Jim's unspoken self-righteousness ("You won't catch *me* giving women the eye"). The hypocrite! It was true she never had caught him at it; she hoped to now. She twisted her body a bit and put one arm behind her back, so that her figure would be well silhouetted for him.

His head was hunched down and forward, and his elbows were out. By the time he was even with her, going at a moderate speed down the middle of the road, she had not caught him so much as glancing at her. How repressed! And his face was so sullen.

"Jim!" she called, not peremptorily but with a faint tremor of anxiety in her voice.

He glanced over his shoulder quickly and turned as smoothly as though he had been planning this maneuver all along. He pulled up beside her, holding the black motorcycle erect, its engine idling with soft rich sounds.

She kept nudging the right handlebar with her belly. "Didn't you see me?"

He shook his head. "Come on. Let's go."

"You mean you didn't notice me at all? I was right here in plain sight."

"I noticed some girl."

"Don't I have an interesting enough figure for you?"

He spat. "If I felt like oggling women, I'd go to a burlesque house and oggle them in the nude."

His moral forthrightness was to her like a miracle: she saw it, had no explanation for what *really* brought it about, and did not credit her eyes. The expression "in the nude" offended her as artificial, and the emphasis with which he uttered it she interpreted as repressively puritanical.

"Goody-goody," she said, deadpan.

He took her "Goody-goody" as ironic congratulation, poking fun at him for being sissy.

"What's the matter with you?" he said. "Don't you even know the first thing about manners? Oggling is rudimentary bad manners. Like I've got to take a leak right this minute. So I'm goody-goody because

I don't unzip my pants and let 'er flicker right here on the street?"

She was a little shocked. She said, in a tone that was meant to be snippy but sounded childish in her own ears, "It's not 'oggle,' it's 'ogle.' "

He mock-ogled her legs, winked, and gave a wolf whistle.

She straddled the seat behind his and put her arms around him, snuggling up to his back more than necessary. She was glad he had not let her catch him this time. Tonight was not the night for that victory; it would have to wait. Still, showing him up for the hypocrite he must be was a project worth keeping in mind for a long time. Meanwhile, she snuggled.

"Let's go to the rose garden," she said.

"What?" he said. "Rose garden?"

"You know, right down the hill in Codornices."

"Roses, for Pete's sake," he said.

"It's a balmy evening, and there's no wind, and lots and lots of the bushes are in bloom. It smells good too."

All true, and when they walked down from the street onto the top terrace of roses, she began chattering away about the beauties at a great rate.

Jim, who wanted only to find out whether she would have him, saw not roses but three or four other couples strolling on the paths. At the sixth bush he balked.

"Look," he said, "we've got no privacy here. We can't talk. Let's go up to the stables."

"Why?" she said.

"There won't be anybody there. Presley doesn't have a summer session, does it?"

"No. But stables!"

"We can pat the horses," he said. "It seems to me people talk better when they're around horses. At least about some things."

"Don't you like roses?" she said.

"But we won't be interrupted there!"

They frowned at each other.

"Please, honey," he said, "it'll be better up with the horses."

"Okay, let's go," she said. "But I'm hungry."

He groaned.

"All I had," she said, "was a bowl of soup for supper. What did you have?"

"Some oranges," he said. "But I'm not hungry. My God, it's too . . . Sybil!"

She took his hand, and they ran up to the motorcycle.

"Down to San Pablo!" she said. "We need hamburgers! The stomach has reasons Reason knows not of!"

403

"Grrr," he said, baring his teeth. He twisted on the seat and kissed the tip of her nose.

They zoomed off.

By chance he stopped at a joint to which she had gone with Leon on several dates, including their first one. So far from objecting to going into the place, Sybil was secretly pleased at the thought of having sentimental memories of Leon revived on this occasion. She insisted on having two hamburgers, French fries, and a chocolate milkshake; Jim ordered one hamburger and coffee. She ate slowly, and when the juke box fell silent asked him to play it. Her animation, though forced, was gay enough to bring him out of his sullenness. Also, he discovered with eating how hungry he was and ordered a second hamburger too.

Sybil kept thinking of Leon, though not comparing him with Jim. Somewhere in the back of her mind thoughts of Leon circulated, obscure, high-charged, generating tension in her. The thoughts as such were not very important. What mattered more was that, even while she was with Jim, she was comparing the easy naturalness she felt in his company with the nervous excitement she had felt with Leon. At the moment she was keyed up at being with Jim because he wanted her to declare herself. Yet somehow the very fact of this tension, which she enjoyed, reminded her of Leon. Jim would not often make her feel this way—alert, on the *qui vive,* restless. She had always felt something was wrong with Leon, and there was nothing seriously the matter with Jim except that he had never excited her in this special way before and probably never would again. He just wanted her to say she would marry him when they could manage it. He was in every important way acceptable. She thought he would make a better husband than any other man she had ever known.

So why should she be thinking, with excitement, of Leon, whose intentions had never been unambiguous and whose proposals had occasionally been dishonorable? It could only be because there was something essentially wrong with her feelings for Jim, with their relationship, and they certainly had no business even thinking about getting married. If she could betray him in her thoughts at such a time as this, what would she not do after they had been married a while? Impossible.

The tension stayed with her up the hill to the deserted campus. Jim parked some distance from the barns, to avoid the nightwatchman. As they walked in silence, he held her hand with a shyness, a confidence, an absence of sensuality which made his touch utterly different from Leon's. Nevertheless, the excitement she was feeling continued, nervous and restless, like the excitement she had felt with Leon. Not even stroking the horses relaxed her, put her "in the mood," as Jim had obviously planned it should.

In a husky voice Jim asked her whether she would marry him.

She was as wrought up as she had sometimes been in advanced stages of petting with Leon. But on those occasions her nervous excitement was heightened by sensual passion, whereas now her excitement with Jim had nothing extra to heighten it, except an unclear sense that it must be wrong of her to be feeling this strange tension on this occasion.

Why did Jim have to make the whole thing so damned moral? Couldn't he just start necking and make her say yes because she wanted to all over? Whose flank was he stroking, hers? No, a mare's!

She gave the mare's shoulder a hard slap that made her toss her head and whicker. Then Sybil stepped aside and folded her arms, intending to get even with Jim. He turned down roses for horses, he wouldn't so much as kiss her first, he was so crude he didn't even tell her how much he loved her, he just came out and asked, bang, like that! All right, she could be dry as dust too, she would begin a long rational argument about the practical obstacles confronting their marriage.

But her tongue betrayed her. Her voice was cool and remote, and her face was without expression or movement, as tenseness made it; but her tongue told the truth.

"How do I know how I'm going to feel a year from now?" she said. "Besides, we won't have any more money then than we do now."

He too stepped aside from the horse. He stood with his head cocked a bit, eyes blinking. Then he seemed to hear whatever it was besides words he had been listening for. He gave her a lopsided smile.

"That's right," he said, "we won't. We'll both have to work. There's just one thing—you mustn't earn more than I do."

"Oh, come on," she said.

"It'll be slim pickings for quite a while, till I pass the bar and get started."

"But I can get a job teaching grammar school," she said. "There's a shortage of teachers, and I want to."

He shook his head. "Nope. Not yet."

"Daddy could help, easily."

He kept shaking his head.

"We could live in the garden cottage," she said hopefully. "We could be as independent as we like there. It's a nice little place."

"What the hell. My folks have a cellar we could live in too. But we aren't going to."

"You're so stubborn. Men are so stubborn." She sighed. "I don't want to live in poverty."

"You won't. Don't worry, you'll always have a toilet to flush."

"Do you have to be so crude?" she said.

"I don't know whether I *have* to be. I *am*."

"And anyway, what do you mean by saying 'we'? I haven't answered yet."

"Let's take a walk," he said. "The eucalyptus smell good on a nice warm night like this."

He took her hand and set off up the hill.

She started to hold back, but he yanked and she went along.

She was determined to balk and complain all she wished, because, she told herself, he was so damned cocksure he knew what he wanted and what was best for her.

Her true feelings were far deeper. She trusted herself to him because he knew what she wanted.

They stopped by a fallen tree. For half an hour he argued with her, scuffling to and fro by the trunk, breaking twigs and pieces of bark off it, flipping the little cone-shaped nuts. Then he sat her down on a place he cleared of stones, half lay beside her, and began rootling at her and grunting, without using his hands.

"Oh, you're so uncouth," she said and pulled his ears.

He grunted into her neck a couple of times, then took her in his arms and kissed her. When he said he loved her, she slid down beside him.

They drew up in front of her house at two-thirty.

"Don't turn off the motor," she said and got off the machine. "It's awfully late."

"You're dirty and dusty," he said.

"And my shoulder blade hurts from that rock."

"Tomorrow night same time?" he said. "You look tired. Sleep late."

"I'm so happy," she said.

She expected him to smile at this and drive off beaming. Instead, he seemed to frown and just sat there looking at her. She kissed his wrinkling forehead, opened the gate, and half ran in.

· 10 ·

In the patio Sybil stopped to listen to the sound of Jim's motorcycle dwindling away. She badly wanted to talk with her mother, but she was reluctant to go into her parents' bedroom for fear her father was there. Had her parents been living together, she would not have

406

hesitated to slip into the room and rouse her mother, but as things stood she could not.

In fact, Beth had awakened at the sound of the motorcycle and was lying in bed wishing she could call to Sybil to come in and talk a while. What she really wanted was to complain about Alfred. With Lizzie she could have done it, in a joking way, but not with Sybil, certainly not at a time when something important was cooking between her and Jim.

Downstairs, Sybil stopped at Nancy's door. Nancy started to turn over, whimpered a little, sighed, and flopped back onto her back. Sybil watched for a minute to make sure she had sunk into sleep again, and went to bed herself.

The moment she lay down, her eyelids flicked open. This made her indignant. She was the one who had to drink cups and cups of coffee and take a Benzedrine just to stay awake one night to study for a final. She was the one who could fall asleep while her roommate was putting her hair up in curlers with the radio playing. And now she couldn't fall asleep at three in the morning alone in the silent dark. But her indignation did not endure.

Her consciousness kept skittering from one subject to another. Her thoughts kept returning not to Jim but to Leon. An image kept recurring, of Parktilden Village across the green valley as she had seen it on her last date with Leon, softened with distance, twinkling, pretty. Actually she loathed the place, the flawless towers and manors and grounds. Everything about it seemed to be on exhibit, including the tidy people. The title to a magazine article on these pseudo-villages that were springing up in or near many of the big American cities had stuck with her: "Museums of the Future." The phrase was intended to be favorable, but it had made Sybil shudder and laugh. Once she had got Jim to cruise around through the Village so that they could look through the picture windows at the living exhibits of engineered progress. Jim had just thought the whole layout was uninteresting, too new but probably comfortable. She had refrained from sharing her opinion with him and murmured yes, they probably were comfortable places to live in. Now the image of the horrid village that came into her mind was the distant one she had shared with Leon, and it was pleasant.

She felt sure of nothing, least of all that she wanted to marry Jim.

She could not remember how she had answered him. They had discussed practical difficulties—which seemed insuperable for years and years to come—and they had necked for hours by the fallen tree. He didn't seem worried, she was pretty sure of that, and now she resented him for it. He acted as though he knew her answer already, better than she did herself.

So intense had the turmoil of her emotions and sensations been in the woods that she was not absolutely positive that she was still a virgin. She had lost her virginity—if indeed she had lost it—by only a few seconds. She no longer cared much whether she was still a virgin or not; either way, it was by a technicality. What did matter to her was being unsure which. She felt neither the serenity of unclouded virtue nor the satisfaction of remembered experience, nor even sharp guilt, but the bungler's self-regarding, toothless, excuse-seeking shame.

At dawn she went to the bathroom and peered into the mirror at her face. The eyes were puffy; the mouth was drawn, somewhat open; the face was not wrinkled or lined, but at least it was not pretty. She did not know what she was afraid of, but she felt a certain relief at seeing that her face was afraid too.

She was seized by the impulse to tell Leon that she was engaged to marry Jim. Should she call Leon up? Go see him? No, she must write. For a quarter of an hour she sat at her desk, chewing her pen, wondering how silly it would be of her to write him a letter. Maybe a telegram would be better? No, she could not dictate the necessary words over the telephone to a telegraph clerk. She owed Leon nothing. Why should he be the first person she told, before her own mother even? What would Jim think if he knew? Finally she dashed off a note, with no salutation:

"I am engaged to be married. He is a wonderful, reliable, trustworthy, serious fellow a couple of years older than I am. He is going to be a lawyer too, and we don't have any money but we are going to make out fine. He is the brother of Kay Ravagli's first husband, who was killed in the war. His name is Jim Sorb. If I have made him sound sort of like Brewster, that is just because I can't find words to describe him adequately. He is utterly different—humorous, thoughtful, *peculiar*.

"Nancy fell on the trampoline yesterday and broke her arm but she is fine now. Because of the accident Daddy and Mother got together for the first time since they were separated. They are so silly, as you know.

"I wish you happiness and success in everything you undertake.

S"

She did not read over what she had written but folded the paper and sealed it in an envelope. Then she could not make up her mind how to get the letter to him. She wanted him to get it right away, but how? She yearned to go put it in his mailbox, or even slip it under his door, but decided that would be too silly altogether. She would have to mail it to him by Special Delivery.

She found two fifteen-cent airmail stamps; thirty cents' worth of extra postage should be plenty, even if they weren't the right kind. She pasted them on the right-hand side of the envelope, well below the regular four-cent stamp. Then she circled them with red ink and printed SPECIAL DELIVERY in heavy block capitals with green crayon. She crept out of the house, opened the garage door as quietly as possible, and started the car—the motor scooter would make too much noise.

The sound of the car awakened Beth. She ran into Alfred's study and peeked out through the slats of the Venetian blind to see what was happening. In the confusion of being startled from a troubled sleep, she hoped it was Alfred who for some reason was taking the car out. When she saw it was Sybil, she worried. She went down to check on Nancy, who was sleeping peacefully. Sybil's room seemed to be in order.

Sybil drove down to Oakland to mail the letter at a substation she had noticed on Grove Street, a few blocks from where Leon lived. On her way home she went by his house to make sure that his car was in its usual place.

Beth lay awake till she heard the car come back into the garage. She went to the window overlooking the patio and watched Sybil cross it; Sybil seemed self-contained as ever. With an effort, Beth restrained herself from catching her in the hallway and demanding to know what was going on. Everything seemed to her so perilously poised that she had better not interfere.

· 11 ·

The Special Delivery letter was delivered to Leon shortly after ten. He stood in the doorway with it in his hand, staring at the envelope as though hypnotized. It had been postmarked that morning in Oakland, the airmail stamps were garishly wrong, there was no return address, the words were printed in childish capitals in pencil and crayon. It was the pencil and crayon that confirmed his terror. He was convinced that, if this letter were a hoax, the jokesters would not have thought to use pencil and crayon on the envelope. It was a genuine threat. It could be nothing else. From some of Harry Evans' conspiratorial comrades. Warning him to leave Chantal alone. "Immolate"— for some reason the word "immolate" appeared among his fears, though he scarcely knew what it meant. Chantal must be allowed to immolate herself for Harry. Otherwise he, Leon, would have to take the consequences.

He was so affronted to be warned off like this that he crumpled the envelope and threw it unopened into the trash basket. They didn't know their man if they thought he could scare so easily. If they had appealed reasonably to him, he could have been persuaded to treat Chantal with even more considerateness than he was already exercising with her. But to a sneaky threat like this, honor permitted nothing but resistance. So far from laying off Chantal, he would press all the harder.

In ordinary circumstances this indignant determination to "show them," and at the same time to do what he wanted, would have satisfied Leon's egoism. But he had lived all his life in a world of political conspiracies and double agents—first the revolutionary Russia which he had heard about endlessly as a child, then the Nazis, then the Cold War spying and betraying, and most immediately Harry Evans and Roy Carver and their shadowy little group of anarchists. Two days earlier, in the library stacks, Peter Hazen had said that one in ten of the members of the Communist Party in the United States was really an agent of the FBI; the going joke was that a chairman would open a CP meeting with the words, "Comrades and agents, the meeting will now come to order." In addition to this general ambience of political suspicion, Leon accepted a psychoanalytic view which characterized motivation as being, if nothing else, devious: mixed in every motive were sexual and/or destructive elements, sometimes open but usually disguised and treacherous.

Therefore, he now began to speculate that they had calculated that his reaction to the letter would be to do the opposite of what it threatened. The trouble with this notion, once the first glow of outwitting them at their own game had faded a bit, was that it led to an infinite regress: they had foreseen his seeing through their first deception. But the second? the third? He was like the once-Communist radicals who had passed through mere anti-communism to a vigorous anti-anti-communism; some even claimed to be anti-anti-anti. What were they for? Leon became feverish.

He began to speculate on who could possibly have sent the letter. He even entertained the notion that Chantal herself might have sent it. Such an action was preposterously unlike her, but still, who could tell what went on in the secrecy of her mind? Why did she have to be so surreptitious? Couldn't she just come out and tell him what she wanted of him?

After a long siege of these suspicions, he took a platform stance, pounded his desk like a trial lawyer, and announced to himself that he was going to pay no attention to all these threats but would do just exactly what he wanted to with Chantal, and she could do whatever she wanted in response, no matter what her connection with the anonymous letter might be. He felt much better for having swept his mind clear, until he asked himself what it was he wanted of Chantal and realized he was not sure.

The crumpled envelope was waiting for him in the wastebasket. He glared at it. The least he could do was to see how the threat had been put. Much might be learned from the wording.

He smoothed out the envelope and slit it carefully with a knife. There was—of course—no salutation or date. The signature, S, meant nothing to him; it was no doubt intended to mystify and alarm him. Then his eye caught the word "Nancy." He began reading from the beginning and blushed.

His embarrassment was so deep that his mouth opened and closed several times as though he were stammering; he waved the letter back and forth, he shrugged and blinked.

He reread the letter. This time he realized not only that Sybil had written it but also that she was getting married. He made himself a cup of instant coffee and sat sipping it, chastened. At first he was relieved that his absurd fantasies about the letter had been groundless. But then his relief was over something much more important, he was not sure what. He looked at the envelope again. What on earth had got into Sybil to put things all over it like this in so many colors? She must have been out of her head. And to mail it in Oakland so early in the morning?

He read the letter a third time. Its language sounded amazingly childish to him. Was she really that childish and he just hadn't noticed before? She must have been terribly upset when she wrote the letter. Maybe she had regressed to an early stage. Nevertheless, it was he, Leon, she had needed to write to at such a time. He was flattered to think he still had so strong a hold over her.

With this thought, he realized that the relief he had been feeling came from being freed of her. Her rejection of him that spring had pained him far more than he had expected it could have done. He had remained tied to her by the very pain. He had never loved her so much as in the losing. He had suffered more over her than over any other woman. He had written her two anguished letters; she had not answered them. He had called her once on the telephone, begging for just one more chance to talk; she had cut him off harshly. He had been thinking that if she would only have him, he would hurry up the divorce with Chantal, reform his whoring ways, and devote himself to Sybil, the only pure, decent, true woman in his life. Now, to learn that she was engaged to marry some other man, and especially that she felt called upon to tell him about it, suffused him with a benign glow. She was still just a girl really, a lovable girl, to be sure, but he had

411

never had any business thinking of her as a mature woman. He must write her a note which would let her off the hook. Then they could become friends. She would grow up and they would be lifelong friends.

"My dear Sybil—

"Nothing could give me more pleasure than to learn that you have found a young man who is beautifully suited to you. I can't tell you how I have worried sometimes whether I might not have been a bad influence on you. The teacher-student relationship is extremely delicate, even when there is no question of class participation. It is not for nothing that such liaisons are frowned upon by custom. Well, I shall never do *that* again, and it is a great burden off my mind to hear how well things have turned out for you. You are a very valuable person.

"Incidentally, I hope you will invite Chantal and me to your wedding. We are going to make our marriage genuine, somehow. It will depend on many things, of course, but I am sure it will happen. Enough.

"Your news about Alfred and Beth cheers me up too. I'm sorry about Nancy's accident. I'll tell Jean-Louis about it this afternoon. He will want to visit her, I have no doubt.

"You must have heard about Robin's illness. It is appallingly tragic. She is being marvelous about it, very courageous. Incredible.

"With my very warmest wishes for you and your husband-to-be,
"Your most sincere friend, who wishes
the best for you, now and always,
Leon"

He read it over with satisfaction, folded the paper, and put it in a stamped envelope, on which he typed Sybil's name and address in black and the words SPECIAL DELIVERY in red. Then he drove to the Berkeley main post office, put a Special Delivery stamp on the envelope, and posted it.

He went by the campus and found Hazen in his office, about to go to lunch. Though Leon did not like Hazen much, he sometimes enjoyed his company, when he wanted to see in someone else a sleazier version of his own faults. He could be severe and yet indulgent with Hazen. Besides, they often had lively arguments.

The day was fine, and they ate on the terrace of the student union. Leon wanted to argue about whether there was anything more to marriage than local customs and the need to get children raised, but Hazen acted indifferent and uneasy when Leon got wound up in his reasoning. Hazen was writing a paper on world overpopulation and the religious barriers to the mass prevention of births, a subject which only depressed Leon.

Then they were joined by a graduate student in economics, a fat, dogmatic lesbian in a frilly dress, whose name Leon could not recall. She began complaining about how difficult money theory was. Hazen and Leon agreed that the economics of money was the least of it, but they fell out when Leon asserted the correctness of the Freudian view that symbolically money was feces. Hazen called this crude reductivism, and the woman asserted that Freudian theory was all very well in psychology but it certainly had no place in economics. Leon was outraged and went at it vigorously with her, until Hazen said that money was obviously all things to all men, whereupon Leon and the woman joined forces in beating up on Hazen, who just laughed his way through their indignation.

When they broke up at two-thirty, Leon thought that Hazen's position, despite the flabbiness of Hazen's arguments, was somehow the strongest. Hazen had kept repeating "money is reality" with a maddening lack of elaboration, and though the notion rankled in Leon's mind, it somehow made more sense than anything he or the woman had said. The trouble with it was that it did not permit of positive action. You couldn't do anything about "money is reality." If you took that position the most you could do was to learn something about yourself from observing the way you actually dealt with money. An untenable state of affairs, for a lawyer especially. One thing Leon resolved: not to let money and love get mixed up, as Alfred and Beth had done so foolishly. Chantal was sensible about money too. So much the better.

At four-thirty, when Chantal came out of the insurance-company building where she worked, he was parked in front waiting for her. He had not surprised her like this before, and she looked pleased as she got in beside him.

· 12 ·

"An unexpected pleasure," she said.

"I wanted to apologize for having skipped dinner last night," he said.

"You explained already! Too much! Besides, you were wise, as it turned out. I made a Quiche Lorraine, and the eggs were no good. At least I presume the eggs. Anyhow, it was a disaster, all told. Tonight we have chicken."

"Robin's visit came just at the dinner hour, and I was too upset when she left."

"Ah."

He had stopped for a traffic signal. He picked at a flaw on the steering wheel.

"Yes," he said, "you see, she's fatally ill."

"*Mon Dieu*! She assured you?"

"Three or four months at the outside."

"Sometimes, you know, hypochondria is very severe."

"I think not in this case," he said.

"You knew her closely, *hein*?"

Leon nodded. Chantal touched his leg. They went the rest of the way home without speaking further, her fingers gently pressing his thigh.

Jean-Louis was in the kitchen, eating graham crackers and milk. "*Bonjour, chéri*," she said to him.

" 'Did you have a hard day at the office, dear?' " Jean-Louis mimicked.

"Heh-heh-heh," she said hollowly.

He giggled, hiding his mouth with his hand.

"You heard about Nancy?" Leon said to him severely.

"Nancy?" Jean-Louis instantly became alert like a squirrel.

"Last evening she fell on the bar of the trampoline and broke her arm."

"You're kidding!" Jean-Louis went pale and glanced from Leon to Chantal and back. "Honestly?"

"Is it bad?" Chantal asked.

Leon nodded.

"I don't know. Alfred just gave me a brief account. I thought Jean-Louis might want to see her."

"May I, *Maman*?" he said. "Now?"

"Why, I don't know," she said. "Why not wait till after supper?"

"No! Her mother will make her go to sleep early. Please, *Maman*?"

"Why don't you phone and see how the land lies?" said Leon.

"Yes!" cried Jean-Louis. "I shall telephone."

"*Tiens*," said Chantal. "We shall see what we shall see. Perhaps it's obligatory that I speak to Mrs. Royce. Eh, Leon?"

He shrugged.

"I shall. Jean-Louis, inquire after Nancy, and then I shall speak to her mother. Leon, go into the living room so we may not be made self-conscious."

In five minutes they rejoined him, Jean-Louis nearly dancing with eagerness, Chantal frowning but smiling secretly.

"What could I do?" she said. "Mrs. Royce was too much for me."

"She said I would do Nancy good!" said Jean-Louis.

"I am sure you will. Tya, tya. Still, how could I refuse?" She turned to Leon. "She insisted that he stay for dinner. She will drive him home when it's time for Nancy to go to sleep. I heard Nancy squall when her mother asked her if she wanted to have Jean-Louis visit. So."

"Squeal, *Maman*. Squall is for babies. Young ladies squeal. Should I wear a tie, Leon?"

In fifteen minutes Jean-Louis appeared, gleaming clean, wearing a freshly ironed shirt without a tie, his good pair of slacks, and the shoes he wore to dancing class. He looked at Leon with such defenseless, speechless appeal that Leon went against his resolve and said he would drive him up to San Jacinto Way. Leon was afraid of running into Sybil, and he wanted to have Chantal to himself alone for as long as possible. But by the gratitude in her glance when he offered to drive Jean-Louis, he saw this errand would be time well spent.

"You are kind," she said to him. At the door she told Jean-Louis to behave himself and to be sure to thank Mrs. Royce for each necessary thing.

Halfway there Jean-Louis said to Leon, "Perhaps you could take me by the rose garden? I have no money, but I would like to take Nancy a flower. Perhaps I can find a rose with a long stem."

"Great," said Leon enthusiastically. "I'll drop you there. I have an errand to run anyway. You can walk up the steps to their place. Okay?"

"Everything is working out splendidly," said Jean-Louis, looking with shining eyes at Leon as at a father.

Neither of them, in such a case, would ever have shaken hands with his father. Nevertheless Leon thought that shaking hands would be the American thing for a father to do with a son at this moment.

"Shake," he said.

"Shake," Jean-Louis answered proudly.

They clasped hands firmly and gave one vigorous pump of their arms. When Jean-Louis got out at the rose garden, Leon gave him a big wink, and he winked back.

"That again?" Chantal said and looked at him coldly. "You are being monotonous. We went through all that already. Once is enough, surely. The subject is closed."

She was so firm and final in her manner that Leon felt crushed. She was not going even to allow him to utter the little speech he had prepared, ending with the words, "My need is desperate." He shrank.

Then, without changing manner, she said, "Anyway, you've brought a bottle of Meursault. I must not divert myself from making a chicken a little bit worthy of such a wine. *Eh, mon ami?*" She walked around the table to where he was sitting and, without having to bend much, kissed him lightly on the forehead, her eyes cold but her lips soft. "Now read to me the next chapter from *Bleak House*. I enjoy Charles Dickens more than any other writer to hear aloud. And lawyers! My God, what he knows about lawyers! They are another species of beings. He is aware of their essence. Here, read."

He looked at the words she pointed to. They were void of sense to him.

"But, Chantal, I mean what I said."

"You are preposterous." She turned from the counter, where she had begun to pick over the lettuce and break the leaves for salad, and spoke intensely. "You're romantic? Very good. But don't mix me up in your tendencies. I am not good for romance, no. I don't know all about your women. They're nothing to me, this way, that way. Do as you please. Pfft. But I know something about them. They are beautiful and they are plural. I, I am singular, one plain skinny French-woman five years older than you, with one breast bigger than the other. *Hein?*"

"Bigger?" he cried. "Much bigger? It's irrelevant. Really? I wish you hadn't told me that."

"It's difficult to have your dreams about an uneven woman, eh? Well, I don't like my body very much either. But it is the one I have. So . . ."

"I still mean everything I said."

"Bah, momentum, nothing but momentum. You got started with sweet talk, you keep going. Now, back to Dickens. I will not have this chicken spoiled."

"But, Chantal—"

"You say one more word, and I put this chicken back in the refrigerator, and you can go to some greasy spoon and eat a hamburger with a milkshake. Blah. Idiot. Back to Jarndyce and Jarndyce. Go. Read."

At quarter past seven, as they were enjoying their coffee and Leon was trying to choose the exact words with which to broach *the* subject again, Jean-Louis telephoned. He spoke to his mother in French, not only because it was easier but also because he did not want to be understood by Nancy or Sybil. Chantal did not say much. Just because she said so little, Leon's French was more or less up to grasping what she said.

What Jean-Louis really wanted—at Nancy's suggestion—was to get a ride home with Jim. The rest of what he said to his mother was for the purpose of overwhelming her so that she would let him stay till ten, when Jim was due to visit Sybil. There was no question of her permitting him to ride on a motorcycle, but if he could keep her from inquiring too specifically, she would never know about it.

He told her everything was in such turmoil at the Royces' that it would really be a kindness for him to stay with Nancy till things calmed down. Sybil had received a special letter that afternoon, about which she had said nothing to anybody; but it was noticeable that she was dreamy and *bienveillante*.

"Sybil?" said Chantal. *"Bienveillante? Non."*

He assured her that it was true all the same. In addition, Mrs. Royce had walked, she herself, to visit Mr. Royce. Another special letter had come while they were eating, from the daughter who was married. It was addressed to both Mr. and Mrs. Royce. Mrs. Royce read it in the other room. Then, looking very strange, she said she was going to take it to Mr. Royce. Nancy was sitting at the table at the time, and Sybil of course. Neither of them knew what to make of it. Who knew when Mrs. Royce would return? Sybil's fiancé was coming for her at ten. He would be able to give Jean-Louis a ride home, if Mrs. Royce had not returned by then. Someone must stay with Nancy. Meanwhile, he and Nancy were playing hearts.

"So, may I stay till ten o'clock?"

"Yes, yes, very well. Oh dear. Good-by, darling. Keep Nancy occupied."

Jean-Louis went back to Nancy's room and sat in the chair by her bed. They looked listlessly at the deck of cards. She shifted position and grimaced.

"Your arm hurts when you move?" he said.

"No. It's all right."

"But you made a face."

"It was just a little pain," she said.

"Where?"

"The other place I hit myself when I fell."

"Where? Here?" He put his hand on his ribs at his side.

"No, not there," she said. "I can't say." She dropped her eyes. *"You* know."

"Oh. I'm sorry." He pulled his chin in and ran his tongue over his teeth. "Say, do you want me to teach you how to play chess?"

"Sure!" she said. "If there's a chess set in the house."

"Shall I ask Sybil?" he said.

"Sure. Syb!" she called. Then she spoke to him conspiratorially. "Put some Billy Boyle on the record player, Johnly, and we'll have lots of fun."

Beth had invented this nickname for him on his last visit. She had drunk a good deal of wine and slurred his name to Johnly, to everyone's amusement. He did not like it very much, but he was happy that Nancy was using it.

Billy Boyle sang ballads about social injustice and faithless lovers, in hillbilly style, to an electric guitar. Neither Nancy nor Jean-Louis would have enjoyed his songs so much had they not annoyed the other members of their households and had not everyone else of their age been raving about him too.

Sybil produced a chess set and board for them. They played seriously. At first they turned Billy Boyle up loud, but then turned him down. They played the same three records over and over without stopping, while they concentrated on the chess board.

Jean-Louis was peremptory about correcting Nancy's errors. The third game he let her win. But he was so effusive in his congratulations that she suspected it had been a put-up job. She determined to get well right away so she could make him jump on the trampoline with her, where she could show him up.

"Your mouth," he said, "looks just like my mother when she is thinking sometimes."

"Oh, is that so," Nancy said and lay back on the pillow. "Let's talk. I'm tired of playing so much."

When Chantal hung up she poured herself another cup of coffee. It was a measure of her preoccupation that she neglected to fill Leon's cup too.

"Jean-Louis will not be home till after ten," she said.

"What is this I heard you say about Sybil being *bienveillante*?" he said casually.

She shrugged. "Some little thing. A letter she received. Who cares? Girls moon around one way or another. Something much more important has taken place, apparently. Mrs. Royce received a letter from Lizzie, and immediately, without telling the children what was in the letter, she went to visit Mr. Royce."

"Good lord," he said as though worried. But in fact he was happy to hear of Sybil's favorable reaction to his letter. Lizzie and Joe were probably having some sort of difficulty, and while he wished them no ill he could not believe they could be in bad trouble. They had all that money, they were on a honeymoon, they were nice decent people. "Did Jean-Louis sound upset?"

"No, no," she said. "He was concerned to keep Nancy from becoming upset."

"Is he in love with her?" said Leon.

"Her? That Amazon? Don't be ridiculous. She is not his type. She is not intellectual in the least. What could they talk about?"

418

He smiled.

"I am being silly, you think?" she said. "Very well, I am silly. Perhaps I am even more romantic than you, about words. I do not like to use the word 'love' "—she shrugged and bobbed her head—"except rarely, very very rarely."

"And I?" he said, affronted. "You mean to say I throw 'love' around loosely?"

"Perhaps you are the least bit promiscuous with it? No? Enough."

"Chantal."

"No. If you cannot hold your peace, you must go home."

He did not speak of love but of his painful fears. She did not tell him again to leave. She stood by him. But she did not let him embrace her. She watched him as from a certain distance. He told her how much he needed her, how her firmness and intelligence could generate in him the order he desperately needed. Her look became a little more distant, but she continued to touch his hair. Then, in a kind of agony, he confessed his dread that he might become sexually depraved. He had gone into law instead of teaching, which he liked very much, so as not to corrupt students, and he told her that he feared he might have corrupted Sybil.

Her look became very remote. She closed her eyes and bent over and kissed him on the mouth, gently but sensually.

He started to put his arm around her waist, but she caught his wrist.

"You understand," she said, "I cannot be abandoned again. If we are eventually to be married, it is without the possibility of divorce. That would kill me, to be abandoned once more. You understand, Leon?"

"I do," he said. "I need somebody about whom I cannot change my mind."

"Oh, you will regret it, have no doubt of that. One does, from time to time. It is just that you must know what you are getting into. You have the habit, my dear, of changing your mind about women, and then changing the women. You may change your mind about me as much as you like. You just may not change me. Understood? You had better learn to change your mind about me back again, because I am here to stay, perhaps. Okay?"

"Okay," he said.

"Otherwise," she said in a softer voice, "I will die. Perhaps kill you first and then die. *Alors*. This is all very fantastic. It's a problem, how does one make love with one's husband without marrying him too? If we weren't such good friends, perhaps rape would be suitable?"

"Oh, Chantal," he said reproachfully.

"No, you are right, rape is not romantic. Still, a little force, out of consideration for my feelings?"

Laughing, he picked her up, carried her into her bedroom, and put her on the bed. He sat beside her and leaned over to kiss her gently, but she pulled him down on top of her, and he gave way to his desire.

For a couple of hours nothing he wanted but she wanted too. Because of this, he wanted nothing of which he would later be ashamed.

"Jean-Louis will be home soon," Leon said.

"He will want to talk a while," Chantal said.

"Let's get dressed and talk with him. I'll tell him that we are married now."

"No!" she cried. "We aren't married."

"But I want to stay with you tonight."

"No, Leon. I made no bargain."

"Aren't we married now?" he said in a hurt voice.

"We are not yet released," she said. "We have our deaths to endure, each a death. I was weak to give way to you tonight." She snuggled into his arms and kissed his throat. "We shall see what we shall see."

"I need you badly," he said.

"Let us see what happens after they die. Who knows what we will need then?"

"You haven't heard from Harry?"

"As I told you." She withdrew a little, turning her head so that she was looking at the ceiling. "Nothing has changed in that quarter."

Her body felt indifferent to his arms. He was not so much hurt as puzzled by her averting her face from him. Because his arms, muscles, body still knew her, he did not feel himself shut out as he had always felt before when she had made such a gesture; he felt her shut in.

He stroked her face with his fingertips, then turned her face toward him again. Without speaking, without smiling, he looked into her eyes. She returned his gaze.

"What illness does Robin have?" she said.

"Hodgkin's disease."

"She has had radiation treatments, of course."

"If so, she never mentioned it to me."

"There is a salesman at the office," she said, "who had radiation for it three or four years ago, and now he is fine."

"You're sure he had Hodgkin's?"

"I am sure. My husband was a doctor."

"But it's fatal."

"Shh," she said, patting his lips with one finger. "Gently, Leon. No doubt the doctors have told her every possibility already. In case she did not understand sufficiently, you must tell her again, of course. Perhaps you may telephone her tonight. But it is not necessary to do so this very instant. Let Jean-Louis come home first."

"But I must," he began. "She may not realize—"

"Come," Chantal said firmly. "You think you can persuade her to save herself if she does not want to?"

"Well," he said, "she may be teetering on the verge and I could—"

"That sentence does not complete itself well, does it, my friend? Only one thing might possibly make her change her mind."

"I can't just leave her there."

"Rhetoric perhaps? You should see the letters I sent to Harry, such eloquence. He has not answered them. He is right. They do not contain the one thing."

They looked into one another's eyes for a little while. He began to caress her again.

"Jean-Louis?" she said.

"Shh," he said, patting her lips with one finger.

When her frown began to melt into a smile, he kissed into her, and she sustained him.

He lay thinking how fortunate he was to have found Chantal, a woman whom he could respect yet who had a dubious past like his own. All his other women he had looked either up to or down upon. Chantal and he were equals. Except that she was so clear about her responsibilities. It seemed to him that he had never been surrounded by so many firm lines before, or felt so free.

At a stifled sound, he tilted her face up.

"Why are you crying, sweetheart?" he said.

"I don't know."

He kissed her eyes. "Regret so soon?"

"In anticipation, perhaps," she said. "I haven't been unfolded for very long, even a little bit. It is strange. Forgive me."

· 13 ·

Dear parents—

When I landed in New York, I decided to come directly here to San Refugio instead of going home. The reason is that I no longer believe in the bourgeois family. In fact, I think that the bourgeois family is probably the worst social institution ever developed in the history of mankind and may well be the main source of the infection which has corrupted Western civilization beyond salvaging. I don't want you to think this is a reflection on you personally. You are both exceptionally wonderful people, individually, and I cannot tell you how grateful I am to you for everything you have given me of a non-bourgeois *human* sort. It is because of what you have given me that I have the strength and will to strike out on my own and make a new life for myself. But you are part of a sick culture, and you have never shown any signs of wanting to get out of it that I ever saw. Nobody in the West can hope to escape that poisonous influence completely, of course, but I want to get out as much as I can. *Within* it, you both do wonderfully. You are the best-functioning invalids I know—much better than I am now, for example, though I am confident that living with the Koyala will make me well. The thing is, though, for the cure to be successful I have to immerse myself in them completely. I don't want you to send me any of my things whatever, not even books and clothes, or any money. Maybe you can send a letter once in a long long time. The Koyala have a saying about Masau'u: "He died to his people." This is when he was the first being to come up from the darkness under the earth where everybody was in the beginning. You must think of me as dead to you. But of course we can write letters back and forth once in a while. I am going to become a Koyala. They accepted Masau'u's offer to join him in his hard life here in the Pueblo world of light, and I am going to too. This means that I am going to live without civilized possessions to speak of, just what they use themselves, and work hard to eke out my living with them. They don't want me, of course, but I shall force them to take me by proving that I can live their life. I will be a slave to them till they accept me. You see, I have no alternative. That is how serious my sickness is.

I have so much to say and I am too turbulent to say it now. I shall write you at greater length when things have calmed down and I have got established in my new life. *Please don't send me anything.* This break must be kept clean.

In a way, Joe has helped me to this. Of course our marriage was a disaster. But just because it was a *total* disaster, I can make a clean break now. I don't hold anything against Joe. In fact, as I just indicated, I am in a way grateful to him. If I had not got to see so clearly just how sick Western civilization is, by seeing how incurably ill it made him, I wouldn't be where I am now. I don't mind looking forward to dying of natural causes, but to see anybody as marvelous as Joe is, in *many* ways, succumbing to the fatal disease which our society *is*, that just opened my eyes for me once and for all. Poor poor Joe, he's just had more than he could take—more than any human being could ever take. And Joe is just human. He is no saint or hero, just a better-than-average man in every way. The list of his troubles is incredible. Of course he hoped for too much from our marriage. (You see? Here we are back to the bourgeois family again. You can't stay away from it.) So when our marriage didn't make his problems disappear, naturally he turned on me. People do. Well, it wasn't *my* fault, any more than it was *his*. It is society's fault. The culture itself is to blame. I tried to make him understand that. He half believed me but he couldn't believe me enough to rescue himself. He kept trusting the Church to save him, which it couldn't and didn't, at all. He just ran away from me one night in the middle of the night, promising to send me money to get home. But he didn't. I haven't heard from him since. I hope he never tries to get in touch with me again. If you hear anything from him, you might mention this to him. If he wants a divorce, he can have one, so long as I don't have to do anything more than sign legal forms. One thing—if I ever get married again, it certainly will not be any kind which has anything to do with bourgeois marriage or divorce. So I just don't care what Joe does about divorcing me so long as he leaves me in peace.

More later,
Lizzie

P.S.—In spite of everything you might think, I truly respect you and love you and am sorry if I hurt you in any way by my decision.

· 14 ·

Beth opened the front door, paused, then stepped back a pace and swung the leather-headed hammer so hard that the gong made a sharp crashing sound before it settled down to reverberating harmoniously.

Alfred and Irma were at the table, eating beef stew and noodles. "Who is it?" Irma called in alarm.

"Me," Beth answered. She walked heavily, on her heels.

"In the dining room," Alfred called.

He rose at his place. Irma half rose, munching nervously.

Beth appeared in the doorway, her lips white, Lizzie's letter in her hand, and paused a moment.

Irma did not know where to look, but glanced from one to the other. "Nancy?" she said hopefully.

Beth gave her head an impatient shake.

Alfred said nothing but stood motionless, looking at Beth with complete readiness.

"A letter from Lizzie," she said to him. "To us both." She walked on the other side of the table from Irma to hand it to Alfred. "We've got to go to her immediately. She's out of her mind. What in God's

423

name have they been teaching her down at that godforsaken University? Here, read this."

When he had telephoned that morning to ask after Nancy, Beth had been brusque, impatient. There was no longer reason for concern over Nancy, and she had rejected the most tentative overture from him, aborting the hope of the night before. He assumed she had done it because she knew about his affair with Virginia, and he had spent the day immobilized with self-reproach, doing busy work in his study.

She, however, had been testing him with her brusqueness. She wanted to find out if his desire to come back to her was hardy enough to last beyond the occasion which had aroused tender sentiments in them both. Obviously he had failed her test. She had been feeling bitter about him all day.

What she said when she held the letter out to him ("What have they been teaching her?") was not directed against him, except generally as he was a professor at the University. But the fearful fury in her eyes and voice was coming in his direction. He was not sure how much she meant it for him. She had never been very good at holding her hostility on target, and more and more often in recent years had swung on him without any other provocation than that he was her husband and was there. He took the letter without saying anything.

When he came to the words "I don't want you to think this is a reflection on you personally," he winced and doubled over a little as from a blow in the belly.

"You see?" Beth said. "Did you ever hear anything so insane? We've got to bring her back."

"It's terrible," he said in apparent agreement, though he did not agree. "Here, I want to read it over carefully." She started to follow him as he moved toward the door to the garden. "No, wait a minute," he said. In the same room with Beth, he would not be able to discover his own reactions to the letter. "I'll be right back in."

Left with Irma, with whom she had never been able to talk for more than two minutes, Beth hid her face in her hands as though in distress too acute to bear, when what she really wanted to be doing was watching Alfred's expression as he read. The spayed old maid, she said to herself and liked the rhyme. The spayed old maid.

"Wouldn't you like some coffee, Beth dear?" Irma said, pouring her a cup.

Beth gave her head a violent shake, but Irma slid the cup in front of her. "I've put in a little cream the way you like it."

Alfred did not think that Lizzie sounded out of her mind; none of her ideas in the letter were new, and her action of going to live among the Koyala was one she had been talking about for a long time. He was dead sure that it would be a mistake for either him or Beth to go to her now, trying to get her to change her mind. Whatever else, she was striking out on her own and needed not to be interfered with. Having failed in her marriage, she had the right to be left alone in this new, peculiar endeavor, though he and Beth might not like it and think it doomed to failure.

His problem at the moment was to divert Beth's wrath. As for his pain at Lizzie's repudiation of them both, he looked at it from a great distance, knowing that it would wait. Meanwhile it did not occur to him simply to tell Beth what he thought and then to withdraw from her. By the fear in her eyes he saw that, however angry with him she might be, she would be grateful to him if he guided her. Moreover, it was for his own sake too that he needed to help her. He believed he should do nothing for Lizzie, but doing nothing was now more than he could bear.

He read the letter again. Lizzie had embraced Beth and him as one, and in the rigor of that embrace he was not disposed to quibble.

He stepped back into the dining room. Beth looked up.

"My dear," he said, "it is clear to me what our first step should be."

"Go get her," she said.

"Later, perhaps. Not yet."

Irma held her napkin to her trembling mouth. Alfred glanced at her with a twitch. For the most part he could pretty well block Irma out, but this one habit of hers never failed to irk him. Involuntarily he shifted his weight onto the leg nearer Beth and with this tiny shift sidestepped Beth's present wrath.

"Before we do anything else," he went on, "we must find out what happened between her and Joe."

"What happened!" Beth cried. "We know the main thing—he deserted her."

"Separation in itself is not necessarily the main thing," he said. Realizing as the words came into his own ears their double application, he began without pausing to throw out filler phrases. "On the other hand, it seems to me, unless I am seriously mistaken, we owe it to her to go talk to Joe's parents and find out what we can from them."

Beth was sufficiently confused by his first general statement about separation not to notice the blurry logic by which he got to the statement about visiting Joe's parents.

"What can they tell us?" she said.

"How do we know that until we ask them?" he said.

"Of course," Irma said, "you might always ask Sybil?"

Beth glared at her. "Sybil has been deliberately vague about Lizzie all along."

425

"We might press her now," said Alfred, seizing the opportunity to get Beth herself to repudiate this notion.

"You can't squeeze blood from a turnip," she said. "Let's go."

"Wait. I'll phone first," he said. "Cyrus Stephen Thompson in San Leandro—right?"

"Right."

Mr. Thompson was home and would be pleased to have them visit. Mrs. Thompson had just left for prayer meeting and would not be home for over an hour.

They walked up San Jacinto Way.

With his hand on the garage door handle, Alfred turned to her. "Are you going to tell Sybil where you're going?"

"Well." Beth hesitated. Then she said with defiance, "No. They never tell me where they're going. I won't tell them where I'm going. Okay?"

"Okay."

He felt her mood changing as they drove.

"Do you want me to do most of the talking?" he said.

She bristled. "What makes you say a thing like that?"

"You have never entered a Negro's home socially before, have you?"

"I was thinking of that," she said in a diminished voice. "Isn't that awful?"

"I thought it might be making you nervous," he said.

"That's putting it mildly. I'm jumpy as a cat. I talk too much when I'm nervous, don't I?"

"Sometimes, my dear."

"And I get myself all wound up in big stiff sentences when I'm talking to social inferiors."

"Once in a while."

"You talk for us both, Alfred. Yes, that's a good idea."

"Don't forget, the Thompsons are probably at least as nervous as you are."

"Aren't you nervous too?" she said.

"But a lawyer needs to be nervous," he said. "It's part of his training to put nervousness to good use. That's why I thought I might do the talking."

He was not a lawyer, he was a professor. He was not calling on the Thompsons as a lawyer but as a relative by marriage. He was so inadequate at handling the jitters that he had had stomach trouble from time to time over the years. She knew all this and felt warm toward him for taking such a palpably silly position in order to comfort her.

426

15

The Thompsons' stucco house was distinguishable from the others in its tract by the perfection of its lawn and bushes and by its spotless whiteness. The curtains on the large arched window facing the street were drawn back, displaying the room. Quite a few pictures and ceramic figurines and vases hung on the walls, none of them awry, and in the center of the table in the window stood a big-bodied pink lamp with a tasseled blue shade.

"Good lord," Beth said.

"Except for the TV antenna," Alfred said, "it could be my Aunt Rosalee's house."

"It's not that far out of date."

"All right—the house she would have if she were still alive. She was a decent woman."

"They can be," said Beth. "So was Cousin Maylayne of Corpus Christi. Decent."

Mr. Thompson opened the door as they were walking up the path. A girl of nine or ten and a boy a couple of years younger were peering around him on each side. He was a white-haired man of medium height with heavy shoulders and large features, dressed in a freshly ironed hickory shirt and tan work pants. The children were much darker than he.

After the introductions he told the children to go outside and play, repeated his apologies that his wife was not home, and asked them to sit on the davenport. After they had seated themselves, side by side, straight, legs not crossed, he sat in a rocking chair to one side of the picture window. It was the one piece of furniture that did not go with the rest. On a small table beside it lay a library book with folded glasses holding the pages open.

"I never expected to meet you folks till the children came back from their honeymoon." He spoke deliberately, without any facial expressions. "I'm mighty sorry things didn't arrange themselves the way we would have liked them to. The good Lord often seems to see fit otherwise."

"Yes," said Alfred, "well, I can't tell you how unhappy we were to learn that Lizzie and Joe have broken up. We thought so highly of Joe, in every way. I was sure he would make a promising lawyer, and he and Lizzie seemed to be devoted to each other."

"They got married in a peculiar way," said Beth.

"Well," said Alfred.

"You know," said Mr. Thompson, "maybe that's a feminine point of view there. Margery said the same thing. She's Joe's stepmother, you know, the mother of my two little ones that I just introduced you to. Joe's mother died fifteen years ago in March. She was a good woman."

"Joe spoke of her with great affection," said Alfred.

"Lizzie had supper with us one time last fall," said Mr. Thompson. "She was real friendly. I could see Joe was interested in her. I had hopes she would make him a good wife."

"We're worried sick about her," said Alfred. "We don't have any idea what went wrong between them, and we just got a letter from her in which she says that she doesn't ever want to come home." He told Mr. Thompson the little he knew, including Lizzie's intention of living among the Koyala. "We don't know what to do. Maybe there's nothing to do, but we hoped you would help us out in any way you can."

"I don't know," said Mr. Thompson. "Joe was the apple of his mother's eye, and we gave him the best Christian education we knew how. He went Episcopalian after she passed on, but that's all right, we're all Christians in the eyes of God. There's a lot more divorcing nowadays than there used to be. People go to church and get divorced anyhow. I just don't know. I worked hard to give Joe all the advantages I was able. I got discouraged back there during the Depression. I even got so low I went on the relief for quite a spell. I just gave up looking for work. It was my own fault, I gave up. But howsomever, we got through that, and Joe went on to college. He was in the war too, you know, and got decorated. He didn't put any stock in metals, he said, but I got it pinned on the wall above my dresser, right beside the picture of him in his Army Uniform. He was in the Air Force. I did everything I could to see he got what I never had. That means the world and all to me, I know you understand. He even got all that money on the TV. I saw him get it. I was setting right where you are now, Mrs. Royce. I can tell you, I was proud of him. I never did figure out why they gave him so much for answering those questions. Of course he always was studious. He'd sooner to bury his nose in a book than play pool any day, like his old man. He explained to me about advertising and the economy and such like, why they give so much money away on the TV, but I reckon I never will understand it rightly. They must have some reason, though, and I am mighty proud of him. He's a good son to me. He sent me some of that money to pay off my mortgage and buy a new car. He said I need never worry about my old age either. Of course we got Social Security and so on from back in the New Deal, but he will look after us too. And now all this trouble."

"What did he tell you?" Alfred asked.

"Yes, he wrote to us from Paris, France. I thought he was in England. He always used to talk about England like it was the promised land. I never rightly understood why. I remember what he wanted for his fourteenth birthday was a big history of England, and I got it for him. It cost ten dollars, and there was two volumes to it. He took it with him when he went to college. I don't know what has ever happened to it. But he went to Paris, France. He gave us an address there. Here." He reached under the book and pulled out an envelope. "Care of American Express, it says. I don't know. That's where he can be wrote to, he says. I was going to do it tonight."

"He didn't say what happened or what he intends to do?" said Alfred.

"No," said Mr. Thompson, "he just said they broke up. Those are his very words, 'We have broken up.' Which don't say much of anything to the point that I can see."

"There's nothing to be done," said Alfred.

Beth began to cry quietly.

"Not till they want us to," said Mr. Thompson. "We got to trust in the Lord. We got to put ourselves in the Lord's hands."

He spoke with a kind of finality.

Alfred stood up and held his hand out to Beth. "Come, my dear. We must go home."

Beth controlled her tears and thanked Mr. Thompson.

As they were standing on the front stoop, saying good-by, a car drew up and Mrs. Thompson got out, saying thank you to the woman who was driving. Mrs. Thompson was a stout, corseted woman in a white dress and a white hat. She walked with a sort of roll, and on her dark brown face was a beaming expression, as though she were bursting with good news. Her upper lip covered its teeth even when she spoke.

"So you're Lizzie's folks," she said heartily. "Why, you come right on back into the house and set a while, and we'll get acquainted. This is surely the time for fellowship. Not but what every time isn't the right time, but this is especially the right time, being a time of tribulation for us all. Cyrus, did you give them any coffee? Shame on you. Now you all come right on back inside."

When they demurred, she said they would hurt her feelings if they did not.

"They're upset, Margery," said Mr. Thompson deliberately. "Mrs. Royce was crying just a little while ago. I think they could stand to be alone."

"Well, now, of course she was crying. She has got something to cry about too. You and I, Mrs. Royce, we can just have a good cry together. Now you go put on the water for the coffee, Cyrus, and Mrs.

429

Royce and I'll just set here on the davenport beside, and we'll have us a good talk. Did he show you the letter that boy wrote to him? No? Well, now, say. When he comes back in here from the kitchen, I'll ask about that. Joe was a good boy, I'll say that much for him. So long as he was staying to home where he was under the influence of the Church of Christ, he was a good boy. Then he took to going abroad in the world, and naturally he changed. You have three daughters. Isn't that right, three daughters? Yes, I knew I couldn't be wrong. I don't forget family, never. So, as I was saying, the world got its hooks into him, and it's Godless nowadays, it has turned its back on God and its face to the Devil. First he went Episcopal, which is the next thing to Catholic, and they are the children of Belial himself. Then he went white, which is all right if you are born white and can't help it, but he wasn't and never will be. How do you think his father felt about that? Where is his father anyhow? Cyrus, what are you doing in there so long?"

He appeared in the dining room. "I was putting the coffee in the pot for you, Margery. I can hear you talking. Just go ahead. I'll come in a minute."

"Joe has such beautiful manners," said Beth, hoping to divert her.

"Manners!" said Mrs. Thompson. "Why, he's a gentleman! Who would ever be able to guess his father is a working man? An honest, God-fearing working man. Now who is it is a gentleman? The Good Book tells us who. It is the Devil. I don't know who Joe has been associating with, you know that better than I do, but you are so right, he is a gentleman. Of course you meant it a different way. Don't deny it, I can see you did. That's all right. And that isn't all—he appeared to do it all by himself. You need help to do a thing like that. You know that. Then the crowning touch, he ups and marries your Lizzie when nobody's watching, in New York City. Do you know what she told us when she joined us in fellowship at our very table here last October? She said she had fallen away from the religion of her fore-fathers. I know how it is, Sister Royce. We are sisters under the skin, aren't we?—and relations on top of that. So it's right I should call you Sister. Anyhow, she went to the University of California and they taught her the ways of this world. You remember who Jesus said was the prince of this world, don't you? 'Now is the judgment of this world: now shall the prince of this world be cast out.' John Twelve, Thirty-one. So be it. Joe knows. He has no refuge, he knows. But he never tried to make his own wife see the light, he just sank right down into her sin with her. You're Christian yourself, so you know." She paused, peering. '

Beth could not respond, quivering between outrage and politeness.

430

"No," said Alfred softly, "we are neither of us Christians. We never go to church and we never made our children go to church."

Mr. Thompson was carrying in the coffee pot and cups and saucers. He did not turn a hair at Alfred's words. But Mrs. Thompson breathed hard and closed her eyes. She lifted her upper lip and rubbed her upper teeth with it as though scraping scum off them.

"That's the root," she said. Then she opened her eyes and jabbed her forefinger at her husband, who was pouring coffee tranquilly. "I told you, Cyrus, and you wouldn't listen. You close your eyes to too much. You say you go around forgiving, they're just poor sinners. *Did Jesus forgive the Devil?*" Beth started to get up, but Mrs. Thompson caught her by the wrist and pulled her back down. "Now you see what befell us with our own children when they shut their hearts to God? They went away. Joe is in Paris, France, which is the Babylon of this generation, it is the city of enticements. The Catholics. And your Lizzie, where is she? Went to live among the pagans, by her own testimony, heathen Indians. You see? Now you listen to me, Brother and Sister." For the first time she incorporated Alfred in her address and glance. "You listen to the Word of God. It is not too late, even at the eleventh hour. Cyrus, why didn't you show them that letter of Joe's? Let them see what it's like where he has gone to. The things he says about his bride of a few months! And him a Christian born and bred. You should know it. What she says about him, I can just imagine, for they are in the same pit—different parts of it, but the same pit. Yet there is repentance even at the last minute. The Lord shall not turn His back even on them who have closed their hearts to Him, if they repent, if only they will repent. The deathbed is not too late, but He does not always grant a slow death."

"That's enough, Margery," said Mr. Thompson firmly.

"All right," she said and sighed. "The letter! You got it. There, Mr. Royce, you take it and read it."

Mr. Thompson was holding the letter in his hand, neither concealing it nor offering it.

Alfred rose from the chair he had been sitting in and took Beth by the arm.

"Thank you," he said delicately to Mrs. Thompson. "I would prefer not to read Joe's letter to his father. We are going now." He turned to Mr. Thompson. "Thank you very much for your hospitality. I hope that our next meeting may be in pleasanter circumstances."

"Amen," said Mrs. Thompson.

16

As soon as they had got onto East Fourteenth Street heading back toward Berkeley, Alfred settled into his seat, gripped the steering wheel till his knuckles turned white, and began swearing steadily. Alone, he would have contained his anger, and there was a time when he would have tried to moderate Beth's, had she begun to rail against Mrs. Thompson as he was now doing. Intending to relieve Beth of some of her burden of anger, he found himself enjoying the cursing for its own sake.

In a while he said, "I need a drink badly."

"So do I," said Beth. "Let's go to Iggy's Igloo."

"What's that?"

"A bar on East Fourteenth where hot-rodders hang out."

"For heaven's sake, Beth."

"Sybil told me about it. I never get to go to bars any more and I hate cocktail lounges. Syb went there with Jackie Devereux before she ran off."

"So what's it got to recommend it?" he said. "Hoods?"

"Nothing," she said. "It's just that it hasn't got anything against it. Nowadays nothing bad is something good. What a vile age we live in."

"You find the place and we'll stop. Meanwhile don't interrupt me. I'm going to consign that blackhearted devil-worshipper to the hell she has taken such pains to outfit for everybody else."

With the word "black" he released the stock liberal attitudes toward bad behavior among Negroes. Beth, rather feebly, began an automatic defense: society is to blame for the faults of its victims.

"Okay, okay," he said. "So why isn't Mr. Thompson a son of a bitch too?"

"How do I know? And anyway," she went on, glad to abandon a line of argument that issued only from the machine part of her head, "what is wrong with him?"

"Wrong with him?" said Alfred. "He seemed like a decent enough man to me. It's his wife that's so awful."

"He married her," said Beth. "He stays with her. He didn't get mad at her this evening."

"Ah."

"What do you mean, 'Ah'? That's more than you did, Alfred Royce. Onetime husband."

"Aha," he said.

"Quit sounding so damned oracular."

"Recently in the book I'm writing," he said, "I've been working on a subject which has turned out to be far more important than I had realized before. It has to do with agentry—not with appointing contractual agents so much as slipping in surreptitious agents when nobody is noticing. I have become convinced that it is a considerably more important legal problem than is commonly appreciated. And more than legal."

"I don't follow," said Beth. "He is her agent?"

"Not at all, my dear. She is his agent. He lets her do his dirty work for him."

They had come to Iggy's Igloo and went in. It was a small old-fashioned bar with red-checked tablecloths and a few booths. There was a middle-aged man at the bar, talking with the bartender, a somewhat bent old man, with spectacles, Iggy himself. In one booth were a young man and two young women, all three dressed identically in black leather jackets, faded blue jeans, and cowboy boots. The five people in the room silently watched Alfred seat Beth at a corner table, then go to the bar and order two double Scotches with ice.

At the table he was able gradually to get back into his ideas about agentry. Beth glanced about occasionally. Suddenly she frowned at him.

"Are you double-talking?"

"What?" he said.

"Are you trying to get at me somehow, with all this talk about agents?"

"What makes you say that?"

"Come on," she said, "you're not a headshrinker, cut the boomeranging. Yes or no. What are you getting at?"

One of the young women went to the juke box, punched three buttons, and put a coin in. Jangles boomed from the machine in uniform clusters. Alfred shrugged and sat back, and Beth began looking around again. In the middle of the third record, a pseudo-Calypso piece which was not quite intelligible, the front door of the bar swung open and a young man stepped inside and stood looking at the three in the booth. He was dressed as they were, except that the tooling on his boots was fancier. The young woman who had started the juke box waved to him to come join them, but he jerked his head, turned, and walked back out. She got up, shrugging to her companions, and followed.

When the music stopped, Beth leaned forward. "I feel like I was on a date."

"I need another drink," said Alfred. "You too?"

She nodded. "You suppose they're really as tough as they act?"

"They're tougher than we are, anyway."

He brought the drinks back, intending to start talking about his book again. But Beth said as he was setting her glass in front of her, "So—am I your agent or you mine?"

She was clearly hostile and skeptical, spoiling for a fight. But the events of the past two days had been too much for him. He could no longer control her or himself, neither avert the fight nor enjoy it. He spoke in an earnest voice, so low that she had to lean forward a little to listen.

He had never thought the painful subject through. He began now from his theory of agentry and gradually narrowed it to their own case. She attended.

"But before I try to define exactly what I think is the case with us," he said, not knowing exactly what he thought, "I must tell you, my dear, that I want to come back home if you will have me back."

"Ah," she said.

"Will you?"

"Nothing has been cleared up."

"Oh, many things are changed," he said.

"So let me hear the rest of your theory."

"I believe," he said, "that the very seed and root of our trouble, the thing that ultimately caused us to separate, had to do with my allowing you to use me as a surreptitious agent in an impossible enterprise."

"Which was?"

"To exorcise you of your family ghosts—furniture, money, and all. But your will was divided. You couldn't let go of them. You wanted an agent to tear them from you by force, or, as it turned out, to blame for your holding on to them. I think it was impossible for you to be separated from them without destruction to yourself, but this may be mere rationalization on my part. What I am sure of is that I mistook my role for that of servant and rescuer." There was a long pause, during which Beth frowned thoughtfully. Then he added, "Ghosts don't fear the agent of a divided self."

"God damn you, Alfred Royce," she said. "May you fry in hell for saying what you just said."

She got up and stalked out. She began walking down the street away from the car. He drove up beside her and opened the car door. First she slammed it shut and strode on. Then, when he opened it again, creeping in low by the curb beside her, she turned and got in.

"If there was a taxi in this godforsaken wasteland . . ." she muttered.

"You believe what I said was untrue?"

"Oh, it may be true, for all I care. That's irrelevant."

"Nonsense," he said.

"You really don't know what you said to me, do you?"

"Yes, I know."

"What you did, then," she said. "What you did was as slick a job of blame-shifting as I ever saw, and you're a real pro at it."

"I said that I allowed you to make me your surreptitious agent."

"And arrogant!" she said. "Christ, how arrogant. You allowed me to misbehave! Jesus Christ almighty, Alfred."

They did not speak again.

When he parked the car in the garage, she snatched the keys from his hand without a word, glaring at him, and stalked into the house, slamming the door behind her.

Nancy shouted to her in an excited happy voice, and Sybil appeared at the foot of the stairs. Beth called that she would be down in a few minutes. She went into the bedroom, threw herself face down on the bed, and beat the pillow.

Alfred walked down the dark street, rising onto the balls of his feet, his head high. A pure, unvengeful rage grew from his guts up through his chest and burst in his head. He could hardly breathe, he had to close his eyes, his ears roared. Fortunately no one saw him as he stood clutching a branch by the side of the road and swaying. He could not have hidden symptoms of his distress, and if somebody had insisted on trying to help him then, he would have knocked that person down. He let himself into his house quietly so that Irma would not hear him and come clucking, as she had done more than once.

When Beth heard Jim arrive on his motorcycle from taking Jean-Louis home, she roused herself and went to greet the young people. It was because of them, it seemed to her, that she refrained from giving way to madness.

· 17 ·

"Well," said Jim, "I hope you're not hungry tonight."

"I'm not," said Sybil, settling herself on the seat behind his. "I want to go for a long ride."

"Great," he said. "Where to?"

"The ocean?" she said.

"Too foggy. Let's go along Bear Creek Road till we find a good fence to climb."

"And sit on the stubble?" she said. "There's lots of foxtails out there too. We need a blanket."

"Softy," he said.

435

"Nut," she said. "I'll get the old gray blanket out of the trunk of the car."

In a pasture at the foot of a hill they found a live oak to spread their blanket beneath.

As soon as she sat down he knelt beside her and began kissing and caressing her.

"Listen," he said, "I've got a great idea. I've been thinking about it all day. It's the solution to everything."

"Mm," she said.

"I mean it. Let's get married right away."

"Right away?" she cried. "Like next week?"

"Sure. Why not?"

"For heaven's sake," she said, kissing him since he had said what she wanted, "you know why not as well as I do. That's all we've been talking about for weeks, it seems to me."

"Aw, honey," he said, bending her back and leaning over her, "who cares whether we can afford it?"

"You do," she said.

"I did," he answered. "We'll make out all right."

"Why are you so different tonight?" she said.

"How different?" he said.

"I don't know. More authoritative."

"Do you like it?" he said.

"Mm."

"A dream."

"A dream?" she said, raising her head.

"Yes."

He tried to close in on her, but she held him off.

"Come on, Jim, what are you talking about? You never lose a chance to say how you have no use for Freud."

"He didn't invent dreams," he said.

"But he invented the way to interpret them."

"All I know is," Jim said, "whatever dreams mean, everything in them comes from inside the dreamer's own head. I don't believe in spirits and devils."

"Don't you now?" she said. "That's a start."

He said nothing.

"I'm sorry," she said, snuggling up to him. "Jimmy? What did you dream?"

"A baseball game."

"Yes?" she said. "Between?"

"The Yankees and San Quentin."

"San Quentin? You mean the prison?"

"Yes," he said, "a team of convicts, and I was the umpire. There was a big crowd in the ballpark. Everybody was rooting for the Yankees, but the convicts kept winning anyway. I was being as fair as I possibly could when I called the strikes and balls and plays, but the crowd kept blaming me. They kept yelling, 'We want the pros! We want the pros!' So did I, but what could I do? Then all of a sudden on the scoreboard all the lights went on and they spelled, 'Send the cons back where they came from.' So I ordered them to go back to jail. I was afraid they would attack me, but they didn't. They just trotted back down into their dugout as docile as anything. Everybody went wild and carried me around on their shoulders like a hero."

"But the Yankees usually do win," she said.

"Oh, baseball," he said with disgust. "What does baseball have to do with anything? It's me, dummy, me, me, me! The cons were winning, so I had to send them back where they belong. Which I did. Now, honey, come on, let's get married."

"What a lovely nut," she said.

"Will you?" he said, making a gesture over his head as though he were about to throw a lasso.

"Yes," she said, "I will."

"Right away?"

She slid herself against him. "Right now."

"If only we could," he said.

"We can."

"Oh, Sybil."

"Can't we?" she said.

"No, you know we can't."

"Hey!" she yelled. "A con's escaped! Let's lock him up. Come on, quick, put him in where he belongs!"

"Why are *you* so different tonight?" he said.

"Am I? How?"

"I'm not sure. Sort of more exciting."

"Really?" she said. "Good. I don't strike you as being worried?"

"Just the opposite," he said.

"Maybe," she said, "it has something to do with a letter I got today." But then she thought it would not be tactful to mention Leon's letter at this point, if ever. "From Lizzie. When somebody I'm close to gets into bad trouble, I feel like I've got to rush."

This time when they kissed they did not unkiss even when he began to take her clothes off.

Jim was squandered before he had properly begun. In humiliation he rolled over with his back to Sybil.

"Well, honey," she said, drawing a finger down his backbone, "one thing is sure. We aren't either one of us pros."

437

He rolled onto his back and said in a small voice, "You don't—"

"Oh, for Pete's sake, don't be a goofball. *Every*thing points in the same direction. We've just got to get married. We're the type. Nothing else will do. Even he thinks so." She patted his penis. "So let's get dressed and go home."

· 18 ·

At two that morning Alfred walked up San Jacinto Way to his home, felt about on the ledge above the garage door, where he found the spare key to the outer door of his study in its accustomed place, and let himself in. He turned on the light in the study so he would not bump into the boxes and odds and ends of furniture that were being stored there, crossed the room, and opened the first of the double doors to the large bedroom.

"Who's there?" Beth cried.

"Me," he said, turning the handle of the inner door.

"Alfred?"

"Yes."

He entered, leaving the door slightly ajar so that he could see by the light from his study.

She was sitting up in bed with something black in her hand.

"What's that?" he said.

He walked over to her and extended his hand. She let him take the revolver. She was trembling.

"Beth, for God's sake!" He put the gun on the table.

"Shh!" she said. "You'll wake up the children."

"All right, then I'll wake them. I've come home to stay."

"Oh, you have."

"And they might as well know it sooner as later."

"What makes you think you've come home to stay?" she said.

"Because I can't get along without you," he said, sitting on the bed beside her. "Tonight after I left you I was so mad I could have killed somebody. And then after I calmed down in about an hour, everything came crowding in on me at once, and I thought I would die."

"Don't be melodramatic."

He blinked at her.

"Nancy's all right," said Beth, "and so is Sybil. She got home about an hour and a half ago and came in and told me she and Jim are going to get married as soon as they can—next week sometime."

"I'll be damned," he said with a kind of awe. "If those two don't make it . . . Do you suppose they will make it?"

"She seems determined to," Beth said.

438

"Where are they going to live?"

"They'll find someplace. They *won't* live in the garden cottage, and they *won't* take money from us."

"What about furniture?" he said.

"What do you mean?" she said, bristling.

"I'm going to sell Thomas's house," he said. "So the kids can have any of the furniture they want."

"Well," she said, "I offered Sybil any of Mother's stuff that isn't being used. She just said they'd see about it. Look here, Alfred, don't you try to trap me with all this sweet talk. I haven't agreed to a thing, and you know it."

"I can't afford to keep Thomas's house," he said. "I've got a five-thousand-dollar mortgage on it already."

"It's not my fault you can't earn a decent living," she said.

"Nobody said it was your fault. And besides, I could earn a lot more money if I chose to. I have chosen not to."

"Why?"

He took a deep breath. "Do you really want to know, or are you being aggressive?"

"Both," she said.

"That's honest, at least," he said.

"Bah. It's obvious. Now—why?"

"Shortly before Thomas died he arranged with Tony St. Clare to have me offered a federal judgeship, at more than double my present salary at the University." He stopped.

"So?" she said.

"I decided not to. There were many reasons."

"There always are. But there is usually *the* reason."

"Yes," he said and rubbed his forehead. He was afraid she would laugh at him if he told the truth and that he would get so hurt and angry with her for laughing that he would spoil everything again. But he would never be easy in his mind about it if he did not tell her the truth now. He decided to be as dry as he could. "Lizzie said in her letter that she was getting out of American society and that we showed no signs of repudiating it. For me, at least, that was only partially true. As a judge I would be more substantively a part of this society than I was willing to be. I did not want to be this society's agent as completely as I would have to be if I were a crucial instrument of the State. To that extent Lizzie was wrong about me. But she was right that I do not really repudiate our society. It is corrupt and so on, but I don't think it is about to disintegrate or to turn into an absolutely inhumane monstrosity. It threatens to do one or the other. I dream sometimes that it happens. Either way, it's the end of the world. Well, *there* is the real reason I don't even try to break out, to break myself off from society—I dream of it, it is that deep in me, I am in it over my ears. So I'll be a part-time professor and write books about law theory. As a professor I am an agent of the State I happened to be born into. As a theorist I aspire to be the agent of the idea of Society."

"What about when they conflict?" she said.

"My head fills up with bad thoughts."

Because he had spoken so rationally at a time of such emotional pressure, she believed him. Nothing he could have done would have won her over more than thus appealing to her understanding: she did not trust him to tell the truth cleanly when he was speaking emotionally, and she never felt more confidence in herself than when addressed intellectually without a hint of condescension.

"Are you cold?" she said.

"I'm shivering some."

"Take off your shoes and lie down under the blanket."

He did, but reared up on one elbow. She lay on her side, facing him, and snuggled her arm under her pillow.

"What sort of bad thoughts come into your head?" she asked.

"About Lizzie. Or Robin. Or the assassination. Whether I made the wrong choice not to be a judge—you know, what's going to hold society together if people of ability desert it? And about us, of course. And money."

"What about money?"

"Well," he said, "we'll sell what property we aren't going to use, consolidate it, invest it safely, make a budget, and live within our means."

"Can we, honey? We never did."

"Oh yes, we did. In fact, we usually did. We've seldom gone into debt."

"I mean," she said, "we never had a budget and stuck to it."

"We never got so slopped up about property before either. I *detest* thinking about money, and this is the only way I know of to free my mind of money thoughts."

"You mean, all our money? Even my inheritance?"

"Even your inheritance, and mine too. The whole works—into banks and blue-chip stocks where we won't have to think about it. Then we'll see to it that we get along on what we have coming in."

"If we only could," she said.

"We not only can, we shall," he said.

She believed him.

"What about Irma?" she said.

"She'll have to forage for herself."

"She has no relatives, poor thing."

440

"A nephew or so in the Midwest someplace."

"Will he take her in?" said Beth.

"I don't think so. I'm not sure, but I doubt it."

"She could live in the garden cottage. We can't just cast her out."

"You can't stand her, Beth, and you know you can't. Thomas left her a trust fund to keep her for the rest of her life. If she settles in the Bay Area I'll go call on her every month or two and we can have her to Christmas dinner. And that is all."

"You're so hard," she said gently.

"I've thought about it," he said. "If you liked her, I could put up with her. But we're going to have enough trouble keeping our head above water as things stand. Irma goes."

"What do you intend to do about Lizzie?"

"Give her what help I can—when she asks for it."

"But, Alfred—"

"And not before she asks for it."

Beth sighed, with little catches like sobs as she inhaled.

"Beth," he said in another voice, "I really can't make it without you."

"You know what an impossible neurotic bitch I am."

"I'm no lily."

"But I'm much worse," she said. "I'm awful. I can't even stand myself."

"Sometimes you're awful, all right," he said. "And I can't stand Mary Louise."

"Well, *I* can't stand Horace and Virginia."

"All right," he said, "I don't like them too much any more myself. I haven't seen them for weeks. I won't invite them to any more of my parties if you won't invite her to any more of yours."

"All right."

He kissed her cheek, and she gave his beard a scratch.

"Who was she?" Beth said.

"Who was who?" he said.

"Your gay lady."

"I told you," he said, "no gay ladies."

"The *femme fatale* you left me for."

"Oh, Beth, I didn't leave you for another woman."

"Won't you even let me have a shred of dignity?"

"Not such a transparent shred as that," he said.

"Why did you leave me? I keep going over what happened, and nothing I can remember seems important enough to break up over."

"I got so mad at you," he said, "that I forgot how much I needed you."

"Can I still make you mad after twenty-three years?" she said.

441

"Can you still make me mad!" he shouted. She shushed him. "You're the most infuriating woman I ever knew in my life, and you get worse instead of better."

"Hm," she said.

"So, wife—I'm back. I'm going to get undressed and get in bed with you now."

"You're already in bed," she said.

"But I'm on top of the sheet with my clothes on, and you're between the sheets with your pj's on."

"Whose agent are you being this time?" she said.

"Tonight I am the agent of my own desire," he said. He pulled the sheet down to their waists and took her in his arms.

"That's pretty grand," she said, resisting. "Oh, what a pompous ass. How can I stand you?"

His embrace did not relax because of her sarcasm. He whispered that he wanted to make love to her and nipped the lobe of her ear with his lips. Her body left off resisting.

"Your beard, Alfred," she said with a giggle, "it's tickling my neck."

He leaned back and stared her down. She returned his embrace.